挑戰
新制多益
閱讀滿分

NEW TOEIC

模擬試題1000題

作者 Choi Young Ken ┃ 譯者 蘇裕承 / 關亭薇

目錄

新制多益介紹

新制多益於2018年3月正式實施

✅ 改制後如下

類別	Part	舊制多益		新制多益		時間	分數
		題型	題數	題型	題數		
聽力	1	照片描述	10	照片描述	6	45分鐘	495分
	2	應答問題	30	應答問題	25		
	3	簡短對話	30	簡短對話	39		
	4	簡短獨白	30	簡短獨白	30		
閱讀	5	句子填空（文法和單字）	40	句子填空（文法和單字）	30	75分鐘	495分
	6	段落填空	12	段落填空	16		
	7	閱讀　單篇閱讀	28	閱讀　單篇閱讀	29		
		雙篇閱讀	20	多篇閱讀	25		
TOTAL		7 Parts	200題	7 Parts	200題	120分鐘	990分

✅ 題型變更重點

聽力測驗

- Part 1, 2 題數減少（**Part 1**：10 題→ 6 題／ **Part 2**：30 題→ 25 題）
- Part 3 題數增加（**Part 3**：30 題→ 39 題）
- 部分對話長度減短、對話次數增加
- 新增三人對話 **NEW**
- 部分對話中將出現母音省略（如：going to → gonna）
- 新增對話、說明加上圖表（表格或曲線圖等）的整合題型 **NEW**
- 新增詢問說話者意圖的題型 **NEW**

閱讀測驗

- Part 5 題數減少（**Part 5**：40 題→ 30 題）
- Part 6, 7 題數增加（**Part 6**：12 題→ 16 題／ **Part 7**：48 題→ 54 題）
- 新增判斷上下文意的題型（句子插入題）**NEW**
  1. 在文章內放入符合上下文意的句子
  2. 將句子放入適當的段落位置
- 新增文字簡訊、線上聊天、通訊軟體多人對話題型 **NEW**
- 新增整合三篇文章的閱讀題型 **NEW**
- 詢問閱讀測驗文章中單字字義的題型
- 新增詢問說話者意圖的題型 **NEW**

PART 5–6 高分策略

PART 5–6 命題趨勢

01 PART 5 從 101 至 130 題，總題數為 30 題；PART 6 從 131 至 146 題，共有四個題組，每組四題。PART 5 的題目為商業情境或日常生活中經常使用到的短句（由 13–25 個單字組合而成），要求填入適當的單字，或符合文法結構的選項；PART 6 的題目則是在信件、電子郵件、備忘錄、報導等中篇文章中放入四個空格，要求考生根據文法和上下文，選填適當的單字或句子。

02 PART 6 每篇文章都有一題要根據上下文，從四個選項中選填適當的句子插入文章中。
扣除這四題，每次多益測驗的 PART 5 和 PART 6 有 40% 屬於詞彙題；60% 屬於時態和文法題。

03 兩大題常見的題型為確認句型結構，並選出正確的詞性（名詞、形容詞、動詞、副詞、介系詞、連接詞）填入空格當中。

04 詞彙題會要求考生從數個意思相似的單字中，根據文意選出正確的答案，此類題型的比例與難度逐漸增加。

05 注意綜合單字、詞性和基礎文法概念（被動語態、不定詞、分詞、時態等）的題型。

PART 5–6 重點題型

多益測驗中，PART 5 和 PART 6 的題型有：

❶ 詞性變化　　❷ 動詞相關題型　　❸ 其他文法概念
❹ 詞彙題　　　❺ 根據文意填入適當的句子。

01 **詞性變化**
此題型的數量少則 6 題，多則 9 題，只要確認名詞、形容詞、副詞、介系詞、或連接詞扮演的角色與放置的位置，就能輕鬆解題。最重要的是，此題型為節省時間的好幫手，可以讓你迅速找出答案並進展至下一題，同時增加 PART 7 長篇閱讀的解題時間。

02 **動詞相關題型**
包含語態、分詞、不定詞、動名詞和時態等動詞變化的題型。只要將文法概念歸納整理，便能輕鬆解決此題型。每個月的句子雖然有所變化，但是基本上都是使用上述的文法概念，因此請務必熟悉此類題型，確保每一題的答題正確率。

其中動詞的「單複數一致」為 100% 必考題型，主詞人稱的單複數必須與動詞單複數保持一致，也是學習英文句型結構的出發點。多益考題中，為了加深題目難度，常在句子中加入修飾語，使得主詞長度增加，讓主詞和動詞的距離變得遙遠，以混淆考生選出正確的動詞。答題策略就是**遮住英文句子中的修飾語**，學會找出句子中的主詞和動詞，確認主詞的單複數，再搭配正確的動詞，此題型為 100% 必考的文法題。

03 其他文法概念

其他文法概念指的是英文基礎文法概念，除了主詞與動詞單複數一致，還有代名詞的三種格（主格、受格、所有格）、不定詞、動名詞、關係代名詞、假設語氣、比較級、倒裝句等。

04 詞彙題

多益測驗中的詞彙題分成四大類

① collocation（選擇常用的搭配詞）
② nuance（懂得區分同義詞的細微差異）
② interchangeable words（選擇實際對話中互相通用的單字）
④ 掌握文意（根據文意選填適當的單字）。

也可以依詞性分成：
①名詞題　②形容詞題　③副詞題　④動詞題　⑤介系詞題。

05 句子插入題

指的是 PART 6 中，要求考生根據上下文，從四個選項找出一個適當的句子插入文章段落的題型。除了基本閱讀理解能力之外，考生還必須具備邏輯思考力，懂得掌握前後文意。

PART 5–6 高分Point

✅ 徹底熟悉各大題必考的文法概念。

✅ 不斷學習單字和其相關用法。

包含介系詞和名詞的用法、與動詞的搭配、動詞各類變化、慣用語等題型。此外，考生必須不斷記憶理解新的單字和用法，因為每個月的考題都會出現新的單字。

✅ 要練習掌握前後文的脈絡。

針對 PART 6 的新題型「句子插入題」，要學習理解前後文的關係，才能將符合文意的句子填入空格中。

PART 5–6 高分策略

PART 5 題型綜覽（句子填空題）

PART 5 的題型要根據句中的文法或是單字，從四個選項中選出一個最適當的答案填入空格中，使其成為完整的句子。新制多益的命題方向不變，但是總題數從 40 題減少為 30 題。

READING TEST

In the Reading test, you will read a variety of texts and answer several different types of reading comprehension questions. The entire Reading test will last 75 minutes. There are three parts, and directions are given for each part. You are encouraged to answer as many questions as possible within your time allowed.

You must mark your answers on the separate answer sheet. Do not write your answers in your test book.

Part 5

Directions: A word or phrase is missing in each of the sentences below. Four answer choices are given below each sentence. Select the best answer to complete the sentence. Then mark the letter (A), (B), (C), or (D) on your answer sheet.

101. The fundraising event recorded such high ------- that there will be more than expected proceeds.
   (A) attendant
   (B) attended
   (C) attend
   (D) attendance

102. Sky Motors offers a variety of training programs to help enhance ------- in the workplace.
   (A) productivity
   (B) produce
   (C) productive
   (D) productively

103. All the employees are asked to report all the expenses incurred ------- business trips.
   (A) during
   (B) so
   (C) meanwhile
   (D) while

PART 6 的題型要根據上下文，從四個選項中選出一個最適當的答案填入空格中，使其成為完整的段落。新增加的題型為「句子插入題」，要求根據文意，從選項中找出最適當的句子填入空格中。新制多益新增了 4 題變成 16 題，每篇文章有四個題目，共有四篇文章。

Part 6

Directions: Read the texts that follow. A word, phrase, or sentence is missing in parts of each text. Four answer choices for each question are given below the text. Select the best answer to complete the text. Then mark the letter (A), (B), (C), or (D) on your answer sheet.

Questions 135-138 refer to the following notice.

Important Notice about Hatter Industries

Please note that the contact information for Hatter Industries changed on March 21. Due to the closure of our Dabbley office and the ----135---- of our operations in Buena, all correspondence concerning our products and services should now be sent to the following address: Hatter Industries, 642 Mandela Lane, Buena, CA. Our employees' e-mail addresses, as well as our website's address, www.hatterindustries.com, remain ----136----.

However, we are still waiting for our new telephone and fax numbers. ----137---- will be updated on our website as soon as the new numbers are assigned as of March 25. ----138----.

135. (A) decision
(B) relocation
(C) suspension
(D) result

136. (A) assigned
(B) even
(C) formal
(D) unchanged

137. (A) Yours
(B) Another
(C) These
(D) Theirs

句子插入題 (NEW)

138. (A) We apologize for any inconvenience and thank you for your understanding.
(B) Refer to the side of the packet for full details of instructions before applying.
(C) Her office location will also remain the same.
(D) For more information about the forthcoming event, visit www.lizard.org.br/events.

PART 7 高分策略

PART 7 找出主題句！

無論是長篇或短篇文章、困難或簡單的單字、屬於舊制還是新制多益的文章和題目，每篇文章的關鍵都只有一個：**主題句**（Topic Sentence）。

PART 7 高分Point

01 **速讀**

新制多益最明顯的特色就是題數增加、文章篇幅變長，同時新增通訊軟體對話以及多篇閱讀。閱讀的分量遠超過解題的時間，因此務必將文章的閱讀重點擺在找出主題句。要有效率地找出主題句，**邏輯式速讀**是解決之道！無關文章的長度和種類，只要找出將眾多句子濃縮成一句精華（simplified）的關鍵主題句，便能在短時間內掌握文意。

02 **掌握文章脈絡**

為了傳達主題句的理念，集合眾多句子而成的集合體稱作「文章」。因此閱讀文章的關鍵並非以句子為單位一句句閱讀，而是要掌握句子和句子之間的走向，也就是「脈絡」。新制多益中新增的題型為**詢問說話者意圖**，以及**完成段落填空**，更加強調掌握文章脈絡的重要性。因此在閱讀多益文章時，不可使用單句翻譯（translation）的方式，執著於單一句子或是單字的意思，而是要**確認文章想要表達的重點理念**，找出主題句，推敲前後文意後，以速讀的方式快速**確認文章的脈絡**，這樣才得以迎戰新制多益的變化。

03 **迎戰新增的題型**

→ 完成段落填空

> We are currently looking for an experienced, creative, and dedicated environmental expert to work in our office in Vienna, Austria. —[1]—. With employees from all over the world, the FOE is a linguistically diverse community. —[2]—. Applicants must also possess a degree in environmental science, hydrology, or biology, and have at least three years of international work experience. —[3]—.
>
> Please e-mail your application with a current resume, a letter of recommendation, and a writing sample to Clifford Samuelson by September 30. —[4]—.

Q. In which of the positions marked [1], [2], [3] and [4] does the following sentence best belong?

"However, English is the working language of the organization and fluency in written and spoken English is a must."

(A) [1]   **(B) [2]**   (C) [3]   (D) [4]

解說 由「With employees from all over the world, the FOE is a linguistically diverse community.」，可以得知此團體使用多種語言。再看到題目句：「However, English is the working language of the organization」，表示此團體的共通語言為英語。本句剛好與前述句子的概念相反，因此可以使用 However 連接兩個句子。

另外，題目句後半的 fluency in written and spoken English is a must 表示必要條件（a must）為精通英文，緊接在後方的 Applicants must also possess a degree in environmental science . . . 中的 also，可知為補充說明應徵的條件。綜合上述，題目句最適合填入的位置為 [2]，故答案為 (B)。

突破解題障礙SOLUTION

01 多次閱讀仍無法選出適當的插入段落

破解此題型要採用速讀技巧（skimming）。請先找出主題句，推敲（guessing）文章的主要內容，並快速檢視文章的起承轉合。經由速讀的過程確認文章的架構後，再依照上下文邏輯順序（logical sequence）找出**前後語意轉折**、**突然轉換主題**或**未完成的段落**，即可在此段落的空格中插入題目句。

02 總是選錯選項

閱讀文章時，請特別留意句子之間的**轉承語**（discourse marker）。轉承語包含連接詞、連接副詞、代名詞、指示代名詞等用語。此類用語在句子和句子間作為連接或轉折的角色，使得文章以主題句為中心，順利延伸出後續的內容。只要擅用轉承語，就能輕鬆掌握句子之間的邏輯關係，例如因果關係、補充說明、語意轉折、突然轉換主題或未完成的段落。

PART 7 高分策略

→ **找出通訊軟體對話「說話者所隱含的意圖」**

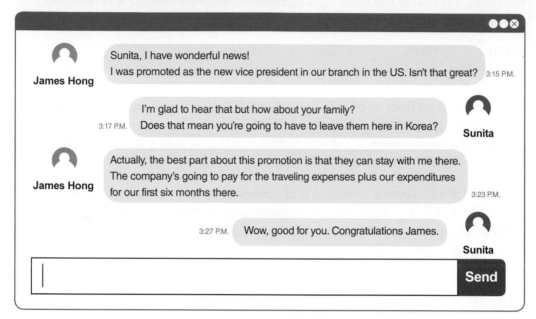

Q. At 3:27, why did Sunita write, "good for you"?

(A) James can work as a CEO in the US.

(B) James can bring his family with him abroad.

(C) The company pays for James' retirement plan.

(D) The company will pay for James' expenses until he retires.

解說 James 可以帶他的家人一同前往國外工作，公司還會提供最初六個月的補助金，令他感到十分開心。聽到此消息的 Sunita 向他祝賀，因此答案為 (B)。

突破解題障礙SOLUTION

01 難以找出隱含的意圖

先刪除選項中不會出現該段對話的相關用詞，再從選項中選出最符合前後對話脈絡的內容。

02 難以找出對話主旨

請注意每段對話開頭的稱呼語（I/we/you/here/there），掌握對話者之間的關係。
由對話者的相互關係可以看出對話內容的重點，進而得知對話的主旨。

→ **多篇閱讀**

The Nature Tour, in Costa Rica, is ideal for anyone who wants to explore the incomparable beauty of Costa Rica's rain forests.

Tour price includes:
- 1 Night hotel accommodations
- Round-trip in an air-conditioned bus between San José hotel and Nature Lodge
- All meals, entrance fees, and activities listed in the itinerary (except for rafting)

San José hotel stays not included in tour price

Itinerary	
Day 1	Transfer from San José to the Nature Lodge. Visit a volcano and natural hot spring along the way.
Day 2	Morning rafting on the Corobici River and then head to Playa Coco on the Pacific Coast.

To Nature Tour:

I saw the ad of your tour service in Costa Rica. I really enjoy rafting so I want to know what I should prepare for this activity in advance. I would like you to call me in person ASAP. I usually work during the daytime. Therefore, is it possible to contact me after 6 PM? I'm looking forward to your response.

Mark Pitt

Supervisor at National Fitness Center

Q. Where is Mark most likely preferred to experience?

(A) Corobici River　(B) Nature Lodge

(C) Pacific Coast　(D) San José

 本題要綜合第二篇行程表和第三篇文章的內容解題。Mark 在信中寫道：「I really enjoy rafting」，而柯羅比西河（Corobici River）的行程包含泛舟活動，因此答案為 (A)。

突破解題障礙SOLUTION

01 難以負荷三篇文章的閱讀分量

多篇閱讀的每篇文章都可以相互連結，因此可以視為一篇文章分割成三篇短文。
練習試題時，請勿忘記這個解題關鍵。先找出第一篇文章的主題句，並徹底掌握文章的脈絡，同時確認各篇章之間的關係。

02 無法整合分散至三篇文章的資訊

在多篇閱讀題型中，會將首篇文章的部分內容，進行補充說明、或是濃縮成重點精華，也可能將首篇文章中的內容轉換成數字或其他名稱，延伸出圖表、電子郵件、表單等第二、三篇文章。由於三篇文章都在闡述**相同的資訊**，通常會用**換句話說**（paraphrasing）的方式，傳達重複的資訊，所以考生不用緊張，只要找到整合三篇文章的共同重點，便能輕鬆找出答案。

Test

答對題數表

PART 5	
PART 6	
PART 7	
總題數	

01

READING TEST

In the Reading test, you will read a variety of texts and answer several different types of reading comprehension questions. The entire Reading test will last 75 minutes. There are three parts, and directions are given for each part. You are encouraged to answer as many questions as possible within the time allowed.

You must mark your answers on the separate answer sheet. Do not write your answers in your test book.

PART 5

Directions: A word or phrase is missing in each of the sentences below. Four answer choices are given below each sentence. Select the best answer to complete the sentence. Then mark the letter (A), (B), (C), or (D) on your answer sheet.

101. All of the new employees receive training packets that ------ details about their duties.
    (A) contains
    (B) to contain
    (C) contain
    (D) containing

102. ------ just two miles remaining in the race, Ms. Kaufman had a sizable advantage over the next runner.
    (A) With
    (B) Though
    (C) But
    (D) Added

103. Mr. Shaw is not able to participate in the committee convention in Shanghai, so Ms. Jeon will attend in ------ place.
    (A) him
    (B) he
    (C) his
    (D) himself

104. The executive director at All Day Department Store is ------ to any changes to the company logo.
    (A) eager
    (B) interfered
    (C) opposed
    (D) anxious

105. The conference center is on Brooklyn Street, ------ across from the new post office.
    (A) directs
    (B) direct
    (C) direction
    (D) directly

106. ------ the rise in steel prices, FTX Builders will most likely revise the bid for the Golden Bridge construction work.
    (A) Given
    (B) Provided
    (C) Namely
    (D) Regardless

107. The office complex ------ on the outskirts of the pedestrian shopping area.
    (A) will be built
    (B) built
    (C) are building
    (D) builder

108. In the past twenty years, clothing designers have become ------ aware of customer needs and preferences.
    (A) increasing
    (B) increased
    (C) increase
    (D) increasingly

109. ------- the last four months, Miracle Theater attendance has improved significantly.

(A) During
(B) Above
(C) Behind
(D) Into

110. Temporary workers from Adrian Recruitment Inc. have proven to be highly ------ employees.

(A) competent
(B) competence
(C) competency
(D) competently

111. Revenue from sale of outdoor furniture has been ------- higher than expected over the last six months.

(A) optionally
(B) considerably
(C) eagerly
(D) informatively

112. Please complete all items on the checklist ------ submitting your entry for the photography contest.

(A) as for
(B) mainly
(C) before
(D) so that

113. Many ------ farmers sell their produce at Pemberton Green Market.

(A) close
(B) around
(C) local
(D) near

114. Owing to predicted bad weather, tomorrow's outdoor concert has been ------- to next Saturday.

(A) postponed
(B) eliminated
(C) prolonged
(D) implemented

115. In order to ensure a timely response, please include your account number on all -------.

(A) are corresponding
(B) correspondence
(C) corresponds
(D) correspond

116. Lunch will be catered by Welco Café ------ Haqri Grill.

(A) but
(B) nor
(C) and
(D) yet

117. Timothy Darlton is highly qualified for the managerial role, ------ requires extensive experience.

(A) whoever
(B) who
(C) which
(D) whatever

118. We'd really appreciate your ------ in the Nathan Apartment Complex improvement survey.

(A) participant
(B) participation
(C) participate
(D) participated

119. Mr. Lopez will assist with the manuscript, so it is not necessary to do all the revisions by -------.

(A) yours
(B) yourself
(C) you
(D) your

120. Midora Manufacturing reserves the right to delay further deliveries ------ the customer has made all outstanding payments.

(A) until
(B) next
(C) then
(D) later

Go on to the next page

121. Blico Marketing Group ------ provides clients with updated information about its services.

(A) equally
(B) perfectly
(C) substantially
(D) regularly

122. Nortize Interiors has quickly gained a ------ for excellence among real estate agents in the city.

(A) pursuit
(B) reputation
(C) center
(D) design

123. The board members of Cistal Inc. ------ to make a hiring decision for the executive officer position by the end of next week.

(A) indicate
(B) allow
(C) assume
(D) expect

124. Please notify the training session instructor of your anticipated absences ------ different dates can be scheduled.

(A) ever since
(B) due to
(C) in spite of
(D) so that

125. Mr. Miller ------- that only the loan advisors should take part in the meeting on new trends in lending.

(A) specify
(B) to specify
(C) has specified
(D) is specified

126. Employees of Leading-Edge Machinery were amazed to receive an ------ bonus in July.

(A) inexperienced
(B) indefinite
(C) equipped
(D) unexpected

127. Ms. Diana must determine ------ or not to submit the proposal to the North American bureau.

(A) whether
(B) neither
(C) either
(D) unless

128. Staff members who have not ------ submitted their time sheets must do so by 5:00 P.M. today at the latest.

(A) only
(B) earlier
(C) yet
(D) rather

129. At last month's company banquet, 11 workers were ------ for having served the company for 25 years.

(A) recognized
(B) advocated
(C) resumed
(D) administered

130. Because of its ------ to major tourist attractions, Casey Hotel in Singapore is frequently fully booked.

(A) proximity
(B) exclusion
(C) efficiency
(D) availability

PART 6

Directions: Read the texts that follow. A word, phrase, or sentence is missing in parts of each text. Four answer choices for each question are given below the text. Select the best answer to complete the text. Then mark the letter (A), (B), (C), or (D) on your answer sheet.

Questions 131-134 refer to the following press release.

Charles Burrow, founder and president of Burrow's, Crosstown's largest clothing retailer,

announced that he ------- $4,000 to the city's new community center. The funds derive from the
131.

sale of tickets to a party held last night at his company's -------. Mr. Burrow will present a check
132.

to the center tomorrow at its opening ceremony.

------- the past thirty years, Mr. Burrow has organized several fundraising events for charitable
133.

institutions and community services. -------.
134.

131. (A) will donate
(B) donated
(C) might donate
(D) donating

132. (A) museum
(B) hotel
(C) residence
(D) store

133. (A) Despite
(B) Over
(C) Between
(D) Beneath

134. (A) The opening ceremony will begin at 10:00 A.M.
(B) The community center offers classes for adults and children.
(C) Last night's event was the most successful thus far.
(D) Mr. Burrow plans to open a new location in London next year.

Go on to the next page

Questions 135-138 refer to the following article.

August 30 — After two years of construction, the largest hotel in Pittsburgh history is almost

ready to open. The Rivertop Hotel, on the banks of the Allegherry River, will have 1,500 rooms

for visitors. -------. The first guests will arrive on September 12 as part of a medical technology
       135.

conference. The project is among four downtown area hotels -------. According to Kristofer
            136.

Walsh, president of the Pittsburgh Hotel & Lodging Association, these new developments are

a -------. "We've had a massive influx of visitors over the past few years," said Mr. Walsh. -------,
 137.   **138.**

almost all the hotels in the city are completely full. Clearly, additional hotel rooms are needed.

135. (A) It is unclear when it will be ready to accept reservations.
(B) Building renovations will begin next month.
(C) It will also have seven meeting rooms for groups of up to 200 people.
(D) There are multiple companies bidding on the project.

136. (A) to construct
(B) are constructing
(C) were constructed
(D) being constructed

137. (A) necessity
(B) nuisance
(C) risk
(D) bargain

138. (A) On the other hand
(B) In other words
(C) In the first place
(D) As a result

Questions 139-142 refer to the following e-mail.

To: Seth Ortega <sortega@xeroxmail.net>

From: Jake Morris <jmorris@fubmanufacturing.com>

Date: May 21

Subject: Factory Manager Position

Dear Mr. Ortega,

You are officially invited to a second interview. This time, I will be meeting only with the top

candidates to determine who is most ------- for the manager position. I believe you possess
139.

many of the ------- we are looking for.
140.

I trust that you remain interested in this job opportunity. -------, would a 3:00 P.M. appointment
141.

next Tuesday work for you? Please prepare a proposal that explains how you would increase

production at our plant without decreasing quality. -------.
142.

Jake Morris

139. (A) suiting
(B) suitable
(C) suit
(D) suits

140. (A) agreements
(B) performances
(C) qualities
(D) promotions

141. (A) Despite that
(B) If so
(C) However
(D) For example

142. (A) I would be happy to write a job reference for you.
(B) My assistant will train you in your new duties.
(C) I look forward to hearing your vision for an efficient workplace.
(D) Your new product ideas were especially informative.

Questions 143-146 refer to the following article.

August 3

By Chris Garneau

The Noxville Transportation Committee (NTC) will hold a public meeting at City Hall on

Tuesday, August 10, at 6 P.M., to discuss its proposal to extend light rail service to Noxville

Industrial Park.

-------. Residents of the community have complained that the extension will cause too much
143.

noise during the rush hours. -------, the NTC has been researching the possibility of installing
144.

noise barriers along the tracks. At the meeting, Alex Khan, Chief Executive Officer of Typhoon

Builders, will explain how much noise reduction the NTC can ------- getting with the barriers.
145.

A ------- by Mayor Charlie Hoffman will follow.
146.

143. (A) The NTC finished the project ahead of schedule.
(B) The rail line will run through a residential area.
(C) The committee chairman will run for mayor election next year.
(D) The NTC has decided to hold monthly meetings.

144. (A) In addition
(B) In time for
(C) In response
(D) In conclusion

145. (A) remind
(B) accept
(C) persuade
(D) anticipate

146. (A) to present
(B) presenter
(C) presenting
(D) presentation

PART 7

Directions: In this part you will read a selection of texts, such as magazine and newspaper articles, e-mails, and instant messages. Each text or set of texts is followed by several questions. Select the best answer for each question and mark the letter (A), (B), (C), or (D) on your answer sheet.

Questions 147-148 refer to the following letter.

We are aggressively looking for a receptionist for a local law firm in Crimson Shore. Duties include connecting calls, welcoming clients, answering telephones, handling meeting schedules, and sending out the daily e-mail. The qualified applicant should have an outgoing personality and be proficient in document preparation software. A university degree is required. Pay begins at $100 a week. Send your résumé to danielhickman@fairlaw.com.

147. What job is most likely available?
(A) Teller
(B) Lawyer
(D) Supervisor
(D) Assistant

148. What type of qualification is NOT included as a requirement for the job?
(A) Accounting
(B) Word processing
(C) Client service
(D) University degree

Go on to the next page

Questions 149-150 refer to the following text message chain.

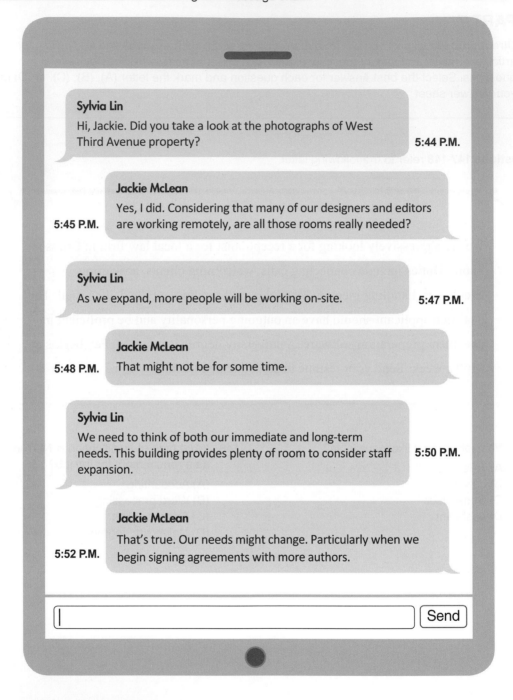

Sylvia Lin

Hi, Jackie. Did you take a look at the photographs of West Third Avenue property?

5:44 P.M.

Jackie McLean

5:45 P.M.

Yes, I did. Considering that many of our designers and editors are working remotely, are all those rooms really needed?

Sylvia Lin

As we expand, more people will be working on-site.

5:47 P.M.

Jackie McLean

5:48 P.M.

That might not be for some time.

Sylvia Lin

We need to think of both our immediate and long-term needs. This building provides plenty of room to consider staff expansion.

5:50 P.M.

Jackie McLean

5:52 P.M.

That's true. Our needs might change. Particularly when we begin signing agreements with more authors.

Send

149. What kind of business do the people probably work for?

(A) A relocation company
(B) A publishing company
(C) A property agency
(D) An exterior design company

150. At 5:52 P.M., what does Ms. McLean most likely mean when she writes, "That's true."?

(A) A different place should be rented.
(B) A new place will be too expensive.
(C) The property may meet the company's needs in the future.
(D) The property needs overall improvements.

Questions 151-153 refer to the following memo.

To: All staff members
From: Dwight Howard, Director of Operations
Date: June 5
Subject: East Wing Closure

This is to inform you that the east wing of the main office building will be temporarily closed at the end of next week. The maintenance staff will be replacing all ceiling lights in the offices and meeting rooms with high-quality fluorescent lights. Safety regulations stipulate that no staff members be allowed in the area while the work is in progress. The work is due to begin Friday, on June 9, and be finished on Saturday, June 10. The affected offices are 200–262. Staff members in these offices should plan to finish assignments at home or, if necessary, use a temporary work area in another section of the building. To reserve a temporary work area, you may contact Administrative Assistant Michael Kane at extension 242. Please note that temporary work areas are limited and requests must be submitted by 5:00 P.M. on June 7 at the latest.

151. What does the memo mainly report?

(A) Staff members are being relocated to new offices.
(B) Meeting space is being added.
(C) A safety inspection is being conducted.
(D) Office lighting is being upgraded.

152. When will the closure begin?

(A) On June 5
(B) On June 7
(C) On June 9
(D) On June 10

153. What are some staff members asked to do?

(A) Call a manager
(B) Work from home
(C) Vacate the offices
(D) Complete work ahead of time

Go on to the next page

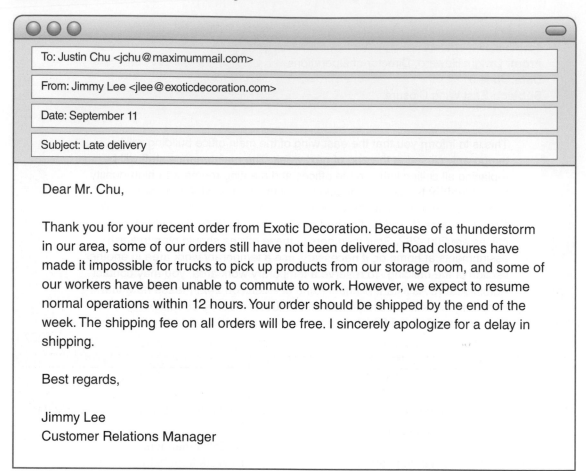

To: Justin Chu <jchu@maximummail.com>

From: Jimmy Lee <jlee@exoticdecoration.com>

Date: September 11

Subject: Late delivery

Dear Mr. Chu,

Thank you for your recent order from Exotic Decoration. Because of a thunderstorm in our area, some of our orders still have not been delivered. Road closures have made it impossible for trucks to pick up products from our storage room, and some of our workers have been unable to commute to work. However, we expect to resume normal operations within 12 hours. Your order should be shipped by the end of the week. The shipping fee on all orders will be free. I sincerely apologize for a delay in shipping.

Best regards,

Jimmy Lee
Customer Relations Manager

154. Why was the order late?

(A) Payment has still not been received.
(B) Severe weather affected the delivery schedule.
(C) The product that was ordered is not in stock.
(D) The firm used an inaccurate mailing address.

155. What will Mr. Chu receive?

(A) A discount coupon for his next purchase
(B) A cash refund
(C) Complimentary shipping on his order
(D) A replacement part

Questions 156-158 refer to the following e-mail.

From:	Tim Daily <tdaily@sunflower.com>
To:	Derek Hamilton <lhamilton@goodcaterer.com>
Date:	June 12
Subject:	Re: Floral centerpieces

Dear Mr. Hamilton,

This e-mail serves as confirmation of our telephone conversation this morning about your request for 12 flower arrangements for your company awards ceremony. You had asked that they be comparable to the floral centerpieces that we made for your last event. However, my supplier for the rose of Sharon has notified me that, due to a delay at the greenhouses, they won't be available until the end of this month.

Because you need the flower arrangements finished by June 17, I think it would be best to select an alternative flower. I recommend the hollyhock, which is comparable in appearance. Please let me know if this is acceptable by replying to this e-mail. I will then fax you the finished agreement and pricing list. If you have any other questions, please contact me at 432-234-2345.

Thank you,

Tim Daily
Manager, Sunflower

156. What is suggested about Mr. Hamilton?

(A) He is a friend of Mr. Daily.
(B) He is preparing a private party at his house.
(C) He has asked for a change to his order.
(D) He has used Sunflower's services previously.

157. Why does Mr. Daily recommend replacing the rose of Sharon?

(A) They are out of stock.
(B) They are the wrong size.
(C) They are not cheap.
(D) They are not fresh.

158. What does Mr. Daily ask Mr. Hamilton to do?

(A) Sign a contract
(B) Talk at the shop
(C) Respond to an e-mail
(D) Send a partial payment

Go on to the next page

The Museum of Fine Arts

The Museum of Fine Arts will host Ed Harrison on Wednesday, April 5, at 6:00 P.M. Mr. Harrison will talk about his most recent book, *The American Dream's Painting*. Published by Neo Publishing, the volume provides a detailed description of the history of art in North America. The talk is open to the public. No reservation will be taken. Guests must arrive at least half an hour before the start time because seats are limited to 100. For additional information, call 287-333-2422 or go to our website.

159. Who is Mr. Harrison?

(A) An author
(B) An artist
(C) A bookstore supervisor
(D) A museum staff member

160. How should seats for the event be obtained?

(A) Online
(B) By telephone
(C) By mail
(D) In person

Question 161-164 refer to the following article.

Expansion Project Moving Forward in Shanghai

July 5 — Roland Technology finished the first stage of its expansion project two weeks ago. Roland Technology, one of the largest manufacturers of components used in computer monitors and projectors, began construction on its three new factories to be built over the next eight years. —[1]—. The first of the factories to be built, in China's Shanghai, is the company's largest factory and will ultimately produce 60% of the company's production quota every year.

The new plant has brought with it a rise in jobs for local citizens. —[2]—. Over 1,500 construction workers were employed to build the large-scale factory and its surrounding structures. Roland Technology President Dakashi Miyuki said, "This is the largest project for our company. When we began construction, we realized that it was going to need plenty of money, resources, and staff. —[3]—. We employed locals to expand the physical plant as well as adding a number of employees to our full-time payroll. We hope to do the same thing in Japan. We plan to start building in Tokyo soon." The company's main office is now located in Tokyo, Japan.

Extra factories will be constructed in Roland Technology's other locations, including in Thailand and Korea. While the remaining plants will not be as large as the Shanghai factory, they will still need resources and labor. —[4]—.

161. What is mentioned about Roland Technology?

(A) It produces monitor elements.
(B) It was recently acquired by its competitor.
(C) It is remodeling its company headquarters.
(D) It sells construction materials.

162. What is inferred about the Roland Technology factory in Shanghai?

(A) It was the third new factory which was built last year.
(B) It is the biggest factory the company has.
(C) It manufactures a quarter of the company's output.
(D) It took over six years to construct.

163. Where will the next Roland Technology factory be constructed?

(A) In China
(B) In Thailand
(C) In Korea
(D) In Japan

164. In which of the positions marked [1], [2], [3] and [4] does the following sentence best belong?

"We were delighted to see the influence the project had on local laborers."

(A) [1]
(B) [2]
(C) [3]
(D) [4]

Go on to the next page

Questions 165-167 refer to the following article.

Situated on the corner of First Avenue and East Street, Variety opened a decade ago and rapidly became a popular eatery. As its name suggests, Variety features a large collection of dishes prepared with several international recipes. Variety had been closed for two months while undergoing an improvement in management. It reopened its doors two weeks ago. The new chef, Matt Shelian, has made a remarkable menu with an even wider selection of gourmet soups, salads, and delicious entrées. Some of his specialties include excellent seafood dishes, such as the smoked halibut with mango and the shrimp with chili sauce. Please be sure to try the outstanding dessert—caramel-apple pie. With so many delicious items to select, Variety is certain to be a new favorite.

165. What is the purpose of the article?

(A) To review a restaurant
(B) To promote a cooking class
(C) To compare two restaurants
(D) To announce a new location

166. What is mentioned about Mr. Shelian?

(A) He is proficient in making seafood dishes.
(B) He uses only local produce.
(C) He has refurbished a restaurant.
(D) He started working at Variety six months ago.

167. What is suggested about the restaurant?

(A) Its management replaced most of the staff.
(B) It serves an excellent dessert.
(C) Its most popular dish is the halibut.
(D) It has relocated to a new building.

Questions 168-171 refer to the following e-mail.

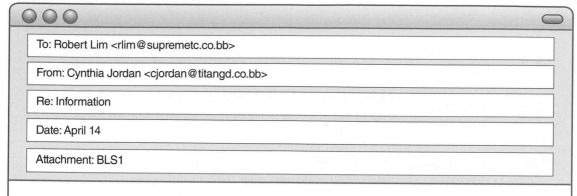

To: Robert Lim <rlim@supremetc.co.bb>

From: Cynthia Jordan <cjordan@titangd.co.bb>

Re: Information

Date: April 14

Attachment: BLS1

Dear Mr. Lim:

I am following up on the Titan Gardening service proposal I sent on 22 March. —[1]—.

We are one of the best in Queensville, and we want to add you to our list of satisfied clients. Our clients include numerous local businesses like hotels, restaurants, and resorts. —[2]—. In the event you overlooked the original proposal, I am attaching it again here.

The proposal is based on the service you asked about, namely the maintenance of the grounds around Supreme Tennis Courts twice a week. —[3]—. If you are interested in more extensive work, such as replacing trees, extra charges would apply.

I'm looking forward to hearing from you. I hope our company will have the chance to be beneficial to you in the future. —[4]—.

Sincerely,

Cynthia Jordan

168. Why was the e-mail written?

(A) To schedule a meeting
(B) To explain new prices
(C) To resend a previous estimate
(D) To send in a corrected proposal

169. What is suggested in the e-mail?

(A) Mr. Lim is a satisfied customer.
(B) Titan Gardening is a new business.
(C) Ms. Jordan had a meeting with Mr. Lim.
(D) Mr. Lim asked Ms. Jordan for some information.

170. What type of business does Mr. Lim probably work for?

(A) A hotel
(B) A tennis facility
(C) A restaurant
(D) A gardening center

171. In which of the positions marked [1], [2], [3] and [4] does the following sentence best belong?

"Additionally, we would reevaluate your requirements on an ongoing basis and relay recommendations to you twice a month."

(A) [1]
(B) [2]
(C) [3]
(D) [4]

Go on to the next page

Questions 172-175 refer to the following online chat discussion.

🔵⬜❌		

	Tyrone Gibson [1:32 P.M.]	Thank you for participating in the virtual sales meeting this morning. Do you have any other questions?
	Judy Chung [1:35 P.M.]	George and I are not certain about how the new sales territory maps influence established customers. Will the new territories apply exclusively to new customers?
	Tyrone Gibson [1:37 P.M.]	Of course not. The new territories apply to first-time and established customers alike.
	Judy Chung [1:38 P.M.]	So, does that mean I will no longer obtain commissions from my French customer, YDV Mechanism?
	Tyrone Gibson [1:39 P.M.]	That's right. All established customers in northern France go to George.
	George Kim [1:41 P.M.]	But why don't I just allow Judy to keep YDV Mechanism?
	Tyrone Gibson [1:42 P.M.]	YDV Mechanism is a big customer.
	George Kim [1:44 P.M.]	Yes, but I want to avoid disrupting a productive partnership. Plus, this customer is unimportant to me.
	Tyrone Gibson [1:45 P.M.]	I don't see it as disrupting, really. However, if you feel strongly about this, George, I might be able to bend the rules if our president approves of it.
	Judy Chung [1:47 P.M.]	Why don't I speak to the customer?
	Tyrone Gibson [1:48 P.M.]	I don't think that's suitable.
	Judy Chung [1:49 P.M.]	Understood.
	George Kim [1:49 P.M.]	All right. We're looking forward to hearing back from you about this matter.

Send

172. Who most likely is Mr. Gibson?

(A) A president
(B) The head of sales
(C) A tour guide
(D) A personnel director

173. What is inferred about Ms. Chung?

(A) She has a good rapport with YDV Mechanism.
(B) She is being relocated to an office in France.
(C) She is delighted with the new territory assigned to her.
(D) She did not take part in the sales meeting.

174. At 1:48 P.M., what does Mr. Gibson most likely mean when he writes, "I don't think that's suitable."?

(A) He is doubtful that Ms. Chung can meet YDV Mechanism's requirements.
(B) He thinks Ms. Chung has misunderstood.
(C) He would like Ms. Chung to visit France.
(D) He doesn't want Ms. Chung to contact YDV Mechanism regarding this matter.

175. What will probably happen next?

(A) Ms. Chung will go over the new map of the sales territory.
(B) Ms. Chung will speak with her customer.
(C) Mr. Gibson will call the company's president.
(D) Mr. Kim will accept a job offer from YDV Mechanism.

Go on to the next page

From: Mary Cho <mcho@dtu.com>

To: Peter O'Malley <pomalley@dtu.com>

Date: June 3

Subject: Worldwide Design Conference

Dear Peter,

Thank you for volunteering to fill in for me at the Worldwide Design Conference in Boston on June 10. I need to stay at the San Francisco main office to meet with some visiting French clients. When I was there last year, I found it extremely worthwhile and was able to make some business contacts with prospective designers.

I've already handled your airplane ticket, hotel, and rental car. These have already been paid for by DTU, and you'll receive $50 a day for meals after you return here. If you decide to take some designers out for dinner, please retain receipts for your records and hand them in to the Accounting Department after you come back for reimbursement.

The timeline for the conference is as follows:

Monday	10 A.M. – 12 P.M. Innovative Graphics
	12 P.M. – 2 P.M. Web Design World and Luncheon
	3 P.M. – 5 P.M. Gigantic Logos 4D
Tuesday	The entire day is scheduled for the design exposition

Best regards,

Mary

From: Peter O'Malley <pomalley@dtu.com>

To: Mary Cho <mcho@dtu.com>

Date: June 10

Subject: RE: Worldwide Design Conference

Dear Mary,

I came back from the conference earlier this afternoon. The Monday morning presentation was canceled because the speaker's flight had been delayed. However, the other presentations went smoothly. I heard and experienced many things and will finish a report in two weeks. I really appreciate your giving me the opportunity to represent DTU's advertising department at the conference.

Sincerely,

Peter

176. Why did Ms. Cho write an e-mail to Mr. O'Malley?

(A) To show her gratitude for his suggestion
(B) To give him some information about a business meeting
(C) To check his conference reservation
(D) To issue him a refund

177. What does Ms. Cho indicate about the conference?

(A) It is renowned for presentations by leading business owners.
(B) It took place in San Francisco last year for the first time.
(C) It offers opportunities to meet business acquaintances.
(D) It is the best location to meet French businessmen.

178. What expenditure will DTU NOT pay for beforehand?

(A) Food expenses
(B) Hotel charges
(C) Airfare
(D) A car rental charge

179. What presentation was called off at the conference?

(A) Innovative Graphics
(B) Web Design World
(C) Gigantic Logo 4D
(D) Design Exposition

180. What department does Mr. O'Malley most likely work for?

(A) Sales
(B) Advertising
(C) Personnel
(D) Accounting

Go on to the next page

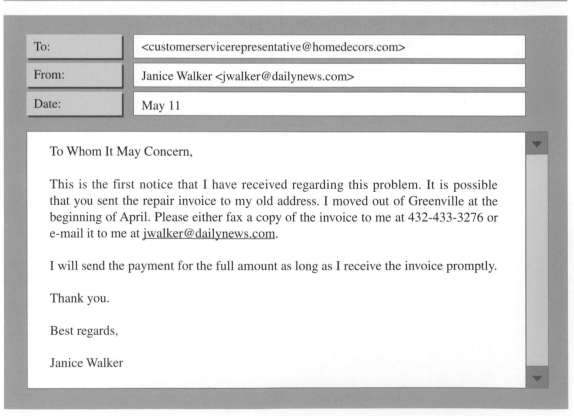

To:	Janice Walker <jwalker@dailynews.com>
From:	Rachel Hunter <rhunter@homedecors.com>
Date:	May 10

Dear Ms. Walker,

According to our database, your account is overdue at the moment. You have a balance of $735.40 for the work done at your residence. Five workers were at your home to fix the hole in the roof on March 13. An invoice was sent out to you on April 5 and was to be paid by April 23. There is a late fee of $50, but if full payment is made promptly, this late fee will be waived. If you have already submitted payment, contact our main office as soon as possible. Would you please send all correspondence to me because I am monitoring your account?

Thank you.

Sincerely,

Rachel Hunter
Account Manager, Home Decors

To:	<customerservicerepresentative@homedecors.com>
From:	Janice Walker <jwalker@dailynews.com>
Date:	May 11

To Whom It May Concern,

This is the first notice that I have received regarding this problem. It is possible that you sent the repair invoice to my old address. I moved out of Greenville at the beginning of April. Please either fax a copy of the invoice to me at 432-433-3276 or e-mail it to me at jwalker@dailynews.com.

I will send the payment for the full amount as long as I receive the invoice promptly.

Thank you.

Best regards,

Janice Walker

181. Why did Ms. Hunter send an e-mail to Ms. Walker?

    (A) To notify her of mistakes in an invoice
    (B) To ask for an overdue payment
    (C) To apologize for an unsatisfactory job
    (D) To charge a late fee

182. What does Ms. Hunter ask Ms. Walker to do?

    (A) Copy a billing statement
    (B) Meet the deadline
    (C) Check her account
    (D) Pay for the invoice in full

183. What does Ms. Walker request that customer service do?

    (A) Send a document of her fees by fax
    (B) Deposit the payment
    (C) Check her current address
    (D) Call her right now

184. What is inferred about Ms. Walker?

    (A) She built a new house.
    (B) She recently relocated to a new home.
    (C) She lost her billing statement.
    (D) She went on a business trip in April.

185. What detail did Ms. Walker NOT include in her e-mail?

    (A) The former residence
    (B) The e-mail address
    (C) The name of the account manager
    (D) The fax number

From: <jasonkang@resisdente.com>

To: <bills@planpower.com>

Date: June 17

Subject: Invoice A893-06

To Whom It May Concern,

Hello, I am writing about my electricity bill for May. The amount due was much higher than I have paid in previous months, which is normally $350. I do not plan on missing the deadline for the payment, but I would like to know why the substantial increase in my bill occurred. If the change is incorrect, I would appreciate an adjustment to my account. I know that my meter is nearly obsolete, so I also wonder if it should be replaced with a new one.

If a technician needs to check it, the best time would be before noon on any weekday. I am at home then and would prefer to be present, if possible, while the work is being done.

With my best regards,

Jason Kang

Service Technician Log Sheet — New Year Residences
June 30

Technician name	Address of service	Start time	Service
Paula Morreja	2249 Keystone Blvd.	10:52 A.M.	Meter repaired
Gini Padovani	2809 Redhill Rd.	12:38 P.M.	Meter replaced
Barak Hilton	76 Ellington Ave.	1:40 P.M.	Meter replaced
Brad Hopkins	8100 Saint Rd.	3:52 P.M.	Meter inspected

From:	<bills@planpower.com>
To:	<jasonkang@resisdente.com>
Date:	June 30
Subject:	invoice A893-06

Dear Mr. Kang,

Thank you for contacting Plan Power. I am writing to let you know that the sudden increase in your bill was caused by a faulty meter. The technician who visited your Redhill residence found out that the old device had registered your use of electricity incorrectly.

The device has been replaced, and this type of problem should not take place again. The malfunction affects your bill for May only; the total amount of $127.18 will appear on your next bill. Should you have any questions, please feel free to contact us.

Sincerely,

Mark Dillon
Plan Power Customer Support

---

186. Why was the first e-mail sent?

(A) To change a deadline extension
(B) To ask for a receipt
(C) To inquire about the amount
(D) To sign up for online billing

187. What is suggested about Mr. Kang?

(A) He correctly identified the problem.
(B) He recently moved to a new place.
(C) He has contacted Mr. Dillon several times.
(D) He plans to close his account with Plan Power.

188. Who visited Mr. Kang's house on June 30?

(A) Paula Morreja
(B) Gini Padovani
(C) Barak Hilton
(D) Brad Hopkins

189. In the second e-mail, the word "registered" in paragraph 1, line 3, is closest in meaning to

(A) attended
(B) permitted
(C) recorded
(D) allowed

190. What does Mr. Dillon indicate in his e-mail?

(A) That the payment is already overdue
(B) That the problem was limited to only one month
(C) That the new service is being provided
(D) That the new meter was ordered

Go on to the next page

Melody Academy of Music
32 Saint Street, Seattle, WA 98105
www.melody-music.ac

Melody Academy of Music is delighted to announce its next season of performances — from classical music to jazz, hip hop, and pop.

Please join us to see all that we have to offer! You can buy all kinds of tickets for the entire season or for an individual performance. Tickets can be purchased at half of the original price for Season Ticket buyers.

※ The Mozart Group gives an impressive jazz performance. 18 – 22 March
※ Eugene Ryu performs his award-winning pop songs. One day only — 7 April
※ The Seattle Ensemble plays classical music. 15 – 22 April
※ Catherine Winslet sings while accomplished by live guitar. 23 – 27 April

---

To: Jane Austin
From: Tylor Yun
Cc: Samuel David
Subject: Your visit to KG Electronics
Date: 29 March

Hi Ms. Austin,

On behalf of the personnel department at KG Electronics, I'd like to let you know how happy we are to adopt the personnel management software you will be teaching us about on 21–23 April. As you requested, I reserved the room and necessary devises such as a desktop computer, projector, and microphone. If you need any further assistance with your presentation, do not hesitate to let me know.

As a token of appreciation, Mr. David, our department head, has made special plans to make your visit more memorable. He made a dinner reservation at a very famous Italian restaurant on the first evening of your visit. On the second day of your visit, we will be able to go to see an outstanding performance at the Melody Academy of Music.

Sincerely,

Tylor Yun
KG Electronics

Tylor Yun's phone

From: Samuel David
Received: 8:45 A.M.

Hi, I just got words from Ms. Austin. Her original flight has been delayed. Therefore, her new arrival time has been changed. However, we're going to still be able to hold the meeting today. She requested that the entertainment be moved to tomorrow, so there is no rush now. If I order the tickets myself rather than have you do it, we can receive a considerable discount. Could you postpone the dinner reservation? If that is not possible, please cancel it. I apologize for the inconvenience this may cause.

191. What is suggested about Melody Academy of Music?

(A) It has an on-site museum.
(B) It is employing a new conductor.
(C) It offers music lessons to young children.
(D) It offers different styles of music performances.

192. How much discount will Season Ticket buyers get?

(A) 20%
(B) 30%
(C) 40%
(D) 50%

193. What is Ms. Austin scheduled to do during her visit?

(A) Revise legal documents
(B) Demonstrate how to use some software
(C) Repair presentation equipment
(D) Conduct a survey

194. What performance was Ms. Austin originally scheduled to attend?

(A) The Mozart Group
(B) Eugene Ryu
(C) The Seattle Ensemble
(D) Catherine Winslet

195. What is Mr. Yun asked to do?

(A) Make a flight reservation
(B) Set a meeting time
(C) Train new employees
(D) Call off a meal reservation

Go on to the next page

Questions 196-200 refer to the following advertisement, online form, and review.

OHQ Containers
Mobile Refrigerated Storage Units

OHQ Containers provides refrigerated storage units to restaurants, cafés, grocery stores, and other businesses that are currently looking for cold-storage solutions.

All the units below include :
1. Lockable door latches, non-slip flooring, and interior fluorescent light fixtures
2. A 20-metre power cable

Service for your business :
Our delivery service is available to any location in Scotland.
All the units are available for short-term, monthly, or annual lease.

Our storage options are:

Unit	Door Type	Length (metres)	Floor Space (square metres)	Internal Capacity (cubic metres)
Economy	Single	3.0m	7.5m²	18.75m³
Standard	Double	6.0m	15.0m²	37.5m³
Supreme	Double	9.0m	22.5m²	56.25m³
Supreme Plus	Plus Double	12.0m	30.0m²	75.0m³

Should you need any help with making a decision, our outstanding customer service representatives will recommend the ideal storage solution for you. For further information, please visit http://www.OHQ.com.

http://www.OHQ.com/inquiry

OHQ Containers—Customer Inquiry Form

Name: Aiden Park
Business: Park's café
E-mail: <parkscafé@plantomorrow.com>
Date: Oct. 14

Hello, I was told about your company from my friend, Bill Folder, who is currently using one of your units for his own business. I am also the owner of a restaurant, and our freezer can no longer accommodate our food storage needs. Thus, we require an OHQ unit that can be placed near the back entrance of the building. We don't need a lot of extra storage space, but we do need a unit with double doors so we can easily load everything in and out. Please tell me which unit you recommend and also the possible date of delivery. Also, I was wondering if your units are equipped with a digital temperature display. We need to be able to closely monitor the temperature at all times.

Thank you.

Customer Review

I have been using OHQ Containers for about four months now, and I am fully contented with my choice. And I was pleased to have my first month's rental fee waived thanks to OHQ's refer-a-friend program, which allowed my friend and me to receive a free month's rental each. I started with a smaller 37.5 cubic-metre storage unit, but it became clear this month that I would need something one size bigger to serve the increasing guests. The day after I called OHQ, a company representative delivered a new unit that meets my needs perfectly. I highly recommend OHQ Containers to everyone that is in need of efficient cold storage for their business.

Aiden Park, Owner, Park's Café

196. What information about OHQ Containers is NOT given in the advertisement?

(A) The total number of doors
(B) The type of lighting
(C) The range of temperature settings
(D) The size of the interior space

197. What is indicated about Mr. Park?

(A) He used to be a coworker of Mr. Folder.
(B) He supports the local community.
(C) He plans to switch to a new delivery company.
(D) He got a discount from OHQ Containers.

198. What is suggested about Park's Café?

(A) It features organic produce.
(B) It is located near OHQ Containers.
(C) It plans to extend its business hours.
(D) Its business continues to grow.

199. Which unit is Mr. Park currently using?

(A) Economy
(B) Standard
(C) Supreme
(D) Supreme Plus

200. In the review, the word "contented" in line 1, is closest in meaning to

(A) pleased
(B) angry
(C) dismayed
(D) astonished

Test

答對題數表

PART 5	
PART 6	
PART 7	
總題數	

02

READING TEST

In the Reading test, you will read a variety of texts and answer several different types of reading comprehension questions. The entire Reading test will last 75 minutes. There are three parts, and directions are given for each part. You are encouraged to answer as many questions as possible within the time allowed.

You must mark your answers on the separate answer sheet. Do not write your answers in your test book.

PART 5

Directions: A word or phrase is missing in each of the sentences below. Four answer choices are given below each sentence. Select the best answer to complete the sentence. Then mark the letter (A), (B), (C), or (D) on your answer sheet.

101. Salespeople at Cedarville Grocery Store receive extra pay when ------ work extended hours.

(A) they
(B) their
(C) them
(D) theirs

102. Ms. Juntasa has been ------ recommended by her former employers.

(A) high
(B) highly
(C) higher
(D) highest

103. The use of high-quality but ------ mechanical components resulted in a decline in costs for Mr. David's factory.

(A) unhappy
(B) incomplete
(C) unaware
(D) inexpensive

104. The publishing conference has been rescheduled ------ tomorrow due to the worsening weather conditions.

(A) in
(B) by
(C) for
(D) out

105. Alpha Tech's most recent software makes it ------ than ever for publishers to create newspapers.

(A) easy
(B) ease
(C) easily
(D) easier

106. A limited ------ of time for questions will be provided subsequent to Mr. Yamaguchi's talk.

(A) amount
(B) number
(C) value
(D) record

107. Customers ------ purchase merchandise from Easy-To-Go.com typically receive their orders within three business days.

(A) whomever
(B) whom
(C) whose
(D) who

108. The ------ of this training session is to provide business owners with the tools to make informed decisions.

(A) guide
(B) experience
(C) objective
(D) solution

109. Ms. Lee is ------ responsible for supervising quality assurance procedures at the Hawksdale facility.
(A) primarily
(B) nearly
(C) slowly
(D) previously

110. ------- for the Valleywood Photography Contest must be received by May 25.
(A) Being entered
(B) Entries
(C) Enters
(D) Entered

111. Riley Textile Corporation reported a 10 percent rise ------ profits last year.
(A) off
(B) at
(C) in
(D) up

112. Because of the decrease in the cost of materials, the price of Supreme Laboratory's cutting-edge microscope will be lower than -------.
(A) anticipated
(B) organized
(C) experimented
(D) inclined

113. Admission to the Maxwell Botanical Garden will be free every Thursday from 10 A.M. to 2 P.M. ------ the spring.
(A) beneath
(B) throughout
(C) without
(D) down

114. All staff members who ------- drilling equipment must wear safety goggles.
(A) operate
(B) operates
(C) operating
(D) is operated

115. A replacement key for your car may be ordered directly from our dealership, ------ you demonstrate proof of ownership.
(A) as though
(B) provided that
(C) regardless of
(D) instead of

116. We encouraged guests to leave ------- for improving the service at our airline.
(A) suggest
(B) suggested
(C) suggesting
(D) suggestions

117. An uncommonly large number of employees in the Accounting Department retired last year, leaving **13** positions -------.
(A) dedicated
(B) hollow
(C) invalid
(D) vacant

118. Kane's in Denversville is a full-service photography studio ------ in family portraits.
(A) specialist
(B) specially
(C) specialize
(D) specializing

119. Larkhill Health Center is always ------ to consider the certified specialists who are interested in joining our organization.
(A) possible
(B) willing
(C) necessary
(D) useful

120. Government ------ on the import of construction materials were temporarily lifted so as to meet increasing demand.
(A) authorities
(B) treatments
(C) restrictions
(D) supplies

Go on to the next page

121. Spring Deli's fruit and vegetable tray is popular now that it is appealing and ------ priced.
    (A) afford
    (B) afforded
    (C) affordable
    (D) affordably

122. Mr. Davidson volunteered to help at the reception desk ------ he has not ever worked directly with clients.
    (A) even though
    (B) or
    (C) until
    (D) so that

123. Smith's Plumbing has eight company-owned trucks, four of ------ are currently in the auto repair shop.
    (A) whose
    (B) other
    (C) whom
    (D) which

124. Hampton Accounting has ------ costs by restricting international travel and encouraging the use of online video conferencing.
    (A) reduced
    (B) stated
    (C) qualified
    (D) examined

125. Dawson Corporation announced in a press conference that it is planning to expand ------ Europe.
    (A) of
    (B) into
    (C) around
    (D) at

126. As ------ a month has passed since the products were sent, we should ask the delivery company for an update.
    (A) nearly
    (B) immediately
    (C) partially
    (D) thoroughly

127. Seeking new sources of revenue, many local orchards ------ catering to tourists in the past five years.
    (A) to begin
    (B) have begun
    (C) will have begun
    (D) will begin

128. Meteorologists forecast three ------- days of rain, which should provide a welcome relief from the unseasonable heat.
    (A) sensitive
    (B) refreshed
    (C) consecutive
    (D) deliberate

129. Caribbean Bay Hotel's kitchen is open 24 hours a day, making sure that you have the dining service you need ------ you desire it.
    (A) wherever
    (B) even if
    (C) whenever
    (D) in order that

130. Jacob Lee told his manager about the complaints from overseas clients, and she promised to ------ the problem.
    (A) look into
    (B) pick up
    (C) show up
    (D) turn off

PART 6

Directions: Read the texts that follow. A word, phrase, or sentence is missing in parts of each text. Four answer choices for each question are given below the text. Select the best answer to complete the text. Then mark the letter (A), (B), (C), or (D) on your answer sheet.

Questions 131-134 refer to the following information.

Hightech staff members who have been working full time for more than two years are -------
131.

to apply for internal transfers and job advancement opportunities within the firm. -------. Those
132.

interested will be considered together with external -------. Staff members who have essential
133.

qualifications to fill the open positions will be given ------- if outside recruitment isn't considered
134.

to be in the company's best interest.

131. (A) eligible
(B) collaborative
(C) exclusive
(D) prominent

132. (A) Staff members who wish to apply
should first meet with their managers.
(B) Actually, all staff members are
required to report their work hours
daily.
(C) For instance, a competitive benefit
package is given to full-time workers.
(D) We are delighted to welcome new
staff members to our Hightech team.

133. (A) factors
(B) candidates
(C) occupations
(D) suppliers

134. (A) preferring
(B) preferred
(C) preference
(D) prefer

Questions 135-138 refer to the following article.

The Michael Theater will be extending its run of Shining Stars, a play by Justine Kay.

Due to an unexpected rise in ------- for the tickets, the last performance will now occur on
                                 135.

March 18. The move comes as something of a surprise, considering the ------- reviews written
                                                         136.

by critics after the show's opening on February 2. -------. However, the show has abruptly
                                     137.

become popular among younger people, most of whom get their news through the Internet.

They are ------- interested in the play's exploration of economic issues and career choices.
     138.

---

135. (A) demanded
    (B) demanding
    (C) to demand
    (D) demand

136. (A) brilliant
    (B) deep
    (C) harsh
    (D) prompt

137. (A) Actors from the show are local
        residents.
    (B) The premiere was attended by local
        business leaders.
    (C) The initial box office sales had also
        been weak.
    (D) Moreover, the theater company has
        been around for several years.

138. (A) apparent
    (B) more apparent
    (C) apparentness
    (D) apparently

Questions 139-142 refer to the following notice.

On April 5, Emerson Radio will celebrate its twenty-fifth anniversary. That's a quarter

of a century of stimulating -------. Over the years, we ------- our listeners breaking news,
                               139.   **140.**

thought-provoking stories, and popular music throughout the world. Now, we encourage

you to celebrate with us during an open house from 7:00 P.M. to 9:00 P.M. on April 5 at our

Charles Avenue studio. Take a tour and see some of the behind-the-scenes magic. Watch a

demonstration of our digital audio equipment. -------. The open house is free, but registration is
                                              141.

required. We hope you can join us for this ------- event.
                                          142.

139. (A) concerts
     (B) development
     (C) programming
     (D) discussions

140. (A) offers
     (B) will offer
     (C) offering
     (D) have offered

141. (A) We hope to merge with another local
         radio station in the coming year.
     (B) You can also meet some of your
         favorite broadcasters.
     (C) This is the second event in our April
         schedule.
     (D) This station continues to be an
         essential part of your neighborhood.

142. (A) special
     (B) specialize
     (C) specially
     (D) specialization

Go on to the next page

To: David Kim <dkim@eleganthotel.com>

From: Albert Lee <alee@eleganthotel.com>

Date: 22 June

Subject: Good Afternoon

Dear David,

I was recently notified of your upcoming -------. Though the new position as general manager
                                              143.

in our New York location formally ------- on 1 August, I wanted to offer my best wishes to you
                                      144.

now.

The transition can be -------, so please don't hesitate to contact me if you need any assistance.
                         145.

Your performance as assistant general manager at the Elegant Hotel here in Singapore has

been outstanding. -------.
                   146.

Congratulations!

Sincerely,

Albert Lee

143. (A) promotion
(B) award
(C) event
(D) trip

144. (A) began
(B) begins
(C) could begin
(D) has begun

145. (A) challenging
(B) challenges
(C) challenge
(D) challenged

146. (A) The New York hotel is bigger and has additional amenities.
(B) I'm presently interviewing candidates for all the positions.
(C) In the meantime, inquire about staff member discounts at the hotel.
(D) I am confident that you will succeed in your new role.

PART 7

Directions: In this part you will read a selection of texts, such as magazine and newspaper articles, e-mails, and instant messages. Each text or set of texts is followed by several questions. Select the best answer for each question and mark the letter (A), (B), (C), or (D) on your answer sheet.

Questions 147-148 refer to the following text message.

From: Montera Hassan
To: Grace Kim

Grace, my smartphone battery is almost dead. I think I left my power cord at the office.
Would you please call my customer and tell him I'll be roughly 20 minutes late?
I'm heading back to the office to get the cord right now.

147. Why did Mr. Hassan send a message to Ms. Kim?
(A) To inquire whether she found his power cord
(B) To ask that she contact a customer
(C) To remind her to recharge a battery
(D) To check the location of an accounting division

148. What will Mr. Hassan probably do next?
(A) Find his computer
(B) Return to his office
(C) Purchase a power cord
(D) Contact the technical support department

Go on to the next page

Dayton Café owner, Brandon Ehret, has signed a lease for a second restaurant at 623 Smithon Avenue.

The building, close to Rolling Concert Hall, previously housed a branch of Carol Financial Group. Mr. Ehret's most recent venture, to be called Tiara Snacks, will begin service on August 1. At first, however, the small restaurant will be open only during the evening hours. The idea is to build a customer base, particularly among concertgoers, prior to adding a lunch service. Mr. Ehret's original restaurant, Dayton Café, is located on First Street, near the Winning Grocery Store bus stop. Executive Chef Jessica Choi will supervise the two locations.

149. What is the article about?

(A) The opening of a new restaurant
(B) An outstanding real estate agent
(C) A change in prices
(D) A restaurant's relocation

150. What is suggested about Tiara Snacks?

(A) It is situated adjacent to a public transportation route.
(B) It is expected to receive business from concert patrons.
(C) It is supposed to start serving lunch on August 1.
(D) It is Mr. Ehret's third restaurant.

Questions 151-153 refer to the following memo.

From: Alex Baldwin
To: Garrison Builders employees
Date: 15 June
Subject: All staff meeting

To all of the employees,

Next Monday, 29 June, we will have a guest speaker at our all-staff meeting in room 304. Dee Ihibramvich is a senior architect at the Extraordinary Firm in Bern, where she has worked for the last ten years. She led the design project of Bern's Bundle House as well as the Titan Skyscraper in Rome. These two buildings received international awards for their innovative designs.

Before making a name for herself in Europe, Ms. Ihibramvich spent six years in San Francisco at the Dynamic Architect Organization (DAO). It was at the DAO that I had the opportunity to cooperate with her on many projects. Ms. Ihibramvich will be here in London for two weeks and has consented to deliver a speech at our meeting about many of her internationally admired design projects.

All employees are required to participate.

151. Why was the memo written?

(A) To announce a plan to open another satellite branch
(B) To employ a new employee
(C) To suggest a construction project
(D) To introduce an architect's accomplishments

152. What does Mr. Baldwin suggest about Ms. Ihibramvich?

(A) She will lead a design project for his company.
(B) She intends to open her own business.
(C) She is a former coworker of his.
(D) She is relocating to a new city.

153. Where is Garrison Builders located?

(A) In London
(B) In San Francisco
(C) In Rome
(D) In Bern

Go on to the next page

Questions 154-155 refer to the following text message chain.

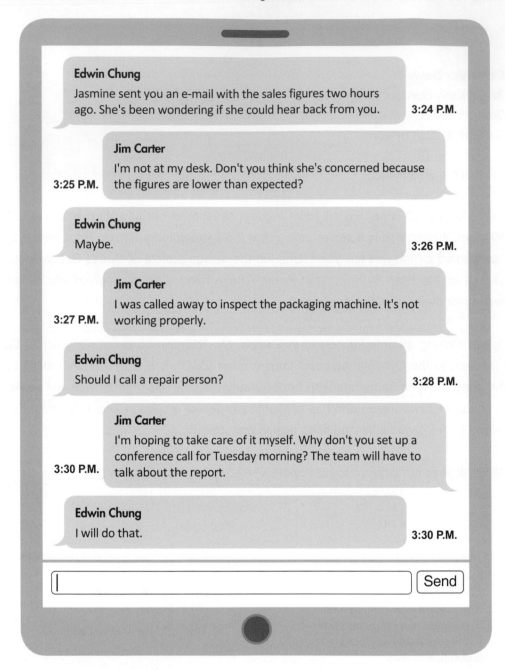

Edwin Chung
Jasmine sent you an e-mail with the sales figures two hours ago. She's been wondering if she could hear back from you.
3:24 P.M.

Jim Carter
3:25 P.M. I'm not at my desk. Don't you think she's concerned because the figures are lower than expected?

Edwin Chung
Maybe.
3:26 P.M.

Jim Carter
3:27 P.M. I was called away to inspect the packaging machine. It's not working properly.

Edwin Chung
Should I call a repair person?
3:28 P.M.

Jim Carter
3:30 P.M. I'm hoping to take care of it myself. Why don't you set up a conference call for Tuesday morning? The team will have to talk about the report.

Edwin Chung
I will do that.
3:30 P.M.

Send

154. At 3:25 P.M., what does Mr. Carter probably mean when he writes, "I'm not at my desk."?

(A) He got off work early.
(B) He will miss a deadline.
(C) He is stopping by Mr. Chung's office.
(D) He cannot reply to Jasmine.

155. What is Mr. Chung requested to do?

(A) Go over documents
(B) Arrange a meeting
(C) Check travel plans
(D) Fix some devices

Rachel Artwork Museum

15 March

Ms. Jennifer Baek

Dear Ms. Baek,

As a Rachel Artwork Museum member, you will shortly be able to make use of our special appreciation deals. —[1]—. From 1 to 28 April, members will receive an additional 30 percent discount on all gift shop products. Members will also be offered a free beverage with their meal in the on-site café. Furthermore, people who become new members no later than 28 April will be offered a 15 percent membership fee discount. —[2]—. So invite your family members, friends, and colleagues to go to our website and register.

—[3]—. The formerly closed fourth-floor galleries, which feature sculptures and paintings by ancient Persian artists, will be open to all visitors until 7:30 P.M. every Tuesday of this month. Images of select artwork from these galleries can be seen on our Web page. —[4]—.

We look forward to seeing you soon.

Sincerely,

Justine Liu
Director of Membership Management

---

156. What is mentioned about the Rachel Artwork Museum?

(A) It has a place to eat.
(B) It will be closed down for one month.
(C) It will have photos on exhibit.
(D) It has a workshop for art courses.

157. What will be different on Tuesdays?

(A) Admission to the museum will be free.
(B) Extra galleries will be open.
(C) Operating hours at the restaurant will be extended.
(D) People will buy some Persian artwork.

158. In which of the positions marked [1], [2], [3], and [4] does the following sentence best belong?

"April is a great time to come by the museum for another reason."

(A) [1]
(B) [2]
(C) [3]
(D) [4]

Notice

September 8 — An article about the upcoming remodeling projects in the public library network, published in our September 7 edition, incorrectly listed the closure date of the library's Kirkstein and Dodgeville branches as October 15. However, according to the library's spokesperson, only the Kirkstein branch will be closed from October 15 through November 20. The Dodgeville branch will keep operating as normal until the Kirkstein branch reopens on November 21. From that date, the Dodgeville branch will be closed until December 25. Please go to the library's website for further information. We sincerely apologize for any inconvenience our mistake may have caused.

159. Where would this notice probably be found?

(A) In a library's yearly report
(B) On a schedule of gatherings
(C) In a remodeling plan
(D) In a local newspaper

160. When will the Dodgeville branch close for the renovation project?

(A) On October 15
(B) On November 20
(C) On November 21
(D) On December 25

Question 161-164 refer to the following article.

Farther Rider is gone!

By Jamal Lopez

On Tuesday, Typhoon Motors, the producer currently manufacturing Farther Rider motorcycles, announced a delay in the launch of the new Fast DM model. Industry rivals responded in surprise at the news. —(1)—. And Farther Rider motorcycle enthusiasts went to its website to express bewilderment with Typhoon Motors for calling off May's eagerly awaited release.

It appears the determination to equip the Fast DM with a hybrid system, which uses gasoline and electric power alike, is to blame. Typhoon Motors admits that the current prototype was rejected due to its huge dimensions and heavy weight. This design of the power system would have needed a larger motorbike body than planned. They had concerns about the durability of its exterior. —(2)—.

Besides the design difficulties, the Farther Rider plant, having been equipped to manufacture previous models, is not ready for production of the Fast DM hybrid. —(3)—. New machines will need to be purchased, and the assembly line will have to be reconfigured.

Two years ago, Typhoon Motors was widely complimented by motorcycle fans after it intervened to save Farther Rider from going bankrupt. What a difference two years has made? —(4)—.

161. What is suggested about Typhoon Motors?

(A) It owns the Farther Rider motorbike brand.
(B) It intends to sell a model at a discounted price.
(C) It is relocating its main office.
(D) It will introduce a new motorbike in May.

162. What is NOT mentioned as a difficulty with the power system?

(A) It weighs a lot.
(B) It isn't cheap.
(C) It isn't strong.
(D) It is too big.

163. Why will the factory be remodeled?

(A) It does not conform to a new regulation.
(B) It has not been updated in over two decades.
(C) It had been outfitted to produce older models.
(D) It is so small that it cannot produce two models at the same time.

164. In which of the positions marked [1], [2], [3], and [4] does the following sentence best belong?

"From now on, they will have to bring back the goodwill of these prospective customers."

(A) [1]
(B) [2]
(C) [3]
(D) [4]

Go on to the next page

Hair Style Salon

9 August — Hair Style Salon had an impressive grand opening earlier last week. Owner and hair stylist Arthur Lee mentioned that the event was well attended, and many appointments in the salon have been reserved during the past week. James Morgan, who came by the salon for the first time yesterday, said that he is not surprised that Hair Style Salon is already popular. "It offers quality cuts," he said, "And it's within walking distance because it's situated on the same street where I and many people in the commercial area work."

In fact, Hair Style Salon is situated on crowded Madison Avenue, down the street from Darlington University. "I selected Madison Avenue as a result of its proximity to the campus, and I want to appeal to university students and faculty members," said Lee at the salon opening.

Another new client mentioned that the rates for the salon's services and hair care items were not that expensive. "I was happy to find a good hair salon that is affordably priced," said Michelle Lin, a satisfied customer. "I will absolutely be returning."

Please don't hesitate to call 031-532-4343 or visit www.hairstylesalon.com for additional information or to set up an appointment.

---

165. What is the purpose of the article?
(A) To inform people of the relocation of a business
(B) To encourage hair stylists to attend an event
(C) To introduce the neighborhood to a new business
(D) To notify students of a special discount

166. What is mentioned about Mr. Morgan?
(A) He works on Madison Avenue.
(B) He owns the Hair Style Salon.
(C) He participated in the salon's grand opening.
(D) He made an appointment through the Internet.

167. Why did Mr. Lee select a particular site for his business?
(A) There is no competition in the community.
(B) There are many parking garages nearby.
(C) The rent is much lower than other locations.
(D) It is adjacent to a university.

168. What is suggested about Hair Style Salon?
(A) It is looking for a new stylist.
(B) It sells hair products at a reasonable price.
(C) It offers a discount to new customers.
(D) It provides complimentary hair care vouchers.

Company World Subscribers!

Right now, you can register to receive personalized e-mails every Wednesday morning with the latest in business and financial news. You can get the same exhaustive coverage you expect from *Company World* magazine each month without having to wait for 30 days. Select your favorites from a comprehensive list of topics and receive various fascinating articles on those topics every week. This service is available exclusively to subscribers of *Company World*.

It's simple to get started. Just go to www.companyworld.com. Click Sign Up for Personalized E-mails, provide your e-mail address, and select your preferences for the service, knowing that you can change them whenever necessary. You can also keep having access to subscription information online.

169. What is being advertised?

(A) A discussion with a financial specialist
(B) A method of paying bills through the website
(C) A weekly online newsletter
(D) A class in corporate investment

170. What is suggested about the service?

(A) It is designed for subscribers of a publication.
(B) It will be available 30 days from now.
(C) It is already popular with business owners.
(D) It is the third in a series of the latest services being offered.

171. What are interested people asked to do in order to receive the service?

(A) Send in an application
(B) Register online
(C) Make a call
(D) Mail a request

Go on to the next page

Dominic Flores

Ms. Han, it looks like there will be a storm tomorrow, so the roof work on your hospital's new east wing will need to be postponed.

2:26 P.M.

Sooji Han

2:27 P.M.

Does that mean no work all day?

Dominic Flores

Absolutely not! My employees can help Tony Lim's workers fix the support beams inside the old building.

2:27 P.M.

Sooji Han

2:28 P.M.

How long will it take to fix them?

Dominic Flores

Let me find out.

2:28 P.M.

Dominic Flores

Tony, how close are you to completing your project?

2:29 P.M.

Tony Lim

Everything was fine until this morning, when the structural engineer visited with some updates. We'll be working overtime for the next ten days.

2:31 P.M.

Dominic Flores

What do you think about my employees assisting you tomorrow?

2:32 P.M.

Tony Lim

That's terrific! Then, we could maybe finish in three days.

2:33 P.M.

Sooji Han

2:35 P.M.

So, will your employees require access to the old building?

Dominic Flores

For tomorrow, yes. Would it be all right for them to park their vehicles in front of the old building?

2:36 P.M.

Sooji Han

2:38 P.M.

Of course. There should be sufficient places near the main entrance. And could you please tell them not to drive their cars on the lawn?

| Send |

172. What does Mr. Flores indicate will disrupt work tomorrow?

(A) A defective machine
(B) Late shipping
(C) Inclement weather conditions
(D) A shortage of employees

173. At 2:31 P.M., what does Mr. Lim most likely mean when he writes, "We'll be working overtime for the next ten days."?

(A) His workers have not been arriving at work on time.
(B) His workers' plan is to get off work early on Thursday.
(C) His workers are needed at two separate work areas.
(D) His workers' construction project was made more challenging.

174. Who most likely is Ms. Han?

(A) A gardening designer
(B) A hospital manager
(C) A transportation supervisor
(D) A construction materials supplier

175. What is one thing Mr. Flores inquires about?

(A) The building entrance for their use
(B) Directions to the newest building
(C) Suggestions for the structure's new wing
(D) Permission to park

Go on to the next page

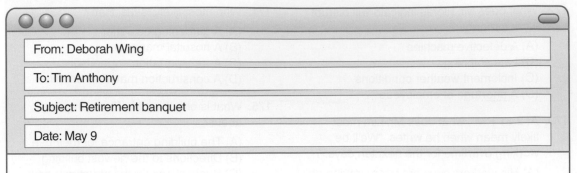

From: Deborah Wing

To: Tim Anthony

Subject: Retirement banquet

Date: May 9

Dear Tim,

As you know, I am on the committee in charge of planning Mr. Dalton's retirement banquet. We want to include a slideshow presentation using photographs taken during diverse corporate events held over the past ten years, and we're seeking someone who wants to create the slideshow for us.

I remember your telling me that you studied photography in college, so I was wondering if you would be interested in doing this. If you accept, I can send an e-mail within three days requesting pictures from those who have them and then get them to you at your earliest convenience. Your assistance would be greatly appreciated. I'm certain Mr. Dalton together with the remainder of the team, would enjoy the show!

Sincerely,

Deborah

From:	Tim Anthony
To:	Deborah Wing
Subject:	RE: Retirement banquet
Date:	May 10

Dear Deborah,

I would like to create the slideshow for Mr. Dalton's retirement banquet. I think we both agree that he's been a great supervisor here. However, I don't think I'm the best person for doing that. I took pictures at one event, but, in fact, I majored in journalism in college. There's a woman whom I want to recommend for creating the slideshow. Her name is Catherine Heinz. I believe she may be interested in doing it. I know she previously created a slideshow for a training session. If Ms. Heinz can't do it for the event, please contact me and I'll recommend another person to you.

Sincerely,

Tim

176. How do Ms. Wing and Mr. Anthony most likely know each other?

(A) They work for the same company.
(B) They attended the same university.
(C) They live in the same apartment complex.
(D) They collaborated on a special project.

177. What does Ms. Wing offer to do?

(A) Order invitations to a retirement banquet
(B) Make a copy of materials for a training session
(C) Gather pictures from employees
(D) Participate in an upcoming show

178. Why does Mr. Anthony say that he studied journalism?

(A) He'd like to relocate to another position.
(B) Ms. Wing needs assistance with an article.
(C) Ms. Wing asked him to confirm his qualifications.
(D) He'd like to correct a misunderstanding.

179. What does Mr. Anthony indicate about Ms. Heinz?

(A) She is more experienced with an assignment than he is.
(B) She is more flexible about a schedule than he is.
(C) She will replace Mr. Dalton after he leaves the company.
(D) She has a university degree in journalism.

180. Why might Ms. Wing contact Mr. Anthony again?

(A) He sets up Ms. Heinz's schedule.
(B) He can enroll her in training sessions.
(C) He takes photographs at all of the company events.
(D) He can recommend other people to assist her.

Go on to the next page

Innovation Centre

Overlooking the shore, Innovation Centre combines a relaxing resort with the services to fulfill your business needs. In addition to 10 meeting rooms for large conferences, the Opal Room and Sapphire Room provide the perfect solution for small groups of a maximum of 10 people.

Innovation Centre has both a formal dining room and a more comfortable eatery. One-, two-, and three-bedroom suites have high-speed Internet access, fax machines, and coffee makers. Guests can also make use of the indoor and outdoor swimming pools. For more information, contact Randy Frederick at 424-2769 or randyfrederick@innovationcentre.com.

TO: Cameron Gee <camerongee@bronzejournal.com>

FROM: Randy Frederick <randyfrederick@innovationcentre.com>

DATE: March 21

SUBJECT: Reservation

Dear Ms. Gee,

Thank you for your partial deposit of $300.00 for a one-bedroom suite for June 12 and June 13. We have reserved the Opal Room for your event on June 13, but we'll need a total deposit of $500.00 by April 1 to put it on hold for you.

Please let us know what equipment you will need for your presentation so that we can prepare the conference room for you beforehand.

Moreover, to talk about the luncheon for your group, you must contact our catering manager, Lilly Pontiac, at 424-4327, extension 22.

Sincerely,

Randy Frederick
Reservations Manager, Innovation Centre

181. Who is the advertisement probably intended for?

(A) Family members
(B) Hotel supervisors
(C) New employees
(D) Business specialists

182. What is NOT mentioned as a feature of the Innovation Centre?

(A) A fitness facility
(B) Restaurants
(C) An indoor pool
(D) In-room fax machines

183. What is indicated about Ms. Gee?

(A) She is the CEO of a large company.
(B) She has stayed at the Innovation Centre before.
(C) She assumed the responsibility for a presentation.
(D) She received a discounted rate for the conference space.

184. What is suggested about Ms. Gee's event?

(A) Full payment for the conference space has been made.
(B) Ten or fewer people will participate.
(C) Attendees will be offered a discount on rooms.
(D) It will be held on April 1.

185. What will Ms. Gee ask Ms. Pontiac to do?

(A) Cancel a reservation
(B) Review her presentation
(C) Prepare a food service
(D) Make a payment

Go on to the next page

Questions 186-190 refer to the following Web page, e-mail, and form.

http://www.middletownoffice.com

| BROWSE | ORDER | **HOME** | GALLERY | CONTACT |

Middletown Office Furniture

Welcome to our Web page! Look around our inventory to visualize workspaces that are stylish and useful. We have been serving Richmond Cape for more than a decade, and you can rely on our high-quality office furniture to satisfy your needs.

We provide the following deals at all times:
- Complimentary shipping and handling for new customers
- Significant discounts to schools and nonprofit organizations (Contact us for further information)

From: James Harley <jharley@standardlawfirm.co>

To: Lemington Chen <lchen@standardlawfirm.co>

Date: 15 April

Subject: Office furniture upgrade

Hello Mr. Chen,

I've completed some research and would like to recommend that we choose Middletown Office Furniture for the desks and other items for our office remodeling. Although we've never bought from them before, they provided references that offered excellent recommendations.

I think we should decide on a larger desk type for our main workspace (15 desks), with corresponding filing cabinets and bookshelves. For the support team and interns who work upstairs, I recommend a simpler desk style.

If you approve of these recommendations, I'd like to place the order as soon as possible so that the products will be shipped while almost all of our employees are away at the meeting in New York.

However, our work areas will seem quite dirty because we will clear out the old furniture and wait for the arrival of the new products.

Please inform me what you think of the plan I have summarized above.

James

Order Number: F2465Z
Contact: James Harley (067) 523-4352
Delivery to: Standard Law Firm, 252 Square Street, San Francisco, CA 94108
Delivery Date & Time: 8–9 August, 11:00–18:00

Quantity	Item Code	Description
15	CDF4524	Dayton Office Desks
15	FCT1275	Prime Filing Cabinets, light brown
6	AA2042	Crystal Bookshelves, light brown
7	GE3182	Versatile Desks

Note: Due to demand, we are out of ITEM AA2042 at our Casey Town store. These products will be shipped to your office directly from our production site, so they will be delivered into San Francisco from Charleston rather than from Casey Town. This might delay the delivery by two or three days. Every effort will be made to have the entire order shipped on the same day.

186. What is suggested about Middletown Office Furniture?

(A) It offers free interior design services.
(B) It provides special discounts to educational organizations.
(C) It has recently expanded its type of products.
(D) It has just opened a satellite branch.

187. What is most likely true about Standard Law Firm's furniture order?

(A) It will be shipped free of charge.
(B) It includes a product which is no longer manufactured.
(C) It was placed too late for shipment in August.
(D) It includes a style selected by the support team.

188. Why does Mr. Harley want to schedule a delivery during the particular period?

(A) He will receive an extra discount.
(B) He requires some furniture for an important conference.
(C) He needs additional time to shop for the new furniture.
(D) He would like to alleviate inconvenience for colleagues.

189. What product will probably be placed upstairs at Standard Law Firm?

(A) Dayton Office Desks
(B) Prime Filing Cabinets
(C) Crystal Bookshelves
(D) Versatile Desks

190. According to the form, where is the furniture made?

(A) San Francisco
(B) Charleston
(C) New York
(D) Casey Town

Go on to the next page

Questions 191-195 refer to the following e-mail, menu, and comment card.

From: Nathan Jerome <njerome@happydiningarea.com>

To: John McNeil <jmcneil@happydiningarea.com>

Date: Tuesday, July 11

Subject: Menu tasting

Hello Mr. McNeil,

It's hard to believe that Ms. Theresa will be here in only two weeks! Since her review will be published in the local newspaper, why don't we make sure that our selections are reflective of the best of the Happy Dining Area? To get advice on the menu we'll be serving her, I've determined we should host a special menu-tasting event on Thursday of next week.

I have several recommendations for what we can serve at the menu tasting. What about arranging a satisfying meatless main dish that can hold its own? That way, we can emphasize our vegetarian offerings. Maybe our baked sea bream would be a good choice, too. However, I insist on providing the new special pizzas we intend to release on our regular menu. Of course, that is assuming construction of the brick oven is finished by that time. Additionally, I think we can serve a minimum of two of our fruit desserts that are popular at all times. However, I have complete confidence in you, as head chef, to finalize the menu choices.

Finally, I want to provide our menu-tasting patrons with an opportunity to visit the kitchen while they are here. Please inform me of what you think about this and how best to prepare for it.

Thank you.

Sincerely,

Nathan

Happy Dining Area Tasting Menu
Thursday, July 20

Baked sea bream in garlic sauce
Beef steak with cucumber salad
Roasted chicken with chili sauce
Cheesecake with walnuts
All of the steamed shellfish in a broccoli soup
Smoked salmon with mashed potato

Tasting Feedback Card

Name: Jessie Jackson

Please remark on your tasting experience at the Happy Dining Area.

I was pleased by the gentle sweetness of the cucumber dish; the sauce was a little sour for my taste, though. The sea bream, on the other hand, surpassed all my expectations. The roasted chicken was tender, yet overall it was not tasty. Concerning the dessert, it was very delicious, although a bit dry. I was very impressed by the useful design of your kitchen. I look forward to tasting the new brick-oven pizzas when they're released. I'm disappointed that you couldn't offer them today.

191. Why is the menu tasting being conducted?

(A) To prepare for a visit from a restaurant reviewer
(B) To choose dishes to enter in a cooking competition
(C) To assess a chef who is applying for a job
(D) To select dishes to add to the daily menu

192. In the e-mail, the word "satisfying" in paragraph 2, line 2, is closest in meaning to

(A) deep
(B) plentiful
(C) gratifying
(D) creative

193. What is mentioned about the tasting menu?

(A) It lists dishes that were provided free of charge.
(B) It includes a dish suggested by Mr. Jerome.
(C) It was served to patrons in the eatery's kitchen.
(D) It isn't available every weekday.

194. What menu item was probably Ms. Jackson's favorite?

(A) The sea bream
(B) The soup
(C) The cucumber
(D) The chicken

195. What is indicated about the brick oven?

(A) It is extremely big for the kitchen.
(B) It has to be fixed.
(C) It didn't pass a safety inspection.
(D) It is still being constructed.

Questions 196-200 refer to the following e-mail, flyer, and text message.

To: Students
From: Jamal Crawford
Subject: Presenter series
Date: May 5

Dear students,

There's good news! Ms. Ito Hirosa has agreed to attend our Presenter Series this summer. As part of your student internship responsibilities, you will have to prepare her lodging here at the university for August 19–21 and get the relevant document completed and approved so that Ms. Hirosa can receive her honorarium. Also, please reserve a room for her presentation. I suggest the Dynasty Auditorium because it can accommodate the most people, but any other presentation room in the business building would be fine as well.

Additionally, if Ms. Hirosa provides her summary, you will have to design a leaflet and post it in the common areas throughout the building. I believe you will be able to assign the job duties among the six of you without any problems.

Thanks!

Dr. Crawford
Professor, Dickson School of Business

Dickson School of Business

Presenter Series featuring

Ms. Ito Hirosa
Vice President, Tokyo Investment, Japan

Establishing Different Finance Relationships
August 20, 6:00 P.M.
True-Blue Room

In the past two decades, numerous financial organizations have limited lending to minimize their risk. This policy, however, leads to unfavorable market conditions. How can banks reduce their risk while still offering ideal funding opportunities to business owners? One possible solution that is becoming popular is "Alternative Finance." I will give an abstract of "Alternative Finance," share some persuasive materials gathered by researchers at Tokyo Investment and Dickson School of Business, and talk about how this worldwide banking change can revive our field.

From: Jim Curry

To: Lisa Presley

Received: May 16, 7:00 P.M.

Lisa, I'm in the media room about to print the leaflet you created, and I've noticed a mistake. Ms. Hirosa's bio was partially omitted from the leaflet! Could you please correct the leaflet promptly and resend it to me? The media room is closing in 20 minutes, and Dr. Crawford emphasized that the leaflets must be posted no later than tonight.

196. What is suggested about the True-Blue Room?
(A) It is not situated in the business building.
(B) It is the place for all events in the Presenter Series.
(C) It is smaller than the Dynasty Auditorium.
(D) It is made available on August 21.

197. In the e-mail, the word "problems" in paragraph 2, line 3, is closest in meaning to
(A) declarations
(B) inquiries
(C) shipments
(D) conflicts

198. What is the topic of Ms. Hirosa's presentation?
(A) The most recent trend in banking
(B) A job opening in finance
(C) Unique methods of collecting materials
(D) Biographies of experienced business owners

199. What difficulty does Mr. Curry mention?
(A) A number has been incorrectly marked.
(B) The leaflet is missing some details.
(C) The leaflet will not be posted online.
(D) The room booked for the presentation is not open.

200. Who most likely is Ms. Presley?
(A) A repair person in the media room
(B) A secretary to Ms. Hirosa
(C) A speaker from the Presenter Series
(D) A student at Dickson School of Business

Test

答對題數表

PART 5	
PART 6	
PART 7	
總題數	

03

READING TEST

In the Reading test, you will read a variety of texts and answer several different types of reading comprehension questions. The entire Reading test will last 75 minutes. There are three parts, and directions are given for each part. You are encouraged to answer as many questions as possible within the time allowed.

You must mark your answers on the separate answer sheet. Do not write your answers in your test book.

PART 5

Directions: A word or phrase is missing in each of the sentences below. Four answer choices are given below each sentence. Select the best answer to complete the sentence. Then mark the letter (A), (B), (C), or (D) on your answer sheet.

101. ------- the heavy snow this morning, the company picnic will proceed as planned.
    (A) Due to
    (B) Despite
    (C) Because of
    (D) Regarding

102. The school ------- was an alumnus of the school, so he is very popular with the students.
    (A) principal
    (B) principles
    (C) principals
    (D) principle

103. In his report, Young-Ho pointed ------- several mistakes that had been made by the developers when building the new Civic Center.
    (A) over
    (B) under
    (C) out
    (D) from

104. If Marsha ------- in charge of the project, we probably would have had more success.
    (A) has been
    (B) is
    (C) was not
    (D) had been

105. John was disappointed because, out of all the reports, the director singled out ------- as needing more work.
    (A) he
    (B) his
    (C) him
    (D) himself

106. After the last class, Mr. Morris had each of the students ------- the test from last year before taking the final exam.
    (A) will review
    (B) review
    (C) was reviewed
    (D) to review

107. The team's performance on the assignment was ------- poor, so two of the team members were fired yesterday.
    (A) unaccepted
    (B) unacceptably
    (C) unaccepting
    (D) unacceptable

108. ------- we work all weekend, we will not likely be able to have the presentation slides completed by Monday morning.
    (A) Even so
    (B) Evenly
    (C) Eventually
    (D) Even if

109. The company gala was in full -------, and all of the employees seemed to be having a fantastic time.

(A) swing
(B) team
(C) moon
(D) party

110. The team leader asked ------- all employees do an exceptional job on the project, as the client is an important one for the company.

(A) what
(B) to
(C) that
(D) where

111. Five of the new hires, in fact all those hired by the Marketing Department, performed beyond expectations last quarter, but the other three new employees -------.

(A) did not
(B) do not
(C) did
(D) will not

112. It is ------- for each member of the sales team to expect large bonuses this year because company profits increased so much.

(A) reasonable
(B) reasoned
(C) reasonableness
(D) reason

113. The passenger was advised to ------- to the check-in counter to have a boarding pass issued.

(A) returned
(B) returning
(C) returns
(D) return

114. ------- this morning, he would have been able to participate in our strategy meeting.

(A) Simon did arrive
(B) Simon will arrive
(C) Had Simon arrived
(D) Simon is arriving

115. After a couple of slow years for our company, our sales really ------- last year.

(A) took off
(B) fell down
(C) took on
(D) outran

116. -------, Nathan submitted the report in time for the meeting, even though he was sick all week.

(A) Undeniably
(B) Rarely
(C) Absolutely
(D) Surprisingly

117. According to Jason, the projector still has ------- the problems that were mentioned by the mechanic last week.

(A) both of
(B) every
(C) either
(D) seen

118. The guest speaker ------- next Monday, so please reach out to him this week to confirm his travel schedule.

(A) has arrived
(B) arrive
(C) is arriving
(D) is arrived

119. The president of the company was excited to have negotiated such a ------- deal, so he let all of the employees go home early yesterday.

(A) terrify
(B) terribly
(C) terrific
(D) terrified

120. Even though Rachel ------- with the company for very long, she is already thinking of moving on to another job.

(A) weren't
(B) hasn't been
(C) could be
(D) will be

Go on to the next page

121. It was strange that Takashi was late to the meeting because ------- he is extremely punctual.

(A) usually
(B) eventually
(C) more
(D) seldom

122. CraneSteel is committed to ------- the highest levels of customer service and is dedicated to its philosophy of social and environmental responsibility.

(A) providing
(B) provision
(C) provided
(D) provide

123. When Janet announced that she will ------- in May, nobody was surprised, given her age and poor health.

(A) have retired
(B) be retired
(C) retire
(D) retires

124. As ------- earlier, we do not intend to talk about issues that we have already covered in previous meetings.

(A) discuss
(B) discussed
(C) discussing
(D) discussion

125. -------, our weekly staff meetings have been very productive, so let's continue to keep up the good work.

(A) This Wednesday
(B) Always
(C) Of late
(D) Soon

126. ------- of the companies is focusing on teamwork, diversity, and trust in this year's workshop.

(A) Every
(B) Many
(C) Much
(D) Each

127. Interviews ------- all day Thursday in the second-floor conference room.

(A) conduct
(B) have conducted
(C) will be conducted
(D) are conducting

128. Makoto has been with the company more than twice ------- any of the other employees, so she is the best person to answer any questions you may have.

(A) as far as
(B) in comparison to
(C) as long as
(D) relative to

129. It is truly ------- that Pro Consulting was not chosen to undertake the advertising campaign, but Amway Design Co. will do just as good a job.

(A) regrets
(B) regretting
(C) to regret
(D) regrettable

130. Mr. Simpson was a horrible -------, so none of the executives had any intention of hiring him.

(A) interviewer
(B) interviewed
(C) interview
(D) interviewee

PART 6

Directions: Read the texts that follow. A word, phrase, or sentence is missing in parts of each text. Four answer choices for each question are given below the text. Select the best answer to complete the text. Then mark the letter (A), (B), (C), or (D) on your answer sheet.

Questions 131-134 refer to the following e-mail.

From: Gordon Iwatani <gordoniwatani@fastermail.com>
To: Recruit Manager <recruit4@mtlanguage.com>
Date: April 14
Re: Japanese language teacher

Dear Sir:

I am writing in response to a notice I saw that said your language school is seeking a Japanese

instructor. As ------- be clear from my credentials, which I have attached to this e-mail, I spent
    131.

most of the last decade as a Japanese language teacher in China, ------- almost eight years as
                                                                    132.

an instructor at the most prestigious language school in Shanghai.

In addition to my work experience and academic qualifications, I enjoy a number of hobbies,

which you may find interesting. I have spent most of my life playing the violin, and I currently

play in an ------- orchestra. I also have a black belt in judo and enjoy going on long runs and
        133.

cycling in my free time. I have a bright personality and adjust well to new environments.

 -------. Please let me know if I can provide you with more information.
 134.

Sincerely yours,

Gordon Iwatani

131. (A) can
   (B) would
   (C) should
   (D) was

132 (A) I spent
   (B) having spent
   (C) will spend
   (D) be spending

133 (A) amateur
   (B) ordinary
   (C) emerging
   (D) odd

134 (A) I appreciate your time in considering my application.
   (B) I look forward to meeting you tomorrow.
   (C) I graduated from high school in Tokyo.
   (D) I very much look forward to meeting my new students tomorrow.

Questions 135-138 refer to the following e-mail.

To: slivingston@kmail.net

From: marsvideos@mars.com

Subject: Your order

Dear sir,

We are in receipt of your e-mail regarding the products you purchased from Mars Videos -------
                                                                                    135.
July. Unfortunately, we have not yet been able to locate the shipment.

Based on our records, you purchased four Blu-ray discs and two DVDs amounting to a total of

$83. Factoring in shipping costs, this amount ------- to a total order of $97. -------.
                                                 136.   **137.**

We would suggest that you do one of the following things. (1) If you hold tight and wait just a

little bit longer, you may receive the products. We have seen instances where bad weather or

other mishaps created delays in shipments. (2) If you would not like to wait, we can cancel the

order now and provide a full -------.
                            138.

Yours sincerely,

Kyle Johnson

Customer Services Manager

---

135. (A) in
(B) on
(C) when
(D) or

136. (A) increase
(B) increased
(C) will increase
(D) has been increasing

137. (A) You are a valued customer, and we will ship your products today.
(B) Our records show we charged your credit card for this amount on July 17.
(C) Please let us know what you think of this policy.
(D) We will go ahead and charge your credit card for the total amount.

138. (A) refund
(B) shipment
(C) order
(D) apology

Questions 139-142 refer to the following notice.

Attention employees:

I have received several complaints regarding usage of the employee break room. This notice
serves as a reminder of the rules we all must follow.

First, please remember to wash, dry, and put away in its appropriate place any plate, bowl,
cup, or utensil that you've used. This should be done immediately after ------.
                                                                         139.

Second, there have been complaints about smoking in the break room. As you all know, we
have a strict policy against smoking in the building. If you want to smoke, you ------ to do so in
                                                                              140.
the designated smoking area on the back patio or elsewhere outside the building.

Finally, please do not take food that is not yours. All food kept in the refrigerator should be
properly ------ with the owner's name. Take only food that is yours. ------.
         141.   **142.**

Grace Ikawa

Manager

139. (A) be used
     (B) using
     (C) use
     (D) to use

140. (A) would request
     (B) requested
     (C) will request
     (D) are requested

141. (A) labeling
     (B) labeled
     (C) label
     (D) to label

142. (A) We will be holding tomorrow's staff
         meeting in the break room.
     (B) We will be shutting down the break
         room beginning next week.
     (C) Let us all enjoy the food in the
         refrigerator together.
     (D) It is important that we keep the break
         room a pleasant place to use.

Go on to the next page

Questions 143-146 refer to the following review.

Maya Gordon's new guide to doing business in the Middle East is an interesting and comprehensive

journey through the Middle Eastern business world.

In this book, readers are provided ------- a unique yet clear understanding of what the business
                         143.

culture is like in several key Middle Eastern countries. Among the many topics covered by Professor

Gordon are essential ones like proper greeting etiquette, proper etiquette during business meals,

the use of business cards, and the intricacies of negotiating with Middle Eastern counterparts.

If you are just getting acquainted with the business scene in the Middle East, this book is

------- reading. No other guide delves into so many critical aspects of Middle Eastern business
144.

conduct in such depth and with such detail. -------, Professor Gordon has organized her book by
                                            145.

business center (including Dubai, Qatar, and Abu Dhabi), allowing readers to focus on the specific

area they are interested in. -------.
              146.

Once you have read *Doing Business the Middle Eastern Way*, you will have no trouble conducting

yourself appropriately in the Middle East.

143. (A) with
    (B) on
    (C) in
    (D) at

144. (A) absolute
    (B) ridiculous
    (C) compulsory
    (D) confident

145. (A) By comparison
    (B) Unfortunately
    (C) Moreover
    (D) As a result

146. (A) The chapter on Dubai is particularly
        enjoyable.
    (B) Professor Gordon has also written on
        Asia.
    (C) This guide is not as interesting as
        some of the others on the market.
    (D) Book critics have been lukewarm on
        the book.

PART 7

Directions: In this part you will read a selection of texts, such as magazine and newspaper articles, e-mails, and instant messages. Each text or set of texts is followed by several questions. Select the best answer for each question and mark the letter (A), (B), (C), or (D) on your answer sheet.

Questions 147-148 refer to the following order form.

MEGA DEPOT, INC.

Taking care of all of your home and office needs

Contents:

  # 2 color ink cartridges

  # 1 black and white ink cartridge

  # 10 packs of letter-size paper (50 sheets each)

  # 1 postcard for re-orders

Use the enclosed postcard when re-ordering these products.

If you would like to speak to a customer service representative, call 301-555-1999 Mon.–Fri. 10 A.M. to 6 P.M.

NOT FOR CONSUMPTION

---

147. What most likely is the reason for buying these products?

(A) To print documents
(B) To place an order for supplies
(C) To write letters
(D) To create artwork

148. What is true about the order form?

(A) It warns people not to eat the product.
(B) It includes a receipt for the product.
(C) It does not describe the contents of the order.
(D) It provides an address for the store.

Go on to the next page

Questions 149-151 refer to the following text message chain.

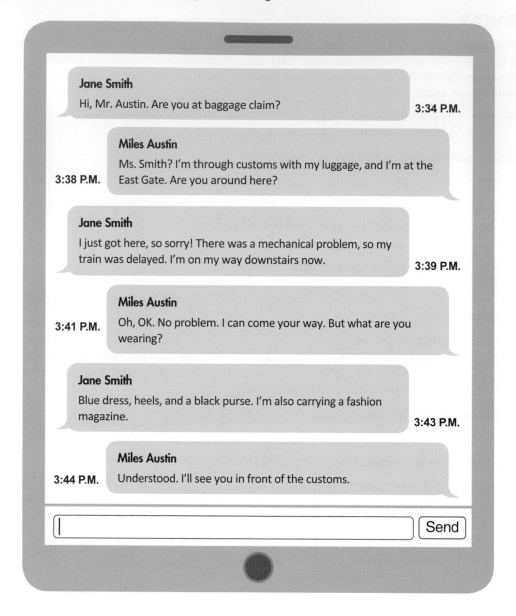

Jane Smith
Hi, Mr. Austin. Are you at baggage claim?
3:34 P.M.

Miles Austin
3:38 P.M.
Ms. Smith? I'm through customs with my luggage, and I'm at the East Gate. Are you around here?

Jane Smith
I just got here, so sorry! There was a mechanical problem, so my train was delayed. I'm on my way downstairs now.
3:39 P.M.

Miles Austin
3:41 P.M.
Oh, OK. No problem. I can come your way. But what are you wearing?

Jane Smith
Blue dress, heels, and a black purse. I'm also carrying a fashion magazine.
3:43 P.M.

Miles Austin
3:44 P.M.
Understood. I'll see you in front of the customs.

Send

149. What is suggested about Mr. Austin and Ms. Smith?

(A) They have never met before.
(B) They have a meeting tomorrow.
(C) They both took trains.
(D) Jane Smith has just bought a magazine.

150. Where is Mr. Austin waiting?

(A) At a magazine stand
(B) At the customs
(C) On a train
(D) Upstairs

151. At 3:44 P.M., why does Mr. Austin say, "Understood."?

(A) He just saw Ms. Smith.
(B) He'll be able to recognize Ms. Smith.
(C) He is also chairing the meeting.
(D) He does not want to be late.

Questions 152-154 refer to the following blog.

February 24

We moved ahead another 25 km on our trek today. My feet are killing me. —[1]—. I really should not have worn my new boots. My knees are a little sore, too, but all in all it was a good day. We got off to a bit of a slow start by sleeping in. Keiko was on alarm duty, so that one is on her! All downhill after that, though. The view was unbelievable. We took tons of photos. I can't wait to show them to you when we're back. —[2]—. We even saw a snow leopard! Those are extremely rare and almost impossible to actually see live. It was hard to see it amidst all the snow—it came into view for about three seconds. It looked beautiful. Keiko missed it—sweet revenge for failing to wake us up in time for the sunrise, ha ha! —[3]—.

February 26

Sorry for not checking in yesterday. It rained all day, and there wasn't much interesting news to tell you. We found a quaint little café and just spent the entire day there. The staff was giving us dirty looks, but they never actually asked us to leave. —[4]—. Well, tomorrow's the last day. I'm really looking forward to seeing all of you the day after!

152. How are the two people most likely traveling?

(A) On roller skates
(B) By motorcycle
(C) On foot
(D) By plane

153. On what date will the blogger return?

(A) March 2
(B) March 1
(C) February 28
(D) February 27

154. In which of the positions marked [1], [2], [3], and [4] does the following phrase belong?

"We ended up just lounging around all day, talking, eating, and playing games."

(A) [1]
(B) [2]
(C) [3]
(D) [4]

Go on to the next page

NON-DELIVERY FORM

Date: 5/16   **Time:** 11:08 A.M.
Delivery person: Sam

Package number: 3494-836636-92
From: General Office Supplies

Reason for non-delivery

   Item too big ☐   **Resident not home to sign for delivery** ☑

   Notes: Item sent by express delivery

Options:

   (A) Dial 1-800-555-2215 toll free 24 hours a day to reach our automated service.
      You will need to have the package number.

   (B) Dial 1-401-555-2216 during office hours (9 A.M.–5:30 P.M., closed on Sundays.)

Remember: *We will keep the package for only five days from the date of failed delivery, after which it will be returned to the sender.*

---

155. Who filled out this form?

   (A) The sender
   (B) An automated service
   (C) A courier
   (D) The resident

156. What will happen after five days?

   (A) Sam will come back with the package.
   (B) The resident will call the delivery company.
   (C) The item will be sent back.
   (D) The resident will come home.

Zebra Car Rental
464 Orange Hills County
Yevon, Collins, ZR2 3HG

Dear customers,

Due to the increasing demands for our cars and vans, Zebra Car Rental is expanding its operations. This will involve a new front yard plus office and warehouse extensions, which will enable us to stock and store more cars and vans.

These changes will take place next month. Especially, we will be closing the warehouse from 8 to 11 of November. However, you can still see a list of our available vehicles for rent online. Please use this website to book a test drive at www.zebracars.com during this period. We hope that you have a good winter and look forward to greeting you at our new facilities in December.

Chris Murphy
General Manager, Zebra Car Rental

157. What is the main purpose of this letter?
  (A) To advise on new prices
  (B) To announce renovations
  (C) To introduce a website
  (D) To offer discounts

158. What is stated about the company?
  (A) It has reduced its stock.
  (B) It sells items from around the world.
  (C) It allows customers to reserve test drives.
  (D) It will be closed throughout the winter.

Tyler Wood [5:10 P.M.]		It's incredible! I love the updated graphics. Much better than the last one.
Sarah Brooks [5:11 P.M.]:		Are you kidding? For $95, they'd better come up with better quality than that.
Tyler Wood [5:11 P.M.]		It is a bit expensive, I know. But I'm sure you were blown away by the soundtrack.
Gavin Ward [5:12 P.M.]		Totally! The music was really great. Didn't you think so, Sarah?
Sarah Brooks [5:14 P.M.]		Well, I wouldn't say "blown away", but it was alright. The thing I did like was the character voice acting. They really stepped it up on that one. It annoys me when a good story just crumbles under terrible performances. Speaking of which, the story was pretty good, too.
Gavin Ward [5:15 P.M.]		Ha ha, I think she might finally be caving, Tyler!
Tyler Wood [5:16 P.M.]		About time. Superior graphics, music, and story—with a solid 80 hours of entertainment, including all of the extra missions. What more can you ask for?

Send

159. What is the conversation most likely about?

(A) A musical
(B) A movie
(C) A video game
(D) A book

160. At 5:14 P.M., what does Sarah Brooks mean when she writes, "They really stepped it up"?

(A) The company did a good job.
(B) The participants walked away.
(C) The users went upstairs.
(D) The performers stopped acting.

Question 161-163 refer to the following article.

Yesterday, both the governor and the state attorney general joined hands in urging for changes to what they called a "broken" public education system in the state. Governor Wayne Johnson and Attorney General Vicki Perez spoke at length about the issue when it was brought up during a debate on education held at Silver Town City Hall yesterday. It was the first time this state has seen the governor and the state attorney general make such a joint statement.

The problems discussed by Mr. Johnson and Ms. Perez can be easily summarized into three key points, which were:

1. The quality of teachers has deteriorated significantly in public schools across the state. Mr. Johnson and Ms. Perez noted the reason for this being that budget cutbacks had been made, which led to teacher salaries steadily decreasing in recent years.

2. Standardized test scores for students across the state have also been steadily decreasing in recent years. The average scores in the state are now below average when compared to other states across the country.

3. The curriculum for middle and high school students has not changed sufficiently over the past decade to keep up with changes being made in other states. Students who have not been exposed to evolved curriculums have been struggling in college when studying with students from schools in other states. The problem starts early on in each student's education and is a fundamental one, Mr. Johnson and Ms. Perez said.

The State Ministry of Education has yet to issue an official response to the statement made by Mr. Johnson and Ms. Perez.

161. What was NOT mentioned about yesterday's statement?

(A) It was about issues with the school system.
(B) Mr. Johnson and Ms. Perez are from different states.
(C) Three key issues were discussed.
(D) The State Ministry of Education did not respond.

162. What is one of Mr. Johnson and Ms. Perez's main points?

(A) The state has too many schools.
(B) Students have been doing better in college.
(C) The quality of teachers is lower than it used to be.
(D) The students are unhappy with the new policy.

163. According to the two officials, what has caused a change in teacher quality?

(A) Teacher salaries are decreasing.
(B) Many teachers are moving to other states.
(C) The teachers are not happy with the schools.
(D) It is the Ministry of Education's fault.

Go on to the next page

Questions 164-167 refer to the following notice.

Sunny Shiny Daycare Center has been caring for children for more than thirty years. Our reputation continues to grow as the center that provides quality learning and playtime in a warm, friendly, and safe environment for children.

We would like to announce the opening of our newest daycare center next month, right here in Orange County. It is planned to be our largest center yet, able to accommodate up to 50 children. Of course, the newest center will have all of the fun-filled game centers and facilities that parents are used to seeing, including a fortress playground, swimming pool, and state-of-the-art computer corner.

We will be holding an open house from January 27 to 31 next year, and all interested parents are invited to join us for a full tour of our facilities and an open dialogue with our award-winning staff. Please don't hesitate to bring your children with you so that they can truly take a "full" tour by immersing themselves in a number of fun activities that will give them a taste of what life at the center would be like every day.

We hope to see all of you in January. If you would like more information, please call 201-555-8765 or e-mail us at sunnyshiny@mnet.org.

At Sunny Shiny, you are always in good hands.

Lucy Mason
Managing Director
Sunny Shiny Daycare Center

---

164. What is NOT a purpose of the notice?
(A) To announce the opening of a new daycare center
(B) To inform parents about an open house
(C) To discuss the history of Sunny Shiny
(D) To provide contact information to parents

165. What is a feature of Sunny Shiny Daycare Center?
(A) A tennis court
(B) A swimming pool
(C) A rock-climbing wall
(D) A water slide

166. How long will the open house last?
(A) 2 days
(B) 4 days
(C) 5 days
(D) 6 days

167. Why might some people call Sunny Shiny?
(A) To talk to their award-winning staff
(B) To buy tickets to the swimming pool
(C) To make a reservation for the open house
(D) To ask for more information

Questions 168-171 refer to the following bulletin.

Devastating wildfires spread throughout California today, causing enormous damage to homes and farmland. —[1]—. Reports show that five people were injured, with hundreds more people having to abandon their residences as fires spread as wide as 8 kilometers and slowly moved towards the city of Los Angeles. David Meyer, Chief Firefighter in the suburb of Annandale, said that this year's fires may be the worst he's seen in his long and storied career, but that his team of firefighters is up to the challenge. "Just the sheer speed with which the fire spread was unbelievable," he said. —[2]—. "My guys have really been battling out there, and we still have a ways to go."—[3]—.

It is not clear how these fires got started. It is usually the case, though, that wildfires are the product of human negligence, such as a careless cigarette or unattended campfire, or of natural causes, such as lightning hitting a dry patch of wood or grass.

—[4]—. Last year, parts of Northern California suffered heavy losses following almost two weeks of rampant forest fires, which ultimately caused injury to three people. Three years ago, the same area saw fires injure 40 people.

168. To whom is Mr. Meyer most likely referring in his comment?

(A) His friends
(B) Other firefighters
(C) His classmates
(D) His sons

169. Which cause of wildfires is NOT mentioned in the bulletin?

(A) Failure to extinguish a campfire
(B) Carelessly dropping a cigarette
(C) Lightning striking dry grass
(D) Someone intentionally starting a fire

170. According to the bulletin, how many people have been injured in wildfires over the last 3 years?

(A) Forty
(B) Forty-five
(C) Forty-eight
(D) Forty-three

171. In which of the positions marked [1], [2], [3] and [4] does the following sentence belong?

"Wildfires have been an annual tradition in California."

(A) [1]
(B) [2]
(C) [3]
(D) [4]

Go on to the next page

Please be advised that our annual company workshop will take place this year on Saturday, April 30. I know many of you will be disappointed that we are holding the workshop on a weekend, but we really had no choice this year. You will be happy to know, however, that all employees may choose any day the week after the workshop to leave work at lunchtime, except Thursday.

Each of you will have received a copy of a report this morning. We ask that you read each of the case studies contained in the report carefully prior to the workshop. Also, this year, we are asking each of the supervisors of the five departments to prepare and give a 10-minute presentation. The presentation should cover the strategies discussed during last year's workshop and how they were implemented throughout the past year.

We will be having a special guest join us this year. Joan Mitchell, whom you all know for having just recently won the Businessperson of the Year Award, will be joining us in the morning to talk about marketing tips that have helped her during her career and to lead group bonding sessions. While you enjoy your lunch, I will be presenting on client management, followed by the presentations from each of the department supervisors.

We are planning to have light cocktails and snacks available at the end of the workshop for those of you who do not need to rush home.

Thanks,
Gregory A. Manning
Manager

172. What is Mr. Manning's main purpose for writing this message?
  (A) To prepare cocktails and snacks for staff
  (B) To introduce Joan Mitchell to everyone
  (C) To ask supervisors to prepare presentations
  (D) To give information about an annual event

173. What is NOT true about this year's annual workshop?
  (A) It is again scheduled to be held on a Saturday.
  (B) There will be refreshments for the employees at the end.
  (C) Client management will be discussed at the workshop.
  (D) A guest speaker will join in the morning.

174. In total, how many minutes will the supervisor presentations take?
  (A) 10 minutes
  (B) 25 minutes
  (C) 30 minutes
  (D) 50 minutes

175. What is suggested about Joan Mitchell?
  (A) She is a department supervisor.
  (B) She was at the annual workshop last year.
  (C) She will be presenting during lunch.
  (D) She has been successful in the industry.

Go on to the next page

Questions 176-180 refer to the following e-mails.

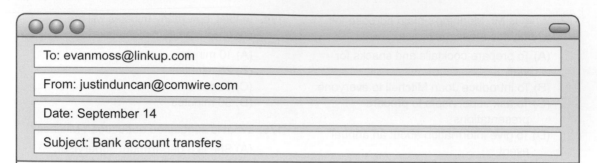

To: evanmoss@linkup.com

From: justinduncan@comwire.com

Date: September 14

Subject: Bank account transfers

Dear Mr. Moss,

Before I temporarily relocated to Hawaii, I asked Linkup Bank to transfer my bank account to the branch here on the island. Although I intended to be here for six months, I have completed my research and will be returning home. Can you now transfer my account back to my initial branch, as from today, September 14? When I return, I would also like to apply for a mortgage. I would appreciate some advice on the most suitable mortgage. I have tried to access the home buying page on your website. However, there is a message that says it is being upgraded at present.

Many thanks for your help.

Yours faithfully,

Justin Duncan

To: justinduncan@comwire.com

From: evanmoss@linkup.com

Date: September 15

Subject: Your e-mail message

Dear Mr. Duncan,

Thank you for your e-mail message yesterday. Please note that your bank account has now been restored to the original branch as you requested. Secondly, we will need to discuss your financial circumstances before we can offer you a mortgage. There are many factors to take into consideration including your income, monthly outgoings and existing loans. May I suggest that you make an appointment to see the mortgage advisor regarding this matter at the Bradford branch when you have a convenient time? Lastly, I must apologize for the error on the website. We are currently upgrading the system and have had to take the page you are seeking off-line until the upgrades have been completed. We hope it will be operational within two days.

Kind regards,

Evan Moss
Customer Service Representative

176. What is the purpose of the first e-mail?

(A) To complain about a transaction
(B) To close an account in Bradford
(C) To transfer money to a third branch
(D) To change an arrangement with a bank

177. What most likely is true of Mr. Duncan?

(A) His permanent residence is in Bradford.
(B) His transfer to Hawaii was for a year.
(C) He is renting an apartment.
(D) He had previously worked for Linkup.

178. What does Mr. Moss suggest that Mr. Duncan should do?

(A) Call the Hawaii branch for advice
(B) Contact the IT department for help
(C) Close his account
(D) Meet with one of the bank's lending officers

179. What is NOT mentioned as a factor that Mr. Duncan should consider in deciding on a mortgage?

(A) His monthly expenditure
(B) The amount of his salary
(C) The number of existing loans he may have
(D) The length of time he would need to repay

180. In the second e-mail, the word "matter" in line 6, is closest in meaning to

(A) concern
(B) substance
(C) result
(D) oversight

Go on to the next page

Sale of the year! DON'T MISS OUT!

You all know it's sale season, and Brady's Bargain Bin is having the biggest sale of them all! You have to see it to believe it! Here are just a few of our bargain deals:

- 50% off our entire line of TVs, featuring the most popular brands in today's market. We have all kinds, from hand-held portable TVs to mega-screen monsters, all for half off! Whatever kind of TV you are looking for, look no further than Brady's.

- Sampson washer/dryers for only $1000. Sound too good to be true? These popular products usually sell for up to $2500, but we're selling them for less than half that price! We have all of the latest models, and we'll even ship them right to your front door free of charge!

- Top-end cameras and camcorders up to 75% off! That's right—75%! All of our stock of recording devices needs to go, which is music to your ears. What's more—if you buy one of our cameras or camcorders, we'll throw in a black canvas bag you can carry it around in.

So hurry on down to Brady's Bargain Bin. These deals will only last for five more days!

From: hjjang@kmail.net

To: jameskim@vogmail.com

Subject: Bought a camcorder!

Hey James,

I just got back from Brady's Bargain Bin. The crowd was unbelievable. I'm not going to visit there again anytime soon!

The camcorders they had left were definitely not top-end—even mid-range is a stretch. The prices were pretty cheap, though. I ended up buying the Morson camcorder, which they were selling for $150. I know the reviews say the Kell camcorder is of higher quality, but I had one before, and it barely lasted me two years before breaking apart—definitely not worth the price, which is more than double that of the Morson. For the tripod, I bought the one that comes with the Kell instead of the matching of one for the Morson. That one looks much better than the one for the Morson.

Anyway, I look forward to seeing you soon.

Best,

Hyuk-Joon Jang

181. Which of the following is true?

(A) The sale will only last for one more week.

(B) Most of the televisions at Brady's are on sale.

(C) The largest discount mentioned in the ad is for cameras.

(D) Products not mentioned in the ad are not for sale.

182. Which sale products also come with free shipping?

(A) Televisions

(B) Washers

(C) Camcorders

(D) Roller skates

183. How much will the black canvas camera bag cost?

(A) $1,000

(B) 75% off of the normal price

(C) 50% off of the normal price

(D) Nothing

184. Why was Brady's Bargain Bin so crowded?

(A) There is a sale at Brady's Bargain Bin.

(B) The store has just recently opened.

(C) People came out to see Mr. Jang.

(D) The store will close soon.

185. Which of the following is NOT true?

(A) Mr. Jang has never owned a Kell camcorder.

(B) Camcorders and tripods are sold separately.

(C) Kell camcorders are more expensive than the Morson brand.

(D) Mr. Jang bought the Morson camcorder.

Go on to the next page

Seeking a General Sales Manager

A leading electronics retail chain is looking to hire a bright, diligent, and motivated person to take the position of General Sales Manager, a role that will have the person be in charge of all 22 of our stores throughout Asia. The successful candidate should have a degree from a prominent business school, as well as at least six years of comparable managerial experience, ideally in the electronics retail industry. We primarily sell high-end electronics, so the successful candidate will be someone who is willing and able to grow the market for such products in the Asian region. Candidates must have a valid driver's license and have some experience living in more than one country, as the position will require quite a bit of travel. For anyone interested in the position, please send your résumé (with photograph) and a list of references to mlinton@kmail.com by no later than March 31.

Name: Daniel Shin
Date of Birth: November 5, 1981
Place of Birth: Seoul, Korea
Nationality: American
E-mail: dshin@kmail.com

Education

1993–1997:	Andover High School
1997–2001:	Harvard University (BA)
2006–2008:	Brussels Business School (MBA)

Work Experience

1995–1997:	Andover Deli (Stockroom)
1998–1999:	Sandwich Center (Waiter)
1999–2001:	Pierre Valentine's (Waiter)
2009–2010:	Xenith Electronics (Assistant Manager, Hong Kong)
2010–2012:	Steinway Electronics (Retail Manager, Singapore)
2012–present:	Self-employed

Other

I hold a valid driver's license, and I am fluent in Mandarin and Korean.

To: Gregory Smith

From: Matt Linton

Re: General Sales Manager (3 attachments)

Date: March 18

Greg,

Thanks again for the wonderful dinner last night. Please also thank Julie and let her know how much I enjoyed the evening!

Anyway, did you have a chance to look at the latest applications for GSM that I sent you this morning? I've attached them here again in case you haven't had time. We have three new candidates. I know we still have some time, but take a look at this Daniel Shin fellow. He looks like he might be perfect for the job. Yes, he's short of one of the requirements from the ad, but he's got everything else and more, right?

The one thing that concerns me is his most recent experience. Self-employed? That has to mean something else. Let's bring him in for an interview and ask him about it. What do you think?

Best,

Matt

186. Which of the following is NOT a requirement for applicants?

(A) A photograph
(B) Relevant work experience
(C) Fluency in Mandarin
(D) A list of references

187. Which requirement is NOT met by Mr. Shin?

(A) He has only lived in one country.
(B) He does not have six years' managerial experience.
(C) He does not have a driver's license.
(D) He does not have a business degree.

188. What appears to be true about Mr. Linton?

(A) He thinks highly of Daniel Shin.
(B) He has not yet met Julie.
(C) He is Greg's boss.
(D) He is from Korea.

189. Why did Mr. Linton attach the applications to his e-mail?

(A) He forgot to send them to Mr. Smith this morning.
(B) He wants Mr. Smith to show them to Julie.
(C) Mr. Shin's résumé does not include a photo.
(D) He thinks Mr. Smith may not have seen them.

190. What does GSM most likely stand for?

(A) General Sales Manager
(B) Greg's Sales Memo
(C) Global Sales Mechanism
(D) General Staff Management

Go on to the next page →

More Improvement Ahead

At Wednesday's city council meeting, the Manchester City Council unanimously voted to explore options for more renovations to be conducted on city infrastructure. According to Michael Mann, the City Treasurer, the recent renovation of the Manchester Public Library surprisingly came in significantly below budget. Council members, therefore, decided to put together a short list of other improvement projects that could be completed with the excess funds.

The most well-received suggestions include adding a wheelchair ramp to Manchester Community Center, replacing broken streetlamps in downtown Manchester, and repairing the parking areas in Manchester Park. According to Mr. Mann, the council has decided to open the decision up to public opinion. Those interested in putting forth their ideas may do so at the next council meeting on Wednesday, April 22 at 5 P.M. or can send an e-mail to City Hall by no later than April 29. After April 29, the city planning committee will put before the council a final list for discussion. A final decision is expected shortly thereafter.

From: sshort@hostmail.com

To: citycouncil@manchester.org

Date: April 24

Subject: Improvement projects

Dear City Council Members,

I understand that you are accepting suggestions for improvement projects to city facilities. I had a doctor's appointment, so I was not able to attend the council meeting on Wednesday, but I wanted to express my strong support for replacing broken streetlamps in the downtown area. I work downtown, and when I get off work late, I've noticed that quite a number of streetlamps are in need of replacement. The dark streets are actually a bit frightening. Brightening the streets again should bring more people downtown and reduce crime. This will benefit all of the residents of Manchester. I hope that you will choose this project.

Susan Short

From: mchoi@hostmail.com

To: citycouncil@manchester.org

Date: April 27

Subject: City projects

To Whom It May Concern,

Finally, a renovation project that was actually completed under budget. Although the public library is open to everyone and people of all ages, it tends mostly to be young adults and parents with young children that go to the library. I was hoping we could use the leftover funds on a project that would benefit the senior citizens of Manchester.

The community center is where most older citizens gather, and it is a crime that there are no wheelchair ramps at the entrance to the center. Many of the citizens that frequent the center are in need of wheelchair assistance and have difficulty or need assistance from others just in order to get into the building. Choosing this as the improvement project would really be applauded by people who didn't feel they gained much from the renovation of the library. It is important that the chosen project benefit the entire Manchester community. Thank you for your attention.

Milton Choi

191. Why does the city of Manchester have funds available?

(A) The city council raised taxes last year.
(B) It received a generous donation.
(C) It cancelled a renovation project.
(D) Its previous project cost less than expected.

192. In the article, the phrase "put before" in paragraph 2, line 7, is closest in meaning to

(A) move fast
(B) do first
(C) provide to
(D) place on top

193. When did Ms. Short have a doctor's appointment?

(A) April 22
(B) April 24
(C) April 27
(D) April 29

194. What does Mr. Choi mention in his e-mail about Manchester Public Library?

(A) It hasn't been renovated for years.
(B) It is used mainly by young citizens.
(C) It has many good programs for senior citizens.
(D) It is in need of further renovations.

195. On what point would Mr. Choi and Ms. Short most likely agree?

(A) The chosen project should be beneficial to the entire community.
(B) The city should save the extra funds instead of doing a project.
(C) The city council should push back the deadline for receiving public opinions.
(D) The downtown streetlamps are not really in need of replacement.

Go on to the next page

Questions 196-200 refer to the following article and e-mails.

Over the past two days, our two local high schools (Grand Park and Fontana) came together to put on a joint fundraising festival to help raise funds for those affected by the recent devastating earthquake that left more than 30,000 people homeless in Ridgewood.

Never before in our community have the two schools joined together to hold a charity event, and it was a smashing success! The schools were able to raise more than $150,000 to help the disaster victims. Mayor Jeremy Irons graciously accepted the money, thanking each member of the two schools who participated in the event, and he promised that the entire amount would go towards constructing new homes for the victims of the earthquake.

Those who attended the two-day festival will have a few memories they will never forget. Groups of students put on quite a show on the stage at Fontana High School, consisting of unforgettable song and dance performances, comedy skits, and dramatic plays. Each performance was done by a group intentionally composed of students from both schools. This was to symbolize the need for all of us to join together in times of difficulty. There was also a basketball tournament that took place at Grand Park High School on Sunday. Non-student members of our community were also free to take part in the tournament, and everyone said they had a blast.

For the most popular event at the festival, however, the karaoke singing competition on the second day. Contestants were staff and students from each school. One of the students from Fontana High School, Mark Saint, ultimately won the competition, and from the sounds of the cheering, you could tell it wasn't close. When speaking at the closing of the festival on Sunday evening, Mayor Irons emphasized how proud he was of the entire Ridgewood community. This paper would also like to thank everyone involved for providing a ray of hope during what would otherwise be a dark time.

From: Jeremy Irons

To: pjones@fontana.co.edu; mthacher@grandpark.co.edu

Subject: Thank you so much!

Date: Tuesday, October 1

Dear Priscilla and Mary,

I wanted to thank both of you again for your incredible efforts and success this past weekend. You have brought so much joy to our community by collaborating on this amazing event. Please take a moment during your next school day to pass on my appreciation to everyone who took part.

Unfortunately, all-day meetings kept me from joining in the festivities on Saturday, but I was told it was a lot of fun—I heard great things about the display of world foods even though I missed it. That was truly a great idea!

I know Sunday was wonderful because I was there to take it all in. Mary, that Mark is quite a talent. Maybe we will see him on television someday! He could make a good musician, and a proud alumnus of Grand Park High School. Anyway, again, my heart-felt congratulations. On behalf of Ridgewood, I thank both of you.

Jeremy Irons, Mayor

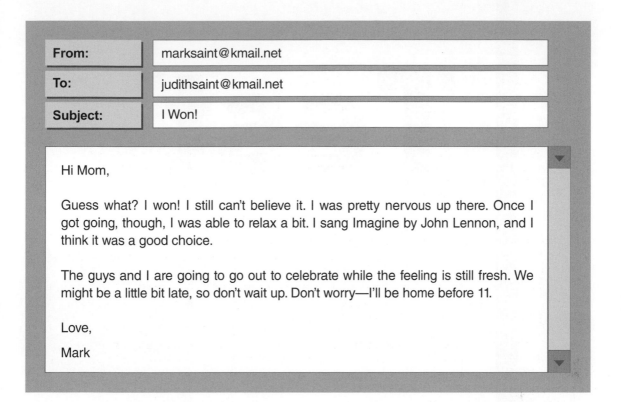

From:	marksaint@kmail.net
To:	judithsaint@kmail.net
Subject:	I Won!

Hi Mom,

Guess what? I won! I still can't believe it. I was pretty nervous up there. Once I got going, though, I was able to relax a bit. I sang Imagine by John Lennon, and I think it was a good choice.

The guys and I are going to go out to celebrate while the feeling is still fresh. We might be a little bit late, so don't wait up. Don't worry—I'll be home before 11.

Love,

Mark

196. In the first e-mail, the phrase "took part" in paragraph 1, line 3, is closest in meaning to

(A) attended
(B) enjoyed
(C) achieved
(D) completed

197. Which of the following happened first?

(A) The mayor, Mr. Irons, attends the fundraiser.
(B) The local residents take part in the basketball tournament.
(C) Mark Saint sings "Imagine" in the singing contest.
(D) A variety of world foods are displayed in the festival.

198. On what day did the event begin?

(A) Tuesday
(B) Monday
(C) Sunday
(D) Saturday

199. According to the article, what mistake did Mr. Irons make?

(A) He thought they had raised only $100,000.
(B) He wasn't able to attend the event on Saturday.
(C) He thought Mark Saint attended Grand Park High School.
(D) He addressed his e-mail to Judith Saint.

200. In the second e-mail, what is implied about Mark?

(A) He is disappointed about not winning the contest.
(B) He was on a TV program.
(C) He has sung "Imagine" before in other contests.
(D) He went out with his friends after the festival.

Test

答對題數表

PART 5	
PART 6	
PART 7	
總題數	

04

READING TEST

In the Reading test, you will read a variety of texts and answer several different types of reading comprehension questions. The entire Reading test will last 75 minutes. There are three parts, and directions are given for each part. You are encouraged to answer as many questions as possible within the time allowed.

You must mark your answers on the separate answer sheet. Do not write your answers in your test book.

PART 5

Directions: A word or phrase is missing in each of the sentences below. Four answer choices are given below each sentence. Select the best answer to complete the sentence. Then mark the letter (A), (B), (C), or (D) on your answer sheet.

101. Because the regular building inspection will be conducted, please use the side ------ to the main lobby for next week.

    (A) entering
    (B) entered
    (C) entrance
    (D) entry

102. National Council of Teachers and Education states that all in-state instructors are dedicated to ------ their students from in-school violence.

    (A) save
    (B) saving
    (C) saved
    (D) safety

103. The marketing department must ------ reliable information to other companies for securing the copyrights they have reserved in their book publishing sector.

    (A) influence
    (B) provide
    (C) register
    (D) remain

104. All the employees must follow the current workplace policies ------ otherwise directed from the manager on-site.

    (A) below
    (B) either
    (C) unless
    (D) while

105. If you have any problems with the purchased items, please contact the technical support team and tell them the current conditions -------.

    (A) most precise
    (B) precise
    (C) more precise
    (D) precisely

106. Applicants who have more than 5 years of experience in marketing will ------ the opportunity to be promoted to a managerial position.

    (A) give
    (B) be given
    (C) be giving
    (D) have given

107. A marketing director at Samhwa Electronics carefully reviewed the terms of contracts with the huge ------ company, Whale Co., known as the leading enterprise in Canada.

    (A) distribute
    (B) is distributed
    (C) distribution
    (D) distributes

108. Ms. Christine submitted two proposals for encouraging employees of Allo-Plus Batteries to create a good working environment, but the management declined to accept -------.

(A) fewer
(B) one another
(C) both
(D) much

109. Standard Property Realty has benefited financially ------ the well-prepared contract with the worldwide development company.

(A) about
(B) as
(C) from
(D) for

110. In order to increase sales figures, employees at Mobby Telecoms ------ to work overtime until they recover the former amounts.

(A) to agree
(B) agreeing
(C) have agreed
(D) agreement

111. ------- who purchased the brand-new smartphone T-Star 7 in advance online can receive a refund in full if the model is sold out in the early stage.

(A) They
(B) Them
(C) Which
(D) Those

112. Over the past seven years, Xvid Clip Productions ------ the rules about reserving the right to protect its own contents.

(A) set
(B) has set
(C) will be setting
(D) to set

113. The total damage caused by inside information leakage is ------ to billions of dollars, which is likely to be a third of annual revenue.

(A) profitable
(B) equivalent
(C) considerate
(D) preventable

114. The candidates have stated that they accept their respective ------ for their promotions to Lecovo Technology's overseas branches.

(A) venues
(B) registration
(C) nominations
(D) suspension

115. Our county offers you exceptional and fantastic attractions such as Sea Land, Character World, and Fun Driving Park, ------ that you have a memorable vacation.

(A) ensure
(B) ensures
(C) ensuring
(D) ensured

116. Employees who have not yet enrolled in the on-the-job training should submit their applications -------.

(A) previously
(B) immediately
(C) closely
(D) roughly

117. Economic analysts have devised three ------ approaches to the current problems related to the long-term financial downfall.

(A) difference
(B) differ
(C) different
(D) differently

118. In an effort ------ sales of newly released items in an e-commerce market, the company has suggested doing viral marketing by using various SNS channels.

(A) increase
(B) increasing
(C) to increase
(D) increasingly

119. Those who get a refund in full should first contact the sales manager ------ they want to receive it by check.

(A) then
(B) if
(C) despite
(D) shortly

Go on to the next page

120. ------- you find any errors in those articles for the next issue, please report them directly to the chief editor before publishing them.

(A) Had
(B) Should
(C) Were
(D) Have

121. We are sorry to inform you that we cannot use the photo that was sent ------ the application in the mail package.

(A) along with
(B) in addition
(C) on account
(D) instead

122. Each division and executive at Hans Corporation has a framework document that contains the ------ of responsibilities and accountabilities for each position.

(A) statement
(B) department
(C) increment
(D) enforcement

123. Giant Mall has newly developed the rapid order processing system to ------ shipping to customers.

(A) obtain
(B) reduce
(C) expedite
(D) increase

124. ------- the firefighters arrive at the scene of the crime, the building will have been totally destroyed by an arsonist.

(A) Because
(B) By the time
(C) In spite of
(D) Furthermore

125. His comments on the article that dealt with the environmental issues ------ the need for the conservation of our ecological environment.

(A) acquire
(B) emphasize
(C) customize
(D) sophisticate

126. Last year, New York Modern Art Supplies was relocated to Macy Avenue beyond 42th Street ------ its previous store.

(A) on
(B) from
(C) with
(D) about

127. Our goal is to attract ------ sensitive customers to the item design when they consider purchasing something.

(A) highly
(B) properly
(C) much
(D) far

128. Many salespeople were disappointed because the sales figures were ------ lower than they expected.

(A) significance
(B) significant
(C) significantly
(D) more significant

129. Before installing the security program on your computer, please delete the former version of any antivirus software as ------ as possible.

(A) quicken
(B) quick
(C) quickly
(D) quicker

130. Giantbook Publishing provided Mr. Dany with a full refund ------ there was a trivial printing error on the cover page.

(A) although
(B) as though
(C) whether
(D) if

PART 6

Directions: Read the texts that follow. A word, phrase, or sentence is missing in parts of each text. Four answer choices for each question are given below the text. Select the best answer to complete the text. Then mark the letter (A), (B), (C), or (D) on your answer sheet.

Questions 131-134 refer to the following article.

EGE buys FilaGas

Exron Gulf Energy announced this morning that it had acquired FilaGas in an effort to gain

entry ------- the Permian Basin oil field. EGE spokesperson Jarvis Meeks said they wanted to
    131.

take advantage of FilaGas' firm foothold in the recently discovered oil-rich area, given FilaGas

already operates half a dozen drilling concessions in the basin. -------.
                                       132.

Ray Littman, an expert in the energy sector, predicts that the acquisition will make EGE the

leader in oil exploration in the Permian Basin, head and shoulders above its -------. EGE's
                                           133.

early move also saved the oil giant millions of dollars, as the cost of buying land in the area

continues to skyrocket. -------, land prices per acre in the Delaware field rose from $14,516 to
    134.

$49,000 in just two years.

131. (A) into
    (B) with
    (C) for
    (D) of

132. (A) FilaGas is still considering the offer.
    (B) All six are drilling at full capacity.
    (C) EGE will acquire more companies soon.
    (D) The purchase cost is higher than EGE expected.

133. (A) buyers
    (B) observers
    (C) investors
    (D) competitors

134. (A) In this instance
    (B) After all
    (C) Despite this
    (D) As a matter of fact

Questions 135-138 refer to the following notice.

We highly recommend early bookings as flights to the remote Finnish village of Ivalo are very

limited. Thomson Airways offers ------- flights to Ivalo direct from the U.K. The rest of the year,
                                    135.

one can take Finnair flights from Helsinki. In case you choose to cancel a flight reservation,

Thomson requires a seven-day notice, while Finnair only asks for three for your ticket ------- in
                                                                                      136.

full. Both airlines serve meals and drinks to first-class travelers for the ------- of the flight. -------.
                                                                            137.   **138.**

135. (A) season
     (B) seasons
     (C) seasoning
     (D) seasonal

136. (A) are refunding
     (B) will be refunded
     (C) to be refunded
     (D) had been refunding

137. (A) length
     (B) degree
     (C) site
     (D) month

138. (A) Frequent flyers to Ivalo can fly year-
         round via Thomson Airways.
     (B) This service does not apply to those
         in the economy class.
     (C) Flights to and from Ivalo can be
         canceled without prior notice.
     (D) We recommend morning flights so that
         they serve meals to all passengers.

Questions 139-142 refer to the following notice.

Industrial Park Gets Go-ahead

Drastic changes ------- to the residents of Fairbank. On Monday, a real estate developer,
139.
Ultima Holdings, announced that its 30-acre Industrial and Technology Park has been given

the go-ahead by the Fairbank Town Council. -------. The park will include the construction of
140.
several high-rise office buildings as well as manufacturing and warehouse facilities. ------- of
141.
the acreage will also be devoted to recreational purposes, such as a golf course and a driving

range. Most local residents protested during talks on the proposed development, ------- it as a
142.
future source of noise, traffic, and pollution.

---

139. (A) will have come
(B) came
(C) are coming
(D) comes

140. (A) The approval was announced on
Monday, June 2.
(B) The plan will be welcomed by the
town's members.
(C) Residents and developers both await
the council's decision.
(D) Nonetheless, Ultima Holdings
withdrew its plans to develop.

141. (A) Some
(B) Many
(C) One
(D) Few

142. (A) see
(B) sees
(C) seeing
(D) seen

July 12

Ms. Amanda Pickwick

Origami Paper Company

278 East Road

Teaneck, NJ 07666

Thank you for your inquiry about purchasing four bottles of Iron Gall Ink from Collins Supply

Company. We are happy to inform you that we have the ink in stock and can ship it to you if

you fill in the enclosed order form today. -------. As you are a regular customer of more than
143.

two years now, we are also pleased to provide you with a 5 percent discount on this and other

------- orders. -------, you can earn store credits with every purchase. When you have -------
144.   **145.**   **146.**

store credits, you can use these to purchase other products. This is our way of thanking you for

your continued patronage.

Sincerely,

Dave Earnshaw

Customer Relations Manager

Enclosure: #Order Form.pdf

143. (A) You may want to choose it from our online catalog of calligraphy inks.
(B) However, we will ask you to return the product in its original package.
(C) You can expect that you can receive your order within 5–7 business days.
(D) Unfortunately, we have no records of any order of Iron Gall Ink.

144. (A) upcoming
(B) preceding
(C) preliminary
(D) sequential

145. (A) However
(B) In addition
(C) Nonetheless
(D) Of course

146. (A) accumulates
(B) accumulating
(C) to accumulate
(D) accumulated

PART 7

Directions: In this part you will read a selection of texts, such as magazine and newspaper articles, e-mails, and instant messages. Each text or set of texts is followed by several questions. Select the best answer for each question and mark the letter (A), (B), (C), or (D) on your answer sheet.

Questions 147-148 refer to the following notice.

The Oregon Prime Association (OPA) is opening a local chapter in Eugene in October. This organization will be gathered on every Friday at the Culpepper, 305 Washington Drive, at 8:00 P.M. It is open to the public at any time.

If you are interested in this and want to use public transportation, Eugene Red Bus leads to the site, two blocks away, at the corner of James Boulevard and Fleming Avenue. If you plan to drive yourself, the parking lot, Hopkins Park, is free for all citizens after 7 P.M.

We have a lot of topics for next year's events for our community, so we hope you will be about to join our activities together. For more information about topics and presenters, visit our website at www.opaeugene.org.

147. Where would the notice more likely be posted?

(A) At a community center
(B) At a parking lot
(C) At a local restaurant
(D) At a residential hotel

148. According to the notice, what is available on the online homepage?

(A) Some videos regarding local promotion
(B) Procedures about local parking
(C) Documents for the registration
(D) Some details about the meeting

Go on to the next page

Sigma Network Corporation: 2018 Biennial Event!
Thank you for your interest in the COD Network Conference at Sigma Network Corp.
Please complete the request form below.

2018 COD Network Conference
Millennium Hotel St. Louis

Conference Registration Form
October 10–14, 2018

Name Badge and Mailing Information (use a separate form for each person)

Name	_____	(for POD database)
Badge Name	_____	(this name will appear on your name badge)
Title	_____	
Department/Unit	_____	
Institution/Organization	_____	
Mailing Address	_____	
City _____	State/Prov. _____	Postal Code _____
Work Phone _____	Fax _____	E-mail _____

Conference Registration

	Early Bird (postmarked by 9/21)	Regular (postmarked after 9/21)	On-site	Registration Amount Enclosed
Member (must have paid 2018–2019 dues)	$180	$220	$240	$ _____
Non-member (includes 1 year membership)	$255	$295	$315	$ _____
Student or Retired	$130	$160	$180	$ _____
One Day Only ___Thurs ___ Fri ___ Sat	$130	$140	$150	$ _____

** If you need to get a temporary parking permit during the conference, please stop by our reception desk and pick it up from our personnel for the event.

149. What is implied about the 2018 COD Conference?

(A) It offers in-advance payers some discounts.
(B) Its members should register for participation online.
(C) It provides the conference with just regular members.
(D) It has been held in St. Louis once a year.

150. What will Sigma Network staff do?

(A) E-mail potential clients their conference details
(B) Accept participants' papers for the conference
(C) Deliver short-term parking permits to attendees
(D) Organize and designate the conference rooms

Questions 151-152 refer to the following e-mail.

To: Sales Associates

From: Richard Steve, General Manager

Date: October 10

Subject: Urgent Issue

Dear Sales Associates,

Our advertisement in the recent issue of *Cal-State Post* has some errors. It indicates that our date for the half-price sale is November 11 instead of November 1. Although a correction of the error appears in the next month's issue of paper copies, our customers cannot be aware of this error on the Web. Therefore, if they ask whether it is November 1 or November 11 for the sale, first apologize for this inconvenience and then offer them a coupon for 10% off any item they want to buy, at both off-line stores and online ones. If consumers have more questions about it, please direct them to the floor manager. Thank you for your understanding.

Richard Steve,

General Manager, Kingswhite Clothing

---

151. What is stated about *Cal-State Post*?
- (A) It publishes articles and advertisements every week.
- (B) It posted an apology for the error of their promotion date.
- (C) It attached a discount coupon on the page of Kingswhite's advertisement.
- (D) It misprinted the date of Kingswhite Clothing's sale.

152. What does Mr. Steve require the associates to do?
- (A) Advise customers to discuss extra issues with a supervisor
- (B) Tell customers about problems with an item's malfunction
- (C) Explain the reason why they made a mistake
- (D) Send the correction of the misprinted date to the magazine

Go on to the next page

ANNUAL SPRING MEETING

Central Pennsylvania University
April 13, 2018

Mellon Board Room
9:00 – 12:00

8:30 – 9:00   Registration & Breakfast
9:00 – 10:30   Panel Discussion: *Expanding the Teacher Toolbox*

Peggy Daniel, Director, Intercultural Communication Center, & Rebecca Oreto, Associate Professor, Carnegie University
   Technology in your hands: using creative materials and building academic fluency

Steve Lin, English Language Program Coordinator, Chatham University
   Highlighting some collaborative group activities in a "Glee" syllabus

Jane Piadget, ESL Teacher & ELL Coordinator, Franklin Regional School District
   Teacher Technology Tips–Using Puzzlelet.com and Mobile Devices

Christopher Pierce, Instructor, Pittsburgh City University, English Language Institute
   Using Jigsaw Puzzle to generate and share vocabulary activities

10:30 – 11:15   Interest Groups Gathering Sessions & Networking
11:15 – 12:00   General Business Meeting and Elections

Free to members of Three Rivers TESOL
$5.00 for non-members

Map: http://www.cpu.edu/campusmap/
Directions: http://www.cpu.edu/about/directions.cfm
Parking at the Terrace Parking Lot

Special thanks to Central Pennsylvania University for hosting our 2018 Spring Meeting!

---

153. For whom is the workshop most likely intended?

(A) Human resources experts
(B) Business analysts
(C) Educational graduate students
(D) New employees at local colleges

154. Whose topic involves web-based learning?

(A) Ms. Daniel
(B) Mr. Lin
(C) Ms. Piadget
(D) Mr. Pierce

155. What is NOT indicated about the workshop?

(A) It is a half-day event.
(B) It includes free lunch.
(C) It introduces new items.
(D) It may require a fee to attend.

Questions 156-157 refer to the following text message chain.

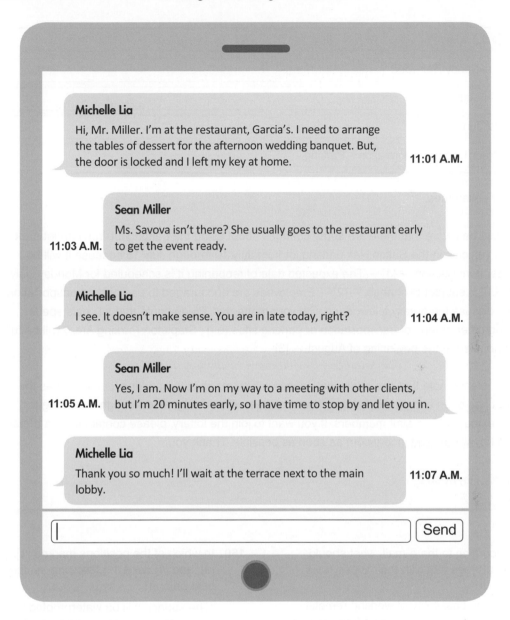

Michelle Lia

Hi, Mr. Miller. I'm at the restaurant, Garcia's. I need to arrange the tables of dessert for the afternoon wedding banquet. But, the door is locked and I left my key at home.

11:01 A.M.

Sean Miller

11:03 A.M.   Ms. Savova isn't there? She usually goes to the restaurant early to get the event ready.

Michelle Lia

I see. It doesn't make sense. You are in late today, right?   11:04 A.M.

Sean Miller

11:05 A.M.   Yes, I am. Now I'm on my way to a meeting with other clients, but I'm 20 minutes early, so I have time to stop by and let you in.

Michelle Lia

Thank you so much! I'll wait at the terrace next to the main lobby.   11:07 A.M.

Send

156. Who most likely is Mr. Miller?

(A) A café waiter
(B) A restaurant manager
(C) A café cashier
(D) A restaurant chef

157. At 11:04 A.M., what does Ms. Lia most likely mean when she writes, "It doesn't make sense."?

(A) Her peer doesn't show up in advance.
(B) She does not understand what Mr. Miller said.
(C) The situation is unsuitable for the event.
(D) Event attendees are already there.

Go on to the next page

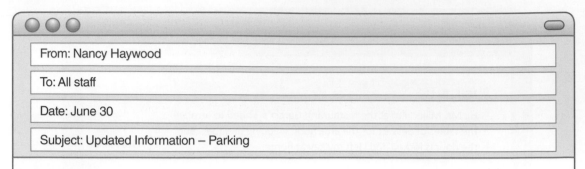

From: Nancy Haywood

To: All staff

Date: June 30

Subject: Updated Information – Parking

Dear colleagues,

Please be aware that there are some changes about using the parking lot. You cannot park your vehicles in the Sutton Hall parking lot from July 10 through July 15 because it will be under construction. —[1]—. The expected date of reopening it is scheduled for Monday, July 16, but is subject to change. —[2]—. Employees are encouraged to use public transportation and discuss temporary teleworking with your managers. Please note that all costs spent using other means of transportation or parking sites (e.g., Stapleton Parking Area) will be fully reimbursed at the beginning of August. —[3]—.

Also, please note that two additional spaces will be made in the parking lot as soon as the work has been completed. —[4]—. These places will be designated through a drawing to interested full-time staff members. If you want to join the lottery, please contact me via e-mail at n.haywood@suttoncorp.com as soon as possible. Thank you.

Nancy Haywood

158. According to the e-mail, what should employees talk with their supervisors about?

(A) The possibility of working remotely
(B) The best alternative parking spaces near the company
(C) How to participate in the parking space lottery
(D) The amount of reimbursed expenses they can get

159. What is implied about the Stapleton Parking Area?

(A) It will be closed on Sundays.
(B) It has the latest equipment.
(C) It was recently expanded.
(D) It charges drivers for its use.

160. In which of the positions marked [1], [2], [3], and [4] does the following sentence best belong?

"The surface will be waterproofed, and safety fences will be constructed."

(A) [1]
(B) [2]
(C) [3]
(D) [4]

Question 161-164 refer to the following online chat discussion.

Chris Paul [3:30 P.M.]	Jim and I are grabbing an early meal after work around 4:00. Anyone want to join us?	
Jeremy Lavine [3:31 P.M.]	Maybe. I still have something more to do on a report for my boss. Where are you going?	
Chris Paul [3:32 P.M.]	We're thinking of going to the Mexican bar on Washington Avenue. It's called TACO Ring.	
Danny Rivera [3:33 P.M.]	Oh, you are unlucky! That place closed last week.	
Chris Paul [3:34 P.M.]	Really? That's too bad. I heard there are a variety of great things to eat there.	
Danny Rivera [3:35 P.M.]	How about Romeo Pizzeria near Carnegie Street? They have a lot of delicious dishes and snacks on Tuesdays.	
Chris Paul [3:37 P.M.]	That sounds great. Does anyone want to go there with us?	
Jeremy Lavine [3:38 P.M.]	OK. But I won't be able to get there until around five, I guess.	
Brad Triana [3:39 P.M.]	It will be great for me. Lavine, I just sent you the modified reporting documents.	

Send

161. What are the chat participants discussing?

(A) The place to go for dinner
(B) The meeting for a weekly sales report
(C) The menu at TACO Ring eatery
(D) The introduction of new members to others

162. What information does Mr. Rivera provide about TACO Ring?

(A) The taste of the food is not good.
(B) The menu is very diverse.
(C) The restaurant has gone out of business.
(D) They are gathered there for a meeting.

163. At 3:34 P.M., why most likely does Mr. Paul write, "That's too bad."?

(A) He cannot go with his colleagues for dinner.
(B) He wanted to eat at TACO Ring.
(C) He has a lot of things to report to his boss.
(D) He has had a delicious meal at TACO Ring.

164. What does Mr. Lavine decide to do?

(A) Join his coworkers for a meal
(B) Request a food delivery
(C) Work overtime on a task
(D) Look for another cafeteria

Go on to the next page

TEST 04

PART 7

Pennwholeissue Co.
We value your opinion!

The Pennwholeissue Corporation has been conducting open polls of the public about current issues for over two decades. All of our questions are based on phone interviews with adults, who are eighteen years of age or older living in our designated polling areas. To ensure the same opportunity for participation for these adults, potential respondents are chosen by a computer at random.

To find information on what people think about recent world issues, please visit our Latest Poll Issues tab on our website. New polls are created weekly, and all of them are saved and accessible through the Internet. If you want to find polls by subject, use the sorting tools for a specific topic or Subject on the banner on the right. Should you want to copy the tables, graphs, charts, or other graphics made by Pennwholeissue, click the Contact Us banner and request them through our Permission Division. You can easily find the information about an easy-to-use online manual form with specifications about how and where to use them. Usually, we can respond to your request within 24 hours after you submit it.

165. What is NOT mentioned about poll participants?

(A) They are interviewed via the phone.
(B) They are randomly selected.
(C) They should be adults.
(D) They should be interviewed in a group.

166. What is indicated about Pennwholeissue Co.?

(A) It publishes books about world-historical issues.
(B) It posts new poll results on the Web every week.
(C) It is seeking new employees for Web management.
(D) It has more branches in other locations.

167. How can readers be permitted to get graphics?

(A) By submitting a paper form
(B) By calling a Web master
(C) By sending a request letter
(D) By contacting them on the Web site

168. The word "current" in paragraph 1, line 2, is closest in meaning to

(A) contemporary
(B) tentative
(C) momentous
(D) appropriate

Need to take a break?

<u>Come along on the Rocky Mountains Trip!</u>
<u>with Bluespruce's Tips for "Best Southwest Vacation!"</u>

Bluespruce Co. Offers:

The Great Outdoors!

See incredible views of oak groves and valleys along the ranges while you breathe fresh mountain air. Over 20 km of off-road biking and riding a cable car to the mountain top, which is offered for an additional fee, is prepared for you. Travel along this beautiful ridge on your own or with a trained guide. The Extreme Sports Activities program allows you to enjoy a variety of sports such as rock-climbing, white-water rafting, and so on. Indoor Unity Day is also provided by having a barbeque party, Bingo game, and live music performance in our condominium. If you want to join us in this group, we offer a special price based on the number of participants in our events. Should you have more questions about our activities and costs, do not hesitate to contact us at 750-8103.

169. What most likely is Bluespruce?

(A) A travel agency
(B) A national park
(C) A recreational area
(D) A sports complex

170. What is indicated about the Rocky Mountains?

(A) They include a variety of waterfalls and lakes.
(B) They are located in the Southwest.
(C) They have a lot of complimentary activities.
(D) They require visitors to get a license for activities.

171. What is offered at an extra cost?

(A) A cable car
(B) A Bingo game
(C) Live entertainment
(D) A rock-climbing activity

TEST
04

PART
7

Hopkins Apparel

Weekly Reports about Management Status, April 7–11
Assigned: Jose Mackerry, Project Manager

This week's achievements:

* Talked with five manufacturing companies in Hochimin, Vietnam, with experience of making handbags. —[1]—. Gave them our brand-new bag designs and asked questions about minimum order amount, costs of production, and shipping and processing time. —[2]—.

* According to initial data about contacted manufacturers, Staple Industries is the most suitable for our needs in terms of time and cost. —[3]—. In addition, Jim Bommer, an account manager, called me first. He was very passionate and professional, and gave us immediate answers to all our requests. I strongly believe that Staple Industries could have a good relationship with us in this business.

* The other companies we contacted were unable to accept our schedule or meet our pricing requirements. —[4]—. Therefore, we do not need to consider them.

Plans for the week of April 15–20

================= [an intentionally blank page] =================

172. What is suggested about Hopkins Apparel?

(A) It has a branch in Vietnam.
(B) It plans to acquire other companies.
(C) Its project manager will retire soon.
(D) It is planning to introduce some new items.

173. According to the report, what did Mr. Mackerry do during the week of April 7?

(A) He chose the best partner possible.
(B) He got a permit to make a product.
(C) He called a shipping company for negotiation.
(D) He held training sessions for new recruits.

174. What is mentioned about Mr. Bommer?

(A) He is willing to work with Hopkins Apparel.
(B) He needs more information about new bags.
(C) He has worked as a project manager at Hopkins Apparel.
(D) He wanted to meet Mr. Mackerry for pricing negotiation.

175. In which of the positions [1], [2], [3], and [4] does the following sentence best belong?

"The company is too small to produce our request, but it is willing to hire additional employees to carry out the work."

(A) [1]
(B) [2]
(C) [3]
(D) [4]

Go on to the next page

Questions 176-180 refer to the following e-mails.

To: Steve Jack <stevejack@fastmail.com>

From: John Dewy <jdewy@aaco.com>

Dear Mr. Jack,

Your application for the managerial position of the Accounting Department at Arizonas Accounting Co. has been carefully reviewed by our department. This year's application process was highly competitive, and we were able to offer a position to only two of those who applied. Based on their recommendation, I regret to inform you that we cannot act favorably on your application and go with you at this time.

If you wish further information regarding this action, please feel free to contact the recruiting division of the Human Resources Department.

Recruiting Office
Telephone: (480) 965-3344
e-mail: recruit@aaco.com
URL: http://recruit.aaco.com/manger-apply

If you wish to be considered for other positions at Arizonas Accounting Co., more information and Web links are available at http://www.aaco.com/departments.

We thank you for your interest in Arizonas Accounting Co. and wish you success in your future endeavors.

Sincerely,

John Dewy
Arizonas Accounting Co.

To: John Dewy <jdewy@aaco.com>

From: Steve Jack <stevejack@fastmail.com>

Dear, Mr. Dewy,

I am writing this e-mail inquiring about your e-mail. I am sorry to hear that the position I applied for was not given to me, but thank you for informing me so kindly. However, I wonder what other departments are dealing with monetary issues at your company. Because I majored in business at the University of Arizona, I can handle any other matters related to accounts, budgets, and distribution management. Would it be possible for me to apply for these relevant positions in your company during this season? If so, please let me know at your earliest convenience.

By chance, the duties that I currently perform for SYSMATIC Ltd. are exactly the same as the responsibilities mentioned above. So, I would like to know very quickly about other job openings at Arizonas Accounting Co.

I look forward to becoming a valuable member of Arizonas Accounting Co.

Regards,

Steve Jack

---

176. For what kind of company does Mr. Dewy most likely work?

(A) A law firm
(B) A financial business
(C) A publishing company
(D) A governmental office

177. In the first e-mail, what is the recipient NOT asked to do for more information?

(A) Send an e-mail to the personnel division
(B) Click some links on the Web
(C) Call the company directly
(D) Post questions on the Web

178. What is suggested about Arizonas Accounting Co.?

(A) It had a lot of remarkable candidates.
(B) It has entered into a partnership with SYSMATIC.
(C) It has increased its sales figures in distribution.
(D) It employed a lot of new employees for the assembly lines.

179. Why was the second e-mail written?

(A) To advertise the applicant's merits to the manager
(B) To negotiate further conditions for the position
(C) To recommend a suitable person for a position
(D) To ask whether other related positions are available

180. What most likely is NOT indicated about Mr. Jack?

(A) He has a bachelor's degree.
(B) He studied business law in college.
(C) He can do various monetary tasks.
(D) He wants to transfer to a new company.

Go on to the next page

Issue 100, June

Table of Contents

Monthly Cover: 100th Issue Anniversary

From: jdoris@royalrecipe.com

To: t-daven@lycoos.com

Date: 20 May

Subject: Contest Winning

Dear Mr. Daven,

I am happy to inform you that your entry of Daven's Sweety & Breeze-to-Make Pudding is the winner of our contest. Your innovative recipe will be published in the June issue of our magazine. However, the title may be shortened by our editors due to limited space in the column of the Winner's Recipes section.

Before we publish your recipe in our magazine, I would like to ask some additional information. In the recipe you submitted, honey could be used instead of sugar as a sweetener. Could you tell me how much honey is used in comparison with using sugar? Is there any other replacement if there is no honey at home? In addition, the recipe shows that the pudding should be frozen in the freezer before eating. What is the minimum amount of time and proper degree for freezing it? Thank you for giving us this information.

It is also usual for us to include a picture of the author when we publish a recipe. Please attach a clear half-length photograph of you in your reply e-mail to this.

Thank you,

Jane Doris

181. Why was the e-mail sent to Mr. Daven?

(A) To point out errors in his submission
(B) To encourage him to register for a cooking class
(C) To tell him about the winning process
(D) To discuss the publication of a recipe

182. In the e-mail, the word "entry" in paragraph 1, line 1, is closest in meaning to

(A) front of building
(B) new staff member
(C) contest submission
(D) lowest degree

183. What does Ms. Dorris NOT ask Mr. Daven to provide?

(A) A modified recipe title
(B) An amount of an ingredient
(C) A length of time for a process
(D) A photograph of himself

184. On what page does Mr. Daven's recipe appear?

(A) 16
(B) 20
(C) 36
(D) 38

185. What can be inferred about the recipes?

(A) The artichoke is cooked with spaghetti.
(B) The Oriental Balsamic Salad has a sweet flavor.
(C) A key to making pudding is the place it is cooked.
(D) All of the recipes are made by head chefs.

Go on to the next page

Questions 186-190 refer to the following Web page, list and article.

[http://www.m-survival.it]

Event Name: Long-Night-Summer Song Festival
Location: Daytona Beach, Florida
Dates: 1–14 August
Contact: Sabrina Anne: sanne@musicsurvival.com

About:

This annual event, in its fifth anniversary, brings in over 100 solo and group contestants from around the southeastern area of the United States of America. In particular, there are a lot of competitive and competent applicants in diverse fields of music. In addition, Music Survival, an organizer of this event, expects that more than 2,000 audience members will be gathered in Daytona Beach, Florida, which is nearly double that of the previous year. This contest has become one of the largest beach events in Florida. Daytona Beach, one of the longest sandy beaches in Florida, is located about one hour from Orlando. During this week, the city of Daytona holds the 40th World Grand Prix Championship, which is internationally recognized in car-racing sports. Visitors can get a chance to attend these fantastic events for free, with just $5 for parking.

The Winners of the Fifth Annual Long-Night-Summer Song Festival

[Solo Section]

Placement	Name	State	Title
1st Prize	Ashton Jane	Alabama	**Cooling Summer Night**
2nd Prize	Justin Moore	Georgia	**The End of the Moon**
3rd Prize	Simon Rick	North Carolina	**Mixed Bowl in the World**
4th Prize	Tyler Smith	Florida	**Catcher in the Lie**

[Group Section]

Placement	Group Name	State	Title
1st Prize	Tina Band	Tennessee	**Don't Bully the Rustic**
2nd Prize	South Life	South Carolina	**Never Stop Exploring**

126

What's New in Northeast Florida?

By Donald Scott

The annual Long-Night-Summer Song Festival took place last week, and it was the perfect way to say farewell to the hot summer season. Because of the beautiful weather, the number of visitors was over double that of the preceding years, even more than the host anticipated.

The contest drew music artists for both the solo and group sections. They introduced themselves to visitors by stimulating their emotions with their great voices. All people on the Daytona Beach fully shared their emotion. I strongly believe that this is the reason why we consider music as one of the composite arts. A feast of songs made the festival more and more exciting and helped everyone to relax.

As a result of this contest, Ashton Jane, with the amusing song, Cooling Summer Night, won the first prize in the solo section, and Tina Band from Tennessee did it in the group section with Don't Bully the Rustic, which deals with anti-social issues. The winning process consisted of both judges and audience members at the rate of fifty-fifty voting.

With the success of this festival, John McKayne, the state governor of Florida, announced that the Department of Culture in Florida will expand the scale of this event all over the country in the near future. By doing so, the state intends to advertise its region to all citizens as one of the most prosperous culture states in the U.S.

186. What is indicated about contestants?
(A) They are from a certain group of states.
(B) They are all professional musicians.
(C) They are requested to register early.
(D) They are all in-state residents.

187. What is indicated about this year's event?
(A) It is the largest festival ever.
(B) It costs $5 per person to join.
(C) It took place in Daytona Beach for the first time.
(D) It was the last event be held.

188. Who is the second prize winner in solo category?
(A) Ashton Jane
(B) Justin Moore
(C) Tyler Smith
(D) South Life

189. What does Mr. McKayne intend to do?
(A) He will develop the event into a nationwide event.
(B) He will never accept the following events.
(C) He will run for election to the National Assembly.
(D) He will change the event into a charitable one.

190. Which song was performed by an in-state participant?
(A) Cooling Summer Night
(B) Mixed Bowl in the World
(C) Catcher in the Lie
(D) Never Stop Exploring

Go on to the next page

Questions 191-195 refer to the following information, e-mail and parking permit.

Borough of Ebensburg
Continuing Education Classes – June

Continuing education classes are open to all residents in the Borough of Ebensburg aged 19 and over. Classes are held at Mount Aloysius College unless otherwise notified. For the registration process, please see page 4 of this brochure. There is more detailed information about tuition, fees, and payment options.

How to Start Your Own Business	
Mondays, 1 P.M. – 3 P.M.	Sutton Hall, Room 101
Instructor : M. Judies, Co-chair of Indiana Retailer Association	

Taking a Photo — Easy and Fun Photography World!	
Tuesdays, 2 P.M. – 5 P.M.	Stapleton Library, Room 202
Instructor : S. Kenneth, Manager of Narin-Arto Pictures	

Become a Real Estate Agent — Preparation for the License Test	
Wednesdays, 1 P.M. – 4 P.M.	Leonard Hall, Room 305
Instructor : K. Peter, President of Jack's Realty Firm	

To Make Your Car Perfect! — Self-Care Tips	
Thursdays, 3 P.M. – 6 P.M.	Lael Auto Lab, Monroeville Campus
Instructor : T. Schenider, Mechanic of Heinz Auto Parts, PA	

TO : Gloria Park (and 12 others)

FROM : Jerry Gebhard <jgebhard@ebensburg.gov>

SUBJECT : [URGENT] Class Canceled

DATE : June 19

To All Class Participants:

Ms. Judies asked me to let every student know the class has been canceled due to an important issue she should attend to, so it will be rescheduled soon. Once we know the date and time, we will inform you of it via e-mail and send a new parking permit too, because your current permit is no longer valid. Sorry for this inconvenience.

Regards,

Jerry Gebhard
Manager, the Department of Local Welfare, Borough of Ebensburg
Telephone: 743-8917

Mount Aloysius College Facility Division

TEMPORARY ONE DAY PASS
FOR TODAY ONLY

SOUTH BLUE LOT
Valid Date: June 22
Time Stamp: 1:30 P.M.

* Please display this permit on the front window of your vehicle so it is visible from the outside.

191. Who most likely is T. Schenider?

(A) A repairman
(B) A council member
(C) A local business owner
(D) An association chair

192. What is NOT indicated about participants in the continuing education classes?

(A) They live in the Borough of Ebensburg.
(B) They paid class tuition and fees.
(C) They should be at least 19 years old.
(D) They graduated from Mt. Aloysius College.

193. What is Ms. Park most likely interested in?

(A) Real estate
(B) Owning a business
(C) Photography
(D) Car maintenance

194. In the e-mail, the phrase "attend to" in line 2, is closest in meaning to

(A) participate in
(B) take care of
(C) bring up
(D) sing up for

195. On what date will the rescheduled class take place?

(A) June 20
(B) June 21
(C) June 22
(D) June 23

Go on to the next page

Questions 196-200 refer to the following article, e-mail and message.

Richmond Daily Post

In Brief 17 March

As reported earlier this year, Giant Hawk Grocery is going to open its additional distribution center. Completion of construction was delayed for a time because there were some problems with the ground conditions at the site. However, these matters have been completely resolved and the 20,000-square-meter area will be fully operational starting on April 5, when the opening ceremony is held with numerous citizens.

The warehouse has a special section with state-of-the-art equipment to wrap up packages with a vacuum pack system. In addition, other equipment can keep foods frozen or cool by applying quick-cooling technology.

The new distribution center is expected to create more than 200 new jobs, according to Chuck Conrad, General Manager of Operations. Due to the size and scope of the work, a variety of new employees will be needed from loaders and drivers to office clerks.

TO:	Chuck Conrad <chuck@gianthawk.co.ca>
FROM:	Mallory Blaniar <mblaniar@gianthawk.co.ca>
SUBJECT:	Notification Company
DATE:	20 April

Dear Conrad,

Thanks for inviting me to the grand opening at the beginning of this month. It's unbelievable that I have seen such a well-organized event. We should get Mr. Andrew something to show our appreciation for preparing it.

I think that it is time to choose a company that sends automatic notifications to employees' cell phones. This service would enable us to deliver messages to our staff promptly and prevent some mistakes. I have the contact information of a company working with customer service at Sending to You. I guess that this is a good company, but Unitas Notification also looks great, and its monthly fees are lower than the former. Anyway, I attached the information for both companies to help you decide. Please let me know what you think.

Regards,

Mallory Blaniar

UNITAS NOTIFICATIONS

2:20 P.M.

To Giant Hawk Employees,

The frozen-item deliveries expected to arrive on Monday will not arrive until Wednesday. Employees who had volunteered to work overtime on Monday and Tuesday night at the Richmond Distribution Center will not be needed. However, we will need help for the overnight shift on Wednesday night. If you are willing to work additional hours at that time, please contact Sue Trinity in the Personnel Division.

196. What is the purpose of the article?

(A) To introduce a start-up venture
(B) To report on a business index
(C) To provide information on a new local issue
(D) To demonstrate the latest equipment

197. What is most likely true about the Richmond Distribution Center?

(A) Its opening ceremony was very impressive.
(B) Mr. Chuck will soon be retired from the site.
(C) Ms. Blaniar is one of the volunteer workers.
(D) Some technical issues took place.

198. What is the e-mail mainly about?

(A) Celebrating the opening ceremony
(B) Organizing the upcoming event
(C) Helping choose a company
(D) Breaking off a business connection

199. What company was selected by Mr. Chuck?

(A) The company that Ms. Blaniar works with
(B) The company that employees want to join
(C) The company that operates an overnight service
(D) The company that is cheaper than another

200. What does the message ask the employees wishing to work extra to do?

(A) Contact the human resources department
(B) Work for another distribution center
(C) Go to the warehouse from Tuesday
(D) Reply to the message within a day

Test

答對題數表

PART 5	
PART 6	
PART 7	
總題數	

05

READING TEST

In the Reading test, you will read a variety of texts and answer several different types of reading comprehension questions. The entire Reading test will last 75 minutes. There are three parts, and directions are given for each part. You are encouraged to answer as many questions as possible within the time allowed.

You must mark your answers on the separate answer sheet. Do not write your answers in your test book.

PART 5

Directions: A word or phrase is missing in each of the sentences below. Four answer choices are given below each sentence. Select the best answer to complete the sentence. Then mark the letter (A), (B), (C), or (D) on your answer sheet.

---

101. Mr. Robertson was concerned that the suggested hotel was not ------- enough to the airport.

(A) close
(B) closer
(C) closest
(D) closely

102. The University of Texas at Arlington provides residents ------- various recreational programs.

(A) for
(B) at
(C) with
(D) as

103. Office supplies should be ------- only for business-related purposes.

(A) purchase
(B) purchases
(C) purchased
(D) purchasing

104. In order to stick to the ------- of Omega Fashions, buyers ought to present a valid receipt when getting a refund.

(A) product
(B) sales
(C) manual
(D) policy

105. Anyone attending the mountain climbing activity has to prepare proper -------.

(A) equip
(B) equipped
(C) equipping
(D) equipment

106. The state-of-the-art program will ------- reduce the amount of time it takes to meet the deadline.

(A) significantly
(B) recently
(C) inappropriately
(D) approximately

107. Promising candidates should possess a license to operate ------- bulldozers and excavators.

(A) either
(B) both
(C) during
(D) after

108. We are scheduled to ------- the final results of the survey conducted last week with our customers on our website.

(A) share
(B) split
(C) ask
(D) improve

109. The department of human resources replaced its chairs with ------- ones to decrease noise in the office.
(A) lightly
(B) lighter
(C) lightest
(D) lightness

110. The schedule for the conference call has been changed, so those involved will attend on Monday -------.
(A) alike
(B) yet
(C) likewise
(D) instead

111. ------- of Mr. Anderson's telephone messages is to be left with his secretary while he has a meeting with his clients.
(A) Everyone
(B) Other
(C) All
(D) Each

112. Given the nature of the meeting, formal attire is considered -------.
(A) useful
(B) appropriate
(C) affirmative
(D) indicative

113. General Electronics plans to start a new business that ------- its customers to access more information.
(A) enabled
(B) enable
(C) has enabled
(D) will enable

114. The managers at Lion Autos award a prize to employees who continuously ------- their expectations.
(A) exceed
(B) command
(C) desire
(D) suggest

115. The recently released film by Astro Enterprises has received customer reviews and ratings that are ------- positive.
(A) except
(B) exception
(C) exceptional
(D) exceptionally

116. At Berkshire Hardaway, managers of each department are chosen based on their expertise and experience in a ------- area.
(A) granted
(B) provided
(C) particular
(D) substantial

117. Valuable, fragile or perishable items would be much more expensive to ship ------- they need greater care.
(A) because
(B) nevertheless
(C) however
(D) even

118. McKain and Mae is a full-service law firm that can help clients with a ------- of specialized legal needs.
(A) kind
(B) range
(C) way
(D) direction

119. The newest version of our computer program for business expenses, ------- contains various functions, is relatively easy to use.
(A) it
(B) which
(C) whose
(D) those

120. ------- you encounter any problems regarding assembly or operation, please call our customer service center.
(A) If
(B) Whether
(C) As
(D) Nor

Go on to the next page

121. The following document details the statistics the government will need for its ------- of next year's budget.

(A) analyze
(B) analyzes
(C) to analyze
(D) analysis

122. ------- a lot of people in Salt Lake City showed interest in the lifelong education program, none have yet enrolled.

(A) Even though
(B) As though
(C) However
(D) Likewise

123. Sales in North America are expected ------- most of the company's profits.

(A) generate
(B) generated
(C) to generate
(D) will generate

124. Lawyers process a sizable number of cases at the same time ------- strict time limits.

(A) near
(B) toward
(C) following
(D) within

125. The feasibility for the construction of the new museum is heavily ------- upon the city authorities' ability to pass the budget.

(A) depend
(B) depended
(C) dependable
(D) dependent

126. To prevent dairy and other ------- products from going bad, all trucks for Andy's food delivery service company are refrigerated.

(A) perishable
(B) pervasive
(C) adverse
(D) solid

127. The Ministry of Finance reported that many small and medium-sized businesses are ------- strapped during their first year of business.

(A) finance
(B) financial
(C) financing
(D) financially

128. Mr. Nakamoto recommends that travel expense reports be submitted ------- after employees return from their trip.

(A) measurably
(B) vaguely
(C) uniquely
(D) promptly

129. After careful -------, we decided to move to a larger location to accommodate more tourists.

(A) deliberate
(B) deliberated
(C) deliberately
(D) deliberation

130. With her outstanding performance, Ms. Ashley has already ------- herself from her colleagues.

(A) differentiated
(B) designated
(C) featured
(D) performed

PART 6

Directions: Read the texts that follow. A word, phrase, or sentence is missing in parts of each text. Four answer choices for each question are given below the text. Select the best answer to complete the text. Then mark the letter (A), (B), (C), or (D) on your answer sheet.

Questions 131-134 refer to the following e-mail.

To: Brian Nixon <bnixon@futuresky.co.au>
From: Jessica Hepburn <jhepburn@cardinalfargo.org.au>

Dear Mr. Nixon,

We have received your application for a photographer at Cardinal Fargo Studio. The ------- is
131.
still available. -------.
132.

I was quite ------- with your previous experience of working at other major studios, so you must
133.
be accustomed to some of the job duties we require. -------, our main business would be quite
134.
different from what you have done before, so you need to spend some time getting to know

about this. I have scheduled a job interview for 15 September at 10:00 A.M. To confirm the

schedule, please call my office at (01) 444-0125. I am looking forward to seeing you soon.

Sincerely,

Jessica Hepburn, Personnel Manager
Cardinal Fargo Studio

131. (A) document
 (B) position
 (C) operation
 (D) appointment

132. (A) Could you give us additional
 information regarding reimbursement?
 (B) To be specific, do you have any
 experience in designing unique styles?
 (C) Directions to the room for the interview
 can be found on our website.
 (D) If you are still interested in this job, an
 individual interview is the next step.

133. (A) impress
 (B) impressed
 (C) impressive
 (D) impression

134. (A) However
 (B) Therefore
 (C) Consequently
 (D) Moreover

Go on to the next page

April 20

Leonardo Cruise
111342 Main Street
Kroger, CA 91101

Dear Mr. Cruise,

We are delighted to inform you of the fact that Kroger Recycling Program will start in our area

on May 1. Residents who would like ------- in the program will be offered a blue container with
                                       135.
wheels. To ------- a container, please call 800-111-1217.
          136.

As scheduled, the program will take place once a week instead of twice a week. -------, this will
                                                                                 137.
reduce greenhouse gas emissions and provide us with a better environment.

If you need further information, such as a list of recyclable materials and maps, visit our

website at www.krogerrecycling.com. -------.
                                     138.
Sincerely,

Dwayne Damon, General Manager
Kroger Recycling Program

---

135. (A) participate
(B) participated
(C) to participate
(D) participating

136. (A) request
(B) reinvent
(C) review
(D) remove

137. (A) However
(B) Consequently
(C) Meanwhile
(D) On the other hand

138. (A) The program has raised significant funds thanks to generous donors.
(B) We hope that you take part in this important program.
(C) You will get the blue container within 10 days.
(D) Please make sure that you do not put fragile materials in your container.

City Mayor Alexandra Smith made the announcement that Robin Williams Tunnel ------- to

139.

better accommodate larger trucks. Drivers using the tunnel have increased significantly over

the last few years due to the growth of freight transportations in this area. It is expected to take

approximately ten months to finish this expansion project. -------.

140.

Jacksonville Road, which runs ------- the tunnel, is to be closed and traffic congestion between

141.

Amitiel and Hennatown will increase during that time. " -------, it is the only possible option we

142.

could have," said mayor Smith.

139. (A) expand
(B) to expand
(C) was expanded
(D) will be expanded

140. (A) Robin Williams Tunnel was completed one hundred years ago.
(B) Those living in Amitiel have complained about traffic jams.
(C) Freight service companies hope to recruit graduates from Hennatown University.
(D) The provisional estimate of eighteen months has been reduced as a result of accurate measurement.

141. (A) along
(B) next
(C) while
(D) over

142. (A) Surprisingly
(B) Accordingly
(C) Therefore
(D) Unfortunately

TEST 05

PART 6

Go on to the next page

To: Sarah O'Connor <sarah_oconnor@pinghwacorp.com>
From: Jim Lennon <jim_lennon@ams.com>
Date: November 11
Subject: AMS
Attachment: AMS Brochure

Dear Ms. Sarah O'Connor,

We would like to express our gratitude for your inquiry on AMS. Our most advanced software

program has helped a great number of companies streamline their performance appraisal

process, ------- time and money.
      143.

We would recommend that you ------- the attached file. It contains information about five top-
          144.
notch companies taking advantage of AMS. As you are aware, the ability to browse through

evaluation sheets based on ratings has been exceptionally helpful to them. -------, they can
           145.
easily find all candidates who are eligible for promotion with our software program. In addition,

after the entire digital sorting process is done, there is no paper clutter. -------.
           146.

If you have any questions regarding this, please let me know.

Sincerely,

Jim Lennon
AMS Marketing Manager

---

143. (A) save
(B) saves
(C) saved
(D) saving

144. (A) review
(B) make
(C) prepare
(D) throw

145. (A) As a result
(B) As long as
(C) In the meantime
(D) In keeping with

146. (A) Our software will be updated next week.
(B) It will be a difficult task for you to sift through qualified candidates for promotion.
(C) All the sheets are well organized in the computerized database.
(D) Candidates should have at least 3 years of experience in a related field.

PART 7

Directions: In this part you will read a selection of texts, such as magazine and newspaper articles, e-mails, and instant messages. Each text or set of texts is followed by several questions. Select the best answer for each question and mark the letter (A), (B), (C), or (D) on your answer sheet.

Questions 147-148 refer to the following text message.

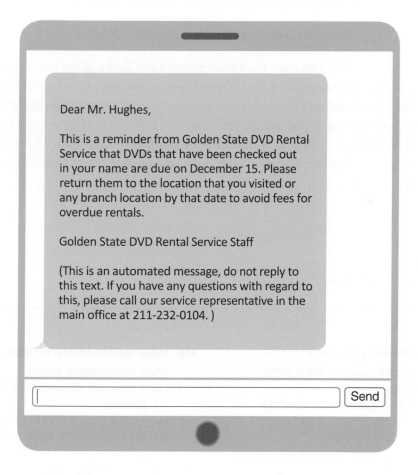

Dear Mr. Hughes,

This is a reminder from Golden State DVD Rental Service that DVDs that have been checked out in your name are due on December 15. Please return them to the location that you visited or any branch location by that date to avoid fees for overdue rentals.

Golden State DVD Rental Service Staff

(This is an automated message, do not reply to this text. If you have any questions with regard to this, please call our service representative in the main office at 211-232-0104.)

Send

147. Why did Mr. Hughes receive the text message?

(A) Because the items that he borrowed should be turned in soon
(B) Because he should pay late fees by December 15
(C) Because the items he requested are already sold out
(D) Because his membership card is set to expire on December 15

148. According to the text message, what could Mr. Hughes do if he has any questions?

(A) Visit the rental service company's website
(B) Speak with a service representative
(C) Send a text message to a service representative
(D) Go to any branch location of the rental service

Questions 149-150 refer to the following e-mail.

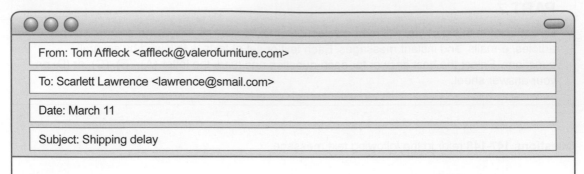

From: Tom Affleck <affleck@valerofurniture.com>

To: Scarlett Lawrence <lawrence@smail.com>

Date: March 11

Subject: Shipping delay

Dear Ms. Lawrence,

Thank you for your recent purchase from Valero Furniture. Some of the items have yet to be shipped owing to the heavy snow in our area. Closures on the roads have also made it harder for items to be delivered from our warehouse. To make matters worse, the snow has caused power failures in our region. We, however, promise that we will get back to normal within 12 hours. Thus, your order will be shipped no later than Wednesday. The shipping fee on all affected orders will be fully refunded. We do apologize for any inconvenience this may cause you.

Sincerely,

Tom Affleck
Customer Service Manager

149. Why was the e-mail written?
(A) To give an update on the weather conditions
(B) To inform Ms. Lawrence of a late shipment
(C) To advertise furniture
(D) To report that some roads have been closed

150. What will Ms. Lawrence receive?
(A) A confirmation e-mail
(B) A discount voucher for a future purchase
(C) Free shipping on her order
(D) An additional new product

New Rules for Trash Collection

Krudenwald City will set a limit on the number of trash bins, which starts on April 25. Therefore, residents can now put no more than three trash bins outside for each curbside pickup, even though the monthly fee for trash collection is still unchanged. The sum of all trash bins should not exceed 100 liters in size.

City officials said that encouraging residents to take advantage of the city's free collection and recycling services for metal, plastic, and paper is part of the city's efforts to reduce the cost of trash collection. This will decrease landfill dumping fees as well.

151. What is the purpose of the notice?

(A) To provide a new service
(B) To announce a policy change
(C) To complain about recycling fees
(D) To recommend a landfill site

152. According to the notice, what can residents use free of charge?

(A) A recycling service
(B) A trash collection service
(C) A trash bin
(D) A landfill site

TEST

05

PART

7

MEMO

To: All employees
From: Christian Diesel, Director of Operations
Date: Thursday, July 28
Subject: West Wing Closure

The west wing of the building will be closed in the first week of August. The maintenance department will be in charge of replacing all the chairs and desks with environmentally friendly ones. According to the safety regulations, the site is off-limits to all employees while the maintenance staff is at work. The replacement schedule will start on Tuesday, August 1, and it will be finished on Saturday, August 5.

The affected offices are 1201–1235. Employees involved should work at home or, if necessary, a temporary workspace can be prepared for them in another part of the building. You may call administrative assistant Natalie Johansson at extension 51 to request a temporary workspace. Please note that we have limited temporary workspaces, which will be provided on a first-come, first-served basis. Thank you for your cooperation.

---

153. What is the reason for the closure of the west wing?

(A) A regular inspection will be taking place.
(B) The headquarters will be moved to a different location.
(C) Office furniture will be replaced.
(D) Space for meetings will be added.

154. Which of the following offices will be temporarily unavailable?

(A) 1200
(B) 1224
(C) 1236
(D) 1240

155. What should employees do if they would like to request a temporary workspace?

(A) Contact their supervisor
(B) Write an e-mail to Mr. Diesel
(C) Apply online
(D) Call Ms. Johansson

Questions 156-158 refer to the following e-mail.

From: Angelina Grant <agrant@lowecatering.com>

To: James Hardy <jhardy@uig.com>

Date: June 11

Subject: Catering service

Dear Mr. Hardy,

This e-mail is to confirm your telephone conversation yesterday with respect to your request for a catering service for the annual corporate conference. My understanding is that it should be similar to what you requested for last year's conference. Unfortunately, my food supplier has notified me of the fact that due to a shortage of beef, they are unable to provide it until next week. As you will hold the conference on June 15, I think it would be necessary to choose a different type of meat. I recommend chicken, which could be ready in time. So, if this is acceptable, please let me know by responding directly to this e-mail. Once you agree to the alternative, I will send you the contract and estimate sheet. If you need more information, please call me at 514-212-0114.

Thank you,

Angelina Grant, Manager
Lowe Catering Service

156. What is suggested about Mr. Hardy?

(A) He is Ms. Grant's colleague.
(B) He is planning a dinner party for his friends.
(C) He has requested a service from Lowe Catering Service before.
(D) He has asked for a change to a service.

157. Why does Ms. Grant recommend replacing the food item?

(A) It is out of stock.
(B) It is very expensive.
(C) It lacks freshness.
(D) It doesn't taste good.

158. What does Ms. Grant ask Mr. Hardy to do next?

(A) Send a contract
(B) Call her immediately
(C) Reply to an e-mail
(D) Cancel a meeting

Go on to the next page

Questions 159-160 refer to the following text message chain.

🔵⬛❌		

Seneca Co. Agent [5:15 P.M.]	Hello, this is Seneca Co. Service Center. What's your problem?
Martin Ford [5:15 P.M.]	I am having trouble with updating the newest version of software for my desktop.
Seneca Co. Agent [5:16 P.M.]	What kind of desktop do you have?
Martin Ford [5:17 P.M.]	It's an XPS 8910. In order to download the software, I have to enter the correct serial number, but I can't find it.
Seneca Co. Agent [5:18 P.M.]	Here's how to find the serial number on your product. It is printed near the barcode on your product packaging.
Seneca Co. Agent [5:18 P.M.]	It could be too small to read, so take a photo of the number with your mobile phone, then zoom in.
Martin Ford [5:19 P.M.]	Yes, there is a ten-digit number on it. Is that it?
Seneca Co. Agent [5:20 P.M.]	Yes, that's right. Is there anything else that I could do to help you?
Martin Ford [5:20 P.M.]	No. Thank you so much.

		Send

159. What is Mr. Ford trying to do?

(A) Find his password
(B) Create an account
(C) Buy a computer
(D) Download software

160. At 5:19 P.M. what does Mr. Ford most likely mean when he writes, "Is that it?"?

(A) He wanted to check what he was looking for.
(B) He didn't understand the agent's idea.
(C) He has not used the online service before.
(D) He wanted to end the online chat.

From:	Bradley Cooper [bcooper@sysco.com]
To:	Robert Gosling [rgosling@sysco.com]
Date:	January 4
Subject:	Donation program

Dear Mr. Gosling,

I have looked into the documents you gave with regard to Sysco's new donation program. —[1]—. At the next department meeting, you should share the information in the documents with our members. —[2]—. Moreover, I will encourage them to check the list of recommended organizations and participate in the program by selecting at least one of these to donate to before the program starts in February. —[3]—.

Please give me a call at your earliest convenience to discuss some issues about the program. —[4]—. Thank you in advance for your cooperation.

Sincerely,

Bradley Cooper
The Department of Human Resources

161. What does Mr. Cooper want Mr. Gosling to do?

(A) Discuss details about the program
(B) Make a donation to some organizations
(C) Reschedule a department meeting
(D) Create a donation program

162. What is suggested about Sysco's new donation program?

(A) It is scheduled to go into effect in February.
(B) It is limited only to employees.
(C) It is held twice a year.
(D) It allows for employees to choose only one organization.

163. In which of the positions marked [1], [2], [3], and [4] does the following sentence best belong?

"This will take several weeks to decide."

(A) [1]
(B) [2]
(C) [3]
(D) [4]

TEST

05

PART

7

Questions 164-167 refer to the following letter.

May 1

Ryan Eastwood
Pinewood Apartment #1299
Orange County, California 562

Dear Mr. Eastwood,

Your Pinewood rental apartment is subject to a regular maintenance assessment. We are scheduled to visit on Tuesday, May 15, at 2:00 P.M. What we request is that tenants be present. Please let us know a time that works for you if this time is inconvenient for you. —[1]—.

During the assessment, we check several important items to make sure that they are working properly, which include appliances, the gas line, and plumbing. —[2]—.

According to our check-up lists, the interior of your apartment has not been painted for five years. If you want your house to be repainted, our maintenance staff will handle the task. We will make the utmost effort to finish the work in a timely fashion. —[3]—. We have a range of colors for painting, and you can see them by visiting our website at www.pinewood.com/colorsforpaint. —[4]—. Finally, our records indicate that the furniture in your house was fully replaced last year, so the replacement is not available at this time.

If you have any questions, please call me anytime.

Best Regards,

Chris Hemsworth
Office Manager

164. Why was the letter sent to Mr. Eastwood?
(A) To provide him with information on a rental promotion
(B) To notify him of a late payment
(C) To inform him of upcoming check-ups
(D) To suggest an annual event in an apartment

165. What is Mr. Eastwood asked to do on the afternoon of May 15?
(A) Visit a Website
(B) Choose paint colors
(C) Reply to an e-mail
(D) Stay at home

166. What home improvement work is Mr. Eastwood currently eligible for?
(A) Painting a house
(B) Changing to new appliances
(C) Fixing doors
(D) Replacing furniture

167. In which of the positions marked [1], [2], [3], and [4] does the following sentence best belong?

"If necessary, maintenance work will be performed."
(A) [1]
(B) [2]
(C) [3]
(D) [4]

148

Questions 168-171 refer to the following form.

Moonlight Questionnaire

Thank you for participating in the preview of the film tentatively named *Moonlight*. As the film is in its final stages, it would be a great help for the final editing if you could give us your opinions about the film. Please take a few minutes to answer to the following questions.

Name: Rachel Jane
Address: 2885 Sanford Avenue Grandville 28912

What was your impression of this film?
I loved it! I enjoyed watching the same characters and scenes that I had imagined when reading the original novel a few years ago. It was a perfect adaptation of the novel.

How about the sound quality? Please elaborate.
It was very clear. Especially, I loved its soundtrack. In general, there was no part where I could hardly understand the dialogue.

If there are any parts that seem too long, please elaborate on this.
It seemed that this film was a bit longer than any other films that I have ever seen. However, all scenes were necessary for its storyline and flowed together smoothly. I would personally recommend not making any cuts.

Do you have any other comments?
Emma Aniston and James Niro gave quite excellent performances. I have never paid attention to Jessica Watson before. This time, she was amazing, and I hope she wins an award for this film. Just one thing I would like to mention is that what she wore in the movie didn't seem true to the original. The film is set in the mid-1880s. I think she should have worn something historically accurate.

168. To whom was the questionnaire given?

(A) Professional writers
(B) Acting class members
(C) Directors in the film industry
(D) Audience members at a film screening

169. What is indicated about *Moonlight*?

(A) It has a relatively short running time.
(B) It is based on a book.
(C) It is filmed in a documentary style.
(D) It was completed a few years ago.

170. What can be inferred about Ms. Watson?

(A) She recently starred in several films.
(B) She dropped out of the film.
(C) She was participating in the preview of the film.
(D) She had an impressive performance in the film.

171. What does Ms. Jane recommend?

(A) Enabling the dialogue to be understood more easily
(B) Making clothing more authentic
(C) Including more soundtracks
(D) Shortening the film

Questions 172-175 refer to the following online chat discussion.

Sandra Lopez [9:02 A.M.]		Good morning. The board of directors approved our company's merger at the December meeting. I would like to know what you heard from the managers' meeting at the headquarters.
Kate Lively [9:03 A.M.]		At first, it caused a lot of confusion, but everything is restored to normal now. People seem to know what is going to happen.
Cameron Winslet [9:03 A.M.]		Employees here are convinced that the merger will lead to changes in personnel. Everybody is expressing concerns about any moves in February. That's because it is our busiest time of the year. When are we going to get detailed information on this?
Cate Adams [9:05 A.M.]		I am not in the right position to answer these questions without knowing more information from the head office.
Sandra Lopez [9:07 A.M.]		I'll keep working on this. I will get more information before long. In February when the four of us meet together, I will make a report.
Cameron Winslet [9:08 A.M.]		It seems that some of our employees will move boxes in March.
Sadra Lopez [9:09 A.M.]		It could be possible. The personnel department is still figuring out which offices will receive employees from the other teams.
Cate Adams [9:10 A.M.]		There must be plenty of decisions to be made.

Send

172. Why did Ms. Lopez start an online chat with the managers?

(A) To cancel a meeting
(B) To announce an upcoming merger
(C) To gather some opinions
(D) To change the date of the relocation

173. At 9:07 A.M., what does Ms. Lopez most likely mean when she writes, "I'll keep working on this."?

(A) She is trying to get an update.
(B) Employees increased substantially last year.
(C) The headquarters will be moved in February.
(D) She is making an effort to get back to normal.

174. When will the managers receive the updated information?

(A) In December
(B) In January
(C) In February
(D) In March

175. What is the personnel department expected to do?

(A) Reshuffle some employees
(B) Provide employees with office supplies
(C) Introduce new employees
(D) Replace the old personnel system

Statewide Insurance Co.

848 Main Street, Fresno, CA 93721-2760

April 8
George Hanks
2451 Inyo Street, Fresno, CA 93721

Dear Mr. Hanks,

Thank you for applying for the position of junior associate with Statewide Insurance Co. We regret to inform you that we decided to select another applicant after much consideration. However, we were very impressed by not only what you have done in the past few years, but also the knowledge and expertise you showed when you interviewed. Therefore, we would like to offer you a vacant position that we believe suits you.

The position that we offer you is a part-time job, unlike the one you applied for. The working hours are from 2 P.M. to 6 P.M. on Tuesday and Thursday, and 3 P.M. to 7 P.M. on Monday, Wednesday, and Friday. Your primary responsibilities will be gathering and analyzing information and data, providing potential clients with tailor-made plans, and planning insurance products.

If you are interested in this position, feel free to call me at 515-217-0121 or email me at markchan@statewideinsurance.com.

| From: George Hanks [ghanks@atmail.com] |
| To: Mark Chan [markchan@statewideinsurance.com] |
| Date: April 10 |
| Re: Your letter |

Dear Mr. Chan,

Thank you for your letter in which you offered me a job. I am very delighted to join Statewide Insurance Co. I am wondering, however, if the company could adjust my business hours.

At the interview session, I mentioned that I have been working as a volunteer with the International Insurance Society (IIS). There could be a scheduling conflict on Monday and Tuesday since I am now working for the organization Monday and Tuesday from 9 A.M. to 3 P.M. So, I would really appreciate it if your company would allow me to work from 4 P.M. to 8 P.M. on Monday and Tuesday.

I am looking forward to hearing from you soon.

Best wishes,

George Hanks

176. For what kind of company does Mr. Chan most likely work?

(A) A law firm
(B) An auto manufacturer
(C) A publisher
(D) An insurance company

177. In the letter, the word "select" in paragraph 1, line 2, is closest in meaning to

(A) go with
(B) receive
(C) depend on
(D) account for

178. What is mentioned about Mr. Chan's company?

(A) It has joined with the International Insurance Society.
(B) It recently signed a great number of clients.
(C) It has never hired full-time employees before.
(D) It offers an insurance planning service.

179. Why was the e-mail written?

(A) To ask for a change of working hours
(B) To make inquiries about benefits for employees
(C) To recommend someone else qualified for the position
(D) To request a pay increase

180. What most likely will NOT be a responsibility Mr. Hanks takes at Mr. Chan's company?

(A) Collecting materials
(B) Counseling customers
(C) Introducing products
(D) Interviewing job applicants

Go on to the next page

New York Media Corporation
Research and Development Team

Annual Performance Appraisal Report
Name: Kim Barrymore
Title: Research Associate

Please write all major events and projects in which you took part this year.

1. Offered four-week course of media law for students at New York University majoring in mass communication (February 2–28)
2. Represented Research and Development Team at the 10th anniversary of News Media Conference, New York City (March 2–3)
3. Acted as a guest speaker, *"Current Status of Internet Media"* at the World Journalism Forum, London, England (May 12–15)
4. Carried out a research project on a new wave of Internet broadcasting (January — November). Study submitted to *Broadcasting Trade Journal*, accepted for publication.
5. Led public tours of new headquarters at New York Media Corporation (December).

NY Media's Kim Barrymore Receives Award

by David Stewart, JSP Journalist

December 17—Kim Barrymore from New York Media Corp. has been named Journalist of the Year for her research project on a new wave of Internet broadcasting.

Margot Green, editor-in-chief of New York Media Corp., mentioned that it is unusual for the award to be given to a researcher. She went on to say, "It is attributable to Barrymore's hard work and dedication. And we're very delighted to have her on our team."

Ms. Barrymore joined New York Media Corp. 10 years ago after earning a doctorate degree in mass communication from New York University. She received her undergraduate education at Brooklyn Latin School in New York.

The award ceremony will be held on 23 December at the New York Conference Center.

181. According to the report, why did Ms. Barrymore go to England?

(A) To report a case
(B) To study mass media
(C) To deliver a speech
(D) To tour a new research facility

182. What does the report suggest happened at New York Media Corp. in December?

(A) An international forum was held.
(B) New courses for university students were given.
(C) A new head office was opened.
(D) The cost for public tours decreased.

183. Where most likely did Ms. Barrymore's article first appear?

(A) A magazine published by New York University
(B) On the website of New York Media Corporation
(C) In an industry publication
(D) In a scientific journal

184. What does Ms. Green imply about the Journalist of the Year award?

(A) It offers both a medal and prize money.
(B) It is presented by New York Media Corp.
(C) It is rarely presented to a researcher.
(D) It is only for New York residents.

185. What is mentioned about the News Media Conference?

(A) It is usually organized by the government.
(B) It was not held for the first time this year.
(C) It gives university students complimentary tickets.
(D) It is held every two years.

Go on to the next page

Honeywell International's Offices to Be Relocated

March 1 — Honeywell International is scheduled to move its offices in Sydney, Melbourne, and Brisbane into company-owned properties. The significant increase in rental costs forced the company to make such a decision.

"We came to realize that building our own offices would result in saving money in many ways," said Elizabeth Lohan, Honeywell International's general director. She also mentioned that sharing space with other businesses has caused discomfort and inconvenience when doing businesses. Construction of its headquarters in Sydney, which began two years ago, will finally be finished this month.

Construction of the other branch offices in Melbourne and Brisbane will be finished in one year, and then employees will be moved accordingly.

A representative of the company said that its entire workforce, which totaled approximately 1,000 employees last year, will be relocated to one of the new buildings no later than July.

TIAA Relocation Services

We will handle everything for you. TIAA makes your move easier.

A relocation consulting service will be provided free of charge. Our consultant will visit your office or your home to give an estimate for the move. We will send you a written estimate by e-mail within two to three days after the visit.

Whenever you need us during the move, we will always be there for you.
• Do you need help packing? Our team members can help you with anything.
• Do you want to move any classified materials? We will arrange a schedule with your security staff to make sure that confidential files and documents are monitored without interruption.
• Do you need some space to hold your belongings? Our strictly-controlled warehouse is prepared for you.

We will fulfill our tasks. We will do our best to make all items neatly arranged.

TIAA Relocation Services Estimate Sheet

Please complete the following request form to schedule a visit for an accurate estimate.

Company Name :	Honeywell International	**Name of contact person :**	Elizabeth Lohan
Telephone number :	128-01-2821169	**E-mail :**	el0800@atmail.co.au
Pick-up address :	680 George Street, Sydney	**Delivery address:**	458 Harris Street, Sydney
Pick-up date :	April 3	**Delivery date :**	April 3

Preferred date and time for an estimate: March 3, 10:00 A.M.

186. In the article, the word "forced" in paragraph 1, line 2, is closest in meaning to

(A) compelled
(B) acted quickly
(C) broke down
(D) made a difference

187. What is inferred about Ms. Lohan?

(A) She was promoted to general director this year.
(B) She has worked for Honeywell International for five years.
(C) She will move to the headquarters in April.
(D) She works in Honeywell International's Brisbane office.

188. What kind of service does TIAA offer?

(A) Constructing buildings
(B) Transporting sensitive items
(C) Maintaining computer systems
(D) Strengthening security

189. What is implied about the Harris Street location?

(A) It will accommodate nearly 1,000 employees.
(B) It was constructed in approximately two years.
(C) It has recently been remodeled.
(D) It is now rented by other firms.

190. What will most likely happen on March 3?

(A) A TIAA employee will visit George Street.
(B) Items will be properly arranged.
(C) Ms. Lohan will check an e-mail to review an estimate.
(D) Classified documents will be moved.

TEST
05

PART
7

Questions 191-195 refer to the following Web page, list, and article.

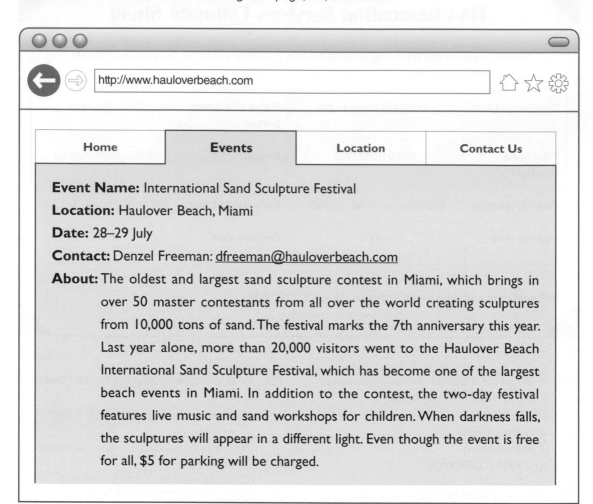

http://www.hauloverbeach.com

| Home | Events | Location | Contact Us |

Event Name: International Sand Sculpture Festival

Location: Haulover Beach, Miami

Date: 28–29 July

Contact: Denzel Freeman: dfreeman@hauloverbeach.com

About: The oldest and largest sand sculpture contest in Miami, which brings in over 50 master contestants from all over the world creating sculptures from 10,000 tons of sand. The festival marks the 7th anniversary this year. Last year alone, more than 20,000 visitors went to the Haulover Beach International Sand Sculpture Festival, which has become one of the largest beach events in Miami. In addition to the contest, the two-day festival features live music and sand workshops for children. When darkness falls, the sculptures will appear in a different light. Even though the event is free for all, $5 for parking will be charged.

Winners of the 7th International Sand Sculpture Festival

Placement	Name	Title of Piece
First Place	Humphrey Washington, England	Dinosaurs
Second Place	Jack Nicholson, Canada	Spaceships
Third Place	Johnny Spacey, U.S.	Castle
Fourth Place	Russel Pitt, Denmark	Pirates and Princesses
Fifth Place	Lonardo Travolta, Argentina	Sea Creatures

WHAT'S NEW IN MIAMI

By Christian Winslet

(1 August)—The 7th International Sand Sculpture Festival was held last weekend and was the best way to enjoy the summer. Due to the exceptionally fantastic weather, the event attracted more visitors than last year. This year, there was a competition for solo masters. They created eye-catching sand creatures and turned mere sand and water into genuine art. Masters depicted everything from sea creatures to castles and even spaceships in a somewhat exaggerated way.

Humphrey Washington from England beat three-time champion Jack Nicholson from Canada with his "Dinosaur" sculpture, which dazzled the judges with its absolute artistic realism. All the sculptures were attractive, but my personal favorite was "Pirates and Princesses," which vividly expressed comic gestures through the characters' arms and faces.

Children could participate in the sand class led by sand sculpting experts who were not participating in the contest. Live music pleased visitors' ears as well. This must be the perfect way to enjoy the hottest season.

191. What is mentioned about the contestants?

(A) They are all amateurs.
(B) They have an acquaintance with Mr. Freeman.
(C) They had to sign up online in advance for the event.
(D) They are from various countries.

192. In the article, the word "attracted" in paragraph 1, line 3, is closest in meaning to

(A) moved
(B) drew
(C) won
(D) participated

193. What is indicated about this year's event?

(A) It cost 5 dollars to attend.
(B) It had over 20,000 visitors.
(C) It took place at Haulover Beach for the first time.
(D) It had adult-only programs.

194. What is indicated about Mr. Nicholson?

(A) He has won the contest before.
(B) He has led a sand class.
(C) He just moved to Canada.
(D) He is a member of a national team.

195. Whose sculpture did Ms. Winslet like the most?

(A) Mr. Washington's
(B) Mr. Nicholson's
(C) Mr. Spacey's
(D) Mr. Pitt's

Go on to the next page

International Financial Investment Forum

Nairobi Conference Center, Kenya
Thursday, November 8

The 1st International Financial Investment Forum in Kenya will be a venue for discussing the current state of financial investment industry. Africa is one of the fastest growing markets in the world. The tourism and building infrastructure have brought a huge influx of money into Africa. World-renowned presenters will bring their expertise, passion, and enthusiasm to their session and share their insights on various issues. To participate in the forum, all involved are required to have their names registered. Anyone who would like to attend, please feel free to visit our website at www.ifif.org and fill in the sign-up form. No participation fee is charged.

Please note that applications for participants will be accepted entirely on a first-come, first-served basis because of the limited number of seats.

Time	Presenter	Title
9:00 A.M.	Keira Jane	Current Status of Africa
10:30 A.M.	Catherine Jones	Economic and Market Outlooks in Africa
12:00 P.M.	Lunch Break	
1:00 P.M.	Clive Gibson	Strategic Investment
2:00 P.M.	George Bloom	Quality Decision-Making Process
3:00 P.M.	Sandra Ryan	Risk Management

From: Sandra Ryan <sryan@ryaninvestmentgroup.com>

To: Megan Diaz <mdiaz@ifif.org>

Subject: November Forum

Date: September 15

Dear Ms. Diaz,

Thank you for giving me the opportunity to be a part of this meaningful forum. First of all, I have to say that the international forum will have a great impact on the industry in Africa, which needs more investment across the board.

I have received the full schedule of presentations. Unfortunately, I have an important commitment in Kenya after the lunch break, so I have to leave the venue by 11:00 at the latest. The schedule indicated that I am the last presenter. Although I already reported the issue to the organizing committee, I want to get a definite answer. So if it is possible to change my presentation schedule, please send me a revised schedule and distribute it to everyone.

Thank you.

Sincerely,

Sandra Ryan
Ryan Investment Group

196. What are participants required to do?

(A) Arrive at the event site 30 minutes early
(B) Register online
(C) Receive name cards
(D) Take a designated seat

197. Who will make a speech on economic forecasts?

(A) Keira Jane
(B) Catherine Jones
(C) Clive Gibson
(D) George Bloom

198. When will Ms. Ryan probably speak at the forum if it is rescheduled?

(A) 9:00 A.M.
(B) 12:00 A.M.
(C) 2:00 P.M.
(D) 3:00 P.M.

199. What is indicated about Ms. Ryan?

(A) She has to go to the airport after her presentation.
(B) She has an appointment during the forum.
(C) She changed her topic before the event.
(D) She is a member of the organizing committee.

200. What does Ms. Ryan request that Ms. Diaz do?

(A) Extend the registration date
(B) Get approval from the hotel
(C) Update an event document
(D) Change a location

Test

答對題數表

PART 5	
PART 6	
PART 7	
總題數	

06

READING TEST

In the Reading test, you will read a variety of texts and answer several different types of reading comprehension questions. The entire Reading test will last 75 minutes. There are three parts, and directions are given for each part. You are encouraged to answer as many questions as possible within the time allowed.

You must mark your answers on the separate answer sheet. Do not write your answers in your test book.

PART 5

Directions: A word or phrase is missing in each of the sentences below. Four answer choices are given below each sentence. Select the best answer to complete the sentence. Then mark the letter (A), (B), (C), or (D) on your answer sheet.

101. As one of the company's events, GLK-Auto provides complimentary auto parts to ------ loyal customers.

(A) they
(B) their
(C) them
(D) theirs

102. Taking advantage of Power-Shoulder to ------ goods can prevent people from getting injured on their shoulders.

(A) achieve
(B) cause
(C) lift
(D) culminate

103. Some ------ coast communities are totally dependent on the shipping and fishing industry to earn a living.

(A) locate
(B) local
(C) location
(D) locals

104. Ruby's Friday restaurant is always ------ to provide exceptional dishes to our customers by hiring professional chefs.

(A) delicious
(B) ready
(C) experienced
(D) complicated

105. If you have a problem with the item, please return it to the nearest store ------ seven days of the purchase to get a refund.

(A) until
(B) out of
(C) within
(D) from

106. A ------ of products targeted for the winter season has been gradually piled into stockrooms in Portland stores.

(A) series
(B) lack
(C) frequency
(D) length

107. According to the monthly financial report, these results of increasing loans on properties accord ------ with predictions in the popular magazine, *Jerry's Economy*.

(A) newly
(B) lately
(C) closely
(D) drastically

108. A policy without any discussion among the management should not ------ the decision-making process regarding expanding their branches internationally.

(A) act
(B) remind
(C) influence
(D) confess

109. Premium Ltd. has made an extensive
------ to its assembly line to increase its
productivity, which had caused a lot of
mechanical problems.

(A) modifying
(B) modification
(C) modify
(D) to modify

110. Mr. Terry has sent the loan application
to several banks for securing funds
displayed on the proof of bank statement
------ to purchase a new house in Austin,
Texas.

(A) require
(B) will require
(C) required
(D) requiring

111. Ms. Yoon has started the research project
on second language writers by -------,
but recently asked peers to help with
collecting reliable data.

(A) her
(B) hers
(C) herself
(D) she

112. ------- this year's annual profits are lower
than expected, the management at
Johnny Index Distributions is not willing to
approve employees' annual pay raise.

(A) Owing to
(B) Given that
(C) With regard to
(D) In case of

113. The Maxi Department Store has attracted
a lot of people due to its ------ to many
urban transportation.

(A) arena
(B) field
(C) proximity
(D) width

114. ------- advance ticket sales number more
than three thousand, Penn Entertainment
uses its main auditorium at Kovalchick
Convention Center in Flint City.

(A) Whether
(B) If
(C) That
(D) Despite

115. Candidates are ------ to submit their
portfolios to apply for the position at Alex
Cooper Appliances.

(A) will ask
(B) asks
(C) asking
(D) asked

116. The award committee of Selex Security
Service nominated the top 10 employees
------- are entitled to get the Employee
of the Year Award at its 20th anniversary
banquet.

(A) those
(B) anyone
(C) who
(D) which

117. The newly installed program for the staff
payroll system will be operational ------
on Friday, March 17, unless otherwise
directed by a general manager.

(A) beginning
(B) to begin
(C) will begin
(D) beginner

118. As of next year, UPT Electronics ------ its
branches into other countries, especially
Eastern Asia, for diverse businesses.

(A) have expanded
(B) are expanding
(C) will expand
(D) is expanded

119. You can easily find the Stapleton Library,
which is located slightly ------ the Oak
Grove on the IUP Campus.

(A) over
(B) among
(C) between
(D) past

120. If you purchase the latest items from
Savannah Electronics, please thoroughly
------ the manual that comes with the item.

(A) program
(B) gather
(C) direct
(D) review

Go on to the next page

121. Whenever ------ with prospective clients, please keep in mind that you should tell them about approaching special offers such as online discounts.
(A) to speak
(B) speaking
(C) spoke
(D) spoken

122. Recruitment experts will help to distinguish a ------ candidate from other applicants by using tools for assessment of aptitude.
(A) selling
(B) promising
(C) reminding
(D) proposing

123. Montgomery Corp. is ------ to confirm that they achieve a diversity of positive results from distribution, exclusive sales, and service sectors.
(A) pleasure
(B) please
(C) pleasing
(D) pleased

124. Working as a senior manager at Punxtwaney City Museum two years ago, Mr. McNab has ------ been in charge of directing main exhibitions.
(A) since
(B) yet
(C) ever
(D) too

125. Premier Investment Co. was forcibly operating inefficient production lines at a deficit, which might be damaging the company's ------ for maintaining its rank in the financial world.
(A) reputation
(B) negotiation
(C) consideration
(D) rotation

126. After parliament members reach an agreement to the amendments, the new regulations will be fully understandable to ------ concerned about the election.
(A) each other
(B) whatever
(C) anything
(D) everyone

127. ------ all the prerequisite courses have been finished, the graduate students should prepare for their comprehensive written and oral test.
(A) While
(B) So that
(C) As soon as
(D) In that

128. The board of directors has already recognized ------- of the issue when all sales figures started to take a downward curve in the budget report.
(A) specifically
(B) specify
(C) specific
(D) specifics

129. Once you submit the application for the position, you are ------ to hear the interview schedule from the Personnel Division.
(A) limited
(B) sought
(C) bound
(D) covered

130. If the item you purchased had been damaged, you ------ to return it to a nearby store for exchange.
(A) would have been opted
(B) would have opted
(C) has opted
(D) is being opted

PART 6

Directions: Read the texts that follow. A word, phrase, or sentence is missing in parts of each text. Four answer choices for each question are given below the text. Select the best answer to complete the text. Then mark the letter (A), (B), (C), or (D) on your answer sheet.

Questions 131-134 refer to the following e-mail.

To: Brad Triana

From: John Fontainne

Date: 17 March

Subject: A request for advice about theater renovation

Dear Mr. Triana,

We have spent a lot of time dealing with the recommendations you gave at the last meeting.

Above all, we ------- a wide black curtain that blocks the noise from the outside of the stage. For
     131.

testing its degree of blocking, our worker stood ------- near the stage, and we couldn't hear any
           132.

sound during pre-practice. We also have plans to comply with your recommendations to expand

the control console, enabling experienced staff to work closely together. -------.
                133.

We are pleased ------- your useful and informative guidelines and look forward to meeting you
      134.

next time.

Sincerely,

John Fontainne

131. (A) purchase
(B) purchased
(C) will purchase
(D) are purchasing

132. (A) shortly
(B) hardly
(C) only
(D) rather

133. (A) This can enable us to manage our lighting and sounds more effectively than before.
(B) The prior curtain is too thin to screen noise from the outside.
(C) There is only one improvement we made among your recommendations.
(D) We want to increase the number of ticket sales for the next performance.

134. (A) to
(B) with
(C) for
(D) on

Go on to the next page

Questions 135-138 refer to the following article.

Indiana Tribune – Business Briefing

Clarion (20 October) – Tyler Srinogil has been promoted to the chief editor of the *Indiana*

Tribune. The board of directors ------- his promotion on Friday. -------. As of next month, he
           135.   **136.**

will supervise the featured columns and inserted images. -------, he will manage the overall
                                             137.

operations for IndianaTribune.com, the company's online website. Tyler Srinogil is an

industrious staff member ------- the improvement of IndianaTribune.com last year.
                      138.

---

135. (A) confirmed
(B) indicated
(C) provided
(D) rewarded

136. (A) Tyler Srinogil has served as assistant editor for two years.
(B) The chief editor position will stay open until filled.
(C) The *Indiana Tribune* has just leased a new building space downtown.
(D) The management is offering him a new position as the webmaster.

137. (A) However
(B) In addition
(C) Meanwhile
(D) For instance

138. (A) who contributed to
(B) that contributes to
(C) whose contributes to
(D) contributing

Questions 139-142 refer to the following information.

Thank you for your order from <u>Elliezon.com</u>. We sincerely hope that you are content with

the quality of our products. If you are not -------, you can return and refund the products with
                                        139.

the original receipts and boxes you received within 10 days of the delivery date. In order to

get a refund, you should complete the form in the box and sent it to us with the items. All

merchandise ------- in the original packaging. -------. This is because a credit card cancellation
              140.   **141.**

takes more time than a cash transaction. We appreciate your business and hope that you will

continue to ------- with us.
          142.

139. (A) satisfying
     (B) satisfied
     (C) satisfy
     (D) satisfaction

140. (A) will ship
     (B) have been shipped
     (C) are shipping
     (D) should be shipped

141. (A) We extend an apology for the
         inconvenience.
     (B) The items you ordered are out of
         stock.
     (C) We have confidence in the quality of
         all the items.
     (D) It takes one or two weeks to process
         the refund.

142. (A) shop
     (B) learn
     (C) place
     (D) compile

Go on to the next page

After three years of ------- growth, Korean smartphone retailer SLP is planning to expand its
         143.

business into the U.S. and Canada. -------. On November 11, SLP's CEO, Jeremy Kim,
         144.

announced that the company intends to open more than 100 branches in North America. -------,
         145.

SLP is looking for passionate individuals with an adventurous spirit and dedication to customer

service to become franchise owners. Future ------- are advised to contact Christine Jung at +82-
         146.

2-333-8282.

---

143. (A) appropriate
(B) advisable
(C) steady
(D) beneficent

144. (A) The U.S. needs to attract more
smartphone users for boosting its
domestic economy.
(B) The company has already operated
many stores in Asian areas.
(C) SLP is recognized worldwide in the
smartphone field.
(D) The weather in Korea is similar to
eastern America in many ways.

145. (A) Moreover
(B) Nonetheless
(C) However
(D) Therefore

146. (A) candidates
(B) residents
(C) experts
(D) architects

PART 7

Directions: In this part you will read a selection of texts, such as magazine and newspaper articles, e-mails, and instant messages. Each text or set of texts is followed by several questions. Select the best answer for each question and mark the letter (A), (B), (C), or (D) on your answer sheet.

Questions 147-148 refer to the following advertisement.

Posting Item: XA-360 Deer Power Lawn Mower
Price: $700
Location: Fairfax, VA

Item Description:
Bought at LEX store a year ago. Paid $1000 for it. Had a two-year warranty.
Fuel box is not working and should be replaced by the buyer.

In good condition. (No image available)
The price is fixed. (Not negotiable)

If you have any questions about the item, please feel free to contact me.
(fairJohn@horrisnet.com)

147. What is NOT indicated about the lawn mower?

(A) A part should be purchased.
(B) A manual is included.
(C) The price cannot be changed.
(D) It is a pre-owned item.

148. What is the seller likely to do?

(A) Respond to an inquiry
(B) Extend the warranty
(C) Attach some pictures via e-mail
(D) Send the item to a buyer directly

Go on to the next page

Johnstown City has planned to recruit a new financial planner in order to replace Mr. Kevin Davis, who has lately expressed his intent to retire. Mr. Davis will hand over his responsibilities on October 31 after holding the role for fourteen years. —[1]—.

The city finance director reports to the city manager and is in charge of supervising the monetary issues of the city. —[2]—. This position is a complex one, requiring the ability to enhance or put into effect a huge range of policies and steps to support the city's aims and to organize and keep the entire city's financial records.

"The new planner will have a lot of things to do," said city manager Cindy Fetterman. "The prospective staff member must have extensive experience managing the finances of an organization or a company."

According to Ms. Fetterman, the application screening period will begin soon, and interviews for the position begin in early September. —[3]—. The new employee will be confirmed at the end of October. —[4]—.

149. What is the information mainly about?

(A) Johnstown City has a plan to rebuild the city hall.
(B) There is a job opening for a city position in finance.
(C) The city's financial issues have not yet been resolved for two consecutive years.
(D) To celebrate Mr. Davis's retirement, city officials organized a banquet.

150. According to the information, what is required for the position?

(A) A master's degree in finance
(B) A willingness to work on weekends
(C) A capacity for finance-related issues
(D) Moving to Johnstown City

151. In which of the positions marked [1], [2], [3] and [4] does the following sentence best belong?

"Applications received after August 20 cannot be considered."

(A) [1]
(B) [2]
(C) [3]
(D) [4]

Questions 152-153 refers to the following article.

Bremerton, March 6 — Bremerton has recently invited local property developers to bid for constructing a business complex on a 30,000-square-meter area in the northern area of the town.

The business complex will be built near 81 Penn Highway, on the site that used to be an industrial complex that formerly included Waxon Generator, Bill's Auto Parts, and Ulus Steel Manufacturing. The new buildings will be equipped with the latest energy- and water-saving systems. The town also plans to erect a small residential section near the area within three years.

"We are pleased about this opportunity to bring new business to our town," said Mayor Gilford Hubric. "The business complex will be located in the best area, adjacent to a national main highway and many popular accommodations." He also mentioned that the space will be distributed among occupants based on their needs after the first blueprint is designed.

Most of these activities in Bremerton have been prompted by the recent expansion of the local sports complex in the Millner neighborhood.

152. What is suggested about the northern area of Bremerton?

(A) It is close to the sports complex.
(B) A variety of metal products were made there.
(C) It is currently a residential area.
(D) Its population has suddenly increased.

153. What characteristic of the business complex is NOT mentioned?

(A) Its location near a major highway
(B) Its proximity to hotels
(C) Its energy-efficient structure
(D) Its country-operated area

Go on to the next page

Questions 154-155 refer to the following text message chain.

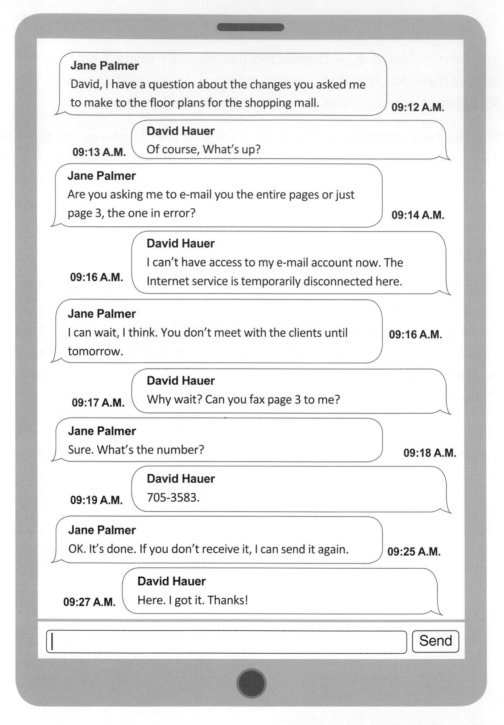

Jane Palmer
David, I have a question about the changes you asked me to make to the floor plans for the shopping mall.
09:12 A.M.

09:13 A.M.
David Hauer
Of course, What's up?

Jane Palmer
Are you asking me to e-mail you the entire pages or just page 3, the one in error?
09:14 A.M.

09:16 A.M.
David Hauer
I can't have access to my e-mail account now. The Internet service is temporarily disconnected here.

Jane Palmer
I can wait, I think. You don't meet with the clients until tomorrow.
09:16 A.M.

09:17 A.M.
David Hauer
Why wait? Can you fax page 3 to me?

Jane Palmer
Sure. What's the number?
09:18 A.M.

09:19 A.M.
David Hauer
705-3583.

Jane Palmer
OK. It's done. If you don't receive it, I can send it again.
09:25 A.M.

09:27 A.M.
David Hauer
Here. I got it. Thanks!

Send

---

154. Who most likely is Ms. Palmer?

(A) A computer programmer
(B) An architect
(C) An attorney
(D) An Internet service manager

155. At 9:17 A.M., what does Mr. Hauer most likely mean when he writes, "Why wait?"?

(A) He wants to get the paper now.
(B) He thinks he had better postpone the meeting.
(C) He asks about the Internet connection.
(D) He needs to download the form.

Questions 156-157 refer to the following letter.

Shirley Eye Care
#203, 151 Fleming Avenue
Bayside, NY 11361
March 17

Heather Lory
#403 West Gate Apartments
333 Lancaster Boulevard
Bayside, NY 11361

At Shirley Eye Care, it is our priority to continuously provide the best service for you. Starting on August 1, all payments will not be made at the time of service but must be paid within 15 business days. Enclosed you will find the details about the reason why we changed the billing policy.

The new policy enables us to continue to offer the best eye care service to you and your family without any rate increases in the upcoming 2 years. If you have more questions about this payment policy, please call our client account manager, Kevin Loyce, at 715-6534.

Sincerely,

Jane Shirley

Enclosure

156. What is the purpose of this letter?
(A) To recruit licensed nurses
(B) To publicize a clinic's service
(C) To inform a customer of a policy change
(D) To make a correction to a billing statement

157. What is suggested about Shirley Eye Care?
(A) It makes an effort to keep service rates low.
(B) It has recently moved to a new area.
(C) It is offering free eye examinations.
(D) It will be equipped with the latest tools.

House and Office Cleaning

The house and office cleaning division of Kane Upper Town Hotel hires 100 team members who are responsible for keeping clean the public spaces in the building in addition to each of the individual rooms and offices throughout the facility.

- Public spaces, such as restrooms, lobbies, ballrooms, the banquet hall, and other visitors' areas are cleaned every day.
- Individual rooms are cleaned in compliance with guests' schedules. Making a schedule for the rooms is outlined further on Page 10 of this recruit manual.
- Office areas are cleaned on Saturdays. Housekeepers will sweep and wipe floors and throw out the garbage. Team members should water the plants in the offices and arrange the desks.
- The cleaning staff must always be standing by ready for public areas that need prompt attention.

158. For whom is the information most likely intended?

(A) Cleaning supply company members
(B) Hotel employees
(C) Travel agents for hotel reservations
(D) Visitors seeking good hotels

159. According to the information, how can readers know the housekeeping schedules of the individual rooms?

(A) By referring to a staff training manual
(B) By talking to the service head in the cleaning division
(C) By calling the reception desk of the hotel
(D) By reading a schedule posted in the staff lounge

160. How often are the floors of the offices cleaned?

(A) Daily
(B) Weekly
(C) Biweekly
(D) Monthly

Question 161-164 refer to the following online chat discussion.

	Cody Silva [10:18 A.M.]	Hello. I want to give you some information regarding yesterday's meeting agenda. Our marketing team suggested that cooling bubble gum would likely be popular in the food market.
	Susan Vivianne [10:19 A.M.]	I know the reason. People want to feel cool in their mouth after eating something.
	Nakata Shunzi [10:20 A.M.]	Not to mention the fact that it cleans your teeth.
	Cody Silva [10:21 A.M.]	Sure. We decided that our company needs to have our own line of special chewing gum with a sugar-free formula. We should get moving fast.
	Susan Vivianne [10:22 A.M.]	Consumers are becoming more concerned about their health, so how about focusing on using organic ingredients? I can find more information about it for our products.
	Cody Silva [10:23 A.M.]	That sounds great! Go ahead!
	Nakata Shunzi [10:24 A.M.]	I like that. But I think we should consider consumer preferences in the flavor. If the taste of the gum is not attractive to prospective clients, the best item we make will just be useless. We need to first conduct market research about consumers' preferred tastes.
	Cody Silva [10:26 A.M.]	Great. Mr. Nakata, could you set up a meeting with the market research team and public relations team? I want to hear what they have to say. How about Thursday?
	Susan Vivianne [10:27 A.M.]	Sorry, but I can't make it then. On Thursdays, I always conduct the on-the-job training for new staff. Can we do Wednesday or Friday?
	Cody Silva [10:28 A.M.]	The end of the week is fine.
	Nakata Shunzi [10:30 A.M.]	Works for me. I'll also outline the questionnaire for the research on our side. Can any of you guys give me possible questions for the survey?
	Cody Silva [10:31 A.M.]	Of course. I will.

Send

161. What kind of business do the chat participants most likely work at?

(A) A grocery store
(B) A hotel restaurant
(C) A marketing agency
(D) A food manufacturer

162. When do the participants plan to meet with the marketing team?

(A) On Tuesday
(B) On Wednesday
(C) On Thursday
(D) On Friday

163. At 10:30 A.M., what does Mr. Nakata mean when he says, "Works for me."?

(A) He is able to attend the meeting.
(B) He will talk with researchers right away.
(C) He plans to lead to the on-the-job training.
(D) He wants to make a new product by himself.

164. What will Mr. Silva probably do?

(A) Meet the president
(B) Taste some gum flavors
(C) Outline marketing strategies
(D) Prepare some questions

Go on to the next page

Questions 165-168 refer to the following e-mail.

From: Jimmy Khermin
To: Staff, Premium Electronics
Date: Monday, December 7
Subject: Week-long training session

You have already been informed that all staff members of Premium Electronics are required to attend the week-long training session each winter, which focuses on our company's goals and provides you with a chance to get to know other staff members. It can give us a lot of benefits for our business. Our employee surveys show that we have made a major impact on our work productivity and cooperation since starting these sessions five years ago.

The dates of the training session have been posted on our intra-bulletin-board since September, and attendance is required. I would like all of you to get ready for the session by selecting various topics that we can talk about. Staff members at all positions should not hesitate to share their suggestions. What you should do is to e-mail me with "Session Topics" in the subject line. —[1]—. You need to use your own transportation to get to Blue Spruce Park, so please remember to submit a travel reimbursement form before the end of the month. It is recommended that you ride together with others in a group. —[2]—. In addition, there are other means of public transportation available, such as a shuttle bus, subway, and city train, which stop near Blue Spruce Park. —[3]—. Whatever means you choose, please be sure that you get there on time and ready to join us. —[4]—.

Jimmy Khermin

165. What is the main purpose of the e-mail?

(A) To announce details regarding an annual event
(B) To encourage staff members to volunteer for an event
(C) To advertise a company's latest item at a fair
(D) To publicize new job openings at an electronics company

166. How are the employees required to get ready for the event?

(A) By updating personal information
(B) By filling out a questionnaire
(C) By promoting a brand-new item
(D) By preparing discussion topics

167. What does Mr. Khermin mention about transportation arrangements?

(A) All expenses will be reimbursed by Premium Electronics.
(B) All employees should take public transportation.
(C) All vehicles are prohibited at the site at certain times.
(D) All staff should get a travel pass from each department.

168. In which of the positions marked [1], [2], [3], and [4] does the following sentence best belong?

"There is even a taxi affiliated with our company that provides a huge discounted price for a ride from the office to there."

(A) [1]
(B) [2]
(C) [3]
(D) [4]

Questions 169-172 refer to the following notice.

SKihut National Archipelago Authority (SNAA)

SKihut National Archipelago includes a main forest, beach areas, and other similar islands. Please be aware that there are some additional tour restrictions during this summer vacation season. If visitors are not accompanied by an authorized guide when they want to take a trip to the islands, they will be restricted from entering these areas. This regulation also applies to those who may want to visit the islands individually by using private boats. These individuals can only see the view of the island from the water and come to anchor on offshore but must not land there.

The SNAA's official cruise tours for visitors to the islands are offered daily throughout the year and move in a cycle with two-hour intervals from 8 A.M. The final tour is available until 4 P.M. except for the winter season from November to February, during which time it can be extended to 6 P.M., depending on weather conditions. Please call +01-319-5225 to make a reservation for the cruise tour. This tour includes some description about the islands' geological and historical features, and attractive aspects of the beautiful view. You can also view a special spot for endangered species by getting an escort from our island rangers.

Payment and Reservations

Tours can be conducted with a maximum of 20 participants per group. If the group is smaller than 15, we reserve the right to add other travelers to your tour. You can purchase a ticket at $30 per person for adults and $15 for children. You are asked to pay a deposit of $5 per person in order to hold the reservation. In addition, you can get our special offer when booking it in advance of 6 months. The deposit amount will be credited to your total admission fees. If your group does not show up at the appointed time, the ending time of your trip will remain the same, so as not to disrupt later trips. Any change of other groups' itineraries cannot be allowed.

---

169. What is the purpose of the notice?

(A) To update information about a fee
(B) To introduce some attractions
(C) To announce the safety rules about a trip
(D) To inform visitors of the trip policy

170. What is implied about visiting SKihut National Archipelago?

(A) Visitors must step into the islands with a guide.
(B) Visitors should comply with their safety rules.
(C) Visitors cannot swim anywhere around the archipelago.
(D) Visitors need to gather groups by themselves.

171. What is NOT mentioned about the SNAA?

(A) Night tours can be scheduled.
(B) The capacity of the group is limited.
(C) Early reservations can be discounted.
(D) Tour times are different depending on the season.

172. According to the notice, what may happen if a group arrives late for the prearranged trip?

(A) It may be reduced in tour hours.
(B) It may be canceled without any notice.
(C) It may be charged an additional fee.
(D) It may be changed into another ending time.

Go on to the next page

Visiting Hershey County
Don't miss the chance to experience a fantastic world!

Chocolate World Tour

Open daily, 10 A.M.–5 P.M. / $5 admission

The Chocolate World Tour brings you the historical scenes of Hershey County by bike-coaster with a lot of stages and figures.

Charlie's Chocolate Factory

Open to the public at no charge, Business Days, noon – 3 P.M.

Constructed by the founder, Mr. John Hershey. Visitors can get a chance to see the chocolate-making procedures and receive some free chocolate items. Guided tours are available for $1 per person.

Hershey Amusement Park

Open daily, 9 A.M.–10 P.M. / $10 admission, $40 unlimited pass for the rides.

This amazing theme park is suitable for the whole family. A lot of fantastic rides are available, including roller coasters. Special discounts for the park are given in specific seasons.

County Chocolate Museum

Open Tuesday to Sunday, 9 A.M.– 4 P.M. / Free of charge, but donations are welcome.

A variety of impressive chocolates are exhibited in chronological order. Also, the Hershey family's history is played on a big LCD monitor on the ceiling. This museum is located adjacent to the North Gate of the amusement park.

173. What is the purpose of the information?

(A) To describe a list of events
(B) To help visitors to tour certain spots
(C) To give directions to local attractions
(D) To announce some special monuments

174. What is indicated about Hershey Amusement Park?

(A) Its admission fee is not the same year-round.
(B) It varies from the opening time periodically.
(C) It uses a mini-trailer for watching the historical movie.
(D) It is only popular with teenagers and children.

175. According to the information, what do the chocolate factory and the museum have in common?

(A) Both charge no admission fee.
(B) Both require guided tours.
(C) Both show historical events.
(D) Both are located near the shore.

Go on to the next page

CAAA's Twentieth-Annual Athletic Equipment Fair, June 1–10
Progressive Convention Center, Cleveland, Ohio

The CAAA(Cleveland Area Athletic Association) invites companies to join this fair, which was attended by over 200 businesses last year. This event is related to effective approaches and methods for using the right exercise equipment.

The CAAA is pleased to offer corresponding benefits based on the degree of corporate sponsorship.

(For inquiries, contact Ms. Gloria Sanders at 932-451-3894. To register, e-mail supports@ caaa.org.)

▶ **Workshop Sponsor — $1,200**
A representative of your company will have a chance to promote your company by speaking as a keynote speaker in one of the workshop sessions.

▶ **Stage Sponsor — $2,000**
At each stage displaying equipment, your company's name will be displayed in front of the demonstration booth.

▶ **Bag Sponsor — $3,000**
Your company's logo and name will be on fabric tote bags that are distributed to all visitors.

▶ **General Program Sponsor — $6,000**
Three executive members of your company will be introduced in a banquet, named "CAAA Night," on the first day of the fair.

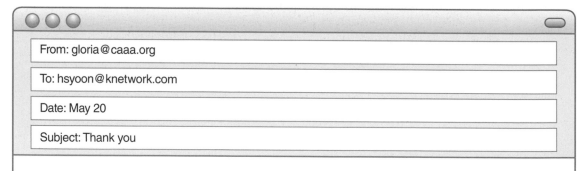

From: gloria@caaa.org

To: hsyoon@knetwork.com

Date: May 20

Subject: Thank you

Dear Ms. Yoon,

I would like to show my appreciation for your registration of the Remote Interval Exercise Program as a supporter of the Cleveland Area Athletic Association (CAAA) Fair. Your sponsorship not only enables us to make this event possible, but also stimulates interest in exercise.

Your donation of $2,000 has been credited to our account. In addition, we are attaching your company's name to the demonstration booth at no extra cost. It is a token of our appreciation for the long-standing support of CAAA and its programs. To finalize the promotional materials, please e-mail me your official CI(corporate identity) or BI(business identity) images.

Gloria Sanders
CAAA Fair Coordinator

176. What is the purpose of the flyer?

(A) To announce the success of these successive events

(B) To encourage participants to try out equipment

(C) To promote the benefits of joining an event

(D) To report financial issues to their sponsorship board

177. According to the flyer, when should a call be placed to CAAA's office?

(A) When additional information is needed

(B) When a donation cannot be processed

(C) When participation is required

(D) When a change is made at their level

178. What will happen on June 1?

(A) An athletic game will be started.

(B) A formal gathering will be held.

(C) New board members will be appointed.

(D) Display stages will be set up at the fair.

179. What is suggested about CAAA's event?

(A) It is intended to promote interest in exercise.

(B) It attracts more than 200 companies annually.

(C) It is partially funded by the Cleveland City Council.

(D) It is held at a different location every year.

180. In the e-mail, what is Ms. Yoon asked to do?

(A) Check the amount of supporting budget for taking part in the event

(B) Send an e-mail including the company's logo designs to the fair.

(C) Organize an event booth to promote their new items at the fair

(D) Call the customer service center to ask more information about the fair

Go on to the next page

To:	berry@linguisticconference.org
From:	customerservice@holidaylodge.us
Date:	25 July
Re:	Reservation TC1270

Dear Dr. Berry,

Thank you for choosing Holiday Lodge Hotel. As requested before, you have made a reservation of 12 rooms for your group. Since you will attend the National Applied Linguistics Forum here this August, you are receiving a special rate of $90 a room per night.

We have you checking in on 3 August, and checking out on 10 August. The room reservations are confirmed under your name. Please be aware of your reservation code, TC1270, which you must use if you need to contact us about these arrangements for any reason.

We are confident that you will enjoy our amazing amenities such as an outdoor pool, a spa, a gym, and a variety of dining options. For a casual dining experience, you may want to try the Romeo's Café terrace, located next to our lobby. If you are interested in dining at Donnatello Restaurant, which was given a 5-star rating from Trip Advisory Guide, we strongly recommend that you make a reservation in advance.

Please let us know if you need more information.

Thank you again for choosing Holiday Lodge Hotel.

Sincerely,

The Holiday Lodge Hotel Staff

To: customerservice@holidaylodge.us

From: berry@linguisticconference.org

Date: 27 July

Re: Reservation TC1270

To Whom It May Concern,

My reservation number is TC1270, and I am writing to correct some errors I noticed in the previous e-mail.

Firstly, the number of reserved rooms is 10, not 12. Also, I will not be arriving until August 4, even though almost all members will get there one day before the conference.

I clearly stated these points on my original reservation request form. Please correct these and contact me in order to confirm that this has been resolved. Thank you in advance for your immediate response to this matter.

Sincerely,

Dr. Bonds Berry

181. What is the main purpose of the first e-mail?

(A) To confirm the details of a reservation
(B) To notify a customer of a change in hotel price
(C) To explain a variety of amenities
(D) To announce a hotel's temporary construction

182. What is suggested about the Donnatello Restaurant?

(A) It was recently opened.
(B) It has been remodeled.
(C) It is usually busy.
(D) It is next to Holiday Lodge Hotel.

183. What information in the hotel reservation is wrong?

(A) That Dr. Berry will check in on August 3
(B) That Dr. Berry has organized the forum
(C) That Dr. Berry has paid for all rooms
(D) That Dr. Berry will depart before the conference ends

184. What is stated about the hotel reservation?

(A) The reservation code is misprinted.
(B) The number of rooms is not correct.
(C) The attendants for the forum are not enough.
(D) The room rates are different.

185. In the second e-mail, the word "matter" in paragraph 3, line 3, is closest in meaning to

(A) situation
(B) substance
(C) material
(D) publication

Go on to the next page

Questions 186-190 refer to the following article, form, and e-mail.

Athens Gazette

Local Companies Need More Staff
by Sophia Lauren

Athens (April 10)—It is difficult for us to seek suitable candidates for a position. To make their hiring process easier, some companies make a request to staffing agencies. By finding part-time employees for the peak season or handling the whole application procedure through these agencies, companies save money and time in many ways.

Jane Foster, the general manager of Hellocrew Recruiting, which is one of the oldest staffing agencies in Georgia, said that a number of companies can get an advantage while hiring temporary staff from the agency. "They have a chance to resolve certain hiring matters. Another benefit is that they can train a potential member before they offer him/her full-time employment," Foster said.

To support local companies through this process, we have posted a list of staffing agencies. You can find it on the upper right-hand side of this page at www.athensgazette.com.

Hellocrew Recruiting
TEMPORARY EMPLOYEE REQUEST FORM

Company Information
- **Name:** Brad Triana
- **Field:** Accounting
- **E-mail:** btriana@mscbiz.com

- **Company:** MSC Business Accounting
- **Phone:** 412-237-9400

Task Information
- **Need number of staff:** minimum 8
- **Expected duration:** 2–3 weeks

- **Opening Position:** office workers

Specifications:

We have a lot of government-led projects on auditing city councils' accounts in many districts. Because of these projects, we have stored up too many documents and files that we need to arrange. These documents and files should be categorized and scanned more quickly in order to meet a deadline. We are seeking meticulous applicants who are able to follow instructions well.

How did you find out about us?
I saw your agency in yesterday's online column in the *Athens Gazette*.

Thank you for your registration!
One of our staffing agents will contact you within 24 hours through e-mail.

From: Brad Triana <btriana@mscbiz.com>

To: Heather Lowry <hlowry@hellocrew.net>

Subject: Thank You

Date: April 15

Dear Ms. Lowry,

I would like to extend my sincere gratitude for your help. It was my first time working with a staffing agency, so, frankly, I did not have confidence in this process. Because of your agency, we are ready to complete our tasks with the temporary employees you matched with us. You responded to my request form within just three hours and made a list of employees available within just a day! The employees you recommended were really industrious, hardworking, and devoted to our assignments. For that reason, we made a decision to interview two of them for offering them full-time positions.

Best wishes,

Brad Triana

186. In the article, what advantage is NOT indicated about part-time staff?

(A) Getting specialized and professional support
(B) Saving more than the company's budget planned
(C) Making the recruiting process smoother
(D) Supporting companies in handling some issues

187. What is implied about Mr. Triana?

(A) He read Ms. Lauren's article on the Web.
(B) His company is included in the list on the *Athens Gazette*'s page.
(C) His company has worked with Hellocrew Recruiting before.
(D) He did an interview with the *Athens Gazette*.

188. In the form, the word "duration" in paragraph 2, line 2, is closest in meaning to

(A) length
(B) strength
(C) growth
(D) path

189. What is the main purpose of the e-mail?

(A) To offer both staff members new permanent positions
(B) To confirm a request the sales team made
(C) To express thanks for an issue they dealt with
(D) To complain about some errors in the article

190. Who most likely is Ms. Lowry?

(A) A part-timer in the MSC Business Accounting
(B) An official in a city council
(C) A staffing agent at Hellocrew Recruiting
(D) A news writer at the *Athens Gazette*

New Local Landmark Construction

At a meeting on Thursday, Hattiesburg officials discussed a local improvement plan that would enable the town to attract more students and visitors. According to Gian Pagnucci, the chair of Hattiesburg College, construction of a multi-complex convention center should be fully considered within both the local council and college's budget. Hence, the city council decided to encourage local companies to join a public bid for this construction project. In addition, local residents are encouraged to submit an entry for a contest to name the center.

Some proposed projects include an outdoor sports park, depending on whether it would be located near the center on Oak Grove Street. According to Mr. Pagnucci, the council will ask all community members to share their ideas. Interested people may bring their opinions to the next weekly meeting on Thursday, 18 June, at 4 P.M. or send an e-mail to the task force team before 22 June. After fully considering extensive opinions from citizens, the planning committee will put forth a final draft to the council for an official discussion. The expected date of the decision is no later than 30 June.

From:	selindiana@stormmail.com
To:	citycouncil@hattiesburg.org
Date:	20 June
Subject:	Additional Projects

Dear Council Official,

I was notified that you are accepting suggestions for the use of the town's budget to build new convention center. Due to another appointment in my schedule, I was not able to attend the weekly meeting for the project, but I would like to express my support for the plan to make our town more attractive. Although the cost of the construction is likely to be reasonable, project planners should fully take into account the effectiveness and proximity to the center, and the benefit of all our community members. This project will be a good source of civic pride and a brand-new landmark where we can enjoy a diversity of activities. Even though it is important for the town's image, its advantages should be evenly distributed among our citizens.

Selin Diana

From: fangyu@solomonunitas.com

To: citycouncil@hattiesburg.org

Date: 21 June

Subject: City Projects

To Whom It May Concern,

I was happy to hear that the new development was decided for our town. Because the town's public facilities are not suitable for a variety of activities for all citizens of all ages, this multi-complex space can give the public many opportunities to enjoy a wide range of events such as NCAA basketball games, local job fairs, and so on. I have just one issue to consider, and it concerns older people.

This project should not just focus on teenagers and young adults. According to the city population distribution data, the elderly form 30 percent of the citizenship in Hattiesburg. Therefore, we should never overlook considering their needs. It would be a remarkable improvement to the town if all of us can enjoy this facility—both young and old—without any inconvenience. Please make sure these benefits are equally shared among all people.

191. Why does the town of Hattiesburg need a new project?

(A) The city council canceled a previous project.
(B) The town has raised tax on property.
(C) The area is planning to attract more people.
(D) Citizens have debated a development issue.

192. In the article, the phrase "put forth" in paragraph 2, line 6, is closest in meaning to

(A) publish
(B) promote
(C) propose
(D) plant

193. When did Ms. Diana have an appointment?

(A) June 18
(B) June 20
(C) June 21
(D) June 30

194. What is the second e-mail mainly about?

(A) Celebrating civilian projects
(B) Questioning the directions to the new facility
(C) Complaining about incorrect information
(D) Raising a potential issue

195. What will happen by June 30?

(A) A final planning outline will be made with public opinions and officials' research.
(B) The city will have a ground-breaking ceremony for the new multi-complex.
(C) The council will announce a competitive bid for the facility development.
(D) Some citizens will instigate demonstrations against the construction issue.

Go on to the next page

From: John Dyson

To: Ben Tannacito

Subject: Trucking Company

Date: March 2

Hello Mr. Tannacito,

I am so glad that you have signed up for deliveries of our furniture — initially a couch for four, a desk in white, two chairs in black, a queen-sized bed — made here at our LINKer Furnishings Factory. I can assure you that you and your customers will be pleased with the products we provide.

Your store is in an area that is new to us, and we are looking forward to delivering our items into a new store. Please let me know if you are interested in this moving service. Our licensed drivers in Stonybrook do not go out to Albany, so a different company should be hired. U-Haul moving company is the best choice that fits your conditions. We would like to work with a company of your choice to keep the service for you as safe as possible.

Sincerely,

John Dyson

ALTOONA HOME DECO SYSTEM

NEW THIS WEEK!
March 20

Items from LINKer Furnishings Factory

Dear Customers,

We would like to call your attention to the latest additions to our product lines. You've asked for durable and inexpensive home furniture, and now we're carrying it. We can bring these items directly to you from LINKer Furnishings Factory, located just two hours from here in Buffalo.

- Family-Size Couches
- White Desks with Durable Wood
- Well-Being Black Chairs
- Various Bed Designs and Sizes
- Mobile Closets
- Antibacterial Area Rugs

Next season, we will develop user-friendly office furniture in our Amherst branch. If you have any questions about the items, please feel free to contact linkercustomer@lffactory.com.

LINKer Furnishings Order Form

Customer: ALTOONA HOME DECO SYSTEM
Order Date: March 25
Delivery Date: April 10

Delivery Details:

Repeat the initial order with the following changes.
- No couch for four. (Couch for five needed)
- Instead of white items, please send me black items.
- Add one more chair

P.S. You asked me to let you know if there were any issues with the U-Haul Trucking delivery. The arrival was on time, the driver was friendly, and the items were in good condition.

196. Why did Mr. Dyson send the e-mail?

(A) To advertise new products
(B) To request a delivery estimate
(C) To announce a policy change
(D) To follow up on an order

197. Where is Altoona Home Deco System probably located?

(A) In Stonybrook
(B) In Albany
(C) In Buffalo
(D) In Amherst

198. In the notice, what is implied about LINKer Furnishings Factory's products?

(A) They are delivered within just two hours of ordering.
(B) They are likely to best suit small houses.
(C) They are reasonably priced.
(D) They are out of stock because of their popularity.

199. What will Altoona Home Deco System probably receive on April 10?

(A) Antibacterial Area Rugs
(B) King-Size Beds
(C) Four Black Chairs
(D) Black Big Desks

200. What does Mr. Tannacito indicate in the order form?

(A) He had a good experience with the trucking service.
(B) The U-Haul service has a lot of clients.
(C) He was disappointed with the items he got.
(D) Some wear and tear could be found in the products.

Test

答對題數表

PART 5	
PART 6	
PART 7	
總題數	

07

READING TEST

In the Reading test, you will read a variety of texts and answer several different types of reading comprehension questions. The entire Reading test will last 75 minutes. There are three parts, and directions are given for each part. You are encouraged to answer as many questions as possible within the time allowed.

You must mark your answers on the separate answer sheet. Do not write your answers in your test book.

PART 5

Directions: A word or phrase is missing in each of the sentences below. Four answer choices are given below each sentence. Select the best answer to complete the sentence. Then mark the letter (A), (B), (C), or (D) on your answer sheet.

101. Felix Armstrong, the owner of the Indonesian restaurant, chose to order flatware and other ------- directly from the producer.

(A) supply
(B) supplies
(C) suppliers
(D) supplied

102. Every Monday, we ------- tours of the production facilities to ensure they are in order.

(A) arrive
(B) visit
(C) conduct
(D) inspect

103. Ms. Grant sees to it that she advises the new workers in order to carry out ------- duties efficiently.

(A) they
(B) their
(C) them
(D) theirs

104. Due to the increase in the availability of mobile technology, landlines have become ------- in many domestic homes.

(A) obsolete
(B) extracted
(C) insolent
(D) contemporary

105. The Dart Entertainer Academy holds open auditions every month for those ------- in participating in the annual singing contest.

(A) interest
(B) interested
(C) to interest
(D) interesting

106. Mr. Spencer has received an appreciation plaque at a retirement ceremony for ------- dedication to the company where he has worked for over 25 years.

(A) he
(B) his
(C) him
(D) himself

107. Cox Industries' latest career announcement ------- notes that the managerial position is only accepting current line supervisors.

(A) specify
(B) specific
(C) specifying
(D) specifically

108. The latest novel from Brian Bennett has had positive ------- from the critics.

(A) matters
(B) repairs
(C) reviews
(D) collections

109. Ms. Cunningham was supposed to purchase the tickets to the concert, but she thought that they were too -------.

(A) expense
(B) expensive
(C) expensively
(D) expensiveness

110. The government has urged everyone to renew their annual tax return online -------- to avoid incurring a financial penalty.

(A) early
(B) hardly
(C) enough
(D) usefully

111. At Mason Hospital, all medical records are strictly ------- and can only be released upon permission of the patient.

(A) confiding
(B) confidence
(C) confidential
(D) confidentiality

112. The results from recent client questionnaires ------- in the file attached to this e-mail.

(A) summarizes
(B) summarized
(C) are summarizing
(D) are summarized

113. Under the ------- of Dr. Owen, the Engineering Department of Patel Precision Industries performs a number of material examinations every year.

(A) prediction
(B) indication
(C) completion
(D) supervision

114. The Cornell Ski Resort employed 12 additional safety guards ------- at its Yellowwoods Valley branch during the hectic winter season.

(A) assists
(B) assisted
(C) to assist
(D) have assisted

115. In its latest newspaper advertisement, Prime Bank ------- the general complaint by the public that its interest rates are too high.

(A) tended
(B) refuted
(C) imposed
(D) recuperated

116. The Health Bureau has assured the public that it will expand the number of medical activities ------- in the following year.

(A) distantly
(B) recently
(C) currently
(D) significantly

117. When checking a safety device, please also ensure that the doors and windows are ------- before leaving the office.

(A) security
(B) securely
(C) securing
(D) secured

118. Workers who make use of company vehicles must ------- a legal and up-to-date driver's license.

(A) expel
(B) assign
(C) specify
(D) possess

119. According to a newsletter published today, a significant ------- of employees welcome the chance to feature their newly developed dietary supplement at the upcoming expo.

(A) major
(B) majored
(C) majoring
(D) majority

120. The fire drill will start at 2:00 P.M. in the Minnesota facility, and its manufacturing process cannot recommence ------- it has been finished.

(A) while
(B) until
(C) that
(D) upon

Go on to the next page

121. To prevent any further delays in the delivery process, the production team had to work ------- to fix the broken machines.

(A) swift
(B) swiftly
(C) swiftness
(D) swiftest

122. Kaur Designs ------- staff satisfaction a top priority since its inception 10 years ago.

(A) has considered
(B) will consider
(C) considering
(D) is considered

123. The Walker's Chicken has a number of chain stores ------- Australia and is planning to extend its business abroad.

(A) behind
(B) among
(C) across
(D) despite

124. It is a ------- procedure to delete all confidential files from your computers at the end of the day.

(A) routine
(B) fastened
(C) difficult
(D) mistaken

125. The Adams Hotel installed energy-saving LED lighting ------- all of its rooms last month.

(A) of
(B) on
(C) in
(D) before

126. The employees ------- intend to undergo an interview for transfer have to apply today.

(A) where
(B) who
(C) whose
(D) when

127. The ------- has announced that cameras will be allowed in the courtroom for the first time.

(A) patron
(B) reputation
(C) spokesperson
(D) outcome

128. Train 404 to Minox County departed two hours ------- than expected due to heavy snow in Foxtown.

(A) late
(B) later
(C) latest
(D) lately

129. ------- the battery runs out quicker than expected after being fully charged, contact our authorized service center.

(A) If
(B) So
(C) Even
(D) Such

130. Any inquiries ------- travel expense claims should be sent to the accounts department.

(A) through
(B) according to
(C) related to
(D) upon

PART 6

Directions: Read the texts that follow. A word, phrase, or sentence is missing in parts of each text. Four answer choices for each question are given below the text. Select the best answer to complete the text. Then mark the letter (A), (B), (C), or (D) on your answer sheet.

Questions 131-134 refer to the following e-mail.

To: John Turner <Johnturner@fastmail.com>

From: Charles Stone <Cstone@walshlaws.com>

Subject: Letter of interest

Date: June 12

Dear Mr. Turner,

Upon reading your letter of inquiry, we ------- in scheduling you for an interview for a career
                                              131.
position with our company. -------. As a result, we would like to consider you for an internship
                            132.
that will run from July 1 to September 30.

The program is intended to develop one's legal research expertise by means of training and

hands-on practice, and if one becomes successful, he or she may choose from the -------
                                                                                133.
positions that we offer after the completion of the program. We advise you to think about this

prospect, and if you wish ------- the internship, please get back to us by e-mail at a time that
                          134.
suits you.

Sincerely,

Charles Stone, Walsh Business Associates

131. (A) interest
(B) interested
(C) are interested
(D) are interesting

132. (A) Your letter suggests that you are looking for a position as a legal associate.
(B) Please submit your application to our legal team by tomorrow.
(C) I think you should reconsider your decision.
(D) We ask for your permission to file your application for future consideration.

133. (A) persistent
(B) permanent
(C) habitual
(D) durable

134. (A) pursuit
(B) pursuing
(C) to pursue
(D) pursued

Go on to the next page

Questions 135-138 refer to the following e-mail.

From: David Watts

To: Marshall Design Studio Staff

Date: March 1

Subject: Mary Ryan's Farewell Party

You may be aware that Mary Ryan is leaving the Marshall Design Studio after having been our

top designer for many years. A celebration in honor of ------- substantial commitment to our
                                                          135.
company is to be held next Friday, March 10, at 6 P.M. in the boardroom.

In my last e-mail, I requested some ideas for a ------- gift for the function. -------. I'm sure that it
                                                136.   **137.**
would make the best gift for her.

In order for us to buy the gift in time for the party, I ask that all donations ------- by Monday,
                                                                               138.
March 6. Please give donations to the associate design director, Claire Lewis, who is located in

the main design studio.

Many thanks,

David Watts

Director of Human Resources

---

135. (A) our
(B) her
(C) your
(D) whose

136. (A) parting
(B) similar
(C) hopeful
(D) gratified

137. (A) We have not decided what we should do with the gift yet.
(B) I will start to search for her replacement.
(C) Everyone is invited, and refreshments will be served.
(D) The general consensus is that you want to give Mary a gold carriage clock.

138. (A) make
(B) makes
(C) be made
(D) will have made

Questions 139-142 refer to the following article.

Canberra (February 22) – Regional airports are planning to ------- the amount of luggage on
139.
board the week after next.

Beginning on March 4, the luggage control will be put in force at every airport from Melbourne

to Sydney. "Banning more than two suitcases will help us to better monitor the amount of

luggage used in order to avoid the congestion that occurs ------- the baggage carousels," said
140.
Director of Services Dorothy Bailey.

Passengers should pack fewer than two suitcases. -------. Alternatively, they can leave
141.
unwanted items in the secure lockers, ------- to hold up to 5kg of luggage.
142.

139. (A) propose
 (B) relate
 (C) enhance
 (D) restrict

140. (A) after
 (B) among
 (C) around
 (D) through

141. (A) All extra boxes will be delivered for
 free.
 (B) Otherwise, they may have to pay extra
 per bag.
 (C) In fact, they have relaxed the
 regulations.
 (D) And the passengers are asked to
 leave their suitcases in the lockers.

142. (A) equipment
 (B) equipped
 (C) equip
 (D) equips

Go on to the next page

Dear Mr. Evans,

I appreciate your interest in ------- our marketing department.
143.

-------. To apply for a position as a service marketing team member with us, you need to send
144.
us your updated résumé, together with a proposal ------- your own marketing approach.
145.

We will be contacting you in two weeks ------- accepting your application to set up an interview
146.
from the materials you sent us about your background and career. You are likely to be an ideal

candidate for the position we talked about before.

Best regards,

Anderson Brooks

Marketing Director, Norton Electronics

143. (A) joining
(B) promoting
(C) evaluating
(D) organizing

144. (A) However, I'm afraid we have already
filled the position.
(B) We enjoyed meeting you at your job
interview.
(C) We would be pleased to receive your
application form.
(D) I'm attaching my résumé as
requested.

145. (A) describe
(B) describing
(C) described
(D) will describe

146. (A) around
(B) until
(C) by
(D) after

PART 7

Directions: In this part you will read a selection of texts, such as magazine and newspaper articles, e-mails, and instant messages. Each text or set of texts is followed by several questions. Select the best answer for each question and mark the letter (A), (B), (C), or (D) on your answer sheet.

Questions 147-148 refer to the following coupon.

Limited Offer

Enjoy Climber Route with your friend for the price of one!

Present this coupon at the ticket booth and you will receive one more ticket for free when purchasing a full-price adult ticket.

Enjoy the scenery and the refreshments – complimentary food and drink are available at our mountain-top café.

– Cannot be used in conjunction with other coupons
– Expires on 31 December
– Children must be accompanied by their parents

147. What is the coupon for?

(A) A sightseeing venue
(B) A cafeteria
(C) A boating site
(D) A sports tournament

148. What restriction is placed on the coupon?

(A) It can be used by adults only.
(B) It can be used on weekends.
(C) It cannot be used before 31 December.
(D) It cannot be used with another coupon.

Go on to the next page

Relocation and Care

When moving animals to a new place, particular care has to be taken to ensure their safe arrival and enhance their ability to fit into their new environment. Always remember they can be very unpredictable. Place them in the designated container, as carrying them without one may allow them to escape. Follow our specific directions on the brochure when relocating animals, as there are a variety of containers for different animals. These leaflets are free and can be found at the cashier.

149. Who is the information most likely intended for?

(A) Storekeepers
(B) Animal owners
(C) Container manufacturers
(D) Safety inspectors

150. What is available at no cost?

(A) Carriers
(B) Written instructions
(C) Containers
(D) Canned food

Questions 151-152 refer to the following receipt.

> **Hawkins Uniforms**
> **DELIVERY RECEIPT**
> ─────────────────
>
> Thank you for your order.
>
> **Order Number:** 452198732
> **Date Placed:** June 21
> **Date Shipped:** June 25
>
> **Customer Name:** Duncan Restaurant
> **Customer Number:** 24
>
> --
>
> _**Item 1:**_ Custom-made shirts, logo on the left sleeve
>   **Color:** Blue /   **Size:** Large / **Quantity:** 13
>
> _**Item 2:**_ Chefs Hats
>   **Color:** White / **Size:** N/A / **Quantity:** 4
>
> _**Item 3:**_ Head Scarves
>   **Color:** Red /   **Size:** N/A / **Quantity:** 27
>
> --
>
> _Visit us online at http://www.hawkinsuniforms.com._

151. How many shirts were ordered?

(A) 24
(B) 13
(C) 4
(D) 27

152. What is stated on the receipt?

(A) The order was made online.
(B) Duncan Restaurant is a regular customer.
(C) Thirteen waiters are working at Duncan Restaurant.
(D) The logo of a company appears on the clothes.

Go on to the next page

	Jeremy Ashton [10:46 A.M.]	Guys, we've got a problem with the dyes again.
	Nancy Parish [10:46 A.M.]	Not again! What's the problem this time?
	Jeremy Ashton [10:47 A.M.]	The 80 purple towels came out in the wrong color. These are more like pink.
	Nancy Parish [10:48 A.M.]	That's terrible. We have to deliver all the towels by tomorrow.
	Dustin Hyde [10:48 A.M.]	I don't think I have enough time to do it over. Is the rest of the order ready to go out?
	Jeremy Ashton [10:49 A.M.]	Yes. All the other colors are ready to go.
	Nancy Parish [10:51 A.M.]	Why don't we send them first so that Lisa's team can start preparing for the upcoming event? In the meantime, you can dye the remaining 80 towels again.
	Dustin Hyde [10:51 A.M.]	That'd save us some time. But we'll have to check the dye before we rework them.
	Nancy Parish [10:52 A.M.]	Sure thing. I'll call Lisa and ask for the color samples.

Send

153. What problem is being discussed?

(A) Some labels were printed incorrectly.
(B) Some dyeing results were unexpected.
(C) An inspector is unavailable.
(D) Some machines are running too slowly.

154. At 10:48 A.M., what does Mr. Hyde imply when he writes, "I don't think I have enough time to do it over."?

(A) The schedule is tight.
(B) They cannot help sending the pink towels.
(C) He doesn't have enough towels to dye again.
(D) The upcoming event should be postponed.

Questions 155-157 refer to the following advertisement.

Reid & Ross Inc. Job Openings

Applications are for the night shift (6:00 P.M. to 5:00 A.M.), unless otherwise stated.

Facilities Manager
Must hold relevant qualifications, in-depth understanding of inventory process, and knowledge of health and safety policies. Also desirable are basic skills in computing and budgeting. Previous experience in mechanical factory work is preferred but not essential.

Forklift Truck Technician
Must be educated to high school level or higher, with two years' experience working in a busy warehouse operating heavy machinery. Must be trained in forklift truck driving. Some day shifts required.

Computer Assistant
Must have a BA degree, with experience of operating SAGE software in an industrial environment. Some day shifts required.

Inventory Assistants and Stock Clerks
Must be conscientious and hard-working. Stock clerks may be required to work the day shift.

Please send résumés to : The Recruitment Manager
Reid & Ross Inc.
472 Southern Lake Drive
Austin, TX 78753

No recruitment agency calls or e-mails.

155. What is a requirement for the facilities manager position?
(A) A degree in finance
(B) Knowledge of health and safety policies
(C) Previous experience in conducting inspections
(D) A valid driver's license

156. What position does NOT involve day shifts?
(A) Forklift truck technician
(B) Stock clerks
(C) Inventory assistants
(D) Computer assistant

157. How will candidates apply for the positions?
(A) By online
(B) By mail
(C) In person
(D) By telephone

Questions 158-160 refer to the following e-mail.

To : All Staff

From : Elizabeth Webster <Ewebster@gilbertfashion.com>

Re : Spring Collection

Date : December 9

On behalf of the management at Gilbert Fashion, I would like to invite you to a special showing of our new Spring portfolio to be held on December 18 from 4 P.M. to 9 P.M. at Silver Hall. —[1]—. We expect every employee to attend and enjoy a buffet meal on the balcony. —[2]—. There will also be entertainment in the form of Ella Kay and her band.

—[3]—. Please note that although this is a free event to preview our new collection, we need to provide numbers for the caterers, so if you can attend, please give your name to Kate Parry or Henry Rhodes by the end of the week. If you have any tunes that you wish the band to play, we welcome any suggestions. —[4]—.

I look forward to seeing everyone on December 18.

Elizabeth Webster
Human Resources Manager

158. What is the purpose of the e-mail?
(A) To invite employees to an event
(B) To ask for volunteers to assist with a party
(C) To encourage employees to hold their show
(D) To order food for a celebration

159. What is NOT indicated about the event?
(A) It is organized by the company.
(B) It will preview a fashion collection.
(C) It will feature live music.
(D) It is held every season.

160. In which of the positions marked [1], [2], [3], and [4] does the following sentence best belong?

"Simply e-mail me with the song choice or for any further information on the event."
(A) [1]
(B) [2]
(C) [3]
(D) [4]

Question 161-163 refer to the following letter.

Emerald Town of Northern Territory

55 Turner Street
Engawala, Australia 0872

February 11
Mr. Ford Lucas
426 Girraween Road
Palmerston City, Australia 0830

Dear Mr. Lucas,

We have received your application at Emerald Town regarding the position that was advertised last week in the *Darwin Times* for a mining assistant. We are sorry to inform you that this position has already been filled. Nevertheless, we are planning to begin mining in another location in April, and we believe that you would be suitable for this position. With your permission, we would like to keep your details on file. The location is not far from our main production facilities in Darwin, but it will require some travel to Pine Creek, Mataranka, and other areas. Please keep checking our website for any future vacancies that arise with our organization. We wish you luck with your job search.

Kind regards,

Jaxon Bates, Personnel Supervisor

161. What is the main purpose of the letter?

(A) To let an applicant know that he failed to meet the qualifications for the position
(B) To ask an applicant for further details of his career
(C) To arrange an interview with an applicant
(D) To inform an applicant that the position he applied for is no longer available

162. Where are the main facilities of Emerald Town of Northern Territory located?

(A) In Darwin
(B) In Pine Creek
(C) In Mataranka
(D) In Palmerston City

163. What does Mr. Bates suggest that Mr. Lucas do?

(A) Check the website for additional job openings
(B) Send in more information about his qualifications
(C) Contact the main facilities for employment changes
(D) Read the job advertisements in the newspaper

Go on to the next page

Questions 164-167 refer to the following text message chain.

Morgan Leek [02:32 P.M.]		Hello, James. I saw several flowerpots in your shop yesterday. Where did you get them?
James Pipe [02:33 P.M.]		Hello, Morgan. You mean the ones on the table by the window?
Morgan Leek [02:33 P.M.]		Yes. They had a lovely, sweet scent and also looked nice. So, I want to put some of those in my apartment.
James Pipe [02:35 P.M.]		From the garden center on St. George Street, next to Thomas' Bakery.
Morgan Leek [02:36 P.M.]		Oh, I know where the flower shop is. By the way, what are they called?
James Pipe [02:37 P.M.]		It slipped my mind. Anyway, they have a lot of wildflowers and herbs. Just take a closer look and check the scent.
Morgan Leek [02:37 P.M.]		But, I don't know much about wildflowers and herbs. Are they easy to maintain?
James Pipe [02:38 P.M.]		Yes, absolutely. They grow well indoors, and they don't need much water.
Morgan Leek [02:39 P.M.]		That's great! I'm not able to be at home every day.

Send

164. What is mainly being discussed?

(A) Ms. Leek's new apartment
(B) Some plants for the Ms. Leek
(C) A bakery on St. George Street
(D) Sowing some herb seeds

165. What does Mr. Pipe suggest that Ms. Leek do?

(A) Stop by the bakery
(B) Meet him at the garden center
(C) Water the flowers every day
(D) Smell the plants

166. At 2:37 P.M., why does Mr. Pipe write, "It slipped my mind."?

(A) He doesn't know how much the plants would cost.
(B) He forgot the names of the flowers.
(C) He thinks Ms. Leek cannot take care of the plants.
(D) He doesn't mind how much water they need.

167. Why would Ms. Leek find the plants suitable for her?

(A) They are inexpensive.
(B) She is going to grow them outdoors.
(C) The flower shop is located near her apartment.
(D) She doesn't need to water them every day.

Questions 168-171 refer to the following article.

BORDEAUX, FR.

May 2 — Alan Debois, President of the Agricultural Union, is to be awarded the Géant Prize on May 10. —[1]—. This is an annual award to a deserving and active member of the Bordeaux business community, whose achievements have enhanced the region.

As a lifelong farmer, Mr. Debois has a keen interest in the local environment and put forward a proposal to the regional government for the installation of flood barriers to prevent crops and livestock from being affected by annual flooding in Bordeaux. Five years ago, his proposal for flood barriers began to be implemented and the Debois Barriers, as they are known, are now a well-known attraction for tourists. The first set was installed three years ago with a grant from the Environmental Agency. —[2]—. Since then, the barriers have prevented crops from being ruined, saved many cattle from drowning, and raised awareness of the dangers of tidal power. Completed last year in Bordeaux, the barrier installation scheme is now being considered by many coastal regions in France.

—[3]—. This program offers funding for apprenticeships to young adults who want to learn how to become farmers and work on the land. So far, over a hundred people have completed the program and have found employment on farms within the region.

—[4]—. The awards ceremony will take place in the Bordeaux Town Hall from 7 P.M. to 9 P.M. All residents of the town are welcome to attend, and details will be posted on the website, www.bordeaux.fr/awards.

---

168. What is the purpose of the article?

(A) To explain why a particular person won a community award
(B) To describe the role of the farming community
(C) To invite the townspeople to a seminar on flood plains
(D) To welcome a new member of the Bordeaux business community

169. What is NOT mentioned as a benefit of Dubois Barriers?

(A) Saving the lives of certain livestock
(B) Drawing travelers in Bordeaux
(C) Organizing a recycling program
(D) Raising awareness of tidal power

170. When was the Dubois Barrier project completed?

(A) Five years ago
(B) Three years ago
(C) The previous year
(D) On May 10

171. In which of the positions marked [1], [2], [3], and [4] does the following sentence best belong?

"In addition, Mr. Debois has also set up the Debois Academy."

(A) [1]
(B) [2]
(C) [3]
(D) [4]

PTZ Component Testing

PTZ Component Testing provides a full testing service for all those involved in the radiology industry, as well as hospitals. We offer extensive testing on all equipment using up-to-date machinery. We consider each application individually, tailoring the testing procedure to each specific client. In addition to being a brand-new testing facility, we also provide a mobile service to test the equipment in your workplace.

Our services:
► Analyzing and testing outcomes of new equipment for hospitals and healthcare facilities
► Examining reports following testing procedures
► Advising and implementing alterations to any equipment offsite or in the facility, if necessary

Facilities and Personnel
Our main facility is located in Shanghai, China, with supplementary offices in West Java Province and Szechuan. We have links with government-run testing firms globally, which enables us to provide an international service not available anywhere else in the country. Every member of our staff is trained to internationally accepted standards, with an average of 15 years' experience in the testing of radiology equipment.

Report
Our software provides results in internationally formatted data reports.
Results are printed in hard copy and provided digitally as well.
All information can be accessed on the website using a client-protected coded password.

For more information, contact Vivian Lawson at vivian@ptzcomponents.com.

172. The word "tailoring" in paragraph 1, line 3, is closest in meaning to

(A) sewing
(B) adapting
(C) presenting
(D) evaluating

173. What service does PTZ Component Testing NOT advertise?

(A) Examining radiology equipment
(B) Providing a mobile service
(C) Inspecting healthcare cleanliness
(D) Analyzing results of some machinery

174. According to the advertisement, what makes PTZ Component Testing unique?

(A) It works with similar companies throughout the world.
(B) It is the oldest company in the industry.
(C) Its scientists graduated from internationally renowned universities.
(D) It has a presence in every major city.

175. What is indicated about the reports generated by PTZ Component Testing?

(A) They are witnessed by independent experts.
(B) They are available online to the public.
(C) They are presented to customers in two formats.
(D) They can be kept on file for an extra fee.

Go on to the next page

From: Nolan Parker <Nparker@toyfactory.com>

To: Khloe Swann <Kswann@toybox.com>

Date: January 25

Subject: Sales update

Attachment: Report-01.xls

Dear Ms. Swann,

I am replying to your inquiry about this month's sales updates. As you can see, I have attached a list of the stock that we sold in December together with a profit and loss spreadsheet. You can see that most of the items sold extremely well. In particular, we sold a record number of the ceramic dolls from Minakawa Inc. The branded stuffed animals from Harpers also continue to be bestsellers, as well as the consoles and electronic games from ELF Ltd. What I find surprising is the lack of sales of the children's wooden building sets. I think the quality was extremely inferior to those of other competitors and we had many complaints that they broke easily. This is shown in the sales figures as refunds.

However, I have sourced a different supplier, so hopefully sales figures for the next few months will reflect this. I am looking forward to meeting you at the annual sales convention next Monday. If you need any further information before then, please let me know.

Sincerely,

Nolan Parker
Sales Manager

From: Khloe Swann <Kswann@toybox.com>

To: Nolan Parker <Nparker@toyfactory.com>

Date: January 26

Subject: Re: Sales update

Dear Mr. Parker,

Thank you for your prompt reply. As you are aware, we have signed a large contract to supply children's toys for the retail stores in Boston and Springfield, both very high-profile areas. From our research, we know that the locals in these areas demand very high-quality merchandise, and they have an even higher than average number of schools and children's clubs. Therefore, I think we should order more stock from Minakawa Inc. Can you supply me with a product list from this company and a contact name and number? I understand the meeting has been rescheduled to Tuesday. Can you confirm this as well?

Khloe Swann
Marketing Manager

176. Why did Mr. Parker send the first e-mail?

(A) To provide Ms. Swann with information
(B) To request a list of available playthings
(C) To supply a new date for a meeting
(D) To respond to a proposed change

177. According to the first e-mail, what items will be provided by a new supplier?

(A) Electronic games
(B) Stuffed animals
(C) Building sets
(D) Ceramic dolls

178. In the second e-mail, the word "locals" in line 3, is closest in meaning to

(A) residents
(B) regions
(C) items
(D) sales

179. What is suggested about the ceramic dolls?

(A) They are expected to sell well in the Boston area.
(B) They are not available during the summer season.
(C) They were purchased from Harpers.
(D) Their price has decreased from last month.

180. About what do Mr. Parker and Ms. Swann have different information?

(A) The date of a meeting
(B) The contact information for ELF Ltd.
(C) The sales figures for December
(D) The refund details of a client

August 15

Customer Service Department

Wells Home Appliances Inc.

22 Saunders Road

San Francisco, CA 94016

To Whom It May Concern,

When my coffee maker (serial code CFM 436) failed to work recently, I took it to the WHA service center in the Morris Shopping Mall, which is listed as one of your repair outlets. I was very annoyed when the shop declined to provide a free repair to my appliance although I have a valid warranty of more than six months. I had to pay for the repairs personally as there are no other local shops listed on your warranty. Here is a list of the charges from the repair center:

Parts :

Filter ··	$12
Power unit ·································	$17
Labor: $10 per hour ··············	$20
Dispenser nozzle ···················	$21
_____	
Total : ·································	**$70**

Please find attached the invoice and my guarantee I received when I bought the coffee maker. If you need any further information, please contact me.

Regards,

Ian Travers

23 Cherrystone Drive

San Jose, CA 95120

Guarantee

Welcome to your new Wells Coffee Maker. We have been supplying quality kitchen appliances throughout the world for over 30 years, and we pride ourselves on our quality and customer service.

All appliances are manufactured to the highest standards of craftsmanship. We offer a two-year warranty that covers the repair and replacement of your appliance in the event of a malfunction of parts. This warranty covers repairing labor and the replaceable parts only; please be aware that we take no responsibility for the damage to the dispenser nozzle or damage incurred by mishandling.

Attached is a list of authorized repair centers. Should you experience any problems with your new appliance, please take it to one of these WHA service centers for repair together with the original receipt and warranty. These centers have all been approved by Wells for the quality of their service and repairs.

181. Why did Mr. Travers write the letter?

(A) To request reimbursement of his expenses
(B) To request a copy of his guarantee
(C) To ask for a replacement for his broken machine
(D) To complain about a mistake on his receipt

182. In the letter, the word "declined" in paragraph 1, line 3, is closest in meaning to

(A) descended
(B) rejected
(C) weakened
(D) modified

183. What does Mr. Travers mention about the WHA service center?

(A) It offered the service at a reduced rate.
(B) It completed the task quickly.
(C) It carried out unnecessary work.
(D) It is an approved service center.

184. What did Wells Home Appliances include with the product warranty?

(A) A customer registration form
(B) A catalog of Wells products
(C) A register of clients
(D) A list of service centers

185. What expense amount reported by Mr. Travers will the warranty NOT cover?

(A) $12
(B) $17
(C) $20
(D) $21

Go on to the next page

City of Jacksonville
Council Office: Street Performer Permit Application

The following applicant seeks a license to perform on the streets of Jacksonville as an "artist" and submits the following information as required:

Artist's Name: <u>Jace Payne</u>

Legal Address of Applicant: <u>2194 Richardson Road, Jacksonville</u>

Location of performance: <u>Ed Austin Park</u>

Completed application forms must be accompanied by:

- Copy of birth certificate issued by Government Births Bureau
- A recording of the applicant playing the relevant instrument or singing
- License fee of $30 for each member, item of equipment, and stage
- A list of all equipment to be used at the venue
- If the music requires an amplifier, please send details of the decibel levels to our noise pollution officer, Mr. Gavin Freeman, to ensure it meets the permitted levels.

The applicant states that the above statement is true and he/she has read and agrees to comply with the provision of Section 44 of the code of the city of Jacksonville as it applies to artists.

Signature of applicant   *Jace Payne*

Date   *July 24*

To: Gavin Freeman <Gfreeman@admin.jacksonville.org>

From: Jace Payne <Jacepayne@bigmail.com>

Date: July 27

Re: Noise permission

Dear Mr. Freeman,

I wish to obtain permission for a street performance to be held at Ed Austin Park from August 1 to 3. I understand that I will need permission to use amplifiers, which are currently capable of emitting 100 decibels maximum. I am planning to use three amplifiers at the event. If you wish to check the noise levels, I'm performing at three venues in the downtown area on weekdays: Marrs Bar, Venure Restaurant, and Streetlife Café. I'll provide free entrance tickets if you want to come along and check that the decibel levels are acceptable.

Regards,

Jace Payne

To: Jace Payne <Jacepayne@bigmail.com>

From: Gavin Freeman <Gfreeman@admin.jacksonville.org>

Date: July 29

Re: Noise Permission

Dear Mr. Payne,

To assess the noise level, I need to operate the measuring equipment on-site. Among the places you've mentioned, Streetlife would work for me. You wrote you are performing on weekdays. When can I come over to see you?

And regarding your application, the person in charge says she hasn't received the recording of your playing yet. If you don't mind, I can record your performance when I visit there to check the amplifiers. Since we don't have much time before August 1, please call me at 500-5157 at your earliest convenience.

Gavin Freeman
Noise Pollution Officer

186. What is Mr. Payne applying for?

(A) A permit to sell drinks
(B) A sound check
(C) A safety certificate from the council
(D) A license to perform

187. Where will Mr. Freeman most likely see Mr. Payne play?

(A) At a park
(B) At a bar
(C) At a café
(D) At a restaurant

188. What required references does Mr. Freeman say Mr. Payne has missed?

(A) A birth certificate
(B) A video clip
(C) A list of equipment
(D) Some money

189. What is the purpose of the first e-mail?

(A) To submit an application
(B) To offer directions
(C) To ask for permission to use equipment
(D) To advertise some venues

190. What will Mr. Payne most likely use at the event next month?

(A) Electric guitars
(B) Microphone stands
(C) Editing equipment
(D) Loudspeakers

International Business Newsletter

MJ Foodville Appoints New Head of Research Team

MJ Foodville (MJF) which has its headquarters in Singapore, has appointed Colton Choi as the new head of its research team. "I am very excited about the new opportunities to open up for me here in Singapore, even though I am sad at having to leave my homeland in Korea," said Mr. Choi in a statement released in the MJF newsletter.

He went on to say that he had been interested in the work done at MJF for many years and is delighted to join the team. His first task once he assumes the position, according to the newsletter, will be to strongly highlight the importance of healthy eating in the Philippines and Indonesia.

Mr. Choi graduated with a master's degree in food and nutrition from the University of London. His previous employment was with Bristol Food Company, where he worked as a research assistant to the company's development director, Julian Baker. He will begin his new role in October at MJF.

To: Colton Choi <coltonchoi@gomail.com>

From: Ariana Rose <arianarose@bfc.com>

Date: September 9

Subject: Congratulations

Dear Mr. Choi,

Well done on your new appointment once again. This is an excellent opportunity for you, and I have no doubt that you will make a valuable contribution to the MJ Foodville. When you resigned, I was asked by Mr. Baker to fill in for your position as research assistant. I intend to accept the offer even though I have not given him an answer yet. I have wanted to join the research team since I began working here last year. I extend my heartfelt gratitude to you for putting me forward for the job.

I would very much like to keep in touch and would appreciate your sending me your new address and phone number in Singapore.

Kind regards,

Ariana Rose
Bristol Food Company

To: Ariana Rose <arianarose@bfc.com>

From: Colton Choi <coltonchoi@gomail.com>

Date: September 11

Subject: Re: Congratulations

Dear Ms. Rose,

I'm very pleased to know that you're accepting the offer. Although we had no chance to work on the same team, I heard a lot about you from your manager, Mr. Cox. I'm sure that your experience in the material division would be a great help to the research team. When I nominated you to the position, Mr. Baker readily agreed to give you the opportunity. So, you should return your thanks to Mr. Baker.

I haven't moved to Singapore yet. I found a house to settle in but still don't have a phone number. And my e-mail is to be changed; you can contact me at coltonchoi2793@mjfgroup. com if you need my advice on your new duties that start next month.

Sincerely,

Colton Choi

TEST

07

PART

7

191. Why was the article written?

(A) To announce the appointment of a staff member
(B) To publicize the findings of a questionnaire
(C) To release information about a new product
(D) To inform staff of an upcoming research project

192. Where are the headquarters of MJ Foodville located?

(A) Korea
(B) Singapore
(C) Malaysia
(D) Philippines

193. What does Ms. Rose ask Mr. Choi to do?

(A) Write a letter of recommendation
(B) Join a research team
(C) Provide contact information
(D) Speak at a meeting

194. What is mentioned about Mr. Choi?

(A) He is currently working for MJ Foodville.
(B) He will replace Mr. Cox for the research assistant position.
(C) He recommended Ms. Rose for his previous position.
(D) He decided to stay in his home country.

195. What is implied about Ms. Rose?

(A) She is a client of MJ Foodville.
(B) She currently lives in Singapore.
(C) She majored in food and nutrition.
(D) She is currently working for Mr. Cox.

Go on to the next page

Hatton Business Update

Trust us for up-to-the-minute news and events

Information to subscribers:

Requests for subscription renewal are sent automatically one week prior to your current subscription's expiration date, subject to the conditions below. If your subscription finishes prior to a renewal request but you wish to continue to renew your subscription within two months of the actual expiry date, you can purchase any missed issues of the business magazine for 25% off the cover price.

Clients who ask for a renewal or extension prior to April 30 will be offered a 10% reduction on a two-year subscription or a 5% reduction on a 12-month subscription. All online offers cease with the expiration of any subscription, including the search-and-find database, which enables you to browse through the past catalogs of previously published *Hatton Business Update* issues. Visit www.hattononline.com for more information.

Hatton Business Update

\-

Account Number: *34073*

Current Login: *March 6*

Previous Login: *February 27*

\-

Hatton Business Update Online Subscription

- **Name:** Austin Crocker
- **Subscription status:** Current subscription expires on March 6.
- **Requested renewal period:** 24 months
- **Payment method:** Bank transfer

Thank you for renewing your *Hatton Business Update* subscription.

Written by: Austin Crocker

Date: March 6

Subject: Subscription Renewal

Dear sir,

I've checked the information about the discount on your website today. I've been very satisfied with your service, so I decided to renew my subscription right away, even though I still have one month left before the expiration date. However, I was surprised to read the message, which states my expiration date is today, March 6. It must be April 6, according to your webpage. Other information on the message seems to be right.

I also checked if I applied for a new subscription instead of renewing it. But it says, "Thank you for renewing your *Hatton Business Update* subscription." Please take care of this issue as soon as possible.

196. What is the purpose of the information?

(A) To announce further discounts on subscriptions

(B) To explain subscription renewal policies

(C) To notify subscribers of changes to online subscriptions

(D) To request that subscribers complete a survey

197. In the information, the word "conditions" in paragraph 1, line 2, is closest in meaning to

(A) ends

(B) proposals

(C) terms

(D) names

198. What is indicated about *Hatton Business Update*?

(A) Its reporters have won several publishing awards.

(B) Its website provides some information to subscribers.

(C) It published its last issue two months ago.

(D) It recently increased its subscription fees.

199. What problem does Mr. Crocker report?

(A) He cannot log on to the website.

(B) He hasn't received any notice about the event.

(C) He got a message with the wrong information.

(D) He wants to get a full refund.

200. How much of a discount will Mr. Croker receive?

(A) 5%

(B) 10%

(C) 20%

(D) 25%

Test

答對題數表

PART 5	
PART 6	
PART 7	
總題數	

08

READING TEST

In the Reading test, you will read a variety of texts and answer several different types of reading comprehension questions. The entire Reading test will last 75 minutes. There are three parts, and directions are given for each part. You are encouraged to answer as many questions as possible within the time allowed.

You must mark your answers on the separate answer sheet. Do not write your answers in your test book.

PART 5

Directions: A word or phrase is missing in each of the sentences below. Four answer choices are given below each sentence. Select the best answer to complete the sentence. Then mark the letter (A), (B), (C), or (D) on your answer sheet.

101. The nutritional instruction program in Addis Ababa was so ------- that some countries are intending to introduce similar initiatives in their cities.

(A) success
(B) successive
(C) successful
(D) successfully

102. Affiliates of Prime.com will now receive unlimited ------- to the organization's exclusive online data pool.

(A) accesses
(B) access
(C) accessing
(D) accessory

103. The brochure highlights the sequence of ------- is happening over the two-day event.

(A) that
(B) what
(C) who
(D) when

104. Two years ago, Mr. Walker ------- college to join his current company.

(A) leave
(B) left
(C) will leave
(D) was left

105. ------- maintenance work on the Kaur Drive, workers at the Mahir Library have to enter via the north entrance to get to work.

(A) Now that
(B) Moreover
(C) Wherever
(D) Because of

106. Those who have ------- about their missing baggage have to visit the claim office located next to the luggage carousel.

(A) features
(B) connections
(C) properties
(D) inquiries

107. Those who feel dizzy in the heat of the day will realize that the best way to make ------- feel better is to drink some water.

(A) they
(B) them
(C) their
(D) themselves

108. The pay increase this year for all employees is the ------- as that incentive last year.

(A) same
(B) repeat
(C) equal
(D) one

109. Farmers in Shamrock are overwhelmed by the enormous demand for ------- organic potato products.

(A) they
(B) themselves
(C) them
(D) their

110. The majority of shoppers at Camden supermarket will readily pay extra for food that is produced -------.

(A) local
(B) locality
(C) locals
(D) locally

111. Although public admission to the Anaheim Society's award ceremony is allowed, the after-party is by ------- only.

(A) collection
(B) invitation
(C) operation
(D) function

112. Company employees have been advised that the new product range's market is highly ------- and will face fierce rivalry from other companies.

(A) competitive
(B) competitors
(C) competition
(D) competitively

113. The customer conference was ------- delayed as the projector had an operational malfunction in the course of the seminar.

(A) enough
(B) many
(C) quite
(D) ever

114. The ------- annual manufacturing costs of the company were estimated to be $12 million as a result of structural renovations.

(A) totaling
(B) totaled
(C) totals
(D) total

115. Visitors ------- to show their passport or photo identification whenever they have to check-in at a hotel.

(A) requests
(B) are requested
(C) to request
(D) requesting

116. The board of directors is considering ------- the headquarters to Vancouver.

(A) to relocate
(B) relocation
(C) relocating
(D) has relocated

117. The Sales Manager, Cody Flynn, insisted that marketing the merchandise ------- online is not a profitable way of attracting young customers.

(A) closely
(B) otherwise
(C) solely
(D) almost

118. Kemp Apparel's second quarter growth rate was higher than originally -------.

(A) anticipates
(B) anticipated
(C) anticipating
(D) anticipation

119. Applicants who passed the initial selection tests for the supervisor position ------- by the company recruiter next week.

(A) will contact
(B) would contact
(C) will be contacted
(D) have been contacted

120. Bainbridge Public Library visitors may check out a total of 5 publications ------- 3 multimedia items per week.

(A) than
(B) just as
(C) so
(D) and

Go on to the next page

121. During their stay, guests have the option of participating in various outdoor activities ------- cycling, fishing, and swimming.
(A) similarly
(B) such as
(C) as far as
(D) likewise

122. Travelers are asked to collect all of their ------- belongings before exiting the train.
(A) personal
(B) accurate
(C) unlimited
(D) believable

123. Changes in LK Telecom's billing policy are ------- determined by how much demand there is.
(A) large
(B) largest
(C) larger
(D) largely

124. The estimate covers all the labor and materials for building a parking ------- on Boulder Road that can accommodate 1,000 vehicles.
(A) structure
(B) structures
(C) structural
(D) structurally

125. Mr. Reynolds should certainly be praised for ------- a welcome reception for the new employees at Orange Software.
(A) correcting
(B) applying
(C) organizing
(D) connecting

126. The retailers on Simpson Street are prohibited from displaying items outside ------- prior consent.
(A) around
(B) without
(C) owing to
(D) as opposed to

127. ------- impresses the board of directors the most is that the White Timber Company has established its presence in the hardwood furniture market.
(A) Nothing
(B) Neither
(C) What
(D) Which

128. While a majority of customers think that the new model is easy to use, those ------- familiar with the original operating system have to look through the user's manual before using the item.
(A) little
(B) none
(C) less
(D) fewer

129. Because of her outstanding performance, Ms. Russell has been ------- to a manager position at Higgins Inc.
(A) promoted
(B) registered
(C) pleased
(D) increased

130. Vending machines containing beverages and snacks are strategically situated ------- the company premises.
(A) between
(B) down
(C) throughout
(D) except

PART 6

Directions: Read the texts that follow. A word, phrase, or sentence is missing in parts of each text. Four answer choices for each question are given below the text. Select the best answer to complete the text. Then mark the letter (A), (B), (C), or (D) on your answer sheet.

Questions 131-134 refer to the following advertisement.

New Exhibition at Sierra Art Museum

In recent years, Sierra Art Museum has been popular in holding exhibitions on Junk art,

innovative art ------- the great artistic talent shown by famous local artist Diego Harding and his
                131.

colleagues.

According to Mr. Harding, his activity would every now and then be termed as "Junk art." -------.
                                                                                        132.

"Junk art," as his work is called, is once-abandoned items ------- are utilized to come up with a
                                                            133.

new creation.

The exhibition will be open to anyone interested from April 1 to June 30. -------, on the evening
                                                                        134.

of Wednesday, March 23, there will be a reception that will include the staff members of the art

center only. A website is also set up in case someone needs more clarification. The website is

at museum.sierraart.org.

131. (A) feature
     (B) featured
     (C) featuring
     (D) features

132. (A) But the materials for those sculptures
         are not junk in fact.
     (B) This was once believed to be possible,
         but Mr. Harding thought otherwise.
     (C) Mr. Harding is now collecting a lot of
         junk to turn his idea into a reality.
     (D) He came up with the idea of utilizing
         the things that people throw away
         every day.

133. (A) what
     (B) that
     (C) how
     (D) each

134. (A) In addition
     (B) Instead
     (C) Thus
     (D) As a result

Go on to the next page

Dear Stellar Store customer,

We appreciate you very much for your interest in joining the Stellar Store Rewards loyalty program. Participating in this program ------- you to enjoy a lot of wonderful rewards. The
135.
benefits of being a member of this program are that you will have early ------- about discount
136.
deals, access to special exclusive occasions, and the opportunity to be awarded a gift certificate worth $50 for every $400 spent on product purchases.

-------. An individual is only required to submit the enclosed application form to the nearby store,
137.
where a membership card can be issued for you. Updates on your account detailing the points you have accumulated and discount coupons you have earned will be provided ------- six weeks
138.
after you start using your membership card.

Membership is free and can be canceled at any time. Welcome and start earning your rewards today!

Sincerely,

Amy Henderson

Customer Loyalty Program Director

Enclosure

135. (A) has allowed
(B) is allowing
(C) allowed
(D) will allow

136. (A) performance
(B) evaluation
(C) information
(D) referral

137. (A) Once you cancel, all your coupons will become invalid.
(B) There are no complications in signing up for this program.
(C) You are not on our customer list; however, we will service you as our most important member.
(D) You'll need to visit one of our affiliates to get an application form.

138. (A) within
(B) since
(C) until
(D) due to

Bangkok (2 April) — Superior Athletics, a prominent Canadian clothing company, will soon

------- its fashion items in Thailand.
139.

Richard Kent, the president of Superior Athletics, declared in an interview with *Thai Business*

News that the company intends to ship its first batch of the newest sports apparel and fashion

accessories to Bangkok, Thailand, in several weeks. Thai ------- can acquire the products in
140.

May, when the goods are put up for sale in the market.

Mr. Kent credited the business move of the company to a ------- demand for sports apparel in
141.

Thailand and its neighboring countries. -------. According to Mr. Kent, the current trend in
142.

Southeast Asia is that more and more people have become interested in workout clothing,

and this is precisely what Superior Athletics aims to provide.

139. (A) recall
(B) market
(C) reduce
(D) design

140. (A) consuming
(B) consumers
(C) consumable
(D) consumed

141. (A) rising
(B) controlling
(C) long-standing
(D) questionable

142. (A) No wonder the company is
withdrawing its business from
Southeast Asia.
(B) He is now worried that the Asian
market might begin to shrink.
(C) As a result, its business may be more
beneficial in European countries.
(D) In particular, its business in the
Philippines was a huge success.

Go on to the next page

Questions 143-146 refer to the following memo.

To: Production workers and inspectors

From: Fred Wilson, Production Manager

Date: February 9

Subject: EZ2Drink Juicer

I am writing to promptly inform you that we ------- several reviews from our customers regarding
143.
the detachable squeezers on our new EZ2Drink Juicers.

-------. While this may seem like an unimportant detail, I feel these complaints would negatively
144.
affect our reputation in the long run. As a reminder, production workers must make sure that

the squeezer is ------- manufactured. Inspectors must also double-check these ------- prior to
145. **146.**
distribution.

Please call me at 764-8314 if you need further details about the EZ2Drink Juicer.

143. (A) will receive
(B) have received
(C) receive
(D) receiving

144. (A) There are no complaints reported by the customers yet.
(B) I'm pleased to know that the newest model is earning favorable reviews.
(C) Despite the poor sales figures, the company has to continue to increase the production.
(D) Some customers are disconcerted as the squeezer does not fit in the body completely.

145. (A) rapidly
(B) comfortably
(C) properly
(D) certainly

146. (A) parts
(B) vehicles
(C) schedules
(D) payments

PART 7

Directions: In this part you will read a selection of texts, such as magazine and newspaper articles, e-mails, and instant messages. Each text or set of texts is followed by several questions. Select the best answer for each question and mark the letter (A), (B), (C), or (D) on your answer sheet.

Questions 147-148 refer to the following notice.

Iron Jones Gym is now due for renovation. The gym is to be closed for two weeks in July for building repairs.

The dates below are important:

June 20 – June 30	Renewal of annual membership
July 1 – July 6	Room refurbishment
July 7 – July 14	External window replacement
July 15	Gym reopening

To check our full calendar for the year, go to www.ironjones.com. Membership can be renewed over the telephone. If you are renting sports equipment, the lending period can also be renewed if you'd like. If not, please return the items before June 20. You may reapply for the equipment on July 15. Even if you are renewing a rental agreement, all equipment has to be removed from your previous lockers by June 30, as they will be changed. Anything left in the lockers will be removed after this date.

Contact us with any questions at 777-4644 extension 14.

147. For whom in the Iron Jones Gym is the notice intended?

(A) Management
(B) Members
(C) Fitness trainers
(D) Gym staff

148. How should membership be renewed?

(A) In person
(B) By phone
(C) By e-mail
(D) Through the website

Questions 149-150 refer to the following message chain.

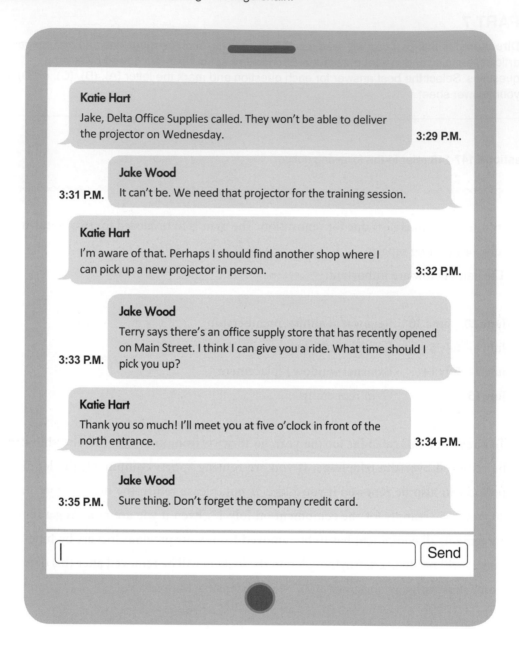

Katie Hart

Jake, Delta Office Supplies called. They won't be able to deliver the projector on Wednesday.

3:29 P.M.

Jake Wood

3:31 P.M. It can't be. We need that projector for the training session.

Katie Hart

I'm aware of that. Perhaps I should find another shop where I can pick up a new projector in person.

3:32 P.M.

Jake Wood

3:33 P.M. Terry says there's an office supply store that has recently opened on Main Street. I think I can give you a ride. What time should I pick you up?

Katie Hart

Thank you so much! I'll meet you at five o'clock in front of the north entrance.

3:34 P.M.

Jake Wood

3:35 P.M. Sure thing. Don't forget the company credit card.

Send

149. What problem are the speakers discussing?

(A) The new projector is not working properly.

(B) They cannot attend the workshop on Wednesday.

(C) An order cannot be delivered in time.

(D) Mr. Wood needs a ride to Main Street.

150. At 3:31 P.M., what does Mr. Wood mean when he writes, "It can't be."?

(A) He can't find another supplier.

(B) He can't fix the projector.

(C) He can't agree to Ms. Hart's opinion.

(D) He can't accept the failure.

Questions 151-152 refer to the following announcement.

Dear Residents of Henderson,

From August, Sunset Station Dance Hall will become known as the Rainbow Paradise Nightclub. There is a major refurbishment taking place, which will include a new dining area as well as an extension to the dance floor to make it larger. The new owner, Larry Stone, will still maintain the same high quality of food and entertainment that you have been used to in the past. We look forward to seeing you again.

151. According to the announcement, what is being changed about the establishment?

(A) Its name
(B) Its location
(C) The menu
(D) The prices

152. What is suggested about Mr. Stone?

(A) He plans to change the menu.
(B) He owns other properties in the area.
(C) He used to work in a nightclub.
(D) He plans to extend a dance area.

Go on to the next page

London Economist
Business News

September 12, London — Ethan Fletcher, Chief Executive Officer at Filton Heating Components, has announced that the company will be expanding within the country over the next six months. He plans to open stores in Glasgow, Leeds, and London. —[1]—.

Mr. Fletcher admitted that the planned expansion is behind schedule due to complications in the manufacturing plant. He said that the recession "had taken everyone by surprise." Following the installation of new advanced machinery in its production headquarters in Bristol, Mr. Fletcher is confident that the company's expansion will merit the investment. —[2]—.

Filton Heating Components was established by the current CEO's father, who began by recycling metal to make the boiler parts. —[3]—. And it has led to a massive rise in market share for the company over the years.

Next year, the company is hoping to expand into the air conditioning market, and the industry will be closely monitoring its performance. The move will be supplemented by an aggressive advertising and marketing campaign. —[4]—.

153. What is suggested about Filton Heating Components?
(A) It has lost significant market share over the years.
(B) Its founder passed the business to his son.
(C) It will expand into the commercial sector.
(D) It closed down its manufacturing plant.

154. In which of the positions marked [1], [2], [3], and [4] does the following sentence best belong?

"This recycling initiative led to cheaper components exclusively for the industrial market."

(A) [1]
(B) [2]
(C) [3]
(D) [4]

Journey in Style through the Highlands with Express Trains

Experience the sights and sounds of a coastal journey along the Highlands route on a three-hour train journey with Express Trains. The 200-kilometer coastal trail encompasses three counties, with beautiful scenery and lush vegetation. Our trip will take you through the high terrain with the option of a tour guide to explain the area. Lunch will be aboard the train passing through the industrial district of the Highlands. Then the journey ends with a visit to a hidden beach where you can see seals and dolphins at play off the coast.

The train leaves the station at 11:30 A.M. from Manchester Station and returns at 2:30 P.M., Mondays to Fridays. Tickets are £40 for adults, £25 for students with valid ID cards, and £20 for children under the age of 12.

For details and a timetable, call
Express Trains
at 0161-334-6259
or
visit our website
at www.expresshighlandstrains.co.uk

Express Trains Trip

TEST 08

PART 7

155. For whom is the brochure most likely intended?

(A) Tour guides
(B) Historians
(C) Train drivers
(D) Tourists

156. The word "hidden" in line 6, is closest in meaning to

(A) restricted
(B) obscure
(C) notorious
(D) crowded

157. How much is the fee for a ten-year-old?

(A) £12
(B) £20
(C) £25
(D) £40

Melrose Business College

If you are seeking an International Master's Degree in business, then contact the Melrose Business College for details of courses.

The college offers a two-year program, beginning in September, and has a range of courses in international relations and business studies. The courses are taught by reputable faculty members, all of whom have significant hands-on experience in international businesses and trade industries. Together with an innovative exchange program with major companies overseas, this has placed the college in the top three educational establishments in the International Business College rankings.

The application fee is $150 for domestic students and $250 for applicants from abroad. If you quote this advertisement, the price will be halved, as long as you submit the application by the end of June. The application deadline for the upcoming course is July 15. There are also a number of grants and scholarships available. For more information and an application form, visit our website at www.melrosebusiness.edu.

158. What is suggested about the International Master's Degree course?

(A) It recently added new faculty members.
(B) It has three enrollment periods.
(C) It has a renowned reputation.
(D) It takes one year to complete.

159. According to the advertisement, what is NOT available to students?

(A) An opportunity to work abroad
(B) Access to lecturers with international expertise
(C) The possibility of getting financial assistance
(D) The ability to take courses over the Internet

160. What is indicated about the application fee?

(A) It is different for national and international applicants.
(B) It will increase next year.
(C) It must be paid by June 30.
(D) It can be paid online or via credit card.

Memo

Irvine Hotel

In an effort to try to reduce expenses, the management of the Irvine Hotel will no longer be supplying free toiletries. Guests must specifically ask for them to be supplied, and there is an additional charge. This is part of our cost-cutting initiative. Please make sure that you inform guests of this change when they check in. However, guests can purchase essential toiletries at a reasonable cost from our shop in the foyer. Guests can pre-order well-selected toiletries to await them when they arrive and the cost of these items will be added to the final bill. Please ensure that this message is clearly stated to any person who books over the telephone. We will post notices of this change in every hotel room and also in the lobby so that the message is clear.

161. For whom is the memo most likely intended?

(A) Hotel guests
(B) Maintenance staff
(C) Housekeeping staff
(D) Hotel receptionists

162. According to the memo, why has a new policy been adopted?

(A) To save the cost of disposable items
(B) To improve training for employees
(C) To use less energy and water
(D) To reduce requests for extra maintenance

163. What are hotel employees instructed to do?

(A) Inform guests that toiletries are not complimentary
(B) Charge guests for any water and electricity used
(C) Provide guests with a variety of items at reception
(D) Notify guests of an increase in room rates

Go on to the next page

April 30 — Designer Carla Whittle of the Whittle Design Agency has made a donation of half a million pounds to the Soweto Town Direct Disability project. This is a huge boost for the charity as funding for the project has been reduced since last year. "We are truly delighted with Ms. Whittle's contribution," commented David Campbell, the director of the Direct Disability program. —[1]—.

Direct Disability was established a decade ago by local businesspeople to help disabled people to use public facilities. Although it was originally supposed to receive a grant from the government, funding was cut earlier this year due to pressure by the Treasury to reduce public spending. —[2]—. The project now relies upon donations.

Last month, Direct Disability began a fundraising campaign targeting local businesses. "Together with requests for donations, we sent pictures of some facilities we have established," continued Mr. Campbell. —[3]—. One of the installations was fitting a wheelchair ramp to the local library, which is frequented by Ms. Whittle's family. "I had no idea that Ms. Whittle's family used the library until she rang and asked if she could assist in some way," Mr. Campbell said.

Supporters and businesses are delighted with the donation, with local councilor Tom Brady praising the work done by the charity to raise awareness and funding for other projects. Ms. Whittle released a press statement saying, "I have loved the library since I was a child, and although I have now moved abroad, I still have fond memories of it. —[4]—. It is not just about installing access ramps. It means that more local people are now able to access the facilities."

Amy Wellington, Local Contributor

---

164. When was the Direct Disability project started?

(A) Two years ago
(B) Three years ago
(C) Five years ago
(D) Ten years ago

165. According to the article, why has the project lost funding?

(A) Local businesses refused to help.
(B) Building material costs increased.
(C) The local population had declined.
(D) The government reduced its financial support.

166. Who is currently NOT a resident of Soweto Town?

(A) Carla Whittle
(B) David Campbell
(C) Tom Brady
(D) Amy Wellington

167. In which of the positions marked [1], [2], [3], and [4] does the following sentence best belong?

"It will certainly help us to install more facilities for disabled people in the community."

(A) [1]
(B) [2]
(C) [3]
(D) [4]

Questions 168-171 refer to the following e-mail.

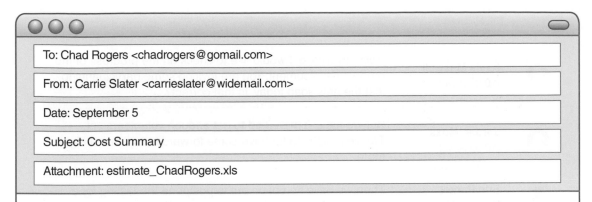

To: Chad Rogers <chadrogers@gomail.com>

From: Carrie Slater <carrieslater@widemail.com>

Date: September 5

Subject: Cost Summary

Attachment: estimate_ChadRogers.xls

Dear Mr. Rogers,

I enjoyed meeting with you last week and hearing your ideas for the expansion of your automatic car wash business. As I mentioned, my financial team has been preparing a financial estimate, which is attached to this e-mail.

You said you plan to open business on the site opposite from the Baxter Building to allow a drive-through car wash service. The team has figured the cost of this into the estimate, including an estimate for the renovations and rental that will be required prior to any agreement. I would still recommend the vacant site next to the Prime Building behind Anton Elementary School as a more viable option. As it has already been renovated, this will reduce your costs.

If you want us to carry out the work, we can begin immediately. Please do not hesitate to contact me with any queries. I look forward to hearing from you soon.

Sincerely,

Carrie Slater

168. Who most likely is Ms. Slater?

(A) A car wash company owner
(B) A building contractor
(C) A financial consultant
(D) A landscaping professional

169. According to the e-mail, what was discussed at last week's meeting?

(A) Designs for a new restaurant
(B) Expansion of a fleet of vehicles
(C) Plans for a business relocation
(D) Potential renovation projects

170. What is mentioned as being included in the attachment?

(A) Detailed blueprints
(B) A breakdown of prices
(C) Receipts for renovation materials
(D) Work schedules

171. The word "figured" in paragraph 2, line 2, is closest in meaning to

(A) exceeded
(B) discounted
(C) incorporated
(D) transformed

Go on to the next page

	Kayla Maxwell [10:01 A.M.]	Hello, everyone. I would like to check on the progress of the product development. You are inviting some participants to test the new soap today. Is that correct?
	Jordan Moss [10:02 A.M.]	But we haven't managed to get enough volunteers yet. Twelve people so far have come forward but we need eight more.
	Erin Parker [10:02 A.M.]	Then we have no option but to postpone the testing for a few days.
	Kayla Maxwell [10:03 A.M.]	Can't we just do it with twelve subjects?
	Erin Parker [10:03 A.M.]	We'd better not. Currently we have only two subjects between the ages of 41 and 50. This can distort the results of the findings.
	Kayla Maxwell [10:04 A.M.]	There's nothing that we can do if it doesn't work. Can you ensure that the testing is carried out as soon as possible, with the results sent directly to me? I will need some sort of written report by the end of next week.
	Jordan Moss [10:05 A.M.]	Yes, it was my general plan. I can assure you that you will receive a report by next Friday.

Send

172. What are the speakers mainly discussing?

  (A) A recruitment drive
  (B) A marketing report
  (C) An advertising campaign
  (D) A product trial

173. What does Ms. Parker tell Ms. Maxwell?

  (A) The test has to be delayed.
  (B) She'll send a report by the end of the week.
  (C) They have to move up the test date.
  (D) She'll proceed with the test with 12 people.

174. At 10:04 A.M., why does Ms. Maxwell write, "There's nothing that we can do if it doesn't work."?

  (A) She doesn't want to volunteer for the test.
  (B) She understands why the test has to be postponed.
  (C) She can help them gather more participants.
  (D) She will work on the research herself.

175. What does Mr. Moss say that he will do?

  (A) Convince Ms. Parker to reschedule the test
  (B) Send the report to Ms. Maxwell by next Friday
  (C) Check the release date of the new soap range
  (D) Advertise for more people in a newspaper

Questions 176-180 refer to the following e-mails.

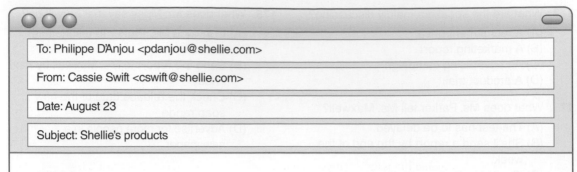

To: Philippe D'Anjou <pdanjou@shellie.com>

From: Cassie Swift <cswift@shellie.com>

Date: August 23

Subject: Shellie's products

Philippe,

I wish to draw your attention to negative feedback posted on a number of websites across Asia and Australia in particular about our Shellie range of windbreakers. You should pay particular attention to www.uniquesales.com and www.ratedornot.au. It seems that there are numerous complaints about the quality of the material used for the items. Shellie is going to be featured strongly in our new advertising campaign, so it is imperative that we find out more about the problem. Could you ask your department to look into this matter? At the same time, could your department undertake some further research into the Shellie range to find out if customers have any other concerns? Please make this a priority and report back to me with your findings by the end of next week.

Many thanks for your cooperation,

Cassie

To:	Cassie Swift <cswift@shellie.com>
From:	Philippe D'Anjou <pdanjou@shellie.com>
Date:	August 30
Subject:	Re: Shellie's products

Cassie,

We have investigated the issues that you mentioned in your e-mail dated August 23. We have discovered that there is indeed a global concern about the quality of the material used in the Shellie range. In particular, it seems to be restricted to the all-in-one item, Shellie XK1. Customers are complaining that the material is too thin and prone to ripping. I would ask your manufacturing department to find a solution to this problem.

Additionally, we have found some dissatisfaction with the Shellie YL bra sets. Customers are uncomfortable about the lack of color choice. The website lists any color other than white as out of stock. I will e-mail you with more details by Friday.

The good news is that the level of satisfaction with both the sizing options and the price are very high. Once we sort out the issues raised by our customers, we will be just fine.

Philippe

176. Why does Ms. Swift write to Mr. D'Anjou?

(A) To promote two new websites
(B) To complain about the quality of an item
(C) To propose a new advertising campaign
(D) To ask him to research a problem

177. In what field does Ms. Swift work?

(A) Manufacturing
(B) Advertising
(C) Customer relations
(D) Product development

178. What is NOT stated about Shellie?

(A) Its products are mainly reviewed on two websites.
(B) Its headquarters are in Asia.
(C) It produces women's clothing.
(D) It has a research-related department.

179. What does Mr. D'Anjou note about Shellie XK1?

(A) The material is of an inferior quality.
(B) The color choices are not as many as customers want.
(C) The price is too high for the customers.
(D) The item is no longer in fashion.

180. In the second e-mail, the word "restricted" in paragraph 1, line 3, is closest in meaning to

(A) reduced
(B) exceptional
(C) limited
(D) confidential

Go on to the next page

Excellence in Technology
Amanti Boost

by Alice Cryer, New Delhi News

April 2 — Amanti is renowned for the quality of its mobile technology, and the New Boost mobile phone — due for launch on April 10 — is no exception. It has the capacity to store approximately 3,000 photos and 20 thirty-minute videos at the same time, and in addition, the external memory card provided with it is able to accommodate up to 5,000 tunes.

As an incentive, contract purchasers of the New Boost will receive a free set of state-of-the-art headphones. They were extensively tested by Amanti's research center, and the sound is far superior to the standard earphones supplied with its mobile phones. Moreover, Amanti is offering a new application that will enable users to download music and films faster and cheaper than before.

The New Boost is all new to us. It has a brighter screen as well as a much longer battery life. The New Boost is expected to supersede the company's previous flagship mobile phones and has a bright future ahead.

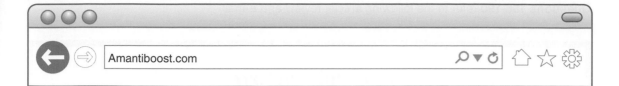

| **Feedback** | **Products** | **Services** | **Purchase** |

User Feedback: Amanti Boost Mobile Phone
User: Ranjit Khan, Mumbai
Posted: 7:12 P.M. May 23

User rating: ★★★★☆

I really like the New Boost, and I have no regrets about waiting in line to purchase it on the day it was launched. I particularly like the headphones that came free with the phone. I also highly recommend the new application that enables you to download music and films for only 100 rupees a month. At the moment, there aren't many options, though I understand from the company that they will resume adding more contents from May 30.

My only real complaint is the new screen. Although it is brighter and bigger than Amanti's previous models, watching movies is a problem as there is a significant glare.

181. What is the purpose of the article?

(A) To announce a company's brand name has been changed
(B) To preview a new mobile device
(C) To explain how to download media onto a memory card
(D) To introduce testimonials from customers

182. What is NOT mentioned about the New Boost?

(A) Its larger screen
(B) Its accessories
(C) Its storage capacity
(D) Its carrying case

183. When did Mr. Khan most likely purchase his New Boost?

(A) On April 2
(B) On April 10
(C) On May 23
(D) On May 30

184. What is indicated about the mobile application?

(A) It is a combined effort between two mobile phone companies.
(B) It is gradually adding more choices to its inventory.
(C) It has been in existence for several years.
(D) It is offered to New Boost purchasers for free.

185. What is Mr. Khan's complaint about the screen?

(A) It is too bright.
(B) It is easily damaged.
(C) It doesn't switch to horizontal mode.
(D) It turns off unexpectedly.

Go on to the next page

FASHION SHOW

Kanta Fashion Show was instrumental in revealing a number of innovations in today's fashion. Since last year, designers have been focusing heavily on natural materials.

"The latest designs from fashion houses are an indication of the new trend. If people had not want the designs, they would not have appeared in the show," commented Ms. Grainger, fashion show organizer.

For some companies, including Essie Sew and Laramar, the show gave them the chance to showcase their portfolio for the first time. Another new company, Pantala, revealed a brand-new concept in outerwear, which earned them the coveted Best in Show award, which has been previously won by Mackowns, who have been exhibiting for nearly five years.

Over 10,000 people attended the show at the Downton Hotel, which is located in the center of the town.

Fashion Review of Pantala
By Suzy Rees

Operating for only twelve months, Pantala produces very well-known designs such as the Oasis Collection. Unlike other start-up companies, the organization is unique in not following the traditional designs of the industry.

Personally, I like the Dress Collection, which is a combination of lace, silk, and hemp — not a common choice but one that certainly attracts attention. The dresses come with a free pair of gloves and a handkerchief of the Grace Silver brand.

Their new collection, Autumn Dream, is the only one that uses leather: up to now, the company has only used soft materials. However, one look at their gorgeous jacket with a leather belt, straps, and silk lining will make you notice its quality.

To: Suzy Rees <Suzyrees@fashiontoday.com>

From: Joanne Kay <Joannekay@pantala.com>

Date: May 7

Subject: Upcoming Event

Dear Ms. Rees,

I'm writing to express deep gratitude for your favorable review on our Dress Collection, exhibited at the Kanta Fashion show last month. The show was the second event we've ever participated in, and I'm so glad to know that our collection has drawn much attention from fashion experts so soon.

In particular, I would like to thank you for your warm reviews about Autumn Dream as well as the Dress Collection. And I would like to invite you to our next event at Hummingbird Hotel, which is scheduled to be held on the 11th of next month. This will be the first fashion show hosted by Pantala, featuring the Autumn Dream collection accompanied by several more collections we are launching for the next season.

Thank you in advance for your time and participation.

Joanne Kay
Senior Designer
Pantala Fashion

186. What did Ms. Grainger imply about the fashion designs made of natural materials?

(A) They have been the only clothes on show.
(B) It is hard to design new trends.
(C) Their prices have been falling.
(D) Interest in them has been high.

187. Which company participated in the Kanta Fashion Show last year?

(A) Essie Sew
(B) Laramar
(C) Pantala
(D) Mackowns

188. What is indicated about the first fashion show hosted by Pantala?

(A) It was organized by Ms. Grainger.
(B) The place of the event has not been decided yet.
(C) It will be held on June 11.
(D) It will be the second fashion event hosted by Pantala.

189. Which design collection received an award at the show?

(A) Oasis Collection
(B) Spring Collection
(C) Autumn Dream
(D) Grace Silver

190. What does the reviewer suggest about Pantala?

(A) It has been operating for over two years.
(B) It avoids using ideas from other companies.
(C) It has relocated to another location.
(D) It uses only natural materials.

Go on to the next page

To: Chloe Page <chloepage@edmonds.com>

From: Kevin Goodwin <kevingoodwin@edmonds.com>

Date: February 17

Subject: Candidate Interview

Attachment: Interview_Schedule.doc

Chloe,

Can I ask a favor of you? Luke Bowden is coming over on Thursday as a prospective candidate for the directorship of the drama school. However, I have double-booked with foreign clients from China at the same time. I cannot reschedule this meeting. Can I swap interview times with you? The original schedule for Mr. Bowden is attached. I hope you can accommodate the changed times.

Mr. Bowden has an impressive résumé, particularly his work with the Oscar Theater, which has been recognized as the top drama teaching academy in the country and is a major rival. I hope he will be a great asset to us. We have also had an excellent reference from Ian Hicks for his outstanding contribution on the board of the Arts and Music Corporation. Mr. Hicks is also coming to join us for lunch.

Thank you,

Kevin Goodwin
Acting Head of Drama
Edmonds Entertainment

Edmonds Entertainment
Candidate Interview Schedule

Candidate Name: Luke Bowden
Potential Position: Director of Drama School
Interview Date: February 20

Meeting	Time	Location
Interview: Chloe Page	11:00 A.M. – 12:00 P.M.	Building A, Room 205
Lunch with Ian Hicks	12:20 P.M. – 1:20 P.M.	Building B, Cafeteria
Interview: Kevin Goodwin	1:30 P.M. – 2:30 P.M.	Building A, Room 303

NOTE: Upon arrival, please show your driver's license to the parking attendant next to the main entrance so that he can check on the necessary information and park your car in a designated area.

To:	Kevin Goodwin <kevingoodwin@edmonds.com>
From:	Chloe Page <chloepage@edmonds.com>
Date:	February 17
Subject:	Interview reschedule

Kevin,

Don't worry about the interview schedule. I'm available on Thursday afternoon. And I also informed Mr. Bowden about the change as soon as I received your e-mail. Upon arrival, he will meet you at Room 303. I have high expectations of him, too. He'd be a great person to work with.

We're going to have lunch together, with Mr. Hicks and Mr. Bowden, right? Then I think Greenwoods restaurant is better than the cafeteria, since this will be the first time for us to meet Mr. Hicks. The restaurant is right next to the company building, so you won't be late for your meeting at 1:30. I'll reserve a table for four.

Good luck with your meeting with the Chinese clients. I'll see you on Thursday.

Chloe Page
General Manager
Edmonds Entertainment

191. What is implied about Mr. Bowden?

(A) He has worked for a competitor of Edmonds Entertainment.
(B) He used to work for Edmonds Entertainment many years ago.
(C) He is being recruited for his acting skills.
(D) He has visited Edmonds Entertainment in the past.

192. When does Mr. Goodwin indicate he wants to interview Mr. Bowden?

(A) At 11:00 A.M.
(B) At 12:20 P.M.
(C) At 1:30 P.M.
(D) At 2:30 P.M.

193. What is Mr. Bowden expected to do?

(A) Leave earlier than originally informed
(B) Book a restaurant
(C) Meet Mr. Hicks at the main entrance
(D) Bring a form of identification

194. Who will meet with Mr. Bowden in Room 303?

(A) Ms. Page
(B) Mr. Hicks
(C) Mr. Goodwin
(D) Ms. Oscar

195. What will Ms. Page likely to be doing at 1 P.M. on February 20?

(A) Taking a tour of the Edmonds premises
(B) Dining at a nearby restaurant
(C) Having a meeting at the company cafeteria
(D) Interviewing Mr. Bowden

Go on to the next page

Peacock Office Supplies

Voted by the Business Times as the best supplier of office supplies!

To celebrate our 5th anniversary in May, we are offering a special service to all our valued customers. On your request, we will imprint your company and personal information on your purchases, including file folders, envelopes, boxes, whiteboards, and all kinds of ballpoint pens. It is completely free!

Please put a checkmark by the items you want on the ordering form. Also, you'll need to fill in the design layout code, which can be checked on our website. And don't forget to update your customer information so that we can imprint them correctly.

Thank you for choosing Peacock Office Supplies!

Peacock Office Supplies

Send order to:
Name: Christopher Dixon   **E-mail:** chrisdixon@foxcox.com   **Company:** Fox&Cox Inc.

Please indicate which information you would like to have on your office products and how you want it laid out.

	File folders	Pens	Business Cards
Company name	✓	✓	✓
Company address			✓
Company logo	✓	✓	✓
Company website	✓		✓
Individual name	✓		✓
Individual phone number			✓
Individual e-mail address			✓
Design layout code	*AD7*	*GK3*	*HL4*
Quantity	*20*	*500*	*100*

After one week of your order being placed, one of our design team members will contact you via e-mail. They will attach a digital copy of the images that you have chosen to go on your office equipment. Please approve these designs or inform us of any changes that you wish to make. We will not go ahead with the order unless we receive confirmation that all images are correct.

Remember to complete the form in its entirety and return it with all the information, including your individual and company details as well as your company logo.

To: Bryan Gibbs <bryangibbs@peakcocksupplies.com>

From: Christopher Dixon <chrisdixon@foxcox.com>

Date: 6 May

Re: Order for Fox & Cox Inc.

Dear Mr. Gibbs,

Having reviewed the information you provided last week, I have decided to change the design layout code of the pens. I would prefer to apply BG33 instead, and add our company website, www.foxcox.com. Once you have made the changes, can you send me the updated version? Everything else is perfect.

Additionally, I am making a presentation at a marketing conference in Berne next month and would like to take some products with the new design with me. Other agencies will be attending, and I want to make an impact. I know your company carries customized corporate items, such as t-shirts, for promotion. Please e-mail me your latest brochure with the prices for these items. In addition, is it possible to add my new choice to this order for one invoice payment, or is it necessary to raise a separate purchase order? Please advise me.

Many thanks.

Christopher Dixon
Marketing Manager
Fox & Cox Inc.

196. What is suggested about Peacock Office Supplies?

(A) It will open a new branch in May.
(B) It will host a marketing conference next month.
(C) It doesn't have a team of designers.
(D) It was voted as the best supplier of office products.

197. Who submitted the order to Peacock Office Supplies?

(A) A manager at a marketing agency
(B) A logo designer of a design team
(C) An office equipment manufacturer
(D) An editor at the *Business Times*

198. What are the customers asked to do to confirm their orders?

(A) Reply to an e-mail
(B) Update their information
(C) Sign an order form
(D) Visit a website

199. In the e-mail, what does Mr. Dixon request?

(A) A copy of the invoice for a previous order
(B) A brochure from Peacock Office Supplies
(C) Shipment of his order to Berne
(D) Changes to the quantities of orders he placed

200. What is suggested about Mr. Dixon?

(A) He has organized an online meeting.
(B) He is designing a new company's logo.
(C) He produced an innovative advertisement.
(D) He hopes to bring promotional items to a conference.

Test

答對題數表

PART 5	
PART 6	
PART 7	
總題數	

09

READING TEST

In the Reading test, you will read a variety of texts and answer several different types of reading comprehension questions. The entire Reading test will last 75 minutes. There are three parts, and directions are given for each part. You are encouraged to answer as many questions as possible within the time allowed.

You must mark your answers on the separate answer sheet. Do not write your answers in your test book.

PART 5

Directions: A word or phrase is missing in each of the sentences below. Four answer choices are given below each sentence. Select the best answer to complete the sentence. Then mark the letter (A), (B), (C), or (D) on your answer sheet.

101. ------- his one year abroad, Mr. Feltman visited London, Amsterdam, and Brussels.

(A) Behind
(B) During
(C) From
(D) Between

102. Luxembourg Electronics has ------- on a couple of selected brand-name appliances each week.

(A) discount
(B) discounts
(C) discounted
(D) discountable

103. Tacoma Computer's in-store promotion ------- customers a selection of cut-price laptops.

(A) recommends
(B) offers
(C) suggests
(D) instructs

104. Mr. Devlin insisted that in order to meet the deadline, ------- must work extra hours together.

(A) no one
(B) someone
(C) everyone
(D) one another

105. What is notable about the Taipei locality is that travelers will take pleasure in eating ------- yet inexpensive dishes and foodstuff.

(A) delicious
(B) hungry
(C) brief
(D) definite

106. The Experimental Design Company produced a range of clothes using silk and leather in an ------- popular fashion statement.

(A) astonishingly
(B) astonished
(C) astonishment
(D) astonish

107. The customer support team checked your purchase and will immediately inform you ------- the product has been placed for shipment.

(A) but
(B) once
(C) than
(D) so

108. Stock of fresh produce should ------- earlier than the market opening time tomorrow morning.

(A) arrival
(B) arriving
(C) arrive
(D) arrived

109. If the fire alarms go off at any time, please contact Mr. Perry in the security office for -------.

(A) assisted
(B) assistant
(C) assistance
(D) assist

110. The committee finally chose the design provided by Interlotze Architecture for their new workplace in Moscow following ------- reviews of the six proposals submitted to them.

(A) cares
(B) careful
(C) cared
(D) carefully

111. In order for Ines Marketing to keep up with competitors, all its departments have to ------- perform to the highest manufacturing standards.

(A) finely
(B) continually
(C) lately
(D) straightly

112. Readers depend upon *Medical Updates Weekly* for ------- information on the latest medical news.

(A) rely
(B) reliable
(C) relying
(D) reliably

113. Although she passed the first examination, Ms. Chan failed to get the job as it ------- to someone with better work experience.

(A) gave
(B) has given
(C) was given
(D) will have given

114. Only after ------- becomes qualified for the accounting certificate is Omar Jenkins subject to promotion.

(A) he
(B) his
(C) him
(D) himself

115. The five fabric conditioners surveyed in the latest ------- were found to have the same effect on clothing.

(A) development
(B) study
(C) history
(D) subject

116. The board of directors chose ------- a leading entrepreneur, Simon Rogers, for his outstanding contribution to the organization.

(A) will honor
(B) to honor
(C) would honor
(D) to be honored

117. If you have any questions ------- our items or carriage services, please do not hesitate to communicate with John's Floral World.

(A) regard
(B) regards
(C) regarding
(D) regarded

118. Because of the complaints filed by foreign clients, Gorden Stanley assured them that he intends to ------- the matter.

(A) go ahead
(B) show up
(C) look into
(D) act out

119. The Santiago Photocopier Company has issued a press release, which is targeted at ------- clients to take their old machines in for repair.

(A) encouraging
(B) to encourage
(C) encourage
(D) encourages

120. Workers require written ------- from their manager in order to borrow equipment.

(A) authorizes
(B) authorized
(C) authorization
(D) authorize

Go on to the next page

121. The Talking Leaves Corporation ------- provides customers with the latest information about its organic syrup products.
(A) perfectly
(B) regularly
(C) equally
(D) considerably

122. The following is a list of the conditions that were most commonly ------- by the employees within the company.
(A) stipulating
(B) stipulated
(C) have stipulated
(D) stipulation

123. Mr. Vasquez will open the Pierce mobile phone's production branch ------- it is fully prepared.
(A) as well as
(B) thanks to
(C) due to
(D) as soon as

124. Owing to the recent oil price surge, all production of excessive stocks ------- until further notice.
(A) are deferring
(B) have deferred
(C) have been deferring
(D) will be deferred

125. When it comes to purchases, Townsend Industries assures its customers that they will receive their items ------- two business days.
(A) through
(B) within
(C) around
(D) behind

126. Thanks to the ------- number of foreign customers, Lloyd Bank is fast becoming one of the most promising financial groups.
(A) growing
(B) unknown
(C) costly
(D) closed

127. Perfect for presents, Allan's Premium Coffee Beans are packaged in a ------- colored case.
(A) bright
(B) brightly
(C) brightness
(D) brighten

128. ------- is especially convincing about the proposed rail link is its proximity to the airport.
(A) Which
(B) That
(C) Why
(D) What

129. Without ------- from the author, no part of the article can be used elsewhere.
(A) permission
(B) reluctance
(C) identification
(D) association

130. The Flying Panda Travel Agency, specializing in honeymoon travel packages, is at its ------- between April and June.
(A) busy
(B) busier
(C) busily
(D) busiest

PART 6

Directions: Read the texts that follow. A word, phrase, or sentence is missing in parts of each text. Four answer choices for each question are given below the text. Select the best answer to complete the text. Then mark the letter (A), (B), (C), or (D) on your answer sheet.

Questions 131-134 refer to the following notice.

The main objective of the Image Nature Stocks publication is to ------- taking photos in the
131.

natural surroundings of the wilderness. -------. Apparatus and methods used to capture these
132.

images are also discussed in this editorial. Hobbyists and freelance ------- are the ones
133.

responsible for submission to this publication, which is issued once every two months.

Snapshots and articles on matters that happened from September are currently being

considered. -------, due to the pressure and the workload that we deal with every day, no
134.

feedback is given to individuals who send materials to us. For more information, please visit our

website at www.imagenaturestocks.com.

131. (A) impress
(B) promote
(C) impose
(D) fund

132. (A) This can be a good piece of evidence supporting industrial evolution.
(B) Those images captured by the space telescope reveal the wonders of outer space.
(C) Remarkable outdoor scenery and wildlife are the main things concentrated on by this publication.
(D) We've been looking for feedback from various users who have rated these magazines on our website.

133. (A) professional
(B) profession
(C) professionally
(D) professionals

134. (A) However
(B) Likewise
(C) For example
(D) Therefore

To: Bobby Wright <wbobby@bigmail.com>

From: International Association of Miners <admin@associationofminers.com>

Date: August 2

Subject: Membership information

Dear Mr. Wright,

The International Association of Miners would like to congratulate you on joining our

organization, which ------- the well-being and security of the global mining community by means
            135.

of conducting numerous programs and services that address the needs of miners worldwide.

Our ------- mission is to make mining construction better by promoting strict safety measures
     136.

in the industry. -------, we offer professionally developed materials for new and experienced
          137.

miners on our website, which includes the latest information on the subject of mining rules and

regulations.

-------. We hope to help you to become a better and safer mining expert.
 138.

Sincerely,

International Association of Miners

---

135. (A) supports
    (B) supported
    (C) having supported
    (D) would be supporting

136. (A) frequent
    (B) primary
    (C) early
    (D) previous

137. (A) However
    (B) By the way
    (C) Furthermore
    (D) As far as I know

138. (A) An application for admission is attached to this e-mail.
    (B) This is the first time that we are offering this exceptional opportunity to local miners in Ghana.
    (C) We want you to join our organization in the future, to keep updated with the latest.
    (D) Attached herewith is a document that outlines the advantages of membership.

Questions 139-142 refer to the following article.

Vice president Randolph Ward has unveiled that his ambitious project, Grand Bloom, is expected to be completed in May in Columbia, Missouri. Presently in the finishing stages of construction, the project consists of a brand-named shopping center and leisure complex.

------- will be located on Olson Boulevard.
  139.

Mr. Ward is organizing a competition to find the best name for the facilities, which will occupy approximately 1,000 square meters and which will have a great ------- of Dawn River.
                             140.

When asked what tips he would give to participants, Mr. Ward commented, "Bear in mind that the premises are surrounded by the river. The successfully-chosen name ------- that." The
                             141.

results will be announced at the end of next month. -------.
                        142.

---

139. (A) Both
(B) Few
(C) Several
(D) Some

140. (A) preference
(B) exterior
(C) appearance
(D) view

141. (A) reflects
(B) reflected
(C) is reflecting
(D) should reflect

142. (A) Mr. Ward is now looking for a site to build this facility.
(B) The prize winner will receive a one-year membership to the complex.
(C) The drawing was held in the new shopping center, and the result was surprising.
(D) The names will be announced at the ground-breaking ceremony.

Go on to the next page

To: Reginald Reed <reginaldreed@umail.com>

From: Aneroid Rental Shop <manager@arentals.com>

Date: Wednesday, August 13

Subject: Overdue DVD items

Our rental records show that the following items were supposed to be returned to the rental shop

on August 5: *Raining Dark Night* and *An Isolated Island*. Please take ------- back here by the end of
                                                                        143.
the week.

-------. However, the items mentioned in the following list are not ------- for the extension: new
144.   **145.**
arrivals, overdue items, and those which have been booked by other rental customers.

------- we have sent you this notification as a reminder, please note that it is the customer's
146.
responsibility to return or renew our items by the deadline.

Thank you.

---

143. (A) it
(B) ours
(C) this
(D) them

144. (A) You may not lease, sublicense, rent, or resell this DVD.
(B) If so, we can renew the due date as long as they are new arrivals.
(C) Remember that rented DVDs can be renewed up to seven days by calling the shop.
(D) It is our responsibility to return the overdue items.

145. (A) eligible
(B) displayed
(C) finished
(D) capable

146. (A) Except
(B) Although
(C) Likewise
(D) In case

PART 7

Directions: In this part you will read a selection of texts, such as magazine and newspaper articles, e-mails, and instant messages. Each text or set of texts is followed by several questions. Select the best answer for each question and mark the letter (A), (B), (C), or (D) on your answer sheet.

Questions 147-148 refer to the following information.

Healing Dream Training Gym Uniforms

Newly appointed personal trainers at the Healing Dream Training Gym will be issued with three uniforms that they must wear when training clients. Two are indoor uniforms, and the third is to be kept for outdoor training. These uniforms are free to employees for the mandatory probation period of two months. However, employees who leave within this time will be required to pay for the cost of them. This money will automatically be deducted from the final paycheck as per our terms and conditions of employment. Uniforms must be kept clean at all times; please note that personal trainers have free access to our on-site laundry, which is located in the basement of the building.

TEST 09

PART 7

147. Where would the information most likely be found?

(A) In a travel brochure
(B) In an expense claim
(C) In an employee handbook
(D) In a clothing store

148. What is mentioned about the Healing Dream Training Gym?

(A) It only offers indoor training.
(B) It has its own laundry.
(C) It manufactures the uniforms itself.
(D) It is closed for two months of the year.

Questions 149-150 refer to the following notice.

7th Used Furniture Fair
with Annual Secondhand Goods Auction

Featuring hundreds of mahogany antique furniture pieces
including chairs, desks, beds, and many more

Saturday, 22 November
32 Reuben Street, Brisbane

Admission: from 11:00 A.M. to 7:00 P.M.
Reception: from 5:00 P.M. to 7:00 P.M.
Auction begins at 7:30 P.M.

Tickets: $5 before 17th November; $7 at the door

For advance tickets, visit our website www.uff.com
or call us at (643) 367-3475.
The ticket price includes the catalog of auction items.

All proceeds of the event go to
Greenslopes Community Hospital.

149. What is the purpose of the notice?
(A) To promote the visit of a famous craftsman
(B) To advertise the sale of unique furnishings
(C) To announce the opening of a furniture store
(D) To publicize a community hospital

150. What is suggested about the event?
(A) There is an additional fee to attend the reception.
(B) Students receive a special discount.
(C) Antique furniture will be displayed beginning at 7:00 P.M.
(D) Tickets cost less if purchased online.

Michael's

665 West Broadway
Vancouver, Canada

February 12	4:31 P.M.
Gym Gear	
Sports Direct: jogging pants	19.99
General Items	
Brand Zest: boxing gloves and pads	16.99
Subtotal	36.98
Tax-8%	2.96
Total	**39.94**
Cash tendered	50.00
Change	10.06

Returns and Exchanges Policy

Unworn items may be returned for a refund or exchanged for credit vouchers within 30 days of purchase. These items must be in like-new condition, and the original receipt of purchase must be included. Items purchased on sale cannot be refunded at any time. These items may, however, be exchanged for goods of the same value and must be accompanied by the original receipt.

TEST
09

PART
7

151. What type of store most likely is Michael's?

(A) A souvenir shop
(B) A sports store
(C) A music store
(D) A rental store

152. What is true about the store's policy?

(A) All exchanges require an original receipt.
(B) All returned items incur an 8 percent restocking fee.
(C) All purchases must be paid in cash.
(D) All sale items must be in original packaging.

Go on to the next page

Questions 153-154 refer to the following text message chain.

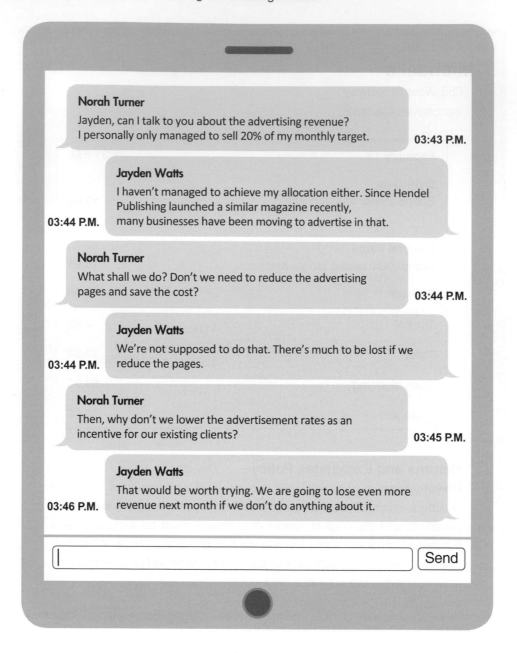

Norah Turner

Jayden, can I talk to you about the advertising revenue?
I personally only managed to sell 20% of my monthly target.

03:43 P.M.

Jayden Watts

03:44 P.M.

I haven't managed to achieve my allocation either. Since Hendel
Publishing launched a similar magazine recently,
many businesses have been moving to advertise in that.

Norah Turner

What shall we do? Don't we need to reduce the advertising
pages and save the cost?

03:44 P.M.

Jayden Watts

03:44 P.M.

We're not supposed to do that. There's much to be lost if we
reduce the pages.

Norah Turner

Then, why don't we lower the advertisement rates as an
incentive for our existing clients?

03:45 P.M.

Jayden Watts

03:46 P.M.

That would be worth trying. We are going to lose even more
revenue next month if we don't do anything about it.

Send

153. What problem is being discussed?

(A) A product's development has been
delayed.
(B) Advertising revenue is falling.
(C) The magazine circulation has been
reduced.
(D) Staff turnover has been increasing.

154. At 3:46 P.M., What does Mr. Watts mean
when he writes, "That would be worth
trying."?

(A) The company shouldn't make any
changes.
(B) He has to cut down the cost by
reducing the pages.
(C) They can offer discounts to current
advertisers.
(D) He wants Ms. Turner to try harder next
month.

Questions 155-157 refer to the following information.

Tapas La Mancha

Sanchez Pietro, Owner
Reviewed by Helene Labore

Overall rating: 3 out of 5 stars ★★★☆☆

Atmosphere: 3 stars
 Sanchez Pietro refurbished the venue last month. —[1]—. It is spacious inside and has a distinct Spanish theme. However, the noise from the kitchen was loud, and there seemed to be a lack of privacy for couples who were dining.

Service: 4 stars
 The service was very good with the serving staff extremely polite and efficient. —[2]—. The food arrived quickly and dishes were cleared as soon as we finished our meal.

Food: 2 stars
 The menu was not very varied and had not really changed from the last time I visited the restaurant, three years ago. —[3]—. I enjoyed the main meal, although the fish was slightly overcooked. The desserts were a big disappointment, as there was little choice and they were tasteless.

Value : 4 stars
 Although some of the items on the menu are overpriced, on the whole, the meals are relatively inexpensive. —[4]—. The wine list is also very pricey, but the main dishes are true bargains.

155. What is the purpose of the information?

(A) To announce the reopening of a restaurant
(B) To summarize the expansion plans of a restaurant
(C) To promote special menus that will be introduced at a restaurant
(D) To assess the quality of a restaurant

156. What is suggested about the restaurant?

(A) Its menu items are overall value for money.
(B) It hosts live musical events.
(C) Its menu has significantly changed over these years.
(D) It is located within a city center.

157. In which of the positions marked [1], [2], [3], and [4] does the following sentence best belong?

"The portions were small, and the tapas starters were not very tasty."

(A) [1]
(B) [2]
(C) [3]
(D) [4]

Alltrue Digital Equipment
355 Tree Drive
Sacramento, CA 94203

16 March

Alexander Soskin
2541 Angel Place
Santa Barbara, CA 93109

Dear Mr. Soskin,

We have enclosed the radio that you returned to us for repair. Unfortunately, we are unable to complete the repairs as the fault to the appliance is not covered under our two-year general guarantee.

We have ascertained that the original sound box has been replaced by a component that is not compatible with our brand of audio equipment. Please see the enclosed report from our repair officer for clarification. Our guarantee is also enclosed, which clearly states that should any part be replaced or altered, the work must be carried out by our repair team using our own approved components. The guarantee does not cover unauthorized tampering with the appliance and, therefore, we are unable to repair this appliance under the terms and conditions of the guarantee. If, however, you still wish to have the item repaired, we can do so at a cost of $100.

Many thanks for your cooperation in this matter and for purchasing an item from Alltrue Digital Equipment.

Yours sincerely,

Kevin Constant
Customer Services Manager
Enclosures

158. What is the main purpose of the letter?
(A) To explain why a request was not fulfilled
(B) To thank a customer for a recent purchase
(C) To request a call back from a repairperson
(D) To request information about digital equipment

159. What is NOT included with the letter?
(A) A guarantee
(B) A findings report
(C) A refund
(D) A radio

160. What is Mr. Soskin advised to do?
(A) Repair the item himself
(B) Pay for repairs
(C) Purchase an extended warranty
(D) Call an Alltrue Customer Service manager

●	**Allison Green** [09:43 A.M.]	Good morning, Timothy. I heard you are meeting our Spanish guests when they come on Monday.
●	**Timothy Moore** [09:43 A.M.]	Hello, Allison. That meeting's giving me a headache.
●	**Allison Green** [09:44 A.M.]	What's the matter? You speak Spanish pretty well.
●	**Timothy Moore** [09:45 A.M.]	As a matter of fact, you know I have to prepare for the sales presentation on Tuesday. I just don't have enough time to take care of the Monday meeting.
●	**Allison Green** [09:46 A.M.]	That must be very hard. Is there anything I can do to help you?
●	**Timothy Moore** [09:47 A.M.]	Hmm . . . I need to find a caterer to provide lunches and some refreshments. Do you have any suggestions?
●	**Allison Green** [09:48 A.M.]	I would say Mortime Caterers. They are very reputable, and they provide an excellent lunchtime buffet. Shall I take care of the food service?
●	**Timothy Moore** [09:49 A.M.]	That would be great. Thank you, Allison. I owe you one.
●	**Allison Green** [09:50 A.M.]	Don't mention it. I can call them now and see if they are available.

Send

TEST 09

PART 7

161. What will Mr. Moore do on Tuesday?

(A) Visit a restaurant
(B) Prepare for a business trip
(C) Give a presentation
(D) Conduct a job interview

162. At 09:44 A.M., what does Ms. Green mean when she writes, "You speak Spanish pretty well."?

(A) She believes Mr. Moore is able to do his job perfectly.
(B) She has a suggestion for Mr. Moore.
(C) She thinks the guests will love Spanish food.
(D) She wants to help Mr. Moore prepare for the Tuesday meeting.

163. What does Ms. Green offer to do?

(A) Provide a buffet
(B) Contact a service
(C) Recommend a restaurant
(D) Purchase a new phone

Go on to the next page

Company Library Cards

The Law Society's library system enables members of the business community to use its facilities.

Employees of businesses within the local area will be eligible for a company library card. The cost is just $40 a year, although the fee is waived for charities and nonprofit organizations.

A company library card can be used by local businesses for research purposes, and employees should take responsibility for any books or papers they might borrow. The cardholder is responsible for any fines incurred for late or lost materials.

To apply for a company library card, you must fill out an application form at the library's reception desk. This must be accompanied by a photo identification, a letter confirming your position at your organization, and the fee to join. We will then provide you with a receipt.

If you have any queries, contact us at the main law office at 555-9284.

164. What is the purpose of the notice?

(A) To explain a service
(B) To propose an idea
(C) To correct a mistake
(D) To announce an opening

165. What is stated about annual fees?

(A) Certain organizations are exempt.
(B) They can be paid by credit card.
(C) They are higher for out-of-town businesses.
(D) They are refunded after a year.

166. According to the notice, what must a borrower do if materials are lost?

(A) Waive their membership
(B) Report the loss to their supervisor
(C) Return their company library card
(D) Pay a fine to the library

167. What is NOT required at the time of application?

(A) Proof of identity
(B) Payment
(C) Confirmation of employment
(D) A signed contract

Manager's Behavior

In his new book, *Etiquette in the Workplace*, Manuel Rodriguez gives advice to managers on how to earn and gain respect from employees by behaving in the appropriate manner. —[1]—. Mr. Rodriguez explains that managers who hold a responsible position should conduct themselves in a manner that befits their status, not just in an office environment but in social situations, especially those organized by the company for which they work.

For example, a manager should be in attendance at a social event such as an awards ceremony where other senior employees are invited. This is part of a manager's role. However, a social event such as a sports tournament with more junior members of staff can be avoided. Nevertheless, managers should decline any such invitations with a polite refusal.

—[2]—. A manager should always appear neat and well-groomed. Punctuality is mandatory. When a manager is attending an event arranged by the company, he or she must acknowledge coworkers who are not seen often and ensure that he or she is familiar with their names as a matter of courtesy. Also, it is compulsory for a manager to praise the organizers of events and acknowledge the effort that has gone into making an event successful for all attendees.

Mr. Rodriguez has been writing online for many years and has been recognized as one of the leading authorities on workplace etiquette. —[3]—. He is a regular contributor to television and his book, *Etiquette in the Workplace*, has already sold over 200,000 copies since its publication six months ago, through Mitchell Hamden. —[4]—. It can be ordered online through www.mitchellhamden.com.

TEST 09

PART 7

168. What does the article primarily discuss?

(A) A book about appropriate behavior for managers
(B) A guide to solving improper workplace issues
(C) A leaflet about organizing social events
(D) A brochure about maintaining employment levels

169. What is suggested about Mr. Rodriguez?

(A) He has worked for the same company for years.
(B) He is a very successful writer.
(C) He will finish writing his book within six months.
(D) He organizes the company's social events.

170. What kind of business does Mitchell Hamden specialize in?

(A) Event organizing
(B) Online design
(C) Employment benefits
(D) Book publishing

171. In which of the positions marked [1], [2], [3], and [4] does the following sentence best belong?

"In addition, a good appearance is essential."

(A) [1]
(B) [2]
(C) [3]
(D) [4]

Gordon Industries

To: All staff
From: Grace Elliott
Date: June 11
Re: Holiday Schedule

Well done for helping Gordon Industries successfully complete its largest contract in the company's nine-year history. As a reward for your hard work, we are organizing a Family Week in the month of July. For one week during the summer vacation, we are holding numerous events to which you and your family are invited free of charge. We hope that the next few years will bring as much success to Gordon Industries, and we are showing our appreciation with the week of events. See below for a day-by-day schedule.

DATE	EVENT	LOCATION	TIME
Monday, July 25	Water play	Magic Springs Water Park	11 A.M. to 6 P.M.
Tuesday, July 26	Family picnic	Hot Springs Park Campsite	All Day
Wednesday, July 27	Outdoor activities	Hot Springs Park (See department notice boards for a breakdown of locations)	All day
Thursday, July 28	Field Day (Basketball, Softball, Soccer)	Park Recreation Center	1 P.M. to 5 P.M.
Friday, July 29	Dance party and children's entertainment	Hot Springs Park Campsite	3 P.M. to 6 P.M.

My personal secretary, Amanda Cole, has already booked the children's entertainment and caterers for the event. Before it reaches the fixed number, please call her at extension 256 as soon as possible. There will also be a barbeque party after the sports competition. To sign up for the tournaments, please give your name to Jared Murphy in management support. There will be prizes for the winning teams.

I hope you are all looking forward to the Family Week, as it will be a chance for you to relax and enjoy the company of your family and colleagues. I hope to see everyone there.

Grace Elliott
President
Gordon Industries

172. Why was the memo written?

(A) To inform employees of management changes

(B) To introduce a week of family-oriented events

(C) To announce the signing of a major contract

(D) To recruit teams for a sporting event

173. How are staff members asked to contact Ms. Cole?

(A) By making a phone call

(B) By registering online

(C) By visiting her office

(D) By sending an e-mail

174. When is the barbeque party?

(A) On Monday

(B) On Tuesday

(C) On Wednesday

(D) On Thursday

175. What is suggested about Ms. Elliot?

(A) She is the founder of Gordon Industries.

(B) She won't be able to join the Family Week.

(C) She has a nine-year-old son.

(D) She wants to reward her employees with a special event.

Go on to the next page

Questions 176-180 refer to the following articles.

Supreme Economy News
Top Gambling Companies See Expansion in Workforce

January 7 — Many of the major gambling companies in the Blenheim district have seen a rapid increase in their workforces over the past six months. These are the findings of a report released yesterday from the Conglomeration of Online Casinos. In total, each of the district's top five companies employed 15% more employees compared to the period between July and December last year.

The leading company is Offshore Developments, currently the market leader in the gambling industry. More than 150 staff members were employed at casinos in Blenheim in the latter half of last year. Most of these employees were headhunted from Blake Soft, a small software company specializing in financial program development, which Offshore Developments acquired last June. Two other companies in the industry, Lucky Thistle and Crown Rooms (both specializing in online poker), also joined forces.

The Conglomeration of Online Casinos only takes revenue from gambling establishments in Blenheim into account when publishing its rankings. Each of the top five companies accrued over $1.2 million in annual revenues. Lucky Thistle generated profits of approximately $1.2 million, with Offshore Developments reporting a $1.3 million net profit.

Marcel Prost

Offshore Developments to Invest in Latest Technology

March 30 — David Carruthers, Chairman of Offshore Developments, is reportedly investing in new software: Marking Up, an online corporate financial program that was tested earlier this year.

This is the first time that Offshore Developments has entered the corporate market. In the past, the company has dealt solely with the individual consumer gambling market. Mark Owen, the business strategy director of Offshore Developments, says, "So that we can develop the technology that will enable corporations to enter the gambling market, we had to hire a number of experts in financial software."

The company has been listed as one of the leading five firms by the Conglomeration of Online Casinos for a number of years, with an average annual profit margin of $1.3 million. This year, the turnover has increased since January with profits of $0.7 million already generated and an additional $4.5 million expected by December.

G. Harker

176. What is the first article about?

(A) New gambling products released in the marketplace
(B) Marketing methods for gambling firms
(C) Employment growth in large gambling companies
(D) Employee satisfaction in the gambling industry

177. In the first article, the word "period" in paragraph 1, line 5, is closest in meaning to

(A) growth
(B) interval
(C) conclusion
(D) exercise

178. What is indicated about Offshore Developments?

(A) It is an Internet-based company.
(B) It sells casino supplies.
(C) It has several international offices.
(D) It took over a software company.

179. What is suggested about Marking Up?

(A) It is the first product designed by Mr. Carruthers.
(B) Almost two million dollars in sales has already been achieved.
(C) It has been designed for the corporate market.
(D) Customers have criticized it for not being user-friendly.

180. How much revenue does Offshore Developments anticipate from January to December?

(A) $1.3 million
(B) $4.5 million
(C) $5.2 million
(D) $6.5 million

Go on to the next page

Questions 181-185 refer to the following e-mail and information.

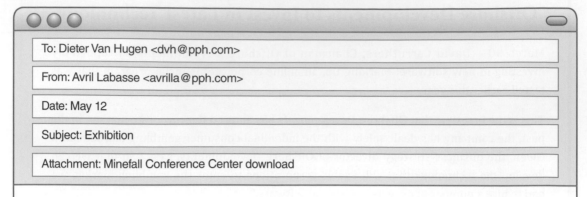

To: Dieter Van Hugen <dvh@pph.com>

From: Avril Labasse <avrilla@pph.com>

Date: May 12

Subject: Exhibition

Attachment: Minefall Conference Center download

Dear Dieter,

Many thanks for your offer to help with PPH Limited's preparations for the forthcoming Technical Exhibition. This year's show will be from June 21 to 24 and, as in the previous year, the venue will be the Minefall Conference Center. For past exhibitions, I have rented the Benton Room, which allowed us to present our new products and stage a number of seminars. Over the four days, we attracted nearly 1000 people, on average 250 a day. We expect the exhibition to be even bigger this year.

In order to prepare for this eventuality, I would ask you to rent a bigger space. Although the room accommodated all attendees comfortably, the presentation facilities were inadequate. We had to rely upon the center's staff to supply and set up the presentation equipment. Although the feedback was excellent for the most part, a number of attendees complained about the quality of the visual material. This must be rectified this year.

Previously, we held a reception for invited guests in the Manila Suite at the end of the week. This time, we prefer to take them somewhere more upmarket. I suggest either Brown's Restaurant or the Quayside Brasserie to avoid self-catering. Please note, I will make the necessary arrangements and forward the details to you.

Please check the enclosed brochure for the most suitable room for our requirements. As the deadline is only two weeks away, you will need to reserve a suitable room with a deposit as quickly as possible.

Please contact me with any questions or problems that may arise.

Avril Labasse

Minefall
CONFERENCE CENTER
ROOM RENTAL

Manila Suite: This is our biggest room, with daylight ingress to three sides. It is able to accommodate up to 400 guests for any celebration or business event. Catering is supplied by the in-house Minefall Catering Department. Costs begin at $300 for morning or afternoon hire, $500 for the full-day hire. Catering costs are additional.

The Fortune Room and Day Room: These are perfect for small private meetings or seminars, with a capacity of 50 people. Equipped for business, these rooms include telephone, computer with Internet access, overhead projector, and dark-colored curtains. Fees for the Fortune Room begin at $200 for a half day and $300 for a full day. The Day Room is slightly larger and has audio facilities. Prices for the Day Room are $220 for a half day and for a $320 full day.

Sentinel Suite: Ideal for large-scale presentations, events, and seminars. This room is equipped with a floor-to-ceiling projection screen, stage, lighting, and an all-around sound system. This luxurious suite holds up to 350 guests comfortably. Prices begin at $500 per half day and $700 per day. There is an added fee for catering services.

Polar Patio: Adjacent to the Sentinel Suite, this outdoor venue is available for receptions and refreshments. The cost is $310 for three hours but comes free with the hire of the Sentinel Suite. There is an added fee for catering services.

181. What most likely was Ms. Labasse's role in last year's exhibition?

(A) She organized PPH Limited's event.
(B) She chose a catering service.
(C) She set up some equipment.
(D) She gave a presentation.

182. How is this year's exhibition expected to be different from last year's?

(A) It will be opened by a celebrity.
(B) It will attract even more visitors.
(C) It will be held at an alternative venue.
(D) It will include additional exhibitors.

183. What problem probably occurred at last year's show?

(A) Some people could not see the presentation screen clearly.
(B) The event location was changed before the exhibition.
(C) The reserved room was too noisy.
(D) A presenter didn't make it in time.

184. Who provided the food services at PPH Limited's reception last year?

(A) Minefall Catering
(B) Polar Patio
(C) Quayside Brasseries
(D) Brown's Restaurant

185. Which space will PPH Limited be likely to reserve this year?

(A) Day Room
(B) Manila Suite
(C) Fortune Room
(D) Sentinel Suite

Go on to the next page

The London branch of Melton Manufacturing is seeking an experienced manager to join the production team!

Melton Manufacturing has been a leading manufacturer and distributor of top-quality automotive parts in the U.K. for half a century. We provide automobile companies both here and abroad with hundreds of car and truck parts.

The production manager will have the responsibility of training and monitoring a production team of 50 full-time staff members as well as many temporary and seasonal workers. The manager is also in charge of the factory environment, ensuring the health and safety of all employees. We are looking for someone with at least four years of relevant experience who has spent one year in the same industry. The successful candidate is expected to work out of hours to oversee deliveries and shipments.

Candidates must be familiar with the production and distribution of materials as well as have a working knowledge of handling requirements. Computer expertise on SPA 43 is also required. Interested parties should send their applications along with a cover letter and references to Tony Beach, Melton Manufacturing, 13 Ryville Crescent, London WR11 4BD.

To: Tony Beach <tonybeach@melton.com>

From: Adam Stern <adamstern@gomail.com>

Date: September 8

Subject: A letter of reference

Attachment: Adam_Stern_Reference.doc

Dear Mr. Beach,

I was surprised by your e-mail. I thought I had enclosed the reference with my résumé; it seems I missed it. I append Mr. Bushell's letter herewith. I'm glad to hear that my résumé is impressive. As to the SPA 43 you inquired about, I qualified for it 5 years ago. I had undertaken an evening course after work for it, and now I am in charge of employee computer training.

Please let me know when I should visit you for an interview. As London is far away from here, I'll need to find a place to stay one night. Again, thank you for considering me for this position.

Sincerely,

Adam Stern

August 27
Mr. Beach
Melton Manufacturing
13 Ryville Crescent
London WR11 4BD

Dear Mr. Beach,

This is a reference for Adam Stern, who is applying for the job of production manager within your organization. I have worked with Mr. Stern for five of his seven years at Packaging Express, where he began as a temporary worker before I took him on full time. Mr. Stern is an extremely competent employee and is currently employed as production supervisor here. He has been particularly instrumental in the implementation and commissioning of new production line equipment that has sped up the production process and reduced wastage.

Mr. Stern is fully qualified for the position advertised and, in addition, has extensive work experience. He has just completed an HNQ in management at Kings Cross College as well as numerous in-house courses.

I have every faith in Mr. Stern's capability for this job, as he has the ability to adapt to any work demands. Please contact me for any further information.

Sincerely,

Trey Bushell
Production Director

186. What is suggested about Melton Manufacturing?

(A) It distributes safety equipment.
(B) It offers computer training.
(C) It recently expanded into the U.K.
(D) It specializes in automotive parts.

187. According to the job posting, what must the production manager be willing to do?

(A) Handle heavy machinery
(B) Hire team members
(C) Work overtime
(D) Sign a one-year contract

188. Why does Mr. Bushell write the letter?

(A) To explain a delay in a shipment
(B) To welcome a new team member
(C) To apply for a new job
(D) To recommend an employee

189. What is indicated about Mr. Stern?

(A) He has experience in overseas sales.
(B) He teaches a course at Kings Cross College.
(C) He is skilled in the use of a computer software program.
(D) He is looking for a part-time position at Melton Manufacturing.

190. What does Mr. Stern ask Mr. Beach to do?

(A) Visit him at his earliest convenience
(B) Write him a letter of reference
(C) Inform him of a date
(D) Send him an application form

Go on to the next page

Questions 191-195 refer to the following e-mails and form.

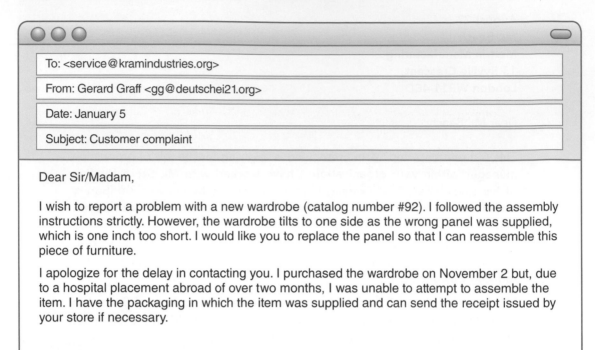

To: <service@kramindustries.org>

From: Gerard Graff <gg@deutschei21.org>

Date: January 5

Subject: Customer complaint

Dear Sir/Madam,

I wish to report a problem with a new wardrobe (catalog number #92). I followed the assembly instructions strictly. However, the wardrobe tilts to one side as the wrong panel was supplied, which is one inch too short. I would like you to replace the panel so that I can reassemble this piece of furniture.

I apologize for the delay in contacting you. I purchased the wardrobe on November 2 but, due to a hospital placement abroad of over two months, I was unable to attempt to assemble the item. I have the packaging in which the item was supplied and can send the receipt issued by your store if necessary.

Sincerely,

Gerard Graff

To: Gerard Graff <gg@deutschei21.org>

From: Joseph Pieters <peiters@kramindustries.org>

Date: January 6

Subject: RE: Customer Complaint

Dear Mr. Graff,

Thank you for the e-mail regarding your purchase. We apologize for the difficulties you have had with assembling this item and will send you a replacement part free of charge. We operate a store policy stating that if the item purchased is less than two months old, it can be returned with the original receipt and in its original packaging. For items bought over two months ago, our policy is that they can only be returned if discovered to be damaged at the time of purchase. This necessitates a Faulty Return Form to be completed. This can be found on our website complaints page: www.kramindustries.org/returns. After the form is filled out and submitted, a Merchandise Return Code will be e-mailed to you. For full details on the policies, please see the website.

I hope this is useful information. We would request that you complete a feedback form attached about your experience with the customer service department. Once completed, you will receive a voucher for 15% off your next purchase with our store.

Joseph Pieters
Manager

Customer Feedback

Name: Gerard Graff
Overall rating: ★★★★☆ (Good)
Comments: I reported a problem with a wardrobe by e-mail, and I received a reply on the following day. I followed the faulty return procedure as informed and got a replacement for the defective part. Thanks to your help, I was able to finish assembling it correctly. However, the illustration on the manual was not very accurate, and I experienced inconvenience in recognizing the problem with the panel. I think that should be corrected as soon as possible. Except for that, I was generally pleased with your service.

191. What problem with the product does Mr. Graff report?

(A) A part is defective.
(B) An instruction manual is missing.
(C) The size is wrong for his bedroom.
(D) It is the wrong color.

192. What most likely is Mr. Graff's job?

(A) Teaching woodwork
(B) Working within a hospital
(C) Preparing meals
(D) Constructing furniture

193. What benefits would Mr. Graff receive from the furniture shop?

(A) A discount coupon
(B) An honorarium
(C) A new piece of furniture
(D) Free delivery

194. In the feedback form, the word "recognizing" in line 5, is closest in meaning to

(A) watching
(B) finding
(C) informing
(D) reporting

195. According to Mr. Graff, what should be revised?

(A) The assembly instructions
(B) The return code
(C) The website address
(D) The packaging

Go on to the next page

Jason Falls
in the center of Urban Melbourne
business, residential, and commercial space to rent

A contemporary, up-to-date structure surrounded by existing shops and businesses. Close to the train station.
Adjacent to the War Memorial with urban park and sports stadium close by.

Residential (Floors 2–7): Two and three-roomed apartments comprising two bathrooms, one en-suite, kitchen-dining room, and living room. For an extra charge, parking is available in the underground car park. Shared rooftop garden as well as on-site laundry facilities.

Offices (Floor 8–14): Large and small offices available. Modular layout with open-plan space that can be compartmentalized. Choice of furnishings.

Commercial (Street level): Four shop fronts. Retail only, each 500 square meters in floor space. No dining establishments.

Details on pricing and availability:
Please direct residential inquiries to Garry Mason, (08) 3014-7610 or residential@jasonfalls.com.au.

Please direct commercial inquiries to Finola Castiel, (08) 3014-7620 or commercial@jasonfalls.com.au.

To: Finola Castiel <commercial@jasonfalls.com.au>

From: Thomas Christian <tchristian@christianbrooks.com>

Title: Jason Falls

Date: 10:01, September 2

Dear Ms. Castiel,

My business has recently expanded, and we will be employing new recruits to help with the future workload. We are currently located close to Jason Falls, but there is not enough space for new employees. I would be interested in finding out if the available office space at Jason Falls is sufficient to house 17 staff members, in Administration and Sales. I will need to see the offices for myself sometime next week.

Many thanks.

Thomas Christian

To:	Elias Innes <e_innes@terralink.org>
From:	Finola Castiel <commercial@jasonfalls.com.au>
Subject:	Urgent renovation work
Date:	11:30, September 2

Dear Mr. Innes,

My colleague Garry Mason referred you to me. I require a quote to remove three internal walls from an office, which are all two meters tall, with one being 20 centimeters thick. The other two are only 15 centimeters wide. These walls were not there originally, but set up by the last tenant's request.

The office is on the twelfth floor of the building, and there's an elevator available. I will need a team of workers who can undertake the work as soon as possible. I have a client who is interested in this office; I think those walls must be removed to accommodate all his staff. I want this renovation work to be done by Sunday.

I hope to hear from you soon.

Regards,

Finola Castiel

196. What is indicated about the Jason Falls building?

(A) It is near a train station.
(B) It is far from the War Memorial.
(C) It is on the outskirts of the city.
(D) It is under construction.

197. According to the advertisement, what is available to residential tenants for an additional cost?

(A) Cleaning facilities
(B) Underground parking
(C) An extra bedroom
(D) Use of a rooftop garden

198. What type of tenant is not allowed to occupy the building?

(A) A law firm
(B) A sales office
(C) A retail store
(D) A restaurant

199. What is suggested about Mr. Christian's company?

(A) It is relocating out of Melbourne.
(B) It recently lost some staff.
(C) It has become increasingly successful.
(D) It is changing its main business plans.

200. Why does Ms. Castiel want to renovate the office so urgently?

(A) She does not work on Sundays.
(B) A tenant will come to see the property soon.
(C) The walls can be hazardous for the new tenant.
(D) A tenant requests to set up some partitions.

Test

10

READING TEST

In the Reading test, you will read a variety of texts and answer several different types of reading comprehension questions. The entire Reading test will last 75 minutes. There are three parts, and directions are given for each part. You are encouraged to answer as many questions as possible within the time allowed.

You must mark your answers on the separate answer sheet. Do not write your answers in your test book.

PART 5

Directions: A word or phrase is missing in each of the sentences below. Four answer choices are given below each sentence. Select the best answer to complete the sentence. Then mark the letter (A), (B), (C), or (D) on your answer sheet.

101. Dinner will be served by Walsh House ------- Hokuto Grill.

(A) but
(B) nor
(C) and
(D) yet

102. Diadora's new running shoe, the Runner Blade, is ------- named for its shape and agility.

(A) suitably
(B) suitable
(C) suitability
(D) suitableness

103. ------- in Davison Restaurant, including the expansion of its parking lot, have attracted more customers.

(A) Improved
(B) Improvement
(C) Improvements
(D) Improving

104. The Nooseburg Society Association will be in charge of tours of historical sites every day ------- Saturday.

(A) other
(B) except
(C) than
(D) some

105. San Marino Steel is now ------- a wide range of steel products for building facilities outside the city.

(A) manufacturer
(B) being manufactured
(C) manufactured
(D) manufacturing

106. Ms. Dennings ------- gives a hand to those in charge of the press conferences.

(A) often
(B) early
(C) less
(D) far

107. You may answer questions ------- the space provided on the enclosed survey form.

(A) up
(B) out
(C) in
(D) of

108. New training methods that could improve productivity -------.

(A) to develop
(B) developing
(C) are being developed
(D) to be developed

109. To receive a full refund, please ------- your items in original condition.

(A) returns
(B) returned
(C) return
(D) returning

110. Both Saitrich and Petrov electronics companies are financially stronger than many of ------- rival companies.

(A) theirs
(B) they
(C) their
(D) them

111. Mr. Vettel broke the record ------- the fastest lap time in the German Grand Prix.

(A) at
(B) within
(C) above
(D) for

112. The energy committee has determined that building a roof in a brighter and more reflective blue color will ------- reduce heat, especially in cities.

(A) significantly
(B) extremely
(C) utterly
(D) countlessly

113. Ashanti Travel Agency provides the ------- flights available from Tokyo to Beijing and Seoul.

(A) cheapness
(B) cheapen
(C) cheaply
(D) cheapest

114. The board of directors ------- approved the plan to make inroads into the overseas market, which was aimed at young adults in Asian countries.

(A) conditions
(B) conditioned
(C) conditional
(D) conditionally

115. Publics Dynamics has three facilities with a combined floor space ------- 51,500 square meters.

(A) processing
(B) totaling
(C) finishing
(D) enduring

116. When requesting full refunds, customers have to show ------- records including the purchase date.

(A) accurate
(B) delayed
(C) accepting
(D) distant

117. Walgreen Alliance deals with a high ------- of claims every day, so it needs capable employees.

(A) set
(B) size
(C) extent
(D) volume

118. Recent research findings for Tisler Cookware's new prototype were ------- encouraging.

(A) well
(B) near
(C) freely
(D) very

119. ------- several suggestions have been made to improve Manchester City's transportation system, none of them is within budget.

(A) Why
(B) Whether
(C) Although
(D) Unless

120. Please check ------- of your order #1282712, which will be shipped by Wednesday.

(A) receipt
(B) receive
(C) received
(D) receiving

Go on to the next page

121. Mr. Shinohara, a plant manager, recently ------- a tour of the facilities for brewing beer for the company's important clients.

(A) conduct
(B) conducted
(C) to conduct
(D) will conduct

122. The owner of Hamilton Art Gallery recruits volunteers who enjoy helping ------- with their need for tour guides.

(A) ones
(B) others
(C) any
(D) that

123. The board of directors interviewed five top candidates before making the ------- decision about whom to choose as a vice president.

(A) final
(B) finals
(C) finally
(D) finalize

124. All fountain pens ------- at Sunday's auction will be open to buyers starting on Saturday at 9:00 A.M.

(A) to be sold
(B) has been sold
(C) is selling
(D) was to sell

125. Official ------- is required for all of the airplanes arriving at the airport.

(A) documentation
(B) administration
(C) freight
(D) agency

126. As the number of travelers visiting China rises, ------- the demand for tour guides to lead them.

(A) as long as
(B) whereas
(C) so does
(D) as to

127. ThermoSafe, a large packaging company, specializes in ------- packaging services for insulated shipping boxes and containers.

(A) absolute
(B) savory
(C) protective
(D) expired

128. Neil Berret's new S/S collection features pants in a ------- variety of colors.

(A) wide
(B) width
(C) widen
(D) widely

129. Unfortunately, research indicated that the increase in oil prices will ------- economic recovery.

(A) interfere with
(B) correspond to
(C) fall behind
(D) rely on

130. All department stores should ------- with regulations regarding sales at special events.

(A) comply
(B) adhere
(C) authorize
(D) follow

PART 6

Directions: Read the texts that follow. A word, phrase, or sentence is missing in parts of each text. Four answer choices for each question are given below the text. Select the best answer to complete the text. Then mark the letter (A), (B), (C), or (D) on your answer sheet.

Questions 131-134 refer to the following e-mail.

To: Maria Gomez <mgomez@samail.com>
From: Taylor Fisher <tfisher@lapubliclibrary.com>
Date: May 5
Subject: Your inquiry

Dear Ms. Gomez,

Thank you for your inquiry about your ------- library book, *The Blossom Girl*. Although the
                                        131.
book is now one week overdue, I renewed it through May 12 so that the library will not keep

charging you a late fee.

I did ask my colleagues to check if they could find it on the shelves, just in case someone

could have found or ------- the book. -------.
                      132.   **133.**

If you cannot return the book by May 12, we will ------- a new one. In that case, you should
                                                134.
bear the expenses.

Sincerely,

Taylor Fisher
Los Angeles Public Library

131. (A) miss
     (B) to miss
     (C) missing
     (D) missed

132. (A) return
     (B) returned
     (C) be returned
     (D) will return

133. (A) All library patrons are issued a
         membership card.
     (B) You can find the location on our
         website.
     (C) Unfortunately, we failed to find it.
     (D) However, we are closed on Sunday.

134. (A) order
     (B) recognize
     (C) acknowledge
     (D) identify

Go on to the next page

TEST 10

PART 6

Questions 135-138 refer to the following article.

San Francisco (March 29) — For two weeks only, Starbean will launch a limited edition of retro packaging for their products, which dates back to thirty years ago, when the brand ------- became popular. This promotion will not apply to Starbean's existing coffee lineup. The
135.
company will be introducing new drinks, including Iced Cinnamon Almond Milk Macchiato, Coconut Milk Mocha Latte, and Caramel Cocoa Frappuccino, ------- the size compared to the
136.
existing options.

Starbean president Kim Perry says the packaging shows the history of the brand. -------. "We
137.
feel this promotion will attract both long-time and new customers," she said. Starbean's retro packaging products will be available in April. And its new ------- will hit stores in May.
138.

135. (A) once
 (B) all
 (C) first
 (D) thus

136. (A) double
 (B) doubles
 (C) will double
 (D) doubling

137. (A) Market analysts predict that it will show disappointing quarterly earnings.
 (B) The price of coffee is expected to steadily increase this year.
 (C) That is why Starbean has become so popular.
 (D) It also appeals to customers who don't have time to enjoy coffee.

138. (A) services
 (B) functions
 (C) equipment
 (D) beverages

Questions 139-142 refer to the following memo.

To: All staff

From: Accounting Department

Date: February 4

Subject: Revised Procedures

Please be aware that the reimbursement program for travel expenses has been changed.

-------, the Travel Expense Form was submitted within one month after the trip. Now, employees
139.

must submit the form within at least two weeks after traveling. All expenses ------- by the
140.

company, providing that they are properly used and have been approved beforehand. Once the

request for travel expenses has been processed, ------- of incurred expenses that have been
141.

approved by the company will be sent to the employee. -------. If you need further information,
142.

please visit our website at www.tesoro.com/reimbursementprogram.

139. (A) Consequently
(B) Exceedingly
(C) Previously
(D) Eventually

140. (A) pays
(B) paid
(C) have been paying
(D) will be paid

141. (A) notifies
(B) notified
(C) notifying
(D) notification

142. (A) Please e-mail this form to the
accounting department.
(B) The company has been encouraging
all staff to travel abroad.
(C) The travel expenses will be
reimbursed by the proper procedures.
(D) Business trips are restricted due to the
financial problems the company has
faced.

TEST
10

PART
6

Go on to the next page

Questions 143-146 refer to the following Web page.

---

www.staplesbestworkplaceaward.com/about

About the Award

Organizations with top performance throughout the U.S. give a boost to the country's economy.

Over the years, we've witnessed that ------- success is mostly attributable to having an
143.

engaged workforce. Enthusiastic employees tend to have a positive impact on their coworkers.

-------. The Staples Best Workplace Award was ------- fifteen years ago to honor successful
144. **145.**

companies whose employees are dedicated to their work. -------, hundreds of organizations
146.

throughout the U.S. have already received the award. If you would like to know about a

complete list of award winners, go to the Recipient page.

---

143. (A) his
(B) when
(C) where
(D) their

144. (A) Sometimes this can cause customer complaints.
(B) The award ceremony will be held in June.
(C) Only large companies are entitled to receive the prize.
(D) This can be seen in higher productivity.

145. (A) established
(B) appealed
(C) asked
(D) inspired

146. (A) Now that
(B) On the other hand
(C) Since then
(D) Nevertheless

Directions: In this part you will read a selection of texts, such as magazine and newspaper articles, e-mails, and instant messages. Each text or set of texts is followed by several questions. Select the best answer for each question and mark the letter (A), (B), (C), or (D) on your answer sheet.

Questions 147-148 refer to the following advertisement.

Nucor Center

- **More than 40 exciting outdoor sports**
- **More than 50 amazing games with reasonable prices**
- **Special music festival all year round**
- **The country's largest indoor food court**
- **A play area designed only for children under five**

Nucor Center is open throughout the year, Monday through Sunday.

Tickets can be purchased online or at the main gate.

Group discounts apply for groups of 12 or more.

---

147. What is being advertised?

(A) A music concert
(B) A competition
(C) An amusement park
(D) A design festival

148. Who is eligible for a discount?

(A) People buying tickets as a group
(B) People visiting more than five times a month
(C) People purchasing tickets online
(D) People under five years of age

TEST 10

PART 7

Go on to the next page

Omnicom S9 Mobile

Thank you for purchasing the Omnicom S9 mobile phone. Your new phone includes state-of-the-art features to make your life more enjoyable. This user manual offers you easy-to-follow instructions for your new mobile phone. If you want to avoid any possibility of damaging your Omnicom S9, please check the list of precautions on page 25 concerning accessories, including battery chargers, phone cases, batteries, and earphones.

149. What is the purpose of the information?

(A) To promote the mobile phone's warranty program
(B) To offer a discount on electronic devices
(C) To advise customers to take a look at the manual
(D) To encourage consumers to buy a new phone

150. What is suggested about mobile phone accessories?

(A) Omnicom S9 includes all of them at no extra cost.
(B) Using them incorrectly might damage the phone.
(C) They come with a one-year warranty.
(D) Authorized dealers can replace the damaged ones with new ones.

Scarlett Portman
51–59 Chester Ave.
Garden City, NY 11530

January 5

Angela West
667 3rd Ave.
Welaka, FL 32193

Dear Ms. West,

I am writing to thank you for your professional reference. I believe that your recommendation letter supporting my application was of great help in securing the position of news interpreter at SBTY.

The experience I have gotten during graduate school, particularly through translating Korean and Japanese into English, made me well suited for this job. Aside from the interpretation, I am now enjoying the challenge of translating medical news program as well.

Again, I really appreciate your help.

Yours sincerely,

Scarlett Portman

151. Why did Ms. Portman write the letter?

(A) To approve some information
(B) To express gratitude
(C) To ask for a translation
(D) To offer a position

152. Where does Ms. Portman most likely work?

(A) At a broadcasting network
(B) At a pharmaceutical company
(C) At a language school
(D) At a hospital

Questions 153-155 refer to the following e-mail.

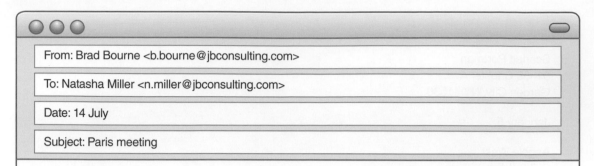

From: Brad Bourne <b.bourne@jbconsulting.com>

To: Natasha Miller <n.miller@jbconsulting.com>

Date: 14 July

Subject: Paris meeting

Hello Natasha,

I'm in Tokyo to supervise the overall inspection process and make sure it is properly carried out, but it's taken longer than I expected. So, I'm going to extend my stay here in Japan for a further two weeks, meaning that I need you to reschedule my appointment on Thursday in Paris.

If you do so, I could prepare for the client meeting with Mr. James next month. And could you send me a copy of the contracts that I drew up? They're probably either in my file cabinet or on my desk. I will not be reachable by phone today. If you need me, please e-mail or message me.

Thank you for your help.

Brad Bourne, President, Bourne Consulting

153. What is the purpose of the e-mail?

(A) To approve a request for an inspection
(B) To summarize a report
(C) To complain about the inspection results
(D) To request assistance in changing a schedule

154. Why is Mr. Bourne most likely in Japan?

(A) To open a new facility
(B) To sign a contact
(C) To oversee a project
(D) To interview a candidate

155. What is suggested about Mr. James?

(A) He is a factory manager.
(B) He is Ms. Miller's administrative assistant.
(C) He is Mr. Bourne's business client.
(D) He helped Mr. Bourne with the inspection process.

Questions 156-158 refer to the following letter.

Aramark Electronics

www.aramarkelectronics.com

Michael Dawson
1C Vestry Road
London, E17 9NH
England

Dear Mr. Dawson,

Thank you for contacting Aramark Electronics for your air-conditioner repair (No. 2912012). To provide the best quality service to our customers, we ask you to take a few minutes to complete the survey. Please send us your completed survey sheet by using the enclosed self-addressed stamped envelope. Thank you for your cooperation.

	Strongly Agree	Agree	Disagree	Strongly Disagree
Aramark Electronics replied to your request quickly.	X			
A service technician precisely explained what the problem is.		X		
Your Aramark Electronics product was immediately repaired and returned.				X

Customer Name: Michael Dawson
Repair Request Number: 2912012

Comments:
It was better to use Q&A's on your website than to chat with a technician. That's because I could get a quick answer about troubleshooting. The answer written by the technician had detailed information about what to do to solve the problems. My air conditioner, however, was not fixed properly and arrived five days later than the estimated shipping date.

TEST

10

PART

7

156. Why was the letter written to Mr. Dawson?

(A) To complain about what he went through
(B) To announce the recall of defective models
(C) To notify him of policy changes
(D) To get information about customer service

157. What does Aramark Electronics offer?

(A) Online assistance
(B) Free shipping
(C) A warranty extension
(D) A troubleshooting manual

158. What does Mr. Dawson mention?

(A) The technician perfectly fixed the air conditioner.
(B) The repair took longer than expected.
(C) The air conditioner was defective at the time of purchase.
(D) The manual was difficult to understand.

Go on to the next page

295

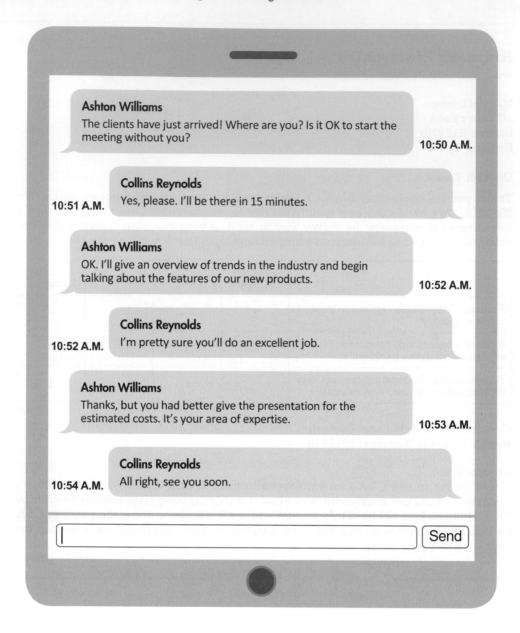

Ashton Williams
The clients have just arrived! Where are you? Is it OK to start the meeting without you?
10:50 A.M.

Collins Reynolds
10:51 A.M.   Yes, please. I'll be there in 15 minutes.

Ashton Williams
OK. I'll give an overview of trends in the industry and begin talking about the features of our new products.
10:52 A.M.

Collins Reynolds
10:52 A.M.   I'm pretty sure you'll do an excellent job.

Ashton Williams
Thanks, but you had better give the presentation for the estimated costs. It's your area of expertise.
10:53 A.M.

Collins Reynolds
10:54 A.M.   All right, see you soon.

[Send]

159. At 10:51 A.M., what does Mr. Reynolds most likely mean when he writes, "Yes, please."?

(A) He needs more information about the product.
(B) He wants Mr. Williams to stay on schedule.
(C) He wants them to take a fifteen-minute break now.
(D) He recommends that the presentation be delayed.

160. According to Mr. Williams, what is Mr. Reynolds most knowledgeable about?

(A) Manufacturing
(B) Product specification
(C) Marketing strategy
(D) Budgeting

Business Inside

Lincoln Bookstore recently has acquired the retail space right next to the store's original location at 877 High Road Leytonstone in London. The popular spot will finally launch an expansion project by using the new space. "Since opening our doors five years ago, we have been on the fast track," says Seth Johnson, cofounder and president of Lincoln Bookstore. "We were told that successful stories for offline bookstores are a thing of the past. —[1]—."

Johnson went on to say that the renovated Lincoln Bookstore will be approximately double the size. "The much-anticipated reopening ceremony will be held on November 8," says Johnson. "—[2]—. We're thrilled with the revamped bookstore. —[3]—. It means we could have many books and host various events like book signings. —[4]—."

161. What is the purpose of the article?

(A) To introduce a local business owner
(B) To announce changes to a bookstore
(C) To advertise a new book
(D) To promote a book signing event

162. Who is Mr. Johnson?

(A) A bookseller
(B) A popular writer
(C) An online book supplier
(D) A real estate agent

163. In which of the positions marked [1], [2], [3] and [4] does the following sentence best belong?

"We have proved that the opposite is true."

(A) [1]
(B) [2]
(C) [3]
(D) [4]

TEST 10

PART 7

Manchester Music Festival

Are you interested in participating in one of the famous music festivals as a committed volunteer while enjoying great music? Then, why don't you volunteer at the 25th annual Manchester Music Festival! This year's festival starts from on 1 and runs until August 5 at the Heaton Park in Manchester, and more than 15 professional groups and 25 talented amateur groups — including local favorites Roland Byrd, Jazzmatazz, Acadia Beat — will show off their great performances during the event.

Volunteers are needed to

- Help with creating, distributing all posters and flyers, and handing out press releases, which starts July 1.
- Greet and interpret for the musicians from July 28 to August 8. All out-of-town musicians will stay at the designated hotel.
- Operate the ticket office and the information desk as well as guide guests to the parking lots during the festival.

To show our appreciation for volunteers' dedication, the rewards are bountiful! Volunteers will receive an official limited-edition Manchester Music Festival T-shirt, VIP invitation to the official after party, a season festival pass, and more.

If you are interested in volunteering, please contact Hilary Roberts at hroberts@manchestermusicfestival.co.uk by June 15.

164. What is indicated about the festival?
(A) It will begin on August 1.
(B) It features various music genres.
(C) It is run by the local government.
(D) It may be postponed due to rain.

165. What is suggested about some of the performers?
(A) They will be donating used musical instruments.
(B) They will be offering autographed CDs.
(C) They will be staying at homes in Manchester.
(D) They will be receiving some interpretation services.

166. What task will NOT be done by volunteers?
(A) Selling tickets for the festival
(B) Transporting musicians to their hotels
(C) Informing visitors of parking locations
(D) Distributing some documents

167. What will volunteers receive for free?
(A) An article of clothing
(B) A voucher for the designated hotel
(C) A ticket for an awards banquet
(D) Food and beverages on festival days

The Renovation of Marine Park

By Jack Davenport

San Diego (April 15) — San Diego's city council has adopted a resolution to renovate Marine Park with unanimous approval. The issue of the renovation project was initially raised three years ago and has been under discussion. After Mayor Natalie Witherspoon took office, the plan was finally approved. She said in an interview, "I told the city that this would be my first act after coming into office, and I plan to fulfill my pledge." —[1]—.

After the park was opened, its two-kilometer trail along the lake became one of the places of interest in San Diego. However, it was not long before residents came to know that the park is not an ideal place for their children. —[2]—.

"We walk the trail on a daily basis, but our kids want to kick a ball around," said city resident Ivanka Aniston. The park is indeed lacking spaces for children to run freely. "We sometimes thought of having lunch at the park, but there are no tables and benches." —[3]—.

As a part of the project, Marine Park will have more green space for outdoor activities. A space will be designed for children to play in safety as well. —[4]—. This was for the convenience of residents who prefer to walk or exercise later in the evening. The renovations will be finished by the end of this year at the latest.

TEST 10

PART 7

168. What is indicated about the park's renovation?

(A) It will end next summer.
(B) Mayor Witherspoon first proposed it.
(C) It will take three years to finish.
(D) All members of the council agreed to it.

169. The word "plan" in paragraph 1, line 5, is closest in meaning to

(A) intend
(B) keep
(C) agree
(D) concentrate

170. How have residents been using the park?

(A) To eat something
(B) To sell their handmade products
(C) To go for walks
(D) To ride a bicycle

171. In which of the positions marked [1], [2], [3], and [4] does the following sentence best belong?

"And the city council has also approved the installation of lampposts along the trail."

(A) [1]
(B) [2]
(C) [3]
(D) [4]

Go on to the next page

Questions 172-175 refer to the following online chat discussion.

Cindy Hilton [9:45 A.M.]	I have to arrange transportation from the airport for our annual conference next week. So, I want you to provide me with flight information. As we are holding the conference for the first time, I sincerely hope there aren't any problems during the event.
Mary Kate [9:46 A.M.]	I've been waiting for this for a long time. Unfortunately, I forgot to reserve a flight. Will the company reimburse me for the travel expenses if I drive my own car? That's because the flights from San Francisco are full.
Ben Ford [9:47 A.M.]	I'll be on Clover Airlines, flight 803 from Dallas to New York at 7:35 A.M.
Cindy Hilton [9:48 A.M.]	Oh, that's too bad, Mary. I'll check on that.
Ariana Crawford [9:49 A.M.]	All flights from Houston were full as well. So, I have no choice but to take a bus to Philadelphia and then fly to New York, arriving at 7:50 A.M. I managed to get the last ticket.
Cindy Hilton [9:55 A.M.]	I've just been told by the finance department that costs of travel by car will not be reimbursed according to the company policy. Why don't you take a train instead? I would appreciate it if you book it immediately and let me know the time of your arrival.
Mary Kate [9:56 A.M.]	Sure.
Cindy Hilton [9:57 A.M.]	Thank you for the information, Mr. Ford and Ms. Crawford. See you then.

Send

172. At 9:46 A.M., what does Ms. Kate most likely mean when she writes, "I've been waiting for this for a long time."?

(A) She is waiting for the details about flight information.
(B) She did not realize flights are fully booked.
(C) She is glad the speakers will finally meet next week.
(D) She has prepared a presentation for the conference.

173. At 9:48 A.M., what is Ms. Hilton going to check on?

(A) A flight ticket from San Francisco
(B) The company's reimbursement policy
(C) Ms. Ford's flight information
(D) The start time of the conference

174. How will Ms. Kate most likely travel to the annual conference?

(A) By car
(B) By air
(C) By train
(D) By bus

175. What is true about the speakers?

(A) They are all flying out of the same city.
(B) They will take the same flight.
(C) They met at the conference last year.
(D) They are all attending a conference in New York.

Go on to the next page

TEST
10

PART
7

Weekly Business Insight:
Trustworthy Brothers

Five years ago, Jay and Gavin Damon set up a company called Trustworthy Brothers, which is truly unique and a game-changing firm in the real estate industry in Barcelona. To renovate older properties, the small firm has much experience working with existing landlords in the city. The brothers have concentrated on an increase in value and rental income potential by effectively evaluating properties and determining what improvements are needed. From building exterior to interior design, Trustworthy Brothers hires skilled and professional laborers to get the project done. Until now, all of their work has been done only in central Barcelona.

One of the local landlords, Jay Manuel, who recently signed a contract with Trustworthy Brothers to renovate his old buildings, said, "Thanks to working with Trustworthy Brothers, I have experienced an increase in tenant demand and rental profits. Furthermore, the renovation has led to cost savings for power and water. Tenants of my building enjoy their leisure time on the new rooftop terrace. I'll definitely recommend Trustworthy Brothers to others."

If you want to contact Trustworthy Brothers, visit their website, trustworthybrothers.com.

From: Michael Keane <mkeane@amail.com>

To: Jay Damon <jdamon@trustworthybrothers.com>

Date: March 24

Subject: New Proposition

Dear Mr. Damon,

I am writing to request a renovation for a building I recently purchased, which is located in a seaside town near Barcelona. I am pretty sure that you would be interested in the renovation project. The building is not currently in good condition because it has been abandoned for several years. So I was able to purchase it at a very low price. The building is, however, very close to a subway station, which I believe is an advantage. I would like to make a request to you to transform my building into a new attractive residence for rent. Please let me know if you are available to talk about it.

Thank you,

Michael Keane

---

176. What does the article NOT indicate about the Trustworthy Brothers?

(A) They have worked in the real estate industry for 10 years.
(B) They improve profits for their clients.
(C) They have worked with landlords in Barcelona.
(D) They employ workers to carry out their plans.

177. What is suggested about Mr. Manuel's buildings?

(A) They attract more tenants than before.
(B) They are new buildings.
(C) The rooftop terrace is not open to the tenants.
(D) Mr. Manuel has to pay more for their electricity bills now.

178. What does the article indicate potential clients should do?

(A) Ask for an estimate
(B) Visit a website
(C) Negotiate the price
(D) Send a request

179. Why was Mr. Keane able to purchase the building at a low price?

(A) It is in a remote area.
(B) It does not have access to a water supply.
(C) It was on sale as a special promotion.
(D) It could not be rented out in its present state.

180. How is Mr. Keane's proposal different from typical works for Trustworthy Brothers?

(A) The work would be done outside Barcelona.
(B) Mr. Keane would like to hire a renowned designer.
(C) The fee for the renovation would be paid after the project is finished.
(D) The project should be finished within a strict time limit.

Go on to the next page

Penske Books
Winter Catalog

Dear Customers,

Please enjoy looking over our latest catalog. If you look at the Cookbooks, Food, and Wine section on page 5, you will find some best-sellers that let you know recipes from famous restaurants. Our Travel and Tourism section on page 7 guides you to enjoy your winter vacation wherever you go. For all the latest in the Science Fiction section on page 9, imaginative writers will lead you into the world of fantasy. Highly experienced writers will tell you about the latest trends in the Business and Management section on page 11. You can also see the best-loved books including Risk Management for Small Businesses, winner of the Jamison Award (page 13).

Please note that this catalog has only a small number of samples. If you want to see a full list of our titles, go to our website, www.penskebooks.com. For those who live in Pennsylvania, please visit our store for a wealth of additional books that you cannot find on our website.

Business Perspective
by Yuri Tielemans and Jane Carter

An impressive introduction to business strategy, full of specific cases and entertaining pictures and illustrations to explain key points. The easy-to-follow instructions will give you a better understanding of the business world.

Condition: Very good. $39.95

Finance Management Analysis
by Thiago Malcom

This book features combining new financial theory with practical examples. Malcom uses real-world scenarios to analyze theoretical principles of finance management. Highly recommended for both businesspeople and students.

Condition: Like new. $25.95.

Risk Management for Small Businesses
by Alicia Dunst

Essential books for small business owners who take care of high-risk situations effectively. The book contains several interviews with owners running a successful business.

Condition: Fair with some wear to corners and edges. $32.95

Encyclopedia of Business Marketing
by Anthony Martial

With more than 5,000 definitions of business marketing terms, this book is a must-have item for those who are starting their own business for the first time.

Condition: Good with signs of cover wear. $49.95

---

181. Based on the note, what book would Penske Books most likely have in stock?

(A) A biography of a famous musician
(B) A history of Africa
(C) An introduction of the new computer models
(D) An information on top vacation spots in East Asia

182. In the note, the word "wealth" in paragraph 2, line 3, is closest in meaning to

(A) value
(B) quality
(C) sense
(D) abundance

183. What is suggested about the catalog?

(A) It advertises used books.
(B) It has a complete listing.
(C) It includes mainly academic books.
(D) It is released twice a year.

184. Who received an award?

(A) Mr. Tielemans
(B) Mr. Malcom
(C) Ms. Dunst
(D) Mr. Martial

185. What feature is NOT mentioned among the descriptions of the books on the catalog page?

(A) Drawings to clarify key points
(B) Interviews with those involved
(C) Examples from real world
(D) Checklists for starting a small company

Go on to the next page

Questions 186-190 refer to the following e-mail, program, and information.

From: James Rodriguez <jrodriguez@ita.com>

To: Brian Mendy <bmendy@altriagroup.com>

Date: December 1

Subject: Invitation for speaker

Dear Mr. Mendy,

I am writing to invite you to be a keynote speaker at the 5th annual Information Technology Association Conference, which is scheduled for May 1-3 in Charlotte, North Carolina. Thousands of business leaders and industry experts will participate in the event, which will be an ideal venue for networking. This conference will be held at the Hyatt Charlotte Hotel, and business leaders will share their insights into the latest trends in the IT industry.

We would appreciate it if you would agree to make a speech on the flexible pricing options you introduced to boost profits for the Internet security program created by the Altria Group. Please let me know your availability.

James Rodriguez
President
Information Technology Association

Information Technology Association Conference Program

(May 1 – Schedules)

8:30 A.M.	**Visual Communication –** A more effective and better way of communicating as well as saving money and effort	
	Speaker: Elizabeth Cohan, Cofounder of Micron Technology	
9:30 A.M.	**Revolutionary Change –** The vice president of Supervalu speaks on how her team brought the company back from near bankruptcy and made the company turn a profit through innovative product design	
	Speaker: Anna Kirby, Vice President of Supervalu	
10:30 A.M.	**Creating a Product –** The secret behind the Altria Group's unique strategy to increase the sales revenues of its computer programs	
	Speaker: Brian Mendy, CEO of Altria Group	
11:30 A.M.	**Leadership in an IT company –** How to react quickly and efficiently to rapidly changing circumstances	
	Speaker: Laurel Allen, Professor of Charlotte Business School	
12:30 P.M.	**Lunch**	

Information Technology Association Conference

Registration fees
Information Technology Association members — $1,000
Nonmembers – $1,500

Registration fees include hotel vouchers for use — during the event as well as meals and refreshments. Registration online in advance is required to attend the conference. Presentation videos will be available on our website to all participants the following month.

186. What is mentioned about the Information Technology Association Conference?

(A) It takes place annually.
(B) An on-site training will be scheduled.
(C) It is a one-day event.
(D) The latest products will be on display.

187. When will product pricing most likely be discussed?

(A) At 8:30 A.M.
(B) At 9:30 A.M.
(C) At 10:30 A.M.
(D) At 11:30 A.M.

188. What is indicated about Supervalu?

(A) It will merge with a rival company.
(B) It has overcome difficulties.
(C) It has changed the company logo.
(D) It moved its headquarters last year.

189. What is a benefit available only to Information Technology Association members?

(A) A private dinner for networking
(B) Free transportation
(C) Upgraded hotel accommodations
(D) Reduced registration fees

190. What will Mr. Mendy receive access to in June?

(A) Recordings
(B) Articles
(C) Receipts
(D) Photographs

Go on to the next page

Discount Coupon

END-OF-SEASON SALE for One Day Only!
Wednesday, 2 April

- 20% off one regularly priced item
- 30% off one clearance item

Thousands of items in stock, including coats, shirts, pants, shoes, accessories, and more. We will extend our business hours for this event: 9:00 A.M. – 9:00 P.M.

This coupon is not able to be combined with other promotions. We limit one coupon per customer. Please note that the coupon is not valid on pants. Once the item is purchased, no refunds or exchanges are allowed. Coupon is valid on 2 April only.

Monstanto

1040 Grand Concourse

Bronx, NY 10456
Telephone: (718) 681-6000

To: Monstanto Employees

From: William Singer, Manager

Date: April 1

Re: Upcoming sale

Today's edition of the *New York Daily* failed to mention that accessories are excluded from the regularly priced items. So, if a customer makes a purchase of the item, please explain the issue and make an apology. And then, please inform the customer of the fact that we'll nevertheless offer 10% discount as a courtesy.

Also, as the promotion has been advertised through all media, more customers are expected to visit our store than usual, especially from 5 P.M. to the closing time. So, we will need more sales associates on duty during that time. Please let me know if you are available for an extra shift.

Thank you.

From: Service Department <service@monstanto.com>

To: Jill Elkins <jelkins@mmail.com>

Date: 2 April, 4:26 P.M.

Subject: Your receipt

Dear Ms. Elkins,

Here is the purchase receipt you recently requested from Monstanto.

Quantity	Item	Price
1	Soft Jacket	$400.00
	30% promotion discount	-$120.00
	Item price	**$280.00**
1	Ring and necklace set	$160.00
	10% promotion discount	-$16.00
	Item price	**$144.00**
1	Long denim pants	$28.00

Total $452.00
Total Saved $136.00

Thank you for shopping at Monstanto.

---

191. According to the coupon, what will happen on April 2?

(A) New product line will be unveiled.
(B) The store will remain open longer than usual.
(C) Additional coupons will be handed out in front of the store.
(D) Customers will be able to see a fashion show.

192. In the first e-mail, what are sales associates requested to do?

(A) Arrive early to work
(B) Volunteer to work extra hours
(C) Hand out flyers
(D) Take an inventory

193. In the first e-mail, the word "advertised" in paragraph 2, line 1, is closest in meaning to

(A) updated
(B) released
(C) attracted
(D) promoted

194. What is suggested about Ms. Elkins?

(A) She purchased a clearance item.
(B) She recently moved to Bronx.
(C) She paid for her purchase with a credit card.
(D) She frequently visits Monstanto.

195. What did Ms. Elkins probably NOT receive when she purchased the ring and necklace set?

(A) A discount
(B) A gift certificate
(C) An apology
(D) An explanation

Go on to the next page

Student Liaison Officer
Chicago University

The university is looking for student liaison officers (SLOs) to work in the Student Support Department. The SLOs will meet two times every month to support international students who make up the Student Committee, taking care of services that can assist with various issues including personal problems, academic issues, accommodation, and career advice. The SLOs will also organize monthly meetings in different places on campus to promote a sense of community.

If you are interested, please send us an e-mail at ssd@chiuni.edu.com.

From:	Bankole Johnson
To:	Robert Rivest
Date:	February 15
Subject:	Welcome

Dear Mr. Rivest,

Thank you for accepting our offer for the position of SLO (Student Liaison Officer). There is some paperwork you should complete before your first day of work. Within a week, you will receive a welcome box containing our university's official documents that you need to fill out by the end of this month. This will also let you know the details about your orientation.

Furthermore, we do need an official transcript from your last university. So please send me an official one by the end of this month as well.

Sincerely,

Bankole Johnson
Director of Student Support Department, Chicago University

San Diego University
Transcript Request Form

Transcripts will NOT be released if:

    Money is not yet paid to the university.

    There is a hold on your student record.

Last Name: <u>Rivest</u>   **First Name:** <u>Robert</u>

Degree Obtained: ☐ Undergraduate   ☑ Graduate (Communication)

Street Address: <u>5801 S Ellis Ave</u>

Post Code: <u>60637</u>   **City:** <u>Chicago</u>   **State:** <u>Illinois</u>

When do you want your transcript proceeded?

☑ Immediately   ☐ Hold for Final Grades

Signature: *Robert Rivest*

---

196. What is the purpose of the notice?

    (A) To recruit international students for a university

    (B) To announce the employment of a new professor

    (C) To solicit applications for an open position

    (D) To publicize the creation of a new organization

197. How frequently does the Student Committee meet with the student liaison officer?

    (A) Once a week

    (B) Once a month

    (C) Twice a week

    (D) Twice a month

198. What will Mr. Rivest do at Chicago University?

    (A) Help relocate the student center

    (B) Help all students select appropriate courses

    (C) Lead the department of student support

    (D) Provide support to international students on campus

199. What will Mr. Rivest receive within a week?

    (A) A package of documents

    (B) A receipt of a payment

    (C) A copy of his school transcript

    (D) A letter of acceptance

200. What is suggested about San Diego University?

    (A) It does not have a medical program.

    (B) It does not have a graduate course.

    (C) It recruits a large number of international students.

    (D) It is the last university Mr. Rivest attended.

TRANSLATION

ACTUAL TEST

PART 5　P. 14–16

◎ Part 5 解答請見 P.457

101. 所有新進員工都會收到訓練資料袋,其中**包含**載明他們職責的細節。

102. **隨著**賽程只剩最後兩哩路,考夫曼女士比起下一名跑者,明顯占優勢。

103. 邵先生無法到上海參加委員大會,所以全女士將代替**他**出席。

104. 全日百貨公司的執行董事,**反對**公司商標有任何變動。

105. 會議中心位於布魯克林街,就在新郵局的**正對面**。

106. **有鑑於**鋼價上漲,FTX 營造公司極有可能會調整金橋工程的競標金額。

107. 綜合辦公大樓**將蓋**在步行購物區外圍。

108. 過去二十年來,服裝設計師**愈來愈**著重顧客需求和喜好。

109. **過去**四個月內,奇蹟影城的來客數有顯著成長。

110. 阿德里安人才招募公司的臨時人員,果然都非常**有能力**。

111. 戶外家具在過去六個月的銷售收益比預期高上**許多**。

112. 報名參加攝影競賽**前**,請完成清單上所有事項。

113. 彭柏頓綠色市集裡,有很多**當地**農民販售自家農產品。

114. 因為預期天氣將會變壞,原訂明天舉行的戶外音樂會將**延期**到下星期六。

115. 為確保即時回應,請在所有的**信件**裡提供您的帳號。

116. 午餐將由好客咖啡館**和**哈克里碳烤提供。

117. 提摩西‧達爾頓非常適合擔綱管理角色,**該職位**要有豐富的經驗。

118. 我們很感謝您**參與**改善納森公寓大樓的問卷調查。

119. 羅培茲先生會協助作業,所以你不需要**獨力**修改所有手稿。

120. 米多拉製造商保有延後出貨的權利,**直到**顧客繳交所有未付款項。

121. 博立刻行銷集團**經常**提供客戶旗下最新的服務資訊。

122. 諾爾台茲室內設計迅速地在這座城市的房仲業界,建立良好**聲譽**。

123. 西絲塔公司的董事會**預計**在下週結束前,決定執行長人選。

124. 務必告知培訓課程講師你預計缺課的時間,**如此一來**才能安排其他日期受訓。

125. 米勒先生**曾指出**,只有融資顧問須參與會議,討論貸款業務的新趨勢。

126. 尖端領導機械公司的員工很驚喜,沒想到會在七月收到一筆**意外**的獎金。

127. 戴安娜女士必須決定**是否**要提交企畫書到北美辦公室。

128. **還沒**繳交班表的同仁,最晚要在今天下午五點前提交。

129. 上個月的公司餐會上,有 11 名員工因為已經任職 25 年受到**表揚**。

130. 新加坡的凱西飯店**鄰近**主要觀光景點,房間常常預訂一空。

PART 6　P. 17–20

131–134 新聞發布

十字鎮最大的服飾零售業者,也就是布洛斯店的創辦人兼總裁,查爾斯‧布洛,宣布將從昨天店裡舉行的晚宴售票所得當中,捐贈四千美元給新設的社區活動中心。布洛先生將在明天活動中心的開幕典禮上捐出支票。

布洛先生過去三十年來，為慈善機構和社區服務舉辦多場募款活動。昨晚的活動是有史以來最成功的一次。

131. Ⓐ 將捐贈
　　Ⓑ 捐贈了
　　Ⓒ 也許會捐贈
　　Ⓓ 正在捐贈

132. Ⓐ 博物館
　　Ⓑ 飯店
　　Ⓒ 住處
　　Ⓓ 店鋪

133. Ⓐ 儘管
　　Ⓑ 在……期間
　　Ⓒ 在……之間
　　Ⓓ 在……之下

134. Ⓐ 開幕典禮將在早上十點開始。
　　Ⓑ 社區中心提供成人和小孩的課程。
　　Ⓒ 昨晚的活動是有史以來最成功的一次。
　　Ⓓ 布洛先生計劃明年要在倫敦展店。

135–138 文章

8 月 30 日——耗時兩年，匹茲堡有史以來最大的飯店即將開張。河頂飯店位於阿勒格尼河河邊，將有 1,500 間客房，還有七間可容納至多 200 人的會議室。第一批賓客將在 9 月 12 日到來，參加醫療科技會議。這項建築計畫是市區四項興建中的其中一項建案。匹茲堡飯店和住宿協會會長克里斯多福‧威爾許表示，這些新開發案有其必要。他說：「過去幾年來，遊客大量湧入。」因此，城裡每一間飯店幾乎都爆滿。顯然本市需要更多的飯店房間。

135. Ⓐ 還不清楚何時開始接受訂房。
　　Ⓑ 下個月將開始大樓翻新工程。
　　Ⓒ 還有七間可容納至多 200 人的會議室。
　　Ⓓ 有很多間公司正在競標這項計畫。

136. Ⓐ 為了建造
　　Ⓑ 正在興建
　　Ⓒ 已完工
　　Ⓓ 正被興建的

137. **Ⓐ 必要性**
　　Ⓑ 麻煩事
　　Ⓒ 風險
　　Ⓓ 便宜貨

138. Ⓐ 另一方面
　　Ⓑ 換句話説
　　Ⓒ 起初
　　Ⓓ 因此

139–142 電子郵件

收件人：塞斯‧歐特佳
　　　　<sortega@xeroxmail.net>
寄件人：傑克‧默里斯
　　　　<jmorris@fubmanufacturing.com>
日期：5 月 21 日
主旨：廠長職位

敬愛的歐特佳先生，

您正式受邀參加第二階段面試。這次我只會和最優秀的應徵者面談，決定誰最適合這個廠長職位。我們相信您具備多項我們正在尋找的特質。

我相信您仍對這個工作機會感興趣。若是如此，您下週二下午三點方便面試嗎？請您準備一份提案，説明您會如何提升工廠產能，同時無損品質。很期待能聽到您對提升工廠效率的見解。

傑克‧默里斯

139. Ⓐ 適合的
　　Ⓑ 適合的
　　Ⓒ 適合
　　Ⓓ 適合

140. Ⓐ 協議
　　 Ⓑ 表現
　　 Ⓒ 特質
　　 Ⓓ 晉升

141. Ⓐ 儘管如此
　　 Ⓑ 若是如此
　　 Ⓒ 然而
　　 Ⓓ 舉例來說

142. Ⓐ 我很樂意為您寫封推薦函。
　　 Ⓑ 我的助理會訓練您適應新職務。
　　 Ⓒ 很期待能聽到您對提升工廠效率的見解。
　　 Ⓓ 您的新商品構想富含資訊。

143-146 文章

> 8月3日
>
> 克里斯・加爾諾撰稿
>
> 諾克斯維爾交通委員會將在8月10日週二傍晚6點，於市政廳召開公共會議，討論將輕軌服務，延伸到諾克斯維爾工業園區的提案。
>
> 路線將穿越住宅區。該社區居民曾抱怨，這會造成尖峰時段過多噪音。對此，委員會研究了沿軌道裝設隔音板的可行性。颶風建設公司的執行長，阿歷克斯・柯翰將與會說明，委員會如果裝設隔音板後，預期能降噪音的程度。緊接著會議之後，市長查理・霍夫曼將進行簡報。

143. Ⓐ 交通委員會提前完成計畫。
　　 Ⓑ 路線將穿越住宅區。
　　 Ⓒ 委員會主席明年將參選市長。
　　 Ⓓ 交通委員會決議每個月召開會議。

144. Ⓐ 此外
　　 Ⓑ 及時趕上
　　 Ⓒ 對此
　　 Ⓓ 總之

145. Ⓐ 提醒
　　 Ⓑ 接受
　　 Ⓒ 說服
　　 Ⓓ 預期

146. Ⓐ 去呈現
　　 Ⓑ 主持人
　　 Ⓒ 正在簡報的
　　 Ⓓ 簡報

PART 7　P. 21-41

147-148 信件

> 我們是緋紅海岸當地一家法律事務所，急徵一名接待人員。職務包括轉接電話、接待客戶、接聽電話、安排會議行程，以及寄發每天的電子郵件。應徵者需個性外向，並精通文書處理軟體及擁有大學學歷。每週薪資一百美元起。請將履歷寄到 danielhickman@fairlaw.com。

147. 該信件最有可能要招募何種職務？
　　 Ⓐ 出納員
　　 Ⓑ 律師
　　 Ⓒ 管理者
　　 Ⓓ 助理

148. 該職缺不需要何種資格條件？
　　 Ⓐ 會計
　　 Ⓑ 文書處理
　　 Ⓒ 客戶服務
　　 Ⓓ 大學學歷

149-150 訊息串

> **希維亞・林〔下午5:44〕：**
> 嗨，賈姬。你看過第三西大道那間房子的照片了嗎？
>
> **賈姬・麥克連〔下午5:45〕：**
> 有啊。考量到我們很多設計師和編輯都在遠端作業，所有房間真的都會用到嗎？
>
> **希維亞・林〔下午5:47〕：**
> 如果我們擴張營運的話，就會有更多人在那裡工作。
>
> **賈姬・麥克連〔下午5:48〕：**
> 短時間內不會吧。

希維亞・林〔下午 5:50〕：

我們必須同時考慮現在和長期需求。那房子裡有足夠的房間，考量之後擴編的話。

賈姬・麥克連〔下午 5:52〕：

說的也是。我們的需求可能會改變，尤其是和更多作家簽約以後。

送出

149. 這些人可能在什麼公司工作？

[A] 搬家公司
[B] 出版公司
[C] 房仲公司
[D] 外觀設計公司

150. 麥克連女士在下午 5:52 的時候寫道：「說的也是。」，她最可能的意思是？

[A] 應該租別的地方。
[B] 新地點太貴了。
[C] 新房子可能滿足公司未來的需求。
[D] 新房子需要全面翻修。

151–153 備忘錄

收件人：全體員工
寄件人：德懷特・霍華德，營運長
日期：6 月 5 日
主旨：東側大樓關閉

本信是為通知您，主辦公大樓的東側樓層將在下週末暫時關閉。維修人員將會替換所有辦公室和會議室的天花板照明，換成高品質日光燈。根據安全規定，施工期間禁止任何員工出入。工程將從 6 月 9 日週五開始，到 6 月 10 日週六結束。受影響的是 200 號到 262 號辦公室，這些辦公室員工應規劃在家工作，必要的話，也可使用本建築其他區域的臨時辦公區。若需預訂臨時辦公區，可聯繫行政助理麥可・肯恩，分機為 242。請留意臨時辦公區空間有限，最晚必須在 6 月 7 日下午五點前提出申請。

151. 這則備忘錄主要是報告什麼？

[A] 員工正要搬到新的辦公室。
[B] 將增加會議室空間。
[C] 安檢進行中。
[D] 辦公室照明升級。

152. 東側大樓何時開始關閉？

[A] 6 月 5 日
[B] 6 月 7 日
[C] 6 月 9 日
[D] 6 月 10 日

153. 部分員工須做什麼？

[A] 電話連絡經理
[B] 在家工作
[C] 清空辦公室
[D] 提前完成工作

154–155 電子郵件

收件人：賈斯丁・朱
　　　　<jchu@maximummail.com>
寄件人：吉米・李
　　　　<jlee@exoticdecoration.com>
日期：9 月 11 日
主旨：延遲寄送

親愛的朱先生：

感謝您近期訂購異國裝潢的產品。由於我們地區遭逢雷雨，部分訂購貨品未能寄出。封路使得貨車無法從倉庫取貨，也讓部分員工不能通勤上班。然而，我們希望能在 12 個小時內恢復正常營運。您訂購的物品將在這週末以前出貨。所有訂單都將免運費。我為延遲出貨誠摯向您致歉。

顧客關係經理
吉米・李 敬上

154. 為什麼訂單晚出貨？

[A] 還沒收到付款。
[B] 天氣嚴重影響出貨時程。
[C] 訂購的產品沒有庫存。
[D] 公司寄錯地址。

155. 朱先生將收到什麼？
- Ⓐ 下次購物可用的折價券
- Ⓑ 現金退款
- **Ⓒ 免運費優待**
- Ⓓ 更換商品

156–158 電子郵件

寄件人：提姆·戴利
<tdaily@sunflower.com>
收件人：德瑞克·哈米爾頓
<lhamilton@goodcaterer.com>
日期：6 月 12 日
主旨：回覆：花卉裝飾

親愛的哈米爾頓先生：

這封電子郵件要向您確認今早在電話裡談過的，貴公司頒獎典禮上所需要的 12 個花卉裝飾。您要求這次提供的花卉設計要比照上次的活動。然而，由於溫室那邊的延誤，木芙蓉的供應商説他們直到本月底才能供貨。

因為您需要所有花卉設計在 6 月 17 日以前完成，我想最好能選擇其他種花替代木芙蓉。我建議外型相似的蜀葵。請回信讓我知道這建議是否可行。我會再傳真最終版合約和價目表給您。如果有其他問題，請透過 432-234-2345 聯絡我。

感謝您，

向日葵花店經理
提姆·戴利

156. 下列何者與哈米爾頓先生有關？
- Ⓐ 他是戴利先生的朋友。
- Ⓑ 他正準備在自宅舉辦私人派對。
- Ⓒ 他要求修改訂單。
- **Ⓓ 他先前用過向日葵花店的服務。**

157. 為什麼戴利先生建議替換掉木芙蓉？
- **Ⓐ 沒有庫存。**
- Ⓑ 尺寸不對。
- Ⓒ 不便宜。
- Ⓓ 不新鮮。

158. 戴利先生要求哈米爾頓先生做什麼事？
- Ⓐ 簽約
- Ⓑ 到店裡談談
- **Ⓒ 回覆電子郵件**
- Ⓓ 支付部分金額

159–160 通知

美術館

艾德·哈里森受邀在 4 月 5 日週三晚上六點，在美術館談他的新書《美國夢之繪》。這本書由新興出版社出版，詳實描述了北美的藝術史。本場講座對外開放。不需要預約座位。由於只有 100 個座位，請各位賓客在演説開始前提早至少半小時進場。欲知更多資訊，可以來電 287-333-2422 詢問，或是上官網查詢。

159. 哈里森先生是誰？
- **Ⓐ 作家**
- Ⓑ 藝術家
- Ⓒ 書店主管
- Ⓓ 博物館職員

160. 如何取得講座的席位？
- Ⓐ 上網
- Ⓑ 用電話
- Ⓒ 寄信
- **Ⓓ 親自到場**

161–164 文章

上海擴建計畫有所進展

7 月 5 日──羅蘭科技兩週前完成第一期擴建計畫。羅蘭科技是電腦螢幕和投影機零組件的製造大廠，日前啟動擴廠計畫，將在未來八年內建設三間新工廠。第一間工廠位於中國上海，是公司旗下最大的工廠，最終產能將達公司年度生產總額的 60%。

新工廠為當地市民帶來就業機會。超過 1,500 名工人受僱來建設這間大型廠房和周邊建築。羅蘭科技的總裁深雪江詩説：「這是公司史上最大的計畫。我們投入建設後，就明白需要大量金錢、資源和人力。我們很高興看到這項計畫對當地勞工的影響。我們聘僱當地人來擴建硬體廠房，也將許多員工轉為全職人員。希望在日本也能比照辦理，很快地我們就會在東京計劃開始新建設。」總公司目前設在日本東京。

更多工廠會建在羅蘭科技的其他據點，包括泰國和韓國。雖然其餘工廠都不比上海這間來得大，但仍會有資源和人力需求。

161. 文中提到羅蘭科技的什麼？
   Ⓐ **生產螢幕元件。**
   Ⓑ 近期被競爭對手併購。
   Ⓒ 總部正在改建。
   Ⓓ 販賣建材。

162. 關於羅蘭科技在上海的工廠，文中可推論出什麼？
   Ⓐ 它是去年蓋好的第三間新工廠。
   Ⓑ 它是這間公司最大的工廠。
   Ⓒ 它的產量是全公司產能的四分之一。
   Ⓓ 它耗時六年多才蓋好。

163. 羅蘭科技的下一間工廠會蓋在哪裡？
   Ⓐ 中國
   Ⓑ 泰國
   Ⓒ 韓國
   Ⓓ 日本

(NEW)
164. 下列句子最適合出現在 [1]、[2]、[3]、[4] 的哪個位置中？
   「我們很高興看到這項計畫對當地勞工的影響。」
   Ⓐ [1]
   Ⓑ [2]
   Ⓒ [3]
   Ⓓ [4]

165–167 文章

多饌飯館坐落在第一大道和東街的交界處。開幕至今已有十載，並迅速累積人氣。店如其名，各種異國料理的餐點是這間店的特色。多饌飯館曾為了改善經營狀況而暫時歇業兩個月，並在兩週前重新開張。新任主廚麥特・薛連推出的菜單讓人驚艷，他推出更多選擇的精緻湯品、沙拉和美味主菜。他的招牌菜包括海鮮盛宴，像是芒果佐煙燻大比目魚和辣醬蝦。也絕對不能錯過出色甜點——焦糖蘋果派。有這麼多美食可供挑選，多饌飯館勢必成為饕客新歡。

165. 這篇文章目的為何？
   Ⓐ **評論一間餐廳**
   Ⓑ 推廣烹飪課程
   Ⓒ 比較兩間餐廳
   Ⓓ 宣布搬到新地點

166. 文中提到薛連先生什麼？
   Ⓐ **他擅長料理海鮮。**
   Ⓑ 他只用在地食材。
   Ⓒ 他整修了一間餐廳。
   Ⓓ 他六個月前開始在多饌飯館工作。

167. 文中提到這間餐廳的什麼資訊？
   Ⓐ 管理部門大換員工。
   Ⓑ 它的甜點非常出色。
   Ⓒ 大比目魚是最受歡迎的菜色。
   Ⓓ 店面搬到新的大樓。

168–171 電子郵件

收件人：羅伯特・林姆
<rlim@supermetc.co.bb>
寄件人：辛西亞・喬登
<cjordan@titangd.co.bb>
回覆：資訊
日期：4 月 14 日
附件：BLS1

親愛的林姆先生：

我來信是向您後續詢問，關於我在 3 月 22 日寄出的泰坦園藝服務提案。

我們是皇后村最好的廠商，想請您加入成為我們滿意顧客清單上的一員。許多當地企業，像是飯店、餐廳和度假中心都是我們的客戶。如果您上次沒注意到初版提案，我在這封信再次附檔給您。

根據您當初所詢問的服務，也就是超凡網球場一週兩次的場地維護，我們做出這份提案。此外，我們也會持續再次評估您的需求，並且每個月提供您兩次建議。如果你需要其他服務，像是栽種別的樹種，則需要再增加費用。

期待您的回信。我希望我們公司未來能有機會為您服務。

辛西亞‧喬登 敬上

168. 為什麼會寫這封電子郵件？
- Ⓐ 排定會議
- Ⓑ 解釋新的價格
- **Ⓒ 重寄之前的估價單**
- Ⓓ 寄出修改過的提案

169. 這封電子郵件提到什麼？
- Ⓐ 林姆先生這顧客很滿意。
- Ⓑ 泰坦園藝是新公司。
- Ⓒ 林姆先生和喬登女士開過會。
- **Ⓓ 林姆先生向喬登女士詢問資訊。**

170. 林姆先生可能從事的行業是？
- Ⓐ 飯店業
- **Ⓑ 網球設施**
- Ⓒ 餐飲業
- Ⓓ 園藝中心

(NEW)
171. 下列句子最適合出現在 [1]、[2]、[3]、[4] 的哪個位置中？
「此外，我們也會持續再次評估您的需求，並且每個月提供您兩次建議。」
- Ⓐ [1]
- Ⓑ [2]
- **Ⓒ [3]**
- Ⓓ [4]

172–175 網路討論區

泰隆‧吉布森〔下午 1:32〕：
感謝你們參加今天早上的線上業務會議。有其他問題嗎？

茉蒂‧鍾〔下午 1:35〕：
喬治和我不太確定，更新銷售區會不會影響到舊客戶。新的銷售區只適用於新客戶嗎？

泰隆‧吉布森〔下午 1:37〕：
當然不只。新舊客戶都適用。

茉蒂‧鍾〔下午 1:38〕：
所以這樣的意思是說，我不能再從我的法國客戶 YDV 機械抽佣金囉？

泰隆‧吉布森〔下午 1:39〕：
對，法國北部的舊客戶之後歸給喬治。

喬治‧金〔下午 1:41〕：
但為什麼我不能讓茉蒂留著她的 YDV 機械？

泰隆‧吉布森〔下午 1:42〕：
YDV 機械是大客戶。

喬治‧金〔下午 1:44〕：
是，但我不想中斷這個良好的夥伴關係。而且，這個客戶對我來說並不重要。

泰隆‧吉布森〔下午 1:45〕：
我不認這會造成中斷。不過，如果喬治你堅持，我們也許可以通融，只要總裁同意的話。

茉蒂‧鍾〔下午 1:47〕：
為什麼不讓我跟客戶說？

泰隆‧吉布森〔下午 1:48〕：
我想這不太適當。

茉蒂‧鍾〔下午 1:49〕：
了解。

喬治‧金〔下午 1:49〕：
好吧。期待知曉您處理的後續消息。

送出

172. 吉布森先生最有可能是？
- Ⓐ 總裁
- **Ⓑ 業務主管**
- Ⓒ 導遊
- Ⓓ 人資經理

173. 文中提到鍾女士什麼事？
- **A 她和 YDV 機械關係良好。**
- B 她正分派到法國辦公室。
- C 她對新分配的銷售區感到開心。
- D 她沒有參加業務會議。

174. 下午 1:48 時，吉布森先生寫道：「我想這不太適當。」，他最可能的意思是？
- A 他質疑鍾女士能否滿足 YDV 機械的需求。
- B 他覺得鍾女士誤解了。
- C 他希望鍾女士拜訪法國。
- **D 他不希望鍾女士就這件事聯繫 YDV 機械。**

175. 接下來可能會發生什麼事？
- A 鍾女士會仔細查看更新的銷售區。
- B 鍾女士會和客戶談談。
- **C 吉布森先生會致電給總裁。**
- D 金先生會接受 YDV 機械的職缺。

176–180 電子郵件

寄件人：瑪麗 · 趙 <mcho@dtu.com>
收件人：彼得 · 歐馬列
<pomalley@dtu.com>
日期：6 月 3 日
主旨：世界設計大會

親愛的彼得：

感謝你自願代理我於 6 月 10 日在波士頓世界設計大會的工作。我需要留在舊金山的總公司和一些從法國來的客戶見面。我去年參加大會，覺得非常值得，而且還可以接觸到有潛力的設計師。

我已經處理好你的機票、飯店住宿和租車。費用已由 DTU 負擔，等你回來之後，還會收到每天 50 美元的餐食費補助。如果你打算和設計師一起共進晚餐，記得保留收據紀錄回來報帳，會計部門會再補貼。

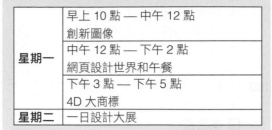

大會日程如下：

星期一	早上 10 點 — 中午 12 點 創新圖像	
	中午 12 點 — 下午 2 點 網頁設計世界和午餐	
	下午 3 點 — 下午 5 點 4D 大商標	
星期二	一日設計大展	

祝好，

瑪麗

寄件人：彼得 · 歐馬列
<pomalley@dtu.com>
收件人：瑪麗 · 趙
<mcho@dtu.com>
日期：6 月 10 日
主旨：回覆：世界設計大會

親愛的瑪麗：

我今天下午提早離開大會。因為講者的飛機延誤，週一早上的演講取消了。不過，另幾場演講很順利。我增廣見聞許多，會在兩週內寫完報告。真的很感謝您給我機會，讓我在會議上代表 DTU 廣告部門與會。

彼得 敬上

176. 為什麼趙女士要寫電子郵件給歐馬列先生？
- A 感謝他的建議
- **B 提供一些商務會議的資訊**
- C 確認預訂參與會議
- D 還款給他

177. 趙女士提到大會的什麼事？
- A 企業領袖的演說讓它聲名大噪。
- B 它去年首度在舊金山舉行。
- **C 它提供與商務人士交流的機會。**
- D 它是認識法國商人的最佳地點。

178. DTU 公司沒有預支的花費是？
- **A 餐食費**
- B 住宿費
- C 機票費
- D 租車費

179. 大會上哪個演講取消了？

    A 創新圖像

    B 網頁設計世界

    C 4D 大商標

    D 設計大展

180. 歐馬列先生最可能在哪個部門工作？

    A 業務部

    B 廣告部

    C 人資部

    D 會計部

181–185 電子郵件

收件人：珍妮斯・沃克
              \<jwalker@dailynews.com\>
寄件人：瑞秋・杭特
              \<rhunter@homedecors.com\>
日期：5 月 10 日

親愛的沃克女士：

我們資料庫顯示，您的帳戶目前有逾期未繳的狀況 —— 居家維修 735.40 美元的欠款。3 月 13 日，有五名工人在您家維修屋頂破洞。費用明細已在 4 月 5 日寄給您，應於 4 月 23 日前繳納。滯納金為 50 美元，但只要即時付款就會撤銷滯納金。如果您已經付款，請儘快聯絡我們的總公司。由於我正在檢核您的帳戶，可以請您把所有相關信件寄給我嗎？

感謝。

家居裝飾帳戶管理經理
瑞秋・杭特 敬上

收件人：\<customerservicerepresentative
              @homedecors.com\>
寄件人：珍妮斯・沃克
              \<jwalker@dailynews.com\>
日期：5 月 11 日

致相關人士：

這是我第一次收到關於逾期欠款的狀況，也許你把維修明細寄到舊地址了。我在今年 4 月初已經搬離格林維爾市。可以把維修明細傳真到 432-433-3276，或是用電子郵件寄給我嗎？我的信箱是 jwalker@dailynews.com。

一收到明細我即刻就會全額付款。

感謝你。

祝好，

珍妮斯・沃克

181. 為什麼杭特女士要寄電子郵件給沃克女士？

    A 提醒她費用明細有誤

    B 詢問逾期未繳的款項

    C 為服務不周道歉

    D 追討滯納金

182. 杭特女士請沃克女士做什麼？

    A 影印帳單

    B 如期繳款

    C 查看她的帳戶

    D 繳清費用

183. 沃克女士請客服做什麼？

    A 傳真繳款文件給她

    B 繳訂金

    C 核對她的現址

    D 馬上打電話給她

184. 文中提到沃克女士的什麼事？

    A 她蓋了新房子。

    B 她搬到新家。

    C 她弄丟了繳款單。

    D 她四月出差。

185. 沃克女士的電子郵件中沒提到什麼？

    A 之前的住處

    B 電子信箱

    C 帳戶管理經理的名字

    D 傳真號碼

寄件人：傑森・姜
　　　　<jasonkang@resisdente.com>
收件人：帳單管理部門
　　　　<bills@planpower.com>
日期：6 月 17 日
主旨：單據 A893-06

致相關人士：

哈囉，我來信的目的是為了我五月分的電費帳單，金額比前幾個月多出很多，平常大概都是 350 美元。我不想錯過繳費期限，但想知道金額為什麼會暴增。如果這是異常變化，我希望帳單可以有所調整。我知道我的電表太老舊，所以我也在考慮是否要替換它。

如果需要技術人員來檢查，週間的每天中午前都可以到府；我會在家，也希望他們作業時我能夠在場。

祝好，

傑森・姜

新年住宅技術人員工作日誌表

6 月 30 日

技術人員姓名	服務地址	服務時間	服務內容
寶拉・莫瑞亞	鑽石大道 2249 號	早上 10:52	維修電表
吉尼・帕多瓦尼	紅丘路 2809 號	下午 12:38	更換電表
巴拉克・希爾頓	艾林頓大道 76 號	下午 1:40	更換電表
布萊德・霍布金斯	聖人路 8100 號	下午 3:52	檢查電表

寄件人：帳單管理部門
　　　　<bills@planpower.com>
收件人：傑森・姜
　　　　<jasonkang@resisdente.com>
日期：6 月 30 日
主旨：單據 A893-06

親愛的姜先生：

感謝您聯繫「有計畫電力」。這封信是要通知您，您的電費暴增是因為電表出錯。拜訪您紅丘住處的維修人員發現，由於電表老舊，因而錯誤記錄了您的用電狀況。

電表已經換新，日後不會再發生類似問題。機器故障只會影響到您五月的帳單；總金額 127.18 美元將顯示在您下個月的帳單上。如有其他疑問，也歡迎向我們反應。

有計畫電力客服專員
馬克・迪隆 敬上

186. 為什麼會寄第一封電子郵件？
　　[A] 展延期限
　　[B] 要求收據
　　[C] 詢問金額狀況
　　[D] 申請網路帳單

187. 文中提到姜先生什麼事？
　　[A] 他正確地辨認出問題所在。
　　[B] 他最近搬新家。
　　[C] 他和迪隆先生接洽多次。
　　[D] 他想關閉在有計畫電力的帳戶。

188. 誰在 6 月 30 日到訪姜先生的家？
　　[A] 寶拉・莫瑞亞
　　[B] 吉尼・帕多瓦尼
　　[C] 巴拉克・希爾頓
　　[D] 布萊德・霍布金斯

189. 第二封電子郵件中，第一段、第三行的「registered」最接近下列哪個意思？
　　[A] 出席
　　[B] 准許
　　[C] 記錄
　　[D] 允許

190. 迪隆先生在電子郵件中指出什麼？

    Ⓐ 繳費期限已過了

    Ⓑ 該問題只發生一個月

    Ⓒ 正提供新服務。

    Ⓓ 已經下訂新的電表

191–195 廣告、電子郵件和簡訊

旋律音樂學院

98105 華盛頓州西雅圖市聖人街 32 號

www.melody-music.ac

旋律音樂學院很高興宣布下一季度的表演——包括古典、爵士、嘻哈和流行樂。

歡迎加入我們觀賞所有演出！您可以買下整季所有表演的票，或是針對特定表演購票。購買全季票的聽眾將享原票價的半價優惠。

* 莫札特團令人印象深刻的爵士樂表演。
3 月 18—22 日

* 歌手尤金·柳的得獎流行音樂表演。
只有一天 —— 4 月 7 日

* 西雅圖樂團的古典樂演出。
4 月 15—22 日

* 凱薩琳·溫斯蕾歌唱與現場吉他伴奏。
4 月 23—27 日

收件人：珍·奧斯丁
寄件人：泰勒·延
副本：山謬·大衛
主旨：KG 電子參訪
日期：3 月 29 日

奧斯丁女士您好：

謹代表 KG 電子的人事部門，我們很開心您能在 4 月 21 日到 23 日，蒞臨指導新的人事管理軟體如何使用。我已如您所要求的，備好房間還有必要設備，像是桌電、投影機和麥克風。如果您的簡報還需要進一步協助，不用遲疑，儘管讓我知道。

為了感謝您，我們的部門主管大衛先生已做特殊安排，將令您本次行程更加難忘。在您蒞臨的第一天晚上，他訂好一間相當知名的義大利餐廳的晚餐。第二天，我們可以一起去旋律音樂學院看場出色的演出。

KG 電子
泰勒·延 敬上

泰勒·延的手機

傳訊者：山謬·大衛
收訊時間：上午 8:45

嗨，我收到奧斯丁女士的消息。她原來的班機延誤了。所以她抵達的時間有變。不過我們今天的會議還是會舉行。她想把娛樂活動延到明天，這樣行程就不會那麼趕。如果由我來訂票，折扣會比你訂票來得多。可以請你把晚餐的訂位時間延後嗎？如果沒辦法，請把它取消。很抱歉造成你的不便。

---

191. 文中提到旋律音樂學院什麼？

    Ⓐ 學院現址還有博物館。

    Ⓑ 正招聘新的指揮。

    Ⓒ 提供小朋友音樂課程。

    Ⓓ 有很多不同風格的音樂演出。

192. 買全季票的觀眾可以拿到多少折扣？

    Ⓐ 20%

    Ⓑ 30%

    Ⓒ 40%

    Ⓓ 50%

193. 奧斯丁女士訪問期間要做什麼？

    Ⓐ 修改法律文件

    Ⓑ 展示如何使用某些軟體

    Ⓒ 修理簡報設備

    Ⓓ 進行調查

194. 奧斯丁女士本來會觀賞的表演是？
　　　Ⓐ 莫札特團
　　　Ⓑ 尤金‧柳的演出
　　　Ⓒ 西雅圖樂團
　　　Ⓓ 凱薩琳‧溫斯蕾的演出

195. 延先生被要求做什麼？
　　　Ⓐ 訂機位
　　　Ⓑ 安排會議時間
　　　Ⓒ 訓練新進員工
　　　Ⓓ 取消晚餐訂位

196–200 廣告、線上表格和評論

> ### OHQ 冷凍櫃
> #### 行動冷凍櫃
>
> OHQ 貨櫃提供行動冷凍櫃給餐廳、咖啡廳、雜貨店和其他需要冷藏空間的行業。
>
> **所有的冷凍櫃都包括：**
>
> **1.** 可上鎖的門扣、止滑地墊、內部日光燈照明裝置
>
> **2.** 20 公尺長的電纜線
>
> **商家服務：**
>
> 冷凍櫃可達蘇格蘭的任何地點。
>
> 所有型號都可以短租、月租或年租。
>
> **可供選擇的型號：**
>
> | 冷凍櫃 | 門型 | 長度（公尺） | 地面空間（平方公尺） | 內部容量（立方公尺） |
> |---|---|---|---|---|
> | 經濟型 | 單門 | 3.0 公尺 | 7.5 平方公尺 | 18.75 立方公尺 |
> | 標準型 | 雙門 | 6.0 公尺 | 15.0 平方公尺 | 37.5 立方公尺 |
> | 超級型 | 雙門 | 9.0 公尺 | 22.5 平方公尺 | 56.25 立方公尺 |
> | 加大超級型 | 加大雙門 | 12.0 公尺 | 30.0 平方公尺 | 75.0 立方公尺 |
>
> 如果對於決定型號需要任何協助，我們出色的客服專員會向您建議最適合的方案。欲查詢更多資訊，可上官網
> http://www.OHQ.com

> http://www.OHQ.com/inquiry
>
> ### OHQ 冷凍櫃──客戶詢問表單
>
> 姓名：艾登‧帕克
> 商家：帕克咖啡
> 電子信箱：<parkscafé@plantomorrow.com>
> 日期：10 月 14 日
>
> ---
>
> 哈囉，我的朋友比爾‧佛德向我介紹貴公司。他的店正在使用貴公司的冷凍櫃。我也是餐廳老闆，而我們的冷凍庫容量，已經冰不下需要的食材量了。所以我們需要一個可放在大樓後門旁的 OHQ 冷凍櫃。容量不需要額外加大，但需要雙門，好方便補貨和取貨。請您推薦我哪個型號合適，並告知可能送達的日期。另外，我也想知道冷凍櫃有沒有溫度顯示的數位面板，我們需要一直嚴密監控溫度。
>
> 感謝。

> ### 顧客評論
>
> 我使用 OHQ 冷凍櫃大概四個月了，讓我十分滿意。我也很高興可以享有第一個月免租費的好友推薦專案，讓我和朋友都享受到免租費一個月的優惠。我一開始用的冷凍櫃是 37.5 立方公尺的容量，不過這一個月下來，很明顯我需要更大尺寸的冷凍櫃，以服務增加的顧客。我打電話給 OHQ 的隔天，公司專員便送來了新冷凍櫃，完美符合我的需求。大家如果需要營業用、而且好用的冷凍設備，我非常推薦 OHQ 冷凍櫃。
>
> 帕克咖啡老闆艾登‧帕克

196. OHQ 冷凍櫃的廣告沒提到什麼資訊？
　　　Ⓐ 門的數量
　　　Ⓑ 照明類型
　　　Ⓒ 可調整的溫度範圍
　　　Ⓓ 冷凍櫃容量

197. 文中提到帕克先生什麼？

    Ⓐ 他曾是佛德先生的同事。

    Ⓑ 他支持當地社區。

    Ⓒ 他想轉業開配送公司。

    Ⓓ 他拿到 OHQ 冷凍櫃的折扣。

198. 文中提到帕克咖啡什麼？

    Ⓐ 特色是使用有機食材。

    Ⓑ 位於 OHQ 公司附近。

    Ⓒ 想要延長營業時間。

    Ⓓ 生意蒸蒸日上。

199. 帕克先生現在使用的冷凍櫃是哪款？

    Ⓐ 經濟型

    Ⓑ 標準型

    Ⓒ 超級型

    Ⓓ 加大超級型

200. 在顧客評論中，第一行的「contented」，
最接近下列哪個意思？

    Ⓐ 滿意的

    Ⓑ 生氣的

    Ⓒ 沮喪的

    Ⓓ 驚訝的

ACTUAL TEST ②

PART 5 P. 44-46

◎ **Part 5 解答請見 P.457**

101. 西達韋爾雜貨店的銷售人員在**他們**加班時，會領到加班費。

102. 洪塔沙女士的前雇主們**大力**推薦她。

103. 大衛先生的工廠使用高品質又**不貴的**機械元件，降低了成本。

104. 由於天氣情況惡化，出版會議改**為**明天召開。

105. 阿爾發科技的最新軟體，讓出版社發行報紙比起以往**更加容易**。

106. 山口先生演講後將會限時開放問答。

107. 從 Easy-To-Go.com 買東西**的顧客**，通常會在三個工作天內拿到訂購商品。

108. 這個培訓課程的**目標**，是讓企業主有辦法做出明智的決定。

109. 李女士**主要**負責監督霍克斯戴爾工廠的品管過程。

110. 谷林攝影大賽的**參賽**收件到 5 月 25 日截止。

111. 芮莉織品企業報告公司去年**在**收益方面成長了 10%。

112. 因為材料成本降低，極優實驗室尖端的顯微鏡價格將比**預期**來得低。

113. 馬克思威爾植物園**整個**春季，每週四早上十點到下午兩點都可免費入園。

114. 所有**操作**鑽孔設備的員工都必須穿戴護目鏡。

115. **只要**您證明車輛的所有權，就可以和我們經銷商直接訂購新鑰匙。

116. 我們鼓勵賓客留下**建議**，讓我們可以改進飛航服務。

117. 會計部門去年不尋常地有大量員工退休，釋出了 13 個**空缺**。

118. 肯恩家是一間位於丹佛斯維爾、提供全面服務的攝影工作室，特別**擅長**拍攝家族照。

119. 雲雀丘健康中心向來都**樂意**請有證照的專業人員加入我們工作團隊。

120. 為因應需求增加，政府暫時取消了建材進口量的**限制**。

121. 春天小館的蔬果盤現在非常流行，既討喜、價格也**實惠**。

122. **雖然**戴維森先生沒有直接面對顧客的經驗，他仍自願在服務台幫忙。

123. 史密斯水電公司總共有八輛卡車，**其中**四輛目前在維修廠。

124. 漢普頓會計公司限制國外出差，並鼓勵使用線上視訊會議，**減少了**公司開銷。

125. 道森企業在記者會中宣布，它計劃拓展**進**歐洲。

126. 產品寄出**幾乎**有一個月了，我們應該追問貨運公司進度。

127. 為了開拓財源，五年來很多當地果園**已開始**迎合觀光客的需求。

128. 氣象專家預測**接連**三天都會下雨，可紓解這季節反常的炎熱。

129. 加勒比海灣飯店的廚房全天無休，確保您在**任何時間**想要用餐，都能享用到餐飲服務。

130. 雅各‧李向經理報告海外顧客的客訴，經理她承諾會**調查**相關問題。

131–134 資訊

高科技公司工作超過兩年的全職員工,都有資格申請內部轉調或晉升的機會。有意願者應該先和主管面談,並且將和外部應徵者一起競爭。如果外部招募不符合公司最佳利益,具備完整資格的內部員工將獲優先考慮。

131. Ⓐ 符合資格的
Ⓑ 合作的
Ⓒ 排外的
Ⓓ 重要的

132. Ⓐ 有意願者應該先和主管面談。
Ⓑ 其實,每個員工每天都需要回報工時。
Ⓒ 舉例來說,給予全職員工更優勢的福利方案。
Ⓓ 我們很高興歡迎高科技公司團隊的新進員工。

133. Ⓐ 因素
Ⓑ 應徵者
Ⓒ 職業
Ⓓ 供應商

134. Ⓐ 偏好的
Ⓑ 更合意的
Ⓒ 優先權
Ⓓ 更喜歡

135–138 文章

麥可劇場將會加演賈絲汀·凱依的戲劇《群星閃耀》的場次。

門票需求的增加超乎預期,最後一場演出如今將在 3 月 18 日登場。之所以加演也是意外,因為 2 月 2 日的開幕場演出飽受評論家的批評,起初門票銷售表現並不好。不過,演出突然在年輕人之間大受歡迎,他們大多都是在網路得知演出訊息。他們對劇中探索經濟議題和職涯選擇的部分,明顯很感興趣。

135. Ⓐ 被需求的
Ⓑ 苛求的
Ⓒ 有所要求
Ⓓ 需求

136. Ⓐ 傑出的
Ⓑ 深的
Ⓒ 嚴厲的
Ⓓ 敏捷的

137. Ⓐ 全部的演員都是當地居民。
Ⓑ 當地企業領袖來觀賞首演。
Ⓒ 起初門票銷售表現也不好。
Ⓓ 不只如此,劇院公司在此已經很多年了。

138. Ⓐ 明顯的
Ⓑ 更明顯的
Ⓒ 顯著性
Ⓓ 明顯地

139–142 通知

艾默生廣播將在 4 月 5 日慶祝 25 週年,這是長達四分之一個世紀且具啟發性的廣播服務。過去幾年來,我們持續提供聽眾即時新聞、發人深思的故事,還有來自全球的流行音樂。現在,我們希望您也來共襄盛舉,一起在 4 月 5 日晚上 7 點到 9 點,前往位於查爾斯大道的錄音室,參觀開放的錄音室並一窺幕後魔法。觀看我們的數位錄音設備,還可以和幾位您所喜愛的廣播員見面。參訪完全免費但需要報名。我們希望您可以參加這特別的活動。

139. Ⓐ 演奏會
Ⓑ 發展
Ⓒ (電視,廣播)轉播
Ⓓ 討論

140. Ⓐ 提供
Ⓑ 將會提供
Ⓒ 正在提供
Ⓓ 已提供

141. A 我們希望在明年和當地另一間廣播電台合併。

B 還可以和幾位你所喜愛的廣播員見面。

C 這是四月分行程的第二個活動。

D 電台會持續成為您鄰里重要的一份子。

142. A 特別的

B 專攻

C 特別地

D 專門化

143–146 電子郵件

收件人：大衛・金
　　　　<dkim@eleganthotel.com>
寄件人：艾柏特・李
　　　　<alee@eleganthotel.com>
日期：6 月 22 日
主旨：午安

親愛的大衛：

我最近接獲你即將晉升的通知。雖然紐約部門的總經理職位正式上任日是 8 月 1 日，我還是想要現在獻上最好的祝福。

職位變動可能頗具挑戰性，所以如果需要任何協助請儘管告訴我。你在新加坡優雅飯店擔任協理時表現一向傑出。我有信心你可以勝任新職務。

恭喜！

艾柏特・李 敬上

143. A 晉升

B 獎賞

C 事件

D 旅行

144. A 開始了

B 開始

C 可能開始

D 已開始

145. A 富有挑戰性的

B 挑戰

C 挑戰

D 受到挑戰的

146. A 紐約飯店更大，而且有更多設施。

B 我目前在面試各項職缺的應徵者。

C 在此期間，向同事詢問旅館折扣。

D 我有信心你可以勝任新職務。

PART 7 P. 51–71

147–148 簡訊

傳訊者：蒙特拉・哈珊
收訊者：葛瑞絲・金

葛瑞絲，我智慧型手機電池的電快用光了。我想我把充電線放在辦公室。

可以請你幫我打電話給客戶，告訴他我會晚大概 20 分鐘到嗎？我現在趕回去辦公室拿充電線。

147. 為什麼哈珊先生寄簡訊給金女士？

A 詢問她有沒有找到他的充電線

B 請她聯絡客戶

C 提醒她要替電池充電

D 確認會計部門的位置

148. 哈珊先生接下來可能會做什麼？

A 找他的電腦

B 回到辦公室

C 買新的充電線

D 聯絡技術支援部門

戴頓咖啡店老闆布蘭登‧艾瑞特，在史米森大道 623 號上簽下了第二間餐廳的租約。

該建築鄰近滾石演奏廳，前身是卡羅金融集團的分部。艾瑞特先生最近的創業——皇冠小吃，將在 8 月 1 日開始營業。不過營運初期只會在傍晚營業，目的是要在開始提供午餐前建立顧客群，尤其鎖定演奏廳的觀眾。艾瑞特先生的第一間餐廳戴頓咖啡店，位在第一街上，就在公車站牌「勝利雜貨店」旁邊。主廚潔西卡‧崔將督管這兩間店。

149. 這篇文章是有關於什麼？
Ⓐ 一間新餐廳開張
Ⓑ 一名傑出的房地產仲介
Ⓒ 價格變動
Ⓓ 餐廳位置搬遷

150. 文中提到關於皇冠小吃什麼事？
Ⓐ 它鄰近公共運輸路線。
Ⓑ 它預期能吸引演奏廳的觀眾。
Ⓒ 它會從 8 月 1 日開始供應午餐。
Ⓓ 它是艾瑞特先生的第三間餐廳。

151–153 備忘錄

寄件人：阿歷克斯‧包德溫
收件人：葛瑞森建築全體員工
日期：6 月 15 日
主旨：全員大會

致全體員工，

下週一 6 月 29 日，將有客座講者蒞臨我們在 304 號會議室舉辦的員工大會。迪‧伊希布拉姆維奇是非凡公司在瑞士伯恩的資深建築師，她在當地已工作十年之久。她領導了伯恩住宅區，以及羅馬泰坦摩天大樓的設計專案。兩項專案都因為創新設計取得國際獎項肯定。

伊希布拉姆維奇女士在歐洲闖出名堂之前，曾在舊金山的動感建築組織（DAO）待過六年。也就是在 DAO 中，我才有機會和她合作多項計畫。伊希布拉姆維奇女士會在倫敦待兩個星期，並答應要來我們會議上演講，談談她多項深受國際推崇的建築計畫。

所有員工都必須參加。

151. 為什麼會有這篇備忘錄？
Ⓐ 宣布開分公司的計畫
Ⓑ 聘用新員工
Ⓒ 提出建設計畫
Ⓓ 介紹一名建築師的成就

152. 關於伊希布拉姆維奇女士，包德溫先生說了什麼？
Ⓐ 她將為他的公司主導一個設計專案。
Ⓑ 她打算開創自己的事業。
Ⓒ 她之前是他的同事。
Ⓓ 她要搬到新城市。

153. 葛瑞森建築位於哪裡？
Ⓐ 倫敦
Ⓑ 舊金山
Ⓒ 羅馬
Ⓓ 伯恩

154–155 訊息串

愛德溫‧鍾〔下午 3:24〕：
茉莉兩小時前發給你一封有銷售數字的電子郵件，她想知道你是否會回信。

金‧卡特〔下午 3:25〕：
我不在位子上。你不覺得她會這麼關心這件事，是因為成果不如預期嗎？

愛德溫‧鍾〔下午 3:26〕：
可能吧。

金‧卡特〔下午 3:27〕：
我被叫去檢查包裝機，它無法正常運作。

愛德溫‧鍾〔下午 3:28〕：
需要我叫維修人員嗎？

金・卡特〔下午 3:30〕：
我想自己處理就好。你何不在週二早上安排電話會議？團隊需要談談這份報告。

愛德溫・鍾〔下午 3:30〕：
好的。

送出

154. 下午 3:25 的時候，卡特先生寫道：「我不在位子上。」他最可能的意思是？
- Ⓐ 他早退。
- Ⓑ 他將錯過截止日期。
- Ⓒ 他將順道拜訪鍾先生的辦公室。
- **Ⓓ 他沒辦法回覆茉莉。**

155. 鍾先生被要求做什麼？
- Ⓐ 查閱文件
- **Ⓑ 安排一個會議**
- Ⓒ 確認旅遊計畫
- Ⓓ 修理一些裝置

156–158 信件

瑞秋美術館

3 月 15 日
珍妮佛・拜克女士

親愛的拜克女士：

您是瑞秋美術館的會員，不久後將能享有特別優惠。從 4 月 1 日到 28 日，會員在紀念禮品店將享額外七折的商品折扣，在館內咖啡店裡用餐還可享一杯免費飲料。此外在 4 月 28 日以前，加入會員的入會費將打八五折。所以邀請您的親朋好友和同事，到我們官網上登記成為會員。

4 月來逛美術館還有一個好康。四樓為古波斯藝術家之雕塑和繪畫的特色展區，原先是關閉的，但從這個月的每週二開始，將全面對外開放到晚間 7:30。該展區嚴選的圖片影像也能在官網上看到。

我們期待您大駕光臨。

會員管理部主任

賈絲汀・劉 敬上

156. 文中提到關於瑞秋美術館什麼事？
- **Ⓐ 有吃飯的地方。**
- Ⓑ 將會關閉一個月。
- Ⓒ 將舉行照片展。
- Ⓓ 有舉辦藝術課程的工作坊。

157. 週二將有什麼地方不同以往？
- Ⓐ 入館免費。
- **Ⓑ 額外開放其他展覽區。**
- Ⓒ 餐廳營業時間延長。
- Ⓓ 大家會選購波斯藝術品。

158. 下列句子最適合出現在 [1]、[2]、[3]、[4] 的哪個位置中？
「4 月來逛美術館還有一個好康。」
- Ⓐ [1]
- Ⓑ [2]
- **Ⓒ [3]**
- Ⓓ [4]

159–160 告示

告示

9 月 8 日——本報於 9 月 7 日當期公告關於公共圖書館將進行分館整修計畫的文章，誤把克爾克絲坦和道奇維爾分館的休館日期寫為 10 月 15 日。然而據圖書館發言人表示，只有克爾克絲坦分館會從 10 月 15 號開始休館到 11 月 20 日。道奇維爾分館將如常運作，直到克爾克絲坦分館 11 月 21 日重新開放後，才會開始休館到 12 月 25 日。欲知詳細資訊，請上圖書館官方網站。若我們的錯誤造成任何不便，誠摯向您道歉。

159. 哪裡比較有可能看到這項告示？
- Ⓐ 在圖書館的年度報告
- Ⓑ 在聚會的行程表上
- Ⓒ 在整修平面圖上
- **Ⓓ 在當地報紙上**

160. 道奇維爾分館將從什麼時候開始休館，以進行翻修工程？
- Ⓐ 10 月 15 日
- Ⓑ 11 月 20 日
- **Ⓒ 11 月 21 日**
- Ⓓ 12 月 25 日

161–164 文章

馳遠騎士車款將停售！

賈邁爾·羅培茲撰文

颱風機車，也就是馳遠騎士車款目前的製造商，週二宣布將延後發布新的快速 DM 車款。同業得知消息紛紛表示驚訝。喜好馳遠騎士車款的熱情用戶也湧上官網，針對颱風機車取消眾所期盼的五月新款發表，紛紛表示不解。

之所以下此決定，似乎是因為他們決意要在快速 DM 車款加裝油電混合動力系統，才會導致問題發生。颱風機車坦承，現階段的系統原型尺寸大又笨重，因此遭到淘汰。這種能源系統的設計，需要一個比預期來得更大的車體。他們對系統外部的耐受度也有疑慮。

不只是設計困難，颱風機車車廠的設備是用來生產前一個型號的產品，目前也沒有準備好生產快速 DM 混合能源型馬達。工廠需要採購新機械設備，產線也需要重新配置。

颱風機車兩年前力挽馳遠車款，助其擺脫破產命運，受到車迷的大力讚揚。這兩年間改變了什麼？而現在開始，他們得再次贏回顧客的信譽。

161. 文中提到關於颱風機車什麼事？
- **Ⓐ 擁有馳遠騎士車款品牌。**
- Ⓑ 有意要以折扣價格販售一個車款。
- Ⓒ 正在搬遷總公司。
- Ⓓ 五月會發布新款摩托車。

162. 下列何者關於動力系統的缺點，並沒有在文中提到？
- Ⓐ 它很重。
- **Ⓑ 它不便宜。**
- Ⓒ 它不夠堅固。
- Ⓓ 它太大了。

163. 為什麼工廠需要改建？
- Ⓐ 它不符合新規定。
- Ⓑ 它已超過 20 年沒有更新了。
- **Ⓒ 它有的是生產舊型號的設備。**
- Ⓓ 它太小了，沒辦法同時生產兩種型號。

164. 下列句子最適合出現在 [1]、[2]、[3]、[4] 的哪個位置中？
「而現在開始，他們得再次贏回顧客的信譽。」
- Ⓐ [1]
- Ⓑ [2]
- Ⓒ [3]
- **Ⓓ [4]**

165–168 文章

美髮造型沙龍

8 月 9 日——美髮造型沙龍在上週初風光開幕。店長兼髮型設計師的亞瑟·李表示，開幕活動的出席很踴躍，過去一週以來也有很多人預約。昨天首次到沙龍的詹姆士·摩根說，他對這間店已廣受歡迎並不感到意外。「剪髮品質很好，」他說，「走路過來也很近，和我還有很多人工作的繁忙商業區在同一條街上。」

的確，從達靈頓大學往下走，美髮造型沙龍位於人來人往的麥迪遜大道上。「我選擇麥迪遜大道，就是因為它鄰近校園，而我想吸引大學生和教職員前來。」李先生在開幕式上表示。

另一名新顧客提到，沙龍服務和美髮保養產品的費用都不算貴。「我很高興可以找到一間價位負擔得起的好髮廊，」對服務相當滿意的顧客米雪兒·林說，「我絕對還會再來。」

欲知更多資訊或預約，請儘速致電 031-532-4343 或上官網 www.hairstylesalon.com。

165. 這篇文章的目的為何？
- Ⓐ 宣告店家搬家的消息
- Ⓑ 鼓勵髮型師參加某個活動
- **Ⓒ 介紹臨近地區有一間新店開張**
- Ⓓ 告知學生優惠訊息

166. 文中提到摩根先生什麼事？
    Ⓐ 他在麥迪遜大道上工作。
    Ⓑ 他是美髮造型沙龍的所有人。
    Ⓒ 他參與了這間沙龍的盛大開幕式。
    Ⓓ 他透過網路預約剪髮。

167. 李先生為什麼替他的店選擇這個地點？
    Ⓐ 這個社區沒有其他競爭對手。
    Ⓑ 這附近有很多停車場。
    Ⓒ 這裡相較其他地點的房租比較低。
    Ⓓ 這裡鄰近一間大學。

168. 文中提到關於美髮造型沙龍什麼事？
    Ⓐ 正在招募新的髮型師。
    Ⓑ 販售價格合理的美髮用品。
    Ⓒ 新顧客可享優惠。
    Ⓓ 贈送美髮護理優惠券。

169–171 廣告

> ### 企業世界的訂戶！
>
> 即刻開始，只要註冊就能在每週三早上收到客製化的電子郵件，提供您最新的商業和財經新聞，還可以得到《企業世界》雜誌月刊每個月的詳盡報導，而不需要再等30 天。廣泛的主題任君隨喜好挑選，每週都可以就相關主題收到好文章。這項服務只提供給《企業世界》的訂戶。
>
> 要啟用服務很簡單。只要上 www.companyworld.com，點選「加入客製化電子郵件」，提供您的電子郵件信箱和選擇服務偏好，您可以隨時依需求更改，也可持續得知相關訂閱資訊。

169. 這則廣告是在宣傳什麼？
    Ⓐ 和財經專家的討論會
    Ⓑ 網路付款的方式
    Ⓒ 每週電子報
    Ⓓ 企業投資課程

170. 文中談到關於這項服務什麼事？
    Ⓐ 它是設計給某個刊物的訂戶。
    Ⓑ 從現在起 30 天都有效。
    Ⓒ 在企業主之間已經很流行。
    Ⓓ 這是最新服務系列中的第三項服務。

171. 感興趣的人要怎麼做才可以取得服務？
    Ⓐ 寄出申請
    Ⓑ 上網註冊
    Ⓒ 打電話
    Ⓓ 寄信請求

172–175 訊息串

> **多明尼克・佛羅雷斯〔下午 2:26〕：**
> 韓女士，看來明天會有暴風雨，所以您醫院新東側建築的屋頂工程需要延後。
>
> **秀智・韓〔下午 2:27〕：**
> 意思是說整天都停工嗎？
>
> **多明尼克・佛羅雷斯〔下午 2:27〕：**
> 當然不是！我的員工會協助湯尼・琳姆先生的工人維修老舊建築的樑架。
>
> **秀智・韓〔下午 2:28〕：**
> 還需要多久才會修好？
>
> **多明尼克・佛羅雷斯〔下午 2:28〕：**
> 我確認一下。
>
> **多明尼克・佛羅雷斯〔下午 2:29〕：**
> 湯尼，你的工作進度如何？
>
> **湯尼・琳姆〔下午 2:31〕：**
> 到今天早上為止一切都很順利，但結構工程師有來看翻修狀況後，我看接下來十天還得加班趕工。
>
> **多明尼克・佛羅雷斯〔下午 2:32〕：**
> 我的員工明天去幫你的話，你覺得怎麼樣？
>
> **湯尼・琳姆〔下午 2:33〕：**
> 太棒了！這樣的話大概可以三天內完工吧。
>
> **秀智・韓〔下午 2:35〕：**
> 所以您的員工會需要進到舊大樓嗎？
>
> **多明尼克・佛羅雷斯〔下午 2:36〕：**
> 明天的話，對。車停在舊大樓門口可以嗎？
>
> **秀智・韓〔下午 2:38〕：**
> 當然。大門附近的空間應該很夠。可以麻煩您提醒他們，車不要壓到草坪嗎？
>
> 送出

333

172. 佛羅雷斯先生指出，什麼會中斷明天的工程？

Ⓐ 有問題的機械

Ⓑ 延後到貨

Ⓒ 惡劣的天氣條件

Ⓓ 缺工

(NEW)

173. 下午 2 點 31 分時，當琳姆先生寫道：「我看接下來十天還得加班趕工。」他最可能的意思是？

Ⓐ 他的工人最近都沒有準時抵達。

Ⓑ 他的工人計劃要在週四提早下班。

Ⓒ 有兩個不同的工地需要用到他的工人。

Ⓓ 他的工人在建案裡將面臨更多挑戰。

174. 韓女士的職業最有可能是？

Ⓐ 園藝設計師

Ⓑ 醫院經理

Ⓒ 運輸業主管

Ⓓ 建材供應商

175. 佛羅雷斯先生問了什麼事？

Ⓐ 建築大門能否讓他們使用

Ⓑ 到最新大樓的路徑

Ⓒ 給予新蓋側翼大樓的建議

Ⓓ 停車許可

176–180 電子郵件

> 寄件人：黛柏拉·溫
> 收件人：提姆·安東尼
> 主旨：退休餐會
> 日期：5 月 9 日
>
> 親愛的提姆：
>
> 你知道，我是籌備道爾頓先生退休餐會的委員會成員。我們想要用過去十年，在各種企業活動所拍攝的照片做成投影片，目前正在找人製作。
>
> 我記得你跟我說過，你在大學修過攝影，所以我想問看看你有沒有興趣做這件事。如果你答應的話，我會再發一封信，請同仁在三天內提供照片，並儘早搜集給你讓

> 你方便作業。感謝你的協助，我很確定，道爾頓先生和團隊裡的其他人，都會很享受這部影片。
>
> 黛柏拉 敬上

> 寄件人：提姆·安東尼
> 收件人：黛柏拉·溫
> 主旨：回覆：退休餐會
> 日期：5 月 10 日
>
> 親愛的黛柏拉：
>
> 我很樂意製作道爾頓先生退休餐會上的投影片。我們都同意他是一位很棒的主管。不過，我並不是最適合做這件事情的人。我確實在一場活動上負責攝影，但事實上，我大學主修新聞。我想推薦你一位適合做投影片的人選，她叫做凱薩琳·海因茲。我相信她會有興趣。據我了解，她之前做過培訓課程的投影片。假如海因茲女士這次不能幫忙，請聯絡我，我到時候再向妳推薦其他人。
>
> 提姆 敬上

176. 溫女士和安東尼先生最有可能是怎樣認識彼此的？

Ⓐ 他們在同一間公司工作。

Ⓑ 他們上同一間大學。

Ⓒ 他們住在同一個公寓大樓裡。

Ⓓ 他們合作過某個特殊專案。

177. 溫女士主動提議要做什麼？

Ⓐ 整理退休餐會的邀請函

Ⓑ 為培訓課程影印資料

Ⓒ 從同仁那裡搜集照片

Ⓓ 參加之後的演出

178. 為什麼安東尼先生提到他學的是新聞？

Ⓐ 他想要調到另一個職位。

Ⓑ 溫女士需要人寫篇文章。

Ⓒ 溫女士請他確認他自己的資格。

Ⓓ 他想要澄清一些誤解。

179. 安東尼先生提到關於海因茲女士什麼事？
- **A** 她在這件事（製作投影片）上比他更有經驗。
- B 她在時間安排上比他更有彈性。
- C 她將接任道爾頓先生離職後的職位。
- D 她有新聞系畢業的大學學歷。

180. 溫女士為什麼還有可能會再次聯絡安東尼先生？
- A 他負責安排海因茲女士的行程。
- B 他可以為她報名培訓課程。
- C 他在公司全部的活動裡都負責拍照。
- **D** 他可以推薦其他人來提供協助。

181–185 廣告和電子郵件

> ### 創新中心
>
> 眺望海岸美景，創新中心結合休閒場所和您所需的商業服務。不但有 10 間大型會議廳，蛋白石會議室和藍寶石會議室也能提供給 10 人以下的小團體使用。
>
> 創新中心有正式的晚宴廳，也有更加舒適的餐館。單人、雙人或三人套房，均配備高速網路、傳真機和咖啡機。賓客也能使用室內和室外的游泳池。欲知更多資訊，請聯絡蘭迪 · 弗瑞德瑞克，電話 424-2769 或是電子郵件 randyfrederick@innovationcentre.com。

> 收件人：卡麥隆 · 杰
> <camerongee@bronzejournal.com>
> 寄件人：蘭迪 · 弗瑞德瑞克
> <randyfrederick@innovationcentre.com>
> 日期：3 月 21 日
> 主旨：訂房
>
> ---
>
> 親愛的杰女士：
>
> 感謝您預訂 6 月 12 日和 13 日的單人套房，並支付 300 美元的部分訂金。我們已為您 13 日的活動訂了蛋白石會議室，不過我們需要您在 4 月 1 日以前支付總共 500 美元的訂金，才能為您保留房間。
>
> 請告訴我們您的簡報需要什麼設備，我們可以提前為您準備會議室。

> 此外，關於您的午餐會，您需要聯絡我們的外燴經理莉莉 · 彭提亞克，她的電話是 424-4327 分機 22。
>
> 創新中心訂房經理
>
> 蘭迪 · 弗瑞德瑞克 敬上

181. 這個廣告的目標對象可能為何？
- A 家庭成員
- B 飯店主管
- C 新進員工
- **D** 商務專業人士

182. 廣告中沒有提及創新中心的哪一項特色？
- **A** 健身場所
- B 餐廳
- C 室內游泳池
- D 套房內的傳真機

183. 文中提到杰女士的什麼事？
- A 她是一間大公司的執行長。
- B 她之前住過創新中心。
- **C** 她負責某項簡報。
- D 她用優惠價格訂到會議室。

184. 文中提到關於杰女士的活動什麼事？
- A 會議室所需款項已經結清。
- **B** 參加人數少於十人。
- C 參與者將享有住房優惠。
- D 將在 4 月 1 日舉行。

185. 杰女士將會對彭提亞克女士要求什麼？
- A 取消訂房
- B 檢閱她的簡報
- **C** 準備餐點服務
- D 付款

http://www.middletownoffice.com

| 瀏覽 | 訂購 | 首頁 | 商品展示 | 連絡我們 |

米德爾敦辦公家具行

歡迎來到我們網站！瀏覽我們的商品清單，想像辦公區可以如此時尚便利。我們在里奇蒙海岬服務超過十年，高品質辦公家具肯定能滿足您的需求。

我們隨時提供下列交易方式：

● 新客戶享有免費送貨到府和包裝服務
● 學校和非營利組織享有大折扣（請聯絡我們獲取更多資訊）

寄件人：詹姆斯·哈雷
　　　　<jharley@standardlawfirm.co>
收件人：雷明頓·陳
　　　　<lchen@standardlawfirm.co>
日期：4 月 15 日
主旨：辦公家具升級

陳先生您好：

我研究了一陣子，想建議我們選擇米德爾敦辦公家具行，來選購辦公室裝修後的辦公桌和家具。雖說我們從來沒向這間家具行採購過東西，但他們的參考資料已經提供了很好的建議。

我們得決定一下，我覺得主辦公室要用比較大的辦公桌型（15 張桌子），還有符合該款式的檔案櫃和書架。至於在樓上工作的輔助團隊和實習生，我建議用比較簡單的桌款。

如果您接受我的建議，我想儘快下訂單，這樣家具就能到貨，此時剛好大多數同仁都出差到紐約開會。

不過，這樣辦公區就會看起來很髒亂，畢竟我們還要把舊家具清空，等新家具來才行。

再請您告訴我，您對上述總結建議的看法。

詹姆斯

訂單號碼：F2465Z

聯絡人：詹姆斯·哈雷 (067) 523-4352

寄件地址：94108 加州舊金山市方形街 252 號，標準法律事務所

寄件日期和時間：8 月 8 到 9 日，11 點到晚上 6 點間

數量	商品代碼	描述
15	CDF4524	戴頓辦公桌
15	FCT1275	一流檔案櫃，淺褐色
6	AA2042	水晶書架，淺褐色
7	GE3182	多功能辦公桌

注意： 由於 AA2042 商品的需求過多，我們位於凱西鎮的店面目前缺貨。這些商品將會直接從工廠送到您的辦公室，所以會從查爾斯敦運送到舊金山，而非由凱西鎮寄送。有可能會延後兩到三天才會送達，我們會盡力讓整筆訂單在同一天到貨。

186. 文中提到關於米德爾敦辦公家具行什麼事？
Ⓐ 提供免費室內裝潢服務。
Ⓑ 對教育機構提供特別優惠。
Ⓒ 最近拓展新產品。
Ⓓ 近期開設分店。

187. 關於標準法律事務所的訂單，下列描述何者最可能為真？
Ⓐ 免運費。
Ⓑ 裡面有已經停產的產品。
Ⓒ 訂單已趕不上八月的配送。
Ⓓ 其中包括輔助團隊所挑選的型號。

188. 為什麼哈雷先生想要在特定時間內讓商品送達？
Ⓐ 他可以拿到額外折扣。
Ⓑ 有場重要的會議需要這些辦公家具。
Ⓒ 他需要額外的時間來選購新家具。
Ⓓ 他想要減輕同仁的不便。

189. 哪個產品可能會被放在標準法律事務所的二樓？
- A 戴頓辦公桌
- B 一流檔案櫃
- C 水晶書架
- **D 多功能辦公桌**

190. 根據表格，家具都在哪裡生產？
- A 舊金山
- **B 查爾斯敦**
- C 紐約
- D 凱西鎮

191–195 電子郵件、菜單和意見卡

寄件人：納森・傑若米
              <njerome@happydiningarea. com>
收件人：約翰・麥可尼爾
              <jmcneil@happydiningarea. com>
日期：7 月 11 日，週二
主旨：試菜活動

麥可尼爾先生您好，

令人難以置信，距離德瑞莎女士到訪不到兩週了！既然她的評論會在當地報紙上登出，我們何不精選菜色，呈現「幸福餐廳」最好的一面？為了得到當天菜單的建議，我決定在下週四舉行一場特別的試菜活動。

對於試菜活動要提供的菜色，我有幾個建議。何不安排無肉但令人滿意的主菜？如此一來，可以強調我們的素食菜色。或許烤海鯛魚也是不錯的選擇。不過，我堅持一定要呈獻新的特製披薩，也就是我們打算在平時菜單上推出的那款。當然，這也得確定到時候磚窯已經蓋好。另外，我想我們可以提供至少兩道總是廣受歡迎的水果甜點。不過我有信心，身為主廚的你，一定能把最終的菜單確定下來。

最後，我想要讓來參與試菜活動的客人，能有機會現場參觀廚房。請告訴我你的看法，還有怎麼準備最好。

感謝。

納森 敬上

TEST 2

PART 7

幸福餐廳試菜活動菜單

7 月 20 日週四

蒜醬烤海鯛

牛排與小黃瓜沙拉

辣醬烤雞

胡桃起司蛋糕

蒸鮮貝花椰菜濃湯

燻鮭魚與馬鈴薯泥

試菜活動意見卡

姓名：潔西・傑克森

請留下您參加幸福餐廳試菜活動的心得。

我很滿意小黃瓜料理溫和的甜味，不過醬汁對我來說有點酸；海鯛則是好得超乎預期；烤雞很嫩，不過整體來說不太好吃；甜點很美味但有點乾。貴餐廳廚房的實用設計讓我印象深刻。我很期待能吃到之後新推出的窯烤披薩。很遺憾今天沒辦法品嚐到。

191. 為什麼要舉辦這場試菜活動？
- **A 為美食評論家的到來做準備**
- B 為了選出參賽用的菜色
- C 為了測試主廚應徵者的實力
- D 為了選出平日菜單要新增的菜色

192. 電子郵件第二段、第二行中的「satisfying」最接近下列哪個意思？
- A 深的
- B 豐富的
- **C 令人心滿意足的**
- D 有創意的

193. 文中提到關於試菜活動的菜單什麼事？
- A 列舉了免費供應的菜色。
- **B 包括傑若米先生所推薦的菜色。**
- C 在餐廳廚房裡供客人享用。
- D 平常日都沒有供應。

194. 傑克森女士可能最喜歡哪一道料理？
- Ⓐ **海鯛**
- Ⓑ 湯品
- Ⓒ 小黃瓜
- Ⓒ 雞肉

195. 文中提到磚窯什麼？
- Ⓐ 對廚房來說太大了。
- Ⓑ 需要修理。
- Ⓒ 沒有通過安檢。
- Ⓓ **還在興建。**

196–200 電子郵件、傳單和簡訊

收件人：學生
寄件人：賈麥爾・克勞佛
主旨：系列講座
日期：5 月 5 日

各位學生：

好消息！伊藤恕沙女士同意在這個夏天出席系列講座。身為實習學生的你們要負責安排她在 8 月 19 到 21 日在校期間的住宿，完成相關文件的核准，讓她順利拿到酬金。也要預約好她簡報所需的場所。我建議朝代演講廳不錯，可以容納最多人，不過，商院大樓裡的其他簡報廳也都可以。

另外，如果恕沙女士提供摘要，請你們設計傳單，並張貼在全商院大樓的公共區域。我想你們六位能妥善分工而沒有有任何問題。

感謝！

迪克森商學院

克勞佛教授

迪克森商學院

特色系列講座
伊藤恕沙女士
日本東京投資副社長

建立不同的金融關係
8 月 20 日，晚上六點
純藍演講廳

過去二十幾年來，很多金融機構都藉由有限的放貸，來讓風險極小化。這項措施卻帶來不利的市場條件。銀行要如何降低風險，又同時提供資金機會給企業老闆？一項可能的方案愈來愈流行，也就是「替代性金融」。我將會概述何謂「替代性金融」、分享從東京投資還有迪克森商學院取得的可信資料，並談談這個全球性的銀行變革，如何振興金融領域。

傳訊者：吉姆・柯瑞
收訊者：麗莎・普萊斯利
收訊時間：5 月 16 日，晚上 7 點

麗莎，我目前在多媒體室準備要印妳做好的傳單，但我發現有錯誤。恕沙女士的介紹有部分缺漏！可否請妳儘快改好重傳給我？多媒體室 20 分鐘後就要關了，但克勞佛教授強調最晚今天晚上要貼出傳單。

196. 文中提到關於純藍演講廳什麼事？
- Ⓐ 不在商院大樓裡。
- Ⓑ 是整場系列講座都要使用的房間。
- Ⓒ **比朝代演講廳來得小。**
- Ⓓ 8 月 21 日那天可供使用。

197. 電子郵件中第二段、第三行的「problems」，最接近下列哪個意思？
- Ⓐ 聲明
- Ⓑ 詢問
- Ⓒ 運貨
- Ⓓ **衝突**

198. 恕沙女士演講的主題是什麼？
　　Ⓐ **銀行業務的最新趨勢**
　　Ⓑ 新的金融職缺
　　Ⓒ 獨特的找資料方法
　　Ⓓ 資深企業主的傳記

199. 柯瑞先生提到什麼困難？
　　Ⓐ 數字寫錯了。
　　Ⓑ **傳單缺少一些細節。**
　　Ⓒ 傳單將不會張貼上網。
　　Ⓓ 準備用來簡報的會議室沒有
　　　　開放使用。

200. 普萊斯利女士最有可能的身分是？
　　Ⓐ 多媒體室的維修人員
　　Ⓑ 恕沙女士的祕書
　　Ⓒ 系列講座的其中一位講者
　　Ⓓ **迪克森商學院的學生**

ACTUAL TEST ③

PART 5 P. 74-76

◎ Part 5 解答請見 P.457

101. **儘管**早上下了大雪,公司野餐行程照舊。

102. **校長**是這間學校的校友,所以很受學生歡迎。

103. 永浩在報告中指**出**,開發商在建設新市政中心時的許多缺失。

104. 如果**當初是**由瑪莎負責這項計畫,我們也許會更成功。

105. 約翰感到沮喪,因為主任在所有提交的報告中挑出**他的報告**仍需加強。

106. 最後一堂課後,摩里斯先生讓每位學生在期末考前**複習**去年度的考題。

107. 團隊在這次任務的表現差得讓人**無法接受**,所以其中兩人昨天被開除了。

108. **就算**我們趕工整個週末,也不太可能在週一早上前完成簡報投影片。

109. 公司晚宴**熱烈進行**,似乎所有員工都玩得很開心。

110. 團隊主管要求所有員工為了這項專案全力以赴,因為這次的顧客對公司來說很重要。

111. 其中五位新進員工——事實上是行銷部門的所有新人,在上一季的表現超乎預期;不過,另外三人卻**沒有如此表現**。

112. 銷售團隊裡每個人今年都期待豐厚的年終獎金,這很**合理**,因為今年公司獲利很多。

113. 乘客接獲建議,請他**返回**登機櫃檯辦理登機證。

114. **如果**西蒙早上有到的話,就能參與我們的策略會議。

115. 業績慘澹了幾年,本公司銷售總算在去年**揚升**。

116. 雖然納森一整週都在生病,他仍及時提交會議報告,令人大感**意外**。

117. 根據傑森的說法,就像技工在上週所反應的,投影機還是有**兩個**問題。

118. 客座講者下週會**來**,請在這週和他聯繫以確認行程。

119. 公司總裁很興奮他談成一筆**很棒的**交易,所以他昨天讓所有員工提早下班。

120. 雖然瑞秋在公司**待得不久**,但她已經在考慮換工作。

121. 隆史這麼晚來開會很奇怪,因為他**通常**非常準時。

122. 起重鋼鐵致力於**提供**最高品質的顧客服務,也矢志貫徹兼顧社會和環保責任的經營哲學。

123. 考量珍妮特的年紀和不佳的健康狀況,當她宣布五月**退休**時,沒有人感到驚訝。。

124. 如同先前所**討論**的,我們不打算再討論之前幾次會議中談過的議題。

125. **最近**我們的員工週會非常有成效,所以讓我們繼續保持。

126. 今年的研討會裡,**每間**公司都專注於團隊合作、多元性和互信。

127. 週四一整天,二樓的會議室都**將舉行**面試。

128. 真琴在公司待的時間是其他人的兩倍**久**,所以如果你有任何問題,問她最合適。

129. 真的非常**遺憾的**,專業諮詢公司沒有中選接下這次的廣告活動,但安路設計公司也一樣會做得很好。

130. 辛普森先生是個很糟的**應徵者**,所以行政主管中沒人有意錄用他。

131-134 電子郵件

寄件人：岩谷高登
　　　　<gordoniwatani@fastermail.com>
收件人：人資經理
　　　　<recruit4@mtlanguage.com>
日期：4 月 14 日
回覆：日語老師

您好：

我看到貴語言中心在找日語教師，所以來信詢問。從我隨信附上的資歷應該可以得知，我過去十年來，多在中國擔任日語教師，其中將近八年在上海最有聲望的語言學校教書。

除了我的工作經驗和學歷，我也有很多嗜好，也許會讓您感興趣。我學了大半輩子的小提琴，現在在一個業餘交響樂團演奏。我是柔道黑帶高手，有空的時候，也喜歡長跑和騎自行車。我個性陽光，面對新環境也能調適得很好。

感謝您費時考慮我的應徵申請。如果需要我提供更多資訊，也請讓我知道。

岩谷高登 敬上

131. Ⓐ 可以
　　　Ⓑ 會是
　　　Ⓒ 應該
　　　Ⓓ 曾是

132. Ⓐ 我花費了
　　　Ⓑ 已花費了
　　　Ⓒ 將花費
　　　Ⓓ 正在花費

133. **Ⓐ 業餘的**
　　　Ⓑ 尋常的
　　　Ⓒ 新興的
　　　Ⓓ 奇特的

134. **Ⓐ 感謝您費時考慮我的應徵申請。**
　　　Ⓑ 期待明天和您相見。
　　　Ⓒ 我畢業於東京的高中。
　　　Ⓓ 我很期待明天見到新學生。

135-138 電子郵件

收件人：slivingston@kmail.net
寄件人：marsvideos@mars.com
主旨：您的訂購

您好：

我們已經收到您所寄的電子郵件，是關於您在七月從火星影視購買的商品。很抱歉，我們目前沒辦法確認商品送到哪裡。

根據我們的紀錄，您購買了四片藍光和兩張 DVD，總額是美金 83 元。加上運費整筆訂單則為 97 元。我們的紀錄顯示，已經在 7 月 17 日從您的信用卡扣款。

我們向您建議兩個方式。（1）如果您願意再等候，就有可能會收到商品。確實有前例是因為天氣不佳，或其他意外導致延後到貨。（2）如果您不想等候，我們可以馬上取消訂單，並予以全額退款。

客服部經理
凱爾強森 敬上

135. Ⓐ 在……期間
　　　Ⓑ 在……時候
　　　Ⓒ 當
　　　Ⓓ 或

136. Ⓐ 增加
　　　Ⓑ 增加到
　　　Ⓒ 將增加
　　　Ⓓ 一直以來在增長

137. Ⓐ 您是很寶貴的顧客，我們今天就會出貨。
　　　Ⓑ 我們的紀錄顯示，已經在 7 月 17 日從您的信用卡扣款。
　　　Ⓒ 您不妨提供對於公司政策的意見。
　　　Ⓓ 我們將繼續進行，並從您的信用卡扣款總額。

TEST 3

PART 6

138. **A** 退款
   B 運送
   C 訂單
   D 道歉

139–142 通知

各位員工請注意：

我已經接到很多關於員工休息室使用的抱怨。本通知提醒大家遵守以下規則。

首先，請記得使用過後，馬上把杯盤、碗和餐具，洗淨、擦乾並且物歸原位。

再者，也有人反應休息室有人抽菸。如你們所知，公司嚴格規定不能在建築物裡面抽菸。如果你想抽菸，需要在特定吸菸區，像是後方露臺或是公司外面。

最後，請不要拿走別人的食物。冰箱內所有食物都應該確實貼上持有人的標籤。你只能取用自己的食物。維持舒適的休息室環境供大家使用，是很重要的事。

經理
葛瑞絲・井川

139. A 被使用
   B 正在用
   C **使用**
   D 去用

140. A 會要求
   B 要求過
   C 將要求
   D **被要求**

141. A 正在貼標籤
   B **被貼標籤**
   C 貼標籤
   D 去貼標籤

142. A 我們明天將在休息室開會。
   B 下週開始我們會關閉休息室。
   C 讓大家一起共享冰箱裡的所有食物。
   D **維持舒適的休息室環境供大家使用，是很重要的事。**

143–146 評論

瑪雅・高登的中東生意指南，綜覽了中東的商業界，既全面也很有意思。

這本書針對幾個中東關鍵國家的商業文化，提供讀者獨特卻清楚的見解。高登教授所著墨的多項主題都很重要，像是適當的招呼禮儀、商務餐敘的用餐禮儀、名片的使用，還有和中東企業磋商的複雜細節。

如果您只是剛開始了解中東的商業界生態，這本書是必讀之作。它深度鑽研中東商業實務許多重要面向，非常詳盡，無人能出其右。不僅如此，高登博士也按照重要商務核心（包括杜拜、卡達和阿布達比）疏理這本書，方便讀者聚焦自己有興趣的區域。其中關於杜拜的章節格外有趣。

只要您讀過《學中東人做生意》，置身中東也可應付自如。

143. **A** 以
   B 在⋯⋯之上
   C 在⋯⋯裡面
   D 在⋯⋯地方

144. A 完全的
   B 荒謬的
   C **必須做的**
   D 自信的

145. A 相比之下
   B 遺憾地
   C **不僅如此**
   D 結果是

146. **A** **其中關於杜拜的章節格外有趣。**
   B 高登教授對亞洲也有所著墨。
   C 這本指南和某些市面上的書相形之下顯得較無趣。
   D 書評對本書的反應冷淡。

147–148 訂購單

> ### 巨得寶股份有限公司
>
> 滿足您家居和辦公需求
>
> **產品內容：**
>
> # 彩色墨水匣兩盒
>
> # 黑白墨水匣一盒
>
> # 標準紙張（每包 50 張）10 包
>
> # 供再次訂購使用之明信片一張
>
> 如需再次下訂產品，請使用隨信附上的明信片。
>
> 如欲和客服人員聯繫，請在週一到週五早上 10 點到下午 6 點間，撥打 301-555-1999。
>
> 產品不可食用

147. 最可能購買這些產品的原因是？
- **A 列印文件**
- B 訂購日用品
- C 寫信
- D 從事藝術創作

148. 關於這張訂購單，何者為真？
- **A 警告民眾產品不能吃。**
- B 隨產品附上收據。
- C 沒有描述訂購的內容。
- D 有提供店址。

149–151 訊息串

> **珍·史密斯〔下午 3:34〕：**
> 嗨，奧斯丁先生。你在提領行李區嗎？
>
> **邁爾斯·奧斯丁〔下午 3:38〕：**
> 史密斯女士？我拿著行李正在過海關，我在東門。妳在附近嗎？
>
> **珍·史密斯〔下午 3:39〕：**
> 很抱歉，我才剛到！我的火車因為機械故障延誤了。我正準備下樓。
>
> **邁爾斯·奧斯丁〔下午 3:41〕：**
> 喔，好的。沒問題，我可以去找妳。但妳穿什麼？
>
> **珍·史密斯〔下午 3:43〕：**
> 藍色洋裝、高跟鞋和黑包包。我手上還拿著一本時尚雜誌。
>
> **邁爾斯·奧斯丁〔下午 3:44〕：**
> 了解。出關那裡見。
>
> **送出**

149. 文中提到關於奧斯丁先生和史密斯女士什麼事？
- **A 他們素未謀面。**
- B 他們明天要開會。
- C 他們都搭火車。
- D 珍·史密斯剛買了一本雜誌。

150. 奧斯丁先生在哪裡等？
- A 在雜誌攤旁邊
- **B 在海關前**
- C 火車上
- D 樓梯上來的地方

(NEW)
151. 下午 3:44 分時，為什麼奧斯丁先生說：「了解。」？
- A 他剛見到史密斯女士。
- **B 他可以認出史密斯女士。**
- C 他也要主持會議。
- D 他不想遲到。

152–154 部落格

> ### 2 月 24 日
>
> 我們今天又跋涉前進了 25 公里。我的腳折磨死我了，我真不該穿我的新靴子。膝蓋也有點酸，不過總體來說今天還是很不錯。起步慢了，因為睡得有點晚。京子負責叫我們起床，所以是她的錯！雖然之後就順利多了。風景美得難以置信。我們拍了超多照片。我等不及回去秀給你們看啦。我們還看到雪豹！牠們非常非常稀有，幾乎不可能親眼目睹。到處都雪，很難從中看出牠來——大概只有三秒鐘看得見。牠很漂亮，京子就錯過了——誰叫她沒叫醒我們，害我們錯過日出，這是甜蜜的復仇，哈哈！

2 月 26 日

抱歉昨天沒有看到部落格。整天都在下雨，也沒什麼有趣的事可以跟你們說。我們找到一間別致的的小咖啡店，整天都待在那裡。店員看我們不爽，但也沒有真的來趕我們走。我們最後只能消磨時間、聊天、吃東西和玩遊戲。明天就是最後一天了。真想在後天趕快見到你們。

152. 這兩人最可能用什麼方式旅行？
    Ⓐ 滑輪
    Ⓑ 摩托車
    Ⓒ 步行
    Ⓓ 搭飛機

153. 這名部落客哪天回家？
    Ⓐ 3 月 2 日
    Ⓑ 3 月 1 日
    Ⓒ 2 月 28 日
    Ⓓ 2 月 27 日

154. 下列句子最適合出現在 [1]、[2]、[3]、[4] 的哪個位置中？
    「我們最後只能消磨時間、聊天、吃東西和玩遊戲。」
    Ⓐ [1]
    Ⓑ [2]
    Ⓒ [3]
    Ⓓ [4]

155–156 表單

寄件未達表單

日期：5 月 16 日   **時間：**早上 11:08
送貨員：山姆
包裹號碼：3494-836636-92
寄件者：大眾辦公用品
寄件未達原因：
商品太大 ☐   住戶不在家未簽收 ☑
備註：此為快遞件

選項：
    (A) 撥打 1-800-555-2215 24 小時免付費電話，使用我們的自動化服務。您需要提供包裹號碼。
    (B) 在上班時間（早上 9 點到下午 5:30，週日休息）撥打 1-401-555-2216。
提醒：寄件失敗後我們只會保管貨品五天，之後將會退還給寄件人。

155. 是誰填寫了這張表單？
    Ⓐ 寄件者
    Ⓑ 自動化服務
    Ⓒ 快遞員
    Ⓓ 住戶

156. 五天後會發生什麼事？
    Ⓐ 送貨員山姆會帶著包裹再次前來。
    Ⓑ 住戶會打電話給快遞公司。
    Ⓒ 包裹將被退還。
    Ⓓ 住戶會回家。

157–158 信件

斑馬租車服務

464 橘丘郡

葉逢，柯林斯，ZR2 3HG

親愛的顧客：

由於小客車和廂型車的需求與日俱增，斑馬租車公司將擴大營運，包括增建前院、辦公室和倉庫擴建，可供我們停放更多車輛。

下個月就會開始動工。特別提醒，11 月 8 日到 11 日間倉庫將會關閉。不過您還是能在網路上看到租車清單。這段期間請用 www.zebracars.com 預約試乘。我們祝福您冬天愉快，也很期待在 12 月，用嶄新設備歡迎您大駕光臨。

克里斯·墨菲

總經理，斑馬租車服務

157. 這封信的目的為何？
- [A] 針對新價格給予建議
- **[B] 宣布要整建**
- [C] 介紹官網
- [D] 提供折扣

158. 文中提到關於這間公司什麼事？
- [A] 將減少停放車輛。
- [B] 販售來自全球的商品。
- **[C] 允許顧客預約試程。**
- [D] 整個冬天都將關閉。

159–160 網路聊天室

泰勒‧伍德〔下午 5:10〕：
好棒！我喜歡新的畫面，比上一版好多了。

莎拉‧布魯克斯〔下午 5:11〕：
你在開玩笑嗎？花了 95 美元應該要有更好的質感才對。

泰勒‧伍德〔下午 5:11〕：
我知道是有點貴。但我確定配樂好聽到爆炸。

蓋文‧華德〔下午 5:12〕：
完全同意。音樂真的很棒！莎拉，妳不覺得嗎？

莎拉‧布魯克斯〔下午 5:14〕：
嗯，我不會說「好聽到爆炸」，但是還行。我喜歡的是聲優的演出。他們真的有更上一層樓。故事好但表現爛真的很惱人。說到這個，這故事也很棒。

蓋文‧華德〔下午 5:15〕：
哈哈，我想她終於淪陷了，泰勒！

泰勒‧伍德〔下午 5:16〕：
也該是時候了。絕佳的畫面、音樂和故事情節—— 80 個小時的充實娛樂，還有所有的支線任務。還能再要求什麼？

159. 這最有可能是關於什麼的對話？
- [A] 一部音樂劇
- [B] 一部電影
- **[C] 一個電玩遊戲**
- [D] 一本書

 160. 下午 5:14 時，莎拉‧布魯克斯寫道：「他們真的有更上一層樓」，她的意思為何？
- **[A] 他們公司做得好。**
- [B] 參加者離開了。
- [C] 使用者上樓了。
- [D] 表演者停止演出了。

161–163 文章

昨天，州長和州檢察長共同敦促，要為他們口中「崩壞的」公共教育體制帶來改變。昨天在銀鎮市政廳舉辦了教育議題的辯論會，州長韋恩‧強森和州檢察長維琪‧培瑞茲議論許久，這也是兩人首度在該州做出聯合聲明。

強森先生和培瑞茲女士討論的問題，可以總結為以下三點：

1. 州立學校內教師的品質明顯惡化。兩人指出原因在於預算縮減，導致近年來教師薪資逐步地下滑。

2. 近年來學生考試成績也逐漸下降，與其他州相比，已低於平均值。

3. 國高中學生的課綱在過去十年來，不像其他州的課綱，充分與時俱進。該州的畢業生沒有接觸到改進後的課程，在大學就學時和其他州的學生競爭就比較辛苦。兩人都指出這是根本問題，在教育學生的早期階段就已經存在。

針對兩人的聲明，州教育部目前沒有做出正式回應。

161. 昨天的聲明中，沒有提到什麼？
- [A] 它和學校體制的議題有關。
- **[B] 強森先生和培瑞茲女士來自不同州。**
- [C] 討論了三個關鍵議題。
- [D] 州教育部沒有回應。

162. 下列何者為強森先生和培瑞茲女士的主張？
- [A] 州立學校太多了。
- [B] 學生在大學的表現更好。
- **[C] 教師的品質比以前差。**
- [D] 學生對新政策感到不滿。

345

163. 根據這兩個官員的説法，什麼改變了教師的品質？
- **A 教師薪資正在減少。**
- B 教師外流到其他州。
- C 教師對學校感到不滿。
- D 是教育部的錯。

164–167 通知

日光閃閃日照中心照顧兒童已超過 30 年之久。我們提供溫暖、友善又安全的環境，給予兒童高品質的學習和休閒時光，不斷累積良好聲譽。

我們在此宣布，下個月將在橘郡開設新的日照中心。它將是我們歷來最大的中心，最多可以容納 50 名孩童。最新的日照中心當然會有樂趣十足的遊戲中心和相關設施，誠如家長所熟悉的，像是城堡遊樂場、游泳池、最先進的電腦中心。

我們將在明年 1 月 27 日到 31 日開放參觀，完整導覽院內設施，歡迎感興趣的家長前來，和本中心曾獲獎的員工對話。儘管帶著貴子弟一起來，「全面」體驗各種有趣的活動，感受未來在我們中心的每一天日常。

我們希望會在一月見到您。欲知更多資訊，可以撥打 201-555-8765 或是寫信到 sunnyshiny@mnet.org 詢問。

日光閃閃給您最全面的照護。

日光閃閃日照中心董事總經理
露西‧梅森

164. 何者並非這篇通知的目的？
- A 宣布新的日照中心要開幕
- B 告知家長參觀日的活動
- **C 討論日光閃閃日照中心的沿革**
- D 給予家長聯繫方式

165. 日光閃閃日照中心有什麼特色？
- A 網球場
- **B 游泳池**
- C 攀岩牆
- D 滑水道

166. 參觀日會持續幾天？
- A 2 天
- B 4 天
- **C 5 天**
- D 6 天

167. 為什麼有些人可能會打電話給日光閃閃日照中心？
- A 想和曾獲獎的員工對話
- B 想要買游泳池的門票
- C 預約參加參觀日活動
- **D 詢問更多資訊**

168–171 新聞快報

今天毀滅性的野火肆虐加州，造成住宅和農地大規模毀損。報導指出火災蔓延了 8 公里，並朝洛杉磯市方向持續緩慢延燒，數以百計的民眾被迫遠離家園，且造成五人受傷。安嫩代爾郊區的消防隊長大衛‧梅耶爾表示，這是他長年服役以來所見過最糟的火災，但消防隊已經準備好因應挑戰。「火災蔓延速度快得難以置信。」他說，「消防隊已經奮戰一段時間了，但距離全面撲滅還有一段路。」

目前還不清楚起火原因。雖然通常是因為人為疏失，像是亂丟菸蒂、無人看管的營火，或是天災所引起，好比閃電打到乾柴或草堆。

加州歷年來都會發生野火災情。去年部分北加州地區為延燒將近兩週的猙獰森林大火所苦，火災最終造成三人受傷。同一地區三年前也發生火災，造成 40 人受傷。

168. 梅耶爾先生發言中所提到的人最可能是誰？

    A 他的朋友

    B 其他的消防員

    C 他的同學

    D 他的兒子

169. 新聞快報中沒有提到哪個造成野火的原因？

    A 沒能撲滅營火

    B 亂丟菸蒂

    C 閃電打到乾草

    D 人為縱火

170. 根據新聞快報，過去三年來有多少人因為野火而受傷？

    A 40

    B 45

    C 48

    D 43

(NEW)
171. 下列句子最適合出現在 [1]、[2]、[3]、[4] 的哪個位置中？

    「加州歷年來都會發生野火災情。」

    A [1]

    B [2]

    C [3]

    D [4]

172–175 訊息

請留意，公司年度研討會今年將在 4 月 30 日週六舉行。我知道很多人對於要在週末舉行研討會感到失望，但今年真的別無選擇。不過，想必您也會很開心得知，所有員工都可以在研討會結束後的下一週，選擇任一天的中午過後進行補休，除了週四以外。

各位今天早上將會收到一份報告副本。我們請您務必在參加研討會前，仔細讀過報告中所提到的每項個案研究。今年我們也將要求五個部門的主管準備 10 分鐘的簡報。其中必須提到去年研討會所討論過的各項策略，和它們在過去一年來落實的成效如何。

今年將有位特別來賓。眾所皆知最近才榮獲年度最佳商務人士獎的瓊安‧米契爾，將會在早上進行演講，分享她從業以來受用的市場策略，以及帶領「團隊凝聚」場次。每位主管報告後，我會在各位享用午餐時，簡報顧客關係管理的情形。

研討會的尾聲，我們也準備了簡單的雞尾酒和小餐點，給不趕著回家的各位享用。

感謝，

經理 格里高利‧A‧曼寧

172. 曼寧先生寫這封訊息的目的為何？

    A 為員工準備雞尾酒和小點心

    B 介紹瓊安‧米契爾給大家

    C 請主管準備簡報

    D 提供年度活動的有關資訊

173. 關於今年度的研討會，何者有誤？

    A 再度在週六舉辦。

    B 結束前會提供茶點。

    C 會討論顧客關係管理的情形。

    D 早上將有客座講者。

174. 所有的主管簡報總共會花多少分鐘？

    A 10 分鐘

    B 25 分鐘

    C 30 分鐘

    D 50 分鐘

175. 文中提到關於瓊安‧米契爾什麼事？

    A 她是一名部門主管。

    B 她去年有來參加年度研討會。

    C 她會在午餐時簡報。

    D 她是業界成功人士。

176–180 電子郵件

收件人：evanmoss@linkup.com
寄件人：justinduncan@comwire.com
日期：9 月 14 日
主旨：銀行帳戶移轉

親愛的摩斯先生：

在我暫時調往夏威夷以前，曾經請聯上銀行把我的銀行帳戶轉移到夏威夷的分行。雖然原訂計畫是我會在這裡待上六個月，不過我已經完成研究準備回家。您能在今天，也就是 9 月 14 日，再把我的帳戶轉回開戶的銀行嗎？等我回去，我也想申請不動產抵押貸款。如果您能給我最適合的建議，我會很感激。我嘗試上您們官網看購屋的頁面。不過上面提到網頁目前還在更新當中。

非常感謝您的協助。

賈斯丁・鄧肯 敬上

收件人：justinduncan@comwire.com
寄件人：evanmoss@linkup.com
日期：9 月 15 日
主旨：您的電子郵件訊息

親愛的鄧肯先生：

感謝您昨天的來信。請留意，您的帳戶已經如您所需，回歸到原先的銀行分行了。再者，在提供您不動產抵押貸款前，我們必須先討論您的財務狀況。您的收入、月開銷和目前所負擔的貸款，都必須列入考量。我想向您建議，如果時間允許的話，是否可以和布拉福分行專職不動產抵押貸款的專員，約時間討論相關事宜？最後，關於官網的問題，我必須和您致歉。系統目前正在更新，不得不把您所查詢的頁面暫時撤下，等到更新完成後會再重新上線。我們希望網頁可以在兩天內回復運作。

祝好，

客服代表
伊凡・摩斯

176. 第一封電子郵件的目的為何？
- Ⓐ 抱怨某筆交易
- Ⓑ 關閉在布拉福分行的帳戶
- Ⓒ 將錢轉給第三方分行
- **Ⓓ 和銀行修改個人設定**

177. 關於鄧肯先生，何者最可能為真？
- **Ⓐ 他的永久居留地在布拉福。**
- Ⓑ 他轉調夏威夷為期一年。
- Ⓒ 他正在租一間公寓。
- Ⓓ 他曾在聯上銀行工作。

178. 摩斯先生建議鄧肯先生怎麼做？
- Ⓐ 電洽夏威夷分行請求建議
- Ⓑ 聯繫資訊部門請求協助
- Ⓒ 關閉他的帳戶
- **Ⓓ 和銀行的貸款專員見面**

179. 鄧肯先生申請不動產抵押貸款，何者不必列入考量？
- Ⓐ 他的月開銷
- Ⓑ 他的薪水
- Ⓒ 他現在有的貸款金額
- **Ⓓ 他還款時間會為期多久**

180. 在第二封電子郵件，第六行的「matter」，最接近下列哪個意思？
- **Ⓐ 關心的事**
- Ⓑ 物質
- Ⓒ 結果
- Ⓓ 疏忽

181–185 廣告和電子郵件

年度特賣！不容錯過！

您熟悉的特賣季來了，貝萊迪特賣區將舉辦超級大拍賣！眼見為憑！這裡提供幾項優惠商品：

◆ 各式名牌電視通通五折，不管是可攜式電視還是超大螢幕，一律半價！不論您在找什麼型號，千萬不要錯過貝萊迪。

◆ 山普森洗／烘衣機只要 1000 元。好得不像真的吧？市售價通常高達 2500 元，我們這邊居然半價不到！這裡有最新型號，甚至免運費送貨到府。

◆ 頂級相機與可攜式攝影機下殺至 2.5 折！沒錯—— 2.5 折！攝錄器材庫存大出清，何其悅耳的好消息。更讚的是，任購一台相機或攝影機，隨機附贈黑色帆布攝影包，方便您外出攜帶使用。

火速趕來貝萊迪特賣區一探究竟。特價只會再持續五天！

寄件人：hjjang@kmail.net
收件人：jameskim@vogmail.com
主旨：買了一台攝影機！

嘿，詹姆斯：

我剛從貝萊迪特賣區回來，人多得難以置信。短期內我不想再去那裡逛了。

他們剩下的攝影機實在不是最頂級的，要我說是中等還嫌太誇張。雖說是很便宜，我最後買了摩森牌攝影機，售價 150 元。我知道柯爾牌的品質評價最好，不過我之前用過，勉強撐了兩年就解體了——它幾乎是摩森牌的兩倍貴，完全不值那個價。至於腳架，我買了柯爾牌用的替代摩森牌，畢竟它看起來好太多了。

總之，期待很快見到你。

祝好，

張赫俊

181. 下列何者為真？
　　Ⓐ 特賣會只會再持續一週。
　　Ⓑ 貝萊迪大部分的電視都在特價。
　　Ⓒ 廣告中提到的最大折扣商品是相機。
　　Ⓓ 廣告中沒提到的商品都沒有特價。

182. 哪些特賣商品免費送貨到府？
　　Ⓐ 電視
　　Ⓑ 洗衣機
　　Ⓒ 攝影機
　　Ⓓ 直排輪

183. 黑色帆布攝影包要價多少？
　　Ⓐ 1000 元
　　Ⓑ 平常價格的 2.5 折
　　Ⓒ 平常價格的 5 折
　　Ⓓ 不用錢

184. 為什麼貝萊迪特賣區擠滿了人？
　　Ⓐ 那裡有特賣會。
　　Ⓑ 店最近才開張。
　　Ⓒ 大家想看張先生。
　　Ⓓ 店很快就要關了。

185. 下列何者為非？
　　Ⓐ 張先生從未擁有柯爾牌攝影機。
　　Ⓑ 攝影機和腳架被分開來賣。
　　Ⓒ 柯爾牌攝影機比摩森牌來得貴。
　　Ⓓ 張先生買了摩森牌攝影機。

186–190 通知、履歷和電子郵件

誠徵銷售總經理

電子零售連鎖業者領導品牌想要找一位正向、勤奮、積極的人，接任銷售總經理職位，掌管全亞洲 22 家分店。合適的應徵者需有著名商學院學歷，且有六年以上類似職務的管理經驗，以電子零售業為佳。我們主要販售尖端電子設備，所以應徵者必須有意願、有能力在亞洲地區，讓產品的市場有所成長。由於該職務不時需要出差，應徵者需持有有效的汽車駕照，並有一國以上的他國居住經驗。有興趣應徵者，請在 3 月 31 日前，將您的履歷（附照片）和相關推薦人名單寄到 mlinton@kmail.com。

姓名：丹尼爾・申
生日：1981 年 11 月 5 日
出生地：南韓首爾
國籍：美國
E-mail：dshin@kmail.com

學歷
1993–1997 安多弗高中
1997–2001 哈佛大學（學士）
2006–2008 布魯塞爾商學院（商管碩士）

工作經歷
1995–1997 安多弗餐館（倉管）
1998–1999 三明治中心（服務生）
1999–2001 皮耶・瓦倫丁的店（服務生）
2009–2010 珊尼斯電子（襄理，香港）
2010–2012 史坦威電子（零售經理，新加坡）
2012– 現在 自營業

其他
我持有有效駕照，中文和韓文也很流利。

收件人：格里高利・史密斯
寄件人：麥特・林頓
回覆：銷售總經理（3 個附件）
日期：3 月 18 日

格瑞格：

再次感謝昨天美好的晚餐，也幫我向茉莉道謝，告訴她我當晚有多愉快！

對了，你看過今天早上寄給你的資料嗎？關於最近幾位應徵銷售總經理職缺的。怕你先前沒有時間看，我在這封信再次附檔給你。我們有三名新的應徵者，雖然還有時間決定，但你不妨看一下其中一位丹尼爾・申。他看起來很適合這份工作，雖然他有一個條件不符合人事廣告的需求，但他符合其餘的要求，甚至比那更好，對吧？

其中讓我很關切的一點，是他最近期的工作經驗。自營業？應該別有所指。我想讓他來面試，談談這個部分。你覺得呢？

祝好，

麥特

186. 下列何者並非應徵條件？
　Ⓐ 照片
　Ⓑ 相關工作經驗
　Ⓒ 流利的中文能力
　Ⓓ 推薦人名單

187. 申先生的哪項條件不符？
　Ⓐ 他只有住過一個國家。
　Ⓑ 他沒有六年的管理經驗。
　Ⓒ 他沒有駕照。
　Ⓓ 他沒有商學院學歷。

188. 關於林頓先生，何者為真？
　Ⓐ 他很看好丹尼爾・申。
　Ⓑ 他沒和茉莉見過面。
　Ⓒ 他是格瑞格的上司。
　Ⓓ 他來自韓國。

189. 為什麼林頓先生要在電子郵件裡面附加檔案？
　Ⓐ 他今天早上忘記一併寄給史密斯先生。
　Ⓑ 他想要讓史密斯先生把資料給朱莉看。
　Ⓒ 申先生的履歷沒有附照片。
　Ⓓ 他覺得史密斯先生可能還沒看過資料。

190. GSM 最有可能的的意思是？
　Ⓐ 銷售總經理
　Ⓑ 格瑞格的銷售備忘錄
　Ⓒ 全球行銷機制
　Ⓓ 人事總管理

191–195 文章和電子郵件

更多整建計畫

曼徹斯特市市議會在週三的會上一致通過，以研擬方案來整治市區的基礎建設。根據市府財政局長麥克・曼恩的說明，最近正在整建的曼徹斯特公共圖書館，其花費出乎意料地遠低於預算，所以市議員決定整理一份短清單，將剩餘經費挹注在其他改善計畫上。

目前最多人提出的建議包括：增設曼徹斯特社區中心的無障礙坡道、更換曼徹斯特市中心壞掉的路燈，以及整修曼徹斯特公園的停車場。曼恩先生表示，市議會決定要再諮詢民意。想進一步表達意見的民眾，可在下週三 4 月 22 日下午五點出席議會會議，或者在 4 月 29 日前寫電子郵件到市府信箱。市政規畫委員會將在 4 月 29 日後彙整一份最終清單，呈報給議會討論。議會將在短期內做出決議。

寄件人：sshort@hostmail.com
收件人：citycouncil@manchester.org
日期：4 月 24 日
主旨：整建計畫

親愛的市議員：

我知道針對市區設施的整建計畫，市議會正在徵詢意見。我當天預約了看診，因此不克出席週三的議會，但我想表達我強烈支持替換市中心壞掉的路燈。我在市中心工作，下班時間較晚的時候，我注意到很多路燈需要換了。街道很暗確實有些恐怖。讓街道更明亮，可以吸引更多人來市區，也能減低犯罪發生。這對曼徹斯特的全體市民都好。希望您會選擇這項計畫。

蘇珊・秀特

寄件人：mchoi@hostmail.com
收件人：citycouncil@manchester.org
日期：4 月 27 日
主旨：市政計畫

此致有關人士：

總算有項整建計畫在預算內完成。雖然曼徹斯特公共圖書館向所有人開放，不分老少都可以去使用，但還是年輕人和帶著小孩的父母居多。我希望我們可以把剩下的預算，用來照顧曼徹斯特年長市民。

社區中心是最多年長市民聚集的地方，入口處卻沒有無障礙坡道，這跟犯罪沒有兩樣。很多去那裡的人都需要使用輪椅，他們經常遇到困難，或必須仰賴他人協助才能進到裡面。選擇這項整建計畫，肯定能讓沒有感受到圖書館整建好處的市民大為讚賞。做出能嘉惠曼徹斯特整體社區的計畫很重要。感謝您的關心。

米爾頓・崔

191. 為什麼曼徹斯特市有預算可用？
    Ⓐ 市議會去年加重課稅。
    Ⓑ 它接獲鉅額捐款。
    Ⓒ 它取消了一項整建計畫。
    Ⓓ 上一個計畫的開銷比預期來得少。

192. 文章中第二段、第七行的「put before」最接近下列哪個意思？
    Ⓐ 快點移動
    Ⓑ 首先做
    Ⓒ 提供給
    Ⓓ 置於最上方

193. 秀特女士預約什麼時候看診？
    Ⓐ 4 月 22 日
    Ⓑ 4 月 24 日
    Ⓒ 4 月 27 日
    Ⓓ 4 月 29 日

194. 崔先生在電子郵件中提到關於曼徹斯特公共圖書館什麼事？
    Ⓐ 已多年未整修。
    Ⓑ 主要是年輕市民在用。
    Ⓒ 提供給年長者很多好課程。
    Ⓓ 需要更多整修。

195. 看起來，崔先生和秀特女士都同意的論點為何？
    Ⓐ 選定的計畫要對社區整體有幫助。
    Ⓑ 市府應該要省下多出的經費，而不是執行計畫。
    Ⓒ 市議會應該延後徵詢民意的截止日期。
    Ⓓ 市中心的路燈不是真的需要替換。

過去兩天，當地的兩間高中（大園和方塔納）聯合舉辦了募款活動，協助募款給最近受到大地震影響、無家可歸的三萬多名里奇伍德的居民。

本社區兩間學校先前從未聯手舉辦慈善活動，這次卻非常成功！學校為受災戶募款超過 15 萬美元。市長傑瑞米・艾隆斯心懷感激收下捐款，向所有參與活動的學校成員致謝，並承諾會把所有捐款拿來替災民蓋新家。

參加這兩天活動的人，肯定留下了難以忘懷的回憶。學生團體在方塔納高中的舞台上表現精采，帶來難忘的歌舞表演、喜劇小品和戲劇。每項演出都是特地由兩校同學所共同參與，象徵人溺己溺、共體時艱的精神。週日在大園高中也舉辦了籃球聯賽。不是學生的社區民眾也開放參加。每個人都說自己玩得很盡興。

然而，最受歡迎的活動莫過於第二天的卡拉 OK 大賽。參賽者是兩間學校的教職員和學生。方塔納高中的同學馬克・聖特最終勝出，從歡呼的聲響，就能得知比數絕非懸殊。週日傍晚活動閉幕式上，市長艾隆斯強調，他為里奇伍德全體市民感到很驕傲。這篇文章也感謝所有與會者，在他人深陷黑暗時，不吝給予希望之光。

寄件人：傑瑞米・艾隆斯
收件人：pjones@fontana.co.edu;
　　　　mthacher@grandpark.co.edu
主旨：非常感謝！
日期：10 月 1 日，週二

親愛的普莉西雅和瑪麗：

我想再次感謝兩位的驚人付出，上個週末很成功。兩位合作的精彩活動，為社區帶來很多歡樂。也請兩位找一天上學日，抽空幫我向所有參與者再次傳達感謝之意。

很遺憾整天的公務會議，讓我沒能參與週六的活動。不過我聽說非常好玩——各國美食展據說很棒。雖然我錯過了，但這真是很棒的創意！

週日好極了，這我就知道了，因為我有幸共襄盛舉。瑪麗，那位馬克真是個人才。也許有一天我們會在電視上看到他！他會成為很好的音樂人，也會是大園高中的傑出校友。總之，我衷心祝福。我也代表里奇伍德向兩位致謝。

傑瑞米・艾隆斯，市長

寄件人：marksaint@kmail.net
收件人：judithsaint@kmail.net
主旨：我贏了！

嗨，媽媽：

猜得到嗎？我贏了！我還是沒有辦法相信。我上場時很緊張。一直到比賽開始，才放鬆了一點。我唱的是約翰藍儂的《想像》，我想這是個好的選擇。

我和大家想趁著開心的感覺還在去外面慶祝一下。可能會比較晚回家，就不要等我了。不要擔心，我 11 點前會到家。

愛妳，

馬克

---

196. 在第一封電子郵件中，第一段、第三行的「took part」最接近下列哪個意思？
　Ⓐ **參與**
　Ⓑ 享受
　Ⓒ 獲得
　Ⓓ 完成

197. 下列哪件事情最先發生？
　Ⓐ 市長艾隆斯先生出席募款活動。
　Ⓑ 當地居民參加籃球聯賽。
　Ⓒ 馬克・聖特在歌唱比賽裡唱《想像》。
　Ⓓ **活動上展示各國料理。**

198. 活動從哪一天開始？
  A 週二
  B 週一
  C 週日
  D 週六

199. 根據文章，艾隆斯先生搞錯了什麼？
  A 他以為募款只募了 10 萬。
  B 他週六沒辦法參加活動。
  C 他以為馬克·聖特是大園高中的學生。
  D 他把電子郵件寄給了茉蒂絲·聖特。

200. 第二封電子郵件提到了馬克什麼事？
  A 他很失望輸掉了比賽。
  B 他上了電視節目。
  C 他之前曾在其他比賽中唱過《想像》。
  D 活動後他和朋友外出。

ACTUAL TEST ④

◎ Part 5 解答請見 P.457

101. 因為要進行例行性的大樓安全檢查，下週請從側**門**進入大廳。

102. 全國教師教育協會表示，州內所有教員都必須致力於**保護**學生免於校園暴力。

103. 行銷部門必須**提供**可靠的廣告資訊給其他公司，以保障他們在出版部門所保留的版權。

104. **除非**管理者在現場給予其他指示，否則所有員工都必須遵守目前工作場所規定。

105. 如果您所購買的商品發生任何問題，請和技術支援團隊聯繫並**確切**告知現況。

106. 有五年以上行銷資歷的申請者，將**給予**機會晉升到主管職。

107. 三華電子的行銷經理細心檢閱和加拿大龍頭企業——威爾**物流**公司所簽訂的合約條款。

108. 克莉絲汀女士提出兩個方案來鼓勵加把勁電池的員工，以創造良好的工作環境，但**兩者**都被管理部門婉拒。

109. 標準不動產公司和一家環球發展公司簽訂了完善的契約，**從**中獲利良多。

110. 為了增加銷售額，摩比通訊的員工**已經同意**加班，直到回復到之前的銷售量。

111. 如果第一批全新智慧型手機 T 星 7 提早完售的話，那些上網預購的**顧客**可以取得全額退款。。

112. Xvid 影像製作公司在過去七年來，**已經制定**規則以保留自製內容的權利。

113. 內部資料外洩所造成的損害，總額**相當於**數十億美元，約是年營收的三分之一。

114. 應徵者均表示，可以接受**提名**指派到樂可沃科技的海外分公司，作為晉升獎勵。

115. 我們縣有超棒絕佳的景點，像是海洋大地、人物世界和趣味駕駛公園，**保證**您有個難忘的假期。

116. 還沒報名在職訓練的員工應該**立刻**提出申請。

117. 經濟分析師想出三個**不同的**方法，來因應當前有關經濟長期不振的問題。

118. 為了**增加**新品在電子商務市場上的銷售，這間公司建議經由多個社群媒體，進行病毒式行銷。

119. 接受全額退費的消費者**若**欲接受支票退費，必須先聯繫銷售經理。

120. **倘若**您發現下一期的文章有任何錯誤，請趕在出版前直接向主編反應。

121. 抱歉通知您，我們無法使用您在信件中**和**申請書**一起**寄來的照片。

122. 漢斯企業裡的每個部門和執行團隊都有一套文件架構，其中包括一份**正式聲明**，寫到每一項職務的責任和擔當。

123. 巨人商城開發了最新的快速交易處理系統，以便**加快**出貨給顧客。

124. 消防員趕到縱火的犯罪現場**前**，大樓將已完全燒毀。

125. 針對那篇討論環保議題的文章，他在評論中**強調**保護生態環境的必要。

126. 紐約現代藝術供應商在去年，**從之前的**店面搬到比第 42 街更遠的梅西大道上。

127. 我們的目標是要吸引購物時，對產品設計抱有**高敏感度**的顧客。

128. 很多業務都很失望，因為銷售數字**顯著地**低於預期。

129. 在你的電腦上安裝安全軟體之前，最好儘**快**刪掉任何之前安裝的防毒軟體。

130. **雖然**只是封面上一個很小的印刷失誤，巨書出版仍給予丹尼先生全額退費。

131–134 文章

艾克隆海灣能源併購斐樂瓦斯

艾克隆海灣能源今早宣布併購斐樂瓦斯，以便取得二疊紀盆地油田的開採權。公司發言人賈維斯·密克斯説，他們想要妥善利用斐樂瓦斯在新發現的產油區所建立的穩定基礎，斐樂瓦斯在當地已經有六座鑽油井，而且六座都全力運作。

能源領域的專家瑞·利特曼，預測這波併購將讓艾克隆海灣能源擠下其他競爭者，成為二疊紀盆地石油勘探的龍頭公司。由於當地的地價持續飆漲，這次的快動作也讓這個石油巨人省下數以百萬的土地購買金額。事實上，只不過在過去兩年內，德拉瓦區的地價就從每畝 14,516 美元，飆漲到 49,000 美元。

---

131. Ⓐ 進到
    Ⓑ 伴隨
    Ⓒ 為了
    Ⓓ 屬於

132. Ⓐ 斐樂瓦斯還在考慮這項提議。
    Ⓑ 六座都全力運作。
    Ⓒ 艾克隆海灣能源很快會併購更多公司。
    Ⓓ 併購案花的錢比預期來得高。

133. Ⓐ 買家
    Ⓑ 觀望者
    Ⓒ 投資者
    Ⓓ 競爭者

134. Ⓐ 這個案例中
    Ⓑ 畢竟
    Ⓒ 儘管如此
    Ⓓ 事實上

135–138 通知

因為到芬蘭偏鄉伊瓦洛的航班非常有限，我們強烈建議提早訂票。湯森航空提供從英國直飛伊瓦洛的季節性航班。其餘月分只能搭乘芬蘭國內線，從赫爾辛基前往當地。如果您要取消訂位，湯森航空須預留七天通知期，而芬蘭航空只要求三天，就能給與您的機票全額退費。兩家航空公司的頭等艙旅客在飛行期間，都有提供餐點和飲料。經濟艙則沒有提供這項服務。

---

135. Ⓐ 季節
    Ⓑ 四季
    Ⓒ 調味
    Ⓓ 季節性的

136. Ⓐ 正在給與退款
    Ⓑ 將被退款
    Ⓒ 能被退款
    Ⓓ 過往一直在退款

137. Ⓐ 期間
    Ⓑ 度數
    Ⓒ 地點
    Ⓓ 月分

138. Ⓐ 經常來往伊瓦洛的乘客，整年都可以透過湯森航空前往當地。
    Ⓑ 經濟艙則沒有提供這項服務。
    Ⓒ 如果要取消往返伊瓦洛的機票，不需要提前通知。
    Ⓓ 我們建議搭早班飛機，因為機上將提供所有乘客餐點。

工業園區獲得許可

白岸鎮的居民即將遭逢劇變。地產開發商天涯海角控股,於週一宣布白岸鎮議會已經給予許可,讓他們建設佔地 30 英畝的工業科技園區。許可案在 6 月 2 日週一宣布通過。園區內將建設幾座摩天辦公大樓、工廠和倉儲設施。部分土地也將作為娛樂用途,像是高爾夫球場和練習場。大多數居民在會議間都反對這項提議的開發案,認為它將帶來噪音、交通和汙染問題。

139. Ⓐ 將已來到
　　Ⓑ 已經來到
　　Ⓒ 正在到來
　　Ⓓ 到來

140. **Ⓐ 許可案在 6 月 2 日週一宣布通過。**
　　Ⓑ 鎮民將會歡迎這項計畫。
　　Ⓒ 居民和開發商都在等議會的決議。
　　Ⓓ 然而,天涯海角控股撤回了開發計畫。

141. **Ⓐ 有些**
　　Ⓑ 很多
　　Ⓒ 一個
　　Ⓓ 很少

142. Ⓐ 認為
　　Ⓑ 認為
　　Ⓒ 他們把……認為
　　Ⓓ 被認為

7 月 12 日
阿曼達‧皮克維克女士
摺紙紙張公司
07666 紐澤西州提內克市
東路 278 號

感謝您來信詢問購買四瓶柯林斯供應商鐵膽墨水。我們很高興知會您本店還有庫存,只要您今天填寫好隨信附上的訂購表單,我們就能出貨。預期您將在五到七個工作天內收到商品。由於您是常客,兩年多來經常購買我們商品,您這次以及未來的交易都將享有 5% 的折扣。此外您每一次的購買,都會得到商家點數,累積的點數可以用來兌換其他商品。這是我們感謝您經常光顧的一份心意。

顧客關係經理
戴夫‧恩蕭 敬上

附檔:訂單表格 .pdf

143. Ⓐ 您或許會想要從我們的線上墨水型錄選購商品。
　　Ⓑ 不過,我們會要求您以原包裝退貨。
　　Ⓒ 預期您將在五到七個工作天內收到商品。
　　Ⓓ 很遺憾,我們沒有任何和鐵膽墨水有關的訂購紀錄。

144. **Ⓐ 即將來臨的**
　　Ⓑ 先前的
　　Ⓒ 初步的
　　Ⓓ 按順序發生的

145. Ⓐ 然而
　　Ⓑ 此外
　　Ⓒ 雖然
　　Ⓓ 當然

146. Ⓐ 累積
　　Ⓑ 正在累積
　　Ⓒ 去累積
　　Ⓓ 累積到

147–148 告示

奧勒岡首席協會十月將在尤金市開設分會。該組織將在每週五晚間八點舉行聚會，地址是華盛頓大道 305 號的科爾佩珀。不論何時，都會對外開放。

如果您有興趣，且打算搭乘公共運輸工具前往的話，尤金市紅巴士會停靠在詹姆斯大街和佛萊明大道的轉角，距離這裡兩個街區的站牌。如果您打算自行開車前往，霍普金斯停車場在晚間七點過後，開放市民免費停車。

明年的聚會我們會討論很多有關社區的話題，所以我們希望您能一起加入活動。如果想要了解更多關於主題和講者的資訊，可以上官網 www.opaeugene.org 查詢。

147. 這則告示最可能貼在哪裡？
Ⓐ 社區中心
Ⓑ 停車場
Ⓒ 當地餐廳
Ⓓ 當地旅舍

148. 根據這則告示，該協會網頁能找到什麼資訊？
Ⓐ 推廣當地的影片
Ⓑ 當地停車的流程
Ⓒ 登記用的文件
Ⓓ 和聚會有關的一些細節

149–150 表格

西格瑪通信公司：2018 年雙年活動！

感謝您有興趣參加西格瑪通信公司舉行的 COD 網路會議。

請填寫以下的申請表格。

2018 年 COD 網路會議

會議報名表格

聖路易千禧飯店
2018 年 10 月 10 日到 14 日

名牌和郵遞資訊（每人須分開填寫表格）

姓名 ＿＿＿＿＿（作為 POD 資料庫建檔使用）

名牌 ＿＿＿＿＿＿＿（將顯示於您的名牌上）

職稱 ＿＿＿＿＿＿＿

部門／單位 ＿＿＿＿＿＿＿＿

機構／組織 ＿＿＿＿＿＿＿＿

郵寄地址 ＿＿＿＿＿＿＿＿

城市 ＿＿＿ 州／省 ＿＿＿ 郵遞區號 ＿＿＿＿

辦公電話 ＿＿＿＿＿ 傳真 ＿＿＿＿＿

電子郵件信箱 ＿＿＿＿＿＿＿＿＿＿＿＿

會議登記

	早鳥 （郵戳早於 9 月 21 日）	一般 （郵戳晚 於 9 月 21 日）	現場 登記	報名金 額總計
會員 （須繳交 2018– 2019 兩年年費）	$180	$220	$240	$＿＿
非會員 （包括一年期會員）	$255	$295	$315	$＿＿
學生或退休人士	$130	$160	$180	$＿＿
只參加一天 ＿ 週四 ＿ 週五 ＿ 週六	$130	$140	$150	$＿＿

＊＊如果您在會議期間需要臨時停車證，請前往接待處找我們的會議人員索取。

149. 文中提到關於 2018 COD 會議什麼事？
Ⓐ 給予提前報名付款的人折扣。
Ⓑ 會員必須在線上登記參加。
Ⓒ 只讓一般會員參加會議。
Ⓓ 一年一度在聖路易舉辦。

150. 西格瑪通信公司的員工會做什麼事？
Ⓐ 寄電子郵件給潛在客戶，提供會議的詳細資料
Ⓑ 接受與會者的開會文件
Ⓒ 給與參加者臨時停車證
Ⓓ 安排會議室

收件人：業務專員
寄件人：李察‧史帝夫，總經理
日期：10 月 10 日
主旨：緊急狀況

親愛的業務專員：

我們在最近一期《加州時報》的廣告有誤，將半價特賣會的日期寫成 11 月 11 日，而不是 11 月 1 日。雖然下個月出刊的紙本會予以更正，但網路上的顧客不會發現這個錯誤。因此，如果他們詢問到底特賣會是在 1 日還是 11 日，務必先向顧客表示，我們為帶來的不便深感歉意，並提供他們九折折價券，任何商品不分線上或實體商店，都可使用這張折價卷。如果消費者有更多疑問，請直接轉接給樓層經理處理。感謝您的諒解。

白王服飾總經理
李察‧史帝夫

151. 文中提到關於《加州時報》什麼事？
    Ⓐ 每週都發行文章和廣告。
    Ⓑ 已經為寫錯促銷日期刊出道歉聲明。
    Ⓒ 在白王服飾的廣告上附上折價券。
    Ⓓ 把白王服飾特賣的日期給印錯了。

152. 史帝夫先生要專員做什麼？
    Ⓐ 如顧客有其他疑問，建議
    他們和主管討論
    Ⓑ 告訴顧客某項產品有何不良
    Ⓒ 解釋為何出錯
    Ⓓ 寄給雜誌修正過後的日期

年度春季會議

中央賓州大學　　　　　　梅隆董事會會議室

2018 年 4 月 13 日　　　　**9:00–12:00**

8:30–9:00 登記＆早餐

9:00–10:30 分組座談：擴充教師的工具箱

● 跨文化傳播中心主任，珮姬‧丹尼爾＆卡內基大學副教授，瑞貝卡‧奧瑞圖

〈科技自在手中：運用創意素材及創建知識暢通性〉

● 查塔姆大學英文學程幹事，史帝夫‧林

〈團康活動重點初探：以《歡樂合唱團》課程規畫為例〉

● 法蘭克林地區學校，英語為第二外語教學教師＆英語學習課程幹事，珍‧皮亞傑

〈教學科技訣竅：使用 Puzzlelet.com 和行動裝置〉

● 匹茲堡市立大學英語所講師，克里斯多福‧皮爾斯

〈運用拼圖來引導、共享詞彙練習活動〉

10:30–11:15 團體討論＆人脈拓展

11:15–12:00 全體商務大會和選舉

三河英語教學的會員免費
非會員 5 元

校園地圖：http://www.cpu.edu./campusmap/
怎麼抵達：http://www.cpu.edu/about/directions.cfm
請將車輛停在露天平台停車場

感謝中央賓州大學提供場地舉行 2018 年春季會議！

153. 這場研討會主要訴求對象是誰？
    Ⓐ 人資專家
    Ⓑ 商業分析師
    Ⓒ 教育研究所學生
    Ⓓ 當地大學的新進員工

154. 誰的主題有談到線上學習？
　　Ⓐ 丹尼爾女士
　　Ⓑ 林先生
　　Ⓒ 皮亞傑女士
　　Ⓓ 皮爾斯先生

155. 關於這個研討會，何者為非？
　　Ⓐ 是個為期半天的活動。
　　Ⓑ 提供免費午餐。
　　Ⓒ 引介新教學方法。
　　Ⓓ 可能需要參加費。

156-157 訊息串

> **米雪兒・萊亞〔上午 11:01〕：**
> 嗨！米勒先生。我已到「賈西亞的家」餐廳。我需要安排下午結婚宴會的甜點桌。不過門鎖上了，我又把鑰匙放在家裡。
>
> **尚恩・米勒〔上午 11:03〕：**
> 薩摩瓦女士不在那嗎？她通常都會提前到餐廳準備活動。
>
> **米雪兒・萊亞〔上午 11:04〕：**
> 我知道，這才奇怪呀。你今天會晚到，是嗎？
>
> **尚恩・米勒〔上午 11:05〕：**
> 對，我現在在路上，要去和其他客戶開會，但我有提早 20 分出發，所以有時間過去一趟讓妳進去。
>
> **米雪兒・萊亞〔上午 11:07〕：**
> 非常感謝你！我在大廳旁的露台那邊等。
>
> 送出

156. 米勒先生最有可能是？
　　Ⓐ 咖啡店服務生
　　Ⓑ 餐廳經理
　　Ⓒ 咖啡店收銀員
　　Ⓓ 餐廳主廚

 157. 上午 11:04 時，萊亞女士寫道：「這才奇怪呀。」她最可能的意思是？
　　Ⓐ 她的同事沒有提前到。
　　Ⓑ 她不懂米勒先生在說什麼。
　　Ⓒ 情況不適合舉辦活動。
　　Ⓓ 參加活動的人已經到場。

158-160 電子郵件

寄件人：南茜・海伍德
收件人：全體同仁
日期：6 月 30 日
主旨：更新停車資訊

親愛的同事：

請留意使用停車場的方式有一些改變。因為索頓大廳停車場進行工程，所以從 7 月 10 日到 15 日，你們不能把車停在那裡。停車場地面要加防水層，還要增建安全圍籬。預計要到 7 月 16 日週一才會重新開放，但也會再變動。建議同仁使用公共運輸工具，或者和主管討論暫時在家工作。請留意，使用其他交通工具或者其他的停車場（像是斯泰普頓停車區），都將在八月初給予全額補助。

另外也請注意，等到整修完畢後，停車場會多出兩個停車位，是專門規劃給有需要的全職員工，以抽籤方式選出。如果想要參加抽籤，請儘快用電子郵件 n.haywood@suttoncorp.com 聯絡我。謝謝。

南茜・海伍德

158. 根據這封電子郵件，員工應和主管討論什麼事情？
　　Ⓐ 遠距離工作的可能性
　　Ⓑ 近公司最適合的替代停車場
　　Ⓒ 如何參加抽籤抽停車位
　　Ⓓ 可以獲得補助的金額多寡

159. 文中提到關於斯泰普頓停車區什麼事？
　　Ⓐ 週日不開放。
　　Ⓑ 設備最先進。
　　Ⓒ 最近剛增建。
　　Ⓓ 駕駛人使用需付費。

160. 下列句子最適合出現在 [1]、[2]、[3]、[4] 的哪個位置中？

「停車場地面要加防水層，還要增建安全圍籬。」

A [1]

B [2]

C [3]

D [4]

161–164 網路討論區

克里斯・保羅〔下午 3:30〕：
金和我工作完要早點出去吃飯，大概四點吧。有人要加入嗎？

傑瑞米・拉文〔下午 3:31〕：
大概吧。我還有報告要交給老闆。你們要去哪？

克里斯・保羅〔下午 3:32〕：
我們考慮要去華盛頓大道的墨西哥酒吧，叫做塔可圈的那家。

丹尼・李維拉〔下午 3:33〕：
喔，你們有點衰！那間店上週收起來了。

克里斯・保羅〔下午 3:34〕：
真的嗎？真不巧，我聽說那裡東西還蠻多不錯吃的。

丹尼・李維拉〔下午 3:35〕：
卡內基街附近的羅密歐披薩店怎麼樣？週二的菜色好吃、點心也不賴。

克里斯・保羅〔下午 3:37〕：
聽起來還不錯。有人要跟我們去嗎？

傑瑞米・拉文〔下午 3:38〕：
可以。但我猜我五點前到不了。

布萊德・崔安那〔下午 3:39〕：
對我來說是好消息，拉文，我剛剛把改完的報告寄給你了。

送出

161. 對話成員在討論什麼？

A 要去哪裡吃晚餐

B 每週銷售報告的會議

C 塔可圈餐館的菜單

D 介紹新成員給大家

162. 關於塔可圈，李維拉先生提供了什麼資訊？

A 食物不好吃。

B 菜色很多元。

C 餐廳不再營業了。

D 他們要到那裡開會。

163. 下午 3:34 分，為何保羅先生寫道：「真不巧」？

A 他無法和同事一起出去吃晚餐。

B 他想去塔可圈吃飯。

C 他還有很多事得報告老闆。

D 他在塔可圈吃過好吃的菜。

164. 拉文先生決定做什麼？

A 加入同事吃晚餐的行列

B 請人外送

C 加班來完成工作

D 考慮其他自助餐廳

165–168 通知

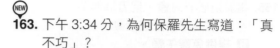

全賓州議題公司

你的意見，我們重視！

全賓州議題公司過去二十年來，持續針對當前議題進行民調。我們所有的問題都是透過電話訪問，訪問住在特定民調區域，18 歲以上的成年人。為了確保每個人公平參與的機會，均由電腦隨機抽選受測者。

想知道民眾對於全球議題怎麼想，可以到我們官網的「最新民調議題」查詢。每週都會舉行新的民調，資料都會在網路上存檔並且公開。如果您想要根據主題查詢民調，使用篩選工具找尋特定主題，也能使用頁面橫幅右方的「主題」。如果您想使用全賓州議題公司所製作的表格、圖表、曲線圖或是其他圖像，請點選「聯絡我們」，並詢問我們的授權部門。您也可以很輕鬆地在網站找到「好用線上手冊」的資訊，關於如何使用和在哪裡使用也有詳細說明。填單繳交後，我們通常會在 24 小時內回覆您。

165. 關於民調參與者，文中沒有提到什麼？
- Ⓐ 他們經由電話訪問。
- Ⓑ 他們被隨機抽選。
- Ⓒ 他們必須是成年人。
- **Ⓓ 他們應該參與團體訪問。**

166. 文中提到關於全賓州議題公司什麼事？
- Ⓐ 它出版和世界歷史議題有關的書籍。
- **Ⓑ 它每週都會在網站上公布新民調。**
- Ⓒ 它想聘人來管理網頁。
- Ⓓ 它有其他分店。

167. 讀者要怎麼樣取得圖片使用許可？
- Ⓐ 繳交紙本表格
- Ⓑ 打電話詢問網頁專家
- Ⓒ 透過信件提出要求
- **Ⓓ 透過網站聯繫**

168. 第一段、第二行中的「current」，最接近下列哪個意思？
- **Ⓐ 當代的**
- Ⓑ 暫時性的
- Ⓒ 重大的
- Ⓓ 適當的

169–171 廣告

想要休息嗎？

來場洛磯山脈之旅吧！
藍雲杉公司給您「最好的西南部假期」！

藍雲杉公司提供：

最好的戶外活動！

呼吸山中的新鮮空氣，享受群山間橡樹林和山谷交織，令人難以置信的美景。加價還能享受超過 20 公里的越野腳踏車之旅，還能搭乘纜車到達山頂。無論是要自行延著美麗的山脊旅行，還是要找經驗豐富的嚮導陪同都行。我們的「極限運動課程」，讓您也能體驗各式各樣的運動，像是攀岩、泛舟等等。在我們的大樓內也提供室內團康活動「室內團聚日」，包括烤肉派對、賓果遊戲或現場音樂表演。如

果您想要入團共襄盛舉，我們會根據參加人數提供不同的價格優惠。如果還有其他關於活動和花費的問題，不用遲疑，馬上打電話到 750-8103。

169. 藍雲杉最可能是什麼公司？
- **Ⓐ 旅行社**
- Ⓑ 國家公園
- Ⓒ 遊樂區
- Ⓓ 運動中心

170. 文中提到關於洛磯山脈什麼事？
- Ⓐ 那裡有各種瀑布和湖泊。
- **Ⓑ 位於西南方。**
- Ⓒ 贈送很多活動。
- Ⓓ 參加活動需要證照。

171. 需要額外花費的是什麼？
- **Ⓐ 纜車**
- Ⓑ 賓果遊戲
- Ⓒ 現場娛樂表演
- Ⓓ 攀岩活動

172–175 廣告

霍普金斯服飾

管理週報，4 月 7 日到 11 日

報告人：專案經理荷西・馬克力

本週成就：

＊ 和越南胡志明市五家有相關經驗製造商，討論手提包的事宜。提供他們新包包的設計，並詢問最低訂購量、製造成本、出貨和物流時間。

＊ 經初步了解各家廠商，史泰博製造最符合我們對時間和成本的需求。這間公司太小，不能滿足產量，但願意配合增僱員工來完成工作。此外，是會計經理吉姆・布默先和我聯繫。他非常熱情，而且也很專業，對於我們的需求即時給予答覆。我深信，史泰博製造在這筆生意中，可以和我們合作得很好。

* 其他聯繫過的公司都不能配合我們的時間安排和定價要求，所以我們不需再多加考慮。

4 月 15 日到 20 日的計畫

[此頁刻意留白]

172. 文中提到關於霍普金斯服飾什麼事？
A 在越南有分店。
B 計劃要併購其他公司。
C 專案經理快要退休了。
D 計劃發布新品。

173. 根據報告，馬克力先生在 4 月 7 日這週做了什麼事情？
A 他挑選可能是最好的合作夥伴。
B 他獲得製造產品的許可。
C 他和航運公司進行磋商。
D 他為新進員工舉行訓練課程。

174. 文中提到關於布默先生什麼事？
A 他很樂意和霍普金斯服飾合作。
B 他需要更多和新包包有關的資訊。
C 他曾在霍普金斯服飾擔任專案經理。
D 他想和馬克力先生見面協商定價的事。

(NEW)
175. 下列句子最適合出現在 [1]、[2]、[3]、[4] 的哪個位置中？
「這間公司太小，不能滿足產量，但願意配合增僱員工來完成工作。」
A [1]
B [2]
C [3]
D [4]

176–180 電子郵件

收件人：史帝夫・傑克
　　　　<stevejack@fastmail.com>
寄件人：約翰・杜威 <jdewy@aaco.com>

親愛的傑克先生：

您申請亞歷桑納會計事務所會計部門經理一職的申請資料，已由我們的部門仔細審查過了。今年度的徵選過程高度競爭，從眾多應徵者中我們只能選出兩人。根據部門建議，很遺憾通知您，我們這次不能如您所願地通過您的申請。

關於這項決定，如果您想了解更多，請您聯繫人資部門的招募處。

人事辦公室

電話：(480) 965-3344
信箱：recruit@aaco.com
URL：http://recruit.aaco.com/manger-apply

如果您還考慮亞歷桑納會計事務所的其他職務，也可以在 http://www.aaco.com/departments 找到更多連結和資訊。

感謝您對亞歷桑納會計事務所的熱忱，也祝福您未來求職順利。

亞歷桑納會計事務所
約翰・杜威 敬上

收件人：約翰・杜威
　　　　<jdewy@aaco.com>
寄件人：史帝夫・傑克
　　　　<stevejack@fastmail.com>

親愛的杜威先生：

我來信是想詢問您上一封的電子郵件。很遺憾聽到我沒有獲取該職位，但謝謝您友善地告訴我這件事。不過，我想了解貴公司哪些部門也處理金融業務。我在亞歷桑納大學主修商學系，能應對不論會計、預算或是物流管理有關的業務。不知道有沒有可能，讓我在這一季應徵貴公司這些相關職位呢？如果可以的話，請儘早讓我知道。

我目前在「體系公司」所負責的工作，湊巧也和上述職務完全一致。所以我希望能儘快知道，亞歷桑納會計事務所其他相關職缺。

我非常期待可以成為貴公司的有力員工。

祝好，

史帝夫‧傑克

176. 杜威先生最可能在什麼公司上班？
- Ⓐ 法律事務所
- **Ⓑ 金融業務**
- Ⓒ 出版公司
- Ⓓ 政府機關

177. 在第一封電子郵件中，收件人如欲獲得更多資訊，不需要做哪件事？
- Ⓐ 寄電子郵件給人事處
- Ⓑ 點選網站上的一些連結
- Ⓒ 直接打電話到公司
- **Ⓓ 到網站上張貼疑問**

178. 文中提到關於亞歷桑納會計事務所什麼事？
- **Ⓐ 有很多優秀的人上門應徵。**
- Ⓑ 和體系公司有合夥關係。
- Ⓒ 在物流方面的銷售量有成長。
- Ⓓ 為生產線聘僱了很多新進員工。

179. 為什麼會寫第二封電子郵件？
- Ⓐ 應徵者向經理宣傳自身的優點
- Ⓑ 協商該職位的後續情況
- Ⓒ 替某職位推薦適合人選
- **Ⓓ 詢問是否有其他相關職缺**

180. 關於傑克先生，何者為非？
- Ⓐ 他有大學學歷。
- **Ⓑ 他在大學學過商業法。**
- Ⓒ 他能處理多項金融業務。
- Ⓓ 他想要換公司。

181–185 目錄與電子郵件

六月，第 100 期

目錄

月刊封面：慶祝發行第 100 期

1 到 10 頁……頂尖主廚

15 頁……食譜索引

16 頁──球狀洋蔥

洋蔥和乳清起司沙拉佐番茄與迷迭香醋油醬

鷹嘴豆、茴香、洋蔥沙拉佐檸檬椰棗醬汁

義大利細扁麵佐新鮮番茄與洋蔥

香米沙拉醃製檸檬、洋蔥和蘆筍

20 頁──培根

嫩雞佐豆子與檸檬

脆蛋佐培根和扁豆

紅酒醬菲力牛排佐鴨肝醬

馬鈴薯、蠶豆和香脆培根沙拉佐薄荷醬

羅馬風味羊排

培根杏仁炒抱子甘藍

30 頁──牛肉

南亞牛肉丸佐凝乳起司

牛肉、焦烤紅蔥派綴花椰菜

牛肉、黃豌豆沙拉佐南瓜子醬

橄欖牛肉捲佐櫻桃番茄

35 頁……冠軍菜單

36 頁──蜜糖微風布丁

體驗食物軟嫩甜蜜的口感和好味道！

38 頁──東方義大利紅酒醋沙拉

熱帶水果沙拉有多種你意想不到的美味食材。

寄件人：jdoris@royalrecipe.com
收件人：t-daven@lycoos.com
日期：5 月 20 日
主旨：獲獎事宜

親愛的戴文先生：

很高興通知您，您的參賽甜點「蜜糖微風特製布丁」贏得我們的比賽。您的創意食譜將會在六月號的雜誌登出。不過，因為「冠軍菜單」的專欄空間有限，菜單名稱可能會被編輯稍微縮短。

雜誌登出您的食譜前，我想向您詢問其他資訊。您的食譜當中提到，可以用蜂蜜替代糖來帶出甜味。可以請您告訴我，如果不用糖，改用蜂蜜需要的量是多少嗎？如果家裡沒有蜂蜜，還能用什麼替代？此外，菜單中提到，布丁在吃之前要先冷藏。最短需要冷藏多久的時間？最合適的溫度是多少？謝謝您提供這些資訊。

刊登食譜的時候，我們通常也會登出作者的照片。請您回覆這封信時，也附上一張您清楚的半身照。

謝謝您，

珍・朵麗絲

181. 為什麼要寄電子郵件給戴文先生？
[A] 指出提交內容有錯誤
[B] 鼓勵他報名烹飪課程
[C] 告訴他贏得比賽的過程
[D] 討論食譜刊登的事

182. 電子郵件中第一段、第一行的「entry」最接近下列哪個意思？
[A] 建築正面
[B] 新進員工
[C] 申請參加比賽
[D] 最低度數

183. 朵麗絲女士沒有要求戴文先生提供什麼？
[A] 改完的食譜名稱
[B] 某樣食材的量
[C] 某項過程的時間長短
[D] 他的照片

184. 戴文先生的食譜將在哪一頁刊出？
[A] 16
[B] 20
[C] 36
[D] 38

185. 文中提到關於食譜什麼事？
[A] 洋蔥和義大利麵烹煮。
[B] 東方義大利紅酒醋沙拉有甜味。
[C] 做布丁的關鍵是製作的地點。
[D] 所有的食譜都是主廚做的。

186–190 網頁、清單和文章

[http://www.m-survival.it]

活動名稱：漫漫夏夜音樂節
地點：戴通納海灘，佛州
日期：8 月 1 日到 14 日
聯絡人：莎柏琳娜・安
　　　　<sanne@musicsurvival.com>

關於這項活動：

這項年度盛事已經是第五度舉辦，帶來 100 組來自美國東南部各地，單人或團體的參賽者。特別的是，參賽者來自各類音樂領域，都很有競爭力和能力。不只這樣，活動主辦方「生存音樂」預期，佛州戴通納海灘將聚集超過 2,000 名聽眾，比去年多出一倍。這項比賽儼然成為佛州最大規模的海灘活動。戴通納海灘是佛州最長的沙灘之一，距離奧蘭多市約一個小時的車程。戴通納市將在這週舉辦第 40 屆國際賽車大獎世界冠軍賽，這是全球賽車的運動盛會。遊客可以免費參加這項很棒的活動，停車費只需要五元。

第五屆漫漫夏夜音樂節的優勝者

單人組

名次	姓名	州	曲目
第一名	艾希頓‧珍	阿拉巴馬	《涼爽夏夜》
第二名	賈斯丁‧摩爾	喬治亞	《月球盡頭》
第三名	西蒙‧瑞克	北卡羅來納	《世界的攪拌碗》
第四名	泰勒‧史密斯	佛羅里達	《謊言捕手》

團體組

名次	姓名	州	曲目
第一名	蒂娜樂團	田納西	《不要霸凌鄉下人》
第二名	南方生活	南卡羅來納	《從不停止探險》

佛州東北有什麼新鮮事？

唐納‧史考特撰文

上週才結束的一年一度的漫漫夏夜音樂節，是告別炎熱夏季的最好方式。由於天氣很棒，訪客超乎主辦單位預期，比去年多出一倍以上。

競賽吸引了個人樂手和音樂團體，他們用美妙的聲音和激昂的情感，向遊客介紹自己，他們的情感渲染了整個戴通納海灘。這也是為什麼，我深信音樂是一種綜合藝術。歌曲饗宴讓音樂節更加好玩，也讓每個人都能放輕鬆。

競賽的結果，由艾希頓‧珍的好玩曲目《涼爽夏夜》拿下單人組冠軍。來自田納西州的蒂娜樂團則是用《不要霸凌鄉下人》，一首處理反社會議題的曲目，奪下團體組之冠。評分過程不只有評審給分，觀眾評分也佔了其中的一半。

由於音樂節大獲成功，佛州州長約翰‧麥凱因宣布，佛州文化部將在不久的將來，把音樂節的規模擴大到全國。這樣一來，佛州就能向全美國人民行銷佛州特色，推廣佛州所擁有的豐富文化。

---

186. 文中提到關於參賽者什麼事？
 A 他們來自不同的州。
 B 他們都是專業音樂人。
 C 他們被要求要提早報名。
 D 他們都是佛州的居民。

187. 文中提到今年漫漫夏夜音樂節什麼事？
 A 是歷年來最大。
 B 活動入場費每人五元。
 C 首度在戴通納海灘舉辦。
 D 這是最後一次舉辦該活動了。

188. 誰是單人組的第二名？
 A 艾希頓‧珍
 B 賈斯丁‧摩爾
 C 泰勒‧史密斯
 D 南方生活

189. 麥凱因先生想要做什麼？
 A 他將把活動發展成全國性的活動。
 B 他不會接受後續活動。
 C 他打算要參選國會議員。
 D 他要把活動轉型為慈善活動。

190. 哪首曲目是由當地參賽者所演出？
 A 《涼爽夏夜》
 B 《世界的攪拌碗》
 C 《謊言捕手》
 D 《從不停止探險》

191–195 資訊、電子郵件和停車證

艾本斯堡區

進修教育課程──六月

所有艾本斯堡區的居民，只要年滿 19 歲都能參加進修教育課程。除非另外通知上課地點，否則都在蒙特阿洛伊修斯學院開課。註冊方式詳參本手冊第四頁，也有更多學費和付費選項的詳細資訊。

如何創業？	
週一下午 1 點到 3 點	索頓大廳 101 室
講師：印第安納零售公會聯合主席， M‧茱蒂斯	

拍張照——簡單又愉快的攝影世界！	
週二下午 2 點到 5 點	斯泰普頓圖書館 202 室
講師：納林歐德攝影公司經理，S·肯尼斯	

成為一名不動產仲介——準備考證照	
週三下午 1 點到 4 點	里昂納德大廳 305 室
講師：傑克房地產公司總裁，K·彼得	

讓你的車超完美——自助保養祕訣	
週四下午 3 點到 6 點	蒙洛維爾校區萊澳汽車實驗室
講師：賓州海因茲汽車零件技師，T·史耐德	

收件人：葛洛麗亞·帕克（和其他 12 人）
寄件人：傑瑞·葛博哈德
　　　　<jgebhard@ebensburg.gov>
主旨：（緊急）課程取消
日期：6 月 19 日

此致所有學員：

萊蒂斯女士請我通知各位，因為她要處理一件重要的事情，課程必須取消，很快會再擇日安排補課。一旦我們知道日期和時間，會儘快透過電子郵件通知你們，並給與新的停車許可證，畢竟到時候現有的這張就會失效。抱歉造成不便。

祝好，

經理，艾本斯堡區地方福利部

傑瑞·葛博哈德

電話：743–8917

**蒙特阿洛伊修斯學院分部
單日臨時通行證
僅限當天**

南方藍停車位

有效日期：6 月 22 日

時間戳章：下午 1:30

＊請將此許可張貼於前座車窗上，以供外部人員辨識。

191. T·史耐德先生最有可能是？
- **Ⓐ 維修人員**
- Ⓑ 市議員
- Ⓒ 當地商家老闆
- Ⓓ 公會主席

192. 關於進修教育課程參加者，文中沒有提到什麼事？
- Ⓐ 他們住在艾本斯堡區。
- Ⓑ 他們要繳交學費。
- Ⓒ 他們最少要滿 19 歲。
- **Ⓓ 他們從蒙特阿洛伊修斯學院畢業。**

193. 帕克女士對什麼可能最感興趣？
- Ⓐ 不動產
- **Ⓑ 創業**
- Ⓒ 攝影
- Ⓓ 維修汽車

194. 電子郵件中，第二行的「attend to」，最接近下列哪個意思？
- Ⓐ 參加
- **Ⓑ 處理**
- Ⓒ 提到
- Ⓓ 報名

195. 補課改到哪一天？
- Ⓐ 6 月 20 日
- Ⓑ 6 月 21 日
- **Ⓒ 6 月 22 日**
- Ⓓ 6 月 23 日

李奇蒙日報

3 月 17 日新聞速報

如同今年初的消息,大霍克雜貨店即將開幕新的物流中心。由於地基的建設問題,造成了工程完工時間延誤。不過,相關問題已經完全解決,而佔地 2,000 平方公尺的新區域,將從 4 月 5 日全面啟用,並舉行盛大開幕儀式,多位市民都能前來參與。

倉庫特別配備最先進的機器,使用真空系統進行包裝。另外也有設備運用快速冷藏科技,能迅速將食品冷藏冷凍。

營運長查克‧康洛德表示,新的物流中心估計將創造超過 200 個工作機會。因應工作規模和領域,將釋出各種職缺,從上貨員、駕駛到公司職員都有。

收件人：查克‧康洛德
　　　　<chuck@gianthawk.co.ca>
寄件人：馬洛妮‧布藍尼爾
　　　　<mblaniar@gianthawk.co.ca>
主旨：簡訊公司
日期：4 月 20 日

親愛的康洛德：

感謝您邀請我參加這個月初的盛大開幕式。沒想到我能見證這麼好的活動安排。我想應該準備一些東西,向籌備活動的安德魯先生表達我們的謝意。

我想是時候找間可以自動發送提醒訊息到員工手機的公司。這樣的服務可以發送即時訊息給我們的員工,也可以避免出錯。我有一間提供這種顧客服務的公司「為你傳達」的聯絡方式。我想這間應該不錯,但是「全體通知」看起來也不差,月租費也相較便宜。總之,我把兩間公司的資訊附給您,再由您決定。再請您告訴我您的想法。

祝好,

馬洛妮‧布藍尼爾

全體通知

下午 2:20

此致大霍克全體員工：

原訂要在週一送到的冷凍配送,將在週三才會送到。所以本來在週一和二晚上自願加班的李奇蒙物流中心的員工就不需要來了。不過,週三晚上我們會需要大夜班的人力。有意願在該時段加班的同事,請聯絡人事部的蘇‧崔納提。

196. 這篇文章的目的為何？
　　Ⓐ 介紹一個新創產業
　　Ⓑ 報告一項商業指標
　　Ⓒ 提供一項在地議題的訊息
　　Ⓓ 展示最先進的設備

197. 關於李奇蒙物流中心,何者最可能為真？
　　Ⓐ 開幕式讓人印象深刻。
　　Ⓑ 查克先生很快就會從那裡退休。
　　Ⓒ 布藍尼爾女士是其中一名自願加班的人。
　　Ⓓ 發生了一些技術問題。

198. 該封電子郵件的主旨為何？
　　Ⓐ 慶祝開幕式
　　Ⓑ 準備即將到來的活動
　　Ⓒ 協助選擇一家廠商
　　Ⓓ 打斷商業合作關係

199. 查克先生選了哪間公司？
　　Ⓐ 布藍尼爾女士工作的公司
　　Ⓑ 員工想去的公司
　　Ⓒ 在大夜班營運的公司
　　Ⓓ 比起另一家廠商更便宜的公司

200. 簡訊中,要求有意願加班的員工去做什麼？
　　Ⓐ 聯絡人資部門
　　Ⓑ 到另一間物流中心工作
　　Ⓒ 從週二開始到倉庫工作
　　Ⓓ 一天內回覆訊息

ACTUAL TEST ⑤

◎ Part 5 解答請見 P.457

101. 羅伯森先生很介意，人家推薦他的旅館距離機場不夠**近**。

102. 阿靈頓的德州大學提供**給**居民各式娛樂課程。

103. 辦公用品的**購買**必須要基於工作用途。

104. 為了遵守歐米茄時尚的**規定**，顧客要退款時需出示有效收據。

105. 任何參加登山活動的人都需要準備合適的**裝備**。

106. 最先進的軟體能趕在截止日前，**大幅**減少所需時間。

107. 有希望錄取的應徵者**都**要有推土機和挖土機駕照。

108. 我們預計在官網上和顧客**分享**上週民調的結果。

109. 人資部門把椅子換成**比較輕的**，來減少辦公室噪音。

110. 電話會議改時間了，所有與會者**改成**下週一參加。

111. 安德森先生和客戶開會時，收到的**每一封**簡訊都會轉給他的祕書。

112. 考量會議的性質，穿著正式服裝才**合適**。

113. 大眾電子打算要開始新業務，**將使**顧客可以獲得更多資訊。

114. 獅子汽車的經理頒獎給表現頻頻**超乎**預期的員工。

115. 星星娛樂公司最近發行的影片，獲得的觀眾評價和評分**特別地**好。

116. 在博克夏爾哈德威公司，各部門的經理都是基於**特定**領域的專業和經驗才能當上主管。

117. 昂貴、易碎或易腐壞物品的運費特別貴，**因為**它們需要更小心搬運。

118. 麥肯和梅是間提供全方位服務的法律事務所，給予有**各式**特殊需求的顧客法律協助。

119. 最新版的營業支出**軟體**擁有多項功能，使用起來相對簡單。

120. **如果**您在安裝或運作時發現問題，請聯繫我們的客服中心。

121. 下列文件詳細記錄了，政府用來**分析**明年度預算所需的統計資料。

122. **即便**有很多鹽湖城居民對終生學習課程表示興趣，卻沒有人註冊報名。

123. 北美區的業務預期將**創造**公司絕大部分的收益。

124. 律師在非常有限的期間**內**，同時處理了大量案件。

125. 新博物館建設能否順利進行，高度**取決於**市府是否通過預算。

126. 為避免乳製品或其他**易腐敗的**產品壞掉，安迪食品運送公司的貨車都有冷藏功能。

127. 財政部報告指出，很多中小企業第一年經營時**財務上**都會資金緊絀。

128. 中本先生建議，員工出差回來後便**立即**提交差旅支出報告。

129. 經過審慎**考慮**，我們決定搬到更大的地點來接納更多旅客。

130. 艾許利女士的傑出表現，讓她在同事中**出類拔萃**。

131-134 電子郵件

收件人：布萊恩‧尼克森
　　　　〈bnixon@futuresky.co.au〉
寄件人：潔西卡‧赫本
　　　　〈jhepburn@cardinalfargo.org.au〉

親愛的尼克森先生：

我們已收到您應徵鮮紅法戈工作室攝影師一職的申請。職缺目前依然開著，如果您對該職位還有興趣，下一階段將進行個人面試。

您在多間大型工作室豐富的工作經驗讓我印象深刻，所以您必然很熟悉我們所要求的某些工作內容。不過，我們的主要業務會和您之前做過的很不同，所以您會需要花些時間了解。我在 9 月 15 日的上午 10 點安排了面試。如果想要確認面試時間，可以撥打 (01) 444-0125 聯絡我的辦公室。希望能很快跟您見面。

鮮紅法戈工作室人事經理
潔西卡‧赫本　敬上

131. Ⓐ 文件
　　 Ⓑ 職缺
　　 Ⓒ 手術
　　 Ⓓ 約會

132. Ⓐ 可以請您給我們關於核銷的額外資訊嗎？
　　 Ⓑ 更精確地問，不知道您有沒有設計獨特風格的相關經驗？
　　 Ⓒ 可以在官網上找到前往面試地點的資訊。
　　 Ⓓ 如果您對該職位還有興趣，下一階段將進行個人面試。

133. Ⓐ 使……有印象
　　 Ⓑ 感到印象深刻
　　 Ⓒ 令人印象深刻的
　　 Ⓓ 印象

134. **Ⓐ 不過**
　　 Ⓑ 因此
　　 Ⓒ 因此
　　 Ⓓ 此外

135-138 信件

4 月 20 日

李奧納多‧克魯斯
91101 加州克羅格市主街 111342 號

親愛的克魯斯先生：

我們很高興通知您，克羅格回收計畫將從 5 月 1 日開始在我們地區實施。我們將提供一個有輪的藍色回收箱，給有意參與計畫的住戶。如欲索取回收箱，請聯絡 800-111-1217。

如同先前所規劃的，這項計畫一週進行一次，而非一週兩次。因此，這項計畫將有效降低溫室氣體排放，並讓我們擁有一個更好的環境。

如果您需要更多資訊，像是回收物品清單或地圖，可以上我們官網 www.krogerrecycling.com 查詢。我們希望您能參與這項重要計畫。

克羅格回收計畫總經理
德偉恩‧戴蒙 敬上

135. Ⓐ 參與
　　 Ⓑ 參與過
　　 Ⓒ 去參與
　　 Ⓓ 正在參與

136. **Ⓐ 要求**
　　 Ⓑ 改造
　　 Ⓒ 複習
　　 Ⓓ 移開

137. Ⓐ 然而
　　 Ⓑ 因此
　　 Ⓒ 同時
　　 Ⓓ 另一方面

(NEW) 138. A 多虧民眾慷慨捐款，這個計畫募得
大量資金。

B 我們希望您能參與這項重要計畫。

C 您將在十天內拿到藍色回收箱。

D 請您確保不會在回收箱內放置易碎
物品。

139–142 文章

市長亞歷山卓拉・史密斯宣布，羅賓威廉
斯隧道將要進行擴建，方便大型載貨卡車
通行。過去幾年來，因為當地貨運運輸的
成長，使用隧道的駕駛也明顯增加。擴建
計畫完工預計大約要 10 個月。經過更精
確的測量後，時間從原來估計的 18 個月縮
短了。

沿著隧道的傑克森韋爾路將會封閉，在這
段期間，阿米提爾和黑娜敦之間的交通將
會更堵塞。「很遺憾，這是唯一可能的選
擇。」市長史密斯說。

139. A 擴建

B 去擴建

C 已被擴建

D 將被擴建

(NEW) 140. A 羅賓威廉斯隧道一百年前就已經
蓋好了。

B 住在阿米提爾的人長久以來都對
塞車抱有不滿。

C 貨運公司希望能招聘黑娜敦大學
的畢業生。

**D 經過更精確的測量後，時間從原
來估計的 18 個月縮短了。**

141. **A 沿著**

B 下一個的

C 當……的時候

D 在……之上

142. A 令人驚訝地

B 相應地

C 因此

D 遺憾地

143–146 電子郵件

收件人：莎拉・歐康諾〈sarah_
oconnor@pinghwacorp.com〉

寄件人：金・藍儂〈jim_lennon@ams.
com〉

日期：11 月 11 日

主旨：AMS

附件：AMS 小冊

親愛的莎拉・歐康諾女士：

感謝您向 AMS 詢價。我們最先進的軟體
程式，已協助大量企業提高評鑑程序的效
率，省時又省錢。

我們建議您詳讀附檔，其中包含五間頂尖
企業善用 AMS 而得利的資訊。如您所知，
用排名來瀏覽績效表單的功能，對這幾家
企業來說特別有幫助。因此藉由我們的軟
體，他們可以輕易找到所有適合升遷的候
選人。此外，所有分類過程數據化後，也
不會有公文凌亂的情形。所有的表單在電
腦化的資料庫中都整理得井然有序。

如果您還有其他相關問題，請讓我知道。

AMS 行銷經理
金・藍儂 敬上

143. A 節省

B 節省

C 節省了

D 節省

144. **A 仔細審閱**

B 做

C 準備

D 丟

145. **A 因此**

B 只要

C 同時

D 與……一致

146.
    Ⓐ 我們的軟體下週將會更新。
    Ⓑ 要從符合資格的人選當中選出晉升者,對你來説是個艱難的任務。
    Ⓒ 所有的表單在電腦化的資料庫中都整理得井然有序。
    Ⓓ 應徵者至少要有相關領域三年的工作經驗。

PART 7   P. 141–161

147–148 簡訊

親愛的休斯先生:

黃金州 DVD 出租服務提醒您,以您的名義租借的 DVD 將在 12 月 15 日到期。請在這個日期以前,到您租借的地點或是其他分店歸還 DVD,以免被徵收逾期費用。

黃金州 DVD 出租服務員工

(這是自動寄發的訊息,請不要回覆。假如您有任何疑問,請撥打總辦公室專線 211-232-0104,由客服代表為您服務)

送出

147. 休斯先生為什麼收到簡訊?
    Ⓐ 因為他借的東西需要儘快歸還
    Ⓑ 因為他在 12 月 15 日前要繳交逾期費用
    Ⓒ 因為他要求的商品已經售罄
    Ⓓ 因為他的會員卡將在 12 月 15 日到期

148. 根據簡訊,如果休斯先生有疑問應該怎麼做?
    Ⓐ 瀏覽出租店的網站
    Ⓑ 和客服代表聯繫
    Ⓒ 傳簡訊給客服代表
    Ⓓ 去出租服務的任何一家分店

149–150 電子郵件

寄件人:湯姆·艾佛列克
                <affleck@valerofurniture.com>
收件人:史嘉莉·勞倫斯
                <lawrence@smail.com>
日期:3 月 11 日
主旨:延遲寄送

親愛的勞倫斯女士:

感謝您近期在瓦萊羅家具購買商品。由於我們地區下大雪,部分訂購貨品未能寄出。封路使得倉庫出貨更加困難。更糟的是,大雪造成我們地區停電。但我們承諾會在 12 個小時內回復正常運作。因此您的訂單最晚會在週三前出貨。受影響訂單的運費將會全額退費。很抱歉可能對您造成不便。

客服經理
湯姆·艾佛列克 敬上

149. 寫這封電子郵件的目的是?
    Ⓐ 更新氣候狀況
    Ⓑ 告知勞倫斯女士寄送延遲
    Ⓒ 推廣家具
    Ⓓ 報告部分道路封閉

150. 勞倫斯女士將收到什麼?
    Ⓐ 一封確認的電子郵件
    Ⓑ 一張家具的優惠券
    Ⓒ 她的訂單免運費
    Ⓓ 額外贈送一樣新品

151–152 告示

收垃圾的新規定

克魯登華德市將從 4 月 25 日開始限制垃圾桶數量。每個月的垃圾清潔費沒有改變,但之後每一次垃圾車來,居民拿來丟的垃圾量不得超過三桶。總容量不得超過 100 公升。

市府官員表示，此舉能鼓勵居民利用市區免費的回收站，以及金屬、塑膠還有紙張的回收服務，為市府推廣降低收垃圾成本盡一份力。同時也能減少垃圾掩埋的花費。

151. 這篇告示的目的為何？
- Ａ 提供一項新服務
- **Ｂ 宣布一個規定異動**
- Ｃ 抱怨回收費
- Ｄ 推薦一個掩埋場

152. 根據告示，居民可以免費使用的服務是什麼？
- **Ａ 回收服務**
- Ｂ 幫忙收垃圾的服務
- Ｃ 垃圾桶
- Ｄ 掩埋場

153–155 備忘錄

備忘錄

此致：所有員工

來自：克里斯提安·迪索，營運長

日期：7 月 28 日，週四

主旨：西翼大樓關閉

西翼大樓將會在 8 月第一週關閉。維修部門會負責把所有桌椅，替換成更環保的材質。依照安全規則，維修人員施工期間，所有員工均禁止進入。更換作業將從 8 月 1 日週二開始，並會在 8 月 5 日週六結束。

受到影響的辦公室是 1201 至 1235 號辦公室，相關員工可以在家辦公，或如果有必要的話，公司也可以在大樓內準備另一間臨時辦公區，供員工使用。您可以透過分機 51，向行政助理娜塔莉·喬韓森提出需求。請留意臨時辦公區空間有限，將優先提供給先行申請的人。感謝您的配合。

153. 為什麼西翼大樓會關閉？
- Ａ 要實施例行性檢查。
- Ｂ 總部要搬到其他地點。
- **Ｃ 要更換辦公家具。**
- Ｄ 要增設會議空間。

154. 以下哪間辦公室將暫時無法使用？
- Ａ 1200
- **Ｂ 1224**
- Ｃ 1236
- Ｄ 1240

155. 如果員工欲申請臨時辦公區，應該怎麼做？
- Ａ 聯繫主管
- Ｂ 寫電子郵件給迪索先生
- Ｃ 線上申請
- **Ｄ 打電話給喬韓森女士**

156–158 電子郵件

寄件人：安潔莉娜·格蘭特
　　　　<agrant@lowecatering.com>

收件人：詹姆斯·哈迪
　　　　<jhardy@uig.com>

日期：6 月 11 日

主旨：外燴服務

親愛的哈迪先生：

這封電子郵件是要和您確認，您昨天在電話中為貴公司年度會議提出餐飲服務的需求。我的理解是，餐食服務的菜色應該要和去年的會議類似。但很遺憾，我的食物供應商通知我目前牛肉缺貨，到下週前都沒有辦法供貨。由於會議將在 6 月 15 日舉行，我想有必要選擇其他種類的肉品。我建議選雞肉，比較能趕上時間。所以如果這項建議可行，請直接回信告訴我。只要您同意替代方案，我會寄合約和估價單給您。如果您需要更多資訊，可以透過 514-212-0114 聯絡我。

感謝，

羅威餐飲服務經理
安潔莉娜·格蘭特

156. 文中提到關於哈迪先生什麼事？
- Ⓐ 他是格蘭特女士的同事。
- Ⓑ 他要為朋友準備晚宴。
- **Ⓒ 他先前曾向羅威餐飲服務提出需求。**
- Ⓓ 他要求更換服務內容。

157. 為什麼格蘭特女士建議更換餐點內容？
- **Ⓐ 它沒有貨了。**
- Ⓑ 它非常貴。
- Ⓒ 它不新鮮。
- Ⓓ 它不好吃。

158. 格蘭特女士要求哈迪先生，接下來怎麼做？
- Ⓐ 寄合約
- Ⓑ 馬上打電話給她
- **Ⓒ 回覆電子郵件**
- Ⓓ 取消會議

159–160 訊息串

> **聖內嘉公司專員〔下午 5:15〕：**
> 聖內嘉公司客服中心您好。請問您遇到什麼問題？
> **馬丁·福特〔下午 5:15〕：**
> 我的桌機無法更新最新版本的軟體。
> **聖內嘉公司專員〔下午 5:16〕：**
> 請問您的桌機型號是？
> **馬丁·福特〔下午 5:17〕：**
> 是 XPS 8910。下載軟體要正確的序號，但我找不到。
> **聖內嘉公司專員〔下午 5:18〕：**
> 要找到產品序號，它就印在產品包裝的條碼旁邊。
> **聖內嘉公司專員〔下午 5:18〕：**
> 可能字太小不好看清楚，所以請用手機拍照，然後再放大。
> **馬丁·福特〔下午 5:19〕：**
> 好，那裡有一組十碼數字。就是它嗎？
> **聖內嘉公司專員〔下午 5:20〕：**
> 是的，沒錯。還有什麼可以幫助您的嗎？
> **馬丁·福特〔下午 5:20〕：**
> 沒有。非常感謝您。
>
> 送出

159. 福特先生想做什麼？
- Ⓐ 找到密碼
- Ⓑ 申請帳號
- Ⓒ 買台電腦
- **Ⓓ 下載軟體**

 160. 下午 5:19 時，福特先生寫道：「就是它嗎？」他最可能的意思是？
- **Ⓐ 他想確定找到的是不是對的東西。**
- Ⓑ 他不了解專員的想法。
- Ⓒ 他從未用過線上服務。
- Ⓓ 他不想再用網路溝通。

161–163 電子郵件

> 寄件人：布萊德利·庫柏
> <bcooper@sysco.com>
> 收件人：羅伯特·葛斯林
> <rgosling@sysco.com>
> 日期：1 月 4 日
> 主旨：捐款計畫
> ─────────────────
> 親愛的葛斯林先生：
>
> 關於西斯科的新捐款計畫，我仔細看過您提供的文件。您需要在下一次的部門會議，和我們同仁分享這份文件裡的訊息。此外，我會鼓勵他們確認推薦的組織名單，並在二月計畫開始前，請他們挑選其中至少一家來捐款以參與這項計畫。這還會花上幾週才能做決定。
>
> 請儘早打給我討論這項計畫的內容。在此先感謝您的配合。
>
> 人資部門
> 布萊德利·庫柏 敬上

161. 庫柏先生想要葛斯林先生做什麼？
- **Ⓐ 討論計畫的細節**
- Ⓑ 捐款給某些組織
- Ⓒ 重新安排部門會議的時間
- Ⓓ 發想一個捐款計畫

TEST 5

PART 7

162. 文中提到關於西斯科的新捐款計畫什麼事？

Ⓐ 計畫將在二月生效。

Ⓑ 只限員工參與。

Ⓒ 每年舉辦兩次。

Ⓓ 員工只許選一家組織捐款。

🆕 163. 下列句子最適合出現在 [1]、[2]、[3]、[4] 的哪個位置中？

「這還會花上幾週才能做決定。」

Ⓐ [1]

Ⓑ [2]

Ⓒ [3]

Ⓓ [4]

164–167 信件

5 月 1 日

萊恩・伊斯伍德

562 加州橘郡松木公寓 1299 號

親愛的伊斯伍德先生：

您所租的松木公寓將實施例行性的維修評估。我們計畫在 5 月 15 日週二的下午兩點拜訪您。我們要求住戶必須在場。如果時間不便的話，還請您讓我們知道適合的時間。

評估過程中，我們會檢查多項重點項目，像是家電、瓦斯或水管管線，確認它們運作無虞。如有需要，就會進行維修工作。

根據我們的檢查清單，您的公寓內部已經五年沒有粉刷了。如果您想要重新粉刷，我們的維修人員也能處理。我們會盡全力以最有效率的方式完工。我們有很多顏色的油漆可供選擇，您可以造訪我們的官網 www.pinewood.com/colorsforpaint 查看。最後，我們的紀錄也指出，您去年才全面更換房裡的家具，所以現階段還不需要更換家具。

如果您有任何問題，請隨時跟我聯絡。

祝好，

辦公室主任

克里斯・漢斯沃

164. 為什麼要寄這封信給伊斯伍德先生？

Ⓐ 提供他租屋促銷的資訊

Ⓑ 通知他帳款遲交

Ⓒ 通知他之後要來檢查

Ⓓ 建議公寓裡辦一項年度活動

165. 伊斯伍德先生在 5 月 15 日下午被要求做什麼？

Ⓐ 查看網頁

Ⓑ 選擇油漆顏色

Ⓒ 回覆電子郵件

Ⓓ 待在家裡

166. 哪一種家居改善方式，目前適合伊斯伍德先生？

Ⓐ 粉刷房子

Ⓑ 換家電

Ⓒ 修理門

Ⓓ 換家具

🆕 167. 下列句子最適合出現在 [1]、[2]、[3]、[4] 的哪個位置中？

「如有需要，就會進行維修工作。」

Ⓐ [1]

Ⓑ [2]

Ⓒ [3]

Ⓓ [4]

168–171 表格

月光問卷

感謝您參加電影《月光（暫名）》的試片。由於本片正在最後收尾階段，如果您願意分享意見，將對本片最後剪輯有莫大幫助。請花幾分鐘回答下列問題。

姓名：瑞秋・珍

地址：28912 格蘭維爾，

桑福德大道 2885 號

您對這部片的印象是？

我好愛！我好喜歡裡面的角色與場景，跟我幾年前讀原著小說所想像的一模一樣。改編得很完美。

音質如何？請詳細說明。

非常清楚。我尤其喜歡原創配樂。原則上，整部片裡沒有一句對白是我聽不懂的。

如果有太冗長的橋段，請詳細說明。

這部片確實比我看過的片子都要來得長一些。不過每個場景，對故事走向來說有它的必要，進行得也很流暢。我會建議不要再多作刪減。

有其他的建議嗎？

艾瑪·阿尼斯頓和詹姆斯·尼洛演得超棒。我先前從沒注意過潔西卡·華森。這次她的演出很驚人，我希望她能因為這部片得獎。只有一件事是我想提的，她在電影中穿得服裝和原著中的不像。電影背景設定在 1880 年代中期。我覺得她應該穿著更貼近歷史的服裝。

168. 這份問卷是給哪些人填的？
- Ⓐ 職業作家
- Ⓑ 演員訓練班學員
- Ⓒ 影視產業導演
- **Ⓓ 試映會的觀眾**

169. 文中提到關於《月光》什麼事？
- Ⓐ 片長相對短。
- **Ⓑ 根據一本書改編。**
- Ⓒ 用紀錄片風格拍攝。
- Ⓓ 幾年前已經完成。

170. 從文中可以推論關於華森女士什麼事？
- Ⓐ 她最近演出多部電影。
- Ⓑ 她退出這部電影的演出。
- Ⓒ 她參加了試映會。
- **Ⓓ 她在電影中的表演讓人印象深刻。**

171. 珍女士建議什麼？
- Ⓐ 讓對話更好理解
- **Ⓑ 讓服裝更寫實**
- Ⓒ 加入更多電影配樂
- Ⓓ 縮短電影

172–175 網路討論區

珊德拉·羅培茲〔上午 9:02〕：
早。董事在 12 月的董事會議上批准了我們公司的併購案。我想知道你們在總部的經理會議上，聽説了些什麼？

凱特·萊芙莉〔上午 9:03〕：
起先是一陣大混亂，但現在所有事情都已經回歸正軌。大家似乎知道接下來的狀況。

喀麥隆·溫斯雷〔上午 9:03〕：
這裡的員工認為併購將造成人事動盪。所有人都很關心二月的任何動靜，畢竟那是一年最忙的時候。什麼時候可以知道詳情呢？

凱特·亞當斯〔上午 9:05〕：
沒從總公司那裡知道更多訊息以前，我不適合回答這些問題。

珊德拉·羅培茲〔上午 9:07〕：
我會持續追蹤這件事，儘快了解更多。等到二月我們四個見面時，再向各位報告。

喀麥隆·溫斯雷〔上午 9:08〕：
聽起來，有些同仁可能在三月面臨調動？

珊德拉·羅培茲〔上午 9:09〕：
的確有可能。人事部門還在安排，看哪些部門將吸收其他團隊的人。

凱特·亞當斯〔上午 9:10〕：
一定還有很多事要決定。

送出

172. 為什麼羅培茲女士和經理線上討論此事？
- Ⓐ 取消會議
- Ⓑ 告知未來併購事宜
- **Ⓒ 收集意見**
- Ⓓ 擇期搬遷

173. 早上 9 點 7 分時，羅培茲女士寫道：「我會持續追蹤這件事。」，她最可能的意思是？
- **Ⓐ 她嘗試要取得最新狀況。**
- Ⓑ 去年員工人數大增。
- Ⓒ 總部將在二月遷址。
- Ⓓ 她努力要讓一切回歸正常。

174. 經理們何時可以得知更新的資訊？
- Ⓐ 12 月
- Ⓑ 1 月
- **Ⓒ 2 月**
- Ⓓ 3 月

175. 人事部門預計會做什麼？
- **Ⓐ 人事洗牌**
- Ⓑ 提供員工辦公用品
- Ⓒ 引介新員工
- Ⓓ 重整人事制度

176–180 信件和電子郵件

> **國廣保險公司**
>
> 93721-2760 加州佛雷斯諾市大街 848 號
>
> 4 月 8 日
> 喬治・漢克斯
> 93721 加州佛雷斯諾市音約街 2451 號
>
> ---
>
> 親愛的漢克斯先生：
>
> 感謝您申請國廣保險公司初級助理的職位。很遺憾通知您，經過多番思慮，我們選擇了另一名應徵者加入我們。但我們對您印象深刻，不只因為您近年的成就，還有您面試時所表現的知識和專業。因此，我們想要提供您一個相當適合您的職缺。
>
> 這是一份兼職工作，和您原先申請的有別。工時是每週二和週四的下午兩點到六點，以及週一、三、五的下午三點到七點。您的主要職責會是蒐集並分析資料和數據，向潛在客戶提供客製化的提案，並規劃保險產品。
>
> 如果您對這個職位有興趣，請儘管打電話給我，號碼是 515-217-0121 或是來信到 markchan@statewideinsurance.com。

> 寄件人：喬治・漢克斯
> 　　　　<ghanks@atmail.com>
> 收件人：馬克・陳
> 　　　　<markchan@statewideins urance.com>
> 日期：4 月 10 日
> 回覆：您的來信

> 親愛的陳先生：
>
> 謝謝您來信提供我工作。我很高興可以加入國廣保險公司。但我在想想貴公司能不能調整我的工作時間。
>
> 我在面試時曾經提到，我至今都在國際保險協會（IIS）擔任志工。由於我目前在那裡的排班是週一和二的早上九點到下午三點，這會和您安排的週一、周二時間有衝突。如果貴公司可以為我將週一和二的班，調整為下午四點到晚上八點，我會非常感謝。
>
> 期待您的回覆。
>
> 祝好，
>
> 喬治・漢克斯

176. 陳先生最可能是在什麼公司上班？
- Ⓐ 法律事務所
- Ⓑ 汽車製造業
- Ⓒ 出版商
- **Ⓓ 保險公司**

177. 在信件中，第一段、第二行的「select」，最接近下列哪個意思？
- **Ⓐ 選擇**
- Ⓑ 接受
- Ⓒ 依賴
- Ⓓ 對……負責

178. 文中提到關於陳先生的公司什麼事？
- Ⓐ 和國際保險協會合夥。
- Ⓑ 最近和大量客戶簽約。
- Ⓒ 以前從未僱用全職員工。
- **Ⓓ 提供保險規劃服務。**

179. 為什麼要寫這封電子郵件？
- **Ⓐ 詢問能否更改工作時間**
- Ⓑ 詢問員工福利
- Ⓒ 推薦其他勝任這個職缺的人選
- Ⓓ 要求加薪

180. 下列何者最不可能是漢克斯先生在陳先生公司裡，所要負責的職務？
- Ⓐ 收集資料
- Ⓑ 向客戶提出建議
- Ⓒ 介紹產品
- **Ⓓ 面試應徵者**

181–185 報告和文章

紐約媒體企業

研發團隊

年度績效考核報告

姓名：金・巴利摩

職稱：研究員

請寫下所有您在今年所參與的重要活動和計畫：

1. 紐約大學，指導大眾傳播科系的學生四週的媒體法規課程（2月2日至28日）

2. 紐約，第10屆新聞媒體會議，研發團隊代表（3月2日至3日）

3. 英國倫敦，世界新聞論壇，「網路媒體的現況」客座講者（5月12日至15日）

4. 執行一項網路傳播新潮流的研究計畫（1月至11月）。研究獲登《傳播業期刊》。

5. 多次帶領紐約媒體企業新總部的公眾導覽（12月）

來自紐約媒體的金・巴利摩

獲獎

JSP 記者 大衛・史都華撰文

12月17日——紐約媒體企業的金・巴利摩，以她研究網路傳播新潮流的計畫，獲頒年度傑出記者。

紐約媒體的主編瑪格特・格林表示，這個獎很少頒給研究者。她說：「這歸功於金・巴利摩的勤奮和奉獻。我們非常欣喜有她在我們團隊裡。」

巴利摩女士十年前取得紐約大學大眾傳播的博士學位後，便來到紐約媒體企業就職。而她大學讀的是紐約的布魯克林拉丁學院。

頒獎典禮將在12月23日於紐約會議中心舉行。

---

181. 根據報告，為什麼巴利摩女士要去英國？
- Ⓐ 報告案例
- Ⓑ 研讀大眾傳播
- **Ⓒ 發表演說**
- Ⓓ 導覽新的研究場所

182. 從報告中可以得知，紐約媒體企業12月發生了什麼事？
- Ⓐ 舉行了一場國際論壇。
- Ⓑ 為大學生開設了新課程。
- **Ⓒ 開設新的總部。**
- Ⓓ 公眾導覽的支出減少了。

183. 巴利摩女士的文章最有可能在哪裡首次刊登？
- Ⓐ 紐約大學的雜誌
- Ⓑ 紐約媒體企業的網站
- **Ⓒ 一份業界刊物**
- Ⓓ 一本科學期刊

184. 針對年度傑出記者獎，格林女士暗示什麼？
- Ⓐ 有提供獎牌和獎金。
- Ⓑ 由紐約媒體企業所頒發。
- **Ⓒ 不常頒給研究者。**
- Ⓓ 只會頒給紐約居民。

185. 文中提到關於新聞媒體會議什麼事？
- Ⓐ 通常由政府主辦。
- **Ⓑ 這不是今年第一次舉辦。**
- Ⓒ 提供大學生免費門票。
- Ⓓ 通常每兩年舉辦一次。

漢尼威國際辦公室即將搬遷

3月1日——漢尼威國際計劃將其位於雪梨、墨爾本和布里斯本的辦公室，搬到公司名下的大樓內。租金飛漲迫使公司做出這項決定。

「我們注意到，自己的辦公室自己蓋，可以從很多方面把錢省下來。」漢尼威國際總經理伊莉莎白・蘿涵說。她也提到和其他企業共享辦公空間，會在辦公時造成困擾與不便。設在雪梨的總部於兩年前開始建設，終於將在這個月落成。

墨爾本和布里斯本的分公司建設計劃將在一年內完成，屆時員工也會搬過去。

一名公司代表表示，全體員工（去年估計約有 1,000 人）最晚將在七月以前，全數搬到其中一間新大樓。

TIAA 搬家服務

通通由我們為您打點。TIAA 讓您搬家更輕鬆。

免費的搬家諮詢服務。我們顧問會親訪您的辦公室或住家，並對搬家進行估價。寫好的估價單會在諮詢後的兩到三天內，用電子郵件寄給您。

不論您什麼時候需要搬家，我們都準備好為您服務。

- 您需要打包嗎？我們人員全都可以幫忙。

- 您需要搬移機密資料嗎？我們會和您的安全人員一起安排行程，確保機密文件和檔案都在監督之下搬運不被干擾。

- 您需要空間保存私人物品嗎？我們準備好嚴密管理的倉庫等您到來。

我們使命必達。盡我們所能讓一切物品整整齊齊。

TIAA 搬家服務估價單

請完成下列需求表格，以便安排現場精準估價。

公司名稱：漢尼威國際	聯絡人姓名：伊莉莎 白・蘿涵
電話號碼：128-01-2821169	信箱：el0800@atmail.co.au
載貨地址：雪梨喬治街 680 號	寄送地址：雪梨哈里斯街 458 號
載貨日期：4 月 3 日	寄送日期：4 月 3 日

偏好的估價日期和時間：3 月 3 日早上 10 點

186. 在文章中，第一段、第二行的「forced」最接近下列哪個意思？
  A 不得不
  B 迅速做出反應
  C 壞了
  D 做出改變

187. 文中提到蘿涵女士什麼事？
  A 她今年升為總經理。
  B 她在漢尼威國際工作五年了。
  C 她會在四月搬到總部去。
  D 她在漢尼威國際布里斯本分公司工作。

188. TIAA 提供什麼服務？
  A 建設大樓
  B 搬運敏感物件
  C 維護電腦系統
  D 強化保全

189. 文中提到哈里斯街地點什麼事？
  A 將要容納近 1,000 名員工。
  B 花了大約兩年來建設。
  C 最近才整修。
  D 現在也有其他公司租用。

190. 在 3 月 3 日這天最有可能發生什麼事？
  A 一名 TIAA 的員工會拜訪喬治街。
  B 東西都會被整理好。
  C 蘿涵女士會收電子郵件查閱估價單。
  D 機密文件會被移動。

http://www.hauloverbeach.com

首頁	活動	地點	聯絡我們

活動名稱：國際沙雕節

地點：邁阿密樂華海灘

日期：7 月 28 日、29 日

聯絡人：丹佐‧費里曼
<dfreeman@hauloverbeach.com>

關於：邁阿密歷史最悠久、規模最大的沙雕競賽，50 名以上來自世界各地的大師齊聚競爭，用一萬噸的沙創造作品。今年已經是第七屆了。光是去年就有超過兩萬名遊客來到樂華海灘國際沙雕節，也成為邁阿密最大型海灘活動其中一項盛事。除了競賽，兩天的節慶期間也有特色現場音樂表演和兒童沙雕工作坊。當夜幕低垂，沙雕也會搭配不同燈光呈現。沙雕節雖然免費入場，但會收取五元的停車費。

第七屆國際沙雕節得獎者

名次	姓名	作品名稱
第一名	韓福瑞‧華盛頓，英國	恐龍
第二名	傑克‧尼可森，加拿大	太空船
第三名	強尼‧史派西，美國	城堡
第四名	盧梭‧皮特，丹麥	海盜和公主
第五名	羅納度‧特拉維塔，阿根廷	海怪

邁阿密新鮮事

克莉斯汀‧溫斯雷撰文

（8 月 1 日）——第七屆國際沙雕節於上週末舉辦，是享受夏日的最佳選擇。因為天氣超級好，參加人數比去年還多。今年有沙雕大師單人賽。參賽者的沙灘創作很吸睛，他們將普通的沙子和水變成真正的藝術。不論是海怪、城堡，甚至是有些誇張的太空船，都是大師描繪的鉅作。

來自英國的韓福瑞‧華盛頓，靠著作品「恐龍」的高超藝術寫實風格，讓評審眼睛一亮，擊敗了奪過三次冠軍、來自加拿大的傑克‧尼可森。所有作品都很吸引人，不過我個人最喜歡的是「海盜和公主」，角色的肢體和表情栩栩如生，別有一番風味。

兒童也可以參加沙雕課，由沒有參賽的沙雕專家領班授課。現場音樂表演也讓遊客一飽耳福。這真是最炎熱季節的最佳享受。

191. 文中提到參賽者什麼事？
[A] 都是業餘人士。
[B] 認識費里曼先生。
[C] 活動前必須先在網路上報名。
[D] 來自不同的國家。

192. 在文章中，第一段、第三行的「attracted」，最接近下列哪個意思？
[A] 受到感動
[B] 被招來
[C] 贏得
[D] 曾參與

193. 文中提到今年的活動什麼事？
[A] 參加要花五元。
[B] 有超過兩萬名遊客。
[C] 首度在樂華海灘舉辦。
[D] 有僅限大人參加的活動。

194. 文中提到尼克森先生什麼事？
[A] 他之前曾贏過比賽。
[B] 他曾教過沙雕課。
[C] 他剛搬到加拿大。
[D] 他是國家代表隊成員。

195. 溫絲雷女士最喜歡誰的沙雕？
[A] 華盛頓先生的
[B] 尼可森先生的
[C] 史派西先生的
[D] 皮特先生的

TEST 5

PART 7

國際金融投資論壇

奈洛比會議中心，肯亞

11 月 8 日週四

肯亞第一屆國際金融投資論壇將討論目前金融投資界的局勢。非洲是世界上其中一個快速成長的市場。觀光業和基礎建設帶動大量資金湧入非洲。揚名世界的講者將在這場論壇，展現他們的專業知識、熱情還有熱忱，並分享對於各類議題的洞見。如欲參加論壇者都須以姓名報名。有興趣參加者，歡迎上官網 www.ifif.org 查詢，並填寫報名表。入場完全免費。

請留意因為座位有限，與會申請將完全採取優先報名，優先入場的機制。

時間	講者	主題
上午 9:00	凱拉・珍	非洲現況
上午 10:30	凱薩琳・瓊斯	非洲經濟與市場展望
中午 12:00	午餐休息	
下午 1:00	克里夫・吉普森	策略性投資
下午 2:00	喬治・布魯	高品質決策過程
下午 3:00	珊德拉・萊恩	風險管理

寄件人：珊德拉・萊恩 <sryan@ryaninvestmentgroup.com>
收件人：梅根・迪亞茲 <mdiaz@ifif.org>
主旨：11 月的論壇
日期：9 月 15 日

親愛的迪亞茲女士：

感謝您給我機會參加這麼有意義的論壇。首先，這個國際論壇將對非洲的產業帶來很大的影響，這裡需要來自全方位更多的投資挹注。

我已接到所有講座的行程了。但很遺憾在午餐休息時間後，我在肯亞有個重要的任務，所以我最晚必須在 11 點離開會場。行程表上顯示我是最後一名講者。雖然我已經向籌辦委員會反應過這個問題，但我

想要一個明確答案。如果可以重新安排我的演講時間，請寄給我一份修改後的行程表，也麻煩將它寄給大家。

感謝。

萊恩投資集團
珊德拉・萊恩 敬上

196. 參加者需要做什麼？
Ⓐ 提前 30 分鐘到場。
Ⓑ 線上報名
Ⓒ 取得名牌
Ⓓ 按指定座位入座

197. 誰將發表預測經濟的演說？
Ⓐ 凱拉・珍
Ⓑ 凱薩琳・瓊斯
Ⓒ 克里夫・吉普森
Ⓓ 喬治・布魯

198. 如果萊恩女士的講座重新安排，可能的時間是？
Ⓐ 上午 9:00
Ⓑ 中午 12:00
Ⓒ 下午 2:00
Ⓓ 下午 3:00

199. 文中提到萊恩女士什麼事？
Ⓐ 她演講完就必須趕到機場。
Ⓑ 她在論壇期間有其他任務。
Ⓒ 她在活動前更改題目。
Ⓓ 她是籌辦委員會的一員。

200. 萊恩女士要求迪亞茲女士做什麼？
Ⓐ 延後報名日期
Ⓑ 取得飯店的同意
Ⓒ 更新活動文件
Ⓓ 換地點

ACTUAL TEST ⑥

PART 5　P. 164–166

◎ Part 5 解答請見 P.457

101. GLK 汽車在活動中贈送汽車零件給**他們的**忠誠顧客。

102. 藉由「強力肩膀」的幫助，人們得以避免**抬**貨時傷到肩膀。

103. 一些沿岸社區的**當地**居民，完全仰賴船運和漁業維持生計。

104. 露比的星期五餐廳聘僱專業廚師，總是**準備**好獻上極佳的菜色給顧客。

105. 如果產品有問題，請在購買七天**內**前往最近的店家退款。

106. 針對冬季推出的**系列**商品，漸漸堆積在波特蘭店的倉庫裡。

107. 根據財務月報，增加的房地產貸款額度和受歡迎雜誌《傑瑞經濟》的預測**密切**一致。

108. 主管之間未經討論的政策，不應該**影響**增設國際分部的決策過程。

109. 優質有限公司為了增加產能大規模**改進**裝配線，它先前造成很多機械故障。

110. 泰瑞先生向數間銀行提出貸款申請，以確保銀行財力證明上有充裕資金，**得以**買得起德州奧斯丁的新房。

111. 尹女士起先是靠**自己**開始研究雙語作家的計畫，但最近開始請同儕幫忙蒐集可信的資料。

112. **考量**今年的年度獲益低於預期，「強尼指標物流公司」的管理階層不想給員工年度加薪。

113. 馬克西百貨公司**鄰近**多個都市交通要點，靠著地緣之便吸引了很多人來。

114. **如果**預購票售出超過三千張，賓州娛樂就會啟用位於弗林特市柯瓦爾奇客會議中心的大禮堂。

115. 亞歷克斯庫柏電器行職缺的應徵者**被要求**提交作品集。

116. 塞雷克斯保全服務公司的頒獎委員會提名十位頂尖員工，**他們**將在二十週年餐會上獲頒年度最佳員工。

117. 最新安裝的員工薪資帳冊軟體將從 3 月 17 日週五**開始**運作，除非總經理另外給予指示。

118. UPT 電子明年**將**到其他國家**拓展**分公司，特別是東亞，開拓不同業務。

119. 要找到斯泰普頓圖書館並不難，它就在賓州印第安納大學校園內，**過了**橡樹林一點點後。

120. 如果您在沙瓦納電器行買了最新產品，請務必完整**詳讀**所附的產品說明書。

121. 每當與潛在客戶**談話**時，務必記得要告訴他們近期內會推出的優惠方案，像是線上折扣。

122. 人資專家運用職能評估工具，就能分辨應徵者是否**有潛力**。

123. 蒙哥馬利企業**欣喜**證實了，他們在物流、專賣和服務部門，取得多樣正向成果。

124. 麥卡納柏先生兩年前開始在龐蘇托尼市立博物館擔任資深經理，**自此**負責督導多項重要展覽。

125. 優質投資公司面臨赤字，還是硬撐著效率不彰的生產線，這可能不利保持他們公司在金融圈的**聲望**。

126. 國會議員對修正案達成共識後，這項新規定將讓**每個**關心選舉的**人**都能夠了解透徹。

127. 研究生修完所有必修課，**就**可以準備資格考和口試。

128. 當預算報告顯示銷售數字開始有下滑趨勢，董事會就已意識到相關議題的**詳細情形**。

129. 一旦您應徵該職位，**就會**知道人資部門的面試安排日程。

130. 如果您買的商品有瑕疵，您**大可**選擇到附近的店面換貨。

PART 6   P. 167–170

131–134 電子郵件

收件人：布萊德・崔安納
寄件人：約翰・馮丹
日期：3 月 17 日
主旨：請給予劇院整修建議

親愛的崔安納先生：

我們花了很多時間消化您上次在會議裡的建議。最重要的，我們買了一個又寬又大的黑布幕，可以用來隔絕舞台外的噪音。為了測試減噪程度，我們的同仁站在離舞台很近，我們排練時也聽不到任何聲音。我們目前也規劃採納您的建議，擴大控制台讓有經驗豐富的同仁可以更密切合作。這會讓燈光和音效的操作比以往更有效率。我們很開心能有您實用又完整的指示，期待下次再見。

約翰・馮丹 敬上

131. Ⓐ 購買
    Ⓑ 購買了
    Ⓒ 將購買
    Ⓓ 正在購買

132. Ⓐ 不久
    Ⓑ 幾乎不
    Ⓒ 只有
    Ⓓ 相當

133. **Ⓐ 這會讓燈光和音效的操作比以往更有效率。**
    Ⓑ 之前的布幕太薄擋不住外來噪音。
    Ⓒ 您的建議裡，我們只採納了其中一項予以改進。
    Ⓓ 我們想要增加下一場表演的售票量。

134. Ⓐ 去
    Ⓑ 有
    Ⓒ 為了
    Ⓓ 在……之上

135–138 文章

《印第安納論壇》——企業簡報

克拉里翁（10 月 20 日）——泰勒・史里諾吉爾晉升為《印第安納論壇》的總編輯。董事會已在週五確認了他的升遷。泰勒・史里諾吉爾兩年來擔任助理編輯。於是他將從下個月開始管理專欄和圖片。此外，他也會管理公司官網 IndianaTribune.com 的整體營運。泰勒・史里諾吉爾是名勤奮的員工，他去年對 IndianaTribune.com 的改進有所貢獻。

135. Ⓐ 確認了
    Ⓑ 已指出
    Ⓒ 提供了
    Ⓓ 獎勵了

136. **Ⓐ 泰勒・史里諾吉爾兩年來擔任助理編輯。**
    Ⓑ 總編輯的職缺會空出來，直到有人補上。
    Ⓒ 《印第安納論壇》近來在市中心租了新辦公空間。
    Ⓓ 管理部門給他一個網頁管理的新職務。

137. Ⓐ 然而
    Ⓑ 此外
    Ⓒ 同時
    Ⓓ 舉例來說

138. **Ⓐ 他對……有所貢獻**
    Ⓑ 它導致……
    Ⓒ 他的貢獻對……
    Ⓓ 貢獻

139–142 資訊

感謝您在 Elliezon.com 下訂單。我們誠摯希望您滿意我們的產品品質。如果您不滿意，可以持原收據和外包裝在到貨的十天內退貨並取得退款。要取得退款，您需要填寫箱子內的表單，並將它和商品一起寄還給我們。所有商品都應該以原包裝運送。退款過程會花上一到兩週。因為取消信用卡交易會比現金來得久。感謝您的購買，也希望您會繼續購買我們的商品。

139. Ⓐ 令人滿意的
　　 Ⓑ 感到滿意的
　　 Ⓒ 使滿意
　　 Ⓓ 滿足

140. Ⓐ 將運送
　　 Ⓑ 已經運送
　　 Ⓒ 正在運
　　 Ⓓ 應該被運送

 141. Ⓐ 我們對造成不便致歉。
　　 Ⓑ 您所訂購的商品目前沒有存貨。
　　 Ⓒ 我們對所有商品的品質很有信心。
　　 Ⓓ 退款過程會花上一到兩週。

142. **Ⓐ 購物**
　　 Ⓑ 學習
　　 Ⓒ 放置
　　 Ⓓ 匯編

143–146 文章

經過三年穩定成長，韓國手機零售商 SLP 正規劃將業務擴展到美國和加拿大。該公司在亞洲區已有很多營業店面。SLP 執行長傑瑞米·金在 11 月 11 日宣布，公司有意在北美開超過 100 家分店。因此，SLP 正在徵求有熱情、具冒險精神、為顧客服務熱忱的人成為分店長。如欲應徵者，請您聯絡克莉絲汀·鐘，電話是 +82-2-333-8282。

143. Ⓐ 適當的
　　 Ⓑ 可取的
　　 Ⓒ 穩定的
　　 Ⓓ 行善的

 144. Ⓐ 美國需要吸引更多智慧型手機使用者，以活絡其國內經濟。
　　 Ⓑ 該公司在亞洲區已有很多營業店面。
　　 Ⓒ SLP 在智慧型手機領域享有全球知名度。
　　 Ⓓ 南韓的天氣和美國東部有很多相似之處。

145. Ⓐ 並且
　　 Ⓑ 雖然
　　 Ⓒ 然而
　　 Ⓓ 因此

146. **Ⓐ 應徵者**
　　 Ⓑ 居民
　　 Ⓒ 專家
　　 Ⓓ 建築師

PART 7　P. 171–191

147–148 廣告

張貼物品：XA–360 鹿力割草機
價格：700 美元
地點：維吉尼亞州費爾法克斯郡

物品描述：
一年前在 LEX 店家以 1000 元購入。兩年保固。燃料箱故障，買家須自行更換。

狀況良好。（未附圖）。
不二價。（不可議價）。

如果您對商品有任何問題，請儘管和我聯繫（fairJohn@horrisnet.com）。

147. 文中沒有提到割草機什麼事？
　　 Ⓐ 有一零件需要購買。
　　 Ⓑ 有附上說明書。
　　 Ⓒ 價格不能更動。
　　 Ⓓ 是二手商品。

148. 賣家可能會做什麼？
    A 回覆詢問
    B 展延保固
    C 透過電子郵件附上照片
    D 直接把商品寄給買家

149–151 資訊

> 約漢斯敦市計劃要僱用新的財務規畫師，來接替最近有意退休的凱文・戴維斯先生。戴維斯先生職掌 14 年，將在 10 月 31 日移交他的職務。
>
> 市府財政局長向市執行官報告，負責管理城市的金融事宜。職務複雜，需要能改進、落實面向廣泛的政策，更要能進一步協助達成市鎮目標，也要安排、維持全市的財政紀錄。
>
> 「新的財務規畫師有很多事情要做，」市執行官辛蒂・菲特曼說，「我們期望的同仁需要有在組織或公司內管理財務的豐富經驗。」
>
> 菲特曼女士表示，很快就會開始篩選應徵申請，將在九月初進行面試。8 月 20 日以後收到的應徵資料將不予考慮。新人員的人選將在十月底確認。

149. 這篇文的主要資訊為何？
    A 約漢斯敦市規劃重建市鎮廳。
    B 市府開出財政相關的職缺。
    C 市府的財政問題接連兩年都沒辦法解決。
    D 為了慶祝戴維斯先生退休，市府官員辦了餐會

150. 根據文中資訊，這個職位有什麼條件？
    A 財經碩士學位
    B 願意在週末上班
    C 處理財政事務的能力
    D 搬到約漢斯敦市

151. 下列句子最適合出現在 [1]、[2]、[3]、[4] 的哪個位置中？
> 「8 月 20 日以後收到的應徵資料將不予考慮。」

    A [1]
    B [2]
    C [3]
    D [4]

152–153 文章

> 布雷默頓，3 月 6 日──布雷默頓近來為了在北區興建佔地三萬平方公尺的商業區，邀請當地的房地產開發商參與競標。
>
> 新的商業區將蓋在 81 號賓州公路旁邊，原來是包括華克森發電、比爾汽車零件、烏利斯製鋼的工業區。新建物將配備最新的節能省水系統。該鎮也計畫三年內在附近設立小型住宅區。
>
> 「我們很高興有這個機會，為鎮上帶來新商機。」鎮長吉爾福德・胡布里克說，「新的商業區將坐落在最好的地區，鄰近全國主要幹道和很多有名的住宿地點。」他也提到等到初步藍圖設計出來，會再根據廠商需求分配空間。
>
> 布雷默頓近來多項建設都是受到鄰近地區，米爾納的綜合運動場擴建工程所啟發。

152. 文中提到布雷默頓的北區什麼事？
    A 距離綜合運動場很近。
    B 曾生產多種金屬製品。
    C 而今是住宅區。
    D 近來人口暴增。

153. 文中沒有提到商業區有何種特色？
    A 鄰近全國主要幹道
    B 距離飯店很近
    C 節能設備
    D 它的公營區域

珍‧帕默〔上午 09:12〕：
大衛，你要求我修改的購物中心樓層規畫，我有一個問題。

大衛‧浩爾〔上午 09:13〕：
好的，怎麼了？

珍‧帕默〔上午 09:14〕：
你是要我寄全部頁數給你，還是只要出錯的第三頁就好？

大衛‧浩爾〔上午 09:16〕：
我現在沒辦法連到信箱看。這裡暫時沒有網路服務。

珍‧帕默〔上午 09:16〕：
我想我可以等。你明天才要見客戶吧？

大衛‧浩爾〔上午 09:17〕：
為什麼要等？妳可以傳真第三頁給我嗎？

珍‧帕默〔上午 09:18〕：
當然。傳真號碼是？

大衛‧浩爾〔上午 09:19〕：
705-3583。

珍‧帕默〔上午 09:25〕：
沒問題，傳好了。如果沒收到，我再傳一次。

大衛‧浩爾〔上午 09:27〕：
有了。收到了，感謝！

送出

雪麗眼睛保健
11361 紐約州貝塞區弗萊明大街 151 號
203 室
3 月 17 日

海瑟‧洛瑞
11361 紐約州貝賽區蘭卡斯特大道 333 號
西門公寓 403 室

持續提供您最好的服務，是雪麗眼睛保健的首要之事。從 8 月 1 日起，服務完不再需要馬上付費，而是可以在 15 個工作天內付款。您可以在隨函附上的詳細說明中，了解我們改變付費方式的原因。

新規定讓我們可以繼續提供您和家人最好的眼睛保健服務，未來兩年內也不會調整價格。如果您對新的付費規定有更多疑問，可以聯絡我們的客戶經理凱文‧羅伊斯，電話是 715-6534。

珍‧雪麗 敬上

附件

154. 帕默女士最有可能是？
Ⓐ 程式設計師
Ⓑ 建築師
Ⓒ 律師
Ⓓ 網路服務經理

155. 上午 9:17 時，當浩爾先生寫道：「為什麼要等？」他最可能的意思是？
Ⓐ 他現在就想收到文件。
Ⓑ 他考慮最好延後會議。
Ⓒ 他詢問網路連線。
Ⓓ 他需要下載表格。

156. 這封信的目的為何？
Ⓐ 聘僱有執照的護士
Ⓑ 宣傳診所的一項服務
Ⓒ 告訴客戶一項規定異動
Ⓓ 修正帳單明細

157. 文中提到雪莉眼睛保健什麼事？
Ⓐ 努力維持低收費。
Ⓑ 最近搬到新地區。
Ⓒ 提供免費的視力檢查。
Ⓓ 配備最先進的設備。

家居和辦公室清潔

肯恩上城鎮飯店的家居和辦公室清潔部門聘用 100 人加入團隊，負責大樓公共空間、設施內的個人房與辦公室整潔。

- 每天打掃公共區域，像是廁所、大廳、舞廳、宴會廳，和其他訪客使用區域。

- 依據房客時間表打掃個人房。如何安排客房時間表，概述在招募手冊第 10 頁。

- 每週六打掃辦公區域。清潔人員會掃地拖地並清空垃圾筒，也為辦公室植栽澆水和整理桌面。

- 打掃人員必須隨時在需要及時留意的公共區域附近待命。

158. 這些資訊最可能是要給誰看的？
- Ⓐ 清潔公司員工
- **Ⓑ 旅館員工**
- Ⓒ 負責訂房的旅行社員工
- Ⓓ 想找好飯店的遊客

159. 根據文中資訊，讀者要如何得知個人房的清理時間表？
- **Ⓐ 參考員工訓練手冊**
- Ⓑ 詢問清潔部門長官
- Ⓒ 致電飯店接待處
- Ⓓ 看員工休息室張貼的行程表

160. 辦公室的地板多久清掃一次？
- Ⓐ 每天
- **Ⓑ 每週**
- Ⓒ 每雙週
- Ⓓ 每個月

寇帝・席爾瓦〔上午 10:18〕：
哈囉。我想給你們昨天會議流程的資訊。我們行銷團隊提議，清爽泡泡糖可能會在零食市場上受到歡迎。

蘇珊・薇薇安〔上午 10:19〕：
我知道原因。人們吃完東西，會希望口腔內感覺清爽。

中田俊二〔上午 10:20〕：
別忘了它還能清潔牙齒。

寇帝・席爾瓦〔上午 10:21〕：
沒錯。我們公司決定，要有自己的產線生產無糖配方的特製口香糖。我們必須加快腳步。

蘇珊・薇薇安〔上午 10:22〕：
消費者愈來愈注重健康，不如我們強調使用有機原料怎麼樣？我可以為產品找出更多關於有機原料的資訊。

寇帝・席爾瓦〔上午 10:23〕：
聽起來很好！就這麼做！

中田俊二〔上午 10:24〕：
我喜歡這個想法。不過，我想也要考慮消費者的口味偏好。如果口香糖的口味不能吸引潛在消費者，我們產品做得再好也沒用。我們得先針對消費者喜歡的口味進行市場研究。

寇帝・席爾瓦〔上午 10:26〕：
好。山田先生，可以請你安排和市場研究團隊與公關團隊開會嗎？我想聽聽他們怎麼說。週四怎麼樣？

蘇珊・薇薇安〔上午 10:27〕：
抱歉，那個時間我不行。週四我都得為新進員工進行在職訓練。週三或五可以嗎？

寇帝・席爾瓦〔上午 10:28〕：
週五可以。

中田俊二〔上午 10:30〕：
我也可以。我也會擬好我們的問卷大綱，供研究使用。你們之中有誰可以給我一些問卷可用的問題嗎？

寇帝・席爾瓦〔上午 10:31〕：
當然。我再給你。

送出

161. 對話成員最有可能是哪一種企業的員工？

[A] 雜貨店
[B] 餐旅業
[C] 行銷代理商
[D] 食品製造商

162. 對話成員打算什麼時候和行銷團隊見面？

[A] 週二
[B] 週三
[C] 週四
[D] 週五

163. 早上 10：30 時，當中田先生寫道：「我也可以。」他最可能的意思是？

[A] 他可以出席會議。
[B] 他會馬上和研究者談。
[C] 他計劃要主導在職訓練。
[D] 他想要自己做新產品。

164. 席爾瓦先生可能會怎麼做？

[A] 和總裁見面
[B] 試吃一些口香糖的口味
[C] 概述市場策略
[D] 準備一些問題

165–168 電子郵件

寄件人：吉米・赫爾明
收件人：優質電子員工
日期：12 月 7 日，週一
主旨：一週培訓課程

您應該已接獲通知，所有優質電子的員工都需要參加為期一週的冬季培訓課程，課程聚焦在更明確了解公司目標，同時也能認識其他同仁。對我們的公司有非常多好處。員工問卷顯示，自從五年前開始培訓課程，對我們公司的工作產能和同仁間的合作都有了很大的影響。

訓練課程的日期自九月起就發布於內部布告欄，大家都必須參加。我希望您們都能準備好各式各樣的主題到課程上討論。所有同仁都可以盡情分享建議。您要做的只是回信給我，主旨請寫「課程主題」。您得自行前往藍雲杉公園，所以請記得這個月底前填寫交通費的差旅核銷單。也建議您可以團體共乘前往。此外，也有很多大眾運輸工具可以搭乘，像是接駁公車、地鐵、市營火車，會停在藍雲杉公園附近。從辦公室到那裡甚至有和公司合作的計程車行，提供非常優惠的折扣。不管您選擇什麼方式前往，請確保能準時到達，而且準備好加入我們。

吉米・赫爾明

165. 這封電子郵件的目的為何？

[A] 宣布一項年度活動的細節
[B] 鼓勵同仁當某個活動的志工
[C] 在商展上推廣公司的最新產品
[D] 公告電子公司開出的新職缺

166. 員工需要為活動準備好什麼？

[A] 更新個人資訊
[B] 填寫問卷
[C] 推銷全新產品
[D] 準備討論題目

167. 關於交通安排，赫爾明先生怎麼說？

[A] 優質電子會補貼所有開銷。
[B] 所有員工都需要搭乘大眾運輸工具。
[C] 該地點在特定時間內完全不能通車。
[D] 每個員工都需要從各部門取得通行證。

168. 下列句子最適合出現在 [1]、[2]、[3]、[4] 的哪個位置中？

「從辦公室到那裡甚至有和公司合作的計程車行，提供非常優惠的折扣。」

[A] [1]
[B] [2]
[C] [3]
[D] [4]

滑雪屋國家群島管理處（SNAA）

滑雪屋國家群島主要有一片森林、還有海灘地區和其他類似島嶼。請注意在這次夏天的度假季中有新的旅遊限制。遊客來到島上旅遊，如果沒有核准的嚮導隨行的話，將被限制出入這些區域。這項規定也同樣適用於自行以私人船隻前往群島的遊客。他們只許從海上欣賞島上風景，在離岸下錨停靠，但不准登島。

由 SNAA 管理處主辦的巡航之旅提供遊客全年服務，從每天上午八點開始，每隔兩小時有一個船班。直到下午四點的末班船為止。但冬季從十一月到二月，將根據天氣狀況延長到下午六點。請來電 +01-319-5225 預約航遊。該行程包含島嶼地質和歷史特色的解說，也能欣賞美麗風景的迷人風貌。您也可以申請島上管理員的陪同，參觀瀕危物種群聚的特別景點。

付款和預約

該行程每團最多能容納 20 人。如果人數少於 15 人，我們保有在行程裡安排加入其他旅客的權利。成人票為每人 30 元，小孩則是 15 元。為保留預約，您需要支付 5 元的保證金。此外，如果提前六個月訂票將享有特別優惠。保證金將計入入場費的總金額當中。如果您的團體沒有按預約時間準時到場，旅程結束的時間仍不會改變，以免影響後續行程。我們嚴禁更改其他團體的行程。

169. 這則公告的目的為何？
- [A] 更新某個費用的資訊
- [B] 介紹一些景點
- [C] 宣布旅程的安全規定
- **[D] 知會遊客旅遊規定**

170. 文中提到關於參觀滑雪屋國家群島什麼事？
- **[A] 遊客登島需要嚮導陪同。**
- [B] 遊客須遵守安全規定。
- [C] 遊客在群島周圍任何地方都不許游泳。
- [D] 遊客需要自己組團遊玩。

171. 文中沒有提到 SNAA 什麼事？
- **[A] 可以安排夜間行程。**
- [B] 團體人數受到限制。
- [C] 早鳥預約享有優惠。
- [D] 航班次數根據季節有所不同。

172. 根據公告，如果團體在已安排好的行程中遲到，會發生什麼事？
- **[A] 旅遊行程時間將減少。**
- [B] 無需通知，行程將被取消。
- [C] 會被額外收費。
- [D] 將更改行程結束的時間。

赫希郡一遊
別錯過體驗夢幻世界的好機會！

巧克力世界之旅
每天上午 10 點到下午 5 點開放，入場費 5 元

巧克力世界之旅帶您乘單車穿越多個歷程和雕像，一覽赫希郡的歷史景點。

查理的巧克力工廠
營業時間平日中午到下午 3 點，免費對全民開放

由創辦人約翰·赫希先生所建立。遊客有機會一窺巧克力的製造過程，並免費獲得巧克力產品。導覽行程向每個人酌收 1 美元。

赫希遊樂園
每天上午 9 點到晚上 10 點開放，入場費 10 美元，無限暢遊所有設施只要 40 美元。

超棒的主題公園適合闔家光臨。包括雲霄飛車的多種極棒的遊樂設施。特定季節入園享有特別優惠價。

郡巧克力博物館
週二到週日，上午 9 點到下午 4 點開放，免入場費，但歡迎贊助。

各種巧克力讓人難以忘懷，依年分順序陳列展覽。天花板的大液晶螢幕回顧赫希家族史。博物館地點鄰近遊樂園北大門。

173. 這則資訊的目的為何？
- Ⓐ 描述一份活動清單
- **Ⓑ 協助遊客參觀某些景點**
- Ⓒ 提供前往當地景點的路徑
- Ⓓ 公告一些特別的紀念館

174. 文中提到赫希遊樂園什麼事？
- **Ⓐ 整年的入場費用並不完全一樣。**
- Ⓑ 營業的時間會定期更動。
- Ⓒ 播放歷史電影的簡短預告。
- Ⓓ 只受到青少年和兒童歡迎。

175. 根據資訊，巧克力工廠和博物館有何共同之處？
- **Ⓐ 都不用入場費。**
- Ⓑ 都需要導覽。
- Ⓒ 都展示歷史事件。
- Ⓓ 都坐落在海岸旁邊。

176–180 傳單與電子郵件

CAAA 二十週年體育器材展，
6 月 1 日到 10 日
俄亥俄州克里夫蘭市，革新會議中心

CAAA（克里夫蘭地區體育協會）邀請各公司參展，去年有超過 200 家企業與會。這場活動讓您更快找到合適的運動器材，並教您正確使用。

根據企業贊助的額度，CAAA 很榮幸給予相應的回饋（如需詢問請洽格洛麗亞・桑德斯女士，電話是 932-451-3894。如需登記，請寄信到 supports@caaa.org）

研討會贊助──1,200 元

您的公司代表將在其中一個研討會中擔任主講人，有機會為您的公司宣傳。

舞台贊助──2,000 元

在所有舞台前的設備，在展示攤位前方都會展出貴公司的大名。

提袋贊助──3,000 元

發送給參展訪客的布製手提袋，全都會印上貴公司商標和名稱。

活動整體規畫贊助──6,000 元

展覽首日的「CAAA 之夜」晚宴上，將介紹貴公司三位的經理人給大家。

寄件人：gloria@caaa.org

收件人：hsyoon@knetwork.com

日期：5 月 20 日

主旨：感謝

親愛的尹女士：

感謝您登記贊助遠距間歇訓練計畫，以支持克里夫蘭地區體育協會（CAAA）展。您的贊助不但讓我們策展順利，也能讓大家對運動更感興趣。

您捐贈的 2,000 元已經成功入帳。此外，我們也會特別將貴公司名稱秀在展示攤位上，不收取額外費用。以此向您長久以來對 CAAA 和我們計畫的支持，致上我們的感謝之意。為確認宣傳用的素材，請您回傳貴公司企業或商業識別的圖片。

CAAA 展統籌
格洛麗亞・桑德斯

176. 這篇傳單的目的為何？
- Ⓐ 宣布一系列的活動有多成功
- Ⓑ 鼓勵參加者試用器材
- **Ⓒ 推廣加入活動的好處**
- Ⓓ 向董事會回報贊助的財政狀況

177. 根據傳單，什麼時候需要打電話到 CAAA 的辦公室？
- **Ⓐ 需要更多資訊時**
- Ⓑ 沒辦法處理捐款作業時
- Ⓒ 需要參加活動時
- Ⓓ 當他們層級有所變動時

178. 6 月 1 日會發什麼事？
- A 一場運動賽事即將開始。
- **B 將舉辦一場正式的集會。**
- C 將指派新董事會成員。
- D 將設置好展覽展示台。

179. 文中提到 CAAA 展什麼事？
- **A 它的目的是為了推廣運動。**
- B 它每年都吸引超過 200 間公司參展。
- C 由克里夫蘭市議會部分贊助。
- D 每年都在不同地點舉辦。

180. 電子郵件中，尹女士被要求做什麼？
- A 確認企業為了參加這活動所贊助的預算金額
- **B 回信附上要參展的公司商標設計**
- C 安排一個展區在展場上宣傳新產品
- D 聯絡客服中心詢問更多有關展覽的資訊

181-185 電子郵件

收件人：berry@linguisticconference.org
寄件人：customerservice@holidaylodge.us
日期：7 月 25 日
回覆：TC1270 預約

親愛的貝里博士：

感謝您選擇度假小屋飯店。如您稍早的需求，為您的團體預約了 12 間房。由於您將到這裡參加八月分的全國應用語言學論壇，您享有每個房間一晚 90 元的優惠價。

我們需要您在 8 月 3 日辦理入住，並在 8 月 10 日退房。房間預約都登記在您名下。請記得您的訂房號碼為 TC1270，當您對這些安排有任何需要聯絡的事，都需要使用這組號碼。

我們有信心您會很喜歡這裡很棒的設施，像是戶外游泳池、水療、體育館和多樣化的用餐選擇。如果想要悠哉一點的用餐環境，您可以嘗試位於大廳旁邊的羅密歐咖啡廳。如果您有興趣在「旅遊推薦指南」中，評等為五星的多那太羅餐廳用餐，我們強烈建議您事先預約。

如果您需要了解更多資訊，請告訴我們。

再次感謝您選擇度假小屋飯店。

度假小屋飯店員工 敬上

收件人：customerservice@holidaylodge.us
寄件人：berry@linguisticconference.org
日期：7 月 27 日
回覆：TC1270 預約

致相關人士：

我的訂房號碼為 TC1270，我來信的目的，是更正我在上一封電子郵件中所發現的一些錯誤。

首先，我預訂的房間是 10 間，而非 12 間。而且，我也要等到 8 月 4 日才會抵達，即便大多數人都會提前在會議前一天到。

我在原來的訂房需求表單裡，已很明確地提出上述這些事項。請予以修正，並和我聯繫確認這個問題已經解決。先謝過您對這件事的即時回應。

龐茲·貝里博士 敬上

---

181. 第一封電子郵件的目的為何？
- **A 確認訂房細節**
- B 提醒房客客房價格有更動
- C 解釋多樣設施
- D 宣布飯店要暫時整修

182. 文中提到多那太羅餐廳什麼事？
- A 最近才開張。
- B 剛整修好。
- **C 通常客人很多很忙碌。**
- D 位於度假小屋飯店的旁邊。

183. 哪個訂房資訊有錯誤？
- **A 貝里博士會在 8 月 3 日入住**
- B 貝里博士主辦論壇
- C 貝里博士已為所有訂房付款
- D 貝里博士會在會議結束之前提前離開

184. 文中提到關於這次飯店訂房什麼事？
- Ⓐ 訂房號碼印錯了。
- **Ⓑ 訂房數量不正確。**
- Ⓒ 出席論壇的人數不夠。
- Ⓓ 客房價格有別。

185. 第二封電子郵件中，第三段、第三行的「matter」最接近下列哪個意思？
- **Ⓐ 情況**
- Ⓑ 物質
- Ⓒ 材質
- Ⓓ 刊物

186–190 文章、表格和電子郵件

《雅典公報》

當地企業需要更多員工
索菲亞‧羅倫撰文

雅典（4月10日）——對我們來說，要找到適合的應徵者並不容易。有些公司為了簡化聘僱流程，會轉往人力仲介找人。公司透過這些仲介尋找旺季的兼職員工，或處理整個應徵流程，多方面省下金錢和時間。

喬治亞歷史悠久的一家人力仲介公司，「哈囉幫人力」的總經理珍‧佛斯特說，很多公司經由仲介聘僱臨時工，並從中獲利。「他們有機會解決某些聘僱問題。另外一個好處是，他們可以先訓練有潛力的員工，再給予他或她全職職位。」佛斯特說。

為了支持當地企業使用這個流程，我們公告了人力仲介公司的名單。您可以在 www.athensgazette.com 網頁的右上角找到資訊。

哈囉幫人力
臨時雇員需求表

公司資訊
- 姓名：布萊德‧崔安娜
- 公司：MSC 商業會計
- 領域：會計
- 電話：412-237-9400
- 電子郵件信箱：btriana@mscbiz.com

職務資訊
- 員工需求數：最少 8 人
- 職缺：職員
- 預計聘僱期間：2 到 3 週

特別說明：
我們接了很多政府計畫，審計市議會多區的帳務。因為這些計畫，我們堆積了太多的文件和檔案需要整理。這些文件和檔案需要分門別類歸檔，並在期限前儘快完成掃描。我們徵求的應徵者需要非常細心，且要能聽從指示辦事。

您如何知道我們的？
我在《雅典公報》昨天的線上專欄看到貴公司。

感謝您的登記！
我們的人事專員將在 24 小時內透過電子郵件與您聯繫。

寄件人：布萊德‧崔安納
　　　　<btriana@mscbiz.com>
收件人：海瑟‧洛瑞
　　　　<hlowry@hellocrew.net>
主旨：感謝
日期：4 月 15 日

親愛的洛瑞女士：

我誠摯感謝您的協助。這是我第一次和人力仲介公司合作，所以坦白說，我對這個流程不是很有信心。因為貴公司所找到的合適臨時工，我們已經快完成工作了。您在短短三個小時內回覆我的需求，而且一天內就提出人員名單！您推薦的人員真的很勤奮認真，對於我們指派的任務也很投入。有鑑於此，我們決定要面試其中兩個人，提供他們全職員工的職缺。

祝好，
布萊德‧崔安納

186. 關於兼職員工，文中沒有提到哪一項好處？
- **A 得到專門或專業的協助**
- B 比公司原先規劃的省下更多預算。
- C 讓聘僱程序更加流暢
- D 協助公司處理某些問題

187. 文中提到崔安納先生什麼事？
- **A 他在網站上讀了羅倫女士的文章。**
- B 他的公司也被列在《雅典公報》網頁的清單裡。
- C 他的公司曾和哈囉幫人力合作過。
- D 他接受《雅典公報》的採訪。

188. 在表格中，第二段、第二行的「duration」，最接近下列哪個意思？
- **A 時間長短**
- B 強度
- C 成長
- D 路線

189. 這封電子郵件的目的為何？
- A 給予兩名成員新的正職
- B 確認銷售團隊所提出的需求
- **C 對於他們所處理的事表示感謝**
- D 抱怨文章中的一些錯誤

190. 洛瑞女士最可能的身分是？
- A MSC 商業會計的兼職員工
- B 市議會的官員
- **C 哈囉幫人力的人事專員**
- D 《雅典公報》的新聞撰稿人

191–195 文章和電子郵件

當地新地標的建設

週四的會議上，哈蒂斯堡的官員討論了一項地方改善計畫，可以讓城鎮吸引更多的學生和遊客。根據哈蒂斯堡學院主席金安·帕格努奇的說法，建設一個多功能綜合會議中心，需要全面考慮當地議會和學院的預算。因此，市議會決定鼓勵當地企業競標這項建設計畫。此外，也鼓勵當地居民報名參加中心命名的比賽。

部分提案提議建設戶外運動公園，但是否選址在中心旁邊、位在橡樹林街上還有待決定。帕格努奇先生表示，議會將請所有當地社區成員分享意見。感興趣的民眾可以帶著自己的意見，於 6 月 18 日下週四下午四點，到議會週例會分享，或在 6 月 22 日前寄電子郵件給任務執行團隊。籌委會將通盤考量眾多的公民意見，並向議會提出最終版草案，進行正式的討論。預計最晚會在 6 月 30 日前做出決議。

寄件人：selindiana@stormmail.com
收件人：citycouncil@hattiesburg.org
日期：6 月 20 日
主旨：附加計畫

親愛的議會官員：

我知道對於使用市鎮預算建設新的議會中心一事，您正在徵詢建議。由於我已有行程安排，不克參加這項計畫的週會，但我仍想表態支持這項可以讓地方更具吸引力的計畫。雖然建設的成本可能還算合理，專案規畫人員還是得全面考量會議中心的成效、地理方便性，還有它對於我們全體在地居民的助益。這項計畫將成為市民驕傲，中心也將會是我們可以享受各類活動的全新地標。即便它對市鎮形象舉足輕重，它的效益還是應該均衡地回饋給所有在地人。

塞林·戴安娜

寄件人：fangyu@solomonunitas.com
收件人：citycouncil@hattiesburg.org
日期：6 月 21 日
主旨：市政計畫

致相關人士：

我很開心我們鎮上有了新的發展方向。因為鎮上的公共設施不足以提供各式各樣的活動，滿足各年齡層的需求，這個全新的綜合空間可以讓大家有更多機會享受更廣泛的活動，像是國家體協籃球聯賽、當地就業博覽會等等。但我只有一個和老年人相關的考量。

這項計畫不應該只著重在青少年或年輕人身上。根據市鎮的人口分布數據，高齡人口佔哈蒂斯堡公民的三成。因此，我們絕對不能忽視他們的需求。如果我們全體，不分老少都能夠便利地享受這個設施，這會是一項了不起的進步。請確保所有人都可以平等共享好處。

191. 為什麼哈蒂斯堡需要新的計畫？
　　Ⓐ 市議會取消了前一項計畫。
　　Ⓑ 鎮上最近提高了地產稅。
　　Ⓒ 該地區計劃能吸引更多人。
　　Ⓓ 鎮民已爭論了一項發展議題。

192. 在文章中，第二段、第六行的
「put forth」，最接近下列哪個意思？
　　Ⓐ 出版
　　Ⓑ 推廣
　　Ⓒ 提案
　　Ⓓ 栽種

193. 戴安娜女士何時有約？
　　Ⓐ 6 月 18 日
　　Ⓑ 6 月 20 日
　　Ⓒ 6 月 21 日
　　Ⓓ 6 月 30 日

194. 第二封電子郵件主旨為何？
　　Ⓐ 慶祝市鎮計畫
　　Ⓑ 質疑新設施的方向
　　Ⓒ 抱怨錯誤資訊
　　Ⓓ 提出潛在問題

195. 6 月 30 日前將會發生什麼事？
　　Ⓐ 根據公民意見和官員研究，完成最終版企畫大綱。
　　Ⓑ 鎮上將為新綜合場館舉行破土典禮。
　　Ⓒ 市議會將為了開發新設施宣布競標。
　　Ⓓ 有些市民將發動抗議，反對建設計畫。

196–200 電子郵件、通知和訂購單

寄件人：約翰．戴森
收件人：班．塔南西多
主旨：貨運公司
日期：3 月 2 日

哈囉，塔南西多先生：

我很高興您登記了我們的家具運送服務，您訂了由我們聯客家具工廠所生產的四人座沙發、白色辦公桌、兩張黑色椅子和一張大號的床。我可以保證，我們提供的產品將讓您和您的客戶感到滿意。

您店面所在的地區，對我們來說是個新地點，我們很期待可以把商品送到新的店家。請讓我知道您是否對這項運送服務感興趣。我們在石溪的合格駕駛員不會派送到阿伯尼，所以會聘請其他公司協助。考量您的情況，優運搬運是最合適您的選擇。我們很願意和您所選擇的公司合作，盡力提供給您安全的服務。

約翰．戴森 敬上

阿爾圖納居家裝潢系統
本週最新！
3 月 20 日
來自聯客家具工廠的產品

親愛的客戶：
我們籲請您注意我們產品線上的最新產品。您諮詢過耐用且價格實惠的家具，現在我們有提供了。這些聯客家具工廠的產品，從水牛城到這裡只要兩個小時車程，就會直達您身邊。

── 家用尺寸沙發
── 耐用木製白色書桌
── 安康黑色椅子
── 各種設計和尺寸的床
── 可移動式櫥櫃
── 抗菌地毯

下一季，在我們阿姆赫斯特分公司，將開發貼近使用者需求的辦公室家具。如果您對這些商品有任何疑問，請儘管聯繫 linkercustomer@lffactory.com

---

聯客家具訂貨表

客戶：阿爾圖納居家裝潢系統
訂單日期：3 月 25 日
配送日期：4 月 10 日

配送內容：
維持原訂單但修改內容如下：
一 沒有四人座沙發（需要五人座）
一 請配送黑色書桌，而非白色的。
一 加一張椅子

備註：您向我詢問優運貨運有沒有狀況。他們準時到貨、駕駛友善，運送抵達時商品的狀況也良好。

196. 為什麼戴森先生要寄這封電子郵件？
　　Ａ 為新產品打廣告
　　Ｂ 詢問運費的估價
　　Ｃ 公告政策異動
　　Ｄ 追蹤訂單

197. 阿爾圖納居家裝潢系統可能位於哪個地方？
　　Ａ 石溪
　　Ｂ 阿伯尼
　　Ｃ 水牛城
　　Ｄ 阿姆赫斯特

198. 關於聯客家具工廠的產品，這篇告示中暗示什麼？
　　Ａ 訂貨後兩小時就會出貨。
　　Ｂ 最適合小坪數房子。
　　Ｃ 價格實惠。
　　Ｄ 因為太受歡迎而缺貨。

199. 在 4 月 10 日，阿爾圖納居家裝潢系統可能會收到什麼？
　　Ａ 抗菌地毯
　　Ｂ 加大尺寸的床
　　Ｃ 四張黑椅子
　　Ｄ 黑色大書桌

200. 在訂貨表格中，塔南西多先生指出什麼事？
　　Ａ 貨運服務使用經驗不錯。
　　Ｂ 優運貨運的客戶很多。
　　Ｃ 他對商品感到失望。
　　Ｄ 產品上有部分刮傷和毀損。

ACTUAL TEST ⑦

PART 5 P. 194-196

◎ Part 5 解答請見 P.457

101. 印尼餐廳的老闆菲力克斯‧阿姆斯壯選擇直接和製造商訂購餐具和其他**必需品**。

102. 我們每週一都會**進行**生產設備巡視,確保它們運作正常。

103. 格蘭特女士一定會給予新進員工建議,讓**他們的**工作執行得有效率。

104. 行動科技的使用愈來愈普及,室內電話在很多家庭已是**淘汰的**。

105. 達特演藝學院每個月舉行公開試鏡,給**有興趣**參加年度歌唱大賽的人。

106. 斯賓塞先生最近在退休典禮上獲頒銘牌,感謝**他**在公司超過 25 年**的**貢獻。

107. 考克斯工業最近的職缺公告**特別地**指出,管理職位只會考慮錄取目前在職的生產線主管。

108. 布萊恩‧班納特新出的小說獲得評論家的好**評**。

109. 坎寧漢女士早該去買演奏會的票,但她覺得太**貴**了。

110. 政府敦促大家**及早**上網更新年度退稅資料,以免被罰錢。

111. 梅森醫院所有的醫療紀錄都是嚴格**保密的**,唯有取得病患同意才能調閱。

112. 近期顧客問卷的結果,**摘要於**電子郵件的附檔中。

113. 帕托精工工程部每年都會在歐文博士的**監督**下檢驗多項材料。

114. 康乃爾滑雪休閒中心黃林谷分店加聘了 12 名保全人員,**協助**冬天旺季的生意。

115. 首席銀行在其最新一期的報紙廣告上,**反駁**民眾批評它的利率太高。

116. 健康局向民眾承諾,會在明年**大幅**增加醫療活動。

117. 檢查保全設施時,也請確保離開辦公室前,所有門窗都**關緊**了。

118. 員工駕駛公司車輛時,須**持有**最新版的合法駕照。

119. 根據今天發布的通訊,絕**大多數**的員工都歡迎在近期展覽會上,主打新開發的營養補充品的機會。

120. 明尼蘇達工廠的消防演習將在下午兩點開始,產線**直到**演習結束前都不能重新運作。

121. 為避免出貨延遲,生產團隊必須**迅速地**修理故障的機械。

122. 考爾設計自 10 年前創立以來,就**視**員工滿意度為第一優先。

123. 沃克炸雞有很多間連鎖店**遍及**全澳洲,並正計劃到其他國家展店。

124. 每天下班前刪除電腦裡的機密檔案是**例行的**程序。

125. 亞當斯飯店上個月**在**所有房間裡安裝了省電的 LED 照明。

126. 有意參加面試、轉換職務的**員工**,必須在今天提出申請。

127. **發言人**宣布,將首次允許在法庭上使用相機。

128. 因為佛克斯鎮的大雪,開往米諾克斯郡的 404 號列車**晚**了兩小時發車。

129. **假如**電池充飽後耗電比預期得快,請聯繫我們授權的服務中心。

130. 和差旅費核銷**有關的**疑問都應轉往會計部門。

131–134 電子郵件

收件人：約翰‧特納
　　　　<Johnturner@fastmail.com>
寄件人：查爾斯‧史東
　　　　<Cstone@walshlaws.com>
主旨：求職信
日期：6 月 12 日

親愛的特納先生：

讀過您的來信，我們有意安排您面試本公司的一項職務。您在信中提到您想應徵的職務是法務專員。因此，我們考慮提供您一份從 7 月 1 日到 9 月 30 日的實習。

這項計畫的目的在於透過訓練和實務操作，培養實習生鑽研法律知識的專業。如果受訓有成，實習生可以在計畫結束後，選擇我們提供的正職。我們建議您考慮這個機會，如果您有意把握這次實習，請在您方便時回信給我們。

沃爾什商會
查爾斯‧史東 敬上

131. Ⓐ 興趣
　　 Ⓑ 感興趣的
　　 Ⓒ 是感興趣
　　 Ⓓ 是很有趣的

132. **Ⓐ 您在信中提到您想應徵的職務是法務專員。**
　　 Ⓑ 請您在明天前向我們的法務團隊提交申請表。
　　 Ⓒ 我想您應該重新考慮一下您的決定。
　　 Ⓓ 我們徵求您的同意，能否讓我們將您的應徵申請留待未來再作考慮。

133. Ⓐ 持久的
　　 Ⓑ 固定的
　　 Ⓒ 習慣性的
　　 Ⓓ 耐久的

134. Ⓐ 追求
　　 Ⓑ 正在追求
　　 Ⓒ 去追求
　　 Ⓓ 追求了

135–138 電子郵件

寄件人：大衛‧華茲
收件人：馬歇爾設計工作室員工
日期：3 月 1 日
主旨：瑪麗‧萊恩的餞別宴

你們應該知道，我們資深的頂尖設計師瑪麗‧萊恩即將離開工作多年的馬歇爾設計工作室。慶祝活動預計在下週五 3 月 10 日傍晚六點在董事會會議室舉行，以茲紀念她對我們公司的巨大奉獻。

我在上一封電子郵件中曾徵詢餞別禮的意見。大家的共識是想送瑪麗一個黃金可攜式時鐘。我確信這會是最適合她的禮物。

為了讓我們可以趕在派對前買到禮物，我要求在週一，也就是 3 月 6 日以前集資完畢。請把錢交給工作室總部的副設計總監克萊兒‧路易斯。

非常感謝，

人資主任
大衛‧華茲

135. Ⓐ 我們的
　　 Ⓑ 她的
　　 Ⓒ 你的
　　 Ⓓ 誰的

136. **Ⓐ 臨別的**
　　 Ⓑ 相似的
　　 Ⓒ 抱有希望的
　　 Ⓓ 感到高興的

137. Ⓐ 我們還沒決定要怎麼處理禮物。
　　 Ⓑ 我會開始找接替她的人。
　　 Ⓒ 每個人都受邀參加，現場會提供茶點。
　　 Ⓓ 大家的共識是想送瑪麗一個黃金可攜式時鐘。

138. Ⓐ 做
　　　Ⓑ 做
　　　Ⓒ 被做
　　　Ⓓ 將做完

139–142 文章

坎培拉（2月22日）——地區機場計劃要從下下週起限制登機的行李數量。

從3月4日起，從墨爾本到雪梨的所有機場將強制實施行李數量控管。「禁止攜帶兩件以上的行李箱，有助我們管控行李的數量，以避免行李轉盤發生阻塞。」服務處處長桃樂絲・貝里説。

旅客不得攜帶超過兩件行李。否則，每件行李須支付額外費用。或者，他們可以選擇把不需要的物品留在安全儲物櫃，可以容納多達五公斤的行李。

139. Ⓐ 提議
　　　Ⓑ 使……有聯繫
　　　Ⓒ 強化
　　　Ⓓ 限制

140. Ⓐ 在……之後
　　　Ⓑ 在……之間
　　　Ⓒ 附近
　　　Ⓓ 穿過

141. Ⓐ 所有多餘的箱子將免費運送。
　　　Ⓑ 否則，每件行李須支付額外費用。
　　　Ⓒ 事實上，規則已經鬆綁。
　　　Ⓓ 而且旅客得把行李箱留在儲物櫃裡。

142. Ⓐ 設備
　　　Ⓑ 備有……的
　　　Ⓒ 裝備
　　　Ⓓ 裝備

143–146 信件

親愛的伊凡斯先生：

感謝您有意加入我們行銷部門。

我們會很高興收到您的應徵申請表。欲成為我們服務行銷團隊的一員，您需要寄給我們您最新的履歷，以及一份描述您自身行銷方式的提案。

收到您的應徵申請後，我們將根據您所寄的背景資料和職場經歷，在兩週內聯繫您安排面試。就我們先前談過的職位，您似乎是非常合適的應徵者。

祝好，

諾頓電子行銷主任
安德森・布魯克斯

143. **Ⓐ 加入**
　　　Ⓑ 推廣
　　　Ⓒ 估價
　　　Ⓓ 組織

144. Ⓐ 然而，恐怕該職位已經有人補上。
　　　Ⓑ 我們很高興與您面試。
　　　Ⓒ 我們會很高興收到您的應徵申請表。
　　　Ⓓ 如您所要求，我將隨信附上履歷。

145. Ⓐ 描述
　　　Ⓑ 描述
　　　Ⓒ 被描述
　　　Ⓓ 將描述

146. Ⓐ 附近
　　　Ⓑ 直到
　　　Ⓒ 藉由
　　　Ⓓ 在……之後

147–148 優惠券

> ### 限時優惠
> **用單人價和朋友共享登山之樂！**
>
> 在售票處購買成人票時，出示此優惠券將免費獲得一張票。
>
> 享受風景和茶點——附贈的餐飲在山頂咖啡廳可供取用。
> — 不可以和其他優惠券併用
> — 12 月 31 日到期
> — 小孩需父母陪同

147. 這是什麼的優惠券？
- **Ⓐ 觀光場所**
- Ⓑ 自助餐廳
- Ⓒ 乘船處
- Ⓓ 運動賽事

148. 這張優惠券有何限制？
- Ⓐ 只有成人可以使用。
- Ⓑ 只能在週末使用。
- Ⓒ 不得在 12 月 31 日前使用。
- **Ⓓ 不得和另一張優惠券一起使用。**

149–150 資訊

> ### 搬移和照顧事項
>
> 搬移動物到新的場所時，需要特別照顧以確保牠們能安全抵達，並加強牠們適應新環境的能力。要牢記牠們非常難以捉摸。將牠們置入特定箱籠，否則可能會導致動物逃脫。為動物搬家時，請遵守手冊上特定的指示，因為不同的動物適用的箱籠都不同。這些手冊可以在結帳櫃檯免費索取。

149. 這些資訊最可能是想提供給誰？
- Ⓐ 店長
- **Ⓑ 飼主**
- Ⓒ 箱籠製造商
- Ⓓ 安檢人員

150. 什麼東西可以免費取得？
- Ⓐ 運輸工具
- **Ⓑ 紙本說明**
- Ⓒ 箱籠
- Ⓓ 罐頭食品

151–152 收據

> ### 霍金斯制服
> ### 送貨收據
>
> 感謝您訂貨。
>
> 訂單號碼：452198732
> 訂貨日期：6 月 21 日
> 出貨日期：6 月 25 日
>
> 顧客姓名：鄧肯餐廳
> 顧客號碼：24
>
> ------
>
> **物品一**：客製 T 恤，商標於左袖
> **顏色**：藍　**尺寸**：大　**數量**：13
>
> **物品二**：廚師帽
> **顏色**：白　**尺寸**：單一尺寸　**數量**：4
>
> **物品三**：頭巾
> **顏色**：紅　**尺寸**：單一尺寸　**數量**：27
>
> ------
>
> 造訪我們的官網 http://www.hawkinsuniforms.com

151. 襯衫訂了多少件？
- Ⓐ 24
- **Ⓑ 13**
- Ⓒ 4
- Ⓓ 27

152. 收據上寫了什麼？
- Ⓐ 這是張網路訂單。
- Ⓑ 鄧肯餐廳是常客。
- Ⓒ 有 13 名服務生在鄧肯餐廳工作。
- **Ⓓ 公司商標秀在衣服上。**

153–154 網路討論區

> **傑瑞米・艾西頓〔上午 10:46〕**：
> 大家，我們又遇到染料問題了。
>
> **南茜・帕里許〔上午 10:46〕**：
> 不會吧！這次是什麼問題？

傑瑞米・艾西頓〔上午 10:47〕：
80 條紫色毛巾的顏色錯了，反而像粉紅色。

南茜・帕里許〔上午 10:48〕：
糟糕。我們明天前得寄出所有毛巾。

達斯汀・海德〔上午 10:48〕：
我想我沒時間重新來過。剩下的訂單全都準備好出貨了嗎？

傑瑞米・艾西頓〔上午 10:49〕：
是的。其他所有顏色都好了。

南茜・帕里許〔上午 10:51〕：
何不先把製好的毛巾寄出，這樣麗莎的團隊就可以開始準備即將到來的活動？與此同時，你可以重染剩下的 80 條。

達斯汀・海德〔上午 10:51〕：
這可以爭取一些時間。但這次重新開始前，我們得先檢查染劑。

南茜・帕里許〔上午 10:52〕：
當然。我會打給麗莎，並詢問看看樣色。

送出

153. 他們正在討論什麼問題？
　　Ⓐ 有些標籤印錯了。
　　Ⓑ 有些染色結果出乎預料。
　　Ⓒ 一名檢查員沒空。
　　Ⓓ 有些機器運作得太慢。

154. 在上午 10:48 時，海德先生寫道：「我想我沒時間重新來過。」，他的意思是？
　　Ⓐ 時程很趕。
　　Ⓑ 他們寄出粉色毛巾。
　　Ⓒ 他沒有足夠的毛巾重新染色。
　　Ⓓ 接下來的活動得延期。

155–157 廣告

里德＆羅斯公司職缺

若無特別說明，職缺均為晚班（傍晚 6 點到早上 5 點）

工廠經理

須持有相關資格，深入了解倉儲運作流程，且熟知健康與安全規定。期望能有計算和制定預算的基本技能。機械工廠工作經驗尤佳，但非必要。

堆高機駕駛技術人員

須有高中以上學歷，並有兩年在繁忙的倉庫裡操作重機具的工作經驗。曾受訓操作堆高機。有若干早班需求。

資訊助理

須有大學學歷，曾在工業環境操作 SAGE 軟體。有若干早班需求。

倉儲助理和倉管人員

須認真勤奮。倉管人員要能配合早班工作。

請將履歷寄給：招募經理
里德＆羅斯公司
78753 德州奧斯汀市南湖路 472 號

謝絕人力仲介來電或電郵。

155. 工廠經理的應徵條件是什麼？
　　Ⓐ 金融學位
　　Ⓑ 健康與安全規定的知識
　　Ⓒ 進行檢查的工作經驗
　　Ⓓ 有效駕照

156. 哪項職務沒有早班需求？
　　Ⓐ 堆高機駕駛技術人員
　　Ⓑ 倉管人員
　　Ⓒ 倉儲助理
　　Ⓓ 資訊助理

157. 應徵者要如何應徵？
　　Ⓐ 線上申請
　　Ⓑ 寄信
　　Ⓒ 面對面
　　Ⓓ 透過電話

收件人：全體員工
寄件人：伊莉莎白·韋伯斯特
　　　　<Ewebster@gilbertfashion.com>
回覆：春裝系列
日期：12 月 9 日

謹代表吉爾伯特時尚的管理階層，邀請您參加我們最新春裝系列的特別秀，將在 12 月 18 日下午 4 點到晚上 9 點於銀廳舉行。我們期待每位員工都可以前來，並在陽台上一起享用自助餐。現場也會有艾拉·凱和她樂團的表演。

請留意，雖然這是一場可以提前觀賞我們最新系列服飾的免費活動，我們還是要提供人數給外燴業者。所以如果您可以出席，請在這週以前向凱特·派瑞或是亨利·羅德斯報名。如果您有什麼歌曲想請樂團演出，我們也歡迎任何建議。只要把選歌用電子郵件寄給我就可以了，或者想知道更多資訊也可以來信詢問。

很期待在 12 月 18 日見到大家。

人資經理
伊莉莎白·韋伯斯特

158. 這封電子郵件的主旨為何？
　Ⓐ **邀請員工參加活動**
　Ⓑ 詢問有沒有人志願幫忙籌辦派對
　Ⓒ 鼓勵員工舉辦自己的秀
　Ⓓ 訂慶祝要用的餐點

159. 關於這場活動，文中沒有提到什麼？
　Ⓐ 由公司主辦。
　Ⓑ 可以搶先看到一個時裝系列。
　Ⓒ 現場音樂表示是一大特色。
　Ⓓ **每一季都會辦。**

🆕
160. 下列句子最適合出現在 [1]、[2]、[3]、[4] 的哪個位置中？
　「只要把選歌用電子郵件寄給我就可以了，或者想知道更多資訊也可以來信詢問。」
　Ⓐ [1]
　Ⓑ [2]
　Ⓒ [3]
　Ⓓ **[4]**

北領地的翡翠鎮

0872 澳洲恩嘎瓦拉市特納街 55 號

2 月 11 日
福特·路卡斯先生
0830 澳洲帕默斯頓市芝拉溫路 426 號

親愛的路卡斯先生：

關於我們上週在《達爾文時報》徵求採礦助理的廣告，我們已收到您寄來翡翠鎮的求職信。很抱歉通知您該職缺已經關閉。不過，我們計劃要在四月開採新礦坑，相信您會是適合的人選。如果您允許，我想把您的詳細資料留檔。新地點距離我們達爾文的主要生產設施不遠，但前往松溪、馬塔蘭卡或其他地區，會花些時間前去。未來請持續關注我們官網所開出的新職缺。我們祝您求職順利。

祝好，

傑克森·貝茲，人事主管

161. 這封信的主旨為何？
　Ⓐ 讓一名應徵者知道他不適合這個職缺
　Ⓑ 詢問應徵者更詳細的工作經歷
　Ⓒ 安排應徵者面試
　Ⓓ **告知應徵者該職缺已經關閉**

162. 北領地的翡翠鎮主要設施位於哪裡？
　Ⓐ **達爾文**
　Ⓑ 松溪
　Ⓒ 馬塔蘭卡
　Ⓓ 帕默斯頓市

163. 貝茲先生建議路卡斯先生做什麼？
　Ⓐ **查看官網後續開出的新職缺**
　Ⓑ 寄出更多關於他資格的資訊
　Ⓒ 聯絡主要設施要求換僱員
　Ⓓ 在報紙上看應徵廣告

164–167 訊息串

> **摩根・里克〔下午 02:32〕：**
> 哈囉，詹姆斯。我昨天在你店裡看到一些花盆。它們從哪來的？
>
> **詹姆斯・派普〔下午 02:33〕：**
> 哈囉，摩根。你是指窗邊桌上那些嗎？
>
> **摩根・里克〔下午 02:33〕：**
> 是的。它們味道很甜美，看起來也不賴。所以我也想要在公寓裡擺設一些。
>
> **詹姆斯・派普〔下午 02:35〕：**
> 是從花卉中心買來的，在湯馬斯烘焙旁邊的聖喬治街。
>
> **摩根・里克〔下午 02:36〕：**
> 喔，我知道那家花店。順便問一下，它們叫什麼？
>
> **詹姆斯・派普〔下午 02:37〕：**
> 我一時想不起來。總之店內有很多野花和藥草。就靠近看看也能試聞香味。
>
> **摩根・里克〔下午 02:37〕：**
> 但我不是很懂花草。照顧起來容易嗎？
>
> **詹姆斯・派普〔下午 02:38〕：**
> 對，很容易。放室內也長得很好，也不需要太多水。
>
> **摩根・里克〔下午 02:39〕：**
> 太好了！我也沒辦法每天在家。
>
> 送出

164. 他們主要在討論什麼？
- A 里克女士的新公寓
- **B 里克女士想要的植物**
- C 聖喬治街的烘焙坊
- D 播種一些香料種子

165. 派普先生建議里克女士做什麼？
- A 順道去烘焙坊
- B 在花卉中心和他見面
- C 每天澆花
- **D 聞聞看植物**

166. 下午 2:37 時，為什麼派普先生寫道：「我一時想不起來。」？
- A 他不知道植物多貴。
- **B 他忘記花朵的名稱。**
- C 他認為里克女士不會照顧植物。
- D 他不在意它們需要多少水。

167. 為什麼里克女士覺得這些植物適合她？
- A 它們不貴。
- B 她要將植物種在戶外。
- C 花店位於她的公寓附近。
- **D 她不用每天澆花。**

168–171 文章

> **波爾多，法國**
>
> 5 月 2 日 —— 農業聯盟主席亞倫・德布瓦，將在 5 月 10 日獲頒巨擘獎。這項年度獎項頒給積極促進波爾多產業界、且其貢獻有益於地區發展者。
>
> 德布瓦一生務農，對在地環境抱有熱忱，推動地方政府設置防洪設施，讓波爾多作物和家畜免於受到每年的洪災波及。他的防洪計畫始於五年前開始執行，也就是現在名聞遐邇的觀光景點德布瓦堤防。第一道堤防在三年前由環境部門出資建設。從那時起，堤防保護了作物免於摧毀，牲畜倖免於難，也提高了當地對潮汐的危難意識。這座堤防去年落成於波爾多後，法國許多沿岸地區也考慮跟進這項堤防建設計畫。
>
> 不僅如此，德布瓦先生還創立德布瓦學院。這項計畫資助訓練有志成為農夫、在地深耕的年輕人。目前已有超過一百人完成課程，並受僱於當地農場。
>
> 頒獎典禮將在波爾多市政廳，晚上 7 點到 9 點舉行。歡迎鎮民蒞臨參加，詳情請見官網：www.bordeaux.fr/awards.

168. 這篇文章目的為何？
- **A 說明特定人物獲社區獎的原因**
- B 描述農業社群的作用
- C 邀請鎮民參加洪氾區的研討會
- D 歡迎波爾多產業界的新進成員

169. 德布瓦堤防帶來的好處，文中沒有提到的是？
- A 拯救某些家畜
- B 吸引觀光客來波爾多
- **C 籌劃一項回收計畫**
- D 提醒民眾小心潮汐

170. 德布瓦堤防的計畫什麼時候完成？
- A 五年前
- B 三年前
- **C 去年**
- D 5 月 10 日

(NEW) 171. 下列句子最適合出現在 [1]、[2]、[3]、[4] 的哪個位置中？

「不僅如此，德布瓦先生還創立德布瓦學院。」
- A [1]
- B [2]
- **C [3]**
- D [4]

172–175 廣告

PTZ 零件測試

「PTZ 零件測試」為放射醫學的業者和醫院提供全方位的測試服務。我們使用最新的儀器測試所有設備，為每一位客戶著想，量身打造適合您的測試流程。不但擁有嶄新的測試機構，我們也提供到府服務，到您的工作場所測試設備。

我們的服務：

- 醫院或醫療設施新設備運作的分析測試
- 測試流程後的檢驗報告
- 如有必要，給予顧客建議，以及提供院內或院外設備的安裝替換服務

設施和人員：

我們的總部位於中國上海，在西爪哇省和四川也設有辦公室。我們和全球各地的政府測試機構有交流，讓我們得以提供當地所缺乏的國際服務。我們全體員工均受符合國際標準的訓練，在放射學的設備測試診斷有平均 15 年的工作經驗。

報告：

我們軟體提供的資料報告均符合國際規格。

測試結果均會印出紙本也能提供電子檔。

所有的資訊都可以在官網上以加密的客戶密碼取得。

欲知更多資訊請透過電子郵件聯繫薇薇安·羅森，vivian@ptzcomponents.com。

172. 第一段、第三行的「tailoring」，最接近下列哪個意思？
- A 裁縫
- **B 調適**
- C 呈現
- D 評估

173. PTZ 零件測試沒有宣傳哪一項服務內容？
- A 檢驗放射醫學的設備
- B 到府服務
- **C 檢查醫療衛生**
- D 分析儀器的結果

174. 根據廣告，什麼讓 PTZ 零件測試獨一無二？
- **A 和遍布全球的類似公司有合作。**
- B 是業界最老牌的公司。
- C 公司裡的科學家都是國際知名大學畢業。
- D 出現於各大城市。

175. 文中提到關於 PTZ 零件測試所產出的報告什麼事？
- A 由第三方專家驗證。
- B 在網路上對外公開給大眾。
- **C 提供給客戶兩種報告格式。**
- D 額外付費可以存放檔案。

寄件人：諾蘭・帕克
　　　　<Nparker@toyfactory.com>
收件人：科勒・史旺 <Kswann@toybox.
　　　　com>
日期：1 月 25 日
主旨：銷售更新
附件：報告－ 01.xls

親愛的史旺女士：

我來信答覆您詢問有關這個月的銷售資訊更新。您可以看到附件中有一份十二月存貨的銷售清單，還有一份損益試算表。您可以看到大多數的商品都賣得非常好。尤其是源川企業的陶瓷娃娃，銷售量破紀錄。哈潑牌的填充動物玩偶也仍為暢銷商品，還有 ELF 股份有限公司的家用遊戲機和電玩也是。令我感到驚訝的是，兒童積木組合的銷售下滑。我想是因為和其他競爭商品相比，我們的商品品質落後非常多，我們也接獲很多抱怨，說它們很容易壞掉。這在銷售數字的退款部分可以見得。

不過，我已經找上另一家供應商，希望幾個月之後的銷售數據可以反應出效果。我很期待在下週一的年度銷售會議上和您見面。如果在這之前您需要更多資訊的話，請告訴我。

銷售經理
諾蘭・帕克 敬上

寄件人：科勒・史旺
　　　　<Kswann@toybox.com>
收件人：諾蘭・帕克
　　　　<Nparker@toyfactory.com>
日期：1 月 26 日
主旨：回覆：銷售更新

親愛的帕克先生：

感謝您迅速答覆。如您所知，我們已和波士頓和春田的零售業者，簽了一筆供應兒童玩具的大訂單，這兩地都是備受關注的

地區。根據我們的研究，我們得知該地區的人對商品品質的要求很高，而且當地有高於平均數量的學校和兒童俱樂部。因此，我想我們應該向源川企業訂購更多商品。可以請您提供一份這間公司的產品清單，還有聯絡人的姓名和電話給我嗎？就我所知，會議已經改期到週二舉行了。您可以同時確認這事嗎？

行銷經理
科勒・史旺

176. 為什麼帕克先生要寄出第一封電子郵件？
　　　A 提供史旺女士資訊
　　　B 要求一份庫存玩具的清單
　　　C 提供會議的新日期
　　　D 回覆一項提議的變更

177. 根據第一封電子郵件，哪項商品將由新的供應商供應？
　　　A 電玩
　　　B 填充動物玩偶
　　　C 積木組合
　　　D 陶瓷娃娃

178. 第二封電子郵件中，第三行的「locals」，最接近下列哪個意思？
　　　A 居民
　　　B 地區
　　　C 商品
　　　D 銷售量

179. 文中提到陶瓷娃娃什麼事？
　　　A 預期將在波士頓地區賣得很好。
　　　B 在夏季缺貨。
　　　C 是從哈潑買來的。
　　　D 售價比上個月低。

180. 帕克先生和史旺女士擁有的資訊，哪一項不一樣？
　　　A 會議日期
　　　B 和 ELF 股份有限公司的聯繫資訊
　　　C 12 月的銷售數據
　　　D 一位顧客的退款細節

8 月 15 日
客服部門
韋爾斯家用設備股份有限公司
94016 加州舊金山市桑德斯路 22 號

此致有關人士：

我的咖啡機（產品序號 CFM436）最近壞了，我把它帶到莫里斯購物中心的韋爾斯服務中心，也是就貴公司列出的其中一個維修門市。我非常生氣，雖然我還有超過六個月的有效保固期，店家卻拒絕免費維修我的咖啡機。因為附近沒有保固證書列出的其他維修點，我只能自己花錢修理。這是維修中心跟我索取的費用明細：

零件：

濾網……………………………………12 元

電源……………………………………17 元

勞務費（每小時）………………20 元

噴嘴管………………………………21 元

總計：………………………………**70 元**

隨信附上我購買咖啡機的發票和保證書。如果還需要更多資訊，請和我聯絡。

祝好，

伊恩・崔佛斯
95120 加州聖荷西市櫻桃石街 23 號

保證書

歡迎新的韋爾斯咖啡機來到您手中。我們在全球供應高品質的廚房電器已逾 30 年，我們以產品品質和顧客服務自豪。

所有的產品都是遵循最高標準的工藝製造。我們提供兩年保固，包括維修和替換故障的零件。這份保固僅涵蓋維修的勞務費用和可供替換的零件；請您留意，噴嘴管的毀損或操作不當造成的損壞，我們一概不負責。

附件清單是我們所授權的維修中心。如果您的新產品有問題，請攜帶原收據與保證書，前往其中任何一家韋爾斯公司的服務中心維修。這些中心的維修和服務品質都經由韋爾斯公司認可。

181. 為什麼崔佛斯先生要寫這封信？
Ⓐ **要求補償他的花費**
Ⓑ 要求取得一份保固書副本
Ⓒ 要求替換他故障的商品
Ⓓ 抱怨他收據上的一項錯誤

182. 在信中第一段、第三行的「declined」，最接近下列哪個意思？
Ⓐ 下降了
Ⓑ **拒絕了**
Ⓒ 弱化了
Ⓓ 修改了

183. 關於韋爾斯公司的服務中心，崔佛斯先生提到什麼？
Ⓐ 它降價提供服務。
Ⓑ 它很迅速完成工作。
Ⓒ 它做了非必要的工作。
Ⓓ **它是經認可的服務中心。**

184. 韋爾斯家電的產品保固包含什麼？
Ⓐ 顧客註冊表格
Ⓑ 韋爾斯的產品型錄
Ⓒ 客戶名冊
Ⓓ **服務中心的名單**

185. 崔佛斯先生所反應的哪項支出，沒有含在保固內？
Ⓐ 12 元
Ⓑ 17 元
Ⓒ 20 元
Ⓓ **21 元**

傑克遜維爾市
議會辦公室：街頭藝人許可申請

下表中的申請人請求傑克遜維爾街頭「藝人」的演出執照，並提交下述必要資訊：

藝術家姓名：傑斯·佩恩

申請人的法定地址：傑克遜維爾市，理查森路 2194 號

表演地點：艾德·奧斯丁公園

完成的申請表格須附下列資料：

- 民政局所核發的出生證明副本
- 申請人演奏相關樂器或歌唱的錄影錄音檔
- 每一名成員、設備和舞台的執照費 30 美元
- 場地所需的設備清單
- 如需使用擴音器，請將分貝等級的細節寄給負責噪音汙染管制的官員，蓋文·弗里曼先生，以確保符合規定。

申請人聲明上述內容皆為真，他／她已閱讀並同意遵守傑克遜維爾市政法第 44 款，適用於藝人的規定。

申請者簽名：傑斯·佩恩

日期：7 月 24 日

收件人：蓋文·弗里曼
　　　　<Gfreeman@admin.jacksonville.org>
寄件人：傑斯·佩恩
　　　　<Jacepayne@bigmail.com>
日期：7 月 27 日
主旨：音量許可

親愛的弗里曼先生：

我想要取得 8 月 1 日到 3 日在艾德·奧斯丁公園舉行街頭表演的許可。我了解我需要得到使用擴音器的許可，它目前的音量最高達 100 分貝。我打算在演出時使用三座擴音器。如果您想要確認噪音等級，我週間在市區的三個地點有演出：馬爾斯酒吧、維紐爾餐廳和街頭生活咖啡店。如果您要前來確認分貝數是否合乎標準，我可以提供您免費入場券。

祝好，

傑斯·佩恩

收件人：傑斯·佩恩
　　　　<Jacepayne@bigmail.com>
寄件人：蓋文·弗里曼
　　　　<Gfreeman@admin.jacksonville.org>
日期：7 月 29 日
主旨：回覆：音量許可

親愛的佩恩先生：

我需要在現場操作測量設備來評估噪音等級。從您先前所提及的地點中，街頭生活對我來說較為可行。您說您週間會演出。那您方便我何時過去呢？

另外關於您的申請，負責人說她沒有收到您演出的影音檔。如果您不介意，我到現場檢測擴音器時可以一併錄影。由於我們在 8 月 1 日前沒有太多時間，請您方便的話，儘早透過電話 500-5157 聯絡我。

噪音汙染部官員
蓋文·弗里曼

186. 佩恩先生要申請什麼？
　Ⓐ 販賣飲料的許可
　Ⓑ 音效檢測
　Ⓒ 議會的安全證書
　Ⓓ 表演執照

TEST 7
PART 7

187. 弗里曼先生最有可能在哪裡看到佩恩先生的演出？
- Ⓐ 在一處公園
- Ⓑ 在一間酒吧
- **Ⓒ 在一間咖啡廳**
- Ⓓ 在一間餐廳

188. 弗里曼先生提到，佩恩先生漏了哪一項資料？
- Ⓐ 出生證明
- **Ⓑ 一段錄影畫面**
- Ⓒ 設備清單
- Ⓓ 一些錢

189. 第一封電子郵件的目的為何？
- Ⓐ 遞交一份申請
- Ⓑ 提供路徑指引
- **Ⓒ 取得使用設備的許可**
- Ⓓ 推廣某個場地

190. 下個月的活動裡，佩恩先生可能會使用什麼東西？
- Ⓐ 電吉他
- Ⓑ 麥克風架
- Ⓒ 剪輯設備
- **Ⓓ 喇叭**

191–195 文章和電子郵件

國際商貿訊
MJ 美食村指派新任研發團隊主管

總部設在新加坡的 MJ 美食村（MJF）最近指派了卡爾登・崔擔任研發團隊的新主管。「我感到很興奮，我在新加坡這裡有了全新的機會，雖然要離開家鄉南韓有些難過。」崔先生在 MJF 通訊的聲明裡表示。

他接著說，他多年來對於 MJF 所做的工作很感興趣，很高興能加入這個團隊。根據本訊，他就任後首要任務，將更重視菲律賓和印尼健康飲食的重要性。

崔先生在倫敦大學取得食品與營養學的碩士學位。他之前在布里斯托食品公司就職，擔任研發部主任朱里安・貝克的研究助理。他將在 10 月開始 MJF 的新職。

收件人：卡爾登・崔
　　　　<coltonchoi@gomail.com>
寄件人：雅瑞安娜・羅斯
　　　　<arianarose@bfc.com>
日期：9 月 9 日
主旨：恭喜

親愛的崔先生：

您又再次獲得很棒的工作，這對您來說是個絕佳的機會，我確信您會在 MJ 美食村有傑出貢獻。當您請辭後，貝克先生請我接替您研究助理的位子。雖然我還沒給他答覆，但我想要接受這份工作。從去年開始在這裡工作，我就想加入研究團隊了。我衷心感謝您推薦我這份工作。

我希望我們能保持聯絡，如果您願意讓我知道您在新加坡的新地址和電話號碼，我也會很感謝。

祝好，

布里斯托食品公司
雅瑞安娜・羅斯

收件人：雅瑞安娜・羅斯
　　　　<arianarose@bfc.com>
寄件人：卡爾登・崔 <coltonchoi@gomail.
　　　　com>
日期：9 月 11 日
主旨：回覆：恭喜

親愛的羅斯女士：

我很高興得知您要接受這份工作。雖然我們之前沒有機會在同一個團隊裡共事，但我從您的主管考克斯先生聽到很多關於您的事。我相信您在材料部門的經驗，對研究團隊會有很大的幫助。我向貝克先生推薦您接任時，他很快便同意要給您這個機會。所以，您應該向貝克先生轉達您的感謝。

我還沒搬到新加坡。我已找到安頓的房子，但還沒有電話。我也會更換電子信箱；假如下個月開始新職務，您需要我的建議的話，您可以透過coltonchoi2793@mjfgroup.com 聯絡我。

卡爾登・崔 敬上

191. 為什麼要寫這篇文章？
   Ⓐ 公告一名新員工就職
   Ⓑ 公布問卷結果
   Ⓒ 釋出新產品資訊
   Ⓓ 通知員工接下來的一項研究計畫

192. MJ 美食村的總部位於哪裡？
   Ⓐ 南韓
   Ⓑ 新加坡
   Ⓒ 馬來西亞
   Ⓓ 菲律賓

193. 羅斯女士要求崔先生做什麼？
   Ⓐ 寫推薦信
   Ⓑ 加入研究團隊
   Ⓒ 提供聯絡資訊
   Ⓓ 在會議中發言

194. 文中提到崔先生什麼事？
   Ⓐ 他目前在 MJ 美食村就職。
   Ⓑ 他會接替考克斯先生擔任研究助理。
   Ⓒ 他推薦羅斯女士接任他之前的職位。
   Ⓓ 他決定待在家鄉。

195. 文中提到羅斯女士什麼事？
   Ⓐ 她是 MJ 美食村的客戶。
   Ⓑ 她現在住在新加坡。
   Ⓒ 她主修食品和營養學。
   Ⓓ 她目前為考克斯先生工作。

196–200 資訊、表格和信件

《哈頓商業最新訊息》

信賴我們帶給您分秒必爭的新聞和事件

向訂戶報告：

更新訂閱的需求，除了會在您現有訂閱過期日的前一週自動通知，也視下述情況而

定。如果您的訂閱在您申請更新前就已經結束，但在過期的兩個月內您還想要繼續訂閱的話，可以用比定價便宜 25% 的折扣，購買您錯過的任何一期商業雜誌。

訂戶如果在 4 月 30 日前要求更新或展延，訂閱兩年期將折扣 10%，12 個月期將折扣 5%。訂閱過期後的所有線上服務，包括可以讓您瀏覽之前每一期《哈頓商業最新訊息》的目錄搜尋資料庫，都將跟著停止。請造訪 www.hattononline.com 取得更多資訊。

《哈頓商業最新訊息》

帳戶號碼：34073

最近登入：3 月 6 日

上次登入：2 月 27 日

《哈頓商業最新訊息》線上訂閱

● **姓名**：奧斯丁・克羅克
● **訂戶狀態**：目前訂閱將在 3 月 6 日到期
● **請求更新訂閱期間**：24 個月
● **付款方式**：銀行轉帳

感謝您更新訂閱《哈頓商業最新訊息》。

來自：奧斯丁・克羅克

日期：3 月 6 日

主旨：更新訂閱

您好：

我今天查看您官網上的優惠訊息。我很滿意您的服務，所以即便距離到期還有一個月，我馬上決定再次訂閱。不過，我收到訊息時很驚訝，上面說我的到期日是今天，也就是 3 月 6 日。根據您的網頁，應該是 4 月 6 日才對。其他訊息裡的資訊看起來都是對的。

我也確認過是不是我按成「新訂戶」，而不是「更新訂閱」。但它寫到「感謝您更新訂閱《哈頓商業最新訊息》。」請儘快處理這個問題。

196. 這則資訊的目的為何？
  Ⓐ 公告訂閱的額外優惠
  Ⓑ 解釋更新訂閱的規定
  Ⓒ 通知訂戶線上訂閱的異動
  Ⓓ 要求訂戶完成問卷

197. 在資訊中，第一段、第二行的
  「conditions」，最接近下列哪個意思？
  Ⓐ 結束
  Ⓑ 提案
  Ⓒ 條件
  Ⓓ 姓名

198. 文中提到《哈頓商業最新訊息》什麼事？
  Ⓐ 它的記者得過很多出版獎。
  Ⓑ 官網提供訂戶部分資訊。
  Ⓒ 兩個月前出了最後一期。
  Ⓓ 它最近漲了訂閱費。

199. 克羅克先生反應了什麼問題？
  Ⓐ 他沒辦法登入官網。
  Ⓑ 他沒有接到任何該活動的通知。
  Ⓒ 他接獲的訊息裡有錯誤資訊。
  Ⓓ 他想要全額退款。

200. 克羅克先生會得到多少折扣？
  Ⓐ 5%
  Ⓑ 10%
  Ⓒ 20%
  Ⓓ 25%

ACTUAL TEST ⑧

PART 5　P. 224–226

◎ Part 5 解答請見 P.457

101. 阿迪斯・阿巴巴的營養指導課程非常**成功**，有些國家也考慮在其都市內引進類似的計畫。

102. Prime.com 的隸屬機構可以無限制地**取得**該組織專屬的線上資料庫。

103. 這本小冊子特別強調這兩天的**系列活動**。

104. 沃克先生兩年前**離開**大學，加入現在的公司。

105. **因為**考爾路的維修工程，梅西爾圖書館的員工必須從北入口進來上班。

106. **詢問**行李遺失的人，必須到行李轉盤旁邊的行李提領處洽詢。

107. 在大太陽底下熱昏頭的人，會發現讓**自己**感到舒服的最佳方式就是多喝點水。

108. 今年度全體員工的加薪，和去年的激勵方式是**一樣的**。

109. 有機馬鈴薯產品的大量需求，使酢漿草農場的農民感到無法負荷。

110. 康登超市的大部分顧客都願意為**在地**生產的食物多付一點錢。

111. 雖然全民都獲准參加安那翰協會的頒獎典禮，但續攤宴會只限受**邀請**者參加。

112. 公司員工被提醒，新產品的市場是高度**競爭的**，且將面臨來自其他公司的強烈較勁。

113. 投影機在研討會上運作失常，造成客戶大會延遲**頗久**。

114. 因為公司大樓結構整修，其年度生產**總**成本預估會是一千兩百萬美元。

115. 訪客在飯店辦理入住時，**會被要求**出示護照或是有照片的身分證件。

116. 董事會正考慮將總部**搬遷**到溫哥華。

117. 業務經理寇帝・佛林堅稱，**僅**在網路上行銷這項商品不能有效吸引年輕消費者。

118. 肯普服飾第二季的成長率比**預期**來得高。

119. 應徵主管職位並已通過初試的人，下週**將由**公司人事招募處**聯繫**。

120. 民眾每週可以在班布里治公共圖書館借出總共五本書**和**三片多媒體光碟。

121. 留宿期間，房客可以選擇參加多項戶外活動，**像是**騎單車、釣魚和游泳。

122. 旅客下火車前，必須帶走所有的**個人**物品。

123. LK 通訊公司開立帳單規定的變動，**主要**根據其需求來決定。

124. 關於建設波德路上可容納 1,000 台車的停車**場**，其估價包含所需的人事和材料支出。

125. 雷諾斯先生為橘子軟體的新進員工**籌辦**了歡迎會，應該獲得稱讚。

126. **沒有**事先取得同意的話，辛普森街上的零售商店禁止在外展示商品。

127. 讓董事會印象最深刻的是，白木公司在硬木家具市場建立了它的一席之地。

128. 即使大部分顧客都覺得新產品操作簡易，還是有**不太**熟悉之前操作系統的人，必須在使用前詳讀使用說明書。

129. 因為表現出色，羅素女士最近被**晉升**為希金斯公司的經理。

130. 飲料和點心的販賣機，策略性地設置在公司內**各處**。

TEST 8

PART 5

409

131-134 廣告

席亞拉美術館新展覽

席亞拉美術館近年來藉著舉辦廢物藝術展大受歡迎。它是創新的藝術，特色標榜知名在地藝術家迪亞哥‧哈丁和他團隊所展現的藝術才能。

根據哈丁先生的說法，他的創作活動有時被稱為「廢物藝術」。他想到要利用人們每天丟掉的東西。「廢物藝術」誠如其名，指的是一度廢棄的物品用來從事新的創作。

展覽從 4 月 1 日到 6 月 30 日開放，歡迎任何感興趣的人蒞臨。此外，3 月 23 日週三晚間將舉行接待會，僅限藝術中心的員工參加。欲知詳情者請參見官網，網址是 museum.sierraart.org。

135-138 信件

親愛的星星商店顧客：

我們非常感謝您加入星星商店的忠誠獎勵計畫。參加本計畫將讓您享受很多優質獎賞。成為計畫會員的好處是可以提早取得優惠資訊、參加獨家活動，每次購買商品消費滿 400 元也有機會贈與 50 元禮券。

加入計畫一點都不難。只需填寫好隨函付上的申請表，並交至鄰近的星星店面，當場就能發會員卡給您。開始啟用會員卡後，就會在六週內提供您帳戶更新的資訊，它會詳列您累積的點數和賺到的優惠券。

免費登記會員，且隨時都能取消。歡迎從今天起開始賺取獎勵！

顧客忠誠計畫主任
艾美‧韓德森 敬上

隨函付上

131. Ⓐ 特色
　　 Ⓑ 有……特色
　　 Ⓒ 以……為特色
　　 Ⓓ 以……為特色

132. Ⓐ 但這些雕塑的材料事實上並非垃圾。
　　 Ⓑ 它一度被認為是可行的，但哈丁先生不這麼想。
　　 Ⓒ 哈丁先生現在蒐集大量廢棄物，來實現他的創意。
　　 Ⓓ 他想到要利用人們每天丟掉的東西。

133. Ⓐ 凡是……的事物
　　 Ⓑ 那東西
　　 Ⓒ 用……的方式
　　 Ⓓ 每一

134. **Ⓐ 此外**
　　 Ⓑ 反而
　　 Ⓒ 因此
　　 Ⓓ 結果

135. Ⓐ 已允許
　　 Ⓑ 正在允許
　　 Ⓒ 允許了
　　 Ⓓ 將允許

136. Ⓐ 表現
　　 Ⓑ 評估
　　 Ⓒ 資訊
　　 Ⓓ 轉介

137. Ⓐ 一旦取消，您所有的優待券就會失效。
　　 Ⓑ 加入計畫一點都不難。
　　 Ⓒ 您不在我們的顧客名單上；然而，我們仍視您為最重要的會員服務您。
　　 Ⓓ 您需要到我們其中一間分店拿申請表。

138. **Ⓐ 在……期間內**
　　 Ⓑ 自從
　　 Ⓒ 直到
　　 Ⓓ 因為

曼谷（4月2日）——加拿大服裝主要品牌「優秀運動」的潮流商品，很快就要在泰國促銷。

「優秀運動」總裁李察‧肯特在《泰國商業新聞》的訪談中宣布，公司打算在幾週內，將第一批最新的運動服裝和時尚配件運到泰國曼谷。商品五月上市，屆時泰國消費者就能拿到貨。

肯特先生認為，這次的商業行動，是因為泰國和其鄰近國家在運動服飾方面成長的需求。特別是在菲律賓賣得非常好。肯特先生表示，依東南亞目前的趨勢，有愈來愈多人對健身服飾感興趣，而這也正是「優秀運動」的目標市場。

139. Ⓐ 回憶
　　 Ⓑ 促銷
　　 Ⓒ 減少
　　 Ⓓ 設計

140. Ⓐ 正在消費
　　 Ⓑ 消費者
　　 Ⓒ 消耗品
　　 Ⓓ 消耗過的

141. **Ⓐ 成長的**
　　 Ⓑ 決定性的
　　 Ⓒ 存在已久的
　　 Ⓓ 可疑的

142. Ⓐ 難怪那間公司正在撤出東南亞的事業。
　　 Ⓑ 他現在擔心亞洲市場會開始萎縮。
　　 Ⓒ 因此，在歐洲的生意或許更有利可圖。
　　 Ⓓ 特別是在菲律賓賣得非常好。

收件人：製造員和品管員
寄件人：弗雷德‧威爾森，生產製造經理
日期：2月9日
主旨：簡單喝榨汁機

我想要立即通知大家，對於新款簡單喝榨汁機的可拆式榨汁器，我們已收到一些顧客的意見。

有些顧客擔心榨汁器不能完整貼合機身。雖然這細節好像不是很重要，但我覺得這些抱怨長遠來看對我們的商譽有害。提醒一下，製造員必須確保榨汁器製造無誤。品管員於配送前也必須再三檢查這些零件。

如果還需要知道簡單喝榨汁機的更多細節，請來電 764-8314。

143. Ⓐ 將收到
　　 Ⓑ 已收到
　　 Ⓒ 接收
　　 Ⓓ 正在接收

144. Ⓐ 尚未收到顧客抱怨。
　　 Ⓑ 我很高興知道最新款商品獲得好評。
　　 Ⓒ 儘管銷售額很差，公司還是得要增加產量。
　　 Ⓓ 有些顧客擔心榨汁器不能完整貼合機身。

145. Ⓐ 很快地
　　 Ⓑ 舒服地
　　 Ⓒ 正確地
　　 Ⓓ 無疑地

146. **Ⓐ 零件**
　　 Ⓑ 車輛
　　 Ⓒ 行程
　　 Ⓓ 付款

147-148 通知

鋼鐵瓊斯健身房預計要整修。健身房將在七月關閉兩週以便建築維修。

幾個重要日期如下:

6 月 20 日—6 月 30 日 年度會員資格更新

7 月 1 日——7 月 6 日 房間翻修

7 月 7 日——7 月 14 日 外窗更換

7 月 15 日 健身房重新開張

如欲查看今年度的全部行事曆,可上 www.ironjones.com。會員資格可透過電話更新。如果您正租用運動設備也能隨時更新租期。如果不需要,請在 6 月 20 日前歸還。等到 7 月 15 日即可重新申請。儘管您更新了租約,但因為將要更換置物櫃,您放在裡頭的所有器材需在 6 月 30 日前清空。任何留在置物櫃裡的東西在 6 月 30 日後將被丟棄。如有任何疑問請致電 777-4644 分機 14 聯絡我們。

147. 鋼鐵瓊斯健身房的通知想要告知的對象是誰?
- A 管理階層
- **B 會員**
- C 健身教練
- D 健身房員工

148. 想更新會員資格應該怎麼做?
- A 面對面辦理
- **B 打電話**
- C 寫電子郵件
- D 上官網

149-150 訊息串

凱蒂·哈特〔下午 3:29〕:
傑克,德塔辦公用品打電話來。他們不能在週三送投影機過來。

傑克·伍德〔下午 3:31〕:
這不行啊。我們訓練課程會用到投影機。

凱蒂·哈特〔下午 3:32〕:
我知道。也許我應該再找一間我可以親取投影機的店。

傑克·伍德〔下午 3:33〕:
泰瑞説,主街上最近新開了一間辦公用品店。我想我能載你一程。什麼時候接你?

凱蒂·哈特〔下午 3:34〕:
非常感謝!我五點在北入口前面等你。

傑克·伍德〔下午 3:35〕:
沒問題。別忘了帶公司信用卡。

送出

149. 談話的人討論到什麼問題?
- A 新的投影機運作失常。
- B 他們不能出席週三的研討會。
- **C 有筆訂購商品不能及時送到。**
- D 伍德先生到主街需要搭便車。

150. 下午 3:31 時,伍德先生寫道:「這不行啊。」,他的意思是?
- A 他找不到其他供應商。
- B 他修不好投影機。
- C 他不同意哈特女士的意見。
- **D 他無法接受貨品未寄達。**

151-152 公告

親愛的韓德森居民:

暮站舞廳從八月起將改名為彩虹天堂夜店。目前正在大翻修,將增建新的用餐區並擴大舞池。新店家賴瑞·史東將維持大家過往所熟悉的高水準餐點和娛樂活動。期望很快與您再相見。

151. 根據公告，工程將帶來什麼改變？
- **A 店名**
- B 地點
- C 菜單
- D 價格

152. 文中提到史東先生什麼事？
- A 他計劃換菜單。
- B 他在當地有其他房產。
- C 他過去曾在夜店工作。
- **D 他計劃擴大舞池。**

153–154 文章

> ### 倫敦經濟家
> ### 商業新聞
>
> 9 月 12 日，倫敦——「費爾頓加熱零件」執行長伊森·佛萊契宣布，公司未來六個月將在全國展店。新店計劃開在格拉斯哥、里茲和倫敦。
>
> 佛萊契先生坦承，擴張計畫因為工廠的複雜問題而落後。他說經濟衰退「嚇了大家一跳」。隨著其布里斯托的製造總部安裝了更先進的機具，佛萊契先生有信心，展店有利於投資。
>
> 「費爾頓加熱零件」由現任執行長的父親所創立，始於他開始回收製作鍋爐的金屬零件。這種回收行動使得市面上的製造零件變得便宜很多。所以公司的市場占有率也在幾年間大幅提昇。
>
> 公司希望可以在明年把業務擴展到空調市場，業界也會密切注意其表現。這項商業行動將搭配積極的廣告行銷活動。

153. 文中提到費爾頓加熱零件什麼事？
- A 市占率在幾年間大幅衰退。
- **B 創辦人把生意傳給他兒子。**
- C 業務將擴展到商業領域。
- D 製造工廠關閉。

154. 下列句子最適合出現在 [1]、[2]、[3]、[4] 的哪個位置中？
「這種回收行動使得市面上的製造零件變得便宜很多。」
- A [1]
- B [2]
- **C [3]**
- D [4]

155–157 手冊

> ### 特快車遊高地的時尚旅程
>
> 沿著高地海岸三小時的特快車行程，體驗視覺聽覺的饗宴。兩百公里的海線軌道穿越三郡，沿途風景宜人，綠意盎然。本行程帶您穿越高地，自由選擇是否要導遊隨行。穿過高地工業區時是車上的午餐時間。旅途的終點造訪密境海灘，沿岸可以看到玩耍的海豹和海豚。
>
> 火車在週一到週五上午 11:30 從曼徹斯特站出發，下午 2:30 回來。成人票價 40 英鎊，學生票持有效證件為 25 英鎊，12 歲以下兒童 20 英鎊。
>
> 詳情與時刻表請致電
> 特快車 0161-334-6259
> 或者
> 造訪我們官網
> www.expresshighlandstrains.co.uk
>
> ### 特快車之旅

155. 這手冊想要告知的對象是誰？
- A 導遊
- B 歷史學家
- C 火車駕駛
- **D 旅客**

156. 第六行的「hidden」最接近下列哪個意思？
- A 禁止的
- **B 隱匿的**
- C 惡名昭彰的
- D 擁擠的

157. 10 歲遊客的車費是多少錢？
   A 12 英磅
   B 20 英磅
   C 25 英磅
   D 40 英磅

158–160 廣告

梅爾羅斯商學院

如果您正在尋找國際商學碩士學位，請聯繫梅爾羅斯商學院了解課程細節。

本學院提供兩年制的課程，課程包括各類國際關係和商學研究，將於九月開學。課程由享譽盛名的教授授課，他們在國際商貿產業有豐富的實務經驗。本院同時也有和海外大公司合作的創新交流計畫，讓本學院在國際商學院評鑑名列前三。

國內學生的申請費為 150 美元，國際學生則為 250 美元。如果您出示這則廣告並於 6 月底前申請入學，申請費將減免一半。新課程的申請截止日期為 7 月 15 日。也有多種獎助學金可供申請。如欲了解更多資訊並取得入學申請表，請上官網 www.melrosebusiness.edu。

158. 文中提到國際碩士學位課程什麼事？
   A 最近來了新進教職員。
   B 有三個註冊時間。
   C 享譽盛名。
   D 一年可以修完。

159. 根據廣告，學生不能得到什麼機會？
   A 到海外工作
   B 修到關於國際專業的課程
   C 取得財務資助的機會
   D 能夠線上上課

160. 文中提到申請費什麼事？
   A 本國人和國際人士申請費用有別。
   B 明年會漲。
   C 6 月 30 日前要付款。
   D 可以線上或信用卡繳款。

161–163 備忘錄

備忘錄
爾灣飯店

為了減少開支，爾灣飯店管理部門將不再免費提供盥洗用品。房客必須特別要求並額外付費，始能提供盥洗用品。這是我們減少成本計畫的一部分。請您於房客登記入住時確實告知這項改變。不過，房客可以在大廳的商店裡，用合理價格買到必要的盥洗用品。房客也能預購嚴選盥洗商品並於抵達時取用，費用將結算在帳單上。請確實、清楚地告知每一位電話訂房的客人。我們也會在飯店全部的房間和大廳張貼異動通知，明確傳達此訊息。

161. 這則備忘錄想要告知的對象是誰？
   A 飯店房客
   B 維修人員
   C 打掃人員
   D 飯店接待人員

162. 根據備忘錄，為什麼要採取新規定？
   A 節省一次性耗材成本
   B 改進員工訓練
   C 節約用水用電
   D 減少其他的維修需求

163. 飯店員工被指示要做什麼？
   A 告知房客不附贈盥洗用品
   B 向房客收使用的水電費
   C 在接待處提供房客多種商品
   D 提醒房客房價調漲

164–167 文章

4 月 30 日 —— 惠特爾設計工作室的設計師卡拉·惠特爾最近捐款 50 萬英鎊，給索維托鎮「直接身障補助計畫」。該慈善活動的捐款自去年起減少以來，這著實是一大捐注。「惠特爾女士慷慨捐獻，我們真的很高興。」「直接身障補助計畫」主持人大衛·坎培爾說。「這確實有助於我們在社區裡，為身障者增設更多身障設施。」

在地商人十年前創設了「直接身障補助計畫」，以協助身障人士使用公共設施。儘管一開始拿到政府補助，不過今年礙於財政部要減少公共支出的壓力，預算在今年初被砍。該項計畫而今仰賴捐款。

「直接身障補助計畫」上個月開始向當地商家展開募款活動。「除了提出捐款要求，我們也寄送我們建設的設施照片。」坎培爾先生繼續說，其中一項設施是通往當地圖書館的無障礙坡道，也是惠特爾女士的家人經常使用的一項設施。「我從不知道惠特爾女士的家人會使用圖書館，直到她打電話給我，詢問能否提供任何協助。」坎培爾先生說。

支持者和企業對於這項捐款均感欣慰，地方議員湯姆·布萊迪也稱讚說，慈善機構的作法連帶提高其他計畫的知名度和募得款項。惠特爾女士在新聞稿發表聲明：「我從小就很愛這座圖書館，即便現在我搬到國外，還是有很多美好的回憶。這不只是裝設無障礙坡道，這意味著如今有更多當地人可以使用設施」。

艾美·威靈頓
在地撰稿人

164. 直接身障補助計畫從何時開始？
Ⓐ 兩年前
Ⓑ 三年前
Ⓒ 五年前
Ⓓ 十年前

165. 根據文章，這項計畫為什麼失去資金？
Ⓐ 當地商家拒絕協助。
Ⓑ 建築材料的成本增加了。
Ⓒ 當地人口減少。
Ⓓ 政府減少資助。

166. 誰現在不是索維托鎮的居民？
Ⓐ 卡拉·惠特爾
Ⓑ 大衛·坎培爾
Ⓒ 湯姆·布萊迪
Ⓓ 艾美·威靈頓

167. 下列句子最適合出現在 [1]、[2]、[3]、[4] 的哪個位置中？
「這確實有助於我們在社區裡，為身障者增設更多身障設施。」
Ⓐ [1]
Ⓑ [2]
Ⓒ [3]
Ⓓ [4]

168–171 電子郵件

收件人：查德·羅傑斯
　　　　<chadrogers@gomail.com>
寄件人：凱莉·史萊特
　　　　<carrieslater@widemail.com>
日期：9 月 5 日
主旨：成本彙總表
附件：估價單 ＿ 查德羅傑斯 .xls

親愛的羅傑斯先生：

很高興上週和您見面，並聽您分享您擴展自動洗車事業的想法。如我所言我的財務團隊已經準備好估價，請參考本電子郵件附件。

您說您計劃要在百特大樓對面設置自動洗車通道。團隊已把成本列入估價，其中包括簽訂任何合約前的整修和承租費用。我仍然建議安東小學後面、一流大樓旁的一塊空地是更佳選擇。因為它已經經過整修，可以降低您的成本。

如果您想要我們執行計畫，我們可以馬上動工。有任何問題都請儘管聯繫我。我期待很快聽到您的看法。

凱莉·史萊特 敬上

168. 史萊特女士最可能的職業是？
Ⓐ 洗車公司老闆
Ⓑ 建築承包商
Ⓒ 財務顧問
Ⓓ 環境美化專家

169. 根據電子郵件，上週的會議裡談了什麼？
Ⓐ 新餐廳的設計
Ⓑ 車隊擴編
Ⓒ 搬遷店面計畫
Ⓓ 可能的整修計畫

170. 關於附件內容，文中提到什麼？
　　Ⓐ 詳細藍圖
　　Ⓑ 價格細目
　　Ⓒ 整修材料的收據
　　Ⓓ 工作進度表

171. 第二段、第二行的「figured」，最接近下列哪些意思？
　　Ⓐ 已超過
　　Ⓑ 已折扣
　　Ⓒ 已併入
　　Ⓓ 已轉變

172–175　網路討論區

> **凱伊拉・馬克士威〔上午 10:01〕：**
> 哈囉，大家。我想確認產品研發的進度。你們正在邀請新肥皂的試用者，對嗎？
>
> **喬丹・摩斯〔上午 10:02〕：**
> 不過我們找到的志願者還不夠。目前有 12 個人會來，但還需要 8 個人。
>
> **艾琳・帕克〔上午 10:02〕：**
> 那我們只好將測試延後幾天。
>
> **凱伊拉・馬克士威〔上午 10:03〕：**
> 12 人難道不能將就用嗎？
>
> **艾琳・帕克〔上午 10:03〕：**
> 最好不要。我們現在只有兩組介於 41 歲和 50 歲間的族群。這會扭曲測試結果。
>
> **凱伊拉・馬克士威〔上午 10:04〕：**
> 我們如果弄不起來就沒輒了。你可以確保測試儘快完成，並將測試結果直接寄給我嗎？我需要在下週末前拿到書面報告。
>
> **喬丹・摩斯〔上午 10:05〕：**
> 是啊，我的大致計畫是這樣。我可以保證讓你在下週五前收到報告。
>
> 送出

172. 對話者主要是在談什麼？
　　Ⓐ 人才招募活動
　　Ⓑ 行銷報告
　　Ⓒ 廣告活動
　　Ⓓ 產品測試

173. 帕克女士對馬克士威女士說了什麼？
　　Ⓐ 測試必須延期。
　　Ⓑ 她會在週五前寄出報告。
　　Ⓒ 他們得提前測試。
　　Ⓓ 她會進行 12 人的測試。

174. 上午 10:04 時，為什麼馬克士威女士寫道：「我們如果弄不起來就沒輒了。」？
　　Ⓐ 她不想自願參與測試。
　　Ⓑ 她了解測試要延期的原因。
　　Ⓒ 她可以幫忙召集更多受測者。
　　Ⓓ 她將自行研究。

175. 摩斯先生說他會做什麼？
　　Ⓐ 說服帕克女士重新安排測試時間
　　Ⓑ 在下週五前寄報告給馬克士威女士
　　Ⓒ 確認新肥皂系列的上市日期
　　Ⓓ 在報紙上刊廣告找更多人

176–180　電子郵件

> 收件人：菲利普・丹朱
> 　　　　<pdanjou@shellie.com>
> 寄件人：凱西・絲薇芙特
> 　　　　<cswift@shellie.com>
> 日期：8 月 23 日
> 主旨：雪莉系列產品
>
> 菲利普：
>
> 我想請你注意一下，亞洲和澳洲的幾個網站上針對雪莉系列風衣的負評。需要特別留意的是 www.uniquesales.com 和 www.ratedornot.au。看起來有很多針對商品材料品質的抱怨。雪莉是我們新的廣告活動打算力推的特色商品，所以有必要找出更多有關問題。你可以請你的部門了解這個狀況嗎？同時，可否請你的部門進一步研究，消費者對於雪莉系列有沒有其他疑慮？請把這視為首要任務，並在下週結束以前回報我你的發現。
>
> 感謝你的配合。
>
> 凱西

收件人：凱西‧絲薇芙特
　　　　<cswift@shellie.com>
寄件人：菲利普‧丹朱
　　　　<pdanjou@shellie.com>
日期：8 月 30 日
主旨：回覆：雪莉的產品

凱西：

我們調查了妳在 8 月 23 日郵件中提到的問題。我們確實發現，雪莉系列的材質品質引起全球的疑慮，特別是雪莉 XK1 多合一那一款。顧客抱怨材質太薄而且容易裂。我會要求妳的生產部門找到解決方法。

此外，我們發現顧客對雪莉 YL 胸罩組也有不滿，就是該產品顏色選擇不多，除了白色，其他在官網上都顯示缺貨。我週五前會再發封電子郵件解釋詳情。好消息是，關於尺寸選擇和價格的滿意度都很高。只要我們處理好顧客提出的意見，應該就沒問題了。

菲利普

176. 為什麼絲薇芙特女士寫信給丹朱先生？
  Ⓐ 宣傳兩個新網頁
  Ⓑ 抱怨產品品質
  Ⓒ 提出新的廣告行動
  Ⓓ 請他研究問題

177. 絲薇芙特女士在哪個領域工作？
  Ⓐ 製造
  Ⓑ 廣告
  Ⓒ 顧客關係
  Ⓓ 產品開發

178. 關於雪莉系列產品，文中沒有提及什麼？
  Ⓐ 主要在兩個網站上討論到它的產品。
  Ⓑ 總部在亞洲。
  Ⓒ 生產女性衣物。
  Ⓓ 有研究相關部門

179. 丹朱先生提及雪莉 XKI 什麼事？
  Ⓐ 材料品質低落。
  Ⓑ 可供選擇的顏色不如顧客期望。
  Ⓒ 價格對顧客來說太高。
  Ⓓ 商品不再時尚。

180. 在第二封電子郵件中，第一段、第三行的「restricted」，最接近下列哪個意思？
  Ⓐ 減少的
  Ⓑ 傑出的
  Ⓒ 限制的
  Ⓓ 機密的

181–185 文章和顧客意見

**科技上的卓越
安馬緹手機**

《新德里新聞》艾莉絲‧克萊爾撰文

4 月 2 日──安馬緹行動科技以品質聞名，即將在 4 月 10 日亮相的 New Boost 新手機也沒有例外。它擁有大容量可以同時存放近 3,000 張照片和 20 支半小時的影片，此外，附贈的外插式記憶卡也能儲存高達 5,000 首歌曲。

作為促銷，簽約購買 New Boost 將隨機附贈最先進的頭戴式耳機。經過安馬緹研究中心大量測試，音質遠遠超過原機標準配備的耳機。不只這樣，安馬緹也提供一個新的應用程式，讓用戶以比先前更快、更划算的價格下載音樂和電影。

New Boost 是一場全新的體驗。螢幕更亮，電池更耐久。New Boost 預計將取代先前的旗艦機種，展望光明的未來。

Amantiboost.com

回饋	產品	服務	購買

使用者回饋：安馬緹手機
使用者：朗吉特．汗，孟買
張貼時間：晚上 7:12，5 月 23 日
用戶評價：四顆星

我真的很喜歡 New Boost，一點都不後悔在上市那天開始排隊搶購。我特別喜歡隨機附贈的頭戴式耳機。我也非常推薦新的應用程式，每個月只要花 100 盧比，就可以下載音樂和電影。現在上面有的選擇還不多，我從公司得知他們將會從 5 月 30 日起加入更多內容。

我唯一想抱怨的是新螢幕。雖然是比以前亮也比較大，但反光很嚴重，看電影時是個問題。

181. 這篇文章的目的為何？
- Ⓐ 宣布公司的品牌名稱異動
- **Ⓑ 提前介紹新行動裝置**
- Ⓒ 解釋如何下載影音到記憶卡
- Ⓓ 介紹來自顧客的使用推薦

182. 關於 New Boost，文中沒有提到什麼？
- Ⓐ 更大的螢幕
- Ⓑ 配件
- Ⓒ 容量
- **Ⓓ 手機殼**

183. 汗先生最可能在何時購買 New Boost？
- Ⓐ 4 月 2 日
- **Ⓑ 4 月 10 日**
- Ⓒ 5 月 23 日
- Ⓓ 5 月 30 日

184. 文中提到關於手機應用程式什麼事？
- Ⓐ 是兩間手機公司的合作成果。
- **Ⓑ 慢慢增加清單上的選項。**
- Ⓒ 已經存在多年。
- Ⓓ 免費提供給 New Boost 的買家。

185. 汗先生不滿螢幕的什麼？
- **Ⓐ 太亮。**
- Ⓑ 容易毀損。
- Ⓒ 不能切換成水平模式。
- Ⓓ 無預警自動關機。

186–190 文章、評論和電子郵件

時裝秀

勘太時裝秀在當今時尚展現大量創新元素上，有舉足輕重的地位。從去年起，設計師非常重視天然材質。

「時裝店最新的設計款式，是潮流的一項指標。如果人們不想要這些設計，那它們就不會出現在這場時裝秀上。」時裝秀負責人格蘭傑女士說。

某些公司，像是艾西縫紉、拉瑞馬爾，藉著這場秀的機會，初次展露它們的作品集。另一家新公司「蜻蜓」展示了外套的全新概念，為它贏得夢寐以求的時裝秀最佳獎。這個獎項之前是由參展將近五年的麥可孔斯所拿下。

時尚秀在市中心的唐頓飯店舉行，有超過一萬人前來共襄盛舉。

蜻蜓時尚回顧

蘇茲．芮意絲撰文

雖然才營運 12 個月，「蜻蜓」生產了非常知名的設計，像是綠洲系列。和其他新創公司不同，這間公司獨到之處，在於不追隨產業的傳統設計。

我個人較喜歡洋裝系列，結合蕾絲、絲和麻——不是常見的選擇，但肯定引人注目。洋裝搭配免費的手套以及優雅銀的品牌手絹。

他們的新系列，秋夢，是唯一用到皮革的系列：到目前為止，這間公司只使用軟性材質。但是只要看一眼他們極好的夾克搭配皮帶、束帶和襯絲，就能注意到它的好品質。

收件人：蘇茲・芮意絲
　　　　<Suzyrees@fashiontoday.com>
寄件人：喬安・凱
　　　　<Joannekay@pantala.com>
日期：5 月 7 日
主旨：下次活動

親愛的芮意絲女士：

對於我們上個月在勘太時裝秀上的洋裝系列，您所寫的精采評論促使我寫這封信表達深切的感謝。那場秀是我們第二次參加這種活動，很高興得知我們的系列這麼快就受到時尚專家的關注。

我尤其想要感謝您給予秋夢系列以及洋裝系列如此熱情的評論。我想邀請您參加我們位於蜂鳥飯店的下一場秀，將安排在下個月 11 號舉辦。這將是由蜻蜓時尚所主辦的第一場時尚秀，以秋夢系列為主軸，同時呈現數個我們下一季要推出的新系列。

提前感謝您撥冗參加。

蜻蜓時尚
資深設計師
喬安・凱

186. 關於時尚設計採用天然材質，格蘭傑女士說了什麼？
　　Ⓐ 是時裝秀上的唯一服裝。
　　Ⓑ 很難設計出新的趨勢。
　　Ⓒ 價格正在下滑。
　　Ⓓ 引發高度關切。

187. 哪家公司去年參加了勘太時裝秀？
　　Ⓐ 艾西縫紉
　　Ⓑ 拉瑞馬爾
　　Ⓒ 蜻蜓
　　Ⓓ 麥可孔斯

188. 關於蜻蜓主辦的第一場時裝秀，文中提到？
　　Ⓐ 由格蘭傑女士籌辦。
　　Ⓑ 還沒決定舉辦的地點。
　　Ⓒ 將會在 6 月 11 日舉行。
　　Ⓓ 這是蜻蜓主辦的第二場時尚活動。

189. 哪一個系列在時裝秀上得獎？
　　Ⓐ 綠洲系列
　　Ⓑ 春系列
　　Ⓒ 秋夢系列
　　Ⓓ 優雅銀

190. 評論家暗示蜻蜓時尚什麼事？
　　Ⓐ 營運超過兩年。
　　Ⓑ 避免使用其他公司的構想。
　　Ⓒ 最近搬到新地點。
　　Ⓓ 只使用天然材質。

191–195 電子郵件和行程表

收件人：蔻羅依・佩姬
　　　　<chloepage@edmonds.com>
寄件人：凱文・古德溫
　　　　<kevingoodwin@edmonds.com>
日期：2 月 17 日
主旨：應徵者面試
附件：面試行程 .doc

蔻羅依：

可以請妳幫忙嗎？路克・鮑登是一位很有潛力的應徵者，週四會來面試戲劇學校的主管職。但是我在同一時間要和兩位中國客戶見面。我不可能重新安排會議。我可以和妳交換面試時間嗎？鮑登先生原訂的面試時間安排如附件。我希望妳可以接受更改後的時段。

鮑登先生的履歷讓人印象深刻，特別是他和奧斯卡劇院的作品。奧斯卡劇院被視為是國內頂級的戲劇教學學院，也是我們的主要勁敵。我希望他可以成為我們的重要資產。對於鮑登先生擔任藝術與音樂企業董事的出色表現，我們也接獲伊恩・希克斯的極力推薦。希克斯先生也會和我們一起午餐。

感謝，

埃德蒙茲娛樂
戲劇學校代理主任
凱文・古德溫

埃德蒙茲娛樂
應徵者面試行程

應徵者姓名：路克・鮑登
應徵職位：戲劇學院主任
面試日期：2 月 20 日

會議	時間	地點
面試：蔻羅依・佩姬	上午 11:00 到中午 12:00	A 棟，205 室
和伊恩・希克斯午餐	中午 12:20 到下午 1:20	B 棟，自助餐廳
面試：凱文・古德溫	下午 1:30 到下午 2:30	A 棟，303 室

提醒：抵達時，請向大門旁的停車服務員出示您的駕照，他才能確認必要資訊，以便將您的車輛停在指定區域。

收件人：凱文・古德溫
　　　　<kevingoodwin@edmonds.com>
寄件人：蔻羅依・佩姬
　　　　<chloepage@edmonds.com>
日期：2 月 17 日
主旨：重新安排面試時間

凱文：

不用擔心面試時間表。我週四下午有空。我在收到你來信的同時，也馬上通知了鮑登先生。他到了就會先在 303 室和你見面。我對他也抱有高度期待。他應該會是個很棒的同事。

我們會和希克斯與鮑登先生一起共進午餐，對嗎？既然如此，我想綠林餐廳比公司自助餐廳更好，畢竟這是我們首度和希克斯先生見面。餐廳就在公司大樓旁邊而已，所以你下午 1:30 的會議不會遲到。我會預訂四個人的位子。

祝你和中國客戶的會議順利。週四見。

埃德蒙茲娛樂
總經理
蔻羅依・佩姬

---

191. 文中提到鮑登先生什麼事？
A 他曾在埃德蒙茲娛樂的競爭者那裡工作。
B 他好幾年前曾在埃德蒙茲娛樂上班。
C 他因為演出技巧而被招募。
D 他過去曾參訪過埃德蒙茲娛樂。

192. 古德溫先生說他想在哪個時間面試鮑登先生？
A 上午 11:00
B 下午 12:20
C 下午 1:30
D 下午 2:30

193. 鮑登先生預期會做什麼事？
A 比原先被告知的時間更早離開
B 預約餐廳
C 和希克斯先生在大門見面
D 攜帶某個證件

194. 誰會在 303 室和鮑登先生見面？
A 佩姬女士
B 希克斯先生
C 古德溫先生
D 奧斯卡女士

195. 佩姬女士在 2 月 20 日下午 1 點，可能在做什麼？
A 在埃德蒙茲建築參訪
B 在附近的餐廳吃飯
C 在公司自助餐廳開會
D 面試鮑登先生

196–200 廣告、訂購單和電子郵件

孔雀辦公用品
《商業時報》票選為最佳辦公用品供應商！

為了慶祝五月的五週年慶，我們向全體尊貴的顧客提供一項特別服務。只要您提出需求，我們將在您購買的商品上刻印公司和個人資訊，包括文件夾、信封、盒子、白板或任一款原子筆。完全免費！

請在訂購單上您想要的商品欄位打勾註記。並且填上設計版型代碼，相關資訊可以在我們官網上查看。也別忘了更新您的顧客資訊，我們才可以正確刻印。

感謝您選擇孔雀辦公用品！

孔雀辦公用品

請將訂購商品寄到：＿＿＿＿＿＿＿＿＿

姓名：克里斯多福・迪克森

E-mail：chrisdixon@foxcox.com

公司：佛克斯＆考克斯股份有限公司

請指明您想要印哪些資訊在您的辦公用品上，以及您期望的版型。

	文件夾	筆	名片
公司名稱	V	V	V
公司地址			V
公司商標	V	V	V
公司官網	V		V
個人姓名	V		V
個人電話			V
個人電子信箱			V
設計版型代碼	AD7	GK3	HL4
數量	20	500	100

下訂單一週後，我們設計團隊的成員將透過電子郵件信箱和您聯絡。針對您選擇要放在辦公用品上的圖樣，他們會附上一份數位設計圖檔。請您同意或者告知我們任何想要修改的地方。除非確認圖樣正確無誤，訂單才會進一步作業。

請記得完整填寫表格，寄回時提供所有資訊，包括您個人和公司的詳細資料和公司商標。

收件人：布萊恩・吉布斯
　　　　<bryangibbs@peakcockssupplies.com>
寄件人：克里斯多福・迪克森
　　　　<chrisdixon@foxcox.com>
日期：5 月 6 日
回覆：佛克斯＆考克斯股份有限公司訂單

親愛的吉布斯先生，

我已經看過您上週提供的資訊，並決定換掉原子筆的設計版型代碼。我偏好用 BG33 取代原來的，並加入我們公司官網網址 www.foxcox.com。您修改後可以寄一份更新檔給我嗎？其他部分都很完美。

還有，我下個月將在伯恩的一場行銷會議上做簡報，我想要帶一些設計好的產品過去。其他代理商都將出席，所以我想讓他們留下印象。我知道您的公司販售很多可用來宣傳的客製化商品，像是 T 恤。請您用電子郵件寄給我最新版、上面有標價的商品手冊。此外，有可能讓我加購的訂單也併入目前這個訂單，用同一張發票，還是有需要另外下單呢？請您給我建議。

非常感謝。

佛克斯＆考克斯股份有限公司
行銷經理
克里斯多福・迪克森

196. 文中提到孔雀辦公用品什麼事？
　　Ⓐ 新分店將在五月開幕。
　　Ⓑ 下個月將舉辦一場行銷會議。
　　Ⓒ 它沒有設計團隊。
　　Ⓓ 被票選為最佳辦公產品的供應商。

197. 誰向孔雀辦公用品訂貨？
　　Ⓐ 一家行銷公司的經理
　　Ⓑ 一個設計團隊的商標設計師
　　Ⓒ 一家辦公用品製造商
　　Ⓓ 一名《商業時報》的編輯

198. 顧客要做什麼來確認訂單？
  Ⓐ **回覆電子郵件**
  Ⓑ 更新資訊
  Ⓒ 在訂購單上簽名
  Ⓓ 造訪官網

199. 迪克森先生在電子郵件中要求什麼？
  Ⓐ 前一次訂單的發票副本
  Ⓑ **孔雀辦公用品的商品手冊**
  Ⓒ 把訂購品運到伯恩
  Ⓓ 修改他的訂購數量

200. 文中提到迪克森先生什麼事？
  Ⓐ 他安排了線上會議。
  Ⓑ 他正在設計公司的新商標。
  Ⓒ 他做過很有創意的廣告。
  Ⓓ **他希望可以帶一些宣傳品去開會。**

ACTUAL TEST ⑨

PART 5 P. 254–256

◎ Part 5 解答請見 P.457

101. 費爾特曼先生過去一年在海外的**期間**，造訪了倫敦、阿姆斯特丹和布魯塞爾。

102. 盧森堡電子每週都會挑選幾個品牌的電器提供**折扣**販賣。

103. 塔科馬電腦的店內促銷**提供**顧客精選的折價筆電。

104. 戴夫林先生堅持，為了趕上截止日期，**每個人**都得加班。

105. 台北成為著名景點，是因為遊客可以愉快享用**美味**又不貴的食物。

106. 實驗設計公司發表一項**驚人**流行時尚宣言，用絲和皮革生產了一系列服飾。

107. 客戶支援團隊已確認您的訂單，**一旦**出貨時馬上通知您。

108. 生鮮農產品的存貨在明天早上**抵達**的時間，會比市場開市來得早。

109. 如果火災警報器在任何時間作響，請聯繫保全辦公室的佩瑞先生**協助**。

110. 經過**仔細**審查六件提案後，委員會最終選用了因特路建築事務所的設計，以打造他們在莫斯科的新辦公場所。

111. 為了讓伊能斯行銷能夠趕上競爭對手，所有部門必需**持續地**以最高生產標準執行工作。

112. 讀者仰賴《醫療週刊新訓》獲得最新醫療新聞的**可靠**資訊。

113. 雖然陳女士通過了初試，她還是未獲錄取，因為這份工作**給**了另一位工作經驗較多的人。

114. 等到歐馬爾．傑金斯取得會計證明，**他**才能獲得升遷。

115. 最近的**研究**發現，五款衣物柔軟精的效果一樣。

116. 考量大企業家西蒙．羅傑斯對組織的傑出貢獻，董事會決定向他**致敬**。

117. 如果您**對於**我們的產品或運輸服務有疑問，請儘管聯繫約翰植物世界。

118. 由於外國客戶提出抱怨，高登．史坦利保證他會**調查**這件事。

119. 聖地牙哥影印公司發布新聞稿，目的是要**鼓勵**顧客拿舊機器來維修。

120. 員工想要借用設備，必須取得主管的書面**授權**。

121. 「說話葉企業」**經常**提供顧客最新的有機糖漿產品資訊。

122. 下列是這間公司員工最常**遵循的**規定。

123. **只要**皮爾斯手機的製造分工廠完全準備好，瓦斯奎茲先生就會讓它開始運作。

124. 由於近期油價上漲，所有過剩商品都先將**暫緩**生產，除非等到進一步通知。

125. 談到買賣，鎮送工業確保其客戶都能在兩個工作天**內**收到商品。

126. 靠著大量**成長的**外國客戶，羅伊德銀行很快成為其中一大前景最為看好的金融集團。

127. 艾倫頂級咖啡豆包裝得**明亮**鮮豔，是完美的贈禮。

128. 這項鐵路網計畫特別有說服力**的點**在於它離機場很近。

129. 沒有作者的**允許**，哪裡都不准使用這篇文章任何一部份。

130. 飛行熊貓旅行社專門規劃蜜月旅行套裝行程，在四月到六月是**最忙的**時候。

131–134 通知

自然圖庫刊物的主要目標是推廣荒野環境的攝影，以出色的戶外風景和野生動物為主。本刊評論也討論拍攝這些影像所需的器材和手法。由業餘愛好者或自由攝影專家負責供稿給這本雙月刊。

九月拍攝的照片和文章目前還在評估。然而，因為每天的工作壓力和負荷，我們將不會個別回饋意見給個人所提供的素材。欲知詳情請上官網
www.imagenaturestocks.com。

131. Ⓐ 給……留下深刻印象
　　　Ⓑ 推廣
　　　Ⓒ 把……強加於
　　　Ⓓ 資助

(NEW)
132. Ⓐ 這可能是支持產業發展的好證據。
　　　Ⓑ 天文望遠鏡拍攝的照片揭露外太空的奧祕。
　　　Ⓒ 以出色的戶外風景和野生動物為主。
　　　Ⓓ 我們查看了眾多讀者在官網上對這些雜誌的評價。

133. Ⓐ 專業的
　　　Ⓑ 職業
　　　Ⓒ 內行地
　　　Ⓓ 專業人士

134. **Ⓐ 然而**
　　　Ⓑ 同樣地
　　　Ⓒ 舉例來說
　　　Ⓓ 因此

135–138 電子郵件

收件人：巴比・萊特
　　　　<wbobby@bigmail.com>
寄件人：國際礦工協會
　　　　<admin@associationofminers.com>
日期：8月2日
主旨：會員資訊

親愛的萊特先生：

國際礦工協會恭喜您加入本協會，我們支持全球礦業同行的安全健康，並為全球礦工的需求進行多項計畫和服務。

我們主要的任務是推廣更嚴格的礦業安全措施，讓礦場建設臻於完善。此外，我們也在官網上，向新進或經驗老道的礦業從業人員提供職業發展的資料，其中包括最新版的採礦法規。

隨信附件說明了會員的權益。希望能幫助您成為更好、更安全的採礦專業人士。

國際礦工協會 敬上

135. **Ⓐ 支持**
　　　Ⓑ 支持了
　　　Ⓒ 已支持
　　　Ⓓ 會支持

136. Ⓐ 頻繁的
　　　Ⓑ 主要的
　　　Ⓒ 早的
　　　Ⓓ 先前的

137. Ⓐ 然而
　　　Ⓑ 順道一提
　　　Ⓒ 此外
　　　Ⓓ 就我所知

(NEW)
138. Ⓐ 電子郵件附上入會申請書。
　　　Ⓑ 這是我們首次給予迦納當地礦工的特別機會。
　　　Ⓒ 我們希望您未來會加入我們組織了解最新狀況。
　　　Ⓓ 隨信附件說明了會員的權益。

139–142 文章

副董事長藍道夫・華德所揭露的遠大計畫「遍地開花」，預計五月在密蘇里州哥倫比亞市落成。計畫現階段已接近完工，包括一棟自有品牌的購物中心和複合休閒中心，雙雙坐落在歐森大道上。

華德先生舉行了命名大賽，要為佔地 1,000 平方公尺、坐擁曙光河美景的建築找到最合適的名稱。

被問到給予參賽者的相關建議，華德先生表示：「要記得這些場所外有河流環繞。命名要反映出這點才有勝算。」比賽結果將在下個月底公布。優勝者將獲得該中心一年份的會員資格。

139. **A 兩者**
　　 B 很少
　　 C 數個
　　 D 有些

140. A 偏好
　　 B 外部
　　 C 外表
　　 D 景色

141. A 反映出
　　 B 反映過
　　 C 正在反映
　　 D 應該反映

142. A 華德先生還在找地點蓋這棟建築。
　　 B 優勝者將獲得該中心一年份的會員資格。
　　 C 新購物中心舉行抽籤活動，結果讓人大感意外。
　　 D 名稱將會在破土儀式上公布。

143–146 電子郵件

收件人：雷吉納德・里德
　　　　 <reginaldreed@umail.com>
寄件人：安納羅伊德影視出租店
　　　　 <manager@arentals.com>
日期：8 月 13 日，週三
主旨：過期 DVD

我們的租借紀錄顯示下列商品：《暗夜風雨》和《孤立島》，應該要在 8 月 5 日歸還。請在這週結束前把它們歸還商店。

請記得您可以透過電話向店家續借 DVD 七天。然而，下列 DVD 並不適用續借規則：新 DVD、逾期 DVD 和其他顧客已預訂的影片。

雖然我們會寄送提醒通知，但請留意準時歸還或續借商品是顧客的責任。

謝謝您。

143. A 它
　　 B 我們的
　　 C 這個
　　 D 它們

144. A 您不應出租、轉授權、租借或轉售這片 DVD。
　　 B 如果是這樣的話，只要是新進光碟，我們都可以續借。
　　 C 請記得您可以透過電話向店家續借 DVD 七天。
　　 D 歸還逾期品是我們的責任。

145. **A 適用的**
　　 B 被展示的
　　 C 完成的
　　 D 有能力的

146. A 除了
　　 B 雖然
　　 C 同樣地
　　 D 以防萬一**

147–148 資訊

夢想療癒健身中心
制服

夢想療癒健身中心將核發三件制服給新進私人教練，為訓練客戶時必穿的服飾。兩件是室內制服，第三件則適合戶外訓練使用。在兩個月的法定試用期期間，這些制服是免費提供給員工的。然而員工如果在這段期間離職，必須支付制服費用。根據我們的僱用條款和規則，金額將從最終薪資單自動扣除。制服必須隨時保持乾淨；請記得私人教練可以自由使用我們地下室的洗衣間。

147. 這項資訊最可能在哪裡看到？
- A 旅遊小冊子裡
- B 索賠單上
- **C 員工手冊上**
- D 服飾店內

148. 文中提到夢想療癒健身中心什麼事？
- A 只提供室內訓練。
- **B 有自己的洗衣間。**
- C 自己生產制服。
- D 今年關閉了兩個月。

149–150 通知

第七屆二手家具市集
暨年度二手商品拍賣

上百件特色桃花木古董傢俱，包括桌椅、床和更多選擇。

週六，11 月 22 日
布里斯本，魯賓街 32 號

入場：上午 11 點到晚上 7 點
接待會：下午 5 點到晚上 7 點
拍賣從晚上 7:30 開始

票價：11 月 17 日前預購 5 元；
現場購票 7 元

預購票請上官網查詢 www.uff.com
或者電話聯絡我們 (643) 367-3475。

票價已包括拍賣會型錄。
活動收益將全數資助綠坡社區醫院。

149. 這則通知的目的為何？
- A 宣傳一位工藝名匠的到訪
- **B 為獨特家具的拍賣打廣告**
- C 公布一家家具店的開幕時間
- D 宣傳一間社區醫院

150. 文中提到這個活動什麼事？
- A 參加接待會要額外付費。
- B 學生享有特別折扣。
- C 古董家具將在晚上七點開始展示。
- **D 網路購票比較便宜。**

151–152 收據

麥可家

加拿大溫哥華市西百老匯街 665 號

2 月 12 日	下午 4:31
運動穿著	
立馬運動：運動用慢跑褲	19.99
一般商品	
品牌興趣：拳擊手套和護墊	16.99
小計	36.98
稅 8%	2.96
總計	**39.94**
收現	50.00
找零	10.06

退換貨政策
未穿過的商品可以在 30 天內退款，或換成有效的現金券。商品必須幾近全新狀態，並附上購買時的收據。特價商品均不得退款，但可以保留原收據兌換其他等值商品。

151. 麥可家最可能是什麼商店？
- Ⓐ 紀念品店
- **Ⓑ 運動用品店**
- Ⓒ 樂器行
- Ⓓ 出租店

152. 關於店家政策，何者為真？
- **Ⓐ 換貨都需要原收據。**
- Ⓑ 所有退貨商品酌收 8% 的入庫處理費。
- Ⓒ 只接受現金交易。
- Ⓓ 所有特價商品都得在原包裝內。

153–154 訊息串

> **諾拉・特納〔下午 3:43〕：**
> 傑登，我可以和你談一下廣告收益嗎？我個人只能達成這個月目標的 20%。
>
> **傑登・瓦茲〔下午 3:44〕：**
> 我也沒能達到額度。自從韓德爾出版最近發行了類似雜誌，很多公司都跑去那裡登廣告了。
>
> **諾拉・特納〔下午 3:44〕：**
> 我們該怎麼辦？我們需要減少廣告頁以節省成本嗎？
>
> **傑登・瓦茲〔下午 3:44〕：**
> 不行，減少頁數的損失太大。
>
> **諾拉・特納〔下午 3:45〕：**
> 那何不降低廣告價格，來吸引我們的現有客戶呢？
>
> **傑登・瓦茲〔下午 3:46〕：**
> 值得試試。如果我們再不採取行動，下個月會損失更多收益。
>
> 送出

153. 他們討論到什麼問題？
- Ⓐ 產品開發的進度落後。
- **Ⓑ 廣告收益下滑。**
- Ⓒ 雜誌發行量下滑。
- Ⓓ 員工一直增加。

154. 下午 3:46 時，瓦茲先生寫道：「值得試試。」，他的意思是？
- Ⓐ 公司不會嘗試任何改變。
- Ⓑ 他必須減少頁數來降低成本。
- **Ⓒ 他們可以提供折扣給目前的廣告主。**
- Ⓓ 他希望特納女士下個月更努力

155–157 資訊

拉曼查小菜

店長桑切斯・彼耶羅
海倫・拉波爾評論

整體評價：三顆星（滿分五顆星）
★★★☆☆

氣氛：三顆星

桑切斯・彼耶羅上個月才整修場地。空間大，西班牙主題風格突出。不過廚房的聲音太吵，情侶用餐的隱私也不夠。

服務：四顆星

服務非常好。服務生有禮貌效率高，出餐很快，我們剛吃很快就清空桌面。

食物：兩顆星

菜單選擇不是非常多，和我三年前來的時候相比沒什麼變化。分量太少，開胃菜味道不太好。我覺得主餐不錯，但魚煮得有點太老。甜點非常令人失望，不但選擇少還沒味道。

價位：四顆星

菜單上有些菜色定價太高，不過餐點整體來說都相對便宜。酒水也很貴，不過主餐真的很划算。

155. 這篇資訊的目的為何？
- Ⓐ 公告一家餐廳重新開張
- Ⓑ 總結一間餐廳的擴建計畫
- Ⓒ 推薦一家餐廳即將推出的特別菜單
- **Ⓓ 評估一家餐廳的品質**

156. 文中提到這間餐廳什麼事？
- **Ⓐ 整體菜色值得這個錢。**
- Ⓑ 舉辦現場音樂活動。
- Ⓒ 菜單在過去幾年有明顯變化。
- Ⓓ 位於市中心。

(NEW) 157. 下列句子最適合出現在 [1]、[2]、[3]、[4] 的哪個位置中？

「分量太少，開胃菜味道不太好。」

A [1]

B [2]

C [3]

D [4]

158–160 信件

全真電子設備
94203 加州沙加緬度市大樹街 355 號
3 月 16 日

亞歷山大‧索斯金
93109 加州聖塔芭芭拉市天使地 2541 號

親愛的索斯金先生：

隨包裹附上您送修的收音機。很遺憾，我們沒有辦法修理它，因為這項機械故障並不含在兩年保固的範圍內。

我們確認原來的音箱已經換成和我們品牌收音機不相容的零件。請參閱附件中維修人員的說明報告。也附上保固書，其中載明如果需要更換或改裝內部零件，必須由我方維修團隊執行，並使用我方核准的零件。未經授權的拆裝將不提供保固，因此根據保固條款，我們無法修理這項產品。但如果您仍想維修，我們會酌收 100 美元維修費。

非常感謝您的合作，也謝謝您在全真電子購買產品。

客服經理
凱文‧康斯坦特 敬上
附件

158. 這封信的目的為何？

A 解釋為什麼沒有辦法達成要求

B 感謝顧客近期的購買

C 請求維修人員回電

D 詢問某個電子產品的資訊

159. 這封信中沒有包括什麼？

A 保固書

B 報告書

C 退款

D 收音機

160. 索斯金先生被建議怎麼做？

A 自行維修商品

B 付費修理

C 付費展延保固期

D 打電話給全真電子的客服經理

161–163 訊息串

艾莉森‧格林〔上午 9:43〕：
早安，提摩西。我聽說你下週一會接待我們來自西班牙的訪客。

提摩西‧摩爾〔上午 9:43〕：
哈囉，愛莉森。這讓我很頭痛。

艾莉森‧格林〔上午 9:44〕：
怎麼了？你西班牙文說得很好。

提摩西‧摩爾〔上午 9:45〕：
事實上，我得準備週二的銷售簡報。我沒有時間準備週一的接待。

艾莉森‧格林〔上午 9:46〕：
這真的很難。有什麼我可以幫你的嗎？

提摩西‧摩爾〔上午 9:47〕：
嗯……我需要找到廠商提供午餐和茶點。妳有什麼建議嗎？

艾莉森‧格林〔上午 9:48〕：
我推薦多食餐飲。他們評價蠻好的，午餐自助吧也很棒。需要我負責處理餐點嗎？

提摩西‧摩爾〔上午 9:49〕：
那就太好了。謝了，艾莉森。我欠妳一次。

艾莉森‧格林〔上午 9:50〕：
不客氣。我馬上打電話問看看他們方不方便。

送出

161. 摩爾先生週二要做什麼？

    Ⓐ 去餐廳看看

    Ⓑ 準備出差

    Ⓒ 做簡報

    Ⓓ 面試

162. 上午 9:44 時，格林女士寫道：「你西班牙文說得很好。」，她的意思是？

    Ⓐ 她相信摩爾先生可以完美勝任這個任務。

    Ⓑ 她想向摩爾先生提出建議。

    Ⓒ 她認為訪客會喜歡西班牙菜。

    Ⓓ 她想幫忙摩爾先生準備週二的簡報。

163. 格林女士主動提供什麼幫助？

    Ⓐ 提供自助餐點

    Ⓑ 聯絡某項服務

    Ⓒ 推薦一家餐廳

    Ⓓ 買新電話

164–167 告示

> **商務圖書證**
>
> 法律協會的圖書館系統允許商會會員使用它的設施。
>
> 當地企業的員工可以申請商務圖書證。年費 40 元，但若為慈善機構或非營利組織則免年費。
>
> 商務圖書證可以讓當地企業基於研究目的使用，企業員工有責任保管借出的書籍或文獻。如有逾期未還或資料遺失，持卡人將面臨罰款。
>
> 如欲申請商務圖書證，您必須在圖書館接待處填妥申請表格。申請需檢附有照片的身分證件、公司就職證明和會費。我們將會提供收據給您。
>
> 如果您有任何疑問，請聯絡法律協會主辦公室 555-9284。

164. 這則告示的目的為何？

    Ⓐ 解釋一項服務

    Ⓑ 提出點子

    Ⓒ 修正錯誤

    Ⓓ 公告開張

165. 文中提到年費什麼事？

    Ⓐ 特定組織得免繳。

    Ⓑ 可以用信用卡付款。

    Ⓒ 外地的企業會比較貴。

    Ⓓ 一年後會退款。

166. 根據告示，如果資料不見，借閱者必須做什麼？

    Ⓐ 取消會員資格

    Ⓑ 向主管回報損失

    Ⓒ 交還商務圖書證

    Ⓓ 向圖書館繳交罰款

167. 申請時不需要什麼東西？

    Ⓐ 身分證明

    Ⓑ 付款

    Ⓒ 確認員工身分

    Ⓓ 簽訂合約

168–171 文章

> **管理者行為**
>
> 曼紐爾・羅德里格斯在他的新書《職場禮儀》內建議管理者舉止合宜，才能贏得員工的尊重。羅德里格斯先生解釋，擔任重責的管理者，其所作所為應該要與他們的地位相稱，不單單只限於辦公環境，也要考量社交情況，尤其是所屬公司安排的場合。
>
> 舉例來說，管理者應該出席社交場合，像是一場邀請了其他資深員工的頒獎典禮。這是管理者職責的一部分。不過，像是大多數由年輕員工參加的運動比賽，則可以避免。然而，管理者拒絕這種邀請時務必婉轉。

另外，外表美觀至關重要。管理者外表要整齊乾淨。準時是義務。管理者參加公司安排的活動，必須認得不常見的同仁，也要禮貌性知道他們的姓名。此外，管理者必須稱讚安排活動的人，讓他們知道他們的努力付出促使活動成功，參加者都很愉快。

羅德里格斯先生在網路上書寫多年，被視為談論職場禮儀的一位重要權威人士。他經常上電視分享，而且他由米契爾‧哈姆登出版公司出版的新書《職場禮儀》，出版六個月以來已暢銷超過 20 萬本。可以在 www.mitchellhamden.com 線上訂購。

168. 這篇文章主要是討論什麼？
🅰 **一本關於管理者舉止合宜的書**
🅑 一本解決不當職場問題的指引
🅒 安排社交活動的傳單
🅓 維持員工職業水準的小冊子

169. 文中提到羅德里格斯先生什麼事？
🅐 他在同一間公司工作多年。
🅑 **他是個非常成功的作家。**
🅒 他將在六個月內寫完書。
🅓 他安排公司的社交活動。

170. 米契爾‧哈姆登專職什麼事業？
🅐 活動企畫
🅑 線上設計
🅒 就業福利
🅓 **書籍出版**

171. 下列句子最適合出現在 [1]、[2]、[3]、[4] 的哪個位置中？
「另外，外表美觀至關重要。」
🅐 [1]
🅑 **[2]**
🅒 [3]
🅓 [4]

172–175 備忘錄

高登工業

收件人：全體員工
寄件人：葛瑞斯‧埃利奧特
日期：6 月 11 日
回覆：假期行程

各位做得好！協助高登公司成功簽下公司九年來，史上最大筆的合約。為感謝您的辛勞，我們將在七月舉辦家庭週。於暑假舉辦為期一週的各式活動，免費邀請您的家人蒞臨參加。希望未來幾年也能為高登工業帶來更多成功，以一週的活動表達我們的感謝。逐日行程如下。

日期	活動	地點	時間
7 月 25 日，週一	水上遊戲	魔術噴泉水上樂園	上午 11 點到下午 6 點
7 月 26 日，週二	家族野餐	溫泉公園露營區	全天
7 月 27 日，週三	戶外活動	溫泉公園（詳細地點請見部門布告欄）	全天
7 月 28 日，週四	運動場日（籃球、壘球、足球）	公園休閒中心	下午 1 點到 5 點
7 月 29 日，週五	舞會和兒童娛樂	溫泉公園露營區	下午 3 點到 6 點

我的私人秘書亞曼達‧科爾已經預約好兒童娛樂活動和活動餐點。指定人數額滿前，請儘快撥分機 256 和她聯絡。運動比賽之後會舉辦烤肉大會。如欲參賽請向負責運動項目的傑瑞德‧墨菲報名。獲勝隊伍將有獎賞。

我希望您們也都引頸期盼家庭週，這將是在家人和同事的陪伴下，好好放鬆享受的機會。我希望可以在那裡見到各位。

高登工業
總裁
葛瑞斯‧埃利奧特

172. 為什麼會寫這則備忘錄？
- Ⓐ 通知員工管理方式有異動
- **Ⓑ 介紹以家庭為主的一週活動**
- Ⓒ 公告簽下一筆大合約
- Ⓓ 為體育活動招募隊伍

173. 員工要用什麼方式聯絡科爾女士？
- **Ⓐ 打電話**
- Ⓑ 線上登記
- Ⓒ 到辦公室找她
- Ⓓ 寄電子郵件

174. 烤肉大會在什麼時候？
- Ⓐ 週一
- Ⓑ 週二
- Ⓒ 週三
- **Ⓓ 週四**

175. 文中提到埃利奧特女士什麼事？
- Ⓐ 她是高登工業創辦人。
- Ⓑ 她沒辦法參加家庭週活動。
- Ⓒ 她有個九歲兒子。
- **Ⓓ 她想要藉特別活動獎勵員工。**

176–180 文章

> **《最高經濟新聞》**
> **多家頂尖博奕公司擴編人事**
>
> 1 月 7 日──線上賭場集團昨天發布的報告中發現，布倫亨區多家主要博奕公司在過去六個月，員工數大幅成長。與去年 7 月到 12 月同期相比，該區的前五大公司多聘了 15% 的員工。
>
> 博奕產業的市場龍頭「離岸發展公司」，是這波聘僱潮的領先者。布倫亨區的賭場去年下半年間，僱用了超過 150 名員工。大多數員工挖角自布雷克軟體公司。該公司在去年六月為離岸發展併購，是一家專門研發財務軟體的小型公司。業界另兩家公司「幸運薊」和「皇冠廳」（均專營線上撲克）也決定聯手。

> 線上賭場集團發布的排名，只考慮布倫亨區賭場事業的營收。前五大公司年營收都超過 120 萬美元。幸運薊總營收大約 120 萬美元，離岸發展的淨收入為 130 萬美元。
>
> 馬歇爾．保魯斯

> **離岸發展將投資最新科技**
>
> 3 月 30 日──據報導，「離岸發展」主席大衛．卡魯瑟斯正在投資新軟體：「增值」，是一款今年初才測試過的企業財務線上軟體。
>
> 「離岸發展」過去只針對博奕市場的個人消費者，這是它首度進軍企業市場。「離岸發展」事業策略經理馬克．歐文說：「我們得僱用幾位財務軟體的專家，如此一來，我們才能發展科技，鼓勵企業投入博奕市場。」
>
> 該公司多年來名列線上賭場集團評比的五大領先企業，年平均淨利潤為 130 萬美元。今年的營業額從一月開始成長，獲益高達 70 萬，預估在 12 月前會再增加 450 萬美元。
>
> G．哈克

176. 第一篇文章主旨為何？
- Ⓐ 市場上出現新的博奕商品
- Ⓑ 博奕公司的行銷方式
- **Ⓒ 大型博奕公司的員工數成長**
- Ⓓ 博奕產業的員工滿意度

177. 在第一篇文章中，第一段、第五行的「period」最接近下列哪個意思？
- Ⓐ 成長
- **Ⓑ 間隔**
- Ⓒ 結論
- Ⓓ 運動

178. 文中提到「離岸發展」什麼事？
- Ⓐ 是間以網路為基礎的公司。
- Ⓑ 販賣賭場用品。
- Ⓒ 有一些國際辦事處。
- **Ⓓ 它接管一間軟體公司。**

179. 文中提到關於「增值」什麼事？

    Ⓐ 是卡魯瑟斯先生設計的第一個產品。

    Ⓑ 銷售額幾乎已達兩百萬美元。

    Ⓒ 設計給企業市場使用。

    Ⓓ 顧客批評不好用。

180. 離岸發展一月到十二月的營收預估為多少？

    Ⓐ 130 萬

    Ⓑ 450 萬

    Ⓒ 520 萬

    Ⓓ 650 萬

181–185 電子郵件和資訊

收件人：迪特·凡·休根
　　　　<dvh@pph.com>
寄件人：艾薇兒·拉巴斯
　　　　<avrilla@pph.com>
日期：5 月 12 日
主旨：展覽
附件：礦瀑布會議中心下載

親愛的迪特：

非常感謝您協助 PPH 有限公司準備即將到來的技術展。本年度的活動日期為 6 月 21 日到 24 日，地點和去年一樣，都辦在礦瀑布會議中心。過去幾次參展我都租用本頓廳來展示新產品和舉辦研論會。我們四天內就吸引了近千人，平均一天 250 人。我期待今年的展覽會比去年更盛大。

為提前做好準備，我想請您租一個更大的空間。雖然本頓廳可以容納所有與會者，但還要放展示設備的話，空間就不太足夠了。我們只能靠中心提供的器材，請中心員工協助架設。儘管大多數評價都很好，還是有些與會者對影像素材的畫質不滿意。今年一定要改正這個問題。

之前我們會在一週行程的尾聲，在馬尼拉套房接待受邀賓客。這次，我們想要帶他們到更高檔的地方。我建議布朗餐廳或是碼頭小館，也不用我們準備餐點。我會把必要的事安排好，再寄給您細節，還請您多加留意。

請看過隨信附上的小冊，選出最適合我們需求的房間。再兩週就要開展了，你需要僅快訂房並支付訂金。

如果還有疑問或遭遇到任何困難，請跟我聯絡。

艾薇兒·拉巴斯

礦瀑布
會議中心
房間租用

馬尼拉套房： 我們所提供最大的房間，三面採光，最多可以容納 400 名賓客，適合舉辦任何慶祝酒會或商貿活動。餐飲由礦瀑布的外燴部門提供。早上或下午的租金為美金 300 元起，全天租用則為 500 元。餐飲需另外付費。

富貴房和日照房： 適合小型私人會議或研討會，可容納 50 人。房間內有電話、可上網的電腦、高架投影機和深色布幕等商務設備。富貴房的租金為半天美金 200 元、全天 300 元。日照房空間稍微大一些，備有音響設備。租金為半天美金 220 元、全天 320 元。

衛哨套房： 舉辦大型演講、活動和研討會的理想場地。房間配備有落地投影螢幕、舞台、燈光和環繞立體音響系統。舒適豪華的房間可以容納高達 350 名賓客。租金從半天美金 500 元、全天 700 元起。餐飲須另外付費。

天極露台：鄰近衛哨套房，適合舉辦歡迎會，或擺設會議餐點的戶外場地。租金為每 3 小時 310 美元，如果租用衛哨套房則可以免費使用天極露台。餐飲需另外計費。

181. 拉巴斯女士在去年的展覽中，最可能扮演的角色是？

Ⓐ **由她安排 PPH 有限公司的活動。**
Ⓑ 由她決定餐點。
Ⓒ 由她架設裝備。
Ⓓ 由她發表簡報。

182. 今年的展預期會和去年的有何不同？

Ⓐ 將由名人開場。
Ⓑ **將吸引更多賓客。**
Ⓒ 將在備用場館舉辦。
Ⓓ 會有額外的展出者加入。

183. 去年的展覽可能遇到了什麼問題？

Ⓐ **有些人看不清楚投影螢幕。**
Ⓑ 展覽前更改地點。
Ⓒ 訂到的房間太吵。
Ⓓ 報告人沒有及時到達。

184. PPH 有限公司去年的歡迎會上，餐點由誰提供？

Ⓐ **礦瀑布外燴部門**
Ⓑ 天極露台
Ⓒ 碼頭小館
Ⓓ 布朗餐廳

185. PPH 有限公司今年可能會預約哪個房間？

Ⓐ 日照房
Ⓑ 馬尼拉套房
Ⓒ 富貴房
Ⓓ **衛哨套房**

186–190 職缺、電子郵件和信件

梅爾頓製造商的倫敦分部正在徵求有經驗的經理加入製造團隊！

梅爾頓製造商半世紀以來，一直是英國高品質汽車零件製造和批發的領導者。我們供應數百個汽車和貨車零件，給本地和海外的汽車公司。

生產製造經理有責任訓練和監督，由 50 名全職員工、臨時工和季節工所組成的製造團隊。經理也要管理工廠環境，確保全體員工的健康和安全。我們正在找的人要有至少四年的相關經驗，且其中一年同樣要在製造業。我們也期待獲選的應徵者，可以加班監督出貨和運送。

應徵者需熟悉材料的製造和批發，也要有處理規定相關的知識，並具備電腦技能 SPA 43。有意的應徵者請將申請書附上求職信與推薦信，寄給湯尼·比奇，地址是 WR11 4BD 倫敦市萊韋爾新月街 13 號梅爾頓製造商。

收件人：湯尼·比奇
　　　　<tonybeach@melton.com>
寄件人：亞當·斯騰
　　　　<adamstern@gomail.com>
日期：9 月 8 日
主旨：推薦信
附件：亞當 _ 斯騰 _ 推薦 .doc

親愛的比奇先生：

收到您的來信讓我很驚訝。我以為我有把推薦信附在履歷上；看來我是忘了。我隨信附上布希爾先生的信。我很高興聽到我的履歷讓人印象深刻。關於您詢問的 SPA 43，我五年前已經取得資格，我之前在下班後的晚間課程研習該軟體，現在也負責員工的電腦訓練。

請讓我知道和您面試的時間。倫敦離我有段距離，我必須找到地方留宿。再次感謝您考慮錄用我。

亞當·斯騰 敬上

8 月 27 日
比奇先生
WR11 4BD 倫敦市萊韋爾新月街 13 號梅爾頓製造商

親愛的比奇先生：

這是一封推薦信，向您推薦亞當‧斯騰，他正在申請貴公司的生產製造經理一職。斯騰先生在打包快遞曾有七年工作經驗，他從臨時工開始做起，直到我讓他轉正職，我們共事了五年。斯騰先生是一名非常稱職的員工，目前在這裡擔任生產製造監督。他曾引進新的生產線設備器材，並讓它順利運作，加快了生產流程也減少浪費。

斯騰先生十分適任貴公司所招聘的職缺，此外，他也有豐富的工作經驗。他最近在王十字學院完成管理學 HNQ 課程，也進修過多項在職訓練課程。

我對斯騰先生有信心，他可以勝任這個職位，因為他能妥善應對任何工作需求。欲知更多資訊，歡迎您聯絡。

生產製造主任
特雷‧布希爾 敬上

186. 文中提到梅爾頓製造商什麼事？
- Ⓐ 批發安全設備。
- Ⓑ 提供電腦訓練課程。
- Ⓒ 最近擴展業務到英國。
- **Ⓓ 專門製造汽車零件。**

187. 根據職缺公告，生產製造經理要願意做什麼？
- Ⓐ 操作重機械
- Ⓑ 招募團隊成員
- **Ⓒ 超時工作**
- Ⓓ 簽一年的合約

188. 為什麼布希爾先生要寫那封信？
- Ⓐ 解釋為什麼延後出貨
- Ⓑ 歡迎新成員加入團隊。
- Ⓒ 應徵新工作。
- **Ⓓ 推薦一名員工。**

189. 文中提到斯騰先生什麼事？
- Ⓐ 他有海外銷售的經驗。
- Ⓑ 他在王十字學院教書。
- **Ⓒ 他擅長使用某個電腦程式。**
- Ⓓ 他想找梅爾頓製造商的兼職工作。

190. 斯騰先生要求比奇先生做什麼？
- Ⓐ 在他方便時儘快前來拜訪
- Ⓑ 為他寫封推薦信
- **Ⓒ 通知他日期**
- Ⓓ 寄給他申請表

191–195 電子郵件和表格

收件人：<service@kramindustries.org>
寄件人：傑拉德‧格拉夫
　　　　<gg@deutschei21.org>
日期：1 月 5 日
主旨：客戶投訴

親愛的先生／女士：

我想要反應新衣櫃（型號 #92）的問題。我嚴格遵循安裝說明，但是衣櫃還是歪一邊，因為有一塊隔板送錯了，它短了一吋。我希望您可以替換這塊隔板，好讓我可以重新把這個家具裝好。

很抱歉我太晚聯絡。我在 11 月 2 日買了衣櫃，但因為被醫院外派海外超過兩個月，期間我沒能組裝它。如果有需要的話，我保有商品運送時的包裝，也可以寄回店家收據。

傑拉德‧格拉夫 敬上

收件人：傑拉德・格拉夫
　　　　<gg@deutschei21.org>
寄件人：約瑟夫・彼特斯
　　　　<peiters@kramindustries.org>
主旨：回覆：客戶投訴

親愛的格拉夫先生：

感謝您的來信說明您購買的商品。針對您安裝商品時遇到困難，我們向您致歉，並且將免費寄給您替換的零件。根據我們所實施的店面營業規定，商品在購買兩個月內，可以持收據和原包裝退貨。如購買已超過兩個月，根據公司規定，要能證明商品是在購買時已有毀損方能退貨。且有必要填寫缺失回報單。該表單可以在我們官網的客戶投訴頁面找到：www.kramindustries.org/returns。填完表單並送出之後，會寄給您一份商品退換碼。如需了解規定全文，還請上官網查看。

我希望這對您有幫助。我們想請您填寫一份隨信附上的客戶回饋單，以了解您對客服部門的經驗感受。填完後，您將收到一張 15% 的折扣券，可供下次在我們的店裡購買時使用。

經理
約瑟夫・彼特斯

客戶回饋

姓名：傑拉德・格拉夫

整體評價：四顆星（好）

意見：我用電子郵件回報了衣櫃的問題，隔天就收到答覆。我按照信中告知的缺失回報流程，並在之後收到了替換零件。感謝您的協助，我才可以順利安裝。不過，手冊上的說明圖示不是非常精確，讓我在找出隔板問題時感到不便。我希望可以儘快改正。除了這點，整體服務讓我很滿意。

191. 格拉夫先生回報了產品的什麼問題？
　A 一個零件有缺陷。
　B 說明手冊不見了。
　C 對他的寢室而言尺寸有誤
　D 顏色錯了。

192. 格拉夫先生最有可能的工作是？
　A 教木工
　B 在醫院工作
　C 準備餐點
　D 製作家具

193. 格拉夫先生從家具店得到什麼好處？
　A 折價券
　B 謝禮
　C 一件新家具
　D 免運費

194. 在回饋表中，第五行的「recognizing」，最接近下列哪個意思？
　A 看
　B 發現
　C 知會
　D 報告

195. 根據格拉夫先生的說法，什麼需要改正？
　A 組裝說明
　B 商品退換碼
　C 官網網址
　D 包裝

196–200 廣告和電子郵件

傑森瀑布

位於墨爾本市中心
公司、住宅以及商業區空間出租

走在時代尖端的建築結構，周遭有多間商店和公司行號。

靠近車站。

緊鄰戰爭紀念碑，一旁還有都會公園和體育場

住宅（2 到 7 樓）：兩房或三房公寓，均有兩間衛浴、一間附衛浴套房、廚房餐廳和客廳。可以使用地下室停車場，需另外繳交停車費。屋頂花園和曬衣場共用。

辦公室（8 到 14 樓）：大小辦公室都有。方塊格局的開放空間可供隔間。辦公家具可供選擇。

商業區（地面樓）： 四間店面。只供租賃使用，每間樓地板面積 500 平方公尺。謝絕餐廳。

租金細節和出租狀況：

如有住宅承租需求請詢洽蓋瑞‧梅森 (08) 3014-7610 或電郵 residential@jasonfalls.com.au.

如有商辦需求請詢問費諾拉‧卡斯蒂爾 (08) 3014-7620 或電郵 commercial@jasonfalls.com.au.

收件人：費諾拉‧卡斯蒂爾
　　　　<commercial@jasonfalls.com.au>
寄件人：湯馬斯‧克里斯丁
　　　　<tchristian@christianbrooks.com>
主旨：傑森瀑布
日期：10:01，9 月 2 日

親愛的卡斯蒂爾女士：

我最近將事業擴大營業，我們會聘請新員工分擔未來的工作。我們目前位於「傑森瀑布」附近，但已經沒有空間容納新員工。我想知道在「傑森瀑布」裡有沒有辦公室空間，可以容納行政部和業務部的 17 名同仁。我需要親自看看辦公室，會在下週找個時間過去。

非常感謝，

湯馬斯‧克里斯丁

收件人：埃利亞斯‧因尼斯
　　　　<e_innes@terralink.org>
寄件人：費諾拉‧卡斯蒂爾
　　　　<commercial@jasonfalls.com.au>
主旨：緊急整修作業
日期：11:30，9 月 2 日

親愛的因尼斯先生：

我的同事蓋瑞‧梅森轉介您給我。我打算要拆除辦公室裡的三面牆，想要跟您詢價。牆壁均為兩公尺高，其中一面 20 公分厚。另外兩面牆則只有 15 公分厚。這幾面牆不是一開始就有的，而是依照上一個承租戶的要求加裝的。

辦公室位於 12 樓，大樓內有電梯。我需要一個可以儘快動工的團隊。有客戶想要這間辦公室，我得拆了這些牆才能容納他所有的員工。我希望整修作業可以在週日前完成。

希望很快能收到您的回信。

祝好，

費諾拉‧卡斯蒂爾

---

196. 文中提到傑森瀑布大樓什麼事？
　　Ⓐ 位於車站附近。
　　Ⓑ 距離戰爭紀念碑很遠。
　　Ⓒ 在城郊。
　　Ⓓ 正在興建中。

197. 根據廣告，住宅區的租戶額外付費的話，可以使用什麼？
　　Ⓐ 打掃用具
　　Ⓑ 地下停車場
　　Ⓒ 額外的寢室
　　Ⓓ 屋頂花園

198. 這棟大樓不允許哪種承租戶使用？
　　Ⓐ 法律事務所
　　Ⓑ 業務辦公室
　　Ⓒ 零售商店
　　Ⓓ 餐廳

199. 關於克里斯丁先生的公司，
文中提到什麼？
    Ⓐ 正要搬出墨爾本。
    Ⓑ 最近失去一些員工。
    ⒸＣ 漸漸發達起來。
    Ⓓ 正在改變主要的商業計畫。

200. 為什麼卡斯蒂爾女士這麼急著想要整修
辦公室？
    Ⓐ 她週日不上班。
    ⒷＢ 承租戶很快要來看租賃空間。
    Ⓒ 對新的承租戶而言，這些是危牆。
    Ⓓ 承租戶要求做些隔間。

TEST
9

PART 7

ACTUAL TEST

PART 5　P. 284–286

◎ Part 5 解答請見 P.457

101. 晚餐將由威爾斯屋**和**北斗碳烤提供。

102. 迪亞朵拉的新款慢跑鞋，照它的外型與機動性命名成「刀鋒跑者」很**恰當**。

103. 戴維森餐廳的**進步**，包括擴建停車場，吸引了更多客人。

104. 努斯堡組織協會負責每日歷史景點的導覽，**除了**週六**以外**。

105. 桑馬利諾鋼鐵目前正**生產**各種鋼鐵製品來興建市外的建築設施。

106. 丹寧斯女士**經常**協助負責舉辦記者會的人。

107. 您可以在附上的問卷表**裡**回答問題。

108. 目前**正在開發**新的訓練方法來提升生產力。

109. **退**貨時請保持商品原貌，以取得全額退款。

110. 塞伊德李奇和彼得洛夫兩家電子公司的財力，都比**他們的**許多競爭對手來得強。

111. 威特爾先生在德國國際賽車大賽打破單圈的最快紀錄。

112. 能源委員會已經證實，用較明亮且有反光效果的藍色蓋屋頂能**大幅**降低室溫，城市裡效果尤佳。

113. 亞香提旅行社提供**最便宜**的東京到北京和東京到首爾機票。

114. 董事會**有條件地**採納了以亞洲國家青年為目標的進軍海外市場計畫。

115. 公眾動態有三座工廠，**總**樓地板面積達51,500 平方公尺。

116. 要求全額退費時，顧客必須出示**正確的**消費紀錄，包括消費日期在內。

117. 沃綠聯盟每天處理大**量**索賠，所以它需要能力很強的員工。

118. 針對提斯勒烹調用具的新產品樣品，近期的研究發現**非常**鼓舞人心。

119. **雖然**為了改善曼徹斯特市的運輸系統已接獲很多建議，但沒半項符合預算。

120. 請確認您 1282712 號訂單的**收據**，商品將在週三前送到。

121. 工廠經理篠原先生為了公司的重要客戶，最近**帶**了釀啤酒工廠的導覽。

122. 哈米爾頓藝廊的老闆聘用了一群喜歡幫助**他人**的志工，滿足他們對導覽員的需求。

123. 在**最終**決定誰是副總裁之前，董事會面試了五名頂尖應徵者。

124. 週日拍賣會上所有**將出售的**鋼筆，都會在週六上午 9 點開放給所有買家鑑賞。

125. 抵達機場的所有班機都需要出示官方**文件**。

126. 造訪中國的旅客增加，帶隊導遊的需求也**隨之增加**。

127. 安熱是一間大型包裝公司，專門為隔熱箱子或容器提供**保護性**包裝服務。

128. 尼爾·柏瑞特新的 S/S 褲款系列，以**多樣**顏色可供選擇為主打特色。

129. 不幸的是，研究指出油價上漲會**干擾**經濟復甦。

130. 所有百貨公司都得遵守**特賣**活動的相關規定。

131–134 電子郵件

收件人：瑪麗亞·戈梅茲
　　　　<mgomez@samail.com>
寄件人：泰勒·費雪
　　　　<tfisher@lapubliclibrary.com>
日期：5 月 5 日
主旨：您的詢問

親愛的戈梅茲女士：

感謝您詢問您所遺失的借閱書本《花開女孩》。這本書現在雖然逾期一週了，但我已更新借閱到 5 月 12 日，所以圖書館不會再繼續收取逾期罰款。

我已請同事確認這本書是否有在書架上，以防有人可能找到它並協助歸還。但很遺憾，我們並沒有找到。

如果您無法在 5 月 12 日前還書，我們將會訂購一本新書。那就必須由您負擔這筆支出。

洛杉磯公共圖書館
泰勒·費雪 敬上

131. [A] 錯過
　　　[B] 去想念
　　　[C] 遺失的
　　　[D] 錯過的

132. [A] 歸還
　　　[B] 已歸還
　　　[C] 被歸還
　　　[D] 將歸還

133. [A] 會員卡會發放給所有來圖書館的訪客。
　　　[B] 您可以在我們官網上找到圖書館地點。
　　　[C] 但很遺憾，我們並沒有找到。
　　　[D] 但是我們在週日閉館。

134. **[A] 訂購**
　　　[B] 認出
　　　[C] 承認
　　　[D] 認出

135–138 文章

舊金山（3 月 29 日）——再等兩週，星豆公司將推出限量復刻版產品，可追溯到 30 年前品牌首度流行的時候。這次活動將不會包括星豆公司現有的咖啡系列。公司將會推出新飲品，像是冰肉桂杏仁牛奶瑪奇朵、椰奶摩卡拿鐵和焦糖可可特調冰沙，容量將是現在的兩倍。星豆公司董事長金·派瑞說，包裝展示了品牌歷史。這正是星豆暢銷的原因。「我們覺得這次的推廣活動，會受到舊雨新知的青睞。」她說。星豆復刻商品將在四月上市。至於新飲品則會在五月開賣。

135. [A] 一度
　　　[B] 全部
　　　[C] 首度
　　　[D] 因此

136. [A] 使加倍
　　　[B] 使加倍
　　　[C] 將使加倍
　　　[D] 使加倍

137. [A] 市場分析師預期，這季的利潤將讓人失望。
　　　[B] 今年咖啡的價格預期將持續成長。
　　　[C] 這正是星豆暢銷的原因。
　　　[D] 這也吸引到沒時間享用咖啡的顧客。

138. [A] 服務
　　　[B] 功能
　　　[C] 裝備
　　　[D] 飲品

收件人：全體員工
寄件人：會計部門
日期：2 月 4 日
主旨：程序更正

請注意最近差旅費的核銷方案有異動。這之前，差旅支出表要在行程結束後一個月內提交。而今，員工最遲必須在行程後兩週內提交。只要合理使用且事先取得許可，所有開銷都將由公司負擔。一旦差旅費申請通過，公司將會寄送核准開銷的通知給員工。差旅費會經由正當程序核發。如果您需要更多資訊，請上官網 www.tesoro.com/reimbursementprogram。

139. Ⓐ 所以
Ⓑ 非常地
Ⓒ 之前
Ⓓ 最終

140. Ⓐ 付款
Ⓑ 已付款
Ⓒ 一直在付款
Ⓓ 將被付款

141. Ⓐ 通知
Ⓑ 已通知
Ⓒ 正在通知
Ⓓ 通知

142. Ⓐ 請將表格以電子郵件寄到會計部門。
Ⓑ 公司一直鼓勵員工出國旅遊。
Ⓒ 差旅費會經由正當程序核發。
Ⓓ 由於公司目前面臨財務問題，商務出差有所限制。

www.staplesbestworkplaceaward.com/about

獎項說明

績效表現頂尖的公司給美國經濟注入了一針強心劑。過去幾年來，我們見證很多成功的公司，其成功大多歸功於員工對工作的投入。有熱忱的員工可為同事帶來正面影響。這可從更高的工作產出上見得。史泰博最佳職場獎於 15 年前創立，為的是獎勵成功企業，他們的員工全心為工作貢獻。從那時起，數百家遍布全美的公司已獲獎項肯定。如果您想知道更完整的得獎名單，可以到「獲獎者」頁面查看。

143. Ⓐ 他的
Ⓑ 何時
Ⓒ 哪裡
Ⓓ 它們的

144. Ⓐ 有時候這會引起顧客的抱怨。
Ⓑ 頒獎典禮將在六月舉行。
Ⓒ 只有大企業會獲頒這個獎項。
Ⓓ 這可從更高的工作產出上見得。

145. **Ⓐ 被建立**
Ⓑ 被訴諸
Ⓒ 被詢問
Ⓓ 被啟發

146. Ⓐ 既然
Ⓑ 另一方面
Ⓒ 從那時起
Ⓓ 然而

147–148 廣告

> ### 紐克中心
>
> - 超過 40 種刺激的戶外運動
> - 50 種以上物超所值的驚奇遊戲
> - 全年度的特別音樂節
> - 國內最大的室內美食街
> - 專為五歲以下兒童設計的遊樂區
>
> 紐克中心週一到週日全年無休。
>
> 可由網路或在大門處購票。
>
> 12 人以上團體享折扣。

147. 這篇是要廣告什麼？
　　 A 音樂會
　　 B 競賽
　　 C 遊樂園
　　 D 設計嘉年華

148. 誰適用折扣？
　　 A 團體購票的民眾
　　 B 單月來訪超過五次的民眾
　　 C 網路購票的民眾
　　 D 五歲以下的民眾

149–150 資訊

> ### 全通 S9 手機
>
> 感謝您購買全通 S9 手機。您的全新手機具備最先進的功能，讓您的生活更好玩。這本使用說明書提供簡單好上手的手機使用說明。如果您想避免全通 S9 受損，請翻閱第 25 頁與配件有關的注意事項，內容包括充電器、手機殼、電池和耳機。

149. 這則資訊的目的為何？
　　 A 推銷手機的保固方案
　　 B 提供電子產品的折扣
　　 C 建議顧客翻閱使用書
　　 D 鼓勵顧客買新手機

150. 文中提到手機配件什麼事？
　　 A 全通 S9 通通附贈。
　　 B 不當使用可能會損害手機。
　　 C 有一年的保固。
　　 D 經授權的經銷商可將毀損的商品換成全新的。

151–152 信件

> 史嘉莉‧波特曼
> 11530 紐約花園市雀斯特大道 51–59 號
>
> 1 月 5 日
>
> 安琪拉‧威斯特
> 32193 佛州韋拉卡第三大道 667 號
>
> 親愛的威斯特女士：
>
> 感謝您的專業推薦。我相信您的推薦信對我應徵上 SBTY 新聞口譯一職，有很大的幫助。
>
> 我在研究所的所學，特別是將韓文和日文翻譯成英文的經驗，讓我勝任這份工作。除了口譯，我也很享受翻譯醫療新聞節目的挑戰。
>
> 再次非常感謝您的幫忙。
>
> 史嘉莉‧波特曼 敬上

151. 為什麼波特曼女士要寫這封信？
　　 A 表示同意一些資訊
　　 B 表達感謝
　　 C 請求翻譯
　　 D 提供職位

152. 波特曼女士最可能在哪裡工作？
　　 A 電視網
　　 B 製藥公司
　　 C 語言學校
　　 D 醫院

TEST 10

PART 7

寄件人：布萊德・伯恩
<b.bourne@jbconsulting.com>
收件人：娜塔莎・米勒
<n.miller@jbconsulting.com>
日期：7 月 14 日
主旨：巴黎會議

哈囉娜塔莎：

我現在在東京監督整個檢驗流程，並確保一切運作正常，不過花的時間比我預期得還要久。所以我想要在日本再多待兩週，這表示我需要你重新安排我週四在巴黎的會議。

如果可以的話，我可以準備下個月和詹姆斯先生的客戶會議。可以請你給我一份我擬好的合約副本嗎？要是它們不在我的檔案櫃裡，就是在我桌上。我今天沒辦法講電話。如果需要跟我聯絡，請寄電子郵件或傳訊。

感謝你幫忙。

布萊德・伯恩，伯恩諮詢總裁

153. 這封電子郵件的目的為何？
- Ⓐ 核准檢驗的要求
- Ⓑ 總結一份報告
- Ⓒ 抱怨視察結果
- **Ⓓ 請求協助更改行程**

154. 伯恩先生待在日本可能是因為什麼？
- Ⓐ 開設新廠
- Ⓑ 簽合約
- **Ⓒ 監督一項計畫**
- Ⓓ 面試應徵者

155. 文中提到詹姆斯先生什麼事？
- Ⓐ 他是工廠廠長。
- Ⓑ 他是米勒女士的行政助理。
- **Ⓒ 他是伯恩先生的企業客戶。**
- Ⓓ 他在檢驗過程中幫助伯恩先生。

愛瑪客電子

www.aramarkelectonics.com
麥克・道森
E17 9NH 英格蘭倫敦教會路 1C

親愛的道森先生：

感謝您聯繫愛瑪客電子來維修您的空調（單號 2912012）。請您花幾分鐘完成問卷，讓我們能夠提供顧客最好的服務。請使用隨信附上的回郵信封寄回您填答完畢的問卷表。感謝您的配合。

	非常同意	同意	不同意	非常不同意
愛瑪客電子迅速答覆您的需求。	✕			
維修技師正確說明問題所在。		✕		
您的愛瑪客電子產品很快修好歸還。				✕

顧客姓名：麥克・道森
修理單號：2912012
其他意見：

在官網上看問題集都比和維修技師溝通來得好。我會這樣說，是因為我從疑難排解就可以迅速知道故障的原因。關於怎麼解決問題，技師寫得很詳細。不過，他沒有修好我的空調，且歸還時間還比預計時間晚了五天。

156. 為什麼會寫這封信給道森先生？
- Ⓐ 抱怨他經歷過的一切
- Ⓑ 公告回收有瑕疵的產品
- Ⓒ 提醒他政策變動
- **Ⓓ 了解有關顧客服務的資訊**

157. 愛瑪客電子提供什麼？
- **Ⓐ 線上協助**
- Ⓑ 免運費
- Ⓒ 保固展延
- Ⓓ 故障檢修手冊

158. 道森先生提到什麼？

    Ⓐ 技師將空調維修得很完美。

    Ⓑ 維修時間比預期還久。

    Ⓒ 空調買的時候就有瑕疵。

    Ⓓ 說明書很難理解。

159–160 訊息串

> **艾希頓・威廉斯〔上午 10:50〕：**
> 客戶剛剛到了！你在哪？你沒到的話我們可以先開會嗎？
>
> **柯林斯・雷諾斯〔上午 10:51〕：**
> 可以啊。我 15 分鐘內到。
>
> **艾希頓・威廉斯〔上午 10:52〕：**
> 好。我會先談整體產業趨勢，再講我們新產品的特色。
>
> **柯林斯・雷諾斯〔上午 10:52〕：**
> 我相信你會做得很好。
>
> **艾希頓・威廉斯〔上午 10:53〕：**
> 謝了，但你最好負責報告估價，那是你的專業。
>
> **柯林斯・雷諾斯〔上午 10:54〕：**
> 沒問題，等等見。
>
> 送出

159. 上午 10:51，雷諾斯先生寫道：「可以啊。」，他最可能的意思是？

    Ⓐ 他需要更多產品資訊。

    Ⓑ 他想要威廉斯先生照進度走。

    Ⓒ 他想要他們現在先休息 15 分鐘。

    Ⓓ 他建議延後簡報。

160. 根據威廉斯先生的說法，雷諾斯先生最熟悉什麼？

    Ⓐ 製造生產

    Ⓑ 產品規格

    Ⓒ 行銷策略

    Ⓓ 預算評估

161–163 文章

> ### 商情內幕
>
> 林肯書店最近收購了原先是零售業者的店面，地點緊鄰它倫敦雷頓斯通高路 877 號原店址。這個熱門地點總算要運用新空間進行擴展計畫。「自五年前開幕以來，我們發展得很快。」林肯書店共同創辦人暨總裁塞斯・強生說。「常常有人跟我們說成功的實體書店是過去式了。我們證明了事實剛好相反。」
>
> 強生繼續說道，林肯書店整修完成後約莫是原店面的兩倍大。「眾所期待的重新開幕儀式將在 11 月 8 號舉行。」強生說，「書店改頭換面讓我們很興奮。這表示我們可以收納更多書，舉行各式各樣的活動，像是簽書會。」

161. 這篇文章的目的為何？

    Ⓐ 介紹當地一家商店老闆

    Ⓑ 宣布書店改裝

    Ⓒ 推銷一本新書

    Ⓓ 推廣一場簽書會

162. 誰是強生先生？

    Ⓐ 書商

    Ⓑ 知名作家

    Ⓒ 網路書籍供應商

    Ⓓ 房仲業者

163. 下列句子最適合出現在 [1]、[2]、[3]、[4] 的哪個位置中？

    「我們證明了事實剛好相反。」

    Ⓐ [1]

    Ⓑ [2]

    Ⓒ [3]

    Ⓓ [4]

曼徹斯特音樂節

您有興趣擔任志工參與知名音樂節，共享音樂盛宴嗎？那您何不自願來第 25 屆曼徹斯特音樂節！今年音樂節將從 8 月 1 日到 5 日，在曼徹斯特的希頓公園舉行，超過 15 個專業團體和 25 個才華洋溢的業餘團體——包括當地人最喜愛的羅蘭·柏德、爵士馬塔茲、阿卡迪亞節拍——都將共襄盛舉，在活動中展現高超表演。

志工需要做的事：

- 協助所有海報和傳單的創作和發放，並從 7 月 1 日開始處理新聞稿。

- 7 月 28 日到 8 月 8 日期間接待音樂家並擔任口譯。來自其他城市的音樂家均住在指定旅館。

- 音樂節期間，管理售票亭和服務台，並引導遊客到停車場。

為了感謝志工的付出，我們提供豐富獎勵！志工將收到曼徹斯特音樂節官方限量版的 T 恤、官方慶功宴的貴賓邀請函、一整季的音樂通行證等。

如果您有興趣擔任志工，請於 6 月 15 日前聯絡希拉蕊·羅伯茲 hroberts@manchestermusicfestival.co.uk。

164. 文中提到音樂節什麼事？
- Ⓐ **從 8 月 1 日開始。**
- Ⓑ 特色是有多種音樂類型。
- Ⓒ 由當地政府舉辦。
- Ⓓ 可能因為下雨延期。

165. 文中提到某些表演者什麼事？
- Ⓐ 他們將捐出二手樂器。
- Ⓑ 他們將提供簽名唱片。
- Ⓒ 他們會住在曼徹斯特的民宅裡。
- Ⓓ **他們會接受一些口譯協助。**

166. 哪項任務不會由志工來做？
- Ⓐ 販售音樂節的票
- Ⓑ **將音樂家送到飯店**
- Ⓒ 告知旅客停車位置
- Ⓓ 發送一些文件

167. 志工可以免費收到什麼？
- Ⓐ **一件衣服**
- Ⓑ 特定飯店的住宿券
- Ⓒ 頒獎晚宴的票
- Ⓓ 音樂節期間的餐飲

海洋公園整修

傑克·戴文波特撰文

聖地牙哥（4 月 15 日）——聖地牙哥市議會全數通過海洋公園的整修決議。整修計畫的議案最早在三年前提出，經過長時間討論，直到娜塔莉·薇斯朋接任市長，計畫才終於通過。她受訪時表示：「我向市民說過這是我當選後的首要任務，我也打算兌現承諾。」

公園開張後，沿著湖邊兩公里長的步道成為聖地牙哥的一大景點。不過，當地居民不久就才發現，公園對他們的小孩來說，並不是個理想的地方。

「我們每天都會使用步道，但我們的小孩只想到處踢球。」當地居民伊凡卡·安尼斯頓表示。公園內確實缺乏讓小孩自由奔跑的空間。「我們有時候想在公園吃午餐，但卻沒有桌子和長椅。」

計畫一部分就是要讓海洋公園有更多綠地，供戶外活動使用。並規劃讓小朋友可以安全遊玩的空間。市議會也通過提案，將沿著步道兩側裝設路燈，方便喜歡在傍晚散步或運動的居民。整修最晚會在今年底完成。

168. 文中提到公園整修什麼事？
- Ⓐ 明年夏天會結束。
- Ⓑ 由市長薇斯朋率先提出。
- Ⓒ 需要三年才會完工。
- Ⓓ **取得議會全體同意。**

169. 第一段、第五行的「plan」,最接近下列哪個意思?
- **A** 有意
- B 保持
- C 同意
- D 專注於

170. 居民如何使用公園?
- A 吃東西
- B 販賣他們的手工商品
- **C** 去散步
- D 騎單車

171. 下列句子最適合出現在 [1]、[2]、[3]、[4] 的哪個位置中?

「市議會也通過提案,將沿著步道兩側裝設路燈。」

- A [1]
- B [2]
- C [3]
- **D** [4]

172–175 網路討論區

> **辛蒂・希爾頓〔上午 9:45〕:**
> 我需要為下週的年度會議,安排從機場到會場的交通事宜。所以我希望你們提供你們的班機資訊。由於這是我們第一次舉行會議,我真心希望過程中不要出錯。
>
> **瑪麗・凱特〔上午 9:46〕:**
> 我期待這會議很久了。但很遺憾我忘了訂機票。如果我自己開車過去,公司會補貼車馬費嗎?因為從舊金山出發的班機都客滿了。
>
> **班・福特〔上午 9:47〕:**
> 我搭乘四葉草航空 803 班機,從達拉斯飛紐約,上午 7:35 抵達當地。
>
> **辛蒂・希爾頓〔上午 9:48〕:**
> 喔,真糟糕,瑪麗。這件事我會再確認。
>
> **亞歷安娜・克勞福〔上午 9:49〕:**
> 從休士頓飛往紐約的班機也都滿了。所以我別無選擇,只能搭客運到費城再轉搭飛機,到紐約的時間是 7:50。我來得及搶到最後一張票。

> **辛蒂・希爾頓〔上午 9:55〕:**
> 我剛才從財務部得知,根據公司政策,自行開車前往不給與補貼。妳要不要改搭火車?如果妳現在馬上訂票,讓我知道妳抵達的時間,我會很感謝。
>
> **瑪麗・凱特〔上午 9:56〕:**
> 當然。
>
> **辛蒂・希爾頓〔上午 9:57〕:**
> 福特先生和克勞福女士,感謝你們的資訊。到時見。
>
> 送出

172. 上午 9:46 時,凱特女士寫道:「我期待這會議很久了。」她最可能的意思是?
- A 她等著知道詳細的班機資訊。
- B 她沒發現班機訂位滿了。
- **C** 她很高興下週講者們終於要見面了。
- D 她準備會議演講已久。

173. 上午 9:48 時,希爾頓女士要確認什麼事?
- A 從舊金山起飛的機票
- **B** 公司的車馬費補助政策
- C 福特先生的班機資訊
- D 會議開始的時間

174. 凱特女士最可能用什麼方式參加年度會議?
- A 開車
- B 搭飛機
- **C** 搭火車
- D 搭客運

175. 關於演講者,下列何者為真?
- A 他們都從同一個城市起飛。
- B 他們會搭乘同一班飛機。
- C 他們去年一起開過會。
- **D** 他們都要參加在紐約舉行的會議。

一週商業洞察：

誠信兄弟

五年前，傑・戴蒙和蓋文・戴蒙創立了「誠信兄弟」，它是很獨特的公司，顛覆了巴塞隆納的不動產業。為了整修老舊建築，這間小公司有和城裡房東合作的豐富經驗。這對兄弟有效評估建築物的價值，並決定需要改善的部份，專注於提高房地產價值和租金潛力。從外部裝潢到室內設計，誠信兄弟聘僱老練專業的工人來完成工程。至今他們所有的工程只集中在巴塞隆納中部。

傑・曼努埃爾是當地一名房東，最近才和誠信兄弟簽約整修他的舊建築。他表示：「多虧了和誠信兄弟合作，我才感受到租屋需求的成長和租金收益的增加。不只如此，整修也節省了水電開銷。我的住戶很享受，閒來沒事就待在頂樓天台。我絕對會向其他人推薦誠信兄弟。」

如果您想要聯絡誠信兄弟，可以上他們的官網 trustworthybrothers.com。

寄件人：麥克・基恩
　　　　　<mkeane@amail.com>
收件人：傑・戴蒙
　　　　　<jdamon@trustworthybrothers.com>
日期：3 月 24 日
主旨：新提案

親愛的戴蒙先生：

我想請求您協助整修我最近新買的房子，它鄰近巴塞隆納的海岸城市。我確信您會對這項整修計畫感興趣。這棟建築荒廢數年，目前屋況並不好。所以我才能低價買下。房子倒是離地鐵站很近，我相信這是個優勢。我想請您改造我的房子，讓它能夠吸引房客入住。如果您有空談談這件事，請告訴我。

感謝，

麥克・基恩

---

176. 關於誠信兄弟，文中沒有提到什麼？
A 他們在不動產業界已工作十年。
B 他們讓顧客的收益增加。
C 他們一直和巴塞隆納的房東合作。
D 他們找工人來完成計畫。

177. 文中提到曼努埃爾先生的房子什麼事？
A 它們較以前吸引更多房客。
B 它們是新建築。
C 頂樓天台沒有開放給房客使用。
D 曼努埃爾先生現在必須替房子負擔更多電費。

178. 關於潛在客戶，文章建議他們怎麼做？
A 請求估價
B 上網查看
C 議價
D 提出請求

179. 為什麼基恩先生能夠用低價買到房子？
A 地處偏遠。
B 沒有供水。
C 特價拍賣。
D 因為它的現況沒有辦法提供出租。

180. 基恩先生的整修計畫，和誠信兄弟之前做過的案子有何不同？
A 這項工程將在巴塞隆納外作業。
B 基恩先生想僱用知名設計師。
C 整修費用要等到完工以後才會付款。
D 計畫必須在緊迫的時間內完成。

潘世奇書店

冬季型錄

親愛的顧客：

請盡情瀏覽我們最新的型錄。如果您看第 5 頁的食譜、飲食美酒類別，您會找到知名餐廳食譜的暢銷書籍。我們第 7 頁的旅行和旅遊類別，帶領您享受各地的冬季假期。第 9 頁有所有最新的科幻小說，充滿想像力的作者引導您進入科幻世界。在第 11 頁的商管類別，經驗豐富的作者將告訴您最新趨勢。您也可以看到倍受喜愛的書籍，包括賈米森獎得主的《小企業的風險管理》（第 13 頁）。

請您留意這本型錄裡的樣書不多。如果您想要看到完整的書目標題，請造訪我們官網 www.penskebooks.com。歡迎賓州居民到我們實體書店來看看，有連官網上也找不到的豐富書籍。

《商業展望》

作者尤里‧蒂耶萊曼斯和珍‧卡特

帶您認識商業策略，引人入勝，充滿具體案例和有趣的圖片插畫，來解釋其中關鍵重點。便於理解的說明，讓您更了解商業界。

書況：非常好。39.95 美元。

《金融管理分析》

作者蒂亞戈‧馬康

本書特色結合實際案例和新的財務理論。馬康用真實世界的場景，分析金融管理的理論原則。強烈推薦給商務人士和學生。

書況：近全新。25.95 美元。

《小企業的風險管理》

作者艾莉西亞‧鄧斯特

小企業主必讀的書，有效處理高風險的情況。本書內有多個商業成功人士的訪談。

書況：一般，書角和書緣有折損。32.95 美元。

《商業行銷百科》

作者安東尼‧馬夏爾

本書有超過 5,000 個商業行銷術語的定義，對於首度投身創業的人，是必定收藏之作。

書況：好，書封有些破舊。49.95 美元。

181. 根據備註，哪本書在潘世奇書店最可能有庫存？
[A] 知名音樂家的自傳
[B] 非洲史
[C] 新電腦模型的概論
[D] 東亞度假勝地的資訊

182. 在備註中，第二段、第三行的「wealth」，意思最接近下列何者？
[A] 價值
[B] 品質
[C] 感覺
[D] 大量

183. 文中提到這本型錄什麼事？
[A] 推廣二手書。
[B] 有完整的清單。
[C] 主要都是學術書籍。
[D] 每年出版兩次。

184. 誰得了獎？
[A] 蒂耶萊曼斯先生
[B] 馬康先生
[C] 鄧斯特女士
[D] 馬夏爾先生

185. 關於書本的描述，型錄頁面上沒有提到哪個特色？
[A] 用圖畫闡明重點
[B] 有關人士的訪談
[C] 真實世界的案例
[D] 創業的勾選清單

寄件人：詹姆斯‧羅德里格斯
              \<jrodriguez@ita.com\>
收件人：布萊恩‧門迪
              \<bmendy@altriagroup.com\>
日期：12 月 1 日
主旨：致講者的邀請函

親愛的門迪先生：

我想要邀請您出席 5 月 1 日到 3 日，於北卡羅萊納州的夏洛特舉行的第五屆資訊科技協會會議，並擔任會議的主講人。數千名商業領導人和產業專家都將出席，這是建立人脈的理想場合。會議將在凱悅夏洛特飯店舉行，商業領導人將分享，他們對資訊科技產業最新趨勢的深入見解。

如果您同意蒞臨演講，談談您為了提高奧馳亞集團網路安全程式的利潤，所引進的彈性定價選擇，我們將不勝感激。請告訴我您能否撥空前來。

資訊科技協會
總裁
詹姆斯‧羅德里格斯

資訊科技協會會議行程
（5 月 1 日行程）

上午 8:30	**視覺化傳播**——更好且更有效率的傳播方式，省錢又省力 講者：伊莉莎白‧科漢，密可龍科技共同創辦人
上午 9:30	**革命性變革**——超價公司副總裁分享她的團隊如何帶領公司，藉由產品的創新設計從破產邊緣轉虧為盈 講者：安娜‧卡比，超價公司副董
上午 10:30	**創造產品**——揭密奧馳亞集團提高旗下電腦軟體銷售量的獨家策略 講者：布萊恩‧門迪，奧馳亞集團執行長
上午 11:30	**資訊產業公司的領導力**——如何即時、有效地因應迅速變動的局勢 講者：羅瑞爾‧艾倫，夏洛特商學院教授
下午 12:30	午餐

資訊科技協會會議

報名價

資訊科技協會會員——1,000 美元

非會員——1,500 美元

報名費包括旅館的消費券——可用於活動期間餐食和點心。欲出席會議須提前上網登記。講座影片將在下個月放上官網，供所有與會者觀看。

---

186. 關於資訊科技協會會議，文中提到什麼？
- **A 每年都會舉辦。**
- B 會安排現場的訓練課程。
- C 是一整天的活動。
- D 會展示最新的產品。

187. 什麼時候最有可能討論到產品定價？
- A 上午 8:30
- B 上午 9:30
- **C 上午 10:30**
- D 上午 11:30

188. 文中提到超價公司什麼事？
- A 將和對手整併。
- **B 它克服困難。**
- C 最近換了公司商標。
- D 總部在去年搬遷。

189. 哪項優惠只提供給資訊科技協會的會員？
- A 人脈拓展的私人晚餐
- B 免費交通
- C 飯店住宿升等
- **D 報名費用減少**

190. 門迪先生在六月可以得到什麼的使用權？
- **A 錄影**
- B 文章
- C 收據
- D 照片

折價券

季末出清，只有一天！

4 月 2 日週三

- 一般價格商品打八折
- 出清商品打七折

數千種庫存商品，包括外套、襯衫、長褲、鞋子和配件等。活動期間我們將延長營業時間，從上午 9 點到晚上 9 點。

本折價券不能和其他優惠活動合併使用。每名顧客限用一券。請留意長褲並不適用本折價券。商品一經購買，就不能退款和換貨。僅限 4 月 2 日當天使用有效。

孟斯坦都
10456 紐約布朗克斯中央大廳 1040 號
電話：(718) 681-6000

收件人：孟斯坦都員工

寄件人：經理威廉·辛格

日期：4 月 1 日

回覆：即將到來的特賣

今天出版的《紐約日報》沒有提到一般價格商品不包括配件。所以如果顧客購買配件，請向顧客解釋清楚並道歉。也請通知顧客為表誠意，我們特別提供九折優惠。

另外，因為廣告已透過媒體宣傳，預期會有比平常更多的顧客到店選購，尤其是下午 5 點以後到關店這段期間。所以到時候，我們將需要更多銷售人員值班。如果您願意加班，請告訴我。

感謝。

寄件人：服務部門 <service@monstanto.com>

收件人：吉兒·埃爾金斯 <jelkins@mmail.com>

日期：4 月 2 日，下午 4:26

主旨：您的收據

親愛的埃爾金斯女士：

這是您向孟斯坦都索取的購物收據。

數量	商品	價格
1	軟夾克 七折特賣折扣 **商品價格**	400.00 美元 -120.00 美元 **280.00 美元**
1	戒指和項鍊組 九折特賣折扣 **商品價格**	160.00 美元 -16.00 美元 **144.00 美元**
1	丹寧長褲	28.00 美元

總計 452.00 美元

總折扣 136.00 美元

感謝您在孟斯坦都購物。

---

191. 根據折價券，4 月 2 日會發生什麼事？
- Ⓐ 揭幕新的生產線。
- **Ⓑ 開店時間較長。**
- Ⓒ 店家門口會發放多的折價券。
- Ⓓ 顧客可以看到一場時尚秀。

192. 在電子郵件中，銷售人員被要求做什麼？
- Ⓐ 提早到班
- **Ⓑ 自願加班**
- Ⓒ 發放傳單
- Ⓓ 盤點存貨

193. 在第一封電子郵件中，第二段、第一行的「advertised」，最接近下列哪個意思？
- Ⓐ 被更新
- Ⓑ 被放送
- Ⓒ 被吸引
- **Ⓓ 被推廣**

194. 文中提到埃爾金斯女士什麼事？
- Ⓐ **她買了一項出清商品。**
- Ⓑ 她最近搬到布朗克斯。
- Ⓒ 她用信用卡付費購物。
- Ⓓ 她經常去孟斯坦都。

195. 埃爾金斯女士買戒指和項鍊組時，可能不會收到什麼？
- Ⓐ 一項折扣
- Ⓑ **一張禮券**
- Ⓒ 一個道歉
- Ⓓ 一個解釋

196–200 公告、電子郵件和表格

學生事務聯絡員

芝加哥大學

校方正在徵求能在教務處工作的學生事務聯絡員。他們每個月要和學生委員會中的國際學生會面兩次，協助他們的各種疑難雜症，包括個人、學業、住宿和生涯規畫等問題。學生事務聯絡員每個月也要在校園各處舉行聚會，來凝聚向心力。

如果您有興趣，請寄電子郵件到 ssd@chiuni.edu.com。

寄件人：班科勒‧強森
收件人：羅伯特‧里弗斯特
日期：2 月 15 日
主旨：歡迎

親愛的里弗斯特先生：

感謝您接下學生事務聯絡員的職務。在您開始工作前，您需要完成一些文書作業。您將在一週內收到校方歡迎您的公文匣，請在這個月底前填完裡面的正式文件。這也幫助您瞭解更多關於迎新的資訊。

此外，我們還需要您在上一間大學的正式成績單。也麻煩您在這個月底前寄給我正本。

教務處主任，芝加哥大學
班科勒‧強森 敬上

聖地牙哥大學
成績單申請表

如果學生沒有向學校繳費，或是學生紀錄有所疑慮，成績單將不予發放。

姓：<u>里弗斯特</u>　　　名：<u>羅伯特</u>
學歷：☐ 大學部　　☑ 研究所（傳播）
住址：<u>南艾力斯街 5801 號</u>
郵遞區號：<u>60637</u>
城市：<u>芝加哥</u>　州：<u>伊利諾</u>
您希望何時發放成績單？
☑ 即刻　　☐ 待最後成績公布
簽名：<u>羅伯特‧里弗斯特</u>

---

196. 這篇公告的目的為何？
- Ⓐ 幫助大學招募國際學生
- Ⓑ 公告招聘新教授
- Ⓒ **徵求職缺的應徵者**
- Ⓓ 宣傳新團體的創作

197. 學生委員會和學生事務聯絡員開會的頻率是？
- Ⓐ 一週一次
- Ⓑ 一個月一次
- Ⓒ 一週兩次
- Ⓓ **一個月兩次**

198. 里弗斯特先生將在芝加哥大學做什麼？
- Ⓐ 協助學生中心搬遷
- Ⓑ 協助所有學生選擇合適的課程
- Ⓒ 領導教務處
- Ⓓ **提供協助給校內國際學生**

199. 里弗斯特先生會在一週內收到什麼？
- Ⓐ **裝有文件的包裹**
- Ⓑ 付款收據
- Ⓒ 成績單副本
- Ⓓ 錄取通知書

200. 文中提到聖地牙哥大學什麼事？
- Ⓐ 沒有醫學課程。
- Ⓑ 沒有研究所課程。
- Ⓒ 錄取很多國際學生。
- Ⓓ **是里弗斯特先生最後就讀的大學。**

答案紙

ACTUAL TEST 01

READING SECTION

ACTUAL TEST 02

READING SECTION

答案紙

ACTUAL TEST 03

READING SECTION

No.	A	B	C	D
101–110	Ⓐ	Ⓑ	Ⓒ	Ⓓ
111–120	Ⓐ	Ⓑ	Ⓒ	Ⓓ
121–130	Ⓐ	Ⓑ	Ⓒ	Ⓓ
131–140	Ⓐ	Ⓑ	Ⓒ	Ⓓ
141–150	Ⓐ	Ⓑ	Ⓒ	Ⓓ
151–160	Ⓐ	Ⓑ	Ⓒ	Ⓓ
161–170	Ⓐ	Ⓑ	Ⓒ	Ⓓ
171–180	Ⓐ	Ⓑ	Ⓒ	Ⓓ
181–190	Ⓐ	Ⓑ	Ⓒ	Ⓓ
191–200	Ⓐ	Ⓑ	Ⓒ	Ⓓ

ACTUAL TEST 04

READING SECTION

No.	A	B	C	D
101–110	Ⓐ	Ⓑ	Ⓒ	Ⓓ
111–120	Ⓐ	Ⓑ	Ⓒ	Ⓓ
121–130	Ⓐ	Ⓑ	Ⓒ	Ⓓ
131–140	Ⓐ	Ⓑ	Ⓒ	Ⓓ
141–150	Ⓐ	Ⓑ	Ⓒ	Ⓓ
151–160	Ⓐ	Ⓑ	Ⓒ	Ⓓ
161–170	Ⓐ	Ⓑ	Ⓒ	Ⓓ
171–180	Ⓐ	Ⓑ	Ⓒ	Ⓓ
181–190	Ⓐ	Ⓑ	Ⓒ	Ⓓ
191–200	Ⓐ	Ⓑ	Ⓒ	Ⓓ

答案紙

ACTUAL TEST 05

READING SECTION																			
101	Ⓐ Ⓑ Ⓒ Ⓓ	111	Ⓐ Ⓑ Ⓒ Ⓓ	121	Ⓐ Ⓑ Ⓒ Ⓓ	131	Ⓐ Ⓑ Ⓒ Ⓓ	141	Ⓐ Ⓑ Ⓒ Ⓓ	151	Ⓐ Ⓑ Ⓒ Ⓓ	161	Ⓐ Ⓑ Ⓒ Ⓓ	171	Ⓐ Ⓑ Ⓒ Ⓓ	181	Ⓐ Ⓑ Ⓒ Ⓓ	191	Ⓐ Ⓑ Ⓒ Ⓓ
102	Ⓐ Ⓑ Ⓒ Ⓓ	112	Ⓐ Ⓑ Ⓒ Ⓓ	122	Ⓐ Ⓑ Ⓒ Ⓓ	132	Ⓐ Ⓑ Ⓒ Ⓓ	142	Ⓐ Ⓑ Ⓒ Ⓓ	152	Ⓐ Ⓑ Ⓒ Ⓓ	162	Ⓐ Ⓑ Ⓒ Ⓓ	172	Ⓐ Ⓑ Ⓒ Ⓓ	182	Ⓐ Ⓑ Ⓒ Ⓓ	192	Ⓐ Ⓑ Ⓒ Ⓓ
103	Ⓐ Ⓑ Ⓒ Ⓓ	113	Ⓐ Ⓑ Ⓒ Ⓓ	123	Ⓐ Ⓑ Ⓒ Ⓓ	133	Ⓐ Ⓑ Ⓒ Ⓓ	143	Ⓐ Ⓑ Ⓒ Ⓓ	153	Ⓐ Ⓑ Ⓒ Ⓓ	163	Ⓐ Ⓑ Ⓒ Ⓓ	173	Ⓐ Ⓑ Ⓒ Ⓓ	183	Ⓐ Ⓑ Ⓒ Ⓓ	193	Ⓐ Ⓑ Ⓒ Ⓓ
104	Ⓐ Ⓑ Ⓒ Ⓓ	114	Ⓐ Ⓑ Ⓒ Ⓓ	124	Ⓐ Ⓑ Ⓒ Ⓓ	134	Ⓐ Ⓑ Ⓒ Ⓓ	144	Ⓐ Ⓑ Ⓒ Ⓓ	154	Ⓐ Ⓑ Ⓒ Ⓓ	164	Ⓐ Ⓑ Ⓒ Ⓓ	174	Ⓐ Ⓑ Ⓒ Ⓓ	184	Ⓐ Ⓑ Ⓒ Ⓓ	194	Ⓐ Ⓑ Ⓒ Ⓓ
105	Ⓐ Ⓑ Ⓒ Ⓓ	115	Ⓐ Ⓑ Ⓒ Ⓓ	125	Ⓐ Ⓑ Ⓒ Ⓓ	135	Ⓐ Ⓑ Ⓒ Ⓓ	145	Ⓐ Ⓑ Ⓒ Ⓓ	155	Ⓐ Ⓑ Ⓒ Ⓓ	165	Ⓐ Ⓑ Ⓒ Ⓓ	175	Ⓐ Ⓑ Ⓒ Ⓓ	185	Ⓐ Ⓑ Ⓒ Ⓓ	195	Ⓐ Ⓑ Ⓒ Ⓓ
106	Ⓐ Ⓑ Ⓒ Ⓓ	116	Ⓐ Ⓑ Ⓒ Ⓓ	126	Ⓐ Ⓑ Ⓒ Ⓓ	136	Ⓐ Ⓑ Ⓒ Ⓓ	146	Ⓐ Ⓑ Ⓒ Ⓓ	156	Ⓐ Ⓑ Ⓒ Ⓓ	166	Ⓐ Ⓑ Ⓒ Ⓓ	176	Ⓐ Ⓑ Ⓒ Ⓓ	186	Ⓐ Ⓑ Ⓒ Ⓓ	196	Ⓐ Ⓑ Ⓒ Ⓓ
107	Ⓐ Ⓑ Ⓒ Ⓓ	117	Ⓐ Ⓑ Ⓒ Ⓓ	127	Ⓐ Ⓑ Ⓒ Ⓓ	137	Ⓐ Ⓑ Ⓒ Ⓓ	147	Ⓐ Ⓑ Ⓒ Ⓓ	157	Ⓐ Ⓑ Ⓒ Ⓓ	167	Ⓐ Ⓑ Ⓒ Ⓓ	177	Ⓐ Ⓑ Ⓒ Ⓓ	187	Ⓐ Ⓑ Ⓒ Ⓓ	197	Ⓐ Ⓑ Ⓒ Ⓓ
108	Ⓐ Ⓑ Ⓒ Ⓓ	118	Ⓐ Ⓑ Ⓒ Ⓓ	128	Ⓐ Ⓑ Ⓒ Ⓓ	138	Ⓐ Ⓑ Ⓒ Ⓓ	148	Ⓐ Ⓑ Ⓒ Ⓓ	158	Ⓐ Ⓑ Ⓒ Ⓓ	168	Ⓐ Ⓑ Ⓒ Ⓓ	178	Ⓐ Ⓑ Ⓒ Ⓓ	188	Ⓐ Ⓑ Ⓒ Ⓓ	198	Ⓐ Ⓑ Ⓒ Ⓓ
109	Ⓐ Ⓑ Ⓒ Ⓓ	119	Ⓐ Ⓑ Ⓒ Ⓓ	129	Ⓐ Ⓑ Ⓒ Ⓓ	139	Ⓐ Ⓑ Ⓒ Ⓓ	149	Ⓐ Ⓑ Ⓒ Ⓓ	159	Ⓐ Ⓑ Ⓒ Ⓓ	169	Ⓐ Ⓑ Ⓒ Ⓓ	179	Ⓐ Ⓑ Ⓒ Ⓓ	189	Ⓐ Ⓑ Ⓒ Ⓓ	199	Ⓐ Ⓑ Ⓒ Ⓓ
110	Ⓐ Ⓑ Ⓒ Ⓓ	120	Ⓐ Ⓑ Ⓒ Ⓓ	130	Ⓐ Ⓑ Ⓒ Ⓓ	140	Ⓐ Ⓑ Ⓒ Ⓓ	150	Ⓐ Ⓑ Ⓒ Ⓓ	160	Ⓐ Ⓑ Ⓒ Ⓓ	170	Ⓐ Ⓑ Ⓒ Ⓓ	180	Ⓐ Ⓑ Ⓒ Ⓓ	190	Ⓐ Ⓑ Ⓒ Ⓓ	200	Ⓐ Ⓑ Ⓒ Ⓓ

ACTUAL TEST 06

READING SECTION																			
101	Ⓐ Ⓑ Ⓒ Ⓓ	111	Ⓐ Ⓑ Ⓒ Ⓓ	121	Ⓐ Ⓑ Ⓒ Ⓓ	131	Ⓐ Ⓑ Ⓒ Ⓓ	141	Ⓐ Ⓑ Ⓒ Ⓓ	151	Ⓐ Ⓑ Ⓒ Ⓓ	161	Ⓐ Ⓑ Ⓒ Ⓓ	171	Ⓐ Ⓑ Ⓒ Ⓓ	181	Ⓐ Ⓑ Ⓒ Ⓓ	191	Ⓐ Ⓑ Ⓒ Ⓓ
102	Ⓐ Ⓑ Ⓒ Ⓓ	112	Ⓐ Ⓑ Ⓒ Ⓓ	122	Ⓐ Ⓑ Ⓒ Ⓓ	132	Ⓐ Ⓑ Ⓒ Ⓓ	142	Ⓐ Ⓑ Ⓒ Ⓓ	152	Ⓐ Ⓑ Ⓒ Ⓓ	162	Ⓐ Ⓑ Ⓒ Ⓓ	172	Ⓐ Ⓑ Ⓒ Ⓓ	182	Ⓐ Ⓑ Ⓒ Ⓓ	192	Ⓐ Ⓑ Ⓒ Ⓓ
103	Ⓐ Ⓑ Ⓒ Ⓓ	113	Ⓐ Ⓑ Ⓒ Ⓓ	123	Ⓐ Ⓑ Ⓒ Ⓓ	133	Ⓐ Ⓑ Ⓒ Ⓓ	143	Ⓐ Ⓑ Ⓒ Ⓓ	153	Ⓐ Ⓑ Ⓒ Ⓓ	163	Ⓐ Ⓑ Ⓒ Ⓓ	173	Ⓐ Ⓑ Ⓒ Ⓓ	183	Ⓐ Ⓑ Ⓒ Ⓓ	193	Ⓐ Ⓑ Ⓒ Ⓓ
104	Ⓐ Ⓑ Ⓒ Ⓓ	114	Ⓐ Ⓑ Ⓒ Ⓓ	124	Ⓐ Ⓑ Ⓒ Ⓓ	134	Ⓐ Ⓑ Ⓒ Ⓓ	144	Ⓐ Ⓑ Ⓒ Ⓓ	154	Ⓐ Ⓑ Ⓒ Ⓓ	164	Ⓐ Ⓑ Ⓒ Ⓓ	174	Ⓐ Ⓑ Ⓒ Ⓓ	184	Ⓐ Ⓑ Ⓒ Ⓓ	194	Ⓐ Ⓑ Ⓒ Ⓓ
105	Ⓐ Ⓑ Ⓒ Ⓓ	115	Ⓐ Ⓑ Ⓒ Ⓓ	125	Ⓐ Ⓑ Ⓒ Ⓓ	135	Ⓐ Ⓑ Ⓒ Ⓓ	145	Ⓐ Ⓑ Ⓒ Ⓓ	155	Ⓐ Ⓑ Ⓒ Ⓓ	165	Ⓐ Ⓑ Ⓒ Ⓓ	175	Ⓐ Ⓑ Ⓒ Ⓓ	185	Ⓐ Ⓑ Ⓒ Ⓓ	195	Ⓐ Ⓑ Ⓒ Ⓓ
106	Ⓐ Ⓑ Ⓒ Ⓓ	116	Ⓐ Ⓑ Ⓒ Ⓓ	126	Ⓐ Ⓑ Ⓒ Ⓓ	136	Ⓐ Ⓑ Ⓒ Ⓓ	146	Ⓐ Ⓑ Ⓒ Ⓓ	156	Ⓐ Ⓑ Ⓒ Ⓓ	166	Ⓐ Ⓑ Ⓒ Ⓓ	176	Ⓐ Ⓑ Ⓒ Ⓓ	186	Ⓐ Ⓑ Ⓒ Ⓓ	196	Ⓐ Ⓑ Ⓒ Ⓓ
107	Ⓐ Ⓑ Ⓒ Ⓓ	117	Ⓐ Ⓑ Ⓒ Ⓓ	127	Ⓐ Ⓑ Ⓒ Ⓓ	137	Ⓐ Ⓑ Ⓒ Ⓓ	147	Ⓐ Ⓑ Ⓒ Ⓓ	157	Ⓐ Ⓑ Ⓒ Ⓓ	167	Ⓐ Ⓑ Ⓒ Ⓓ	177	Ⓐ Ⓑ Ⓒ Ⓓ	187	Ⓐ Ⓑ Ⓒ Ⓓ	197	Ⓐ Ⓑ Ⓒ Ⓓ
108	Ⓐ Ⓑ Ⓒ Ⓓ	118	Ⓐ Ⓑ Ⓒ Ⓓ	128	Ⓐ Ⓑ Ⓒ Ⓓ	138	Ⓐ Ⓑ Ⓒ Ⓓ	148	Ⓐ Ⓑ Ⓒ Ⓓ	158	Ⓐ Ⓑ Ⓒ Ⓓ	168	Ⓐ Ⓑ Ⓒ Ⓓ	178	Ⓐ Ⓑ Ⓒ Ⓓ	188	Ⓐ Ⓑ Ⓒ Ⓓ	198	Ⓐ Ⓑ Ⓒ Ⓓ
109	Ⓐ Ⓑ Ⓒ Ⓓ	119	Ⓐ Ⓑ Ⓒ Ⓓ	129	Ⓐ Ⓑ Ⓒ Ⓓ	139	Ⓐ Ⓑ Ⓒ Ⓓ	149	Ⓐ Ⓑ Ⓒ Ⓓ	159	Ⓐ Ⓑ Ⓒ Ⓓ	169	Ⓐ Ⓑ Ⓒ Ⓓ	179	Ⓐ Ⓑ Ⓒ Ⓓ	189	Ⓐ Ⓑ Ⓒ Ⓓ	199	Ⓐ Ⓑ Ⓒ Ⓓ
110	Ⓐ Ⓑ Ⓒ Ⓓ	120	Ⓐ Ⓑ Ⓒ Ⓓ	130	Ⓐ Ⓑ Ⓒ Ⓓ	140	Ⓐ Ⓑ Ⓒ Ⓓ	150	Ⓐ Ⓑ Ⓒ Ⓓ	160	Ⓐ Ⓑ Ⓒ Ⓓ	170	Ⓐ Ⓑ Ⓒ Ⓓ	180	Ⓐ Ⓑ Ⓒ Ⓓ	190	Ⓐ Ⓑ Ⓒ Ⓓ	200	Ⓐ Ⓑ Ⓒ Ⓓ

答案紙

ACTUAL TEST 07

READING SECTION

101	Ⓐ Ⓑ Ⓒ Ⓓ
102	Ⓐ Ⓑ Ⓒ Ⓓ
103	Ⓐ Ⓑ Ⓒ Ⓓ
104	Ⓐ Ⓑ Ⓒ Ⓓ
105	Ⓐ Ⓑ Ⓒ Ⓓ
106	Ⓐ Ⓑ Ⓒ Ⓓ
107	Ⓐ Ⓑ Ⓒ Ⓓ
108	Ⓐ Ⓑ Ⓒ Ⓓ
109	Ⓐ Ⓑ Ⓒ Ⓓ
110	Ⓐ Ⓑ Ⓒ Ⓓ
111	Ⓐ Ⓑ Ⓒ Ⓓ
112	Ⓐ Ⓑ Ⓒ Ⓓ
113	Ⓐ Ⓑ Ⓒ Ⓓ
114	Ⓐ Ⓑ Ⓒ Ⓓ
115	Ⓐ Ⓑ Ⓒ Ⓓ
116	Ⓐ Ⓑ Ⓒ Ⓓ
117	Ⓐ Ⓑ Ⓒ Ⓓ
118	Ⓐ Ⓑ Ⓒ Ⓓ
119	Ⓐ Ⓑ Ⓒ Ⓓ
120	Ⓐ Ⓑ Ⓒ Ⓓ
121	Ⓐ Ⓑ Ⓒ Ⓓ
122	Ⓐ Ⓑ Ⓒ Ⓓ
123	Ⓐ Ⓑ Ⓒ Ⓓ
124	Ⓐ Ⓑ Ⓒ Ⓓ
125	Ⓐ Ⓑ Ⓒ Ⓓ
126	Ⓐ Ⓑ Ⓒ Ⓓ
127	Ⓐ Ⓑ Ⓒ Ⓓ
128	Ⓐ Ⓑ Ⓒ Ⓓ
129	Ⓐ Ⓑ Ⓒ Ⓓ
130	Ⓐ Ⓑ Ⓒ Ⓓ
131	Ⓐ Ⓑ Ⓒ Ⓓ
132	Ⓐ Ⓑ Ⓒ Ⓓ
133	Ⓐ Ⓑ Ⓒ Ⓓ
134	Ⓐ Ⓑ Ⓒ Ⓓ
135	Ⓐ Ⓑ Ⓒ Ⓓ
136	Ⓐ Ⓑ Ⓒ Ⓓ
137	Ⓐ Ⓑ Ⓒ Ⓓ
138	Ⓐ Ⓑ Ⓒ Ⓓ
139	Ⓐ Ⓑ Ⓒ Ⓓ
140	Ⓐ Ⓑ Ⓒ Ⓓ
141	Ⓐ Ⓑ Ⓒ Ⓓ
142	Ⓐ Ⓑ Ⓒ Ⓓ
143	Ⓐ Ⓑ Ⓒ Ⓓ
144	Ⓐ Ⓑ Ⓒ Ⓓ
145	Ⓐ Ⓑ Ⓒ Ⓓ
146	Ⓐ Ⓑ Ⓒ Ⓓ
147	Ⓐ Ⓑ Ⓒ Ⓓ
148	Ⓐ Ⓑ Ⓒ Ⓓ
149	Ⓐ Ⓑ Ⓒ Ⓓ
150	Ⓐ Ⓑ Ⓒ Ⓓ
151	Ⓐ Ⓑ Ⓒ Ⓓ
152	Ⓐ Ⓑ Ⓒ Ⓓ
153	Ⓐ Ⓑ Ⓒ Ⓓ
154	Ⓐ Ⓑ Ⓒ Ⓓ
155	Ⓐ Ⓑ Ⓒ Ⓓ
156	Ⓐ Ⓑ Ⓒ Ⓓ
157	Ⓐ Ⓑ Ⓒ Ⓓ
158	Ⓐ Ⓑ Ⓒ Ⓓ
159	Ⓐ Ⓑ Ⓒ Ⓓ
160	Ⓐ Ⓑ Ⓒ Ⓓ
161	Ⓐ Ⓑ Ⓒ Ⓓ
162	Ⓐ Ⓑ Ⓒ Ⓓ
163	Ⓐ Ⓑ Ⓒ Ⓓ
164	Ⓐ Ⓑ Ⓒ Ⓓ
165	Ⓐ Ⓑ Ⓒ Ⓓ
166	Ⓐ Ⓑ Ⓒ Ⓓ
167	Ⓐ Ⓑ Ⓒ Ⓓ
168	Ⓐ Ⓑ Ⓒ Ⓓ
169	Ⓐ Ⓑ Ⓒ Ⓓ
170	Ⓐ Ⓑ Ⓒ Ⓓ
171	Ⓐ Ⓑ Ⓒ Ⓓ
172	Ⓐ Ⓑ Ⓒ Ⓓ
173	Ⓐ Ⓑ Ⓒ Ⓓ
174	Ⓐ Ⓑ Ⓒ Ⓓ
175	Ⓐ Ⓑ Ⓒ Ⓓ
176	Ⓐ Ⓑ Ⓒ Ⓓ
177	Ⓐ Ⓑ Ⓒ Ⓓ
178	Ⓐ Ⓑ Ⓒ Ⓓ
179	Ⓐ Ⓑ Ⓒ Ⓓ
180	Ⓐ Ⓑ Ⓒ Ⓓ
181	Ⓐ Ⓑ Ⓒ Ⓓ
182	Ⓐ Ⓑ Ⓒ Ⓓ
183	Ⓐ Ⓑ Ⓒ Ⓓ
184	Ⓐ Ⓑ Ⓒ Ⓓ
185	Ⓐ Ⓑ Ⓒ Ⓓ
186	Ⓐ Ⓑ Ⓒ Ⓓ
187	Ⓐ Ⓑ Ⓒ Ⓓ
188	Ⓐ Ⓑ Ⓒ Ⓓ
189	Ⓐ Ⓑ Ⓒ Ⓓ
190	Ⓐ Ⓑ Ⓒ Ⓓ
191	Ⓐ Ⓑ Ⓒ Ⓓ
192	Ⓐ Ⓑ Ⓒ Ⓓ
193	Ⓐ Ⓑ Ⓒ Ⓓ
194	Ⓐ Ⓑ Ⓒ Ⓓ
195	Ⓐ Ⓑ Ⓒ Ⓓ
196	Ⓐ Ⓑ Ⓒ Ⓓ
197	Ⓐ Ⓑ Ⓒ Ⓓ
198	Ⓐ Ⓑ Ⓒ Ⓓ
199	Ⓐ Ⓑ Ⓒ Ⓓ
200	Ⓐ Ⓑ Ⓒ Ⓓ

ACTUAL TEST 08

READING SECTION

101	Ⓐ Ⓑ Ⓒ Ⓓ
102	Ⓐ Ⓑ Ⓒ Ⓓ
103	Ⓐ Ⓑ Ⓒ Ⓓ
104	Ⓐ Ⓑ Ⓒ Ⓓ
105	Ⓐ Ⓑ Ⓒ Ⓓ
106	Ⓐ Ⓑ Ⓒ Ⓓ
107	Ⓐ Ⓑ Ⓒ Ⓓ
108	Ⓐ Ⓑ Ⓒ Ⓓ
109	Ⓐ Ⓑ Ⓒ Ⓓ
110	Ⓐ Ⓑ Ⓒ Ⓓ
111	Ⓐ Ⓑ Ⓒ Ⓓ
112	Ⓐ Ⓑ Ⓒ Ⓓ
113	Ⓐ Ⓑ Ⓒ Ⓓ
114	Ⓐ Ⓑ Ⓒ Ⓓ
115	Ⓐ Ⓑ Ⓒ Ⓓ
116	Ⓐ Ⓑ Ⓒ Ⓓ
117	Ⓐ Ⓑ Ⓒ Ⓓ
118	Ⓐ Ⓑ Ⓒ Ⓓ
119	Ⓐ Ⓑ Ⓒ Ⓓ
120	Ⓐ Ⓑ Ⓒ Ⓓ
121	Ⓐ Ⓑ Ⓒ Ⓓ
122	Ⓐ Ⓑ Ⓒ Ⓓ
123	Ⓐ Ⓑ Ⓒ Ⓓ
124	Ⓐ Ⓑ Ⓒ Ⓓ
125	Ⓐ Ⓑ Ⓒ Ⓓ
126	Ⓐ Ⓑ Ⓒ Ⓓ
127	Ⓐ Ⓑ Ⓒ Ⓓ
128	Ⓐ Ⓑ Ⓒ Ⓓ
129	Ⓐ Ⓑ Ⓒ Ⓓ
130	Ⓐ Ⓑ Ⓒ Ⓓ
131	Ⓐ Ⓑ Ⓒ Ⓓ
132	Ⓐ Ⓑ Ⓒ Ⓓ
133	Ⓐ Ⓑ Ⓒ Ⓓ
134	Ⓐ Ⓑ Ⓒ Ⓓ
135	Ⓐ Ⓑ Ⓒ Ⓓ
136	Ⓐ Ⓑ Ⓒ Ⓓ
137	Ⓐ Ⓑ Ⓒ Ⓓ
138	Ⓐ Ⓑ Ⓒ Ⓓ
139	Ⓐ Ⓑ Ⓒ Ⓓ
140	Ⓐ Ⓑ Ⓒ Ⓓ
141	Ⓐ Ⓑ Ⓒ Ⓓ
142	Ⓐ Ⓑ Ⓒ Ⓓ
143	Ⓐ Ⓑ Ⓒ Ⓓ
144	Ⓐ Ⓑ Ⓒ Ⓓ
145	Ⓐ Ⓑ Ⓒ Ⓓ
146	Ⓐ Ⓑ Ⓒ Ⓓ
147	Ⓐ Ⓑ Ⓒ Ⓓ
148	Ⓐ Ⓑ Ⓒ Ⓓ
149	Ⓐ Ⓑ Ⓒ Ⓓ
150	Ⓐ Ⓑ Ⓒ Ⓓ
151	Ⓐ Ⓑ Ⓒ Ⓓ
152	Ⓐ Ⓑ Ⓒ Ⓓ
153	Ⓐ Ⓑ Ⓒ Ⓓ
154	Ⓐ Ⓑ Ⓒ Ⓓ
155	Ⓐ Ⓑ Ⓒ Ⓓ
156	Ⓐ Ⓑ Ⓒ Ⓓ
157	Ⓐ Ⓑ Ⓒ Ⓓ
158	Ⓐ Ⓑ Ⓒ Ⓓ
159	Ⓐ Ⓑ Ⓒ Ⓓ
160	Ⓐ Ⓑ Ⓒ Ⓓ
161	Ⓐ Ⓑ Ⓒ Ⓓ
162	Ⓐ Ⓑ Ⓒ Ⓓ
163	Ⓐ Ⓑ Ⓒ Ⓓ
164	Ⓐ Ⓑ Ⓒ Ⓓ
165	Ⓐ Ⓑ Ⓒ Ⓓ
166	Ⓐ Ⓑ Ⓒ Ⓓ
167	Ⓐ Ⓑ Ⓒ Ⓓ
168	Ⓐ Ⓑ Ⓒ Ⓓ
169	Ⓐ Ⓑ Ⓒ Ⓓ
170	Ⓐ Ⓑ Ⓒ Ⓓ
171	Ⓐ Ⓑ Ⓒ Ⓓ
172	Ⓐ Ⓑ Ⓒ Ⓓ
173	Ⓐ Ⓑ Ⓒ Ⓓ
174	Ⓐ Ⓑ Ⓒ Ⓓ
175	Ⓐ Ⓑ Ⓒ Ⓓ
176	Ⓐ Ⓑ Ⓒ Ⓓ
177	Ⓐ Ⓑ Ⓒ Ⓓ
178	Ⓐ Ⓑ Ⓒ Ⓓ
179	Ⓐ Ⓑ Ⓒ Ⓓ
180	Ⓐ Ⓑ Ⓒ Ⓓ
181	Ⓐ Ⓑ Ⓒ Ⓓ
182	Ⓐ Ⓑ Ⓒ Ⓓ
183	Ⓐ Ⓑ Ⓒ Ⓓ
184	Ⓐ Ⓑ Ⓒ Ⓓ
185	Ⓐ Ⓑ Ⓒ Ⓓ
186	Ⓐ Ⓑ Ⓒ Ⓓ
187	Ⓐ Ⓑ Ⓒ Ⓓ
188	Ⓐ Ⓑ Ⓒ Ⓓ
189	Ⓐ Ⓑ Ⓒ Ⓓ
190	Ⓐ Ⓑ Ⓒ Ⓓ
191	Ⓐ Ⓑ Ⓒ Ⓓ
192	Ⓐ Ⓑ Ⓒ Ⓓ
193	Ⓐ Ⓑ Ⓒ Ⓓ
194	Ⓐ Ⓑ Ⓒ Ⓓ
195	Ⓐ Ⓑ Ⓒ Ⓓ
196	Ⓐ Ⓑ Ⓒ Ⓓ
197	Ⓐ Ⓑ Ⓒ Ⓓ
198	Ⓐ Ⓑ Ⓒ Ⓓ
199	Ⓐ Ⓑ Ⓒ Ⓓ
200	Ⓐ Ⓑ Ⓒ Ⓓ

答案紙

ACTUAL TEST 09

READING SECTION

Questions 101–200, each with answer bubbles Ⓐ Ⓑ Ⓒ Ⓓ

ACTUAL TEST 10

READING SECTION

Questions 101–200, each with answer bubbles Ⓐ Ⓑ Ⓒ Ⓓ

ANSWER KEY

TEST 1

101. (C)	121. (D)	141. (B)	161. (A)	181. (B)
102. (A)	122. (B)	142. (C)	162. (B)	182. (D)
103. (C)	123. (D)	143. (B)	163. (D)	183. (A)
104. (C)	124. (D)	144. (C)	164. (C)	184. (B)
105. (D)	125. (C)	145. (D)	165. (A)	185. (C)
106. (A)	126. (D)	146. (D)	166. (A)	186. (C)
107. (A)	127. (A)	147. (D)	167. (B)	187. (A)
108. (D)	128. (C)	148. (A)	168. (C)	188. (B)
109. (A)	129. (A)	149. (B)	169. (D)	189. (C)
110. (A)	130. (A)	150. (C)	170. (B)	190. (B)
111. (B)	131. (A)	151. (D)	171. (C)	191. (D)
112. (C)	132. (D)	152. (C)	172. (B)	192. (D)
113. (C)	133. (B)	153. (B)	173. (A)	193. (B)
114. (A)	134. (C)	154. (B)	174. (D)	194. (C)
115. (B)	135. (C)	155. (C)	175. (C)	195. (D)
116. (C)	136. (D)	156. (D)	176. (B)	196. (C)
117. (C)	137. (A)	157. (A)	177. (C)	197. (D)
118. (B)	138. (D)	158. (C)	178. (A)	198. (D)
119. (B)	139. (B)	159. (A)	179. (A)	199. (C)
120. (A)	140. (C)	160. (D)	180. (B)	200. (A)

TEST 3

101. (B)	121. (A)	141. (B)	161. (B)	181. (C)
102. (A)	122. (A)	142. (D)	162. (C)	182. (B)
103. (C)	123. (C)	143. (A)	163. (A)	183. (D)
104. (D)	124. (B)	144. (C)	164. (C)	184. (A)
105. (B)	125. (C)	145. (C)	165. (B)	185. (A)
106. (B)	126. (D)	146. (A)	166. (C)	186. (C)
107. (B)	127. (C)	147. (A)	167. (D)	187. (B)
108. (D)	128. (C)	148. (A)	168. (B)	188. (A)
109. (A)	129. (D)	149. (A)	169. (D)	189. (D)
110. (C)	130. (D)	150. (B)	170. (C)	190. (A)
111. (A)	131. (C)	151. (B)	171. (D)	191. (D)
112. (A)	132. (B)	152. (C)	172. (D)	192. (C)
113. (D)	133. (A)	153. (C)	173. (A)	193. (A)
114. (C)	134. (A)	154. (D)	174. (D)	194. (B)
115. (A)	135. (A)	155. (C)	175. (D)	195. (A)
116. (D)	136. (B)	156. (C)	176. (D)	196. (A)
117. (A)	137. (B)	157. (B)	177. (A)	197. (D)
118. (C)	138. (A)	158. (C)	178. (D)	198. (D)
119. (C)	139. (C)	159. (C)	179. (D)	199. (C)
120. (B)	140. (D)	160. (A)	180. (A)	200. (D)

TEST 2

101. (A)	121. (D)	141. (B)	161. (A)	181. (D)
102. (B)	122. (A)	142. (A)	162. (B)	182. (A)
103. (D)	123. (D)	143. (A)	163. (C)	183. (C)
104. (C)	124. (A)	144. (B)	164. (D)	184. (B)
105. (D)	125. (B)	145. (A)	165. (C)	185. (C)
106. (A)	126. (A)	146. (D)	166. (A)	186. (B)
107. (D)	127. (B)	147. (B)	167. (D)	187. (A)
108. (C)	128. (C)	148. (B)	168. (B)	188. (D)
109. (A)	129. (C)	149. (A)	169. (C)	189. (D)
110. (B)	130. (A)	150. (B)	170. (A)	190. (B)
111. (C)	131. (A)	151. (D)	171. (B)	191. (A)
112. (A)	132. (A)	152. (C)	172. (C)	192. (C)
113. (B)	133. (B)	153. (A)	173. (D)	193. (B)
114. (A)	134. (C)	154. (D)	174. (B)	194. (A)
115. (B)	135. (D)	155. (B)	175. (D)	195. (D)
116. (D)	136. (C)	156. (A)	176. (A)	196. (C)
117. (D)	137. (C)	157. (B)	177. (C)	197. (D)
118. (D)	138. (D)	158. (C)	178. (D)	198. (A)
119. (B)	139. (C)	159. (D)	179. (A)	199. (B)
120. (C)	140. (D)	160. (C)	180. (D)	200. (D)

TEST 4

101. (C)	121. (A)	141. (A)	161. (A)	181. (D)
102. (B)	122. (A)	142. (C)	162. (C)	182. (C)
103. (B)	123. (C)	143. (C)	163. (B)	183. (A)
104. (C)	124. (B)	144. (A)	164. (A)	184. (C)
105. (D)	125. (B)	145. (B)	165. (D)	185. (B)
106. (B)	126. (B)	146. (D)	166. (B)	186. (A)
107. (C)	127. (A)	147. (A)	167. (D)	187. (A)
108. (C)	128. (C)	148. (D)	168. (A)	188. (B)
109. (C)	129. (C)	149. (A)	169. (A)	189. (A)
110. (C)	130. (A)	150. (C)	170. (B)	190. (C)
111. (D)	131. (A)	151. (D)	171. (A)	191. (A)
112. (B)	132. (B)	152. (A)	172. (D)	192. (D)
113. (B)	133. (D)	153. (C)	173. (A)	193. (B)
114. (C)	134. (D)	154. (C)	174. (A)	194. (B)
115. (C)	135. (D)	155. (B)	175. (C)	195. (C)
116. (B)	136. (C)	156. (B)	176. (B)	196. (C)
117. (C)	137. (A)	157. (A)	177. (D)	197. (A)
118. (C)	138. (B)	158. (A)	178. (A)	198. (C)
119. (B)	139. (C)	159. (D)	179. (D)	199. (D)
120. (B)	140. (A)	160. (A)	180. (B)	200. (A)

TEST 5

101. (A)	121. (D)	141. (A)	161. (A)	181. (C)
102. (C)	122. (A)	142. (D)	162. (A)	182. (C)
103. (C)	123. (C)	143. (D)	163. (C)	183. (C)
104. (D)	124. (D)	144. (A)	164. (C)	184. (C)
105. (D)	125. (D)	145. (A)	165. (D)	185. (B)
106. (A)	126. (A)	146. (C)	166. (A)	186. (A)
107. (B)	127. (D)	147. (A)	167. (B)	187. (C)
108. (A)	128. (D)	148. (B)	168. (D)	188. (B)
109. (B)	129. (D)	149. (B)	169. (B)	189. (B)
110. (D)	130. (A)	150. (C)	170. (D)	190. (A)
111. (D)	131. (B)	151. (B)	171. (B)	191. (D)
112. (B)	132. (D)	152. (A)	172. (C)	192. (B)
113. (D)	133. (B)	153. (C)	173. (A)	193. (B)
114. (A)	134. (A)	154. (B)	174. (C)	194. (A)
115. (D)	135. (C)	155. (D)	175. (A)	195. (D)
116. (C)	136. (A)	156. (C)	176. (D)	196. (B)
117. (A)	137. (B)	157. (A)	177. (A)	197. (B)
118. (B)	138. (B)	158. (C)	178. (D)	198. (A)
119. (B)	139. (D)	159. (D)	179. (A)	199. (B)
120. (A)	140. (D)	160. (A)	180. (D)	200. (C)

TEST 7

101. (B)	121. (B)	141. (B)	161. (D)	181. (A)
102. (C)	122. (A)	142. (B)	162. (A)	182. (B)
103. (B)	123. (C)	143. (A)	163. (A)	183. (D)
104. (A)	124. (A)	144. (C)	164. (B)	184. (D)
105. (B)	125. (C)	145. (B)	165. (D)	185. (D)
106. (B)	126. (B)	146. (D)	166. (B)	186. (D)
107. (D)	127. (C)	147. (A)	167. (D)	187. (C)
108. (C)	128. (B)	148. (D)	168. (A)	188. (B)
109. (B)	129. (A)	149. (B)	169. (C)	189. (C)
110. (A)	130. (C)	150. (B)	170. (C)	190. (D)
111. (C)	131. (C)	151. (B)	171. (C)	191. (A)
112. (D)	132. (A)	152. (D)	172. (B)	192. (B)
113. (D)	133. (B)	153. (B)	173. (C)	193. (C)
114. (C)	134. (C)	154. (A)	174. (A)	194. (C)
115. (B)	135. (B)	155. (B)	175. (C)	195. (D)
116. (D)	136. (A)	156. (C)	176. (A)	196. (B)
117. (D)	137. (D)	157. (B)	177. (C)	197. (C)
118. (D)	138. (C)	158. (A)	178. (A)	198. (B)
119. (D)	139. (D)	159. (D)	179. (A)	199. (C)
120. (B)	140. (C)	160. (D)	180. (A)	200. (B)

TEST 6

101. (B)	121. (B)	141. (D)	161. (D)	181. (A)
102. (C)	122. (B)	142. (A)	162. (D)	182. (C)
103. (B)	123. (D)	143. (C)	163. (A)	183. (A)
104. (B)	124. (A)	144. (B)	164. (D)	184. (B)
105. (C)	125. (A)	145. (D)	165. (A)	185. (A)
106. (A)	126. (D)	146. (A)	166. (D)	186. (A)
107. (C)	127. (C)	147. (B)	167. (A)	187. (A)
108. (C)	128. (D)	148. (A)	168. (C)	188. (A)
109. (B)	129. (C)	149. (B)	169. (D)	189. (C)
110. (C)	130. (B)	150. (C)	170. (A)	190. (C)
111. (C)	131. (B)	151. (C)	171. (A)	191. (C)
112. (B)	132. (D)	152. (B)	172. (A)	192. (C)
113. (C)	133. (A)	153. (D)	173. (B)	193. (A)
114. (B)	134. (B)	154. (B)	174. (A)	194. (D)
115. (D)	135. (A)	155. (A)	175. (A)	195. (A)
116. (C)	136. (A)	156. (C)	176. (C)	196. (D)
117. (A)	137. (B)	157. (A)	177. (A)	197. (B)
118. (C)	138. (A)	158. (B)	178. (B)	198. (C)
119. (D)	139. (B)	159. (A)	179. (A)	199. (D)
120. (D)	140. (D)	160. (B)	180. (B)	200. (A)

TEST 8

101. (C)	121. (B)	141. (A)	161. (D)	181. (B)
102. (B)	122. (A)	142. (D)	162. (A)	182. (D)
103. (B)	123. (D)	143. (B)	163. (A)	183. (B)
104. (B)	124. (A)	144. (D)	164. (D)	184. (B)
105. (D)	125. (C)	145. (C)	165. (D)	185. (A)
106. (D)	126. (B)	146. (A)	166. (A)	186. (D)
107. (D)	127. (C)	147. (B)	167. (A)	187. (D)
108. (A)	128. (C)	148. (B)	168. (B)	188. (C)
109. (D)	129. (A)	149. (C)	169. (D)	189. (C)
110. (D)	130. (C)	150. (D)	170. (B)	190. (B)
111. (B)	131. (C)	151. (A)	171. (C)	191. (A)
112. (A)	132. (D)	152. (D)	172. (D)	192. (A)
113. (C)	133. (B)	153. (B)	173. (A)	193. (D)
114. (D)	134. (A)	154. (C)	174. (B)	194. (C)
115. (B)	135. (D)	155. (D)	175. (B)	195. (B)
116. (C)	136. (C)	156. (B)	176. (D)	196. (D)
117. (C)	137. (B)	157. (B)	177. (A)	197. (A)
118. (B)	138. (A)	158. (C)	178. (A)	198. (A)
119. (C)	139. (B)	159. (D)	179. (A)	199. (B)
120. (D)	140. (B)	160. (A)	180. (C)	200. (D)

TEST 9

101. (B)	121. (B)	141. (D)	161. (C)	181. (A)
102. (B)	122. (B)	142. (B)	162. (A)	182. (B)
103. (B)	123. (D)	143. (D)	163. (B)	183. (A)
104. (C)	124. (D)	144. (C)	164. (A)	184. (A)
105. (A)	125. (B)	145. (A)	165. (A)	185. (D)
106. (A)	126. (A)	146. (B)	166. (D)	186. (D)
107. (B)	127. (B)	147. (C)	167. (D)	187. (C)
108. (C)	128. (D)	148. (B)	168. (A)	188. (D)
109. (C)	129. (A)	149. (B)	169. (B)	189. (C)
110. (B)	130. (D)	150. (D)	170. (D)	190. (C)
111. (B)	131. (B)	151. (B)	171. (B)	191. (A)
112. (B)	132. (C)	152. (A)	172. (B)	192. (B)
113. (C)	133. (D)	153. (B)	173. (A)	193. (A)
114. (A)	134. (A)	154. (C)	174. (D)	194. (B)
115. (B)	135. (A)	155. (D)	175. (D)	195. (A)
116. (B)	136. (B)	156. (A)	176. (C)	196. (A)
117. (C)	137. (C)	157. (C)	177. (B)	197. (B)
118. (C)	138. (D)	158. (A)	178. (D)	198. (D)
119. (A)	139. (A)	159. (C)	179. (C)	199. (C)
120. (C)	140. (D)	160. (B)	180. (C)	200. (B)

TEST 10

101. (C)	121. (B)	141. (D)	161. (B)	181. (D)
102. (A)	122. (B)	142. (C)	162. (A)	182. (D)
103. (C)	123. (A)	143. (D)	163. (A)	183. (A)
104. (B)	124. (A)	144. (D)	164. (A)	184. (C)
105. (D)	125. (A)	145. (A)	165. (D)	185. (D)
106. (A)	126. (C)	146. (C)	166. (B)	186. (A)
107. (C)	127. (C)	147. (C)	167. (A)	187. (C)
108. (C)	128. (A)	148. (A)	168. (D)	188. (B)
109. (C)	129. (A)	149. (C)	169. (A)	189. (D)
110. (C)	130. (A)	150. (B)	170. (C)	190. (A)
111. (D)	131. (C)	151. (B)	171. (D)	191. (B)
112. (A)	132. (B)	152. (A)	172. (C)	192. (B)
113. (D)	133. (C)	153. (D)	173. (B)	193. (D)
114. (D)	134. (A)	154. (C)	174. (C)	194. (A)
115. (B)	135. (C)	155. (C)	175. (D)	195. (B)
116. (A)	136. (D)	156. (D)	176. (A)	196. (C)
117. (D)	137. (C)	157. (A)	177. (A)	197. (D)
118. (D)	138. (D)	158. (B)	178. (B)	198. (D)
119. (C)	139. (C)	159. (B)	179. (D)	199. (A)
120. (A)	140. (D)	160. (D)	180. (A)	200. (D)

挑戰
新制多益
閱讀滿分 模擬試題1000題

作 者	Choi Young Ken
譯 者	蘇裕承／關亭薇（前言）
編 輯	林晨禾
校 對	王婷葦／劉育如／吳思薇
主 編	丁宥暄
內文排版	謝青秀／林書玉
封面設計	林書玉
製程管理	洪巧玲
出 版 者	寂天文化事業股份有限公司
電 話	+886-(0)2-2365-9739
傳 真	+886-(0)2-2365-9835
網 址	www.icosmos.com.tw
讀者服務	onlineservice@icosmos.com.tw
出版日期	2019 年 9 月 初版再刷 (160104)

挑戰新制多益閱讀滿分：模擬試題 1000 題 /
Choi Young Ken 著 . -- 初版 . -- 臺北市：寂天
文化 , 2018.06
　　面；　公分
ISBN 978-986-318-704-2(平裝)

1. 多益測驗

805.1895　　　　　　　　　　107008323

郵撥帳號 1998620-0 寂天文化事業股份有限公司
劃撥金額 600 元（含）以上者，郵資免費。
訂購金額 600 元以下者，請外加郵資 65 元。
〔若有破損，請寄回更換，謝謝。〕